Siren's Curse

Content Warning

Welcome to Prisma Isle, a realm not for the faint of heart.

Humans may not exist, but that doesn't mean villages don't have any fucked up shit happening inside their walls. We would warn you of everything, except the list is extensive. And we could be here far longer than necessary. All you need to know is that shit gets bad and escape isn't always possible.

On the brighter side, because let's face it, there has to be one. There's a lot of sex to counteract all that dark.

Balance is the necessity of life.

Dedication

To our number one fan.

Siren's Curse

PRISMA ISLE™ SERIES
BOOK FOUR

BRIGIT ROSÉ & NIKKI HARAS

TWO REALMS PUBLISHING LLC

TERMINOLOGY

Adolescent: term in shape shifter culture for children ten years of age to twenty years of age

Allimos: the soulmate of an Atlis

Atlese: the language of the Atlis, often learned by the Atlis's Allimos

Aphros [af-rows]: the second cycle of the Vernal Equinox (the spring)

Antekilio [ant-E-keel-oh]: library of the Sirens

Atlis: an offshoot of the sirens created by Demeter, but with far more power, the ability to jump between realms and planes, and one purpose: to serve the gods and goddesses who granted them their powers and helping those who cannot help themselves

Celestimo: magical book sealed and protected by the Atlis, containing every prophecy ever known to exist and details regarding the crystals that make up the Prism believed to create balance in the magic of Prisma Isle

Chicane Village: village of the guilers

Chimera: a lion-like with a snake-like mane, horns, hind legs of a ram, front paws of a bird, a beak-like jaw, and large feather wings

Cycle: approximately one month or from one full moon to the next

Demeter [dee-MEE-ter]: the goddess of fertility, earth, and harvests; protector of marriage and social order; daughter of Cronos and Rhea; mother to Persephone; and creator of the sirens

Draconis: the language of the dragons

Drakes: the tiniest and cutest of the dragon species; these creatures have limited flight access to magic and are often attracted to creatures of great power

Full-fledged: term in shape shifter culture for adults; those twenty years of age and older

Galenus [gah-LEE-nus]: male, canine shape shifter, deceased

Glory: elevated status given to a partner by a dragon, creating a magical connection between the pair; done once in a lifetime

Guiler [guy-lure]: a humanoid species with elemental abilities

Hades: the Greek god of the underworld; sometimes used as a sort-of curse word by the shape shifters

Informant: soldier to the shape shifter king, Markham

Julunna [jew-lew-na]: the first cycle of the Luminos Equinox (the summer)

Kriah [KREE-uh]: a female nymph who lives in Migas Village

Lacuna [la-KEW-na]: an hour of time

Luminos Equinox [lum-OH-nose]: summer

Manticore: a lion-like creature with a scorpion tail and dragon or bat-like wings

Marana: the second cycle (month) of the year

Matriarch: highest position in the Draconic society; another term for the Queen of the Dragons

Métamorphe [met-a-mor-fey]: the shape shifter village

Migas Village [MEE-gahs]: the hidden hybrid village and a place of sanctuary

Mindlink: a telepathic connection between twins and some mates

Nestling: term in the shape shifter culture for children one year of age to five years of age

Newling: term in the shape shifter culture for newborns to one year of age

Penumbra(s) [pah-num-BRAH]: week(s)

Pteryina [ter-EEN-uh]: home of the sirens; adjacent to The Clouds

Regent: an advisor to the Queen of the Dragons

Saint Beast: the largest of the dragons, possessing the greatest raw physical strength and magical power. Unlike typical sky dragons, they have several rings of fangs

Safe Juice: water

Sciphinx [SEF-IŋKS]: a creature with the head and front torso of a bird (sparrow), back torso and tail of a lion, and gold beak; they are battle-intense creatures created for the warriors of Migas Village

Seitadi AKA Dark Sirens: birthed by Clytemnestra, daughter of Nemesis; in their current form, they appear as large birds with dark brown feathers, beady black eyes, and a gold beak; they stand at three-feet in height at the shoulder; their screech can temporarily paralyze a person (lesser forms), as well as burst eardrums; they can control wind, generating great torrents and creating tornadoes

Seplugh: the third cycle of the Luminos Equinox (the summer)

Siren: these bird-like creatures were created by Demeter. From the thighs up, they have the body of a human female/male; from the thighs down, their legs narrow into those of a sparrow with talons for feet

Solaris: year, which comprises sixteen cycles (months) for the inhabitants of Prisma Isle

Umbra(s) [um-BRAH]: day(s)

Vasilia [vuh-SILL-ee-uh]: female siren that is the Elder of the sirens and lives in Pteryrina

Verdant Grove: home of the fae

Vernal Equinox [ver-NAL]: spring

Youngling: term in shape shifter culture for children five years of age to ten years of age

Zancle's Rock [Zan-kuls rock]: bar and restaurant in the marketplace run by Ambrosia; known for their venison stew

Chapter One

Seplugh, the 22nd day, Year 1027

"I don't mean to embarrass you further," Seru said, his voice faltering. "But if there's ever anything I can do to help with your siren pheromones, or anything else." He smiled clumsily. "Please, don't hesitate to ask."

As a searing flash of heat coursed through her, she felt a sudden rush of warmth and her temperature spiked rapidly. Her cheeks flushed. She pulled back slightly, her eyes meeting his. "I ... um..." Thalasia's gaze dropped for a moment. While she knew what was happening with her body, she couldn't very well tell him that. Not without explaining everything. Considering she'd learned about sex at the ripe age of ten, she didn't want to dredge that up. The conversation had been short and somewhat disturbing at that age. "You might notice them before me. I don't know what will happen exactly." She bit her bottom lip. "Seru, I'm untouched."

He tilted his head, with a questioning expression on his face. He buried his face in the curve of her neck. Nestling into her, he trailed his fangs along her skin before he placed a light kiss on her neck.

Her lids lowered. His hot breath sent a shudder through her body. Thalasia licked her lips and raked a hand through his mane.

Seru raised his eyes and looked back at her, his gaze locking with hers. "You smell and taste just fine to me."

She brushed a soft kiss across the skin closest to his ear and whispered, "That goes both ways."

A contented rumble left his mouth. Touching nose to nose with her, he couldn't stop grinning. He stared into her eyes longer

"Guess we should tend to the severely wounded before getting some rest? We can deal with minor injuries in the morning."

A nod followed her smile, wider and brighter than it had been since their first encounter. Not that she could say for sure, but she thought her eyes might have glowed just a touch. Warmth radiated from behind her irises. "We can decide on our next move then, too."

He dipped his chin in approval, but didn't budge, taking both her hands in his.

Thalasia canted her head, her gaze fixed on his captivating blue eyes and the emotions swirling within them. She thought back to Aurelia's comment about her drifting. Her visions had always been a part of her, and she couldn't change that. What did that mean for them? "What are you thinking about?"

"Ah..." He blinked a few times. "I was just thinking," Seru paused, "about us."

"Me, too." She chewed on the inside of her cheek, debating how much to tell him. No part of their road would be easy. But she couldn't hide everything forever. Then she remembered something her father once told her after their many moves. The corners of her lips lifted into a small, almost imperceptible, smile. "We have a lot of obstacles ahead. That's for sure. And I don't know that I'll ever have one place to call home, but that doesn't mean *we* can't have one. When I was little, my father told me, 'Home isn't a place you lay your head; it's a feeling you have with someone.'"

His eyes lit up. "Hmm, I like your father already." Seru kissed her forehead.

"He was a good man." Both of her parents had been good people, strong and faithful. Even in the short time she'd had with them, they had taught her a lot.

"You must miss them terribly," Seru said, drawing her into a tight embrace. He rested his chin on top of her head.

With her hands clasped around his waist, she could feel the steady thrum of his heart. "It's easier when I don't think about them. I can't always stop the memories, but I never want to forget them."

"Do you see them? In your visions, I mean?"

"No. I don't see the past, only the future where I'm meant to go." Funny. Of all the things she'd seen over the years, the night of their murders—it was the one vision she'd never received.

"I'm sorry," he murmured into her hair.

Thalasia wiped at the unshed tears, her shoulders slumping slightly as she took a slight step back. She inhaled and exhaled a deep breath. "I can't change the past, but I can choose to focus on the present and the future."

Seru squeezed his eyes shut. The lines in his forehead creased and his skin rippled.

Oh, this wasn't good. It couldn't be, yet it seemed like his beast was trying to escape. She never wanted to do this without his permission, but she had to gain control of the situation quickly. Thalasia cupped his face, the feel of his skin soft beneath her fingers, and started singing a love song from her childhood. It didn't respond well to her charm. His eyes snapped open. An electrifying pair of blazing-white orbs met her gaze as a ferocious snarl escaped Seru's mouth.

She stopped singing. That didn't work the way she'd hoped, leaving her with one other option. Thalasia clenched his arms, her thumbs gently caressing his skin as she stared into his eyes. "I know you want out. And you're beautiful when you're free. I want you free, too. But right now, I need him here with me. I need you to work with us. I can't help him if you take over. Please, please let him come back."

The beast growled low, its tongue flicking between its teeth. Scales in varying shades of white and gray traveled up his arms where she touched. Seru tilted his head.

At least it looked like her male. If she didn't count the change in his eye color, his altered skin, or even the way he eyeballed her. Almost as if it couldn't decide whether she would make a tasty snack or if it wanted to nuzzle her with affection. As she preferred the latter, she continued stroking his arms where the scales appeared. "I enjoyed our time in the sky earlier. It's something I'd like to do again soon. Right now, I need Seru back. He needs you to share with him. Can you do that? Can you let him come back for now? And we'll go flying again soon."

The beast snapped at the air, irritated. It lifted its nose, inspecting her scent. Somehow, her words had broken through. Whether it was the promise of flight or something else, she couldn't say for sure. The reptilian eyes, once rimmed with yellow, faded back to Seru's standard blue, though they remained unfocused. As the beast recoiled, Seru's body went limp in her arms, his muscles refusing to hold him up without the beast's assistance.

Thalasia held him as much as her strength allowed. She slowly lowered them both to the ground and stroked his head. They could just sit here for a minute while she figured out how to get him settled somewhere—without giving all of her power away or the truth of her family line.

The gemstone Aurelia had given Seru glowed through his clothing. His breaths came slowly and raggedly. "Sorry," he apologized, still unable to regain full control of his body.

"It's okay. We can sit here for a bit. I'm just glad you're back." She brushed a soft kiss across his forehead, feeling the warmth of his skin, and continued to stroke his head. There must have been some kind of internal struggle she hadn't seen Seru go through with his beast. She also didn't know what brought the beast forward to begin with, but they could address that later. Right now, it was more important he regain enough strength for them to get back to the village. The other option, she carried him to the top of the closest tree to rest.

"I... once I can stand," he amended. "I need to go away. For just a little while." Seru still had trouble catching his breath. However, his extremities moved a little.

"Oh, okay." Right. He needed to regroup. Even though she didn't like the idea of being apart, she could understand it. She eyed the collar. They hadn't thought this all the way through, had they? Aurelia knew how to deal with it. She didn't. One obstacle she'd spoken of earlier.

It took effort, but he sat up. "I've neglected feeding—eating," Seru corrected, "for far too long."

With a nod, Thalasia brought her braid over her shoulder, her fingers finding comfort in the rough texture of her hair's ends. "I noticed you didn't eat the fruit. I take it that's not part of your diet."

He offered her a smile; the sweetness laced with a hint of sadness. "Not exactly." Reaching over, he calmed her fidgeting hands. "Saint beasts thrive on battlefields, not in everyday life." He frowned, unable to look her in the eye. "While dragons—like Aurelia—survive on a diet of fish and occasional fruits and vegetables, I can't."

She cupped his jaw and lifted his gaze to hers. "Please don't hide. Not from me. I knew you were different, but it's part of what makes you... well, you. If we gain our strength a little differently, then that's okay."

"That's easy to say when your dinner doesn't die screaming." He grimaced, giving her hand a light squeeze.

That wasn't what she had expected. It didn't bother her as much as it bothered him. Scooting a little closer to him, she opened her mouth and snapped it shut. She glanced over her shoulder toward the village, realizing nature provided in unique ways, and then she faced him. "How much sustenance do you think a dark guiler would provide?"

He glanced at her out of the corner of his eye. "Not much," he said. "Maybe if there were a thousand of them." He paused for a moment before offering a small smile. "Besides, I think that one is more likely to give me indigestion and heartburn rather than sustenance. Mac would never let me live it down if I ate him. Not to mention, the villagers would recognize me for what I am. And that could pose more trouble than the invasion from Candescent Isle."

She chuckled. "Maybe if you didn't have a siren at your side, one who's fantastic at manipulation, if I say so myself."

He bumped shoulders with her. "You're magnificent. But wiping away the most basic instinct of true unbridled fear in any-one—much less an entire village—is a very tall order. You'd be altering who they are, and I'd never ask you to bear that burden."

"Not quite what I had in mind. Manipulate the guard's memory and keep the others asleep." She nudged him. "Just a thought, you know." She beamed, quite proud of her idea, since it was still nighttime.

"I appreciate it," Seru said. "But I don't think there's even a viable source nearby. These people have lost so much already. They couldn't spare the livestock. And attacking another species is out of the question."

She laid her head on his shoulder. It left little in the way of options. "You could hunt here in the forest, but I keep thinking about what Mac said... fae."

Seru nodded.

"How much of the forest belongs to them?" She was unfamiliar with the terrain, not entirely at least, and the map couldn't help her with that, although she didn't believe it covered the entire island.

He reached out, panning his palm across the treeline. "They reside primarily in the western and southern sectors of the isle. They're a secluded species—not unlike the dragons and sirens. Tricky little bastards," he muttered. "Always watching, always lis-tening."

Her shoulders slumped a little. They had been in the forest a good hour or longer. And shared a lot. "So then, if you head east, you should find something."

"More shape shifters and chimeras," Seru said, continuing to mark the land with his hand. "To the northeast are the manticores. Just north, the half-breeds and farther north in the sky are the true sirens—like you." He smiled. "There is an abundance of lesser species, but most of them cohabitate with the major species."

Yeah, a true siren, like me. If only he knew. His mention of the half-breeds reminded her of the war that had occurred between them and the *true* sirens, forcing them apart. Snickering at her thoughts, she laced their fingers together. "But there should be stock for hunting. You just have to keep from being seen."

"I'm as large as a mountain in my beast form. You'd have to be blind, deaf, and really dumb—" He shook his head. "I'll likely go out to sea. It's a risk, especially with the dark guilers in play, but it's safer than going inland and disappearing."

She raised an eyebrow at him. As if she could forget all about his size. "I think you're perfectly stunning." Fishing. Although in his case, maybe the bigger mammals would be better. It had been a while since she'd been along the ocean, dragging her feet and fingers through the water.

Seru's eyes widened, his expression one of shock and surprise. He spun away.

Lifting her head, she studied him for a moment. He had once told her he was like a spectator. His reaction said otherwise. She caressed his cheek, her fingertips tracing the softness of his flesh. "Did you hear what I said to your beast?"

He leaned into her touch. "I did, but I couldn't act on it," he whispered. "The beast has a mind and will of its own."

"I kind of figured. It's why I just tried to talk to him and get him to work with us. Being up there with both of you, I think it helped. We may have a mission here, but that doesn't mean we can't take time for *us*, including him." It might be the only answer they had at the moment. Eventually, she'd get the collar off, and they needed to prepare for the aftermath before they got there.

"It doesn't scare you?" His words were barely audible as he pressed her knuckles to his lips.

"No. Not at all. No part of you scares me." She straddled him and rested her hands on his shoulders, wanting to ensure he understood exactly what she was about to tell him. "I could bury my fingers in your mane, run my hands over your smooth scales, and even wrap my arms around your powerful neck as wide as they'd go. You're gorgeous, no matter which form you're in."

"What... are you?" Seru asked her in disbelief. His hands found her hips, drawing her closer.

Oh, that was such a loaded question. She beamed at him, and a shiver trickled down her spine. Her fingers dug into his shoulders ever so slightly as the feathers on her wings ruffled. "I'm just me."

"In all my years, I've encountered nothing like you," he said, kissing her forehead once more.

She wrapped her arms around his neck and ran her fingers through his dark hair. For the first time, she felt like there could be more to her life, that maybe what her parents had, she could have, too. "It goes both ways."

Seru pulled back, clearing his throat, a visible shudder running through him. "I really should hunt down dinner before my beast decides you look like a very different meal."

"And I should check on the villagers. See if there are any that need healing." She sighed. "Then I'm going to find a tree big enough for two."

Seru smiled as he reached into his pocket to retrieve the crystal. "Here, take this with you." He pressed it into her palm, closing her fingers around it and bringing her fist to his lips. "I'll find you when I return."

Tucking the crystal into her pants pocket, she dipped her chin. While she had one other place to put it, she couldn't do it without drawing attention to her purse. "You better." Thalasia grinned as she climbed out of his lap and held out a hand to help him up.

He took her hand, though she suspected it wasn't really necessary. Seru rose to his feet, stretching his weary limbs, then enveloped her in one last, lingering embrace.

Demeter. She didn't think she'd ever tire of being in his arms. Thalasia wrapped her wings around him, inhaling his familiar scent as she closed her eyes and listened to the steady thrum of his heartbeat.

"Be good," Seru told her as her wings unfurled from around him. He took a few steps back before shifting into the clouds and disappearing into the night.

"Be safe," she called after him, though she quickly brought her attention back to the present. There was work to do, so she turned and flew toward the village.

Chapter Two

Parthenia frowned, groaning inwardly. This meeting had gone on for hours, well into the night. And this was day three. How was it possible there could be so many contentions to consider when so few of them remained?

Five families total. Fifteen sirens altogether, including their Elder, remained. And only seven of them had a say, plus their Elder. Yet none of them could agree on how best to approach a truce with the other species of the land. At least three sirens felt they shouldn't even be considering an accord, but they couldn't go on like this. Their numbers were extremely low, their food supply wasn't growing normally, and the Reflection Pools had almost dried up. That didn't even include the recently broken barrier, which no one had mentioned once in this discussion.

There was so much they needed to know about the species below. They'd spent so much time keeping to themselves that they knew next to nothing. At least most of them. She'd sneaked down for many years. Not to mention her mate was a shape shifter, although only one of them knew that.

Parthenia ran a hand through her mahogany waves and sighed. She couldn't take the arguing any longer. "This isn't complicated. Two of us go down and visit with the hybrids first, and then we travel to the other villages, going counter-clockwise."

"Oh? Any reason you suggest beginning with the *half-breeds*?" Fagonia sneered at the word as she neatly folded her hands in her lap.

"We have the longest history with them. Regardless of how dark our past is, if we reach out to them first, the other species will be more likely to accept our wishes to work together." It wasn't like they had a choice at this point. Everything in their home was falling apart. How had it gotten this far? How had they gone this long without action?

Easy. No one wanted to face the truth. If only they all knew how deep their ignorance ran. Something she had learned six months ago when she and Gavin shared their first kiss.

Or attempted to, anyway.

Parthenia ran a finger lightly across her bottom lip. Their kiss had lasted all of two seconds, if that. His lips were soft as silk and as warm as the sun. That hadn't changed. Although they'd never shared that two-second kiss again, his lips had been on other parts of her body.

Some force had thrown them apart. Since then, they'd attempted to avoid anything that caused it to happen. It had certainly been enjoyable for them to discover exactly what they could and couldn't do. Good Demeter. She was ready to figure out how to break this curse and have him completely. A soft groan escaped her lips.

Cipriana elbowed her, but it didn't deter her thoughts from her mate.

They still knew little about the force, except that a goddess had cursed her species at some point. All the books in the library had proven useful just last month. It referenced a map that led to the location of a secret book, but she hadn't found this so-called map. *Demeter, help me. I need to find that map.* She didn't care—

"Do you agree, Parthenia?"

She blinked at the question. *Agree? With what?* Glancing to her right, she raised an eyebrow at Cipriana. What were they talking about? She'd been so lost in her thoughts that she had heard nothing after her last comment.

"I'm sure she does, Elder Vasilia. She and I would make the perfect ambassadors," Cipriana said.

Ambassadors? Was she out of her mind? They'd be required to sit with the leaders of every village, including the shape shifters. To hide her panic, Parthenia swallowed, her mouth suddenly dry. Her relationship with Gavin was supposed to be a secret for a reason. Even if her Elder changed the law, his King hadn't. The King had already forced her mate out of his village. Not to mention, his king knew about their relationship. What would he do if she showed up at the border of his village? With Gavin's scent all over her body? None of this. She couldn't reveal any of this.

Plastering a smile on her face, she swung her gaze to the Elder, and she bowed her head. "Of course, Elder Vasilia. It would be an honor to serve in such an esteemed position."

"Elder Vasilia, I implore you to reconsider this decision. While I understand we need to make some changes, I still do not agree that we need to reach out to the other species for aid. Nor do I believe these two young females are the best choice as our ambassadors. If we must send someone, then it should be someone with better diplomatic skills," Fagonia said.

Parthenia's brows knitted together. The older female had a lot of nerve, insinuating they couldn't be diplomatic. She worked well with her half-sister.

Their Elder narrowed her almond-brown eyes as the feathers in her wings ruffled ever so slightly. "They are the perfect choice, Fagonia. It is their generation being affected the most by our dwindling numbers, the depletion of our vegetation, and drying pools. They can ascertain the most appropriate actions based on what they learn from the other species."

Cipriana nodded her head at their Elder. "Thank you, Elder Vasilia. Parthenia and I both appreciate the compliment. We're humbled that you think so highly of us."

"I have witnessed your actions among our people. I am certain most would agree the two of you balance one another out well." The female tilted her head and offered a tender smile to them both.

Sure, most would agree. Most didn't include Fagonia. Or her mother. The two of them had always pushed back with anything she attempted to do to save their people. The bottom line—they had run out of options. All they had left was reaching out to the species below. Pteryrina's resources were dwindling quickly.

Still, she would've preferred anyone else to serve as an ambassador, even if she was the most logical choice next to Cipriana. If she didn't go, it would force one of the other females to go in her stead. She glanced over at the faces of the small circle they created between themselves. Her gaze flicked from her mother to Cipriana's mother and on. As much as she wanted to dispute the point their Elder had made, she couldn't.

Aside from her, Cipriana, and Fagonia, everyone else either wasn't old enough yet or were mothers with responsibilities. Although Fagonia protested a lot, she doubted the female could be diplomatic with other species. The female's face revealed disgust at the idea of speaking to someone other than another siren.

This was the best option. She'd just have to warn Gavin, which meant they'd have to figure out how to handle the shape shifter village. One issue at a time.

"Excellent. As we are *all* now in agreement, the two of you should make preparations for your departure tomorrow morning. This meeting is adjourned," Elder Vasilia said.

Everyone stood and flew out of Demeter's Temple. Before she took off, their Elder held out her hand. "I would like you both to hang back a moment, so we may speak privately."

Biting the inside of her lip, Parthenia eyed her half-sister. She didn't like the sound of this. Hopefully, it had something to do with the mission and not the barrier. Or her law-breaking tendencies. Forcing another half-smile, Parthenia sat down on the stone staircase. Cipriana followed suit.

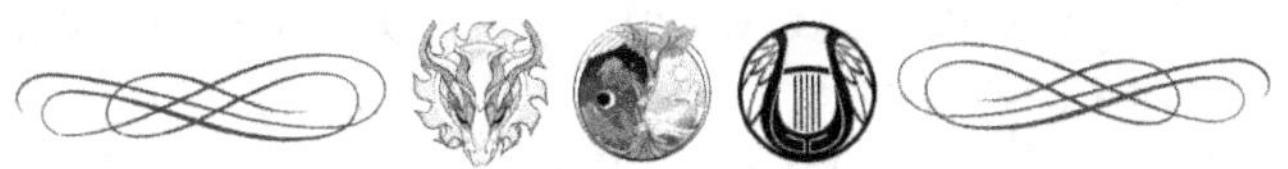

Sitting next to her sister, Cipriana patiently waited for the other sirens to clear out. What further need could their Elder have of them? Did it have something to do with the mission? Or maybe Vasilia noticed how she nudged Parthenia? She swore that ever since her half-sister had found a mate, the female's head had been more and more in the stars.

It was bad enough Parthenia no longer spent evenings in Pteryrina and had completely moved out of her mother's home. Her actions had affected things around here as well, such as the lack of treatment remedies readily available. No one tracked the loss of the Poppy Fields any longer. Nor had anyone continued to monitor the water levels of their Reflection Pools.

"Thank you both for staying behind," Vasilia said. "The reason I asked to speak with the two of you is that I have decided who the next Elder shall be."

"The next Elder? But Elder Vasilia, you still have many *solaris* before a new Elder would even need to be trained." Even if she had decided, what did that have to do with—Cipriana's gaze flicked to Parthenia. No. Not one of them? Surely, that couldn't be it. They had both only just celebrated their nineteenth birth year. They were both too young for such a role.

"That may be. However, I have a feeling it is imperative I name my successor before you two leave."

"Of course, Elder Vasilia." Parthenia bowed her head. "If that is your wish, we shall certainly bear witness."

"You will, Parthenia." The female smiled. "I, Vasilia, the current Elder of the Sirens in Pteryrina, under the first waxing gibbous moon of the fall, name my successor as Cipriana."

Her eyes widened. Had she...? No, no way. Absolutely not! She didn't hear the female say that. Cipriana opened her mouth, but no words came out. She couldn't figure out what to say. *Repeat the proclamation. Say it again. What was that? Any of the above will do.* Nothing. Again, nothing came out of her mouth.

Parthenia cleared her throat. "Elder Vasilia, I don't mean to speak out of order, but are you certain this is your wish?"

"Yes. I believe Cipriana will make an excellent leader for our species." Vasilia picked up a piece of parchment paper and spread it out across the altar for the females. "Cipriana, you need to sign here acknowledging your acceptance, and Parthenia, you will sign here as a witness to this auspicious occasion."

"You're serious?" Cipriana finally asked. Look, she found her voice. It still existed. "I'm only nineteen. Why not pick one of the other older females?"

"What you do not have in *solaris*, you make up for in heart. I have seen the way you care for everyone here. The way you tend to the sick. Or help those in need; even if they do not deserve it; you still offer aid. These are the qualities of a good leader. I have faith you will ensure the laws that require changing are addressed, and our people will survive and thrive because of you."

Cipriana blinked, a salty taste in her mouth as she swallowed the sudden lump in her throat. How did she argue with logic like that? She couldn't think of one way to counter what Vasilia had said. Lifting her gaze to the quill and pot of ink pushed in her direction, Cipriana shakily accepted the quill and penned her name on the parchment. Slowly, she held the items out to her sister.

With a slight nod, Parthenia penned her name to the parchment and returned the quill and pot of ink to their appropriate locations.

"Perfect. Now, as my successor, I have two items to present to you. These are passed down from Elder to Elder. It is of the utmost importance that you protect these artifacts at all costs. They hold valuable information. First, there is the Vlépoun Map. It simply means 'all-seeing.' The map keeps track of all sirens born here in Pteryrina. You can also see the boundaries of each territory and who the current Elder is of each species. Second, there is Ginosko, which is a journal of knowledge containing information on the differences between species of the isle, plus facts about every Elder who has ever lived. The only exception is the shape shifter Elder, Markham. Do not cross those borders under any circumstances. I cannot protect you there. You must still speak with him, but stay outside the territory." She presented both artifacts to Cipriana, who reluctantly took them.

"Now go, both of you. You have a long, trying journey ahead of you."

"Of course. Thank you, again, Elder Vasilia." Parthenia bowed her head and hooked her arm under Cipriana's. Carefully, she helped her to her feet, and they strode together toward the exit.

It wasn't the instructions they'd been given for their mission running rampant in her head. *Elder. I was just named the next Elder.* She really needed to focus. They had a mission to prepare for. Cipriana rubbed her forehead. Good Demeter, how had this happened?

"Are you okay?" Parthenia whispered as they left the temple.

No. No, she wasn't okay. Nothing about this news was okay. She was nineteen years of age. By the gods and goddesses, how was she supposed to be the next Elder? "Yes. I'm just... in shock, I suppose. I'm so young."

"That may be true, but it isn't like you'll take over right away."

"Right." That was a fair point. Once they completed this task and established a few peace treaties, she would certainly have time to study under Vasilia. She could learn what she needed as the future Elder. Cipriana dragged a hand down her face. For now, she had to think about the mission ahead. "I'm going to pack these to take with us. They could be useful as we meet with each of the elders."

Parthenia frowned. "I don't know if that's the wisest idea, but I trust your judgment." She paused and lowered her voice. "I need to go see Gavin, but I'll be back in the morning."

"You better."

"I would never allow you to go alone."

"Be safe." With a small dip of her head, Cipriana split off and headed toward her own home. The next in line as Elder. She inhaled and exhaled a deep breath. She had to stop thinking about this. There was a lot that needed to be done to prepare for the journey ahead. Planning the route they would take, not just as they left the gates, which no one had opened in hundreds of years. The burden of her people's fate felt immense as she exhaled a deep sigh.

Some had said more than once in the course of the last three days that their people were suffering. She stopped halfway to her home and glanced out across the village. They weren't just suffering; they were dying into extinction. Most of the older females were past their final reproductive cycle, and even if they had one remaining, there wasn't anyone to reproduce with. The Poppy Fields were dying off one section at a time. The Reflection Pools had been slowly drying up. Barely two of the nine remained functional. Their gardens hadn't grown at the normal rate, either.

It was these things that Vasilia had been worrying over as the years went on. This was an opportunity to change the course of her people's survival. Not just for herself, but for her younger sisters and half-sisters as well. They depended on her and Parthenia to establish these peace treaties with the other species on the isle.

Cipriana turned toward the houses and continued on her way.

Who knew? Maybe it would mean mates for the remaining sirens in Pteryrina. Sunlight seemed to dance on her upturned lips, her eyes sparkling with unrestrained delight. It would be nice to see them all happy instead of just going through their daily routines. After all, Parthenia had found joy with a shape shifter mate.

Chapter Three

What the hell? Easing out of her glide, Thalasia lowered herself closer to the salty water. Between the two isles sat an empty boat. It didn't appear to fit over three or four people. Had the prisoner used it as part of its escape? She stared at it for a moment and studied the direction it pointed. It floated back toward Candescent Isle. Son of a bitch. This could only mean one thing: the guiler that had gotten free, along with his companions, were somewhere on Prisma Isle.

"Shit." This wasn't good. Not good at all. Thalasia turned around and flew toward Prisma Isle. Fuck, she hoped Seru got back soon. They really needed to figure out what to—her body shook and pain speared her frontal lobe.

In her mind's eye, she saw a brown-headed female and a red-headed male as they stood in front of a hut, speaking to one another. As quickly as the image appeared, it disappeared. It took a moment for her eyesight to return to normal. Thalasia tossed the vision around. The female was obviously a siren, but the male didn't look like a full siren. He had the bird-like feet they all did, but no wings she could see. Half-breed.

Plus, they still had to find—a bolt of lightning stirred her from her thoughts and forced her to pull mid-way back to the shore. Her gaze flicked back and forth as she scanned the shoreline. She'd left a short time ago. A smile crossed her lips, and she flew back to the shore as if her next breath stood in front of her.

Once she had him in her sight, it didn't take her long to get to her destination. Her initial intention had been to wrap herself around him, but something seemed off. Not to mention there was an enormous pile of grain next to him. What the—she frowned. Only one explanation came to mind. She slowed her approach and landed less gracefully than she should have, sand churning beneath her talons. "Dare I ask?"

Seru threw up his arm to shield his eyes against the sand kicked up by her descent. The particles clung to an exposed wound. A hiss escaped him as he lowered his arm to inspect it. His gaze shifted from his arm to her as he reached out and took her by the hand. "I think it's time we find that tree," he said. "We need to talk."

Her gaze fell upon the blisters running the length of his arm. "You're hurt." That bothered her more than she expected. Her eyes flicked to the stone creature next to them. Did it have something to do with his injury? And if it resulted from another guiler—they had definitely found their way across.

Seru, disregarding her words, drew her in and inhaled deeply, burying his nose in the curve of her neck.

She hadn't been able to stop her arms from coming around him. Biting her bottom lip, tingles ran the length of her spine. She didn't think she'd ever get used to that.

"We need to get off the beach," he said.

"I scouted for the tallest tree while I was out. It's along the edge, so we should be able to avoid the fae. Theoretically."

"It'll have to do," he replied, running a hand through his mane.

Standing there in front of him, it occurred to her that he was naked. Very naked. Despite her curiosity, she kept her eyes on his face and broad chest. Nope. She wouldn't look—she had to focus. He was wounded, and there was a lot she had to tell him. Plus, he seemed to have information to share as well. "I don't suppose you left your clothes and things stored somewhere nearby. Not that I don't enjoy you like this—minus the injury."

His eyes shifted to regard her for the first time fully since she'd landed. He studied her silver eyes and couldn't help but offer a strained smile in response. "Like what exactly?" His voice came out a touch raspy but mostly teasing.

A slight flush touched her cheeks as she stared at him. They had talked about her so-called pheromones, and that hadn't embarrassed her. She had told him she was a virgin, and *that* didn't embarrass her. Yet somehow, talking about him standing there, completely nude, made her blush. "Without clothes," she replied huskily as tingles ran down her spine. She bit her bottom lip, and unintentionally her gaze dropped lower and lower and lower until she forced her eyes back to his.

Seru squeezed her hand with a low chuckle. "You go ahead. I'll keep an eye on you from here. Once you make it safe, I'll circle back for the supplies and follow." He traced a finger along her jawline before placing a kiss on her cheek.

"Okay, but I'm taking care of that arm as soon as you get up there." Geez, she needed to get it together. He hadn't been the only man she'd seen naked. It was just flesh. Right? Right. Focusing on what they needed to accomplish, an ever-growing list, she flew into the air toward the tree she had seen on her scout for the missing prisoner.

She glanced over her shoulder once or twice so she could monitor him. His injury really concerned her. Although she knew little about his healing capabilities, it seemed to keep getting worse.

He turned back down the beach. It didn't take long for him to reclaim the items he'd stashed, along with some of his clothing. Slipping a small collection of objects into the folds of his pants, he hoisted the remaining bundle on his back.

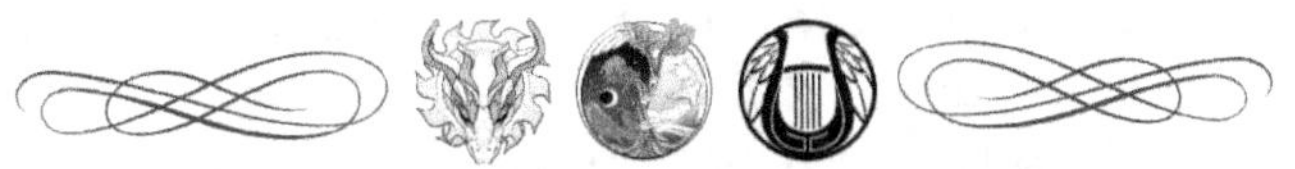

Parthenia's gaze didn't leave the ground as she continued making her way toward the treehouse. Usually, she would have flown, but her mother's last words echoed in her mind, distracting her from the journey. *You are no daughter of mine.* The trip had likely taken a little over an hour between the mix of flying and walking.

Why couldn't she just get out of her head? Sharing the news of the meeting she had been in for three days was bad enough. Now, she had to go to her mate with this on her shoulders, too? What had she ever done to deserve this? Chewing on the inside of her cheek, she lifted her gaze long enough to recognize she'd arrived at the tree. With a gentle push, she took off into the sky and flew to the top.

Gavin had been at the entrance before she even reached it. She hadn't fully landed before he drew her into his arms and buried his face in the crook of her neck. He took a deep breath, her scent filling his nostrils. "I missed you."

"I missed you, too." She stroked the back of his head, her fingers grazing over his ears as her wings wrapped around him tightly. There was no doubt he had felt her rollercoaster of emotions over the last few days. More than once, she could've used him there, simply for moral support. Gods, she didn't want to move from his arms. Eventually, she'd have to share what happened—all of it—but for now, she just wanted to stand here and let his aroma, warmth, and love wash over her.

As they breathed together, she took in his familiar scent, their breaths matching like music. A soft purr emanated from her mate as her fingers slowly stroked his head. Several minutes passed before he uttered a word. "I know you have news," he said, gently nuzzling her neck. "May we stay like this while you tell me?"

"Gods, yes." Maybe it would be easier to tell him if they remained like this, in one another's arms. No, it wouldn't. She just needed to light the match and tell him what had occurred. Because tomorrow morning would come too soon, and she'd agreed to return so she and her half-sister could leave together. Part of that worried her for more than one reason. Not just having to figure out how to meet with Markham without meeting Markham, but how to spend that much time away from her mate. These last three days alone had been unbearable. She was certain she hadn't slept since the last time they parted ways.

An entire trip around the isle to visit several other Elders would take days. Time, she didn't know if the barrier would remain open. Or if they would figure out how to break the curse. If they even had to break the curse. So many variables and just not enough time to sift through them all. Really? What she and Cipriana needed, a way to divide and conquer. Then maybe everything she and Gavin had dreamed of for months would come to fruition.

It wasn't what they had, but she could pray for it to happen. Heavily, she sighed. "The law is being changed. The restriction against sirens engaging and mating with another species is being abolished." Parthenia bit the inside of her cheek. Good news first. That was always the best way, right? Gods, she hoped so, because there was no way around the next bit of information. "My Elder... she is sending ambassadors to visit with the other species."

Gavin froze. He didn't move, except for the deep breaths he took. "They chose you."

"Cipriana and I, yes." Not that having her half-sister there made the situation any better. Parthenia's hand stilled for a moment on his head before she returned to stroking her fingers across his ears and along the nape of his neck. There had to be a way around this. There had to be. One she hadn't thought of yet. Or one she hadn't yet come across. She sighed again because nothing more about this part got better. It no longer seemed necessary to draw it out. "We leave tomorrow morning."

Gavin inhaled and exhaled several long breaths. Other than that, he stayed right where he was, holding her to him, his face buried in her neck. "Okay, alright." Another deep breath. "Where do you two plan to go first?"

That was a simple enough question to answer. Although she hadn't noticed it on the map Devin had finished for her; the half-breed village had appeared on the one Vasilia had given them. Her glimpse had been brief, but she'd seen enough to gather the name of the current Elder. She suspected Cipriana would well use the artifacts presented by their Elder. Talk about—nope, she couldn't focus on that now. Information first, then she could tell him everything else. "Migas, the half-breed village. We'll travel counterclockwise, which will leave the shape shifter and manticore villages last. I'm praying for another solution to present itself before then. One that will keep me away from Métamorphe. I know this isn't the outcome we had hoped for, at least not altogether, but I'm," she let out a deep breath, "trying to have faith that another option will present itself."

Gavin said nothing. No words left his mouth. Silence stretched between them. "What would happen if you did not go to see him? Markham? Is there a way to avoid that? It will make no difference. He will not change. Meeting with him would change nothing."

"If it was just me, I could easily avoid it." But it wasn't that simple. Not only was Cipriana accompanying her, but her half-sister had also been named the next Elder. It was like dropping one bomb after another. Gods, how were they supposed to get through all of this? Just like they had been. One minute at a time. One issue at a time. Even if they all bled together at the moment, they could only tackle one problem at a time. "You and I both know it will make no difference, but Cipriana—she was named the next Elder of my species. I can attempt to convince her to skip Métamorphe, but as the next in line, I don't know that she will."

Gavin blinked a few times. "The next in line? Wow... um..." His words trailed off. "What if I spoke to her? Who better than?" He shrugged. "Someone like me? Someone who knows the dangers of his laws, of breaking them, of who he is, and what he does. I know how set he is in his ways, for lack of a better wording. If what he does to his people is any sign... He would have no interest in speaking to anyone of another species. Be it Elder, Elder-to-be, or otherwise. It would not change who he is, his ways, his decisions. He has tortured and killed his own for the same thing. Not to mention what he would do to—no, what he had done to someone like me. Like us." Gavin pulled back just a touch and lifted his gaze to hers. Bringing his hand to her face, he caressed her cheek. "You cannot go," he whispered. A tear pricked the corner of his eye, and he blinked it back furiously. "Please, there has to be... there has to be another way."

She swallowed the fear and leaned into the gentle comfort of his touch. His emotions were running as rampant as her own. She could feel it, although she could tell he tried to bury his concern over what the days would bring. Maybe the information that he provided Cipriana would suffice. Visiting the shape shifter village was days away. There were a few other Elders to speak with in be-tween. Her eyes widened ever so slightly as their gazes held. "What if you joined us? For now. Maybe what you tell her about Markham will convince her to avoid Métamorphe. Vasilia stated to stay on the boundaries, but I know that wouldn't do any good. As it would be amongst the last, whatever you can teach her, it might be enough."

He stood there quietly. Although his arms remained wrapped around her body, he stilled. With his thumb, he stroked her cheek as he softly pressed his forehead to hers. "There would be much danger in that, for the both of you. My scent would follow you. If we traveled during the day, there would be a possibility of running into his Informants. I know I am still hunted. Markham would not give up his search. But... if you think I would have a chance of convincing her... that could be an option. I could stay camouflaged and stick to the trees as often as possible. And... we would get to stay together."

Was it selfish of her to ask him to journey with them? It had been torture being so far away for so long. But she would rather deal with that than risk his life. She needed him alive and healthy. Not that she had any idea what they would cross in their travels. Everything she knew of the other species had all come from books. This was completely different. "These past three *umbras* have been like death. I don't wish to be away from you any longer. And I also believe you may be the only one to convince her of the importance of staying away from the shape shifter boundaries, but I loathe the idea of even risking your life."

"My life is at risk every single *umbra*, my love. As it was in that village, and even more so now. Neither of us knows what the future holds, not tomorrow or even the next *lacuna* from now. It has been... absolute misery to be parted from you. Every moment gets more and more difficult to bear. If we can eliminate that, if we can be together and possibly convince her of the dangers of associating with him in any way… it would be more than worth it." He nodded a little, not moving his forehead from hers. "I would like to go. I do not want to be away from you, not a single moment longer."

"Me, either. I told Cipriana I was staying here tonight, and we would reconvene in the morning." It wasn't as if she had anything left to go back to Pteryrina for, anyway. Yes, she had left many things in her apothecary, but she had tucked the most important items in the treehouse a while ago. Anything she wished to take with her when they left was here. Her fingers lightly skimmed the nape of his neck as she continued to hold on to him. Truly, he was all she needed. Everything else was just material, which she could replace. He couldn't. "I'll show you how to get to the front gates. That's where Cipriana and I will leave from."

He nodded, a small smile growing on his face as he arched his neck into her touch. "Okay. Good. This is good. This will be good. We will stay together, and we will continue to figure out everything together. That is the only way I want to do anything, together with you. And perhaps I will even be able to convince Cipriana about Markham as well."

"Maybe we'll run into that siren we saw. She may know things we haven't found. And this way we learn everything at once. Yes, I like this plan much better." And she might actually sleep. She had gotten the sense that he had slept little, if at all, in the time that they'd been apart. She pressed a soft kiss to his forehead, nose, and either side of his mouth. No matter what happened, she would return to Pteryrina one last time. Then they would take their leave of this isle and be free to be together. Or so she prayed.

He let out a low rumble. "I like it, too." Gavin kissed her forehead, either side of her mouth, and then the side of her neck. "Come and sit with me," he said. "Your heart has been heavy today."

Parthenia nodded. It was funny. Of everything she had to tell him, she thought the Elder naming her as one of their ambassadors would be the most difficult. It wasn't. Her mother's last words to her haunted her memory. She may have only heard them in the last couple of hours, but it felt like she'd heard them all her life. She had known for a long time Amara didn't care for her, but until today, it had never been confirmed. "Yes, let's sit. I'd like that."

Gavin laced their fingers together as he led her to the bedding pallet. Sitting down first, he tugged her until she sat sideways in his lap. He wrapped his arms around her, rested his head on her shoulder, and softly stroked her arm. "What has saddened you, my love? What did she do?"

Of course, he knew whom her thoughts were about. She shrugged the knapsack off her shoulders and set it aside. Draping her arm across his back, she ran her fingers up and down his spine while chewing on the inside of her cheek. Honestly, it shouldn't be so difficult to recount her mother's words, yet it was hard to say them aloud. Amara had had no issues, not that it should surprise her. The female had made it clear they weren't family. The room spun around Parthenia as her mate's fingers traced her arm, a silent plea escaping her lips for a strength she was desperate to find. "She never loved me. Because my father... because he loved me more than her. How is it possible for a mother not to love her child?"

"I do not know. I cannot fathom how it could ever be possible. But I am so very sorry, my love. I wish there were more I could say than that." Gavin moved his head just a touch and stared down at her, his fingers still stroking her arm. "I know it hurts. I know how that feels. But truly, nothing she says means anything. If that is how she feels about you, she is not worthy of your thoughts, your sadness. She does not deserve you." He pressed a soft kiss to the top of her head, then laid his own back on her shoulder. "Family does not have to mean blood. And family, love... we can find it in all kinds of unexpected places. It does not have to be in the place we grew up, with the people we grew up with. Though I know right now, that may not lessen the pain or the sadness any, it does not make it any less true."

His words—she had told herself the same thing since Amara's last declaration. *You are no daughter of mine.* Those last words replayed in her mind again. Parthenia sighed. "I know I shouldn't give her words power. It isn't anything I haven't known, but to have confirmation, an actual declaration that I'm not her child..."

"The painful words have the most power over us, and they are the hardest to overcome. I remember my father saying that to me. Not in those same words, but enough that I knew what he meant. Sometimes, it still hurts, the knowledge that when we leave this place forever, he will not miss me. That he does not miss me now. But I try to think of those in my life who love me, no matter what. They may be few, but those connections mean more to me than he ever could. For me, it is enough to find comfort in that." He placed a soft kiss on her neck. "I wish I could take this heartache from you, love."

He was right. They held a lot of power, but she didn't want to give them power. Maybe that was the key. Not just to think about those who loved her, whom she loved in return, but that the words only held power if she allowed them to. A soft smile fell upon her face as she leaned her head against his. She could make a choice not to let her mother's words hurt her. Her mother intended those words to hurt her, but she didn't have to listen to them, think about them, or even remember them. Parthenia stroked the nape of her mate's neck. "I think you have, my love. I think you have."

A soft purr left him. "Did I?"

"Yes. You reminded me words only have power if we let them. She made her choice, and I choose not to let her have the power. I have a wonderful mate, whom I adore, and a new sister." It had been weeks since they'd last spoken. It was safer for Gabby, as well as Gavin, if she steered clear of the treehouse. But with the barrier broken... "Soon, the four of us will leave this isle altogether, and we'll make a new life somewhere together. That's all the family I need."

"And that is all the family I need as well, my love." He nuzzled her neck. "I am looking forward to that *umbra* more than I can say."

"Me, too." Maybe they could just stay like this. Forego traveling to the other Elders entirely. No. As much as she wanted to spend her life with Gavin, she needed to do this. Not just for her species, but for the two sisters in Pteryrina she actually cared about. Cipriana and Fantasia both deserved the chance to find love, as she had. They were the reason she'd take this journey. That, and it might give her and Gavin the answers they needed to break the curse.

Chapter Four

When Thalasia got to the tree she had selected for her and Seru; she sat down cross-legged. There was plenty of room for both of them, sitting up or even lying down together. Had she really ogled him? To be fair, she had mentioned the ways they could take time for themselves while they focused on what they had to accomplish. Not that it meant she had to eye his perfectly formed body. What she assumed was an impressive body. She had nothing to compare it to. Or that she even knew anything about—why was she thinking about this?

Inhaling and exhaling a couple of deep breaths, she attempted to stop her thoughts from going any further. First thing, he needed to be treated. They could talk while she did that. She peered over the branches to check his progress. At the tree base, Seru located nearby shrubbery to conceal the bundle on his back before he began his ascent. The wide trunk boasted plenty of robust limbs that quickly became sturdy handholds and footholds.

While he climbed, she could do what was necessary to keep her secret. Scooting back so she was out of sight, she dropped the glamour from her feet and removed her boots and socks. The sirens here had talons. It meant she had to have them, too. In that way, she played the part. With her shoes off, she untied the purple purse attached to her jeans and stowed the boots and socks away. Pulling the glamour back on, she drew the strings of her purse shut tight and hung it up out of the way.

By the time Seru reached her—patiently waiting from her perch—he'd resorted to relying solely on his uninjured arm. "I'm surprised you haven't started nodding off up here."

"I don't think the things going on in my head right now would allow that to happen." She wasn't sure if she'd sleep at all throughout the night. His nakedness had offered a brief reprieve from the concern that had settled the second she had spotted that empty boat. Well, canoe really. It hadn't been big enough to carry many dark guilers. That wasn't the point.

She tilted her head and nodded to the wrap around his wounded arm. Once he had gotten himself situated, Thalasia moved closer until she sat next to him. "Care to share how this happened while I heal it?"

"You shouldn't touch it," he replied, unwinding the now soaked and sticky bandage. "I don't want it to burn you or spread. Whatever it is... my body should have healed it already, but it's sapping my magic. The dark guiler who gave it to me... it escaped." He admitted bitterly. "It wielded an earth magic that it used to create these... these masks, these puppets. They looked and sounded real. Three girls. From the village. It wore their faces to trick me. To watch me. If there are more like it, we can't trust our eyes or ears. If they're hiding among the villagers or disguising themselves as our friends, our allies..."

"And here I thought the escaped prisoner was going to be the bad news of the night." She inspected the skin, noticing its angry red color and the way it was raised. Maybe it was a good thing her powers were growing and that she'd inadvertently healed the burns on that guiler without touching him. "I don't think I'm going to need to touch it. At the very least, I'm hoping this works again. I'll explain in a second."

"Escaped? The fire starter. He's gone?" Seru asked in disbelief.

That was the least of her concerns at the moment. Although he kept his arm away from her, she could see how bad it had become, even from this angle. Her mind once again returned to how easily she'd healed the burns on that guilder in the village. Certain it resulted from her powers, she had to test her theory. She removed the crystal from her pocket and tucked it between the two of them. "Just hold out your arm."

His teeth sank into his talon. He slowly withdrew the pointed nail from between his lips. Hesitantly, Seru ultimately abided by her command and extended his trembling arm.

Inhaling a deep breath, she focused on the injury itself, hovered one hand above his forearm and the other hand below it. The same silver that had covered her body earlier now coated her hands. With careful placement, she created a connection on each side of his arm.

With unwavering concentration, Thalasia saw the silver light softly entering the injury, cleaning it while slowly mending the damaged skin.

A shaky sigh escaped Seru's mouth. "New trick?"

Thalasia didn't speak until the wound had fully healed. Once it had, she leaned back against the tree. It had been pretty deep. While she felt slightly tired, it wasn't to the degree she expected. Her powers were growing, which would make it harder to hide the truth of her species from him. "Honestly, I don't know. I did the same thing earlier with a guiler that had gotten badly burned. It was like second nature, as if my body, my hands, just knew." She had to lie, but gods it felt wrong. With a sigh, she pinched the bridge of her nose, the pressure a slight comfort. "For a second, I thought it had to do with the crystal you gave me to hold, but I just took it out of my pocket. Something else happened, too, but let me back up a second."

Thalasia sat up. "Yes, the fire starter escaped. I came up to a dead guiler, the guard I put to sleep earlier when I got back. His body..." She paused a minute. There had to be a simple way to describe what had happened. "It disintegrated before my eyes."

"Like crumbling ruins or the ash from a dead tree being carried away on the breeze?"

"Neither. It was more like he bubbled into a puddle." She frowned as she thought back to how the guiler had died.

He remained silent for some time. After a while, he reached over and invited her closer while they both struggled to process the newfound information. "What about your... power? Have you noticed any negative side effects? Anything we should be concerned about?" His expression softened as he turned to her.

Quickly, she tucked the crystal back into the pocket of her pants. Leaning against him, her head on his shoulder, one hand on his chest, she thought back to the vision she had as she flew over the ocean. No strange side effects at all. It was as if she were more energized than she'd ever been before. "No. It just seems like my powers are getting stronger. I had a vision while I was over the water. Normally, they knock me back, force me to my knees, like the one I had on the bridge. This one... it was just the flash of images with less kick. If I've figured it out right, we need to head to the half-breed village before we seek the manticore."

Seru buried his nose in her hair, allowing his fingers to play along her skin. "What's in the half-breed village?"

"I saw a siren, a normal-looking one, talking to a half-breed. At least I believe he's one. He had the same feet but no wings that I could see. I know you've said the sirens hadn't left Pteryrina for years, so if one is going to be down here on the isle, she may be the one who gives us a way in." As much as she didn't want to have to go some place her ancestors had left hundreds of years ago, she knew it was inevitable. They had to find the book. Yeah, they had the lyre, but without the book, their knowledge about the barrier was minimal. Plus, the one prophecy she needed to find... make sure she fulfilled it right.

"Do you think it's the same siren that's been seen in the forest?" Seru asked, displeasure seeping into his tone.

She had nearly forgotten someone had referenced one as having been seen. If that was the case, why would she be talking to a half-breed? Unless—was it possible the sirens knew about the barrier? As it seemed to be created by the sirens, it made sense. "Maybe, but it doesn't explain why she'd go to the half-breed village. I'm not even sure anyone here even knows the barrier existed."

Pausing a moment, she focused on the sound of his words versus the words themselves. "You don't sound like you're happy about going to the half-breed village."

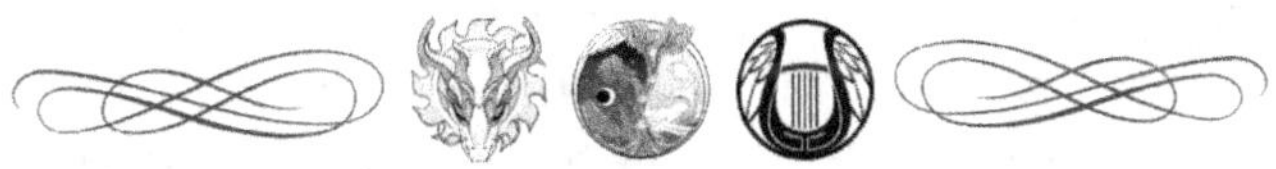

"I wouldn't be so sure," Seru mumbled against her hair. He took a steadying breath before responding. "The dragons—much like the sirens—are purists. Purity breeds strength. Co-mingling promotes weakness, not just in blood or magic, but of the body and mind. It's a corruption of the..." he closed his eyes, searching for a common tongue substitute.

"The essence," he decided. "The Matriarch didn't just target the earthbound. She set us after the mixed breeds, too. I've slaughtered many of their ancestors. Eliminated an entire species for Her new world. They're enemies. So, no, Thalasia. I don't look forward to encountering former *friends* from that time, or their offspring. You'll be surprised how long spilled blood sours relations."

Was it hypocritical of him to relish the thought of plucking a few Phoenix quills from that half-breed siren? Especially now. As he held a full-blooded siren in his arms?

Yes, yes, it did. Somehow, that thought didn't sit well with him. Soft static buzzed across his exposed arms, down his chest. Another deep breath of Thalasia's scent. He forced the agitated energy back down.

Taking a deep breath, she rearranged her head a little and snuggled a little closer. A few minutes passed before she uttered a word regarding his admission. "Maybe we won't be there long. Or, we come across her outside the village, except... the half-breed who gave me the information about this village... maybe she can point us toward the manticore." Thalasia swept her hair over her shoulder and played with the ends of it. "Not to mention, it'll give us the chance to deal with two at once. See if they know anything about the barrier."

"It's my experience outside the safety of the market; the more species that come together, the more trouble that comes with it," Seru grumbled. Putting age-old differences aside was an uphill battle. *Up the side of an extremely steep cliff,* he thought. "But we'll do what we can, though we may have to improvise our initial plan."

He thought back to their former conversation about posing as an interspecies couple to infiltrate the half-breed village. If a full-blooded siren and the Phoenix siren were present, their ruse would be up the moment they set foot in the village. He and Santos hadn't exactly left things on positive terms. Killing the half-Phoenix for the sake of curiosity and stealing his quills left them open to hostility, especially if Santos kept his status of leadership within the community. He wondered idly if killing him again would solve half their troubles. Santos would revive, after all. Not that he'd come across a way to kill off his species, much like he hadn't come across a way to end his imprisonment in nearly 800 years. Seru fidgeted with his collar. One complexity after another. Their problems continued to grow.

"Do you think it would be better if I went in alone?" Thalasia continued to play with the ends of her hair. "I mean, we've known there was the possibility that other species would know what's going on. But, getting a vision of a siren interacting with species on this level when you said they hadn't left Pteryrina in hundreds of years... something is going on. Maybe even beyond just the barrier." She shook her head. "I can't explain why, but I feel we need to go there together, as we planned."

"I don't think it's safe for you to go alone. Entering enemy territory solo is rarely a good idea. You're outnumbered should their intentions be less than peaceful. That said..." Seru swallowed. "If the half-breed in your vision is who I think he is... he'll recognize me on sight. Not just as the Matriarch's Regent, but as a saint beast." Worse didn't cover the implications. He refused to let her go in blind, even if it meant revealing the uglier truths about himself.

"Well, if it is... maybe he won't say anything." Thalasia frowned. "Or do you two have a history?"

Seru did everything in his power to avoid looking at her as he answered. "I may have killed him. Once. Just for fun. I wanted to see what happened when he regenerated. It seemed like an entertaining way to pass the time." There, he'd said it. He cringed. He could only imagine how that must have sounded to her.

Thalasia blinked. She opened her mouth and snapped it shut. Then, softly groaning, she rubbed her forehead. "Okay. Well, we'll... at the moment, I feel like praying he doesn't remember *that* isn't much of an option." She sighed. "I know the consequences of turning away from a vision. We just have to play this out. They've never steered me wrong, and I can't believe they'd start now."

Seru shrugged. "We aren't defenseless. Worst case, we *let* them take us prisoner and see if he ousts me. Aurelia wouldn't like it, but the only way they could kill me is through an alliance with the reaper. That's unlikely. And I won't let them harm you. No matter the consequences." He inclined his head, thoughtfully looking up into the canopy. "Or you could deliver me as a prisoner." His eyes shifted back to her. "Pretend you're on their side. The siren is likely only a visitor. Santos wouldn't have been to their homeland any more than we have. He wouldn't have reason to suspect you're not from Pteryrina."

Bolting upright, Thalasia's head whipped in his direction. "I'm not delivering you as a prisoner. You can forget that, right here, right now." Her words were firm. She ground her jaw. "Depending on how long ago he was reborn, it wouldn't be hard to tell I'm not from Pteryrina. One, the siren I saw him talking to was wearing attire from there. Two, I may still have the dress, but honestly, after what happened in the shop, I'm a little wary of wearing it. Three, Aurelia may not like color; sirens don't, either. Finally, even if I had been born on the isle, they would've never allowed me to live in Pteryrina."

"It would only be to gain their trust. I can break free should things get too out of hand. Perhaps the glowing stone Aurelia gifted us can aid in our disguise." Seru lifted his chin. "Make this match your wings. Imbue it with your silver magic, and it should be enough to call up Verie's residual magic still stored inside. If we believe Mac's prophecies, the sirens should revere you. If we bolster the illusion with me as your captive, they should believe you seek to work with them—against one of their more formidable enemies. Though it may cause trouble for the Clouds later. We'll worry about that when we get there."

She shook her head. "I'm *not* offering you up as bait. I don't care if you can break free or not. It's not happening." Thalasia dragged a hand through her blue hair. Pulling her knees up, she leaned forward and smirked. "If the half-breeds I ran into at the bar are any indication, they won't care that I'm a siren. They didn't seem to care then." With a heavy sigh, she shifted her gaze to Seru. "What do you know of this half-breed elder?"

Seru nestled into her neck and smiled. "He's not nearly as beautiful or nearly as tasty as you." He kissed along her neck and her shoulder.

She visibly shivered. As she glanced at him over her shoulder, a soft chuckle, like a gentle breeze, drifted from her mouth. "Thank you, but that doesn't tell me much."

"Mm, maybe I'm just not trying hard enough," he replied, drawing her closer.

She was practically in his lap, as close as they were now. Her body warmed beneath his touch. "Oh? And if you tried harder, what would that tell me?"

"That depends," Seru mused, enjoying her reaction. "Do you trust me?"

"Implicitly."

At her word, he pulled her to her feet. Taking both her hands in his, he guided her to the center of the hollow. Seru felt her intense eyes on him, waiting for a sign of what he was up to. "What would you do to keep this?"

Tilting her head at him, she stared into his eyes. "Anything."

"Good." His eyes lingered on her a moment longer before regarding what little he could see of the heavens through the dense canopy. His connection to what lay overhead wasn't nearly as deep as Aurelia's. He could sense the stars, but couldn't truly see them. He aligned her opposite the sun. Not as good as aligning her with her natural ruler, the moon. But since that wasn't possible in broad daylight, he'd make do. He gave her hands a gentle squeeze, bending forward to place a kiss on her brow.

"Remain standing." Looping a finger through the string securing her top, he unfastened the tie at the base of her neck. He traced from that point off her shoulder along her collarbone, hoping to set her at ease with the clearly delineated path. He followed his touch with kisses.

Biting her bottom lip, Thalasia shivered again as her wings slowly extended.

As he dipped into the divot of her collarbone, he appreciated the entire span of her wings and the way she responded to his touch. Steadying her with his hand on her back, he loosened the remaining ties of the piece of cloth that matched her wings. He continued to trace a slow path downward, only stopping once his lips met her soft midriff. He gently nuzzled her, careful to guard his fangs from her belly as he bathed in her warm, intoxicating scent.

Her hands settled on his shoulders as her fingers gently played with his mane. Goosebumps crawled across her skin beneath his slight touch. Still, she continued to stand there without question.

When he got to her waistband, he felt along its edge, exploring the strange material. "Your homeland has an interesting choice in clothing, Thalasia," he breathed against her abdomen in a breathless laugh. His fingers clumsily discovered the button and unfastened it. The material was strangely thick, rough, and durable, excellent for someone constantly on the move. Challenging to remove.

A soft chuckle left her mouth as she smiled down at him. "I can't say I've ever heard that before. Then again, every realm I've ever been to is unique in its own way."

Her phrase caught him off guard, halting his progress as he pulled the pants down her legs. He looked up at her; an expression that rarely touched his face broke past his usual calm composure. "What's a *realm*?" He felt suddenly lightheaded as he attempted to think through the heady mixture of heat and smell her body was throwing off. *Was she really affecting him that much?*

Thalasia's eyes widened ever so slightly at his question. "Um, well, this would be one. Different worlds, I guess, would be another way to describe it. Of course, this isn't the only world in existence." Her brow creased in a frown. "The universe is far larger than anything we could imagine, but they are all connected. Some lines allow me to travel between worlds, guided by my visions."

He seemed to accept her answer before lowering his lips back to her exposed skin. The kisses were coming slower, but just as surely as before. His mind struggled to process her revelation. It surprised and concerned him. He did his best to push down his instinct's response, promising to return to the subject at a later time.

Right now, he needed to focus on crowning her while the opportunity presented. She might not be so open and willing later. Even though it felt so natural with her, he still wasn't sure how much of their affection for one another was permanent, and how much was potentially a result of the pheromonal reaction Mac had hinted at. Would siren pheromones even work on another species? Did that explain his recent lack of focus when she was around?

As he sank onto his knees, the expanding pool of questions swirling inside him seemed to vanish in the face of her standing bare before him. Her scent, no longer contained beneath her clothes, drew his attention to her completely. The rest of the world slipped away in a haze of sweet aromas and her taste in his mouth.

Thalasia's eyes met his, a soft shine to her silver eyes. She completely stilled. Heat radiated from her body as she bit her bottom lip.

The sudden spike in heat did precisely what it was meant to. Seru's hands held fast to her thighs as his beast stirred, rising to the surface at the taste of magic and the promise of sex.

His mouth hovered just above her lower belly; fangs pressed against her as he felt the beast staring out from his eyes. It wasn't seizing control but waiting, wondering why its human counterpart was laying claim to a creature with feathers rather than scales. She smelled good, but different. It forced a questioning rumble from between his lips, vibrations across her sensitive skin.

He hoped it stayed subdued as he guided her thigh up and over his shoulder. There was a soft shine in her silver eyes as a slight gasp passed between her lips. Traditionally, the ceremony required dragons to shed their human form to stake their claim. Here, that wasn't an option. And usually, it was the female who claimed the male, assuming his worship of her met her approval. He was improvising on the spot and hoping beyond hope that the earlier feeding kept his beast in check. He needed the beast to accept Thalasia as worthy, on the same level as he did.

With a steadying breath, he grazed the fangs down her thigh and resumed kissing, from just above the knee, upward to the apex of her thighs.

The feel of her fingers interlaced in his mane triggered a response from the beast. It hummed against the sweet spot between her thighs. He felt the brush of feathers on his arms and back as Thalasia encircled them with her beautiful, blue wings. They played along his skin, and the beast pressed outward in response, not to escape but more of an attempt to mark her with its scent. A sparkle of iridescent scales surfaced where they touched.

Her knee clutched a little tighter to his shoulder. She gasped again as her fingers tugged a little harder on his mane. A soft moan escaped her mouth. Her wings continued to stroke his arm and back, drawing him closer.

Both Seru and the beast relished the sound of her pleasure as their lips parted and their tongue drove into her sex. Keeping a close guard on their fangs as the beast encouraged his efforts proved challenging. Its desire for more of her special song pressed them deeper into her, intensifying the building rhythm as they explored her, determined to taste all of her.

His grip tightened, rising to just beneath the exquisite curve of her ass, before the tips of his talons bit into her flesh. A tangy copper was joining the mix. He used his hold on her to burrow even deeper into her, a warning growl reverberating through him. If left unchecked, the beast would unwittingly ride her into oblivion with its eagerness and raw power fueling their pursuit of those musical sounds.

Another moan passed her lips as her grip on his mane tightened, and one of her talons gently scraped along his shoulder blades. Her head fell back as her thighs tensed and her orgasm gushed out, coating his tongue; a silver glow covered her from head to toe as she cried out in ecstasy.

Seru forcibly reined in his beast as she cried out for them. He pulled his mouth from her with some reluctance. Its instincts drove it toward more, uncomprehending of the limits of her softer flesh. They weren't finished. Blue electricity danced in Thalasia's silvery glow, his collar glowing in tune with hers. Their magic, though vastly different—one dangerously electrifying and one soothingly healing—joined for the first time. The soft halo enveloping her signified the moon's presence and served as a confirmation of her being crowned his glory.

He relocated some of the beast's strength into supporting Thalasia above them as its demands overruled his carefully constructed control. With this stage of the ceremony completed, Seru allowed the beast a bit more freedom. Not that he had much choice as it forced their muzzle back to her delicious center. Its tongue slowly savored her, leaving none of her untouched, untasted. Once it achieved contentment that every inch of her belonged to them, it continued, reclaiming her with zeal.

Her hands left their hold on his mane and grabbed onto his arms. The silver beads in his mane sounded a nearly imperceptible tinkling as her hands freed their grip. Never-ending moans left her mouth, louder each time one passed her lips. More and more orgasms rocked through her body.

The beast kept at her relentlessly, refusing to part with her until her body gave out. Licking clean their maw, it receded, satisfied with the unexpected meal the siren provided. Its serpentine visage and scaly hide soon followed.

Seru sighed, a sense of relief washing through him. He'd felt some remorse at releasing his beast on her that way. She was young and extremely naïve. And he'd relied on their shared ability to overwhelm her. Not fully knowing if he'd be able to retain enough control to keep the beast from turning the sexual ritual into a feast. He spared no small thanks that the beast had accepted her worth and, for once in far too long, done as he'd required. Cradling Thalasia against him, he nestled his thigh between her legs. He allowed her a reprieve, closing his eyes as he listened to her breathing.

For reasons he couldn't describe, his heart sank as he retrieved the stash of supplies from the folds of his pants. The roll of leather housed herbs, makeshift tools, and a small collection of shells from the ocean. He reached into her discarded clothes, recovering the knife she always carried with her, and added it to his arsenal.

Reassessing her shallow breaths, he ensured her deep slumber before setting to work. He first selected a slender, black needle he'd broken off a spiny sea creature coated in a natural toxin. In small animals, it served as a paralytic, immobilizing them until they could be devoured. He hoped it would serve as a numbing agent in a siren, though he wasn't sure of her metabolic rate and how quickly the toxin would pass through her system. Resolving to make this quick and painless, he captured the delicate spine between his teeth as he reached for her wing.

Seru gently probed the area he thought housed the metal charm until he found those trademark dark-blue features indicative of its location. He felt beneath them along the soft skin, and found the smoother, sleeker scar tissue. He held his place with one hand while positioning the spine in his other. Glancing down momentarily at her sleeping face, he offered a quiet apology before finding the slender object a home in her flesh.

While the toxin worked its magic, he ground the herbs into a thick paste before setting it aside. He unsheathed and heated the blade of her dagger. It needed to be clean and sharp. Once he was confident the toxin had seeped into the desired spot on her wing, he removed it. Carefully, he parted the feathers, baring the site to the blade's waiting steel. A small, deep cut along the edge of the scar tissue, where the skin offered less resistance, blossomed red with blood. He prayed her slumber remained undisturbed, and that she rested in blissful ignorance through his surgery on her wing.

Seru set the blade aside, its purpose served. He gently found purchase around the metal embedded in her skin, massaging the site until little by little the bloodstained object emerged. It dropped into his palm with relative ease. Turning it over, he inspected it. Some form of a string instrument. A few strands were missing or snapped. He placed it in a shallow recess in the tree where a pool of rainwater had collected.

Repositioning her against him, he gave them both a more comfortable angle as he moved to suck the tainted blood from her wing. A few small mouthfuls were enough to rid her blood of the putrid taste of the metal's poison. He spat out the foul-tasting liquid, unable to abide the flavor. Suffering through the taste, he reclaimed the spine. Free of the toxin, it served as a companion to the small spool of silk, which he used to mend and close the wound. He wasn't sure how much their shared experience had drained her, and though he was confident she could heal the wound on her own, especially after her earlier hands-free show with his arm, he still felt wrong leaving it open and untended.

Polishing off his handiwork, Seru cleaned and restored the blade to its proper resting place, discarding the remaining tools in their tiny pouch over the side. He knew tasks awaited him, but before he tackled them, he'd find solace in her company, feeling the warmth of their bond.

Chapter Five

Mac eyed the sea below as he soared above the clouds. His green wings blended well with the midnight-blue night sky. He hadn't ever ventured this far out of the village. Most of his training occurred in the forest, but never beyond that. At least he had one thing going for him; he knew where on Candescent Isle Felix would be. Getting there would be the problem. Taking a second to ensure his companion wasn't far off, he continued toward the western region of the isle. Landing close to the earth element would be their safest bet.

With a good cluster of mountains and large mounds in sight, Mac flew in that direction. Keeping an eye out for arrows, he began his descent and frowned. From this distance, the jagged edge appeared barren and bleak. Was it supposed to look like that? No matter. It was likely the best they'd get without scouting the entire isle over the next few hours. Trying to land closer to the central region would be too dangerous. Tucking his wings in tight, he dove beneath the clouds, only checking once to see Aurelia follow behind him toward the surface.

Once he got within fifty feet of the ground, he spread his wings and neatly landed with the skill of a dancer. Not that the appearance lasted. Long, black tendrils billowed outward around their ankles.

Aurelia wrinkled her nose, shaking the chilling vapors off her person. She stumbled; a rough landing didn't do it justice. Palms splayed as her knees impacted the jagged mountainside.

Trying to take in a breath, Mac coughed several times. Good stones, what was that stench? Why was the air so damn thick? It burned the back of his throat the more he tried to breathe through the mass of darkness. They couldn't stay here. Tears pricked the corners of his eyes as he sought Aurelia. He weaved slightly over to where she sat, hacking up her lungs. Then, forgetting all about his aversion to touching anyone, he hefted her up by her arms and started her forward. "We need to move."

Clutching at her chest, she attempted to croak out a reply. Nothing but wheezing in response to the toxic fumes. The world around them swam on the icy rapids, careening back and forth with dark, inky splotches.

The last thing he wanted was to have any female close to him. Anyone really. He hated having to aid her, but there wasn't any choice. He needed her help with this rescue.

Good gods, this place was nothing like what Felix had described. But, then again, the male hadn't been born here, and from what he'd been told, the male's father, who had come from here, had died a couple of hundred years ago.

Pushing forward, Mac sought cleaner air for the two of them as he carried more of Aurelia's weight than he liked. If this had gone his way, they would've walked next to one another six feet apart. That way, there'd be no chance they'd ever touch. Unfortunately, he didn't know how far they'd have to go before the dark tendrils would release their vise grip around the two of them.

He found a place out of the worst of the air, and somewhere that was... 'fresh' wasn't the word he'd used to describe it. But the foulness was undoubtedly less than where they'd first landed.

Aurelia reclaimed her footing and shoved herself off his chest. "Hands off, emerald knight."

He didn't need to be told twice to get off. Backing off, Mac put a few feet between them. "I'll remember that next time you're hacking your lungs up."

"Wasn't hacking my lungs up," she grumbled. "I was acclimating to the... whatever the fuck you want to call this black bullshit this place is infested with." Each breath steadied her a little more than the last until everything seemed back to normal.

"You got me there, princess." He glanced around, his senses still burning from the magic that had been used for such ill intent that it had stained the isle. There was no other explanation. The guilers there had used so much of their elemental magic that it not only caused them further deformity, it had leached into the isle itself.

This was nothing like what he'd heard about. Lush forestry, trees as far-reaching as the sky, radiating warmth—he felt none of it.

And this was only the outer edge. They had to go further inland to the central region. If he hadn't been worried over Felix's chance of survival before—he was more so now.

"Can we just get on with this?" Aurelia asked, fists poised on her hips. Without waiting for an answer, she strode down the slope. She navigated the rocky terrain expertly.

Good fucking gods. He asked for her instead of Thalasia. Why? Oh yeah, pheromones. Not that one was proving better than the other. Then again, he wouldn't have to deal with the blue siren's sexual awakening. Mac grinned just a little. *Have fun, Seru.* Idiot deserved it. With a slight smirk, he followed Aurelia. "We're heading east, by the way."

"Toward the gaping abyss at the center," she said, not bothering to slow her pace. "Roger that, Captain Obvious. Let's go kick some guiler ass, grab your grandpa, and get back before the blue bitch and my love-struck lightning rod destroy your village with their kinky interspecies fuckery."

Oh, she had spunk. Yep. He got the better end of the bargain. Mac chuckled. "Unless he knows something about sirens, he won't get very far." As for his village, he expected to find it a little less disastrous when they returned. The fae would show up to render aid.

"Seru knows a lot about pretty much everything..." she trailed. A shit-eating grin spread across her face as she called back, "I wonder what she'll do when she figures out he's roughly 800 years older than her. You sirens don't live very long. That makes Seru old enough to have fucked her great-grandparents, their parents, and..." Aurelia lowered her voice as she skidded to a stop.

"Considering someone cursed the sirens over a thousand *solaris* ago, I highly doubt that." Leave it to a dragon to use fancy terms instead of the common tongue word. Whatever. He probably shouldn't have admitted what he had, but it didn't bother him any. Unless Seru knew about that, he wouldn't get far with Thalasia. And that kind of amused him.

Aurelia shifted her attention back to him for a moment. "Did some crafty wizard decide to shish kebab a siren on his magic broomstick or something?" She raised her eyebrows, a hint of delight sparkling in her violet eyes.

Ignoring her question for a moment, he scanned their immediate surroundings. As dark as it was, and with the addition of the guiler's magic, it looked like shadows moved in the distance. Was it just him? Or was there something unseen watching them? He had to be seeing things. No telling what all was on this isle, but the only thing he'd ever been told about was the guilers. Surely if there were other creatures to worry about, Felix would've said something. Right? Smirking, he looked back at her. "What? You think the only ones who curse people are wizards? Wow, you're really small-minded. Try Nemesis. Apparently, a siren pissed off the goddess of revenge. At least that's what I was taught."

"No, we just don't believe in your weird, moody gods and goddesses." Aurelia shrugged. "We look to the stars for our divine." She pointed skyward. Switching gears, she redirected his attention. "You see that cluster of guilers over there?" She inclined her chin in their direction.

He quickly overlooked the star comment, as he knew Felix had used the star charts for many years. At least until a couple of months ago when that shape shifter had shown up. Had Aurelia shivered? Was she picking up on something else, too? No, it was just this place attempting to unsettle him. The ethereal darkness was trying to find a way in and extinguish his fire. That's all it was. Nothing more.

His gaze flicked in the direction she pointed. Demeter, he didn't like that. Not one bit. That they were gathering—bothered him on a whole new level. What reason would they have to gather? Unless... were they planning an invasion? "Yes, I can see them."

Aurelia shifted next to him. "You sense your gramps? Or am I free to incinerate them?"

"No, Felix isn't among those dark, earth guilers. Though I'll take a second to point out, it'll draw attention to us if you incinerate them. Something to consider, princess." Not that he expected she'd listen. Not this one. At least if she was going to destroy a few, she could wait until they were on their way out. Not when they didn't know how long it would take them to even get to the central region or what they would face once they were there.

"Isn't that the point?" she asked, deadpan. "Draw them here and away from the old man. You swoop in and rescue while I keep their attention." Her eyes narrowed at him. "Look, if you've got a better plan, I'm all ears."

"Yeah, we keep moving and cause some damage on the way out. Otherwise, we take the chance that killing the first guilers we see is a warning signal and not a distraction, like you hope, princess." Mac smirked. Really. Shouldn't she know that? Or was she just determined to kill every guiler they came across?

Aurelia rolled her eyes, freezing briefly. "You're sounding like Seru." She groaned. "'Exercise patience and attack only when you need to.' If I'd known you were gonna be such a buzzkill, I'd have let you take the blue bitch instead."

"I resent the fact that you just compared me to the boyfriend." Mac crossed his arms and scoffed. Her split-second freeze hadn't gone unnoticed. If she hadn't sensed something else out there besides the guilers, then she might've just then. But why wouldn't she say anything? Probably for the same reason he hadn't. Wonderful. For that alone, he almost wanted to let her have at them. Unless they responded the way he expected, it would take more work for them to rescue Felix. He was a good fighter, but he was no healer.

"Why? What's wrong with Seru? Other than his sudden obsession with blue?" Aurelia asked. "Whatever," she said before he could respond, exasperated and barely containing her laughter. "You lead."

"At least we agree on his poor choice of females." He snickered. "Other than that, I don't know the male." Not that he had any interest in getting to know him, either. He'd seen how Thalasia attached to Seru. For that alone, it made him hate the guy. Not that he'd ever admit that. He had no reason to be attracted to Thalasia to begin with. It wasn't like she was his type or anything.

"Exactly," Aurelia retorted. "How do you hate someone you don't know?"

"Pretty easy to form an opinion when choices are shoved in your face." A judgment could be formed quickly. She'd probably spent more time with Seru and Thalasia than he had, but from the moment he'd met the male... he couldn't stand him. Okay, maybe it had something to do with Thalasia. He didn't *want* to be attracted to Thalasia. He didn't *want* to be attracted to anyone. "Although I could ask you the same thing. You seem to hate Thal, and I don't imagine you know her all that well, either." Mac smirked. Then again, he didn't think she liked anyone. She hadn't exactly been all too eager for anything when she and her company had approached his village.

"You say her name like you're besties," Aurelia commented, annoyance in her tone. "She brought down the barrier and brought these guiler invaders to our door. Which got your village torched and your grandpa condemned to everlasting paradise." She gestured to the decaying landscape around them.

Mac stifled a chuckle. He didn't care if Thalasia stayed or went. And the dragon could blame Thalasia for the barrier all she wanted.

Destiny couldn't be changed. "I have no desire to be friends with her, but you can't change what was meant to happen for centuries. That barrier was always going to come down. One way or another."

"Plus, she's distracting my Regent. I healed her without knowing her, and she's still an insufferable bimbo who thinks she's *special*! Besides, do you really think when it comes down to it, she'll stick around? For you or him?"

Glancing at her out of the corner of his eye, he scanned their surroundings to pick up any slight variation in the surrounding abyss. Whether Aurelia was concerned about it, it bothered him. "I honestly don't care if she sticks around. No sweat off my back. Though I get the feeling that's what concerns you, princess. You finally came across someone not automatically bowing at your feet, just because it's what they *should* do."

"Whether she sticks around, he'll grow bored with her, just like all the others. Lightning fried bird or birdie go poof. It makes little difference how she goes. Just that she does sooner rather than later."

"If someone wants something badly enough, they'll make it happen." Maybe he hadn't been alive as long as she had, but even *he* knew that. Then again, perhaps those two, once left alone, would decide they didn't like the other's company. "Ever think he may not? Or have you considered that as the only option?"

"No."

Slipping away from where they watched the guilers unseen, he started down an unmarked path leading away from the earth guilers and toward the center of the isle. "I'm sure we'll get to kill something on the way, princess. We just have to be smart about it and work together."

She rolled her shoulders as they pressed on. "Unlike you birds, dragons don't operate on a 'flock' mentality. We prefer to solo our kills. Not to worry, though, green bean. I will pay you back so we can call it even."

His eyebrows knitted together. "Flock mentality? Do you see me in a flock? Because last I checked, it takes more than two to make up a flock. Not to mention, I don't exactly fly in the same circles as this so-called flock."

"Your village might not be all bluebirds and emerald finches, but they're still your flock. Don't pretend you don't see that. They'll follow you if anything happens."

No, she was the *only* one he depended on at that moment. To a degree, but he didn't want to point that out. He hadn't missed her slight movements as they headed forward. There was something out there. "You feel it, don't you?"

Her eyes flicked briefly behind him, followed by a curt nod as she continued forward. "I don't feel a thing." She shrugged nonchalantly.

Yeah, she didn't sense it, alright. He frowned as he thought more about what she said regarding his people. That wasn't something he wanted to overthink. They'd get Felix back, and things would go back to normal. "Are you trying to say your people won't follow you?"

"My people aren't followers by nature, but they'll do as I command."

There were tons of prophecies, and he'd only mentioned the one that mattered most. He glanced over his shoulder, certain something was watching, but what was it waiting for? His muscles tensed at the growing shadows that seemed to surround them from all angles. "As for the guilers invading... aren't you dragons accustomed to war? Or do I have my history wrong?" Yeah. He figured out the leader she was. Not the worst kind, but not the best kind, either.

Aurelia glared at him. "Yes, though not under my rule," she responded curtly.

"Oh? So, you're changing it, then?" Yeah, he could tell that was happening. The female was all gung-ho to kill any guilers they came across. The hair on the back of his neck rose. Mac rolled his shoulders, balled up his fist, and ruffled his feathers. He despised the way this place felt.

"Trying to..." she grumbled, a hint of embarrassment creeping into her voice.

It wasn't like they knew what was going on—his ears twitched at a low growl not far behind them. Whatever it was, it definitely wasn't a guiler. The sound had barely been above a whisper. He didn't bother asking his companion if she had heard it. Still, he readied himself to leap into action.

"Getting a tad twitchy over there, birdbrain?" Aurelia asked, giggling at his expense.

The growl behind them came a little louder this time. He slowed his pace and turned, just as an enormous wolf covered in thick, black fur and gleaming, red eyes jumped out and swiped at him. The creature's claws caught him in the side, knocking him to the ground. He slammed his fist into its muzzle, throwing it a few feet back.

Blood seeped into the fibers of his t-shirt. Great. He got back up on his feet, pounded his fists together, green flames licking up his hands and arms. "You can't tell me you don't fucking see it now!"

"Don't!" Aurelia shouted. She cast a spell she must have been silently weaving while she'd pretended not to notice the creature stalking them. A bright halo of light encircled the beast. The runic symbols were taking form beneath its feet. Then, just as the creature stood and lunged in Mac's direction, it froze, suspended by the magic. Even the shadowy miasma engulfing the creature ceased moving.

He watched the flames die down before crossing his arms and staring at the creature. What the fuck did she think they were going to learn from it as it snarled? And it kept coming in his direction even when she'd frozen it mid-air. "Does it think I'll taste better or something?"

Aurelia crept closer, circling the creature. Studying it. She cracked a grin. "Do you *really* want me to answer that?"

The creature registered as canine, large and muscular. The shadows seeped from its every pore. After several minutes of examining it, she reached out to touch the dark patch of fur on its forehead. The taint receded in the wake of her touch, billowing backward and out, revealing slightly lighter coarse fur beneath. "Whoa..." Aurelia dragged her hand back, marveling at the bizarre phenomenon.

Like she'd care if it ate him. He stood there and watched for a moment. His eyebrows knitted together at the revelation before them. "What in the world?" Mac closed the distance between him and the creature, flicking his gaze to Aurelia. "How is that even possible? It looks completely animalistic." Kind of like the seitadi he'd learned about back on Prisma Isle. The creatures had no humanity left.

Aurelia glanced at him out of the corner of her eye before returning her attention to the creature. Fangs bared in a ferocious snarl. Her talon traced the ivory fang closest to her. She let out a sigh. Then, with one hand on her hip, she turned to Mac. "Get your silly green ass over here before I change my mind," she said, pointing to the spot beside her.

Change her mind? Oh, gods. She was going to do something like what she'd done to freeze the creature in place. Mac pinched the bridge of his nose with a heavy exhalation. He might regret this, but right now, he needed her help to get Felix. Whatever she intended to do... he was mainly on board with. He crossed over to where she stood and stopped next to her. "Do I even want to know?"

She gave him an annoyed roll of her violet eyes, batting his arm out of the way as she stopped to inspect his wound. "Just quit your squawking and keep your feathers to yourself, will ya?" She peeled back his shirt, only annoyed further by his obvious discomfort. She hovered her palm over the wound, bathing the deep gashes in radiant light. Her magic warmed the space between her hand and his abdomen. Slowly, the magic found the damaged skin and began remaking the flesh anew, knitting it back together piece by piece, until finally he was whole again. Aurelia let out another sigh. Her brow furrowed. She straightened with a deepening scowl. "What the fuck is with you and personal space?" she growled. "It's not like I have unkempt scales or tiny bugs living in my—actually, you birds *might* like those!"

For a moment, he thought about throwing it out there that she had called him over to her, but she had healed something that would've usually taken several hours to stitch back together on its own. A gesture of kindness. And then she had to open her mouth, ruining it. With a shake of his head, he took a step back and inspected the new skin. He dropped the shirt back in place. "You know, with your pleasant attitude, I'm shocked that more people don't cater to your desires a bit more willingly." He waved off her snide remark regarding bugs. Not his forte, but she associated him with a tiny creature with wings instead of a siren. "Sweetheart, nothing could make you attractive in my eyes. Not even if you were naked." He scoffed. "Now what do we do with this thing?"

"I've asked no one to cater anything to me. Thank you very much," Aurelia retorted. Her gaze shifted back to the creature. Her hands found her hips again. "I don't know. Pick at it, pull it apart? See how it works. Like a proper experiment."

"And I was thinking you differed from the rest." Gods, he was wrong. So wrong. *Pick at it. Pull it apart.* They were here on a rescue mission, and she was trying to get her science on. He dragged a hand across his face. Regardless of how she felt, they had a specific timeframe to think about. "Do you plan to take it along with us as a pet? Because in case you haven't noticed... we aren't exactly protected enough for you to play with it like a toy." Mac gestured to the dying trees surrounding them scattered across the barren wasteland they were currently traversing.

"I am," Aurelia insisted, still cringing from her own description. "But I also want to learn more about... All *this*." She gestured at the creature, the shadowy ilk infesting it and subsequently killing everything around them before taking a hand through her golden mane. "I—we," she gestured between them, "can't rescue or protect anyone to any lasting end—until we understand what *this* is. What's causing it. Where it came from. Will it spread to us? To our isle? This is so much bigger than just doing a quick fly-in, fly-out to save your grandpa, bird boy!"

"Yes, it can spread," he said matter-of-factly. How she didn't realize that baffled him. Then again, she didn't look too far past the end of her nose, like most species on the isle. Or at least a few of them. "What *this* darkness specifically is, or maybe I should say what it was, because obviously, it wasn't always like this. I can't say. The short answer is yes. The dark guilers carry disease with them."

"Who don't look like that," Aurelia countered, though that might just be a matter of exposure. "Aren't you the least bit curious? What happens once someone in your village ends up like this? Would you be content just to say, 'I can't say'? Because I, for one, am not willing to go back to say I don't know when this turns into a bigger, longer-lasting problem than just foreign invaders with a chip on their shoulder."

He didn't have to be curious. He'd been there twice when they had a guiler who went dark. It didn't happen often. Not that he was sure how much he could trust her with that information. She'd been ready to kill the others they'd crossed not that long ago. "One, this isn't a dark guiler. I can confirm that much. In fact, if I didn't know better, I'd say it was an infected shape shifter. But as far as I know, the only shape shifters are the ones on our isle."

"Does it matter what species it is? Clearly, whatever this... stuff is..." she pressed her hand in close to the creature, causing the shadow to recede. "It's not just taking up residence in your guiler pals. I trust our firsthand experience over your source any day, flyboy." Aurelia withdrew her hand and crossed her arms.

Though Felix might have lied to him. It wouldn't be the first time. "Two, *when* we have a guiler go dark, we handle it. They don't get outside our borders and further into the isle. They're quarantined until the issue is resolved." It probably wouldn't satisfy her since he didn't explain *how* they handled the situation. But that stone in his pocket—he didn't think it could handle much more.

"You 'handle it?'" she repeated. "That's not an answer—and only a temporary solution. Resolved *how*? Your Band-Aid solution won't hold forever. What are you going to do when it breaks past your borders and finds another species or village to call home?"

"We don't just slap a half-assed answer on it." With a groan, he crossed his arms. He trusted her enough to help rescue Felix. Plus, she'd healed him, not that she had to do that, either. "We'd pull the darkness from them and reeducate. If the situation became terminal, then they wouldn't survive." He didn't think she'd require more of an explanation. And if she did, too bad. It was as clear as he was going to get. "Is that enough of an answer, princess?" He shook his head. "You're acting like the guilers are the cause, and they aren't. And it isn't like they pass it by touch. It has to actually get into the land, parts of the isle, to pass onto other species."

Aurelia remained silent for a moment, her mouth moving to form words her brain hadn't yet decided on. "You don't call *that* a half-assed answer? 'Pull the darkness from them? Re-educate them'—so it has degenerative effects on their minds? You didn't think to mention that *before* we came here? So, the two options are torment and torture? That's just great." She shook her head. "I never said they were the cause, but clearly they're faring better than our fun new friend over here." She pointed to the shifter, still frozen mid-motion. "If they have a higher resistance—it's important."

"Torment and torture?" He scoffed. "That's what you got out of that? Wow! Really, a one-track mind. No. We educate them on the balance that they have to maintain, since they use the surrounding elements to power their magic. The guilers here..." Crossing his arms, Mac scrubbed his face. That was pretty clear to see. At least it was to him.

"Well, you didn't exactly go into specifics. So, how should I have taken it?" Aurelia grumbled.

If the darkness had become a part of the isle, it would naturally latch onto other living things. He gestured to the shifter in front of them. "Even if we pull the darkness from him, we don't know how this has impacted his essence. If he'll even be like he once was." Did that mean they didn't try? He had the stone with him, which was what Felix had been using for years. "I suppose we could give it a shot."

She gritted her teeth; her mane was now wholly disheveled. "How do you intend to pull the darkness from him?" Aurelia craned her neck. "Since you seem to have all the answers," she added under her breath.

About as much as you do, he thought to himself. Fuck. He didn't know what would happen if he used the stone in his pocket to pull the darkness from this creature. Or if it would be successful. "Say I have a way to remove the darkness. What exactly do we do with him afterward?"

"You all but said so yourself." She scrutinized him. "It's your magic trick. Pretty sure my guesses are all supposed to be bullshit. Makes it more... special." She forced a grin, more a baring of teeth and a show of fangs. "So, can we just skip that part?"

"You mean the part where we act like we trust each other?" Yeah, he'd noticed it, but he didn't trust anyone. And honestly, he kind of got the feeling she didn't trust any easier than he did. Still, the longer they stood there arguing over this trivial bullshit, the more time they wasted.

Mac scrubbed his hand across his face, pulled the partially orange stone, a nice chunk of citrine, from the pocket of his pants, and got closer to the creature suspended mid-air. To all the gods, he prayed this didn't become a decision he regretted. "If he kills me, I will haunt you."

The instant the crystal emerged from his pocket; Aurelia became completely alert. Her eyes narrowed, not leaving the sparkly, partially tainted stone. "Where'd you get that?" She forced a breath through her nostrils and crossed her arms. "I never intended to let it kill you."

"Does it matter where it came from?" He raised an eyebrow. "All you need to know is that I've been given a task with it, and I intend to see it through to completion." Even if it meant his going somewhere, he wasn't looking forward to going.

Without another word, Mac reached through the barrier she had infused around the canine shape shifter. It was kind of warm and sent tingles up his arm. Strange. Whatever. It didn't hurt, so that was all that mattered to him. He pressed the stone to the shifter's forehead; in the place she'd already touched twice before. The shadows formed around the creature shrieked as the stone started pulling the darkness into it.

"And what's that? You shouldn't experiment with things you don't fully understand." Aurelia watched his little trick.

"Anyone ever tell you that you're quick to make assumptions?" He shook his head as the stone continued to remove the darkness from the creature; the shape shifter's snarl eased as more of its natural appearance was revealed. It took longer than it had with any of the guilers they'd used it on in the past. This creature had probably been living with it for years.

"If that's what you think, maybe you shouldn't leave so many blanks in your story," Aurelia bit back.

"If you feel you absolutely must know, I've been charged with seeing that the stone is cleansed." As the stone kept working, Mac glanced over his shoulder at her. She was doing exactly what he expected. Asking a lot of questions. Staring at the stone a lot. Even watching his every movement. And she wondered why he didn't trust her? "Why are you so interested in it?"

She settled a bit as the creature became more recognizable. Less shadowy death machine and more of a large, furry woodland creature. "Gemstones hold great importance in Draconic culture," Aurelia replied. "Magically potent artifacts call to us."

It was a surprise she hadn't noticed it earlier. While he hadn't openly hidden it, he also hadn't openly put it out on display, either. Not that he intended to give it to her either way. He glanced over his shoulder and smirked. Her information offered little. "And you talked about my half-assed answers." With a slight shake of his head, he held the gemstone in place until all the darkness was gone from the shifter. A large, gray wolf with a black strip up its muzzle and several across its back and belly emerged. Its ears twitched as it looked from Mac to Aurelia and back again.

Aurelia fanned out her fingers, balling them into tight fists and back out again. "Yeah, well, when your guiler friends took you in, I don't think they carried the same motives the Silver Queen did when she culled all the female hatchlings and forced us through trials from the moment we were born, bathed us in sweet lies and battered us into the ground until she discovered what she was looking for." She heaved a breath as her talons sliced through her mane. Her eyes shifted to the creature.

"We all have a sad tale, princess. It's what you do with your past that makes all the difference." With the darkness gone from the shifter, and its eyes flicking back and forth between the two of them, he shoved the stone back in the pocket of his pants. If she thought for a second, he'd feel sorry for her, she was wrong. However, he empathized with how she felt about it.

"If that's the case, get off my ass, beak boy," Aurelia grumbled.

Nothing in their situation could change their destiny. That much he'd accepted a long time ago. But that didn't mean they didn't have choices. After all, they'd all been given free will. Taking a step back, Mac crossed his arms and raised an eyebrow at the shifter. "I don't know how long you've been like that, but I know you can talk in this form. You have a name?"

The wolf snorted once, then a second time. He rolled his shoulders and grunted. "No... No... Nomad."

"Yeah, lucky you," Aurelia said, flashing him a smile. "Guess you like the taste of bird, huh?" Her eyes dropped to his paws, still stained with Mac's blood. Fresh and crimson, even against the black and gray fur. She reached into a hidden pocket and produced a handful of meat and berries, tossing them at his massive paws. "Here."

Why did he even bother? Even when he tried to be nice, he couldn't keep the sarcasm out of his tone. But really? Boo fucking hoo. She experienced a horrible upbringing, and someone forced her into a role she didn't want. Seemed amongst the standard for those of the sky. He didn't have to talk to another siren to know he was the *last* male siren on the isle, which meant the species' survival fell to him.

The wolf barely glanced at the food before he scarfed it down. Licking his chops, he focused solely on Aurelia and snorted. It took him a minute to get a single word out. "More..."

"Yeah, because bird is really scrumptious." Mac dragged a hand through his dark hair. They needed to get moving. He flicked his eyes over to Aurelia and shook his head. That female didn't know what she was doing.

Aurelia cringed at the wolf's table manners, but obliged by retrieving more meat. But she didn't toss it down as she had before. "What happened here?" She tossed the food to the wolf. "He volunteers for sacrifice if you'd prefer a fresh meal." Aurelia threw her thumb and sarcasm towards Mac, giving the wolf her best smile.

Mac smirked. She wondered why the boyfriend had chosen Thal over her. Gee, he didn't. "You wound me, princess. Here, I thought you were beginning to like me." Not that he cared one stone how she felt about him. But he cared about the fact that they were wasting time.

Snorting, the wolf tilted its head. Nomad caught the meat midair, quickly scarfing it down. He groaned again, his ears twitching. "Darkness... took... isle... many... fell...."

"Before or after the war?" Mac asked. He didn't know what Aurelia was trying to find out. Or exactly how much the shifter could tell them. Despite what he'd seen with the female that had come to his village a couple of months back, this shifter had a hard time communicating. Though he supposed that could result from the darkness.

"After... after..." Nomad snorted, his ears twitching.

"Any idea where it came from? What started it?" Aurelia pressed.

Nomad stared at her expectantly. When no more food came to him, he shifted his gaze to Mac, his tail flicking back and forth.

Now, this was an interesting turn of events. Uncrossing his arms, Mac pulled a plum from his pocket and tossed it at the wolf's paws. Well, wasn't this fun? He glanced at Aurelia and scoffed.

The wolf bit into the plum, which took longer to eat than everything else had. As soon as he finished, he licked his chops and snorted again. "En... En... Enchantress... Enchantress."

Aurelia subdued a laugh, which quickly fled her as the wolf answered. A grimace and a scowl replaced the merriment. "Let's go," she grumbled, turning on her heel and all but stomping her way toward their destination.

His eyebrows knitted together. *Enchantress?* What the fuck was it talking about? Did Aurelia understand? Or know something? Something she wasn't sharing. Mac frowned as they started walking, with Nomad in tow. "Do you know what he's talking about?"

Her energy coalesced around her like a multi-hued cosmic heatwave. The intensity spiked into a raging inferno at the question. "What do you think?!" she snarled.

"I think you need to take a deep, calming breath. Otherwise, you're going to draw *a lot* of unwanted attention to us," he hissed. That was the last thing they needed. Between the stone he carried, the newly freed shape shifter, who was rather old, and who he didn't know how they intended to get off the isle... Fuck! Things that neither of them thought through. Mac shoved a hand roughly through his hair. If this kept up, he'd lose a few strands before they returned to their own isle. Good stones, they'd created a mess. He hadn't expected to end up with a shape shifter tagging along. One that spoke little or had trouble forming words. This ought to be interesting.

Aurelia's steps halted their procession. A strong, scorching gust billowed outward from the dragon. Her eyes danced with the celestial flames. "You keep sharing your epiphanies, greenie, and my next breath is going to set you and everything across this desolate slab ablaze!"

He raised his hands, and like Nomad, slowly backed up to give her space. "Whatever you say, princess." They could make the rest of this trek in silence for all he cared. Obviously, Nomad presented some specific issues that they could figure out later. But as she didn't seem too quick to follow through with her initial intentions, he really wasn't sure at that point. He needed to develop a Plan B for after they got Nomad back to the other side. Sure as shit, he wasn't leaving the male behind.

"Call me 'princess'... One. More. Fucking. Time." Aurelia fumed.

"We'll just walk back here. Give you your space." Demeter, help him. Moody-ass female. And she wondered why he refused to share everything with her. Yeah. She knew *exactly* what Nomad had been talking about. She just had no intention of expanding or explaining. If he could draw one conclusion from all of this... the dragon-shifters were involved.

Chapter Six

The shape shifter was taking his sweet time. How long had she been waiting in this tree now? Fagonia scowled. She could've always found someone else on the isle to work with. Or manipulate. Her seitadi had been following that bluebird at a distance since she landed. It was only a matter of time before she was alone.

That was precisely what she needed.

A moment where she could rid herself of that bluebird. Then she'd ensure the siren line remained pure. And they couldn't create any more abominations like the half-breeds in that village. If only she could find it, then she could set her seitadi loose on it. Unfortunately, the damn thing was too well hidden.

Good Demeter, where was that damn bear? Wasting her time like this.

With a slight groan, she eyed the position of the sun. This male was taking way too long for her liking. If she didn't need that self-imposed nightmare, she'd just leave. Or if only she knew more about the creatures that the bluebird was traveling with. And with the recent decisions of her Elder, it was best to get this over with.

Markham stepped through the trees in his cloaked form. His robe swayed around him, seemingly alive in the stillness, as if an unseen current moved it. He stood there staring upward, then rolled his eyes. "Are we speaking like this today, or are you ever going to come down from that tree?"

She preferred the branch. His stench affected her much less this way. "I believe we shall speak like this. It does not change the news either way."

"Then proceed."

"The barrier has come down and remained such. I believe I have located the one responsible," Fagonia said. They'd spoken of the barrier the last time they met, a day or two ago. That had only been so she could gain his trust. As much as she didn't like it, she needed the use of his... Informants. She didn't have much of an army at her disposal.

"Have you? So, what now? Are your *seitadi* in pursuit?" The corner of his lip lifted in an irritated silent snarl.

"They continue to watch and follow at a distance. It would seem the four have split up. She and the one male are staying on the isle, which will aid in our desire to rid ourselves of her. And gain control of the barrier." She didn't mention that she'd left one of her seitadi to wait for the return of the male siren. He was what she wanted. The bluebird needed to die.

"Once she has served my personal purpose for her, *then* we can get rid of her. Not before. What I need her for, I can accomplish with no other. Have you learned anything more about her companion?"

"Of course. As agreed," Fagonia paused. Not that she cared what he wanted the bird for. She needed him only for his forces. She thought over the information her seitadi had shared with her. "Not much. They took to the skies earlier, above the clouds, where my seitadi could not follow without being seen. He may be a dragon, much like the other female who has left their side." Or something more. The male had a strange collar around his neck. What did it do exactly? What purpose did it serve? Fagonia offered a small smile. "Though he seems quite taken with the bluebird. I do not believe he will leave her side. The dragons are purists. Like so many others, they may seek refuge in the half-breed village."

"The half-breed village is the one place on this isle I cannot penetrate. We must capture her before that occurs. The other two they have parted ways with—did it appear they would rejoin back together at some point?"

"Neither of us can penetrate the half-breed village. It is well guarded, well-protected. By one that is even older than you." Fagonia smirked. Maybe she couldn't gain access, but she had a rough idea of where it was located. "It does not appear they will rejoin the party in the immediate future. I believe we may yet have a few *umbras*."

"I know who guards the place. If a few *umbras* are not enough, what do you plan to do to proceed? I only have so many Informants; my numbers have dwindled of late."

"As it would seem, my Elder sent ambassadors of ours out to the village Elders to negotiate a peace treaty." With a wide grin, Fagonia jumped from the branch, the air rushing past her as she slowly landed on the ground. It truly pleased her to no end to rat out her niece. Especially if the time would come that she could prove it. By then, the female would have no one to save her. "I believe one of them is involved with one of yours."

Markham tilted his head a bit. "I see." He paused momentarily. "Which one?"

"I am uncertain, though I have plans for a seitadi to follow the ambassadors until he reveals himself." Patience had always served her well. She'd waited for eighteen years after killing the male siren's parents for him to reappear. She could certainly wait for the days to pass until her plan came to fruition. "If I am correct, then we will have the perfect bait for the bluebird. She will not stand by without attempting to rescue a fellow siren."

"Good. Be sure to tell me when you know. I am interested in seeing if my suspicions will be confirmed." He snickered. "So. A peace treaty. They will find no peace with me. I wonder if they would enjoy my welcoming party." His chuckle was soft. "Perhaps you should warn them not to cross my border and to meet with me at the boundary line. If they come into my territory, they are fair game." He sneered. "While I am partial to hearts, my Informants are always up for a snack."

"Of course, I will. I am quite intrigued to see who it turns out to be." Fagonia clasped her hands at the small of her back. "I think perhaps I will forget to tell them." She cackled.

He grimaced. "All the better. Perhaps I will damage their wings and see how long it takes my Informants to catch them when they cannot flutter away."

"I do not care what you do with them. That is your business." Fagonia offered him a grin. "Should we meet here again when I have news?"

"Yes. How soon do you expect that to be?"

"They begin their journey tomorrow. I expect to know more once night falls."

"Tomorrow at nightfall, then?"

"Yes." Fagonia paused. "If you are looking for the few who may have gone to the half-breed village, I would suggest sending your dogs toward Mosina Falls." With that, she took off into the sky.

Her gaze flicked to the stairs of Demeter's Temple as her sister approached. Parthenia plastered a smile on her face and prayed to the goddess nothing got picked up with her mate's scent, even if it was only Cipriana.

The grin on her sister's face wavered as she approached. Her nose wrinkled slightly. "Which side is he on?" she asked quietly through gritted teeth.

With a quick nod of her head, Parthenia indicated her left side. It had been the shoulder his hand remained on the entire time they walked. From their vantage point, they could see the bright silver gates, the lyre symbol gleaming above. She'd never noticed the intricate carvings of wings adorning the sides of the lyre. It matched the one they'd seen on the bridge. The decorative gates featured poppies, with their delicate petals and stems carved in exquisite detail. Another sign that they were children of Demeter. A female siren stood on either side of the forty-foot-high pillars, each decked out in a golden suit of armor holding tight to long silver spears.

Forcing a grin onto her face, Cipriana moved to the opposite side of where Gavin stood and walked side by side with Parthenia. "We will discuss this once we leave," her sister muttered.

Not that it would change the outcome. Her mate was by her side, and she wasn't going anywhere without him. Not anymore. As they made their way to the gates, a few sirens gathered to send them off. Fantasia, Echo, and Blair. If any of them caught a whiff of Gavin's scent, no one said anything or appeared to show they had.

Of those who came to see them off, none hugged them. Instead, they each curtsied low and wished them well on their journey. The two females, Ariadne and Khrysis, at the gates struck the bottoms of their spears against the ground twice, which caused a spark. Glowing on the awning, the lyre illuminated as the locks along the seam of the gates rattled. The sides spread out, resembling wings, as if preparing to take flight.

In all her life, she had never once witnessed the opening of the gates. It was quite a glorious sight. Once they had parted, they descended the white, pearlescent staircase, its smooth surface cool beneath their feet, on their way to the bottom of the isle.

When they reached the bottom, Gavin rubbed his head against her. Based on where his head came to on her body, he must have shifted back to his animal form. "I apologize, Cipriana, if my presence caused you any distress. We just do not wish to be parted from each other."

"Stop talking. Not until we are at least a mile into the forest," Cipriana hissed, her words kept low.

Parthenia frowned and glanced over her shoulder as she stroked along Gavin's head and rested her hand on his back. Weren't they far enough away to be out of earshot? Her gaze flicked back to her sister. "No one can hear us."

"I prefer we didn't take any chances." Without a word, her sister turned from the staircase, the rasping of her talons on the sand preceding her as she headed toward the treeline.

"Okay." That went well. Parthenia sighed. "Come, my love." She followed Cipriana.

"I truly did not mean to upset her," he whispered.

"I don't think she's upset, just concerned." At least, that was the impression she had gotten. It wasn't as if Cipriana had stated differently. She assumed her sister would understand, but she certainly didn't expect this kind of reaction.

With her arm draped across Gavin's shoulders, they continued treading through the warm sand until they made it into the forest. Silence stretched between the three of them for the first mile.

"I'm sorry, but there are too many with extensive hearing. That includes a few that are against this new law and this mission," Cipriana said.

"I understand. Probably more than many, to be honest. No apology is necessary."

"That's good." Cipriana sighed heavily. "I get that you two don't want to be apart. Par, I've watched how you've been at the meeting these last few *umbras*. It was like you were broken, no matter how involved you tried to be, which I appreciate. I know how long we have needed this. I'm hoping we accomplish a good treaty with the other Elders."

"Yes, well, that's the other reason Gavin came along. We don't think we should visit the shape shifter village for multiple reasons." Hopefully, her sister would listen to all of them. It surprised her a bit to learn the female noticed her difficulty in the continuous meetings. Although treaties with the species they could reach were necessary.

"Very well. We can discuss that, but save it for when we make camp for the night," Cipriana said.

"We can do that. Did you have a plan for today?" She'd looked at her own map the night before and had her suspicions about the direction they would go. But it wasn't her decision.

"The marketplace first. I expected there was something there you wanted to see or stop in; then we'll continue to Migas, the hybrid village. We'll leave there and then head for Chicane Village."

A smile tugged at the corners of her mouth. Her sister was going to hear them out. It was a start. "Sounds good to me."

"Thank you. For your understanding and for listening," Gavin replied.

Cipriana nodded but said nothing else on the matter.

He stroked Parthenia's wing with the tip of his tail. "She never said, but do you think the hybrid village is the place that Devin found?"

"It's possible." Devin had suggested she couldn't know where the information had come from when she had spoken of the barrier, if she recalled correctly. She didn't know any other village Elder that might've helped. Beaming, she ran her fingers along Gavin's shoulders. Maybe she couldn't see him, but he was close, and she had enough of a sense of where he was that it made it easier to stay connected. Something else occurred to her, something they'd both stated in the first days of their meeting. Back then, they'd both wanted to go to the hybrid village. They'd always said that one day they would go there.

"It will be nice to see it." He continued to stroke her wing, a low purr rising out of him. "If you get tired, love, you can always ride me."

"I have a better idea," Cipriana interjected before Parthenia had the chance to respond. "I'm presuming that being invisible doesn't hinder your ability to run. So, we can cut our travel time down if we fly and you run or...." Her gaze shifted to Parthenia. "You do whatever, so the two of you can stay close. We'll be cutting through the forest, staying outside manticore boundaries until we reach Haggle Road. If my calculations are correct, it should put us about ten miles from the marketplace."

Parthenia smiled. Even though her sister would shrug her off, she wanted to throw her arms around Cipriana and hug the female. "For what it's worth, I think Vasilia made the right choice for new leadership."

"Thank you, but it doesn't mean I still feel confident about it. Now, does this work for both of you?"

"Yes. I think it works fine. We'll stay close." They had proven time and time again that Gavin's ground speed far surpassed their flight speed. She knew her sister wouldn't go easy, but she wouldn't go so fast as to exhaust herself, either.

"Thank you. I will not go at full speed, so we do not lose sight of you." He stroked Parthenia's hip with his tail.

"Okay." Cipriana took flight into the trees, staying below the lowest branches to navigate through the forest easily.

Parthenia stroked the top of her mate's head. "I promise to hold on tight." A second later, with a hand on his shoulder, Gavin had lowered his body, and she climbed on as they had done before. She could've flown, but she simply wanted to be close to him, no matter how they traveled.

"You always do, my love. And I enjoy every minute." With his tail wrapped around her leg, he stood up and sprinted across the ground, kicking up dust.

Chapter Seven

Thalasia stirred from what had to have been the deepest slumber she'd ever had. Slowly, her eyes fluttered open as she felt around for Seru. She bolted upright. What the fuck? She blinked as her gaze flicked all around. Aside from her clothes set aside in the tree's hollow, she was utterly alone.

Not exactly what she expected after the shared experience from the night before. Although it certainly left a lot to be explained as memories danced in her head. Some of which she didn't think Seru could offer any kind of answer. How the fuck had her body glowed? Was that normal? Was it a siren thing? An Atlis thing? A sexual thing? Nothing like this had ever come up in conversation with her mother. But then again, she had been ten. Back then, males were still gross.

Getting to her feet, she collected her denim capris and tugged them on first. As she got dressed, she thought back over the years. Her opinion of males hadn't changed all that much. However, last night had been the first time she'd ever seen anyone naked. And really looked. Seru had gotten hurt, so her focus shifted quickly, even if he had teased her about it.

She adjusted her wings a little as she tied her top in place and frowned. Her left wing. Without a second thought, she extended the wing that had housed the lyre. It wasn't necessary to feel along where the feathers had grown back darker. She could sense the difference in the weight of her wing. No matter how slight, it was one thing all sirens knew.

It wasn't the only thing that was different. Her hand patted gingerly from the top of her head to the end of her braid. Her hair had been down when they arrived in Chicane, even last night when she had passed out. There was also a slight weight there, but it didn't feel as if it belonged to the beads or the flowers—why did she have flowers in her hair? And beads? She shook the questions bubbling in her mind away. The fact remained that whatever item the slight weight belonged to wasn't either of those things. Not that she could feel it. Whatever it was, it had gotten buried in the braid.

Her one concern—the lyre. She poked her head over the side of the tree. No Seru. Seriously, what the fuck? Had he, well, whatever he'd done to her body, had he done it as a distraction? No, that couldn't be it. Even last night, it had felt like something more. Like they'd claimed one another. Was that it? Had they done that?

Dragging a hand down her face, Thalasia groaned. She had so many questions. And the one person she should be able to get at least some answers from had disappeared. Where the fuck had he gone? To be certain everything else was where it belonged, she checked for the dagger in its sewn-in sheath in her pants. Still there. Then she checked for the purple pouch she had hung up on a branch. Also still there. A sigh of relief left her mouth.

Aside from the bit of money she had, it also contained all the clothes she owned, several magical items, a blue gemstone, books, and more. But she couldn't think about any of that. Not today. There were too many things to accomplish.

Leaving the hollow, she leaped into the surrounding forest and flew above the trees. There was a reason she had picked that place to rest. All she had to do to see anything was to fly a little higher, and she could see most of the shoreline and the village. She scanned the village first. Nothing. He wasn't anywhere around. Then, her gaze flicked to the coastline outside the village. It took a minute for her to locate him, and he wasn't alone.

A small hiss escaped her mouth as she took off in Seru's direction. So as not to draw immediate attention to herself, she soared toward him and minimally flapped her wings. She didn't know who the blue-haired chick was that he was talking to, but he was going to damn well give her some answers. She could always—no, she couldn't. The very thought of leaving him behind was like a stab to the chest.

It wasn't a feeling she understood. Though, with Seru, there was a lot she didn't understand. None of which she had time to inspect too closely at the moment. Her flight toward the two of them had been quiet. Thalasia ensured her landing was anything but. The soft sand kicked up ever so slightly as her feet touched the ground.

She crossed her arms as her gaze flipped from the back of Seru's head to the chick in front of him.

The female greeted her with a toothy smile, her amusement self-evident. Giving her a once-over, the female turned back to Seru. The woman's voice came in a musical series of garbled sounds. An edge of laughter to them. She spoke with a relaxed familiarity, completely at ease and undeterred by her entrance.

Seru's response was a rapid succession of harsh tones, blending seamlessly into one another. He turned enough to regard her with his gaze, and a slight nod. He didn't let the woman opposing them out of his range of view.

The female offered a curt reply. Her sharp claws were playing with a large gemstone adorning her long neck on a glittering chain. It refracted the sunlight, playing blue-green shadows across the sand.

Thalasia frowned. It wasn't uncommon for her to come across a dialect she didn't understand. She had been to several realms where that occurred. This trip had proven to be unlike any other. She bit her tongue to keep her words to herself. Though she was positive her anger was showing, certain her silver eyes flared. If she wasn't pissed before, she sure as hell was now. And once whoever the fuck this chick was left, well, Seru was going to see a side of her he'd never seen before.

"Hello, pretty siren," the female spoke in a heavily accented common. "Why so angry? Didn't you sleep well?"

"I slept fine," Thalasia spat out. "Not that it concerns you."

A smile played over the female's lips, a flick of tongue behind her fangs. She seemed to delight in their banter, though the reasons weren't immediately obvious.

"Leave her be, Cyon," Seru warned.

The tone of his voice said it all. Her gaze flicked from Cyon, was it... to Seru. Then back again. The flowers, the beads in her hair. The female recognized something she didn't. What the fuck had he done? Her arms remained crossed, and her tightly-balled fists revealed her tension. No. No. This wasn't like that. It wasn't like that. Closing her eyes for a moment, she shoved the memory back that tried to break through. It was in a box for a fucking reason. Everything tucked back where it should be; she looked between the two of them again. "I'm sorry, Cyberg. I'm sure he doesn't mean to be so rude."

Cyon threw her head back in laughter. Her lush, blue waves bounced with the movement. "Oh, darling, I'm more than used to his stormy moods. They've only improved with time."

Seru gave a derisive flare of nostrils and a show of fang but stayed quiet at her jab.

Lovely. Of all the people they had to cross, it had to be one of them. It made her hate the female on principle alone, which made no sense. No matter what she assumed about what happened last night, the fact remained: she wasn't staying on this rock. Again, the very thought felt like death. She wanted to remain with Seru, but she didn't think her visions would allow that to happen. "Joy," she mumbled. Inhaling a deep breath, she smirked and bit back the comment on the tip of her tongue. She looked at Seru. "Is there anything more you need her for? If so, I can certainly go deal with stuff at the village before we leave. I mean, it isn't exactly like I'm part of the conversation."

"Actually," Cyon interjected. "We were talking about you." She tossed her mane to one side, running her fingers through as she spoke. "If you can abide," Cyon turned to Seru. "I'd like a few words with your... Glory." Before he could refuse, the female turned to her. "We won't be long." The female raised her arms, flashing her empty hands. "I'm not armed. She won't do either of us any good dead." Her aquamarine eyes sparkled.

"It's her choice." Seru sighed dismissively, though the idea clearly didn't thrill him.

Oh, even better. She was the subject. What a fucking—did the female say 'glory?' Thalasia narrowed her eyes at Seru and ground her jaw. Maybe she wouldn't have minded whatever the fuck *glory* he had made her, but she'd woken up alone with no explanation at all. Oh, yeah. He had a lot of fucking explaining to do. She didn't think it was possible to be this pissed. Yet, there she stood, her nails digging into the palms of her hands. Her gaze flipped back to Cyon. "Go right ahead, Iceberg."

"Are you always this pleasant, or are you feeding off his bad mood?"

Most times she was nice, but there was something she inherently didn't like about the female. Probably didn't make her any better than Aurelia. There was one significant difference. She could keep the snide remarks to herself. For the sake of finding out what Cyon wanted. "Just get to the point."

"You should show more gratitude. You may not see it, but he's taking substantial risks for you. Though I'm not yet sure why."

That made two of them. Not that she'd admit it. Surely that wasn't what the female wanted to discuss. "Questions regarding our relationship are off-limits. If that's what you want to talk about, then this conversation is over."

Cyon flashed another smile. "Not at all. Seru doesn't always say what he's thinking, but everything he does, he does with a purpose. If you can't learn to trust that blindly, whatever you think you have with him won't work out. Be it business or something more personal. What I want to know is what you hope to gain here, siren. What is it you want from this isle and its people?"

She glanced over at Seru. That was part of the problem. "Trust goes both ways." He didn't just ask if she trusted him, but he had to trust her, too. Releasing her fingers from her palms, she flicked her gaze back to Cyon. Yeah, like she was going to share all of that with someone she'd just met. She hadn't even told Seru her *reason* for being here on Prisma Isle. Though it was feeling like more than one. "I don't have those answers yet. My purpose isn't always made clear, but I believe it will soon." A lot of damn pieces to the puzzle. Although she knew at least one part, she didn't have enough of the picture yet to understand everything. Probably why she'd been here longer than most places.

Cyon narrowed her eyes ever so slightly. "You sirens love your riddles."

Thalasia raised an eyebrow. What was confusing about her answer? She'd received several visions since her arrival. Even before then. But they were snippets. Not the entire picture. "I'm not really a fan of them, but from what I was taught, sirens are the keepers of secrets and prophecies. Any more questions?"

"I thought you might."

"Have questions? Not for you." No, her questions were for Seru. He was the one who needed to answer them. Simply put, trust could be broken. Though it was more confirmation than a question. She could feel the difference in weight distribution. Not just in her wings, but in her hair. The flowers just made her smell like a mix of Seru and potpourri. Interesting combination.

"Suit yourself." Cyon shrugged.

"Please tell me there's more to this entire conversation. Or were you just trying to get me to ask you my questions instead of him?" She paused. Really? All of this? Wait. She had a question. "What did he tell you about me?"

The corners of her mouth twitched upward. "Nothing. You spoiled his mystery when you showed yourself."

Her anger ebbed just a little. Every action taken had a purpose. There had been a reason her visions had brought her here. Whatever it was with Mac, she had assumptions, but no confirmations. The Manticore... an item she had to take, not that she knew why. Thalasia nodded. "Usually, when I come to a realm, it's to fix something or prevent it. I don't know enough about this isle yet to determine which is the right answer."

Cyon ventured a glance Seru's way, a curious tilt of her head. "Best wishes stopping him." With that, Cyon turned and disappeared into the waves.

Thalasia turned to Seru. "She's fun." Shaking her head, she started back toward the village. Despite the sleep she'd gotten, she was suddenly exhausted. Maybe a couple of pieces of fruit on the way out would perk her up.

"She seems to think so," Seru sighed. He followed a few paces behind. After a moment, he reached over her shoulder, offering her a plum. "You should eat."

She accepted the plum and bit into it, her brain churning over everything before she spoke. That one word was sticking out to her. There were a lot of risks being taken. Even if he didn't know the ones running through her head. "That glory thing she mentioned... that has something to do with last night... my hair..."

"Yes."

"You moved the lyre." It was a statement, not a question. She didn't need to ask him. But it pissed her off. Not because he moved it. Or that he'd done something without explaining himself. It was the fact that he hadn't asked. "Did you think I wouldn't consent? Did you even think about asking me beforehand?" She stopped and glowered. "Because if that's the case, then it doesn't matter how much I trust you if you can't trust me."

"I concealed it in your hair," Seru answered, sounding almost bored, if not distracted. "It's safer there. You're safer. Do I need your permission to protect you and the things you hold dear? Your distrust of me put you on the beach, in plain sight of someone who could target and hurt you. Take your lyre. It was careless."

"I didn't come looking for you because I don't trust you. I came looking for you because I woke up alone after a night that felt like placing a claim on each other. Maybe that's common in your culture, but it sure as fuck isn't in mine." She bit back the tear that threatened to free itself. They had fought to stay together. Why? She wasn't sure she understood at the moment. Swallowing the lump in the back of her throat, she turned back toward the village and took a bite of the plum.

"It isn't." Seru wrapped his arms around her waist. "The ceremony is only once in a dragon's lifetime. If refused, that's it. There is not another." He nestled into the curve of her neck. "It's not a decision I made lightly. I did it to protect you. You were already on Aurelia's shit list. And you just offered yourself up to the sea. I don't know if it will be enough, but at least with access to my power, you'll stand a chance of surviving your stay on Prisma Isle." He pulled back. "I don't know what will happen when you... Leave to other realms." He strode past her, capturing her tear on his finger. "Do plums always make you cry?"

She inhaled a deep breath. Yeah, well, they wouldn't be the first enemy she's ever made. Just add them to her collection. "I don't know that I am leaving." Things had become... complicated. "Sirens only take one mate. The pain of being separated from them... it's unbearable. Like death."

"Just because I crowned you, my glory, does not mean we are... Mates." Seru said, using the heel of his hand to rub his eyes. "It just means that you may use what you require from me. A glory gains strength in her own right as well. You're aligned with your celestial ruler. That grants you tremendous power. I wasn't even sure it would work. It's never been shared with anyone outside the Draconic community."

Right. It was to protect her. Pain... it was an old friend. She nodded. Inhaling and exhaling a deep breath—no one had a love like her parents. She couldn't talk about this anymore. "We should get going."

"You're the queen." Seru motioned her forward.

"I'm no queen." Not a word she'd ever associate herself with, nor would she want to be. Taking a bite of the plum, she pushed on. There was still a lot ahead of them. Demeter, she hoped Mac and Aurelia were faring well on their mission.

"If you say so." Seru managed a small smile.

She finished the plum and offered Seru a soft smile. "Thank you for the plum, by the way." They really needed to start for the half-breed village. She didn't know how long it would take them to get there or which way they were going.

Seru nodded. As they walked, he stooped down to pluck a blade of grass. With his other hand, he reached into her hair, retrieving the clamshell containing the lyre. He'd attached it with a piece of sinew. He held out the blade of grass to her. "You have to tickle it under the chin." He ran his talon under the smooth scalloped surface. "Or it won't open."

"I imagine many people don't know that." It wasn't necessary to open. She'd meant it when she said she trusted him, aside from the fact that she could sense the lyre. It was strange, but it had always been like that. She'd always believed it was because it had been the last connection she had with her mother. Although it could be her connection with the magical item as an Atlis. It was the same with the blade tucked away at her back. At least she knew what kind of shell it was now.

"Not too many. Maybe the mer-people, but they're not seen on land anymore. You don't even want to try it?"

Her curiosity was something that had often gotten her into trouble. Not that this would be troublesome. She plucked the blade of grass from his fingers and stopped long enough to tickle it where he'd indicated.

The clam wiggled before springing open to reveal the golden charm safely tucked inside.

Seru helped her coax it closed and returned it to the safety of her braids.

It shouldn't have surprised her he'd moved it. He'd made his concerns known when she'd shown him where she'd stowed the lyre. She expected it to be moved, but she also thought it would happen while she was awake. "Why were you talking to her? About me."

He stood there in silence for a moment. "I guess I hoped she'd get the message that attacking you is off-limits. The sea dragons will not take Aurelia's side. Cyon only confirmed what I suspected. That when the guilers truly make a move to invade, the sea will side with them. It's how they've made it across so smoothly. And another part of me foolishly hoped your involvement might spur enough interest to coerce Marius to the surface. As you can see, it didn't. Cyon came alone." There was an inflection of sadness in his tone at the last words, overshadowed by a deeply rooted bitterness. "Depending on how things go, we need allies to choose from. The sky and the sea are two of the most powerful allies one could hope for."

Great. She pinched the bridge of her nose. "The guilers are already moving inland. When I went looking for the prisoner, I saw an empty boat about halfway out to sea." She shook her head and squeezed his arm. "Maybe my unexpected arrival there will change that. And we still don't know what allies we may find down here. I know Aurelia discounts the land species, but that doesn't mean we should."

"The guilers we've encountered so far are scouting or operating under specific criteria—they have a mission to complete. There are many, many more waiting for the opportunity to attack the isle when we're at our weakest. If Mac and Aurelia fail in rescuing Felix, and he divulges whatever secrets he possesses... That won't bode well for the species that call the isle home, especially the land species. Their ability to swim and fly is limited, and even if they could, the sky dragons would sooner see them drown. Aurelia's help will only come when it benefits her and the Clouds. Not before. Marius and Cyon rule the seas, even those beyond the isle. Their motivations are still self-serving but a bit more... flexible. They've long disagreed with the Clouds' way of rule with the isle under the thumb. They no longer believe the sky can safely be brought back into the fold—and they may be right. You've seen how deeply rooted Aurelia's hatred is. She's significantly more open-minded than the Cloud Court and the Sky Temple. Should you need to flee the isle and take others with you, we might persuade them to give you safe passage. I'm not discounting potential alliances with the other species. Putting into motion scenarios that will yield us concrete options. We guarantee nothing in war, and even those you think are your friends can turn on you if the right offer is made. I know the dragons well enough that we should have at least one of them backing us, regardless of what else we accomplish. A variety is certainly preferred."

"If these are just scouts, I've seen their numbers. I spent a couple of weeks on the other side trying to find and get to the bridge. As well as staying out of sight. Easier said than done." Among other things, but she didn't think it would bode well if she told him about the good guilers she'd hidden in a cave on Candescent Isle. She sighed. Her purpose? "I'm getting more visions than I normally do. There's more at work here than just an imminent invasion. It's like... I don't know... my arrival was to set things in motion."

"Let us hope your ancestors or the half-breeds can offer us clarity about what exactly has been set in motion. Otherwise, we're fighting blind."

"Maybe when we find the book, we'll get some actual answers." At least, she hoped. Her visions never offered much of anything. And there were a few things she would've liked to have been warned about. Not once in all her travels had she ever been attracted to another soul. That's what she had liked about Seru. What she saw in him. Her nose twitched as she thought back to his earlier words. "What happens if Aurelia finds out about this?" She gestured to the flowers and beads in her hair. "To you, I mean."

His gaze shifted to her, then forward toward their destination. "She'll notice almost immediately. She'll be displeased. Then, angry. After that, we'll see. A lot depends on how successful their trip to Candescent Isle is."

A lot of consequences. Some she knew and understood, but that had been on her. Some he knew and understood, but that was on him. They had decided. There was no going back. Not that she regretted it. Just meant she'd have to make the most of her time with him. After all, they weren't mates. It was the most common term. Not that the term she used would make a difference. She rubbed at the ache in her chest and shook it off. "That place is a wasteland." She frowned. The barrier. It had kept them out. Why would it need to come down and give those things the chance to invade? Unless it hadn't been part of the plan.

"Maybe it's the universe's way of giving the leaders of Prisma a wake-up call," Seru said softly.

"That would be great if they knew it existed. We know Mac at least knew because of Felix. I don't think any other species know of its existence. Not even the fae." Something that led her back to one of her concerns. That none of them knew how bad it could get. Maybe that was why she was here. To help prevent it from getting there. Seru had mentioned some problems that the other species were seeing. If the magic of the isle was failing, how did that involve her?

"The fae were the original peacemakers, though they seem content to have retreated to their forest in more recent years. And who can blame them? Unfortunately, you can't save or reform those who don't wish to be remade."

"That just depends on how far gone they are. Some... you're right... are so far that the only way to help those beneath them is death." It wasn't something that ever happened lightly. She had taken a life before. Most only in dire circumstances. Just like those on the beach on Candescent Isle. Others... well, that wasn't a time she liked to think about.

"You'd think they'd be tired of war. The death and destruction." Seru sighed.

"It's not like this everywhere. Some places, they just have a few rotten apples, while most people thrive." Those had been easy journeys. She just offered a little guidance.

"I don't even know what a world like that would look like."

"Colorful. Vibrant. Lively. I wish I could show you, but that's about the best I can describe it."

He chuckled. "That's not ironic."

She rolled her eyes. "It's nice to know I can amuse you." The last place like that she never wanted to leave. Then she had her first vision that had led her here. The first of many. And the guardian of that realm didn't want her to stay.

"You're a breath of fresh air, Thalasia. In a place that's long been rotting." He frowned.

"Thank you, but not everyone thinks like you." If he thought this was rotting, he hadn't seen the worst yet. But then again, he'd seen more of the problems with Prisma Isle than she had. "My presence may end up leaving a bigger impact than we know at the moment." She inhaled and exhaled a deep breath. "You know, I go to all these places, see all these things, but the one thing I never know, how it changes after I've accomplished my task."

"You've never been back?"

"Unless something takes me back—no." She hadn't returned to any of them. At least one she didn't want to go back to, but that was neither here nor there.

"There's something to be said for that, I suppose."

"Then please tell me what it is." She swallowed the lump in the back of her throat. "Having to move around so much, it gets lonely. Even if you make friends, you're constantly leaving them behind. Never seeing them again. You wonder why I do everything not to make connections? That's why. Not to mention... there's less to lose."

"They may not go with you physically, but you take them with you." He paused. "Aurelia would trade places with you in a heartbeat. She hates being cooped up, forced to stay in one place all the time. But as Matriarch, that's her duty. Much like yours is to travel and help where you can."

"If I could trade with her, I would. Not that I think it would ever be possible." She hadn't talked to anyone about any of this before. It was strange. "Visions... even the lyre... they skip a generation in my family. My grandmother and great-great-grandmother had them. I know it goes further than that... for centuries. Same with the lyre. I used to just think it was a family heirloom." That was only partially true. Of course, it was a family heirloom, but she'd known all along of its magical propensity. Not that she could tell him that.

"It sounds like a tremendous responsibility."

"Yeah." On some days, she could do without. Having anything normal, stable in her life, here she was, making it *even* better. Her eyes lifted to his. "Why do you keep protecting me? You've done it since we met." She paused. "You don't have to answer."

"Can't you just give it away? It sounds like one of them did just that with the book. Pass the burden onto someone else." He considered her question for a moment. "You deserve to be protected. More than anyone else I've met."

She raised an eyebrow at him. That was unexpected. And she didn't know how to process his response. But she could focus on the question regarding the lyre. Or at least a partial truth. "I've thought about it many times. There's only one problem with it. Well, two really. One, I've always felt a connection to the lyre. I used to think it was because it was a family heirloom. Now I understand that differently. Two, even if I could pass the lyre to someone else... it wouldn't stop the visions. When I'm not acting on them, they come more fiercely. Almost to the point of becoming painful."

"Mmm..." Seru replied.

Magic was strange that way. It affected everyone who possessed it in different ways. "It's not a pain I would wish on anyone."

Chapter Eight

P arthenia beamed as the marketplace came into view. Already she could see a variety of species bustling about, purchasing many items. Some went into shops, while others negotiated with vendors along the way. There were so many. Merfolk, satyrs, dwarves, and more. She bit her bottom lip as she felt a kiss on her neck from Gavin before his hand slipped from hers and moved to her shoulder. As excited as they both were to take this trip together, she wished he didn't have to hide, so to speak. Or that they weren't on such a time limit. It would be nice to truly explore the marketplace with him and see everything it offered.

Watching as her sister disappeared into the crowd, she scanned a moment until she found her standing at a fish vendor. A soft giggle left her mouth at the look on the dwarf's face. Not that it lasted long. The robust and scruffy male quickly recovered. As planned, once her feet hit the cobblestone ground, she strode directly for Mystique Herbs. She couldn't wait to see everything the apothecary had in store.

Several times, her pacing slowed as Gavin moved out of the way before someone bumped into him. Or so she presumed. He kept his hand on her shoulder the entire time he followed behind her to Mystique Herbs.

The scent of herbs filled the air as she stepped farther into the apothecary, her eyes widening. "Holy poppies," Parthenia mumbled. So many things filled the shelves lining the walls. The sharp scent of the herbs she knew contrasted with the subtle fragrance of the unknown. Although she noticed the nymph staring at her from the counter, she paid it little attention. Drinking it all in, her shoulders relaxed as her jaw slackened. It was so wonderful. Slowly, she strode into the store a little farther, inhaling the earthy scent, and her gaze fell upon a variety of mushrooms known for their healing properties.

There was some money in her knapsack. It wasn't much—just what her father had left her. She collected those as they could come of use. Wandering around more, her gaze scanned the variety of items here. As her eyes fell on a crate of prepackaged seeds, she paused. Poppy seeds. How was that possible? Pteryrina was the *only* place on the entire isle that poppies grew. And she should know. The Poppy Fields were her responsibility. She moved to head for the counter and inquire about them when Gavin gave her shoulder a gentle squeeze. Parthenia turned. Not that she wanted to—her eyes landed on Devin.

"What in Hades's name are you doing here?" Devin smiled as she crossed the room.

With a bright grin, the two of them hugged. "Oh, how to answer that? Um, well, short story. Our Elder sent my sister and me to negotiate a peace treaty as ambassadors." Right. Short story. At least, she got it all out quickly and without interruption. To make sure that Devin understood she wasn't alone, Parthenia discreetly tapped her fingers on the hand on her shoulder that remained hidden. With the nymph watching behind them, it wasn't like her mate could talk.

Devin glanced up over Parthenia's shoulder and grinned, then looked back at her. "That is... wow... exciting. Good news, right? I would love to know what brought that on. And I am thrilled I ran into you; I was planning to come and look for you. But I have... news. I was not sure if you would know or not." She raised her eyebrows for a moment in question. "I just had to come and get a few things here first."

"Is it good news? Yes. And I... we know. We might have been around when it happened." Which meant they both knew something. She raised a finger. "Let me buy this really quick, and then maybe we can go somewhere and talk for a few minutes?" Not that she had any idea where they could discuss everything. Plus, they couldn't go too far. Cipriana would come seeking them out any time now.

"Yes, of course. I have missed you. I just need a few moments myself." Devin squeezed her hand, then moved around the room.

Parthenia nodded, and while Devin collected the items required, she took her mushrooms over for purchase. She could easily spend a long time here, but they had a journey to continue and information to share. Despite the nymph's wide-eyed stare, the transaction went quickly. She tucked the mushrooms in her knapsack along with the other items she had brought along and almost forgot about the poppy seeds. To comfort the nymph, Parthenia smiled brightly and gestured to the basket. "I was curious where the poppy seeds came from." Her voice had a bit of a melodic lilt to it. She preferred not to use her manipulation powers, but this was something that demanded honest answers. She didn't think she'd get them any other way.

"Someone was kind enough to donate them a few hundred *solaris* ago. Since then, we've been able to produce them ourselves."

Interesting. But not really enough information. "Any idea who the person was or their species?" Not that she was confident that knowledge would help. Nor did she have a clue who she could share it with *if* she got a name or species. Her sister maybe.

"No. They didn't give their name."

"Alright. Thank you." Well, that was... disappointing. Next to nothing for her to go on or to pass along. With a slight frown, she turned toward the door and cast a glance at Devin. "I'll just be outside." With that said, she left the shop, her mate still right there with her.

As soon as they stepped into the open air, Cipriana approached. "Get everything you want?"

"Actually, it'll be a few minutes. I ran into a friend, and there's some information we need to share." Yeah. This was going to go over well. There was *a lot* she hadn't told her sister.

"A friend? How is that even possible?"

"Just come with us when she comes out, and I promise to explain everything." Please, just let her accept that.

"Fine." With a grumble, her sister set the small bag of fish down at her feet.

Devin exited the shop a couple of minutes later and went up to them. She nodded to Cipriana. "Hello. My name is Devin."

"Cipriana." Her gaze flicked to Parthenia. "You're just full of surprises, aren't you?"

"I get it. I haven't been all that forthcoming." She sighed. Her sister was being difficult. "Devin and I need to talk. You agreed to come along."

Grumbling again, her sister nodded. "Then let's get a move on."

Parthenia turned to Devin. "Do you know someplace private where we can talk?"

"I think so. Come this way." She led them through the market-place, dodging people as they wound around to an alley next to a food place. Even from where they stood, wonderful scents wafted in their direction. As Devin knocked on the back door, she looked over her shoulder at them. "Either Jacques or Bruce, the trolls who work here, will probably answer the door. They're both very large, but both gentlemen." The door opened, and a tall, green-skinned male with bright-red hair glanced out at them.

"Hey, Jacques," Devin said. "Do you think we could use Ambrosia's office for a private discussion?"

"She's not here, but I don't imagine she'd mind. Come on in." The male offered a slight dip of his chin.

Parthenia took it all in as they followed behind Devin. There were some interesting aromas in the kitchen as they walked after a troll larger than her mate. She'd never seen a creature like him before. But then again, she expected to see a lot of that over the coming days.

Once they got into the office, Cipriana set the bag of fish she'd purchased aside and leaned against a wall as the door was shut. "Okay. So, please tell me what this is all about?"

"Well..." Parthenia glanced at Devin and back at her sister. "You know there's a barrier around the isle, right? You've seen the fog from the sky."

"I didn't know it was a barrier, but I can accept that."

"It kind of went down. Gavin and I noticed it." She glanced over her shoulder. "It's been... what... six *umbras*?"

Gavin wrapped his arms around her waist and laid his head on top of hers. "Yes, about that long."

"Really? I met someone at the bridge, and they said it had been several *umbras*. This is the first *umbra* I have left the territory in almost a *penumbra*. I have tried to lie as low as possible, not to ruffle any fur unless necessity demanded it," Devin said.

"Yes. We were in the treehouse talking about a meeting I had with my Elder when we noticed the change. We might've gone to check it out." Before Cipriana could even utter one word, she eyed her sister. "We were both invisible. And we didn't stay long." Resting her hands on Gavin's, she returned her attention to Devin. "Wait, tell me you didn't approach the guard?"

"No, I did not approach." She bit her lip. "More like I made what many would say was an unintelligent decision, out of my desire to get information, and got approached." She held up her hand, cutting off questions. "Everything went fine, and I was not harmed. I just came from there."

"Thank the gods you weren't harmed." Parthenia frowned. She had warned Devin about the dragon-shifters. Sirens had wings, even though they were lesser beings. She pinched the bridge of her nose. "Let me rewind to the *umbra* the barrier fell. Gavin and I saw a blue-winged siren along with some dragon-shifters as they inspected the bridge like we did. We think she's the one who caused the barrier to fall. Then we went back the next morning. That siren, along with what we believe, are two dragon-shifters. Well, they headed toward the forest. If the barrier is still down, that means they are somewhere on the isle. We may have a chance to actually leave."

Cipriana's jaw slackened. "Wait a minute. You aren't just talking about leaving Pteryrina. You mean to leave Prisma Isle? Period."

"That is what we prefer, yes."

Her eyes widened. "I get named the next Elder, and you're going to leave me?"

Parthenia reached forward and grabbed her sister's hand. She gave it a gentle squeeze. "You don't need me here to serve as a sounding board or even to help guide you. You have Vasilia, as well as your mother. They'll be there to help."

Dragging a hand down her face, Cipriana groaned. "I can't believe we're having this conversation. Me, yeah, okay, I'll have help, but you need to figure out how to tell Fantasia. You know how attached to you she is."

"And I will."

Devin refocused on Parthenia. "You must keep all of this to yourself. I received the information only because I promised not to speak of what I learned to anyone, but I let him know there were a select few that I could not keep from telling. They do not want others venturing there out of curiosity or to be blamed for what happened. He even spoke about the possibility of a war starting. Tensions seem very high right now, so please do not go back to the bridge again. I was explicitly warned not to do so. Something about the Matriarch, whatever that is, would not be as kind as the one that I spoke to if they caught me. He spoke of a bizarre bird with unique colorings. That must be the blue siren you two saw. He confirmed she was the one who brought the barrier down, but she did not come alone. Invaders followed her."

"The Matriarch is their Queen, Elder, whatever word you'd like to use as the equivalent. Aurelia, according to the journal. The female took on the role in the last *solaris,* if I remember it correctly," Cipriana stated as she dug two items out of her knapsack. She pulled out a scroll and a thick leather-bound journal. She set the scroll on the desk and opened the journal. "Yes. Aurelia."

"'Invaders?'" Parthenia questioned. They had seen nothing; then again, they hadn't stayed long, either. Her gaze flicked back to Devin. "If we can't leave by the bridge, then there's got to be another place we can leave from, but how? And we'll say nothing."

Devin crossed over and peered at the journal as she answered Parthenia. "Yes, 'invaders' are what he called them. By his description, they may not be distinguishable from the guilers I saw in Chicane Village, except they attacked without provocation. According to him, they look like flesh and blood, but they have, as he stated, strange appendages. And they have elemental magic, like the ones I saw in Chicane. With the barrier down, they may enter by other means than the bridge. For example, they could have boats or magical means to cross over the water. Just be careful on your travels, though I know that goes without saying." She looked over at Parthenia's sister. "How much information is in this?"

"A lot, actually. It goes back hundreds of *solaris* with information on nearly all the Elders across the entire isle. Métamorphe is the exception. Most of what we have is on Markham's predecessor, not much on Markham himself or how he gained leadership," Cipriana said. She glanced at her sister. "I can trust her, right?"

"Yes, very much. Devin has helped Gavin and me with a lot of information." Parthenia leaned against her mate. Invaders meant it would be even harder to leave. If that was the case, why hadn't the other siren closed the barrier behind her? If those guilers were similar to the ones Devin had seen and possessed the same elemental magic, why were they viewed as invaders? At least it answered one question. There was something beyond the bridge.

Cipriana's nose twitched a little as she flipped to the pages in the journal about the leaders of Métamorphe and shifted it in Devin's direction. "Like I said, not much. Don't suppose you have someplace you could hide this, do you?"

Gavin gave her a gentle squeeze and caressed her arm with his thumb.

"How is so little known about him?" Devin questioned. She scanned the pages, running her finger across several lines. "This alone has more history than anyone in my village knows about our species, outside of Markham himself, I am sure. Our history is completely absent and has never been taught, at least in my short lifetime. I believe it is somewhere on the isle. I just have never found it." She read a little more, mouthing something from the journal.

Lip reading wasn't really a specialty of hers. Parthenia bit the inside of her cheek. Not that she was paying much attention to what Devin had mouthed. Just enough to know if she needed to chime in on something.

"Well, I do not know his past, but I can tell you some about his powers and where I believe a good majority of them stem from. That he is a purist is most definitely accurate. It is a law of his, but that is as much as I know about it. Even mixing the forms within our species is forbidden. He has punished and killed many for it, and the young...." Devin's words trailed off. "Avoid at all costs; probably the best advice I could give you regarding him." She flicked her gaze to Cipriana. "I have a place where I hide things. No one has ever been there. If you need this to be hidden for you, I would be more than willing. It is definitely not something you would want to fall into the wrong hands."

"Well, he isn't the only purist on the isle. It seems to be something many of the species have in common. Perhaps something that is killing us off as well." Cipriana sighed. "Any information I can add to this would be most helpful. And yes, a good hiding place. I wouldn't have brought these things with me, but something told me I couldn't leave them in Pteryrina."

Parthenia just listened to her sister and Devin talk. She was comfortable in her mate's arms. She squeezed his hand in return. It was nice just to be here, and for once, not to have to worry over something. Maybe this was precisely what Cipriana needed.

"Markham does a good job of killing us off on his own. The smallest thing can invoke his wrath, and he rarely cares who is in his way. If you have time now, I would be happy to fill you in on as much as I know about him, or we can meet up somehow after the completion of your journey. That may be a better option, depending on how much time you have right now. While I know barely anything about him, there is a lot I could tell you. Gavin could as well, though I have discovered some things he may not be aware of."

"What did you find out?" Gavin asked.

Devin tapped her forehead. "His crown. He has a crystal inside of it." She glanced up from the book at Cipriana. "If your instincts were telling you that, there is probably an excellent reason, even if you do not know what it is just yet."

"A crystal, huh?" Cipriana's eyebrows furrowed. "There are a couple of references in here about crystals with other species and that they are what—for lack of a better word—powers Prisma Isle." Her gaze shifted to Parthenia, and she just shook her head. "No. I don't know where the one for the sirens is located. According to Vasilia's notes, it was lost some time ago." She peered back at Devin. "Honestly, it depends on how long you think it would take. We're heading toward Migas, and though Santos isn't expecting us, we still have another fifteen miles left on our journey. So, it might be best for afterward since we need to cover almost the whole isle."

A slight frown crossed Devin's face. "So, every species *has* one? I discovered that the one Markham carries is where he's gotten at least some of his powers from. I do not know how he came to possess it, though, or if he has always had it. He has powers that I have seen in no one else, certainly no other shape shifter. What he does with those powers is unnatural. Evil. And after is fine." Devin strode across the office and collected a knapsack from a bookcase against the wall. Pulling out a piece of parchment and a pen, she scribbled out a note and left it on the desk. "I am in the marketplace at least once a week, specifically here. If you do not see me here, ask to speak to Ambrosia. She runs this place and is a very dear friend of mine. She can get a message to me. Unless Markham spontaneously bites the dust—one can only hope—do not seek me out at the shape shifter territory. I could be killed just for associating with you on a friendly level. I would honestly not advise going anywhere near that place, period, and certainly not over the border. Markham has killed before when someone just lost their way."

"Yes, if what the journal states is accurate, then every species has one. Or at least should. Our current Elder stated not to go beyond the borders." Cipriana nodded to Parthenia and Gavin as she closed the journal. "They were going to talk to me about it later. I feel they would say the same thing, with full indication we shouldn't even go near the borders at all."

"I'm sorry, Cipriana, but you're right. Especially the two of us. He'd smell Gavin on me, and Gavin is already being hunted." Maybe she shouldn't have told her sister that, but she had to know. Their lives hung in the balance with Markham. She wouldn't take that risk.

Her sister groaned. "I feel you've put me in a horrible position, but I'll consider everything you're saying."

Devin looked at Cipriana. "Please do so. Parthenia stated they had sent two as ambassadors to negotiate a peace treaty. I can tell you with full confidence that with Markham that will be complete-ly pointless, extremely dangerous, and potentially deadly. Peace is way too far from his agenda if the way he treats others is any indication. I have not seen him actively go after other species unless they cross over into the territory, but that does not mean he does not do so." She glanced over at Parthenia and Gavin. "Those two, well." She flicked her gaze back to Cipriana. "Markham would kill Gavin, and it would not be a swift death. Parthenia would likely be killed as well. Either Markham would choose to do so because of Gavin's association with her, or she would be killed defending him or trying to save his life. With the powers he possesses and the Informants he has control over, escape would be impossible. I understand that puts you in more than a difficult position as, if I heard you correctly, you become the next Elder of your species. That does not change those facts, though."

"Yes, that's correct. Not that I think I'm necessarily the right person or even old enough to be considered, but that's what our current Elder decided." Cipriana shook her head and shifted her gaze to Parthenia. "The last thing I want is to endanger you. You're my sister. I'd never forgive myself if something happened to you and I could've prevented it." She inhaled and exhaled a deep breath. "We'll skip Métamorphe." She turned her attention back to Devin. "I'd appreciate your hiding these until we can meet back up here."

"Absolutely." Devin took the journal and the scroll and tucked them both carefully into her bag. "I am glad about your decision. I am working toward a solution to the problems of Métamorphe. Unfortunately, the result is proving a little difficult to get to. I am close, though. If his downfall comes to pass, I will let you know as soon as possible. Perhaps then, a peace treaty would be a possibility. Time will tell." She glanced briefly down at her bag, then looked back at Cipriana. "Tell me no, but would it be too much to ask if I read through the parts that concern Métamorphe? I am merely curious about the ones who came before, is all."

Cipriana regarded her for a moment. "For Métamorphe alone, yes, but nothing else. The same with the scroll. That should stay closed. It's more applicable to Pteryrina than anything else."

Devin nodded once. "Of course. I will not look at the scroll, and will look no further in the journal. Thank you." She crossed the room, giving Parthenia and Gavin a group hug. "Please be careful. All three of you. And please do not leave without saying goodbye."

"We will not, so long as we can help it," Gavin replied. "Thank you for everything you have done for us, Devin."

"You are more than welcome. I would not have had it any other way. I only wish I could have done more."

"You did more than enough. More than you had to. We will not forget it."

Devin smiled softly. "Stop it. You are making it feel like this is the last we will ever see of each other. Your mother is well enough. She has not left Métamorphe, but I do not think that will come as a surprise."

"No. It does not," he said sadly. "Gabby?"

"Is doing well. She left a few *umbras* ago and is staying with Derrick in a well-hidden cabin," Devin responded.

Her mate breathed out a sigh of relief. "Oh, thank the gods for that."

Parthenia took her friend's hands in her own and squeezed them. "You helped a lot, Devin. Please never shortchange yourself. I know you do so much for everyone else, but don't forget to do it for yourself, too. You deserve that. And yes, if it's possible, we will say goodbye before we leave." The news about Gabby made her happy. It was good to know she was safe. She'd been afraid the female would never leave. "If you see them soon, please ensure they know we're traveling together and hope to see them soon as we make arrangements."

"I guess this means we're ready to continue toward Migas?" Cipriana asked.

"I will do so. Find me afterward, or Logan in Migas Village. His mate, Ambrosia, is the one that runs this place. Any of us can give you directions to the cabin or can get word to them on where to meet you." Devin gave her hands another squeeze. "Be safe, all of you. I will walk you out."

"We will." Parthenia smiled. This was good. Fantastic. They had a way to get to Gabby and Derrick so they could all leave together after this was over. "Be safe as well." She nodded to her sister. Then, with no further words between them, they all left the privacy of the office, went out the back door they'd come through, and returned to the alleyway before they all parted ways.

the
Sirens

Chapter Nine

Mac gripped the back of his neck as he, Nomad, and Aurelia crouched down behind a grouping of half-dead trees. From where they hid, he could see nearly every angle of the compound. Four solid walls, two guilers at the entrance, and another six walking along the edge of the wall above the gate. How were they supposed to even get in there?

That was before he considered all the superstructures, most of which appeared empty. Only one seemed to be occupied, and it sat near the back of the complex. So, there wasn't any way to see the number of guards protecting the one building. Or even how they'd get into it, provided they got inside the complex to begin with.

It was bad enough it had taken them much longer than he expected it would to get to the center of the isle. The darkness threatened to consume them, and they had to stop repeatedly to fend it off. They'd crossed a few guilers here and there, but none of them engaged unless they were directly in their path. The less attention they drew to themselves, the easier this mission would be.

At least, that was exactly what he'd told her as they continued to the current location. The sun had risen maybe a few hours ago, give or take a minute. Now they had a whole new slew of problems. Not to mention the issues that having Nomad with them created. Mac glanced at Aurelia. "Any thoughts?"

"Why are you asking me? Thought you said you didn't want fireworks," Aurelia replied calmly.

"Because you might see more than I can. We don't want fireworks unless you just want to announce, 'Hey, we're here,' and that might just give them a reason to kill him." With a sigh, Mac dragged a hand through his thick hair. Good stones. Why did she have to be difficult?

"Of course, I can see more than you can," Aurelia said. "I can see all of them—inside and out—and their magicality. Guessing the one without the darkness is your old man."

Mac scrubbed a hand down his face. He'd picked her over the bluebird. Why? Oh, right, pheromones. "You think?" He crossed his arms with a smirk. Okay, she could see—wait, all of them? All the guilers. *That's pretty handy*, he thought to himself. "How many are there? Total in the complex."

"At least thirty apiece, assuming you think you can keep up."

Well, that, indeed resolved one problem. And made the most sense. If they left Nomad in their current position, they could get him before they left. Mac sat and dragged a hand across the top of his head. That was a lot. Considering there'd be various elements coming at them, there was no way they could take them all out. They'd get Felix killed in a heartbeat. He stood by his original stance. The two of them needed to sneak in unnoticed. He was more physical than a female siren, and he had a few tricks, just like he was sure she did, also, but even that would be too much for them to tackle on the way in.

At least on the way out, they could cause some damage. Then again, if Felix was weak, they couldn't leave a string of bodies in their wake. "Can you see a way for us to sneak in? Tunnel access? Or something from underground? That's our best bet. Then we come back for Nomad on our way out."

Aurelia folded her arms, shifting her weight to one hip. She turned her laugh into a cough. "There," she pointed to the slender opening at the base of the wall. "A way back from the main entrance. Judging by the stench, it's their sewage system."

Great. Just what he wanted—to wade through crap—just to sneak inside. But Felix was worth it. He blew out a heavy breath. "If that's what we have to do." Not that he'd stop her from looking for another way in, but if the situation remained unchanged, then they'd do what they have to. Whatever they did, they couldn't waste time. It had already taken too long to get here.

She scoured the walls and the interior layout of the city. She frowned, retracing the walls, streets, and alleyways. Aurelia sighed. She shook her head in dismay. "Let's just get closer. Maybe we'll see an alternative, or something I've missed." She started down the slope. The bright, flickering flames of the guilers moved back and forth along the routes of their posts. If it weren't broad daylight, they could find a hole in their patrols and slip over instead of under.

"Stay here, Nomad. We'll come back for you. Okay?" After the shape shifter gave a simple head nod, Mac rose and pursued Aurelia, his talons scraping against the soil as they descended. So many things that they could cross. Had she even seen what they were all capable of? He smirked. It would be nice if he could switch his looks, but something was preventing him from doing that. It had to be the crystal that he dug up at Felix's request, hours before they'd gotten hit. Almost made him think the male knew the guilers were coming. Mac eyed the stone walls as they moved closer. They were thick; definitely guiler made.

Aurelia glanced back, a hint of irritation in her tone. "You realize you're leaving tracks? For someone living on land for most of his life, that seems like a gross oversight."

Stopping in his tracks, he glimpsed over his shoulder. Inhaling a deep breath, Mac blew out the breath he'd taken, and the wind shifted the sand covering the trail he'd left behind. He looked back at Aurelia. "Better?"

She shrugged, her gaze shifting forward. She continued along the wall; eyes peeled for an alternative entrance. Nothing but polished black stone for infinity. Her eyes lifted skyward. She wrinkled her nose. "Can't we just drop in from above? They don't appear to have many airborne scouts," Aurelia groaned. "Before long, the sun will be at the highest point in the sky. The lack of clouds will ensure that those on the ground are blind to everything directly overhead."

"They may not have what you can see as airborne, but that doesn't mean they won't shoot things from the sky. I'd rather not chance it, but you're welcome to, princess." He smirked. Yeah, someone like her would be too good for crawling through the sludge.

"What? Those glorious green feathers of yours no good as a shield? Or are you just too slow to avoid projectiles?"

"Like I said, princess, go to the sky. I'll crawl through the muck." He grinned widely. "It doesn't bother me."

"Suit yourself," Aurelia said, lip recoiled in disgust.

Mac nodded as he continued his way toward the side. She'd pointed out the direction of the sewer access moments ago. "Then I'll see you on the inside, princess."

"You're kidding." Clearly, he wasn't. She pushed her taloned hand through her golden mane, letting out a low growl. "Alright. Alright!" she exclaimed. "Come here, you idiot."

Raising an eyebrow, he turned around. "You planning on hugging me?" He didn't want her anywhere near him. Helping her to her feet the day before had been the closest he'd been to any person in years. That was exactly how it was going to stay.

"What? No, are you fucking retarded? Why would I hug you?" Aurelia shook her head. "I'm taking us straight to the center. Unless you insist on smelling like a guiler's ass for weeks to come."

Gods, not really. He'd lived with guilers his whole life. He knew how bad it could get. With a groan, Mac ran a frustrated hand through his hair. Yeah. He probably wanted her touching him about as much as she wanted him touching her. At least this way, they'd get it over with. They'd already wasted enough time. "Fine." It took every ounce of willpower he had to close the distance between them.

Aurelia rolled her eyes. "What's your hang-up? I'd say 'I don't bite,' but we both know I'd be lying."

"What? You're the only one who's allowed to have issues with others touching them?" He snickered. Yeah, apparently, her feelings were the only ones that mattered in this world. Princess, all about her.

"I don't 'have issues,'" Aurelia clarified. "It's not permitted. By law. You just make it all…" She threw her hands up, exasperated. "Weird. It's not like I'm contagious or something."

"Let me guess, by your law." Mac nodded. Yeah, princess. "Whatever. Let's just do… whatever you intend to do."

"I didn't make the stupid law. I'm just expected to live by it," Aurelia sneered. "Just hold still and shut up." She paused long enough to narrow her eyes at him. "I'm gonna take your hand now, so try not to lose your head, chicken boy."

"Yeah, but I feel you can change it." He grinned and winked at her before she took his hand. If he'd known it was just that, this conversation would've been a lot shorter.

"You're so hot and cold, it's not even funny," she mumbled, closing her eyes. Taking a slow, shallow breath, she held it as she concentrated. She swallowed nervously, clenching his hand. She breathed out and in again. As she breathed out a last time, everything about their current location shifted and slowly disappeared.

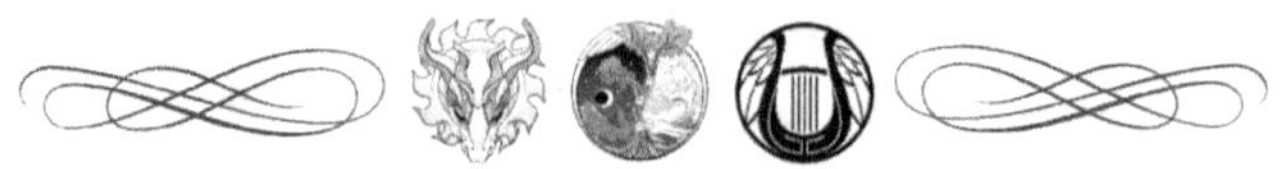

Hand in hand, Thalasia and Seru stared at what appeared to be nothing but an endless forest. She glanced to the right, confirming the existence of the apple trees not far off in the distance. This had to be the right place. A breeze swept through, rustling the leaves and causing the branches to creak and reform into an archway before she could utter a word.

"Guess that answers that question," she mumbled as the two of them stepped through the entrance. If she hadn't been clear about how little her visions provided, this certainly spoke volumes. At no point had she seen anything about a shape shifter. Her body tensed a bit. She might've squeezed Seru's hand. Thalasia swallowed, trying to dislodge the heavy feeling in her throat. It wasn't a bear, so she could deal with it. Especially since the male appeared attached to the siren she needed to talk to. Her eyes flicked to the other male in her vision. So, that was Santos, huh? Fortunately, they were granted entry.

Santos bowed his head to both her and Seru, but only for a moment. "Parthenia, my child, I believe they are here for you."

"Me?" The siren's brown eyes widened.

"Seru, I expect you will be on your best behavior," Santos said. He glanced over his shoulder. "Delenia, will you please show our guests somewhere they may speak privately?"

"Yes, Santos," Delenia said.

Baring his fangs, Seru rolled his eyes. He leaned close to Thalasia. His whisper came out as a snarl. "I guess the plan where he isn't included is out." He snorted.

"Just be nice, and maybe this is as far as it goes," Thalasia whispered. Not that she liked that much, either. Of all the places they had to end up.

Santos smiled at the other full-blooded siren and gestured toward a nearby hut. "Shall we?"

"Yes, thank you," the female said, moving in the specified direction. She offered one glance over her shoulder at the other siren and shape shifter before disappearing inside.

Santos paused just outside the hut, and his eyes fell on Seru and Thalasia. "Oh, Thalasia, be a dear, and ensure when you leave, you take Seru with you." He grinned one last time and stepped inside the hut.

Thalasia squeezed Seru's hand again. Multiple reasons, really. One, to keep him from going after the phoenix. Two, how the fuck did he know her name? Three, the phoenix had ground on her nerves.

"If the four of you will follow me," Delenia said.

The shape shifter tucked the siren closer against his side, which kind of amused her. Well, their relationship anyway. Not that she'd ever dare call a siren... a bird. It was quite insulting. Even if the female was with a feline. Still, Thalasia watched as he kept his hold around... Parthenia... that's what the phoenix had said was her name.

A few feet remained between the four of them as they followed a female whose species she couldn't identify. Strange. Monitoring the shape shifter, Thalasia glanced at Seru. It was a good thing she had a firm hold of his hand. It might be the only thing that stopped him from clawing out the phoenix's throat and parading his corpse around the tight-knit community they'd stumbled upon. On some level, Seru's response to Santos was unexpected. On another, it made perfect sense. Thalasia readjusted her hold on him, wrapping her arm around his waist. One, she needed him to calm down. Two, being even this close to a shape shifter was making her skin crawl. It meant the ones she'd seen back in the market hadn't been shape shifters. This one had fur covering its entire body. She preferred the ones she couldn't tell apart. Not that she should blame the other male; it was her past. Three, the siren kept looking over in their direction. It was unnerving her a bit.

Delenia led them to a couple of benches close to a set of barns, out of sight from the villagers. "You may speak here." With a slight bow of her head, she left the four of them alone.

The black panther shifter kept his arm around Parthenia, keeping her tucked against his side and still keeping several feet between them. "What is it you wish to speak to her about?"

Seru's glowing gaze settled on the male. "We want to know more about sirens. We hear she's somewhat of an expert." He failed in forcing a smile; his voice held some growl. His arm wove around Thalasia's shoulders loosely.

"That hardly answers the question about why her specifically. Nor how you came to find us in this place," the feline said.

Parthenia's gaze focused on Thalasia. "Exactly how unique are you?"

Yeah, no way in hell was she offering information regarding her visions. How they found out about the other siren wasn't all that important. Nor how they found them. And the question that Parthenia just asked was one question she really shouldn't answer.

"I will tell no one if you are truly *that* unique," Parthenia said.

Thalasia narrowed her silver eyes. "It would seem you indeed are an expert."

"I wouldn't call myself that, but I do like to read." Parthenia smiled.

"What do you know of a book called *Celestimo*?" Seru seized the provided opportunity. A shared love of books and knowledge might prove beneficial.

Parthenia's gaze flipped to the panther shifter. Pulling her knapsack around, she dug into it and removed a piece of parchment. She held it out to them. "It's hidden. There's supposed to be a map amidst the ancient texts in Antekilio, though we have yet to locate it, and we've combed through most of them."

Accepting the folded letter, Thalasia opened it so both she and Seru could read it. Not that it was the only thing she was curious about. She didn't recall Mac mentioning the name of the book. So, how did Seru know it? Then again, he'd known about the curse she hadn't mentioned, either. Not that it impacted her, but no way he could know that.

The letter read: *The truth of the siren history is not protected within these walls. To prevent any further information regarding the history, prophecies, and more, Celestimo—the one book with all the answers—has been hidden. If you have found this letter, a map has been separately placed amongst the ancient texts that will direct you to Celestimo. Should you locate the map, take precautions, as the journey was not made to be easy. -A-*

After reading the letter once, Thalasia traced the elegant loops and flourishes of the handwriting. She had seen it before, but she wouldn't mention that right away.

"How did you hear of it?" the shifter asked.

"I have my ways." Even if he hadn't directed the question at her, she'd answered it anyway. She certainly didn't expect—

"I also like to read," Seru said. "Who's 'A'?"

Well, he'd proven her wrong. Not that he offered any more of an answer than she had. Thalasia smirked, leaving Seru's question unanswered, although she knew it. She recognized the handwriting well. Though it certainly surprised her to find anything that belonged to her family on this isle. Even if she'd been told stories as a child.

Parthenia shrugged. "No idea. I've searched our archives, and there's not enough there to decipher their identity. Whoever it is, they went to great lengths to ensure the book remained hidden."

Thalasia folded up the parchment, but didn't return it. "You said you'd been looking for the map, though. Correct?"

"Yes. There are still more books to go through in Antekilio. I suspect it may be in one of them."

"Do you know of a way to sneak into Pteryrina to get to the library and continue the search? I'd like to find the book." Again, she wouldn't state why. But it was beyond necessary for them to find it.

"If you allow us to assist in your search, I may use your letter," Seru indicated the parchment lingering in Thalasia's hand, "to help track down the map. Dragons have heightened vision attuned to magically imbued texts. Not to mention our ability to follow scents... though I'd be surprised if your—" He looked at the silent panther. "Mate. Hasn't given that a try."

Parthenia raised an eyebrow, and half smirked. "I have, and Celestimo isn't in the library. However..." Her nose twitched a little as she eyed Seru and Thalasia. "I know a way in, and I'll help you get there to find the map. On one condition?"

"Which is?" Thalasia asked.

"If you're truly the one prophesied, then you can help us get off this isle. Promise to take us with you, as well as two others, and I'll tell you how to get in." Parthenia grinned widely.

Oh, fuck no. Demeter, please, for the love of the goddess, tell her she didn't have to rescue another one? Her vision *had* led her to Parthenia. Dammit, whether she wanted to believe it, this was likely the reason. Here she just hoped it would be to get answers. Well, fine. If she was meant to help them, so be it. "Done."

"There's a secret passage hidden by willow leaves hanging from a ridge. It's about fifteen miles along Haggle Road if you travel through the marketplace. But you'll need a couple of things." Parthenia dug around in her knapsack again and pulled out three vials. Two with a clear liquid and one with a blue liquid. "These two are an invisibility potion. You'll have about a *lacuna's* use, so make the most of it. The other one is a cleansing potion. It won't completely mask your scents, but it should help."

The shape shifter nodded his head once in Thalasia's direction. "Thank you."

Seru hesitantly accepted the proffered vials, holding them up in the sunlight to better discern their hues and contents. "I didn't realize your species relied so heavily on its sense of smell."

"We use all our senses," Parthenia said.

He handed off a pair of vials to Thalasia. "When the time comes, I drink first." It wasn't so much a question as a statement. He watched the panther closely. "What's got you so scared, kitty?"

Inhaling and exhaling a deep breath, Parthenia looked at Thalasia. "Do you think we can speak privately for a moment? Perhaps while we do that, Gavin can educate your mate on exactly how much the dragons have distanced themselves from the ongoing issues amongst those on the isle."

Tucking the vials, along with the parchment, into her purse, she glanced from Seru to Parthenia. "Yes, of course."

Squeezing the panther's hand, Parthenia nodded to him. "We won't go far, my love."

He dropped a kiss on her cheek, then on the back of her hand. "Alright, love."

Chapter Ten

C old stone materialized beneath Mac's and Aurelia's feet. All sound disappeared, if only for a moment, absorbed by the high walls. Shivers coursed through his entire body as they faded and reappeared. Mac, disoriented, momentarily lost his footing as they emerged into an enclosed room. After he settled into a position, his eyes swept over the room, absorbing the details. At last, his eyes rested on the simple bedding where Felix lay, his fragile form barely covered by a thin sheet. Shaking the sensations off, Mac rushed to the male's side. He'd been the father he remembered. His parents had been killed so long ago, he barely recalled them anymore. Mac dropped to his knees. "Father?"

Felix's eyes slowly fluttered open; their whites revealed. "My son, is that you?" His voice was hoarse and rough.

Aurelia stepped back to give them space.

"We've come to rescue you," Mac said. The male was weak. He could see it in his labored breathing. Felix's breath came out slow and shallow, barely stirring the air. How were they supposed to make it out with him? Even if Aurelia did the same thing as she'd done before—no... there was no way Felix would survive that.

"We? Have you... brought... *her*?"

'Her?' Mac glanced over his shoulder, and around the room until he found Aurelia. It was possible Felix heard her movements, but there was no way the male could tell the one with him was a female. "I have someone with me, yes."

"Is it *her*?" Felix asked.

"Sorry to break your heart, Gramps, but bluebird elected to stay behind," Aurelia said with a cringe, and her voice echoed in the chamber. She stepped closer. Her voice fell to a hush. "She's got her priorities all out of sorts. Maybe we can take a message."

Felix blindly reached out for the female. "Come closer, child."

Of course, his father would've hoped to meet Thalasia. She was supposed to be important to the sirens. She had already proven her worth to him, provided she helped his people as promised. But what did Felix want with Aurelia?

"I said, I'm not her," she repeated. "I'm not the blue siren you're looking for. She's back on the isle. In your village."

"Oh yes, I can sense the difference," Felix said, still reaching for her.

Mac dragged a hand down his face. They'd been gone long enough; they'd be lucky if bluebird and her boyfriend were still there. He flicked his gaze to Aurelia. Gods, please just let her humor him. "He's blind, not deaf."

"And you're afraid of girls! Bite me, you giant kiwi," she hissed, edging closer. "What do you want from me?"

Again, he chose the princess. Why? A low rumble settled in his throat. Gods, if he hadn't needed her help. Mac narrowed his eyes at Aurelia. Insensitive, cold, dead fish. That's what she was, but to appease his father, he kept his mouth shut.

Felix grasped Aurelia's hand. His strength was fading. "Their choices are their own, but he cannot save his people without her."

"Father, what are you talking about?" It was one of those damn prophecies again. The male had shared them with him his whole life.

"Leave while you can," Felix said.

"His people are your people, unless you're talking about more sirens. In which case, no thanks." Aurelia pulled back her hand.

"They are not the same, young dragon," Felix said.

"Enough with the riddles, father. We need to get you—"

"I will not make it. You must leave me." Felix took a shaky breath.

It wasn't the first time the male had interrupted him, but he didn't like the direction this conversation had taken. The withered fingers that had curled around his hand loosened their grip. "Father..."

"You... must... leave..." Each word came out on a gasp. Felix's eyes drifted shut. The male took one last sharp, wheezing breath and exhaled. His hand fell away from Mac's grip and landed on the bedding platform.

Aurelia said nothing.

Mac stared at Felix's body. He'd seen enough death in his life to know what would happen next. He sat back on his talons and rested his hands on his knees. There would be time for tears later. Right now, he was ready to kill some guilers on their way out.

Felix's body withered into a pile of ash. A breeze came out of nowhere and carried the small grains through the slight gap at the bottom of the only door in the room.

"If you tell me that's a sign, we should go out that door. I'm gonna smack you," Aurelia warned. She shook her head.

"I see just how little you know about guilers." Felix's body disintegrated in a manner befitting an air guiler. Mac rose to his feet. They'd come in quietly, but no reason to go out the same way. "But if you want to kick a little ass on the way out, I'm game."

"Not to worry, you can fill me in on the way home," Aurelia smiled. "A little? I came to burn this entire isle to cinders! And all the little guilers with it."

He didn't know if that was a good thing or not. Yeah, she had powers he didn't. Although he could carry his own, no way he'd be able to take *that* many out. He wasn't a fool. Nor did he expect it to be as easy as she had expected. Right. He planned to take a few out and stay alive. Balling his fists up, he pounded his knuckles into one another, and a green flame crawled over his hands. "Kill what you can, but be smart about it. There are still things on our own isle to take care of."

"I like the knuckles." Aurelia nodded at his fiery palms, sounding more than a little impressed.

"I don't really care." He withdrew the flames. She'd done something to the door when they'd first gotten in here, not that he'd seen exactly what she'd done. There was some shuffling outside the door. Hmm, the question... which element was outside? It could be air with their immediate surroundings. Or fire if there were lanterns lighting the hallway.

"What? You want me to kiss it all better? I'm sorry you lost your old man. It's not like we didn't try..." Her words trailed off. Their time for talking was over.

"Well, princess, you ready to do some damage?"

"Fuck, yeah!"

"The only thing you need to do right now, princess, is kill some shit. Nothing..." He smirked. His gaze focused on the concrete walls as he reignited the flames over his fists. If they'd been smart, it would be—an explosion of the earth went off behind them.

Aurelia snatched Mac by the wrist, and in an instant, phased them out into the hall behind their attackers. She matched his emerald flame with her own, taking out those nearest her before turning back to Mac.

Grinning, with a dazzling white smile, fangs and all, she called back, "Six," before phasing into the next cluster a few rooms over. At this rate, they'd torch the entire complex in a matter of seconds and be onto the next encampment.

Alright, he'd give her props for the element of surprise. As long as no others had left the isle, they'd accomplish what she wanted. He didn't move through them as fast as she did. Although he lit a few on fire with the flames, he also slammed his fists through a couple of heads. "Do... you... really... need... to... count?" He grunted the words as he pounded on another one from his side, one he was sure was the earth guiler.

Her laughter echoed through the black stone halls. "Worried you might lose, green bean?" she called affectionately. "How about I give you a head start by... Oh, say, 100... Will that do?"

Half lifting a wing, he spun on his foot, and quill-like feathers shot from his appendage into oncoming guilers. A feather nailed each in the neck, blood gushing all over the floor. "I'm thinking I should've brought the bluebird."

"And here I thought slow and sensuous wasn't your style. You and beasty love the motherly types. That's unfortunate," Aurelia replied. "Eighteen."

"It isn't!" He called out as he trailed behind her, but then again, he didn't want any female. He just didn't care about the competition. Taking a life shouldn't be thought of as something to compete over.

Hopefully, any that were good, like the ones he lived with, had fled. Or were in the process of, but he figured they'd more likely be the ones in the outer villages. Honestly, it was kind of nice to take some out in the opposite direction of the dragon.

"C'mon, you know it's going to be boresville once we get back," Aurelia said.

"'Boresville' for whom? You? I have a village to rebuild, people to take care of, and apparently, I have to figure out what Felix was talking about with bluebird." Nevermind the stone in his pocket. He still didn't know what to do with it. All his father had mentioned when he dug it up was that it had become tainted over the years and needed to be purified in Pteryrina. The male never mentioned what to do with it once he had cleansed it. And now, bluebird, although he had a feeling, he knew what Felix meant; he didn't want to do it. So what if he found her attractive? The female looked at him with utter disdain. Kind of the same way the dragon did.

He smirked as he waded through dark guilers. Their black blood covered the ground, his clothes, even a little on his wings. It didn't make him any less weighed down than he'd been when they first arrived. He focused on what was in front of him—from behind, a golem grabbed hold of his arm and flung him down the hallway. He hit the floor with a resounding thud. Pain lanced across his shoulder and wing. With a hiss, his eyes darkened and he jumped to his feet.

"All the more reason you should focus on enjoying yourself while you can," she commented. She checked in the opposite direction. Her face fell in disappointment as she threw up her hands. "Why do *you* get the big one?"

"Find the guiler!"

In the same instant, just as the words left his mouth, a spout of water doused the dragon.

That had been worth the five-second delay. He flew down the hall at the golem. Big one! Good stones, this fucker would keep coming and not drop until they took its controller out. Mac reignited his flames as he landed behind the golem and hopped on its back. The blind spot would only get him so far. He slammed his fists repeatedly into the back of its head.

"That one's mixing elements!" Aurelia shouted. "Fire!" she gasped.

Did she say it was mixing elements? Oh, shit. Hmm, maybe there was another way around this. He could beat the golem's regenerated head only so many times before he tried something different. Not like he could grow or spew fire. But he could try to make use of his own flames, which were nothing like hers. So, using his talons to dig into the golem's back, Mac pressed his hands on either side of the golem's new head and sent his green flames down the body of the golem toward its core.

It was a long-shot chance it would reach back to its creator, but if the guiler in question had both fire and earth—it could be used to their advantage. Something he'd learned a few years back. His flames were poisonous to fire guilers. He strengthened his hold as the golem bucked to throw him off its back. He didn't need to know exactly which guiler it was—a small smile crept onto his face as his flames reached the golem's creator.

The golem continued to buck, and he truly wasn't sure he could hold on much longer. Not that he could see what was going on with Aurelia or pay the princess much attention. "A little help!" Mac maintained his hold and continued focusing his flames toward the one guiler. He couldn't see the impact, but he could hear the screams coming from the creature; still, it wasn't enough. It would take both of them to kill the fucker.

"Not gonna say please?" Aurelia asked.

It would've been great if he could see what she was doing. But all he heard was the wailing of the guiler as his flames, through the golem, shot through to its veins, likely threatening them to the point of bursting. "Today, princess!" For fuck's sake, what was she doing? His grip on the golem loosened. Before refocusing his attention on the flames, Mac slammed his fists twice against its head, the sickening crunch of stone filling the air. In those small fragments, the flames had rescinded just a little and offered the guiler a brief reprieve. Not that it lasted.

Mac landed on his feet as the golem disintegrated beneath him. He wiped the black blood from his hand on his pants. He rounded the corner and strode toward Aurelia. "Still think we can battle a whole isle of those fuckers?"

"I *know* I can burn them," Aurelia replied, slinging the black sludge from her talons, inspecting them for damage. "Next time," she informed him, turning to brush past him. She stood tall, her head held high in a proud stance. "I get the big one."

"Fire doesn't work on all of them, princess, but if you're determined to get us killed, then let's just go back in the direction we came. I promise we will run into more golems where the earth guilers live." He smirked. Yeah, she was definitely going to get them both killed. Her arrogance was something that left a foul taste in his mouth.

Aurelia turned her head in a flash of blonde waves to regard him with an unfriendly glare. "I'm fearless. Not stupid. And certainly not ill-prepared for this brief *excursion* of ours. I understand you mourn the loss of your father. I'd offer you sympathy, but we both know I wouldn't mean it. Not truly. We don't regard death as the end. Not most times anyway," she amended. "I don't care to fight with you, Mac. Or against you. I simply wish to restore balance to our lands and *our* people. Respectively." Her violet gaze fell. "I want to ensure this isn't what we become. No matter the reason. Be it hatred. Be it black magic. Or something worse altogether. Unless you desire to say your peace for your father, let us be done with this place. Return to Prisma Isle. I'll provide aid, numbers, and guards for you to rebuild your village." With that, she strode down the maze of halls in search of daylight.

For a moment, she surprised him. The last thing he ever expected from her was aid—of any kind. She'd been reluctant to go with him. At least, that was how it had appeared. Mac sighed heavily. Maybe he'd been a little too harsh with his earlier words. "I learned that death is just a natural part of life a long time ago." And he'd never been the same. Even he could acknowledge that. He followed her. He had a lot on his plate to deal with back home. "I appreciate the offer. The fairies and Seelie have been good to us over the *solaris*, and I suspect that relationship will continue, even in Felix's absence." Mac paused for a moment. "I don't want to see Prisma Isle become this wasteland, either, but very few have been willing to work together since the war. Maybe we're the ones who change all that."

It took a few moments before she responded. "Will you take his place? Your father's, I mean."

That was a good question. Mac gripped the back of his neck. "I suppose so." No one had ever mentioned it. Although in some small way, maybe that was part of what Felix had groomed him for over the years. His responsibilities had grown since the male had taken him in. Yes, he was technically a siren, but he didn't imagine ever living in the sky amongst the other sirens. Nor could he ever truly fill Felix's shoes. The guidance the male had given, even to people who weren't his own—how was he supposed to do that?

"Will they just accept that?" Aurelia's eyebrows knitted together as she continued the long trek to the proper exit. She kept her shoulders square, posture straight. "Is that what you *want?*"

"Honestly, I don't know. Most of them treat me now as if I'm... next in line... I guess. As for what I want... I don't want to leave. Felix took me in when my parents were killed." He failed to mention that he'd witnessed it. Not that he remembered much more than a lot of blood. A memory occasionally he tried to recall more of but always failed. "Part of me feels like I owe it to him to stay and make sure *our* people are taken care of. Someone has to look out for them."

Her eyes narrowed ever so slightly. As they emerged from the fort into an expanse, presumably the courtyard, she inhaled deeply. Her skin crawled with amethyst scales. "Can your people not muster the same strength as..." her words ceased as her taloned hand caressed the open space before them.

"My people are different. Of those trained as warriors, only a handful can call on more than one element. All of them can use their element at will, but they also give back to their element to maintain the balance." Something he'd been reminded of on more than one occasion. His physical training never outweighed his philosophical training.

"You said, 'more than one.' There are those that can wield more than two elements." It wasn't a question. "What about all four?"

"One or two, but Felix is the only one who has ever mastered all four."

For the first time since their words in the main hall, she turned to face him fully. "Give back? What happens if they don't give it back? What happens if they take it all—forge it into one potent attack?"

He tilted his head at her last question. Oh, right. She didn't really understand guilers. "It doesn't mean they give back after every use. It just means that either before or after they are done with the full use of their element, they offer something to their element. If they throw the balance out for any reason, they have the potential to... well, become like the ones we've seen here. That's not something Felix nor I have ever allowed."

"You can prevent this?" she pressed, stepping in closer.

"If they aren't too far gone, yes. I can prevent them from losing themselves." He took a step aside. She was just a little too close for his liking.

She settled back on her heels. Her gaze never left him. "How? Why didn't they?"

"I believe Felix used the stone before he took me in. I was a teenager when I discovered my flames. They... cleanse the darkness from those who haven't truly lost themselves. For those that have, it's toxic." Something he and Felix stumbled upon by accident. At least one dark guiler had lived in the encampment for some time. If he'd used it on Nomad, the shifter would've been killed. It happened a second time with another guiler in Chicane, except it had the opposite effect.

Aurelia's face fell. A deep frown was obscuring her features. Finally, she broke their eye contact. Relaxed her posture.

"From what I understand, those who escaped to Prisma Isle after the war made a choice. There may even still be some here, but most of those that are here, the darkness has swallowed them. It's like a disease... one that will spread. I may have used the stone to remove it from Nomad, but even it has its limitations. We can't save all of them." It was impossible. He could count the number of times he'd come across Felix muttering to himself over those star charts he'd given away. Constantly trying to find an answer. One that didn't exist.

"The one you saw descend into... This... Darkness," she paused. "How did it progress? Walk me through it from start to finish."

"No one in our village has ever fully descended. For those who begin the descent, it's as simple as they use their element and don't offer something in return. They do it again and again, and then they end up with a deformity. Like I told you, Felix or I would step in, resolve the darkness that had wormed its way in and re-educate them. They're watched closely to ensure it doesn't happen again." None had ever started repeating those issues. They'd saved a few over the years that way. All this talk about the darkness made him curious.

"That can't be all," Aurelia stated.

A small smile tugged at the corners of his mouth. "It really is that simple. Their ability to manipulate elements is the same as any other power. They maintain a balance. Otherwise, they get consumed by it."

"You expect me to believe... *You* seriously believe they created all *this*... And just up and decided one day that they'd abuse their power, destroy the balance, and succumb to—turn into—this. What for?" At some point, her voice had risen with her frustration. "It makes little sense," she said more quietly, allowing her hand to fall by her side as she took in their surroundings. The structures weren't just shoddy huts like in his village. They were advanced marvels of architecture. The guilers came from a society of knowledge and innovation. Aurelia glanced back, scouring the center. She started off. "You go ahead. I'll catch up."

With a shrug of his shoulders, he took a few steps and stopped. Mac turned and faced her. She was trying to make it out to be complicated. When the truth of the matter was, it was never as complicated as it sounded. It all boiled down to desire. "The guilers in my village want to live their lives peacefully. Do you ever think that those here built all of this so that one day they could exact revenge? I mean, revenge is a powerful motivator, and it can darken even the purest of hearts."

"Revenge on whom? On what?" she called back. "They're the predominant species."

"But they weren't always," he said and spun on his heel, continuing on his way toward the gates. Pausing for a moment, he glanced over his shoulder at her. "I'll be waiting with Nomad. We can't leave him here, not with how he is now."

That alone should be a reminder that, although the dark guilers there may currently be the predominant species, things had changed. It wasn't hard to see the guilers who'd been manning their stations had disappeared. Either they'd left, or they had been among the many killed over the last hour. Not that it mattered much. The fact remained: no one stood between him and the exit.

In all her questions, it bothered him just a little that she'd forgotten all about the war. He hadn't been around for them, but Felix ensured he knew about them. Both the war between all the species and the one that had taken place in Pteryrina.

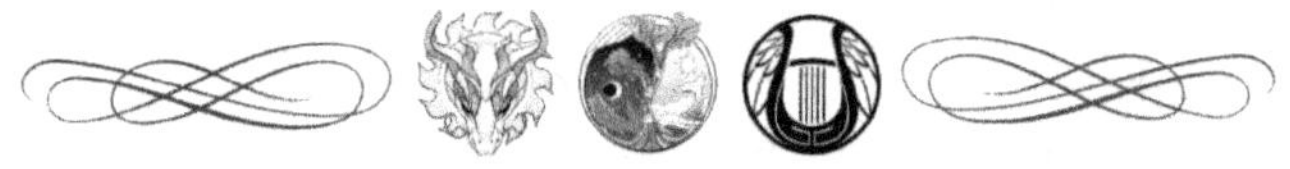

"I apologize for taking you from your mate like this, but I thought it was something we best speak of privately," Parthenia said.

Thalasia stopped herself from interjecting and making it clear Seru wasn't her mate. The admission was there on the tip of her tongue. She glanced over her shoulder at him. It wasn't the word her particular breed of sirens used, but she couldn't admit that, either. Not that she thought that description applied, despite the way he watched over her. Something she still didn't quite comprehend. "It's okay. I'm sure he understands."

"Well, that's good. But with our species, we seem to require a mate who is understanding and patient, truly."

"What do you mean?" She had a pretty good idea what the female meant, but hearing it from a siren's perspective differed from hearing about it from Seru's perspective.

Stopping where they stood, Parthenia canted her head at Thalasia. "The curse."

Bingo. Just where she hoped the conversation would go. Parthenia had already talked to her and Seru together about the barrier and the book. The curse? Seru had said it was rumored. If she'd been honest with him, she could've confirmed its existence. Not that she had all the details. The more she knew, the easier she could portray a regular siren. "I don't know what you're talking about."

The female inhaled and exhaled a deep breath. "My mate and I, shortly after we met, discovered there were certain things we couldn't do. So, I did some research at our library. After some *cycles*, I found out the goddess Nemesis cursed sirens."

Yeah. That much she knew. A male siren had done something stupid over a century ago. "What is that you couldn't do? Do you know what caused Nemesis to curse us? Or how to break it?"

Parthenia folded her hands at the small of her back. "We're limited in what we can do sexually. To be specific, we can't kiss, like on the mouth, and from what we've discovered, we can only partake in oral sex. I don't know all the details of what led Nemesis to curse us, but something to do with actions taken by a siren hundreds of *solaris* ago against her. As for breaking it, I'm hoping you'll find that in *Celestimo* as well."

No kissing. No full-on sex. Just oral sex. Thalasia blinked and chewed on the inside of her cheek. So, as long as Seru didn't know the complete truth about her, then she had to limit a lot of what they did. She'd never been intimate with anyone until last night. The memories of what Seru had done to her body with his tongue sent a blast of heat straight to her core. The way his shoulders bunched up between her thighs. Or the tinkling of the beads every time she grabbed and released that mane of his. Good gods, she had to stop thinking about that. She glanced over her shoulder again at Seru and lowered her voice as she returned her attention to Parthenia. "So, you have some experience with oral then? Like you've..."

With a slight nod, she leaned in close. "Tasted him? With my mouth?" Parthenia grinned. "Yes, I have sucked his dick."

"Yeah, that." That was rather blunt. Still, she took it in stride. "I have more theoretical knowledge than an experienced one." Although her mother had covered the basics when she was young, she'd gotten a little more information as a teenager. Mostly from books and watching public exchanges between couples. If memory served her, the humans called it a public display of affection. Kind of like what she and Seru did when they held hands, or he kissed her forehead or cheek.

"Your mouth is great for suction, but you can use your tongue to tease him. You can suck his balls, too. Males really like that." Parthenia winked.

Listening to Parthenia's description of limitations, she thought back to what had happened the night before with Seru. Was there typically more to it? She hadn't thought of asking him. Not that she could tell him she was unlike the other sirens in more ways than one. She'd been honest with him about her sexual experience.

Thalasia peered at him again and bit her bottom lip. She'd never truly appreciated how handsome he was before now. Well, she was surprised a little less. Maybe a little less shy. "What about my hands? Can I use those, or am I just limited to my tongue and mouth?"

"You have to be careful about where you place them. We haven't tried my hands on that part of him, but when he even got close to that part of me, it was a shock that went through both of us." Holding up a finger, Parthenia shrugged off her knapsack and dug out a small black book. She held it out to Thalasia. "Try reading that. It's a siren's journal. She writes about everything she and her mate ever tried. Obviously, there are some things you won't be able to do, but it'll help with the stuff you can."

That should prove interesting. She had learned a lot from other books and people watching, but reading something from a siren's perspective would be new. She raised an eyebrow as she accepted the journal. "Are you sure about this?"

"Oh, yeah." Parthenia wiggled her eyebrows with a wide grin. "I promise you'll be surprised at all the things we can do with our wings."

"Really? Our wings?" The female had her curious. She opened the book and scanned a few of the pages. Words here and there popped out at her, but what got her attention were the diagrams. There were so many diagrams. Exactly how many positions had this couple tried? Thalasia tilted her head at one as she held the book up. Was the female upside down? How was that even possible?

Parthenia smiled at her mate and nodded. "Absolutely. And I promise your mate will enjoy them, even with our current limitations. I can tell just by the way he looks at you, the way he watches you, and the way you keep stealing looks at him, you two truly love each other."

Her eyebrows knitted together as she closed the book and faced Seru. Neither of them had uttered one word about love. Yes, they cared for each other, but love? Did the female see something she didn't? Maybe Parthenia was just blinded by her own love because Seru had made it clear they weren't mates. It wasn't her term, but it was the most common. But Parthenia hadn't just said *mate*, she had said *love*. Shaking the thoughts from her head, Thalasia smiled. "I'll take your word for it. Thank you for this, though. When we find the book, I'll look for a way to break the curse."

"Thank you! Thank you! Thank you!" Parthenia threw her arms around Thalasia in an excited, warm embrace.

That was unexpected. She patted the female on the shoulder and eased out of her grip. "You're welcome." Pulling the purple pouch from inside her gray-denim capris, she tucked the journal safely away, adding it to the small collection of things she had inside the purse with no end. "So, really quick, with the vials you gave us, am I to assume one is drunk, and the other isn't?"

"Oh yes, the cleansing potion. You just pour a small amount into your hands and run it along your arms. Don't do that until you've gotten into the staircase, and then you can drink the invisibility potion."

"Good to know." Though Seru had already made it clear, he would use them first before she did. It didn't take a genius to understand he was being protective. Something she wasn't accustomed to. As they headed back toward their males, she glanced out of the corner of her eye at Parthenia. "Have you and your mate attempted anything other than oral?"

"Well, yes. We found out about the issue when we tried to kiss. It was an amazing two seconds that was followed by a kind of shockwave. It threw us apart, and he ended up falling out of the tree we were in."

Thalasia covered her mouth as she stifled a chuckle. She really shouldn't laugh. Though it made her more curious. They were more affectionate than she'd ever seen any couple. Definitely *way* more affectionate than she and Seru were; not something she wanted to change. She couldn't ever see calling him some kind of cutesy nickname. The thought alone made her shudder. "How long have you two been together?"

"Close to six *cycles*, I believe. We met in the spring. We both knew right away we were each other's other half."

"Oh?" Had her parents ever told her how they met? Had it been like that with them? She couldn't recall.

"Yes. Our eyes glowed, but even if they hadn't... just one look... it was just something I saw in him and I knew I couldn't be without him." Parthenia let out a satisfied sigh.

Slowing her pace, Thalasia stopped. "With as long as you two have been together, has it only been your eyes that glowed? Not your body?"

"Just our eyes."

Just their eyes. She had to be different all around. Completely different. Why? Maybe it was an Atlis thing. Maybe she could find something in the journal she had from her predecessors. "Are the birth records and family archives in Antekilio?"

"Of course, they are. We keep everything there. Historical records like that are cordoned off. Only those with a key have access to it."

"It's good to know they're kept safe." And that they were in a locked room, which meant, unless it was magical, she could pick it. Her family records. Yeah, those didn't need to stay there. The two of them walked back to where their males had been conversing and watching her and Parthenia.

Chapter Eleven

When the two females had walked off a bit, the feline shifter turned and eyed him for a minute before answering. "I am not afraid. Just… wary, as my instincts are leading me to be. We know neither of you, so how can we know if we can trust you? For all we know, you could get what you want, and we could never see you again. If that happens, we will find another way, but that will certainly not make things any easier. And there is too much at stake for us."

Seru readjusted his position to keep his eyes on Thalasia while still facing the shifter enough to assess him. "You can't," he replied plainly. "We can't trust you, either. The only difference is we have less to lose. We'd… she'd…" Seru amended, praying he and Thalasia weren't nearly as annoyingly affectionate as this pair. "Be stupid to help you so readily and without knowing what you're really fleeing from, which I strongly suspect is much more than just your species' rejection of interspecies relations. However, Thalasia isn't one to make false promises. If she said it, she'll help you. She will move mountains to do so." He watched her as he spoke that last. Observed her regard of the other siren. They appeared to be getting along well enough, though he wasn't sure what to make of their "girl talk." He frowned at the prospect. "She's a genuine woman. Be sure you and your mate don't rob her of that." He paused. "Why do you shifters and sirens refer to your partners as 'mates?'" he asked no one in particular. "It sounds so primitive." His frown deepened. "Clearly, you cherish one another, and with the curse in place, it's not like you're reproducing. Not that biology would rule in your favor even if…" Gods, he was rambling. He let the train of thought drop, realizing belatedly that his out-loud musings were serving the sole purpose of distracting him from entirely focusing on Thalasia. He promptly forced his gaze away.

"As we will not be traveling together, at least not yet..." the panther shifter paused, "...the dangers we face are ours. Neither of us would ever have intended to harm another. But if she truly will help us, I assure you we will not take that lightly." He tilted his head a bit in question. "Is that not a familiar term? I do not ask that to be rude; I just know very little about other species." He turned to gaze a little more in the other siren's direction, still eyeing him from the side. "The physical connection is not the important part. My soul and hers are connected. They are two halves of a whole. We knew it as soon as we met. Even when we are apart, we feel each other in ways that I have never known with another, even being a twin. Her happiness becomes mine, the same with her sadness, anger, or pain. I know it is the same for her. Sometimes, I think my heart beats only because hers does. Being apart from each other is painful, and we cannot imagine a future that is not spent together. Without each other... everything else is meaningless." The panther looked over a bit more at him. "I know there are many who would say that needing another to survive would make us weaker. But it has truly done nothing but strengthen us."

Seru pondered the panther's words. "'Mate' in our culture is a breeding partner," he explained. "It's unnecessary for love or connection. It's for producing offspring. The Matriarch seldom grants her subjects permission to reproduce. It's a privilege. Not a right. The term doesn't encompass any relationship beyond that between a male and a female. It's very specific. Limited. I'd never name Thalasia as my 'mate.' It feels... degrading." He continued to wonder over the man's description and the depth of his feelings toward his partner. Which title in the Draconic hierarchy best suited that description? Was there even a suitable all-encompassing equivalent? He idly responded to the latter statements, if only to validate the other man's feelings for the tidbit of info he continued to chew on. "If you meet your match, there's no shame in admitting it. It should make you twice as strong."

The shifter frowned a bit. "Where I am from, so-called matings are mostly false. It is what they are called, but the two share no love or genuine connection. It is based solely on the male's desire, then only if the..." his nose scrunched up and the tip of a fang showed, "*king* allows it. The number of offspring is not controlled, at least not to my knowledge, but the type is." A smile crossed the male's face. "I would never be ashamed to admit how I feel about her. Despite how most of my species view the word 'mate,' I have always thought of what we have together as what a *true* mating should be. One based on love and affection, how deeply we care for each other, how we balance each other. Not what we can... bring to the table, so to speak. Even if the curse is never broken, I know our love for each other will never change. She will always be my other half, even long after the gods have decided our time on this earth is at its end." The feline looked back at him. "I can understand, with your culture the way it is, why you would shy away from using that term. Regarding your feelings towards her. Is there a term that would be more appropriate?"

Seru listened intently to the panther's explanation. A false mating sounded like a miserable affair. Worse than an arranged marriage. Draconic matings were for status and power, sure. But the arrangements were often short-lived. Not lifelong torment like what the panther described. The number of restrictions, or lack thereof, sounded awful. The males could literally breed their women to death with no one to stop them. He understood most species didn't revere their women in the same way the dragons did. Hell, the dragons only revered females within their own community. Why would any self-respecting king allow such a thing? Surely, it would decimate the population. Create less healthy, weakened offspring. In time, it could deplete their numbers entirely.

It made little sense.

Was the shifter king mad?

"Your Markham has no honor. He is no king. A fool in a paper crown, perhaps."

He thought for a moment. "I don't know. Dragons live extremely long lives. Their partners change with the seasons. The concept of loving only one person over a thousand *solaris* or more... that's a tall order. No matter your species. Climates change, and people change with them. Can you truly say you love all sides, all versions of a person without ever truly knowing them?"

The shifter raised his eyebrows slightly. "You say that not even truly knowing the half of it. But you are right. He is no king. Though he wears a crown." Gavin snorted. "He is a destroyer, and he appears to find full enjoyment in it. What he does to his own people, to all of them, and what he allows to happen..." The male sighed and shook his head. "With my love for her, I can say with no doubt, yes. Though I feel as if I truly know her, we discover new things about each other all the time. Before meeting her, I had been empty my whole life without ever knowing why. When we met, it was as if my soul had found what it had always been searching for. She is truly my other half, the one who completes me. I could not fathom ever feeling what I do for her, not even anything close, for anyone else. Nor would I want to."

A Destroyer. Seru knew all too well what it meant to be a weapon; a tool used to destroy. He'd done more than his fair share of tearing apart the lives of innocents. And for a while, he'd enjoyed it just as much as his brothers had. Was he any better than this false king? He didn't wear a crown or claim a high station. But wasn't he just as much a pretender?

His belly tightened in response.

Did he deserve to bask in the temporary sliver of sunlight Thalasia cast his way? Or was he simply taking advantage of another unfortunate soul too naïve to know the truth, the depth of his shadows, and what hid within them?

"Do you believe yourself worthy of her?" The question left his lips before he could think to stop it. Seru closed his eyes, a shallow sigh of regret escaping him. It wasn't like him to be so careless. Why was he even pursuing this silly train of thought? He knew where it ended. No answer the other man could provide would change that. Their lives demanded they separate. Now or later made no difference. The result was the same.

The male frowned a bit. "Honestly, I do not know. I never really thought of that. If you were to ask my father, he would say I am not worthy of anyone." Gavin shrugged. "But the way she looks at me, the love I feel from her, she makes me feel as though I am worthy of everything. We have shared dreams of a future we want to give each other, a future that would mean nothing to either of us if we did not seek it out together. So, even if the curse is never broken, though I hope it is, I would still want to spend every moment of the rest of my life with her by my side. I want to ensure she never goes a moment without something she wants or needs. That she spends every moment in joy, that nothing ever holds her back from anything she ever wants to accomplish. I have done nothing in my life so spectacular as to deserve someone like her. And I have done nothing evil toward another person. But even if I were the most worthless person on this earth, I feel as though she would still love me the same." The male shrugged again and glanced back at him. "I know people who refuse to seek their own happiness because they do not feel as though they deserve it; they do not feel as though they deserve anything good. They may put on a cheerful face, but inside they are miserable. That is not how I want to live my life. For whatever reason, whether it was a conscious choice or whether it was fate or the gods pushing us together, she chose me, and she loves me with her whole heart. I would be the biggest idiot alive if I threw that away, or turned my back on it, simply because I did not think I deserved it. The gift she has given me is too rare, especially considering where I come from, for me to ever think of walking away from it."

Séru's brow creased in response. "What happens when the universe decides your time together has ended? That your 'mate' isn't your 'mate.' Or, worse, when your false king discovers your secret? What will you do then? Every time you meet, you take a risk, not just with your life, but hers as well. Surely, you've recognized that by now. Your desire and pursuit of it may one day condemn the one you cherish to death; can you live with that when the time comes? If he shows you clemency, but only after he separates her from you by granting her the most painful death imaginable." The male wouldn't be able to protect or save her in that scenario. He'd be powerless. Since, clearly, he hadn't overthrown the false king. Nor had anyone else. And their respective friends wouldn't likely try to save them, either.

"I do not think the universe would decide that. Instead, it led us to each other. I believe it will not part us until death does, and even then, I believe our souls would find each other in the afterlife." The shifter sighed. "The risks that come with our being together have always been there. And she has known them since the beginning. She shared them as well within her own species. So, though my death is more likely to occur than hers, we both know it is a possibility for both of us. Markham would never be lenient with me; it is not in his nature. If he were to catch up to us, he would kill me. But that would be true whether or not he found me with her. That is why we travel as carefully as we do. I would do anything and everything to save her from any kind of pain. And staying apart to avoid being caught together *is* probably the wiser choice. But the pain of separation... each time it grows worse and worse. It is a pain worse than any death for her as well as me. What kind of male would I be if I put her through that pain? If I stayed away from her to keep her a little safer, knowing it was not what she wanted and knowing how much pain it caused her."

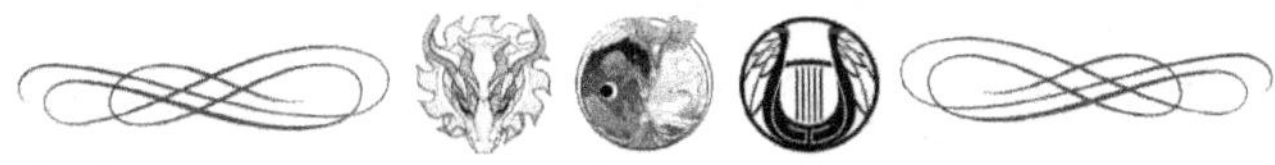

"Of course, they would be," Parthenia said. "It would be irresponsible of us if anyone could gain access."

Thalasia simply offered the female a smile. Her gaze focused on Seru and the shape shifter. She hadn't heard what they'd spoken. She had focused more on her conversation with the siren. It was not only pertinent to the tasks ahead but also to her own... desires. Shaking her concerns off, she looked back at Parthenia as they continued their approach. "You said that you've already searched through some books, correct?"

"Yes. The bottom row in the last aisle is the only one we haven't gotten to. The area is marked, so you shouldn't have any issues finding the section."

"Thank you; that's helpful." Also meant she'd have time, if the woman's calculations of the invisibility potion were correct, to dig for something that didn't belong there. Her eyes flicked again to Seru and the panther shifter as they returned. "You boys have a pleasant conversation?"

Seru merely shrugged in response, too deep in his thoughts to bother with a proper answer. His gaze remained downcast.

Okay, Thalasia thought. That worried her a bit more. She reached out and gave Seru's arm a gentle squeeze. Obviously, he was lost in his head somewhere. Something they both had a tendency to do, him more than her. It was dangerous for her to get lost in her thoughts. For a moment, she considered saying something but decided against it, given their company. If nothing else, she hoped the tender touch would let him know she was there for him. Not that it stopped her focus from staying on him and less on the idle conversation the siren and shape shifter were having.

Seru laid his hand over hers, squeezing back before letting them fall between them. He blinked a few times to clear his head. "'Good' comes when we've left this place and obtained the book. Not before."

Yeah, as if that didn't speak volumes about the conversation he'd had with the shape shifter. And after their situation this morning... nope, she couldn't go there. Thalasia nodded. "We have everything we need from her. We just need to find one more person on our way out."

Dropping her hand, Seru grumbled, "Let's get this over with and take our leave before the almighty Santos graces us with his presence."

Thalasia flicked her gaze to Parthenia and the shape shifter. They didn't really need them any longer. The one she had to find was a half-breed. And whatever conversation occurred between Seru and the panther. Yeah, she wasn't sure *pleasant* was how she'd describe it. "Do you guys mind? I need to talk to him alone for a second."

Parthenia glanced from them to her mate. "Sure."

Once they were far enough away, Thalasia stood in front of Seru, gripped one of his arms again, and cupped his cheek. "Okay. Do you want to talk about the whole three-sixty? We don't have to do it here, but I know something happened. Whatever it is, I just need to know you're really..." 'okay' seemed like an inadequate word to use, but she wasn't sure she had one better, "...okay."

Seru squeezed shut his eyes, taking in a deep breath through his nose. "I want to raze this village to the ground and pick that irritating phoenix apart a feather at a time." He'd trapped her hand beneath his and was squeezing painfully tight. He immediately loosened his grip.

Thalasia grimaced, but nothing more. "Does he really get to you that much?" Okay, yeah, he'd gotten angry, and she'd been a little annoyed herself. Somehow, the male had known her name. That bothered her, seeing as she couldn't explain it, though part of her wondered if it didn't somehow involve her great-great-grandparents. There was a bigger picture, and she just didn't see it yet.

"Yes."

She wished she had a simple answer for him. But honestly, there wasn't one. Thalasia continued to stroke his cheek with her thumb. "He's not worth thinking about or even focusing on. He doesn't deserve any of your attention." She would've prevented them from coming here if she could've, but it hadn't been plausible.

"No, but you do," Seru said, bringing the back of her hand to his lips.

He was constantly worried about her. She lifted her eyes to Seru's exquisite, blue orbs and focused on them. Was Parthenia right? Was there something there she hadn't seen? "I think you give me more attention than you know." She wasn't overly concerned Santos knew her name. That a piece of her family history was there. It had meant one thing—they lived here. Even though it didn't last, she knew the possibilities of her coming up in a vision... well... that wasn't something she planned to touch on there.

"Do I?" he asked, using his thumb and forefinger to massage his eyes.

"Yes. And you won't hear me complain about it. It's... I'm just not accustomed to it." She hadn't been the focus for a long time. Not since... her parents.

"Good," he offered her a sleepy, lopsided grin. "Because it's not likely to change. At least for as long as you stick around."

That was the key right there as long as she was around. And it was getting harder by the second—the idea of leaving him behind. They still had so much to do, and he needed rest. She may not be sure about anything else, but she could see that. "Let's go find the female half-breed and get out of here," she said, still cupping his jaw.

"Too bad we can't just pick and choose," he mumbled, taking her hand in his. "You lead, boss lady."

She raised an eyebrow at him as they started walking. "Pick and choose what?"

"A female half-breed," he clarified with a sweep of his arm.

Thalasia chuckled. "Wouldn't that be a thing?" It would certainly prove interesting. Plenty surrounded them. None in their immediate vicinity looked to be their target, of course.

"Your way sounds more interesting," Seru commented.

"At least I'm not in a position to be the subject of a bet this time." A few days ago, it annoyed her. Then again, maybe it had been the debate with Aurelia. The rest, it had been in good fun. She scanned the area as they strode along. Her gaze fell on two half-breed females talking by a collection of chairs in the clearing. One... she tilted her head. Yeah, that was the one she was looking for, and the other—was that a half-donkey? That was definitely new. She nodded toward those two females. "There."

Seru followed her line of sight to the pair. "Any thoughts on how you want to approach this?"

Oh yeah, she had an idea. A small smirk settled on her face. "Hey, barkeep," she called out as they got closer.

The female with the burgundy hair in a ponytail glanced over her shoulder. "Songbird." The half-siren female looked back at her companion. "I'll catch up with you later, Ina."

Ina nodded, giving them a clearer view of her appearance. The top half of her body was human-like. She had long, light-brown hair and dark-brown eyes. Her lower half was covered in short fur, and she had the hooves of a donkey.

The half-siren faced Thalasia. "What brings you to my neck of the isle?"

Seru remained silent as the other half-breed walked away.

"Hoping for some information again," Thalasia said. The female had been helpful before, and she was taking a shot that it would happen once more.

She stood there for a moment and scrutinized the two of them. "You've upgraded your company, I see." Her fingers settled on the necklace around her throat. "What're you looking for?"

"Aside from the obvious, a place to find manticores."

The half-siren smirked. "That's easy. Belly of the Beast."

"Is that in the marketplace?"

"Sort of." She sighed. "There are some back alleyways, but you can't miss it. The name fits."

Thalasia nodded. "Thank you. You've been a big help."

"Mind if I ask you a question?"

Before Thalasia responded, Seru seized her by the wrist, pulling her along in a sudden hurry to follow the half-breed the barkeep referred to as Ina. What the fuck? Okay. Something was going on. As much as she wanted to ask what had caught his attention, she figured she could find out later.

Another female had stopped Ina somewhere along the way.

"Ina!" Seru called out, ensuring he stopped some distance away from the other half-breeds.

Frowning, Ina peered over her shoulder at Seru and canted her head. Her gaze flicked from him to her. Then, Ina turned her attention back to the female she'd been speaking with. Even from this distance, Thalasia could hear the niceties in the half-breed's voice. With a single nod, Ina turned and approached the two of them. "Is there something I can help you with?"

That was a good question. One she couldn't answer. Thalasia eyed Seru.

Seru opened his mouth to speak, but couldn't seem to formulate words. After a moment or two, he finally spoke. "Yes," he said, shaking his head. "Maybe... I think so."

"Are you certain? You do not sound confident in your response," Ina replied. "If you have a request for jewelry, my mother is better suited for that."

Thalasia glanced from the half-donkey-creature to Seru and back again. Something was definitely up. It worried her a bit. He didn't always have this kind of trouble finding his words. Most of the time. Maybe she could help in some small way. Not that she was positive about that. If nothing else, she could stall while he figured out what he wanted to say. "If that was the case, where would we find her?"

"She is currently at her shop in the market. The Four Muses."

"Oh? Can we get any jewelry there?"

"Yes. She customizes each piece. No two are alike."

"I don't want jewelry," Seru said, his expression one of confusion. "I'm looking for a weapon. Gilded with rubies." His hands moved to size the weapon for reference.

"Oh, we do not sell weapons." Ina paused and frowned. "There is a family heirloom, though I do not know my mother would part with it. Again, you would need to check with her. If there is nothing else."

"Thank you." Seru reluctantly gave up his unexpected and impulsive task. For the moment, anyway.

"You are welcome." With that, she gave the two of them a nod and returned to the female she'd been speaking with before.

That was strange, Thalasia thought. "Tell me you actually got something out of that."

"Ah... Something, yes. Though I'm not sure what." He turned to her and squeezed her hand. He leaned in to kiss her cheek. His breath was hot and hushed against her skin. "We'll talk more once we're on the road."

Another flash of heat speared her body, and her scent blossomed. Even she could smell the change. Her breathing became slightly erratic. Oh, gods. She swallowed to wet her parched throat. Thalasia attempted to shake the sensations coursing through her veins.

His nose wrinkled, a hiss escaping him as he pulled back enough to look at her. "We're going to have to be more conscious of your pheromones, or we're going to be in trouble," he rasped.

The way he was looking at her right then—it didn't help. She bit her bottom lip. Good gods. She took a step back by sheer force of will and put a sliver of distance between them. "Just... uh... just... give me... a minute," she said, her voice husky. Thalasia closed her eyes and focused internally on the heat setting her body ablaze. It was a kiss on the cheek, for crying out loud! Or maybe it was Parthenia's words getting stuck in her head. Crikey. She had to clear her thoughts. Get her body to quiet and settle. It required several deep breaths and much longer than she expected to get the fire stirring inside of her calm. This wasn't good. Not good at all. She swallowed again once it had stilled and opened her eyes.

"You all right?" Seru asked, a little wary.

"Better. How long did I stand here?" Her body was cooler. At least she didn't feel like she was in her own personal inferno.

Seru laughed. "Not long at all," he murmured.

"Well, that's good." She might have lied just a teensy bit about what she knew of the pheromones. If she hadn't stood there too long, then they were still controllable. A bundle of desire wasn't something she needed to be. It wouldn't help either of them.

"I *need* to speak to that half-breed's mother at the Four Muses," Seru prompted.

"Okay. Well, we need to hit the marketplace, anyway. At least we don't have to run all over the place." She inhaled and exhaled one last deep breath and squeezed his hand. If she hadn't dropped his hand, they were definitely still controllable. "Let's get out of here."

He took the lead, careful to keep at least a little distance between them. "You're certain you're alright?"

"Yes." She had to tell him. "I can control it to a degree. That might not be the right word. Extinguish... that's more accurate, but it's going to get worse each time." She kept trying to think of how her mother had explained it. In the end, it would lead to one thing. At that point, there was no controlling it. There was no cooling down. But that was a whole other ordeal that she wasn't even prepared to explain.

"You can push it down for a time. Like I can with the beast," Seru said, bringing his free hand to his chest. "The other siren is right. We need to find the answer to this curse. We can't allow it to get to that point."

Yeah, exactly. Not that the curse had anything to do with it. Although she already knew how to break it. She'd simply chosen something other than her mission, but she couldn't tell him that. "We do. I know we won't find the book in the library, but the map..." Something that tied back to her family. Why was it always her family line involved in things like this? Like she really had to ask that. "Knowing him..." she grumbled. "That we'll find there."

"Him?" Seru asked.

"A," she said. Yeah. She knew who he was alright. "I'll tell you once we're outside these walls."

They brushed shoulders as they walked, sending a shiver down their arms. Seru cursed. She tensed for just a moment as the shivers passed and another jolt threatened to light up inside her. Good news. Later, she'd put the book Parthenia had given her to use. It would help quiet everything charging between them. Temporarily. Other good news: she didn't have to let him know those curse limitations didn't apply to her.

As they approached the exit, she glimpsed Parthenia sitting in the shape shifter's lap. She'd never quite understood the purpose. No matter how many species did it. The branches and leaves reconfigured into the archway as it had upon entry. Her attention reverted to getting out of there.

Chapter Twelve

Ensuring they put some distance between them and the half-breed settlement, Seru walked quietly, hand-in-hand, with Thalasia through the forest until they crossed the dirt path leading toward the Marketplace. He pulled her to a stop just inside the cover of trees and brush. "The onocentaur's mother," he started in a hushed whisper, regretting being unable to speak to Thalasia in a dialect other than common. He didn't want this information getting out to any listening ears, so he opted to keep the specifics to himself. "I'm hoping she can tell us the location of the weapon I mentioned. The gilded dagger decorated with rubies."

He looked troubled as he continued, uncertain where the compulsion had come from and why the memory had suddenly resurfaced. The thought of someone playing around inside his memory bank unsettled him to no end. For any species, even a dragon, to cast a spell powerful enough to affect a saint beast—not just in the moment, but over time—was an incredible feat. Dangerous and worrisome. Beyond the Matriarch, who had that level of power?

Verie hadn't known the truth of the missing dagger's whereabouts. Of that, he remained certain. It had also been kept secret from his brothers. Who else would be so bold as to desire to conceal a part of the most powerful holy weapon? The sea dragons? Marius would have taken it beneath the waves. Seru shook his head. Why could the onocentaur keep the weapon in the first place? The magic imbued in the seven holy weapons forged a connection to their keepers. The only beings resilient enough to maintain control of them were him and his brothers. They degraded, corrupted, and shredded apart the minds and bodies of any others who dared to lay hands on them for more than a few moments.

"Okay. I'm guessing this is important, and something about her made you think of it?"

"Critically," Seru confirmed. With a tilt of his head, he ventured to ask, "Is something troubling you? More than the obvious."

Thalasia dropped her gaze to the ground, her sigh echoing in the stillness. "My family line is pretty involved. I'm just not sure how deep the roots go."

"You're not responsible for their actions—good or not." He took her by the chin to ensure she met his gaze. "You're a good woman. With a good heart."

Her silver eyes stared into his, searching for something. "Thank you." A small smile crossed her face as she gripped his forearm and squeezed tight. "Let's get to the marketplace. We've got some items to collect and a manticore to find."

Seru wasn't sure he'd made her feel any better. It was significantly less confident she wasn't closing herself off to him. He remained silent and tried not to let it bother him. But it did, just like everything else about her. It got to him with little effort and stayed there, burrowing into him like a dwarven burrow rat hunting for precious stones. It showed no signs of stopping until it had fulfilled its purpose. Since he didn't know what that could even be, he resigned with a grumble. "That we do."

Back to their never-ending list of chores.

Her features relaxed, and a gentle sigh drifted from her as her eyes softened. "I *want* to explain everything. Just not out in the open like this. Maybe... after we're done for the day... we get a few rooms at the inn and talk?"

He nodded. He hated being this moody. It was better when everyone else could see and feel it, and he couldn't. He shoved a hand through his mane. "Of course." His head was splitting with a terrible headache. He was sure it would only get worse the more pieces of the puzzle they tackled and tried to solve. "Let's grab your manticore first."

Her arms came around him; her wings followed suit.

This time, her presence soothed him. He curled his arm around her shoulders, hugging her in closer. "Suddenly unconcerned with your pheromones, or just feel like testing your limits?" A sly smile crept over his face. He concealed it in her hair, nestling into the crown of blue.

"Unconcerned," she said. "Testing is for later." A small giggle escaped. She buried her face ever so slightly against his chest and pressed a tender kiss to his pectoral, over his heart.

Seru wrinkled his brow a bit at that response. Teasing for later, huh? "You're growing bold. Should I be worried?" He tried and failed to subdue the shiver that ran through him. This time he didn't shy away, tightening his grip. "You realize I suffer. You succeed, too, don't you?" he asked in a playful growl.

"Worried, no. Intrigued, yes." She paused. "Mmm, sounds like something to look forward to."

He snuffled atop her head. The smile widened with her words. "You're being mischievous and secretive."

"You love it, and you know it."

"Do I?" Seru feigned disinterest. Her little game brightened his spirits.

"Oh yes. Yes, you do. Just as much as I do." She gently dragged her fingers up his spine, across his shoulder blade, and over his biceps.

The beast stirred, a shimmer of scales in the wake of her touch. "Alright," Seru proclaimed a tad too excitedly, capturing her by the wrist. The second statement was sterner, not unlike the tone he'd used more times than he cared to recall when Aurelia's play got out of hand. "That's enough. We don't need a scaly... snake blocking the road." He narrowed his eyes at her a bit, voice softer, more playful.

Her lips twitched and broadened into a smile. "Right. Save it for later."

He returned the smile despite himself. Her warmth penetrated his shields, brought down his defenses, even amid the tension and frustration that threatened to consume him. She didn't deserve his agitation or his rage—that he'd reserve for Marius. He'd more than earned the harsh, verbal lashing their earlier exchange imparted and so much more pain than that which had flitted over his reflected features. Marius deserved the full brunt of the burden he left Seru to carry. Alone. His disgust at the ever-changing, far-off promises of a shared future twisted like a molten blade in his chest.

He gritted his teeth, determined not to let the sea dragons get the better of him. He forced his mind from the past and back into the present. The feel of Thalasia next to him helped restore his focus. "Is there anything we should look out for? Regarding this manticore of yours. They tend to be volatile. The females, especially. We need to tread cautiously."

Thalasia raised an eyebrow at him, which quickly turned into a slight smirk. "Well, she has something that I need to collect. From what I've seen, it should be easy to convince her to turn it over to me."

"Easy?" he repeated, massaging his temples. "Have you ever actually met a manticore? I think you're underestimating their tenacity and belligerence." He gave her a wary eye. "And how do you intend to manipulate her? A direction, even a general one, would be most helpful. Especially if I'll have to jump in and save you." He didn't relish being amid a full-fledged brawl between two females of different species. Of their available options, the manticores challenged the dragons in terms of aggression and brute force. Establishing dominance and superiority seemed to go a long way in cultural displays. However, the same tendencies bred infighting and war. And if perchance a chimera got involved, that didn't soothe his scales. The two species were renowned for the deeply rooted hatred they harbored for one another. Stepping between them sounded like a great way to send feathers and fur flying or even a great way to lose a digit or limb. Injuries weren't just likely—they were guaranteed. Severe ones if they didn't have a good plan and exit strategy in place.

Unfurling her wings from around him, she knitted her eyebrows together. "Never underestimate the power of my voice or soothing touch. It works well. And if that doesn't work, I have other tactics. Either way, I'll be walking out with what the vision showed me."

He missed the brush of her feathers as soon as they fled. "Don't take this personally," he grumbled with a heavy sigh. "But I'm really beginning to loathe your species' knack for prophecies and the 'oh, I'm sorry I forgot to mention the unforetold danger lurking somewhere out of sight.'" The entire vision reeked of complications, blind spots, and promised anything but smooth sailing. They were diving straight into the heart of the storm. "Do I at least get to know what we're taking from her, or is this intended as a trust exercise?" He grimaced as those words left his mouth. He could hardly judge her for withholding details and information when his entire life revolved around hoarding them. As much as he loved discovering and stowing away secrets and other valuable tidbits, he hated going into any situation blind. Lack of information grated on him, driving him insane like unintelligible whispers carried by the wind.

Thalasia crossed her arms and frowned at him. "Does it matter what we're taking from her?"

"No, I suppose it doesn't," Seru growled, throwing up his hands. All the emotions he'd been struggling to contain rushed forth in a crackling rage. "I'm less concerned about her and more concerned about us." He flinched at the truth in his own words. The thoughts had been gnawing at him, persistent and angry. Their time together only fed the voracious swirl, expanding it until... *this*. He hated that he cared so much. Hated it more that it bothered him so much. To the point it was getting the better of him... and while he knew it, he still wasn't able to squash it. It insisted on spilling forth and raining its hot, blue embers on both of them.

"Do you think I would rush us into something that we can't handle? Do you think I don't give a shit? Because if that's the case, you are dead wrong, Seru. You are all I care about. I'm sorry that I can't tell you everything, but right now, it's for both of our safety that I keep it to myself," she snapped. "Yes, it means you have to have a little faith. That in the end, every step we take will get us closer to getting off this isle without looking back." With a groan, Thalasia shook her head. "I *want* to tell you everything. I *want* to show you everything, but I can't do any of that here."

"Are you really so naïve that you believe this has a happy ending, where we fly off into the sunset together?! It doesn't matter what you tell me or when. We're just playing out our roles, and when it's all said and done, none of it will matter. It never does. One side wins. The rest lose. The dead are held prisoner on this damned isle. It's just one endless cycle of misery and death. I'm so sick, so tired of pretending, deluding myself into believing that's going to change." For him, that was the worst unspoken secret. The inescapable truth.

"No, but I'm pretty damn stubborn, and determination benefits me." She dropped her hands to her hips. "Or are you just so ready to accept that there's no alternative? Finding anything that could give us answers is pointless. Our fight to stay together was pointless. Your attaching yourself to me was pointless. That convincing me not to give up on this life was pointless." Tears welled in the corners of her eyes. "You told me that my 'extra' sight might show me many things, but it 'didn't show me all.' For all the knowledge you have, Seru, you don't know everything. So, unless you are so determined to resign yourself to your imprisonment, then wake the fuck up and stop acting like you are alone in this."

"It's not pointless... for *you*." His lightning lashed back at him. The angry bolts were slicing into his skin. At the sight of the unshed tears glistening in her eyes, all his hatred and contempt turned inward.

He deserved to be alone.

The ache in his chest resonated through him. Her words were rebounding in the hollow space like a pebble thrown down a well. Their impact was repeating, rising in volume, crashing into his depths. "I've fought my entire life, Thalasia. All eight-hundred-twenty years. So, *please*," he hissed. "Don't lecture me on giving it my all and the power of not giving up, when the only things I care about care more for their station, their power, and their purpose than they'll ever care for me. I'm a fool to have ever allowed myself to expect any more. I'm a shadow of a man who has nothing more to offer." Thunder sounded. The clouds were churning overhead. Blue lightning sliced through the darkening storm clouds as they threatened rain. "I'm through waiting!"

Thalasia closed the distance between them. She reached up and thrust her fingers into his mane, a silver glow forming all over her body. "You don't get it. I see everything you offer because I see you. I've seen it since we met on the bridge. Protecting me is pointless if you're not there. I can't survive without you. I'll break. So, leaving you here isn't an option. Not for me. So, you plan on continuing to hurt yourself, and then you might as well take me down, too."

She saw him, huh? Call it petty. Seru opened himself up just enough to allow the beast's protective armor through. Its magic cloaked him. He faded away from her silver glow to vanish before her eyes.

"Now, what do you see?" he growled in her ear. "Nothing but a passing storm." She'd survived far worse. And she'd continue to. She was stronger than she knew and refused to break of her own accord. His words of comfort in the woods did nothing compared to her own will. "You've got at least another hundred and fifty years before you're allowed to call it quits. You inspire gratitude and affection in everyone your visions allow you to save. I'm not in your visions or your prophecies. You're wasting your time trying to save me. My heart is not your burden."

Her gaze dropped to the ground. Taking a step back from what she couldn't see, Thalasia waved a hand in front of her legs. Her talons disappeared, revealing legs, feet, and a pair of black boots. Her silver eyes lifted, a storm brewing behind them. "I don't see you in my visions because of how close you are to me. And you don't know if you're in any of the prophecies, unless you've already magically found *Celestimo*. Not that I know everything my great-great-grandparents did to protect it. And you think I inspire gratitude and affection... it hasn't always been like that. At one point, I was the monster, leaving a trail of bodies behind. As for your heart... it's never been a burden. *You* have never been a burden. You just refuse to see what's right in front of you, staring you in the face. Just like you can't see the beauty in a storm. You may have eight hundred years on me, but the only one of us that's blind at the moment is you."

Seru reappeared a few steps behind her. "What does how close I am have to do with any of it?" his breath came hot on her neck. He regarded her new boots with mild curiosity and nothing more. She was Thalasia, regardless of her outward appearance. She still smelled the same sweet scent. "Emotions have no place in Draconic society. They're not a thing of beauty. They're weaknesses. In a species that relies solely on strength, they are a burden. Always." As far as blindness went, he saw with more clarity than he had since long before they'd met. He'd allowed himself to succumb to his greatest weakness. Marius merely took the liberty of disillusioning him with the false future he'd painted. A small kindness in an ocean of pain. He couldn't expect her to understand. She thought she felt toward him the same way he felt toward Marius. Even though she'd only known him for a few days. Days were seconds compared to centuries. "I've spent hundreds of years serving a wicked queen, doing every dark deed she commanded. I spent several more discovering and succumbing to these foolish emotions. Let them blind me into corrupting men, women, young girls... It didn't matter who I manipulated, maimed, or killed. Even in that dark abyss, I knew what it was for. Even if I couldn't get *this*..." he looped a thumb through the metal band. "From around my throat, it was okay. Because I believed it would take care of itself. In time, it would cease to matter. I raised and trained a young girl, stole her dreams, and forced her to do the one thing I could not. Kill my mother. Take her place. Loosen the noose around my neck. All while I plotted against her, worked my own plans into the puzzle without her knowledge or consent. Convinced her to trust you. Because she trusted me."

She removed the crystal that had been in her pants pocket and untied the purple pouch from her pants. Dropping the crystal into the purse, she turned around to face him and dropped it on the ground between them. "Like strength, emotions serve a purpose." Taking two steps back, a silver glow emanated from her right hand. "Take rage, for example. It can harness power." She threw the blast at a nearby tree, turning it to ash. "Make others fear you." Thalasia smirked as silver light crackled across her hands as she created a single bolt. "Fear is a great motivator. Force people to do what you want out of self-preservation. Out of anger." She hurled the bolt at a group of trees away from them, shards of bark splintering as they exploded apart. "Sadness... jealousy.... they're unpredictable. But love... only those who fear it see it as a weakness. It's the most powerful of all the emotions." Her entire body glowed, a silver light forming a halo around her, her features softening as she stepped back toward him. "If you were just trying to convince Aurelia to trust me, then why do I need your protection? Why link me to you for a lifetime? Or were you just manipulating me to fit into your plans?"

He watched her display as the trees disintegrated and split, mimicking his lightning. Her healing magic twisted into bitter weapons. A solemn expression settled over his features. She'd made her point. Silence, save the storm overhead. "You weren't part of the plan." He looked up at the sky. The first raindrops fell. The gentle patter of water striking over leaves filled the space between them. "You need nothing from me, Thalasia," his voice came low, barely above a whisper, lost in the rain. She asked a lot of very valid questions. Some he wasn't sure how to answer. The gray expanse above seemed endless, distant. "I don't know anymore."

She picked up the purple purse and tied it to her pants. Her gaze settled on him as the silver light from her body fell away. She closed the distance between them. "Whether you want to believe it... there is something else at work here. Something between us... fate... destiny... I don't know... I just know you weren't originally part of my plan, yet here you are, standing in front of me, and I can't see any plan where you don't fit in."

"You shouldn't put all your eggs in one basket, siren," Seru said, closing his eyes as the rain fell heavier than before. "Especially this basket."

"Maybe, but there are some things that are out of our control." Wrapping a hand around his neck, she rose on her tiptoes and brushed a soft kiss across his lips. "And no matter how hard you fight it—it always plays out the way it's meant to in the end."

He scrutinized her, studying her features. The blue waves hung heavy, plastered to her face by the rain. Her expression held tenderness. The sparkle in her eyes showed nothing but sincerity, a conviction in her words. An adoration of him despite his ugly outburst. The rain soaked through both their clothes. His were ruined, and hers were... revealing. He couldn't meet her eyes. "You're drenched."

She shrugged. "Just a little water."

His eyes shifted back to her, then back toward their destination. "Maybe we should get those rooms sooner rather than later."

"Yeah, we should."

"Let's skip the trolls this time," Seru said, taking her hand and starting them back toward the market and the inn. "And the lake."

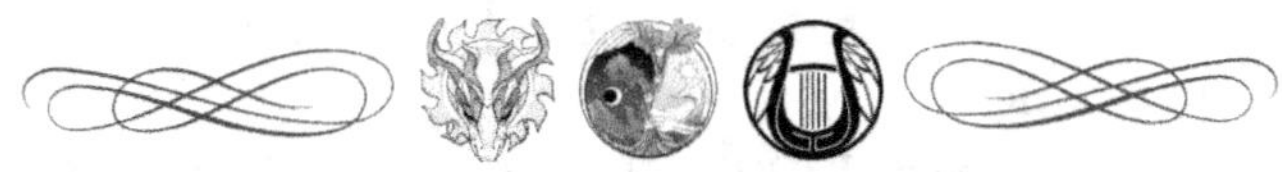

A sigh of relief escaped her mouth. Gods, it felt so good to feel her toes as they walked. She didn't know how any siren enjoyed any kind of travel except flight on those talons. "Um, yeah, definitely."

He nodded his agreement. His eyes were falling to her feet as they walked. "Are your new legs coming into town with us?"

"Oh, no. I'll put the glamour back on before we get there. One thing in private." Though she probably should've put it back on before they started moving, it had been nearly two weeks since she'd felt her toes. "Easier to blend in with the sirens here if I have talons."

"Like the vampire drakes," he mumbled. "They use their magic to appear harmless, to lure in those that see them. Mostly shifters. They're too quick for other creatures."

"Yeah, I guess you could say that." Hers was more done for protection, but it was along the same idea.

"Does it actually change your legs, or is it just an illusion?"

"Bit of both. I'd go through a lot of shoes if it was a physical change. It's an illusion, but it feels real to anyone touching them, even to me. Ensures the movement is accurate."

"Does it work on other parts of your body?"

"Yes, but I've mostly just hidden my feet." That wasn't entirely true. She'd done full glamour in the past, changing her hair color, facial features, even hiding her wings, amongst other things.

"Can you do it to others?"

She shrugged. "Possibly. I've never tried it on anyone else." There had never been a reason to do so.

"Might make sneaking into the library easier... seems more trust-worthy than..." He reached into his shirt to pull out the invisibility vial the siren from the half-breed village had gifted them both.

Yeah, but what would they look like? Other sirens? "Possibly, but there are a lot of unknowns with that. Like, how many sirens even remain in Pteryrina? If there aren't many, it would only take one person to find us there to realize we don't belong. If we used known faces, like the two we saw in the half-breed village, then we run into another issue. We don't know if they were coming or going, maybe, and what if I can't glamour us both?" Of course, the idea was not to get caught. She needed to break into the family archive area. Thalasia bit her bottom lip. "It might be worth a shot to try the glamour first." They still had to track the manticore down. "See if it would even hold."

"You forget, most won't look any closer if their senses agree with a quick glance. Most don't question I'm a dragon, so long as I look and act the part."

"Yes, but acting like a specific person who we don't know differs from acting like a species."

"The more general, the better. They'll see what they wish. Besides, remember the female you spoke with didn't seem to sneak—except for her mate—and her companion seemed in peace talks. They can't just leave if they're brokering peace with the half-breeds."

"Let's just hope no one discovers us. Glamouring like furniture is highly uncomfortable." She rolled her shoulders with a slight shudder. Something she had done once and refused to do again.

Seru shrugged. "Discomfort in the face of years of physical punishment is minor. I've seen your scars just as you've seen mine. Your glamour can't hurt more than that."

If he intended to get her to stop talking, he'd succeeded. He'd only seen a portion of her scars. Even removing the lyre from her wing and braiding it in her hair. No way he'd seen how many physical scars she had. Not that it mattered. It wasn't a time in her life she talked about.

"They're not something you should be ashamed of. They're proof you fought and won." He didn't entirely understand the discomfort the subject brought her.

"Is that what you think of yours?"

He shrugged. "I did."

"Has that changed?" It was easier to focus on his than it was on hers. Then she didn't have to think about her past or what led to them.

"Yes... and no. I don't really remember the time when I didn't have them. They created my brothers and me to fight. And we did. Not just on the battlefield, but with each other. Once Mother became suspicious of us, she tried to beat her version of the truth out of us before setting us against one another."

"No good 'mother' would beat the truth or pit her children against one another." She gave his hand a gentle squeeze. They didn't receive them in the same way. Not that it devalued his suffering any less. If he even saw it that way. "Scars—they're one of two things, a badge of honor if they were earned in valiance or proof you survived genuine horrors in your life." Her gaze shifted from him back to the road ahead. "Nothing more," she whispered as she swept a hand across her legs and engaged the glamour once more.

"She was Mother in title only. We're each shadows of her heart, the undesirable pieces she cast out with magic." He paused. "Survival is valiant in the face of the worst horrors, isn't it? It takes more courage to come back from the brink than it does to fight fairly under a set of predetermined rules, where there's someone to oversee your wellbeing."

"Then why would you call her 'Mother?' It is a title that is undeserved." She shook her head. "Regardless of how your existence came about, no one deserves to be treated that way. No one." She wouldn't have called her survival valiant. Nor would she claim courage. If she had had her way back then, she would've died. But she hadn't been allowed that luxury. Too many people... too many innocents suffered for her decisions.

"The Matriarch is also given the title of All-Mother—she's mother to all dragons and saint beasts," he said, frowning at that last. "Her cruelty doesn't make us less a part of her."

His words had a sense of irony. They could strip titles in many cultures, especially to those who had no honor and didn't deserve them. She had rescued countless children from their parents. They may have birthed them, but that didn't make them parents. "It also doesn't mean she earned the right to that title. The creation, or birth of a species, doesn't make one a mother. It makes them creators. Or a breeder. Nothing more."

"Hmm. The dragons are far too traditionalist to entertain that argument. Far too resigned to their ways and beliefs. The Heavens appoint a worthy female as Matriarch, bless her with exceptional gifts and, in return, she sacrifices to serve her people. Verie defied her purpose, corrupted the role. However, until the gods saw fit to bestow the power on another, she remained the All-Mother and would have remained so if she'd had her way. Her people cannot defy her. She's life. Without a Matriarch, the dragons wither and die. Only a reaper or a Rising Matriarch can depose the Reigning Matriarch. Others don't possess enough magic or resistance to stand much chance."

Traditionalists... another word for old-school, out-dated. She smirked. "It almost sounds as if Aurelia is doomed to follow the same archaic path as her predecessor. If dragons can't accept that traditions change as the world grows, then their only true enemy is themselves. Which means they must accept any failures as no other fault than their own." Though it made her wonder. "Is that the only way for you to gain your freedom?"

Seru plucked a colorful leaf from a low-hanging branch. "If she chooses," he said. "Aurelia resents the silver queen and the matriarchy, the entire Cloud Court. She'll either bring their end or a new beginning." He idly turned the leaf. "Through Aurelia? It would seem so. I've had no success in breaking free on my own. I can't tell you how many times I've tried. I've hoarded more knowledge than anyone in the kingdom—and I still don't understand enough about the magic Verie cast to make us, me. The complexities of the magic that fuse this collar and her power directly into my magic are secrets she kept close and destroyed all evidence of."

Her opinion of Aurelia wasn't all that high. Though she had gone off with Mac to rescue someone she saw as beneath her. That said something. Even if the woman hated her with every fiber of her being, it still said something. Maybe her initial assumptions were incorrect. For Seru's sake, she prayed it was the truth. As for Verie... she knew her type... all too well. Power hungry. Reminded her of... Thalasia swallowed to bite back the memories that threatened to spill-free. Chewing on the inside of her cheek, she focused her gaze on what was ahead of them. "Are you certain it was destroyed and not just well hidden?"

"Yes, Verie destroyed much in her reign. I told you before; she rewrote history. That can't be done without first obliterating the original, not just in form, but from the memories of all her people. Most of them don't seem to remember a time when they were connected to the isle. The earth or the sea. They're so full of pride, and most won't even consider another way of life. Any that answer to the harsh penalties imposed by the court, which for centuries has been convoluted by the noble houses, who achieve and retain their power through coupling with the Matriarch, and priests of the Sky Temple." He cringed.

If memories hadn't been altered, she could see her suggestion as a possibility. But that had changed things. It was something she'd be able to do at some point. It sounded as if the court needed to be dismantled. That would be the only way for change to occur. She'd seen it done with other species. "For breeding." She smirked and shook her head. "When my line was created, we were given free rein to choose our Allimos. I believe it was to make us as strong as possible, given our role in the universe. Not that it's helped."

"That's what you call your partners? 'Allimos?'" Seru asked. "The Matriarch doesn't have that luxury. Not in the same way. It's Her responsibility to select her partners based on what's best for the next generation—to ensure their strength and success."

Her gaze flicked to him. "Yes. The rough translation is soulmate or other-half. Demeter believed it would strengthen us." She raised an eyebrow at him. "As in multiple? Does she require her own harem? And if she chooses multiple partners, how does she determine the accuracy of the genes that are contributed?" She shook her head. "I'm fine with one."

"Her advisors and court officials are more than happy to play matchmaker," Seru gave a rueful smile. "Bloodlines are important to the dragons. The families with the strongest claim to power, usually through magic, are often the same individuals who comprise the high court. If the former Matriarch did her duty, the newly risen would have a list of suitable partners—as in multiple—to choose from. If the coupling produces a strong heir, the match is favored. The Matriarch is more likely to retain the partner and utilize him again in the future. If met with failure, she may dismiss him or lower his status. If an undesirable is produced, there are certain... expectations if the male is to redeem himself and his line for hopes of future consideration." He ventured a glance in her direction. "What happens if your one, your Allimos, fails you in that regard? Your line would cease. I don't imagine your kin would take that lightly."

"I have no kin. It's just me; the end of the line. I'm the only one in existence. Unless Demeter saw fit to bestow the same powers and duty to one deserving, one for me to pass my knowledge to, then it would all end with my death." If her life ended like all the rest before she could pass everything on, then the world would suffer for it. No realm would be safe. "But there are many ways for an Allimos to fail. They aren't simply there for breeding or reproduction."

"Is that why you hesitate to return to Pteryrina? What would be your Allimos's duties when you select him?"

It somehow seemed to slip from his mind that the only sirens in Pteryrina were female. Nevermind the fact that she stated they could be *any* species. If she was limited to a siren only—Mac—that limited her choice to him. Yeah, that's the attitude she'd want to deal with for the rest of her life. *No thank you,* she thought. Besides, she accepted she had already chosen her Allimos. "Aside from sexual gratification, emotional, spiritual, and physical support. That's the most basic explanation." She bit her bottom lip. "My duty isn't easy, not just on me, but on my Allimos. Between the rigorous training, the depth of knowledge we have to attain, and the moral compass we carry, knowing that every decision impacts the livelihood of another species. Their strengths complement my weaknesses. They serve as a sounding board, sometimes accepting truth in what they cannot see, someone to lean on when a mission goes awry, sometimes to push me forward when my emotions become a hindrance." She chanced a glance in his direction. Was he running through everything she said? Countering every word in his head? Stopping before they even had a chance? "There isn't a set standard. No list of duties somewhere. It doesn't work like that. But that's what I saw in my parents. A partnership where they leaned on one another and worked together to solve problems. They made it look effortless." A small smile crossed her face. "I will not say every pairing is like that." She chuckled softly as some of her great-great grandmother's entries came to mind. "Our hearts make the choice for us; there's no rational decision to make. Even if we don't immediately see it... Or it seems like the strangest pairing in the entire world."

"You're banking a lot on chance. Doesn't that bother you?"

"No. Knowing that there are people out there that suffered the way I did, that bothers me. Power-hungry people bother me." Every action she took was a chance. A chance that she could wind up dead like all the rest. The only choice she had made for herself... he'd convinced her it was wrong. And she'd made it upon the realization that no matter how many lives she saved, it would never be enough to atone for the lives she'd taken.

"You crash-landed on the wrong isle in the last territory one would visit if they sought to avoid those hungering for power."

Thalasia frowned. "I didn't say I avoided them. I said they bothered me. It's not my job to avoid them. It's my job to help the people they torment, to set them free, and deal with the rest accordingly."

"Everyone seeks power in life, Thalasia. Be it the power to control their own destiny or to help others achieve their own. The power to protect those people or possessions they value most. There are only differences in perspective and those methods enacted to obtain the desired result. Even the worst tyrants believe they're doing the right thing. Who's saying who's right and wrong? To be the judge of what and how each individual utilizes the power they've obtained."

"That doesn't mean people should suffer because of it." She thought back to the way he'd described the dragon court. And the choices that would be made for another. Along with the outburst he had days ago when they'd first begun their journey. "Do you think the traditions of the court are right? If so, why would it matter if Aurelia changed the way things were run?"

"I know. They're all pretentious fools." His lips recoiled into a snarl. "I'm not a dragon, so I don't get a voice at court. I'm Seru, the treacherous snake with his fangs in the crown and his head underwater."

"And therein lies the problem with tyrants. They care less about the needs of their people than they do about their own power. Their people... are disposable." They're the ones often put into slavery, forced to fight in ways they should never be subjected to. People of any species have basic needs that should be fulfilled. "No one is disposable, especially those who truly carry a society. It doesn't matter whether it's matriarchal or patriarchal. It only matters how people are treated."

"You believe all people are equal or should be treated so. That's not by nature's design."

"I believe people should be free to choose who they can love and to live their lives supporting their species, without fear of repercussions."

"Isn't that idealistic?"

"Is it? Or is it simply understanding that while people of all species aren't perfect, most have kind souls and can thrive if given the opportunity?" Maybe that was the problem... neither of them thought they were inherently good. Not that it would stop either of them from building something.

"It is. You give up the chance to live that way yourself. So how can you be sure it really exists in any measure of permanence? There will always be those with goals, motives, and ambitions that counteract your own. Do you really want to spend your entire existence fighting someone else's battles with the hope they'll eventually take up the sword for themselves?"

Of all the conversations she ever thought they'd have; a philosophical debate certainly wasn't one of them. Not that they had locked horns. It was a conversation with questions she wasn't positive he really wanted all the answers to. Or that she could provide. "There can't be light without dark. That is indisputable. But there is a difference in the levels of dark, and true darkness. It can overrun hope, squash it. My purpose, it's simply to do a part in preventing the world from being swallowed by it." She paused. "As for living my life that way, you didn't seem to care too much for my alternative." Even if the decision had been for reasons, he couldn't... She recalled the words he had screamed. He was tired of waiting. "Besides, I can't bear to watch any more innocent lives taken because of my inaction," she said, her voice low.

"Inaction or death? Don't you want more than that? At what point do you allow yourself the same happiness and peace you're so insistent on *forcing* upon others?" There was a smile in his voice as he teased her with his last remark. "I don't know or pretend to understand how many 'realms' there are out there. But if they all need an outsider to come fix them, they don't really sound like they're much worth saving. Has there ever been a world you haven't needed to save?"

Her gaze settled on him. Part of her wanted to throw his question right back at him. At what point was he allowed to be happy? Not that she forced it on anyone. "Thousands of realms, even more species, and yes. The realm I came from. I just had to find someone and push them in the right direction."

He pinched the bridge of his nose. "I'm sorry. Let's just... get those rooms and go from there. I'm not making fun of you. I'm just struggling to understand. Your life. The way you live."

She sighed as she gripped the back of her neck. Gods, she just wanted fresh clothes and a hot shower. "How is the way I live my life any different from your being what you need to be and doing what you have to do to placate those who choose to see you as beneath them? That's what you said. You do what you must to survive amongst a species who—to be a little crass—seem to have constant sticks up their asses. Do you think that's better?"

"Not at all," he replied. "But it's all I can do aside from rolling over." He stumbled a little, catching himself just as quickly.

Thalasia stopped short. At least the marketplace wasn't far now. They could get the rooms, she'd shower, he could rest, and she could handle the manticore situation alone as long as he didn't object.... though if she had to, she'd wait for him to pass out. Maybe she could even get the piece he described from the onocentaur. They had a shop in the marketplace. That's what the other female had said.

"I'm fine," he insisted before she could even ask. "I'm also working on it. My plans with Marius may have fallen through, and I may not be certain what that leaves, but I'll let you know when I figure it out. Right now, I'm just... at a loss."

"For what?"

"Direction. What comes next?" He swallowed. The storm overhead threatened to intensify.

Yeah. That made two of them. Her eyes lifted to the sky above. That resulted from his emotions. She just wished she understood it better. Shifting her gaze back to him, her eyebrows knitted together. "Maybe things will become clearer after you get that dagger."

"The dagger has nothing to do with Marius," he sighed, blinking rapidly. "It belonged to one of my brothers. I need to get it back. If anyone else gets their hands on it, it'll be one more catastrophic problem for us to solve."

"All the more reason, it seems, for us to split up. Exhaustion is wearing on you. You can deal with that; I'll go deal with the manticore. We can meet back up at the inn. It makes the most logical sense." Whatever decision they had to make, it needed to be made soon. The marketplace didn't appear as empty as she expected it might with the storm. Though she expected they were staying in places as much as possible.

"You really think splitting up is wise?" With a sharp intake of breath, he forced out a reply. "Whatever you think is best."

Did she think it was wise? No, not really. Was it the right thing to do? Maybe not. She didn't know anymore. All she knew was that at the rate he kept pushing her away... she needed to get used to the heartache. He was the only one. And she wasn't sure she could convince him or even how to convince him... unless she had to share the very darkest part of herself. And she didn't know if she was ready to share what led to it. Because if she went into the detail of one... there was no way to leave off the other. Thalasia swallowed the lump in the back of her throat. "It may be our best option right now."

"Let's freshen up first, get some rest, and revisit after we're both in a better state." He rubbed the back of her hand with his thumb in languorous circles.

"Yeah, okay. A hot shower sounds good."

"What, not satisfied?" he asked, gesturing to the sky with his free hand. A hint of playfulness barely touching his exhaustion as a yawn escaped him.

She shook her head with a small chuckle. "Oh yeah. I absolutely love getting drenched in water and having my wet clothes cling to my body like a cold wrap." With a smirk, she extended her wings and ruffled her feathers, flinging water everywhere.

"At least it'll keep you from flying away from me for a little while longer," he replied.

Thalasia blinked. She didn't know how to respond to that. The last thing she wanted to do was leave him behind. To leave him, period. But some things he'd said had already been made quite clear. Aurelia was going to throw a shit fit when she found out about the link he'd created between them. If the cloud courts didn't accept him, no way in hell would they accept her, even if she wasn't bound by her visions. Even if there was another way to put the barrier back up, a life without him—it was no life at all. "I'd stay forever if I could," she whispered.

"I'd never let you," he said softly, drawing her to his side.

Gods, she was going to have to get him off the isle. He wanted her to be happy. He was the only way that happened. Even when they were arguing... She felt... alive. Something she hadn't felt in a long time. She returned his affection with a soft nuzzle, their clasped hands warm between them. The inn was just ahead. "Come on, let's get dried off."

Chapter Thirteen

Parthenia's gaze flicked toward the hut where her sister still negotiated a peace treaty.

The same diminutive female from earlier stepped out of it and headed toward her and Gavin. The female bowed her head to them. "Would you care to step inside out of the coming rain?"

Both Gavin and Parthenia turned their gazes from the strange, sudden storm overhead to the female.

"Oh yes, please," Gavin said. He helped Parthenia to her feet and then stood, wrapping his arm around her as they followed behind the female to the hut. "Thank you."

"Yes, thank you." Her wings appreciated it. It wasn't as if they couldn't handle water, but she hated dealing with the aftermath of being in a storm. Her feathers would be slick and would require a lot of attention.

"You are quite welcome." The female nodded and escorted them through a maze of halls to a room with a single couch and table. She gestured to the entryway. "I shall return momentarily with a few refreshments."

As they followed along, Parthenia glanced around. She didn't see Cipriana or Santos anywhere, but there were a couple of other doors, one of them closed. It would make sense for them to complete the treaty in private. "Thank you. That sounds wonderful."

"Yes, it does. Thank you very much." He nodded to the female and then tilted his head. "Would you like to sit while we wait?"

"That sounds good." She walked next to him and sat down on the couch. They had nothing like this back in Pteryrina. Even the bedding she'd created had been of her own feathers. It was quite plush. She glanced over at the empty doorway. Hmm, the female had said nothing else, just disappeared. The deafening sound of lightning cracking in the sky made her shift her gaze to the roof. "Is it just me, or does that sound strange?"

Sitting down next to her, Gavin rubbed his arms before wrapping one around her. "Strange. It feels strange, too. Just unnerving."

Parthenia curled up to him, tucking her talons behind her. "It feels unnatural. Like no storm I've seen or heard on the isle before. What do you think is causing it?"

"I do not know." He wrapped his other arm around her and held her close, stroking her arm. "I have never seen or felt a storm like this, either. 'Unnatural' is a good word for it. I dislike it." He kissed the top of her head. "I hope things are going alright with your sister, the meeting."

That made two of them. She didn't like the storm, but she also hoped things were good with the peace treaty that was being negotiated. As long as it was taking, it would seem so, but until they saw her sister again, she couldn't say that for sure. Parthenia opened her mouth just as the other female returned with a tray of refreshments.

The female set the tray down on the table. There was a plate of rolls with some kind of icing on them, a bowl of brown balls, and a pitcher of tea. "Take what you like." She bowed her head to them and left, passing Cipriana on her way out.

"Santos has suggested we stay here until the storm passes," Cipriana announced, her voice filled with a hint of worry as she entered the room.

"That makes sense. We won't get far in our travels with the way it's...." Parthenia's words trailed off as droplets of rain pounded against the roof.

"That was kind of him. I do not think any of us want to be out in this storm." His nose twitched. Gavin stroked her arm and then picked up the tray to offer her the food first.

Parthenia eyed the food. It smelled interesting, but those brown balls worried her just a little. She picked up one of the bread items and three cups, along with the pitcher of tea. Without asking, she poured them each a cup. "How did the meeting go?"

Taking a seat across from them, Cipriana let out a long sigh, the sound echoing in the room. "Good. We got everything sorted."

"That's good. Anything in particular we need to know about?" Hmm, intriguing. The bread had a bit of an orange scent to it, along with something... sweet. She couldn't quite put her finger on it. She tore off a small piece and placed it in her mouth. The zest of orange, the sweetness of vanilla and... was that cinnamon... the mixture of those flavors exploded on her tongue.

"Well..." Her sister's words trailed off.

Oh, she didn't like this. Not one bit. But the roll in her mouth made it impossible to form words.

Gavin sat the tray back down and picked up one thing of bread. "What is it? Is everything alright?" He sniffed it before taking a bite, chewing slowly.

"I might have mentioned something about the barrier and the possibility of invaders." Cipriana picked up a cup and took a sip of tea.

"I'm sorry. You did what?" Her eyes widened. They hadn't intended to say anything about that. Why? Why would her sister do something like this? They'd agreed it was best not to mention it to keep Devin safe. Parthenia glanced at her mate. He had to be thinking the same thing. Gavin was already worried enough about Informants finding them. This was the last thing they needed to worry about.

"I had a decision to make, and I felt it was best if he knew, for the safety of his people."

Gavin slowly lowered the bread in his hand. He took a deep breath and let it out slowly. "Did you tell him who told you the information? About the invaders?"

"No, but he seemed to be aware of it already. It mattered little that I told him, although he told me he appreciated my honesty." Cipriana shrugged and took another sip of the tea.

"I'm glad you didn't say where it came from." The last thing she wanted was Devin in more danger than she already faced. Parthenia ripped off another piece of the bread thing in her hand and popped it in her mouth. Wow. That was great. "Though it makes me wonder how he knew."

"The isle is quite large, with many people on it. She cannot be the only one that wanders, for lack of a better term. And we have known about the barrier for quite some time. It was pretty obvious when it fell. I cannot imagine we were the only ones to have noticed it," her mate said.

"I don't know. He didn't say how he knew, and I didn't ask. I don't know if he travels, but even those of us in Pteryrina never mentioned it in any part of the meeting we had over the past few days." Her sister sighed.

Yeah, she'd do that, too, if she had to think about that meeting again. It had been an event she pushed to the furthest recesses of her mind. Parthenia swallowed the piece of roll in her mouth. "I thought that was strange, as well. I figured someone would bring it up."

"Me, too. If anyone, I thought the Elder might, unless she just didn't want to worry those who remain there."

"I didn't think about that," Parthenia replied. It made sense, though. They already had enough to worry about. That just made one more thing. Not that it was a small thing in the least. Even compared to everything else they worried over; it was a rather large issue.

"If they did not mention it, do you think they may not be aware of it?" Gavin wrapped his arm around her and took another bite of the bread.

"I can't see how they wouldn't. I mean, we clearly saw the fog even from the sky. It wasn't hard to miss when it disappeared," Cipriana responded.

Taking another sip of tea, Parthenia laid her head against her mate's chest. While she couldn't imagine Vasilia hiding anything from them, she was still fairly certain the female had known all along she was sneaking down to land. If that was the case, it was something their Elder had kept to herself. Why would this be any different? "Unless they didn't recognize it for what it was. That could also be a reason."

Cipriana shrugged. "I suppose."

Gavin finished the roll and then took a drink of tea. "Maybe she just did not want to worry everyone, then." He laid his head on top of hers and stroked her arm.

"Any of the above is possible. I probably should've consulted the journal to see if anything was in there, but there wasn't time." Cipriana frowned.

Leaning against her mate, Parthenia turned her gaze to the roof. As the rain intensified, the sound grew louder. "I wonder how long this will go on for."

"Hopefully, not too much longer," her mate said.

Parthenia hoped so, too. It created a delay they didn't need. The longer this unnatural occurrence went on, the more she worried about what lay ahead for them.

Running a hand across the top of his head, Mac stepped out of the hut he'd set up for Nomad. Thankfully, the male required little. Food and blankets for the floor. At least the darkness hadn't returned while they made their trip back across the salty shores. Although it would've been nice if Aurelia had hung around while he got the shape shifter settled. Then again, who was he kidding? He'd be shocked if she actually returned later with the dragon-shifters as she promised.

With a heavy sigh, he started toward the center of the village. There was still a lot to address. Yes, cleanup and repairs had begun in his absence, but they'd lost another life. Maggie hadn't wasted time when he returned and told him what Thalasia had found. And how she'd kept her promise and healed their wounded. That female really was something else.

She'd clearly made other choices. He shook his head. That wasn't something he wanted to think about at the moment. Sighing again, he gripped the back of his neck and lifted his gaze to Maggie, who quickly approached him.

"Did you get the shifter settled?"

"Yes, he's got plenty of food, water, and everything he should need." Not that he knew what to do with him beyond that.

"We cannot keep him in that hut forever. Have you given thought to how to help him? At least beyond what you are doing now?"

Yes, and no. He'd given it a lot of thought, and he had very few answers. It wasn't like he knew any shape shifters, well, except that one that visited the village a couple of months back. Based on what Felix had told him about that conversation, it stood to reason he couldn't exactly escort Nomad to the shape shifter village. Mac frowned. Maybe there was another option. "Has Milla come by yet?"

"No. I expect we should see her before dinner, though."

"If I remember correctly, she has shape shifters in her family. From what I've been able to discern, he's going to require aid we're not equipped to offer, but she might." And if nothing else, she may have a better idea of how to help him. According to what the male had told him, he'd been stuck in his animal form for the better part of a century. And words had become nothing more than guttural sounds for a while now. At least until today.

"Good. I was quite concerned when you returned with him."

"I know, but I couldn't leave him there." It had taken a little convincing of Aurelia to carry him back from the other isle. Mac rubbed his eyes. He hadn't been back in the village very long and already he was exhausted. "I'm going to go for a walk. Do you think you can handle things while I'm gone?"

"Of course." Maggie bowed her head and walked off.

Gripping the back of his neck, he bit back a groan. He wouldn't get used to the whole head-bowing thing. Never, even if he remained the village elder. A position he didn't really think he had the right mindset for. Shaking his head, he shoved his hands in the pockets of his pants, strolled through the clearing and left the village.

Some part of him knew exactly where he needed to go. It wasn't a place he'd visited in a long time. Then again, he hadn't ever had the desire to return to somewhere with such... dark memories. He didn't like thinking about that day. Though he couldn't quite get it out of his head.

Hiding in a tree. Doing his best to keep quiet. Nevermind all the blood that splattered and seeped into the ground as someone killed his parents. It had been... gods, had it really been seventeen years? Yes, it had. To this day, he didn't know the person who'd taken them from him. Of course, he'd been six when it happened. And the female who'd been in the tree, comforting him, made sure he didn't look, either. Not that it had been difficult. He'd turned his face away, unable to bear watching.

Still, from time to time, he made his way toward that tree. Hoping one day he might actually remember the face of the one responsible for their deaths. Not that he knew why he so desperately wanted to know anymore. It used to be so he could avenge his parents' deaths, but having lost Felix now, too... Killing all of those dark guilers didn't make him feel better. Getting revenge wouldn't bring any of them back.

Mac stopped in front of the tree. Extending his wings, he flew up and sat on the branch he'd hidden on so many years ago.

"Back again?"

He practically jumped out of his skin. Mac frowned and looked up at the female whose shadow fell over him from the branch above. While he didn't think he hated any living creature, he sure as shit questioned that emotion often with sprites. They spent most of their time in their true size, which meant they stood no higher than twelve inches. However, some could transform to what they called normal size.

The sprite that had kept him safe seventeen years ago was one of them. She hadn't changed in the number of times they'd crossed paths since then. Her red-and-blonde-ombre hair cascaded down her back. Her light-blue, translucent wings folded back as she brushed her hands down her satin gown. Mac frowned. "Must you always do that?"

"Really? You have to ask that?"

No, he really didn't. He already knew how much she enjoyed startling him. Of course, she hadn't done it when he was younger. Though he supposed that had more to do with his age back then. In fact, the first time he recalled her doing it, he'd been a teenager. He shook his head. "Lilac... I'm thinking you have nothing better to do than to wait around here for me."

"Of course, I have better things to do, but I always seem to know when you plan to visit."

"Are you a mind reader?" Or was there something else she wasn't telling him? Either way, there was definitely more to this story. She'd always been at the tree whenever he came by for a visit. Maybe she lived in the tree. Though he didn't think that was accurate. Most of the sprites lived closer to the lake. Not all of them, but most.

"Something to that effect."

Which just meant she wouldn't give him a truthful answer. Mac swung his leg over the branch, leaned back against the rough trunk, and gazed at the forest floor. Although they had long cleaned the blood from his parents' bodies, he could still see it as if it had just happened the day before.

"Are you still trying to remember?"

"Yes, and no." He paused. It really was that simple. "I can't forget what happened to them. I still see it... like I'm that little boy, hiding in the tree, trying not to be seen. But no matter how hard I try; I never see the culprit's face."

Lightly dropping from the branch, she moved to the one he sat on. "Have you ever considered that you blocked that out of your mind for a reason? Not just because you were a young boy?"

"I'm not trying to avenge their deaths. After today... I've realized it doesn't help with the pain. I just... I don't understand why someone would kill them. They were good people." And that was the truth. No, they hadn't ever lived with other sirens, but he didn't think it was necessary. A guiler had raised him, and he'd turned out fine. He still understood everything about his heritage.

"Maybe there is no real reason. At least... not one that would really make sense."

Mac opened his mouth and snapped it shut. She had a point. Even if he learned the why, it may not be something that would ever make sense to him. His gaze flicked back toward the ground. He didn't need to come to the tree to be close to them. The memories he had of his parents were enough. He looked back at Lilac. "You're right."

"While I would miss these chats... I hope this means you don't come back. You don't want this to be your legacy. You have your whole life ahead of you."

Yeah, his whole life. A life where he now had to figure out how to lead nearly a hundred guilers. But Felix had believed in him. So had his parents. That was something he'd never forget. He scrubbed a hand across his face. "You're right. This shouldn't be my legacy. Thanks, Lilac."

"Anytime. Now, go on. Get out of here."

A small smile appeared on his face as he swung his leg back over the branch, the forest's scent rushing up to greet him as he took off. If he was going to start his legacy off right, then he needed to find Thalasia.

Chapter Fourteen

Thalasia glanced up from the Atlis journal she'd scoured for the last hour. Specifically, she'd searched through her great-great grandmother's notes. She was certain that her family had at one point lived in Pteryrina. 'A' may have signed the letter, but she recognized the handwriting. She'd seen it all throughout her training as a child. Any information Adina's notes could've provided about the isle would be useful.

Noting Seru's fitful rest, she closed the book, set it in the chair, and stood. His muscles bunched into knots, his hands reflexively clawing at the feather pillows. His leg kicked out from beneath the sheets. The linen twisted around him, restricting his movements. It threatened to tear as it became tighter with each successive movement. The current flowing through him intensified, vibrant bolts sporadically lashing out across the room.

She crossed over to the bed, propped up a couple of pillows, and sat down. Resting a hand on his back, she gingerly stroked along his shoulders as one of her wings hugged around him.

The tension eased from him at her touch. Her soothing strokes along his back loosened his grip and steadied his breaths. The ragged snarls slowed and transformed into a deep slumber.

Stretching out her legs, her other wing alongside them, she inhaled a deep breath and ran her fingers through his dark locks. Nothing about his broken sleep had resulted from their earlier shower. No, there had been something more going on. It hadn't been difficult to recognize that he was having a nightmare.

They had once been part of her own nighttime routine. It had taken years to overcome. Every day she prayed they would never return. Her gaze flipped to her purse on the nightstand next to her dagger. Carefully, she dug into the purple bag and pulled out the small black journal Parthenia had given her. Maybe not the best option, given the circumstances, but she was too curious to find something else, and the Atlis journal was too big. At least in its full form. She could reduce it to get it into the purple purse.

Thalasia had gotten through perhaps half of the journal Parthenia had given her, though she'd paused a few times to keep her pheromones in check. Seru needed to sleep. His mood had been proof of that. Not to mention the argument they'd gotten into earlier. It certainly had her revealing truths she hadn't intended.

She crossed one ankle over the other, the hem of the button-up shifting with her movement. Once again, her gaze drifted from the journal in her hand to the closed Atlis journal in the chair. Written in Altese, only other Atlis would understand the language. However, there were some images in there from visions and faces of creatures met along the road, and those would be identifiable. Still, so many unanswered questions, even with the entries she'd read.

Seru shifted beside her. His nose brushed her thigh. A low growl left him as he pressed into her. His clawed hand grasped her thigh. The points of his talons pressed against her supple flesh.

Her focus shifted back to him. She set aside the journal in her hand, face down on her other thigh. Bending slightly, she brushed a soft kiss across his forehead, her hair hanging down around them. "I'm not going anywhere," she whispered. "I'm right here."

Maybe Parthenia had seen something Thalasia didn't immediately notice. If this told her anything, there was no way they'd be able to fully separate. He may not have realized it when he was awake, or he wasn't prepared to admit it, but she could see it in the way he clung to her.

His breathing relaxed. His hand went limp on her thigh. The claws receded, and his lips lowered over his fangs. His shallow breaths kissed her thigh as he nestled close. He settled into an easy slumber once more. Warmth spread from him to her, a flush flowing through her, warmer where his skin met hers.

A shiver ran down the length of her spine. She inhaled and exhaled a few deep breaths as she straightened. This certainly didn't help her pheromone levels any. Thalasia rolled her neck a little, the beads in her hair tinkling from the movement. Her feathers ruffled a bit as her body slowly settled.

Seru's hand slid up her thigh. He let out a huff.

She raised an eyebrow. What was going on in his head? Maybe next time, she'd have to put on more than just a button-up and underwear to sleep in. There was a first time for everything.

Getting another shiver running through her body under control, Thalasia returned to gently stroking her fingers along his shoulders as she picked the siren's journal back up. Although the siren had never mentioned her partner's name or his species, the two had been quite adventurous. Not to mention creative.

In an instant, Seru's electric blue eyes flew open, and he jolted upright. His talons pierced her thigh. As she fought back the pain, the journal slipped from her grasp and landed with a soft thud. Fuck, that hurt. Not that she hadn't been through worse. Exhaling through her nose, she balled her hand into a fist. She nearly told him to take a deep breath, except that probably wasn't the wisest idea. No matter what she uttered, he wouldn't be happy with himself. "Whatever you do, move slowly, Seru."

They were going to have to talk about his nightmares. It would be the only way for him to get past them. To actually sleep without them causing him turmoil. Or causing her physical pain.

Seru's eyes darted about. With his jaw locked, rigid with tension, his head jerked in her direction. His glowing eyes dulled as they found her face. A deliberate exhale. His muscles relaxed, if only slightly, triggering his talons to retract. "Are you alright? There's blood," he asked, breathless. Worry colored his tone.

The breath she hadn't realized she'd held released. With a small nod of her head, she inhaled and exhaled a few deep breaths as she eyed the wound. It was deeper than she thought. It would heal, but it would be hours before it closed. There was no choice. It would have to be stitched. She had all the items in her purse. First, it would need to be cleaned. "I'll live." Thalasia swung her legs over the side of the bed, forgetting all about the journal. She picked up her purse from the nightstand and made her way toward the bathroom.

Seru knit his brow in confusion. He leaped off the bed, racing to her side. He sidled up next to her, with a tender grip on her elbow. "I hurt you," he said. It wasn't a question. "Let me help you." The words were a plea. A desperate desire to help, to erase the horrible glaring mistake he'd made. His blue eyes shone with concern, and behind that, pain and guilt lurked.

She offered him a small nod; her gaze held nothing but forgiveness. "It was an accident." Nothing he told her would change her mind on that; it was a fact. But she could relinquish her usual independence to allow him to help. He had no reason to feel guilty.

Though if she had hurt him, even if it was unintentional, she'd feel the same way. "Just help me to the bathroom. I've got things to really clean it out and stitch it up in my bag. You can take one end, and I'll start at the other."

Without warning, he scooped her up in his arms and carried her back to the bed, setting her on the edge. "You shouldn't need stitches." He kneeled before her. "I'm not a healer like you. I'm a shifter—at least in part. Shifters possess innate regenerative abilities. You're my glory. Take what you need from me."

"They will heal on their own. It'll just take a few hours." The point of stitching would be just to close them. The bleeding had already slowed. Taking from him, even if it was something small, didn't seem like the wisest idea. She couldn't heal herself in the same way she healed him, but her body would do it naturally.

"It's a drop in an ocean's worth of magic to heal a wound that minor. Try it," he urged. "It'll take practice. But in time, you should be able to borrow from my magic whenever you're in need. The collar is to temper my beast. You don't have one, so it should be alright, if that's what you're worrying about."

"I'm less concerned about your beast than I am about you." She didn't think his beast would pop out; she just didn't want him exhausted as he had been. But if nothing else, he understood his body and his kind more than she did. Thalasia scratched at her temple and dropped her eyes to the puncture wounds in her left thigh. "I wouldn't even know where to begin. I've never had to borrow someone else's power before."

She thought back to some of her training. Out of nowhere, she heard her father's voice. *You are not concentrating, Thalasia. Your power is there. Now, close your mind and try again.* She had been five back then. And certainly not trying to heal. Her father had walked a slow circle and waited behind her for the tenth time as she attempted to create her first bolt. It would take one more after that before she'd succeed, but her father's advice still rang true.

Seru offered a strained smile. "I'm a saint beast, not a fairy. I'm much less delicate than you imagine. My talons pierced your skin, not your heart." He maintained his hold on her knees. "When I crowned you, my glory—and you accepted—we forged a metaphysical connection. If you close your eyes and concentrate, you'll find it. Follow it down," he gestured at some unseen string connecting them, drawing it between them and down into his core. "Reach in and scoop out what you need. Draw it back along the connection. Channel it through you." He touched her chest with his finger, trailing down until he almost touched the first puncture on her thigh. "To here."

Thalasia set her hands on Seru's shoulders and closed her eyes. She focused first on completely clearing her mind and shutting everything around them out. The bustling noise outside the window, the gentle breeze flowing through the room, the soft sound of his breaths. She silenced all of it then focused on their commingled powers, her silver and his blue.

She found the concentrated link. It was quite beautiful. She almost got lost in just how exquisite it was, but her purpose overrode that. Scooping out just a small bit, as it wouldn't take much at all, she slowly followed the connection between them. It took a few minutes, perhaps longer, as she carried the small piece through her body until it reached her thigh. A soft hue of blue and silver glowed from her thigh as the wounds repaired themselves.

"Just like that," Seru approved, taking her hand and leaving a gentle kiss on her palm. "Now, this time, try it with your eyes open and without physical contact."

He swiftly drew the blade across her palm, cutting a consistently deep gash through the center.

What the fuck? Her eyes flew open to the gash in her palm. Obviously, he'd retrieved the dagger from the nightstand as she'd tended to her thigh.

He sat back, just out of reach. His eyes never left hers. The concern laced with guilt from earlier had vanished, replaced by a distant calm. They gave nothing away, daring her to rise to the challenge.

And the distance now between them. Just like her father, pushing her harder each time. Inhaling a deep breath, she focused on him as she once again cleared her mind. It had been quite some time since she'd had to train like this. It was different finding the connection between them with her eyes open. She had to see the unseen. It didn't take as long as it had the first time to quiet everything around her and find the link. A small gasp left as it appeared before her. It really was stunning. Just as she had before, she plucked a small piece and directed it toward mending her hand. This time, instead of the glow coming from her hand, it came from her eyes. They sparkled like diamonds in the night sky.

Seru nodded, a small smile of approval playing over his lips as he closed the distance between them. He wiped the blade clean on the mangled sheets, offering it up to her hilt first. "I knew you could do it," he said, resting his head in her lap with a contented sigh.

She set the blade aside, pressed a kiss to the top of his head as she draped her arms across the back of his shoulders. "It's been a long time since I've had to do anything like that."

"We can't relax here. Even though things appear calm, it's often a temporary deception. It's important that we stay diligent. Always on our toes," he stated, amusement slipping in as he held her feet. "Or talons."

A single word kept repeating in her mind. Concentrate. Her gaze shifted momentarily from him to the Atlis journal in the chair. Had she missed something? She smirked a little at his joke. She much preferred her toes to the talons. Typically, she removed the glamour only in private, but he'd already seen it. She wanted a little comfort.

His arms snaked around her middle, pulling her off the bed and into his lap. "I want you to enjoy your time here, but I also want you to be prepared and safe..." he trailed, following her gaze. "What's wrong?"

Running her fingers through his mane, a small grin fell upon her lips. "Nothing's wrong. I just think I missed something in my research."

"Can I see?" he asked, rubbing slow circles over her hips.

"Yes." Her fingers gripped ever so slightly in his locks. "You may not understand the language, though there are some images in there."

He brought her with him to retrieve the book from the chair. Passing it to her, he returned to the bed.

It was much larger than the one she'd been reading in bed. She had to dig around to move it from beneath her legs. She set it aside with her pouch and the dagger on the nightstand. The leather-bound Atlis journal covered her entire lap. She flipped it open somewhere in the middle. "This is the Atlis journal. It's passed down from the previous Atlis to the next. I told you in the beginning, I'm not like any other siren. Do you know the history of how sirens were created?"

Seru wrapped his arms around her from behind and nestled into her neck. "I've heard and read what I could find on the isle. There are variations among species, but I believe your goddess Demeter's daughter, Persephone, disappeared. Sirens were created to search for the missing girl."

Well, he was right about the variations. Crossing one ankle over the other, she rested one hand atop his and flipped to the first entry in the journal. "Yes, Hades kidnapped her. The first sirens were Persephone's companions, nymphs. Demeter gave them wings to aid in her search for Persephone, which lasted nine days. The tenth day is when she was told by another god what happened. Demeter created the Atlis on the eleventh day. It's said that she went to the gods and goddesses and collected a power from each of them. Once she finished, she built a female to her desire and imbued it with all that she had received from the other gods and goddesses. She called that creation Atlis. Because we look so much like sirens, that's what we've become known as. Apollonia was the first of us."

She gestured to the page in the journal. It looked like a mix of glyphs and half-circles, making it illegible. "This is Apollonia's initial entry where she speaks of the quest given to her by Demeter herself."

"Judging by her name, she was aligned with the sun. Like you are with the moon." He peered at the pages over her shoulder. "So, the Atlis escaped the curse placed on the sirens? Because while you were both created by Demeter, you weren't created the same. Your gods and goddesses favored you. They are not."

"Yes, I've known that the curse existed, but not all of its details because of one entry in this journal. That's how I knew to glamour the talons. I know this isn't the only place where sirens lived. It surprised me to find my family had lived here at some point." She flipped the pages again, several pages from where she'd original-ly started. "The letter that Parthenia gave to us, which was only signed by 'A,' was written by my great-great-grandfather, Aegeus. I thought there might be something in here amongst my great-great grandmother's entries, but she never mentions where they are at any point."

"Is that typical? Or could she have been intentionally hiding her whereabouts for fear she might be discovered?" He ran his fingers over the page, taking in the textures of the ink and parchment.

"Knowing my great-great grandmother. Either. Although now that I think about it... she may not have, but my great-great-grand-father may have." She set the enormous book aside, reached over, and snagged her pouch from the nightstand. Peering aside, she stuck her hand in and moved a few things around. It was there somewhere. Maybe underneath... "Where—oh! There you are." Her arm plunged down, and her fingers found the cool, smooth texture of the deep-brown, leather journal.

Thalasia pulled out a book that was a quarter the size of the one on the bed. Placing her pouch next to the Atlis journal, she tapped the book in the middle with her forefinger three times, and it expanded to the same size as the other one. "The Allimos have a journal as well. It's a little different from the Atlis journal. Since an Allimos can be of any species, it's most commonly written in whatever language that particular Allimos is most comfortable. However..." She opened the journal to the first page and with the silver light of her forefinger drew the outward shape of the full moon in the center. The letters slowly rearranged into a language they both understood.

"Nifty," Seru mumbled, kissing her exposed neck.

She glanced at him over her shoulder and stroked his cheek with her fingers. "If you really want to know the responsibilities of an Allimos, this would be the best way to understand. According to what my father told me; it's supposed to serve as a guide, I guess you could say." Maybe more than that. An Allimos had unique experiences separate from an Atlis.

"A guide," he echoed, captivated by the new book. Her touch drew his vibrant blue eyes back to her. "Should you be showing me this?" There were honest traces of remorse in his tone. "I'm not an Allimos. Nor a siren."

"Sirens aren't supposed to know we exist." Her gaze drifted back to the book. He didn't think he was, but maybe it was because he was resigned to their parting ways when this was all over. The fact remained; her heart had chosen him before she'd even realized it. By all rights, it belonged to him. "It's my choice who I show it to. My choice of who I give it to."

Seru cast his eyes away from her, disentangling himself from her. He climbed out of the bed. "Put it away." He crossed the room to the far side, where he peered out the partially opened window at the dreary, rain-soaked town.

Thalasia closed the book and set it aside. She drew her knees up to her chest, wrapped her arms around her legs, and stared at his back. How long was he going to fight this between them? He didn't want her to go off by herself so he could keep her close to him, but as far as he was concerned, this only ended one way.

Seru huddled with his arms over his chest, leaning against the wall for support. "You *can't* trust me with something like that," he finally said in a harsh whisper.

"Why? Give me one good damn reason." He wanted her to trust him completely, but not with something like this. With personal thoughts of men long dead. He had done nothing to make her feel like she couldn't trust him. And she certainly couldn't judge him by his past, not unless she expected him to reciprocate.

"Because I deal in information, Thalasia. That's the only thing that's kept me alive. And while you'd like to believe I'm trustworthy, I'm not." He swallowed, not once turning to look at her. "On the beach, I wasn't talking to Cyon about *you*. I was giving her details about the *lyre*, the charm I cut out of your wing." He paused briefly. "I don't know how, but... the sea knows about your charm. Marius sent Cyon to make an offer—an exchange. I may not have given them everything... but I gave them enough. Enough to quench her curiosity and enough to keep Marius off my back—at least for a little while longer. I was buying time." Another pause. "I crowned you as my glory, gave you the first set of Draconic marks, to get Marius's attention—and I got it. He reached out to me while we were in the half-breed village."

It wasn't because of him, Thalasia thought to herself. She shook her head. She knew how. Rumors of her particular line had been shared across realms for hundreds of years. That was why she was the only one left. They'd all been hunted... killed... Cyon's words... it wasn't the first time she'd heard them in her life. "And what exactly are they hoping to accomplish with all of this information? Or you with Marius's attention?"

"I don't know. Like me, I'm sure Marius won't show all his cards until the end. Initially, I thought he stayed away simply because he... feared me. As time went on, I realized it wasn't just me he feared, but the marks I might place on him. I met Marius entirely by chance, while Verie was still focused on waging her war with the earthbound of the isle and the dragons of the land. He'd become injured in a storm. I found him washed up on the beach. Too badly wounded to make an escape and too new to the ways above the waves to fully imitate our human disguises. He'd clearly observed the dragons or the saint beasts at least once or twice before, enough to pull off a mortal form except for a few key details."

In that moment, a smile flickered across his face, extinguishing back to his somber expression just as quickly. He tucked part of his mane behind his ear. His gaze still carefully averted out the window. "He couldn't get the ears right. Still had... fins, here. Intrigued... I pulled back my hair—just as I have here—and he caught on enough to fix the mistake. He still couldn't walk and refused to speak to me for months. I concealed him in the caverns beneath the cliffs. Kept him safe. Away from Verie, my brothers, and the war. Over time, we grew close... even without a common tongue. I became so fascinated, so attached... that I kept him there long after his injuries had healed. I wanted to learn more about the dragons beneath the waves, more about the sea. At least, those are the excuses I made to justify it, then..." He got quiet for a moment.

"He wasn't a king, then. Just a man. Someone I wanted to talk to, to open up about all the things I usually kept under lock and key, guarded by magic. They just spilled out of me when I was with him. I could trust him. He wasn't from our world. The way of the Clouds and the dragons of the isle meant nothing to him." He stalled again. "Eventually, I had no choice but to let Marius return to the sea. I visited him there for a while whenever I could sneak away unnoticed. Our... relationship became more and more... Intense. It got to a point where I... frightened him. Not long after, he introduced Cyon into the mix. He hoped she'd act as... a buffer. A barrier between us. I consented, hoping she'd be a comfort to him. Though I've never really cared for her... I... let her in, hoping to appease him and regain his favor. But it's never been the same. It got worse. When the Sea King finally passed and Marius rose to take his place, I thought things would change. They'd go back to how they used to be. Surely, the new Sea King could rival the Matriarch in the Sky and free me from her hold."

His fingers traced the smooth, chill, metal band of the collar. "Marius grew more and more preoccupied with his duties. Our time together became less and less. Even though he sent his servants to offer his apologies and beg my forgiveness, I didn't... I couldn't see... through the smoke. I didn't want to believe he was pushing me away. Not when we were so close to being able to challenge Verie and get this thing off my neck. When he stopped meeting me voluntarily, I snuck in. Our encounters became more and more desperate. My pent-up frustrations and... these emotions drove me toward aggression. Then the Sky attacked the Sea, but not before I could warn Marius of Verie's plan."

He began fidgeting with his sleeve. "When the Sky and the Sea clashed, nothing happened how it was supposed to. Marius's regiments held their own, but Verie easily saw through to the truth. She knew someone had betrayed Her. That somehow the Sea had known about the attack—before it happened. They'd been prepared. That first betrayal set in motion the series of trials that pitted my brothers and me against one another. It's why they're dead."

In all her travels, she had come across many who had relationships she didn't initially understand. Though after even a few hours, she could see how they fit together. It had never been difficult for her. There were obviously things he left out, details... nothing she needed to pull from him. She wouldn't judge him for that. People found attraction where they found it. Of everything she gathered, it wasn't hard to see Marius was playing Seru. Even if Seru believed it was the other way around. "Is that what you hope to accomplish by telling them about the lyre? To get the collar off? To be free? Something I told you I would help you with, anyway?"

Seru frowned, his hands stilling. "Marius can't remove the collar. That hope vanished when he confronted Verie. Her magic was far superior to anything the Sea offered. Even Marius couldn't hope to stand against Her."

"Then did it ever occur to you that he's playing you? That he always has been? Taking advantage of the emotional connection that developed between you? Whether or not you say it, I can read between the lines."

"No." That one word full of contempt streaked across the room as a hot blue bolt. Just before it struck her, it fragmented, breaking into white lines. The branches skittered away, searing into the floorboards in jagged black lines. The room stank of burned wood. Seru gripped his arms, his talons digging into them. "You're wrong," he said through clenched teeth.

"Am I? Or are you just too blind to see it?" Despite the way his emotions formed, she didn't react to them. She didn't back down from the blow. She tilted her head. "What did he say when he reached out in the half-breed village?"

Seru closed his eyes, pursed his lips. "He asked about the marks. He felt them... the backlash, the recoil from them."

"Explain, please."

He regarded her from the corner of his eyes, only slightly less hostile than when he'd turned on her moments earlier. Though this time, there was some evidence of emotion behind the guardedness. "He expressed relief," he stated with disdain. "Though he couldn't meet my eyes when he said it." Seru watched the raindrops as they slowly slid down the panes in the window. "It hurt him, but he was relieved. He turned the conversation back toward business. Emphasized how, by placing marks on you, I'd made the right choice. Bringing you and your knowledge of the lyre closer was the best decision. I knew that before I decided it myself. I didn't want or need to hear it from him." His voice became harsher, more agitated as he continued. "Whatever else he intended to say, I cut him off. I got angry about personal problems that had—and have—no place amid what we're trying to accomplish. He promised we'd be together soon—that they're readying to mount another offense against the Sky. That all the pieces will come together soon. I just need to be patient—wait a little longer and it will all bear fruit. I threw apples into the barrel and stormed off." He shifted.

Thalasia chewed on the inside of her cheek. If Marius hadn't been able to look him in the eye, it was a ploy. Plain and simple. That he'd created distance between him and Seru to begin with spoke volumes. Though it sure as hell made her wonder what he felt for her. Maybe he just hadn't let his pain go from Marius. She smirked. That was the case. Saying nothing, she closed the Atlis journal and tapped both journals to shrink them back down. Once she had, she dropped them both back in her pouch, along with the small black journal she'd set aside on the nightstand.

Thalasia climbed off the bed and stood. She narrowed her eyes at Seru. "Personal emotions don't go away, regardless of what you're trying to accomplish. They will keep making themselves known until you deal with them. Nothing... nothing will change that. As for his promise that the two of you would be together... I call bullshit. If he really wanted to be with you, nothing would've stopped him from doing it before now. He would've looked you in the fucking eye and been straight up honest with you. He wouldn't have pushed you away."

She got closer and shoved her finger at him. "You want to know how I know? Because *you* keep trying to push me away, then *you* pull me closer and push me away again. And I'm still here. *You* have just openly admitted to using me, and yet, I'm still here. That despite everything you've told me, anything that could make you less in my eyes, I'm still here. People who care, they fight, Seru. They fight for one another. To be together. Stay together." Thalasia crossed her arms. "Do you even know what you're fighting for anymore? To be with him? To bide your time with me? For your own freedom? Or are we all just pawns in a chess game with no goal?"

He wrinkled up his nose. "What's 'chess?'"

His question threw her off and tempered her anger, if only for a moment. Of all the things he had to say, that was what he went with. Right. Different exposures. "It's a game of strategy played between people with pieces and a board."

"This isn't a game, Thalasia," he said, shaking his head. "You don't know him. There's still much you don't know about me. Or this isle." His words had lost their heat. The excitement in his tone dropped only to be replaced by a resigned bitterness. "You're a peacemaker at heart; I'm a warrior, a murderer. Which of us do you truly think better understands the way of war? I've been fighting all my life with nothing in between. Even Marius has several hundred years to your twenty. Do you not think if there were an easier, more sure way, we would've taken it by now? There are always plots and ploys, a vast web of deceit and treachery to wade through. Every step you take can be in the right direction, and you could still miss out on it all. All for one unpredictable variable you don't see coming. No matter how careful or how thorough you are, you'll still lose if you win. All you're buying in the end is more time, more misery for every victory. I'm beyond tired of fighting. It really doesn't matter how it ends. Just that it does, one way or another."

Thalasia shook her head. She was tired of fighting with him. Tired of arguing the same point repeatedly. Yeah, she was a peacemaker alright. Her ass. The image of a pile of bodies flashed in her mind, but she quickly squashed it. "You know nothing about me," she whispered. She walked back over the bed, dug into her pouch and pulled out a pair of boots, socks, a denim skirt, another halter top, and a denim jacket. With her back to him, she unbuttoned the long-sleeved top she had on. "Warriors have two sides. The side that goes into battle, that fights when necessity deems it, and the side that understands waging war isn't always the answer."

Showing him her destructive powers had meant nothing. Telling him the truth about her existence meant nothing. He would never understand. Not until he got past his own demons. His own internal battle. Shrugging the shirt off her shoulders, she tossed it on the bed and picked up the halter. She pulled it on, hooking it around the neck and at the back. Thalasia glanced over her shoulder at him. "Age is just a number, and it bears no reflection on the lifetime I have lived in those short years. So, stop trying to use it as an excuse." She tugged on the skirt, zipped and buttoned the front before she sat down on the bed to put on her socks and boots.

"What about when it isn't a necessity? Fighting for the sake of fighting." He eyed her from his spot by the window, unable to keep his eyes off her. "Where are you going?" he asked, daring to stand before her as she pulled on her boots.

"Then you find a way to move forward when it's finished. We all have light and dark inside of us, a possibility for both. That's just the way it is." With both boots on, she tightened the strings on the pouch and tied it to one of the belt loops on her skirt. She picked up her jacket and stood. "I have a manticore to find. Last I checked, you're not responsible for me or my actions. The only person *I* have to answer to is me. Something you've made abundantly clear."

He grabbed her arm. "Don't answer to me, then. I'm still not letting you go in there alone."

Yanking her arm from his grip, she gritted her teeth. She could quite take care of herself, and she was damn tired of proving it. She had things that needed to be done. "Then follow if you like, but keep your distance. Because right now, I need space from you."

He stepped back from her, allowing his hand to drop. He gave her a curt nod. "As you wish."

Whether she wanted it to show, there was hurt in her eyes. No, it wasn't a game, but it was feeling like that's how he treated it. She shrugged the jacket on, two holes in the back for the tops of her wings to rest comfortably through. Biting the inside of her cheek, she walked past him to the door of the suite and paused with her hand on the knob. She wiped the tears in the corners of her eyes and steeled herself. It was no time for her emotions to come through. She'd be damned if they kept playing a front when all it did was cause more pain in the long run. It was his issues that kept putting this divide between them... sadly... what he would lose... would be painful to them both.

Her shoulders sagged as she opened the door and walked out.

Chapter Fifteen

Parthenia held the map out between her, Gavin, and Cipriana. The sun had set about an hour before. The beautiful pink-and-orange hues changed to a deep blue. It always looked like that after a magnificent storm. Even though it had a strange sensation attached to it. Almost as unusual as the destruction they'd seen of a small group of trees on their way here. Well, wherever here was. It was hard to tell with only the stars and the moon to light the map. With a deep sigh, Parthenia threw up a hand in frustration. "Let's face it, we're lost."

"We're *not* lost. We just can't find what we're looking for," Cipriana said.

"That means we're lost." Maybe if they had a little more light, they could read this better. Why hadn't she and Devin gone over the map more? Devin had certainly filled in a lot of space, but not all of it. This village was supposed to be one of the easiest ones to find.

Gavin wrapped his arms around Parthenia from behind. "It will be alright, love. We will find our way." He kissed her cheek. "There must be a path to the village somewhere, right? And you said it should be between Migas and the fae? So, we should be headed in the right direction."

"You would think we were, but we haven't found the path that Devin referenced, and it's already nightfall." Maybe they should find some place to make camp for the night and start over in the morning. If only that damn storm hadn't kept them in Migas longer than they expected. Although it gave her and Gavin a chance to speak with the Elder. Their backup plan was in place.

"What was the name of the path again?" Cipriana asked.

"Crow Skull..." Her words trailed off as her mate tensed behind her. Parthenia glanced over her shoulder at him.

Gavin put a finger to his lips then turned, putting his body between her and Cipriana. He sniffed the air when a breeze wafted. "Four. I do not know what they are. We need to get moving, or hit the trees. Or, in your case, the sky. I can only go so far up." He shifted to all-fours.

Parthenia quickly shoved the map into her knapsack and slipped it from her shoulders. "I'm not leaving you." They hadn't spent all that time practicing using her feathers as quills for nothing. She set the knapsack aside, tucking it into a nearby hollow.

"Great," Cipriana muttered as she set her own knapsack aside.

Nuzzling up against her for a moment, Gavin shook himself into focus.

The creatures stepped through the trees, but they weren't like anything she'd ever seen or heard of before. Gavin faced the two that came from the left, while she and her sister faced the two that came from the right. What in Demeter were these things? They almost resembled the guilers Devin had spoken of, but not to the same degree. Each of them looked different. The farthest to the left was tall, like Gavin in his humanoid form. It had protrusions from one of its shoulders, the bottom of both of its legs, and its right arm. The creature didn't hesitate to pull a fireball into the palm of its left hand and took aim.

The other one facing Gavin appeared quite gaunt, its skin tight, nearly to where it looked skeletal. Neither of the other two were the same. Blue scales covered one, and the other had inky tentacles for arms. The only similarity between the four was the scowl on each of their faces.

Parthenia gave herself plenty of room as she extended her wings. Unfortunately, that it had scales bothered her. Exactly how strong were those things? She half glanced out of the corner of her eye, first to check on Cipriana, who'd called on her water ability, and then Gavin. She trusted in her mate's abilities to fight the two he'd opted to take, though it took everything in her not to help.

There was no way to focus on anything other than the creature in front of her. As she'd practiced with her mate many times, she used her wings and shot quill-like feathers at the scaly creature. Every quill she shot at the creature bounced back, the points glancing harmlessly off its hide.

Parthenia caught a flash of movement out of her periphery. Using his claws, her mate ripped out the back of the skeletal creature's throat and threw it at its companion. A sudden rush of water slammed into her chest, propelling her backward with surprising force. She landed on her back; the impact sent a searing pain through her spine and wings. *That hurt.* With a slight groan, she took long enough to absorb the collective scene as she got to her feet.

An unknown male siren touched down behind the larger creature that faced Gavin. He slammed a flaming fist into the lower back of the spiked creature and yelled at her mate, "Help them!"

As for her sister, Cipriana seemed to hold her own as she faced off her own water control with the other creature that had the same power.

With a new tactic in mind, Parthenia unleashed her siren song, the sound bending the air around the creature and immobilizing its arms. The scaly creature wiggled and struggled against her control. As long as she held her song and didn't get—she got pelted with another blast of water and knocked to the ground again. The second throw left her gasping for air. It took a little longer for her to catch her breath and get back on her feet this time around. Her eyes settled on her mate.

Gavin leaped at the scaled creature she'd been fighting. He growled as he hurled the creature into the ground, closing his jaws around its throat. His fangs scraped against the scales at his neck, one coming just slightly loose. Her mate anchored himself to the ground by digging his claws as deep into the ground as they would go. He grunted when a blast of water hit his shoulder and midsection. Biting down harder, he tore at the thing's chest, ignoring the blasts of water that hit him until one threw him back to the dirt. Leaping to his feet, he spat the scales out that had come off in his mouth and prepared to attack again.

As she rose to her feet, she winced. She must've done something to one of her wings when she landed this last time. She could figure it out afterward.

The male siren had taken out the big one with lots of protrusions all over its body. He'd rushed off to help Cipriana with the other water creature.

This left the scaly creature to her and Gavin. Parthenia noted the missing section of scales. She glanced at her mate. With a quick nod, she spun on her heel and used her one good wing to shoot out several quills at the scale-free area.

Her quills sunk in deep, right into its heart. The creature's body gave a slight jerk, and it stumbled back. Not taking things to chance, Gavin lunged, sunk his fangs deep in its neck, and yanked it down to the earth. Blood gushed out of the wound, but he didn't let go until the creature's heart stopped beating.

By the time she and Gavin dispatched the scaly-creature by them, her sister and the male siren had killed the other water manipulator. At least they were all dead, and they no longer had to worry about fighting anymore. Something she definitely wasn't completely cut out for. Her quills would've worked if that thing hadn't had scales to protect it. Either way, it was something that was good to know.

"Is everyone okay?" the male siren asked.

"I think so." Parthenia closed the distance between her and her mate. As she wrapped her hands around his neck, a sharp pain shot through her left shoulder, making her wince.

Gavin nuzzled against her and then shifted to his humanoid form. He cupped her face, staring down into her eyes. He wrapped his arms around her, careful of her injuries, and kissed the top of her head. "Thank you for your help," he said to the male, then looked down at Parthenia. "Are you sure you are alright, love?"

"Yes. It could've been worse. What about you?" Gods, he was standing there. He was alive, albeit with a few wounds, but she'd take those over the complete loss of him. Although she hadn't seen it, she'd momentarily felt his pain when he'd kissed her head. Parthenia inhaled his scent and let it flood her senses for a bit.

"A few minor scratches, but I will be alright, love."

She glanced over her shoulder with another grimace to her sister and the male. A small grin settled on her face.

The male and Cipriana stared at one another; each of their eyes had a slight glow to them.

"Look at them," she whispered to her mate.

Gavin kissed the top of her head, inhaling deeply. "Well, would you look at that," he whispered. "Kind of reminds me of when we first saw one another."

That it did. Parthenia beamed and snuggled into her mate's arms for a moment. She'd let the unknown male and Cipriana have a second, especially as he was the first male siren she'd seen since her father passed. Where had he come from?

Thalasia didn't know how long she walked, how many directions she'd gone, but, sure enough, the half-breed was right. One definitely couldn't miss *Belly of the Beast*. Her gaze fell upon the ominous building shaped like the head of a beast. More like a monster. It wasn't the lion's face with a large beak-like jaw she'd have to step through that bothered her; it was the eyes and the way they stared at her. They burned bright red, almost the color of blood, and seemed to bore right into the depths of her soul. Shivers ran down her spine.

Seru closed the gap between them. "What's got you spooked?" He looked up at the ominous, roaring face. "It's just a figurehead. A chimera and manticore couple built the Belly of the Beast. The lion represents the chimera half of the equation." He gestured to each half with his talon extended.

She swallowed. Although it looked nothing like Mistress and she'd told him of her time with the bear-shifter, the eyes bore into her, reminding her of a time long ago. A time full of memories she didn't want to dredge up. That woman had been a veritable monster. Pure evil. Thalasia shook her head. "I'm okay."

That was all she said before she pushed forward toward the front door. She entered the building and drank everything in, including the din of people ordering and drinking. The scent of food, commingled with sweat, filled her nostrils. Her gaze first settled on the bar and grill, then shifted to a dance floor teeming with bodies. Wait. This wasn't quite what she expected. And the faint scent of copper—it was coming from behind the roped-off section. A bouncer stood guarding it. It wouldn't be her first time manipulating someone to get what she wanted.

With a light tap on her arm, Seru pointed toward the bar. "Loose lips might make for the best place to scope out the scene, meet the regulars, and pick up any hype on new participants in the ring. Gamblers love to boast about their winnings and up the stakes." He flashed a few shiny gold coins and pressed them into her palm.

She tightened her grip on the coins and narrowed her eyes at him. "Exactly how naïve do you think I am?" It was absolutely fucking wonderful that he could make such assumptions about her lack of world knowledge. Like this was her first time in a bar. Or that she hadn't been around idiots betting their money away. Grinding her jaw, she stormed off to the bar and hopped up on a stool, shrugged her jacket off her shoulders, freeing her wings, and made herself partially comfortable.

Out of the corner of her eye, she saw Seru as he took up a post at the opposite end of the bar among a pair of burly men. He leaned back on his elbows, and directed his attention elsewhere, but toward her.

Thalasia smirked. She had chosen this halter because it had a peekaboo in the front and offered cleavage. Although she'd complained about the dress that Aurelia had given her only a few days ago to wear, it hadn't been her first time in something that revealing. Come to think of it, she'd worn worse. But those two had needed to believe certain aspects of the vibe she'd given off.

Leaning across the bar, she flashed a smile to the barkeep. She looked visibly over the well-toned, six-foot, dark-haired Seelie. Although he didn't initially seem interested, it wouldn't take much to manipulate him into thinking otherwise.

"What do you have that's good here?" she asked with a slight lilt to her voice, the seductive nature of her tone seeping into the Seelie's body.

He set his hands on the bar. A smile tugged at the corners of his lips as his gaze raked over her. "There are a lot of good things here, sweetness."

She returned the smile, leaned a little closer, and licked her lips. "Well, if I'm restricted to the menu, a shot will do."

"Any spirit you prefer?" The barkeep winked.

"Surprise me," Thalasia said.

She didn't miss Seru working the muscles in his neck and between his shoulders.

Setting her ass back on the barstool, Thalasia glanced over her shoulder toward the bouncer and the section roped off, away from the stench of—was that sex? Oh, hell. That was the last scent she needed in her nose right then. Thank the gods she had to get past the bouncer to the caged ring. Her vision had told her that much. Although she'd kept the information previously general with Seru, she'd known roughly where to go to find the female manticore. And what she had to get from the female. Not that she yet understood why.

When the barkeep returned with a shot of white liquid, she grinned wide and easily knocked it back. "Mmm," she moaned the word and bit her bottom lip when a flush crept into the male's cheeks. Exactly what she hoped to accomplish. She wiggled her finger forward to draw him closer and leaned across the bar again. This time, she got her lips close to his ear, purposely pressing her breasts against him. "What's a girl gotta do to get into the fight ring back there?"

He pulled back just a touch and cleared his throat. "The, uh...VIP section?"

"Yeah. The VIP section." She swept her tongue across her bottom lip. That was exactly where they needed to get. And if she could get access from the bartender, then it would make one less person she had to seduce.

"I could get you in," he grinned at her.

Yeah. Although she couldn't leave Seru behind, could she? Or let him find his own way in? Maintaining her seduction of the Seelie, she bit back a serious internal eye-roll. "I'd really like that, hot stuff." She paused and waited for him to hand her a VIP badge. Wrapping her fingers around the lanyard, she leaned forward and brushed her lips across the male's cheek. Sensing the heat coming from him, she drew back a bit. "Do you think I could get one more hot stuff? For my friend over there?" She nodded in Seru's direction, who was definitely looking past her. What had caught his attention?

"Him? You're with him?"

"Don't worry, hot stuff. He's just a friend. Bodyguard really." A pain in the ass, actually. An irritating, stubborn pain in her ass.

"Yeah... I could... I, uh... I could do that." The barkeep cleared his throat and handed her another VIP pass.

She wrapped her fingers around the second lanyard, brushed another kiss across the bartender's cheek, and hopped down from the barstool. "Thanks, hot stuff."

Seru huffed as he passed behind her. He whispered, a heated breath in her ear, "Why don't you call him *hot stuff* just once more for good measure?" He strode past her toward whatever had caught his eye.

It took everything in her not to slap him. Not that it would do any good. He just seemed determined to piss her off. Unless—was he jealous? Because she was flirting with a Seelie? She smirked. Well, if he wanted to encourage her, then so be it. Thalasia stood there for a moment as he walked over to some female. Grabbing her coat, she leaned across the bar top and set the coins there for the barkeep. "Thanks again, hot stuff." She winked at him.

With the lanyards in hand, she tossed her coat over her shoulder and strode over to the top table against the far wall where Seru stopped, giving her hips a bit of an extra sway as she walked. Really, she could've done many things to get the pass to him, but this gave her a chance to check out the female in an emerald-velvet cloak.

Thalasia shoved the VIP pass into his hand. "Take your time." Smirking again, she slipped her pass over her neck and sashayed over to the roped-off section. The bouncer barely glanced at her pass as she disappeared into the back, the smell of sweat and anticipation leading her toward the fight ring.

Demeter, she prayed he took his damn time. Arrogant ass with his comment about her calling the barkeep 'hot stuff.' Yeah. He wasn't the first and surely wouldn't be the last. Too damn stubborn for his own good. Her attitude certainly came through as she sashayed her way through the throng of people. She paused a little closer to the caged fight ring and crossed her arms. Pretending to watch the ongoing fight, Thalasia scanned the crowd for the female manticore she needed to find.

The manticore was sitting in the bleachers, a few rows up, but she needed a plan before she went over there. A slight disturbance behind her made her look over her shoulder.

Seru's energy lashed out at the bodies pressing too close. Unfriendly static turned tangible sparks. The patrons parted in response. The creature to his left gave a sharp yelp, swallowed by the raucous shouts. Seru growled through his teeth when the man turned to confront him. Their gazes met, and he continued toward her. A dangerous live wire in such close quarters.

Gods, he was annoyed. Great. Whatever. Not her problem. Unless he made a big scene. Damn it. With a groan, she spun around and met him halfway. "Are you trying to cause a scene?"

"No," Seru answered, hissing through his teeth. Short, clipped. Though his voice did not betray him, the muscles in his face were taut, his expression gaunt. His fists clenched. "Find your manticore quickly so we might leave this fucking hole."

Inhaling and exhaling a deep breath, she gripped his shoulder and tangled her fingers in the ends of his mane. "You need to take a deep breath. I need you calm." And not distracted. "Deep breath." This female had something of value to them. There was no telling what they'd have to go through to get it. Even with the plan formulating in her head, things could get derailed.

"Breathing in this filth and being surrounded by these abhorrent creatures isn't exactly calming," Seru hissed at her. He squeezed shut his eyes and calmed himself before he spoke again. "Please," he pleaded. "Just find who you came for."

With a small snicker, she shook her head and released her grip on his shoulder. He insisted on following her, protecting her, and he handled crowds worse than she did. Thalasia turned around and scanned the mass of bodies again. Her eyes landed on a raven-haired female with horns atop her head sitting on the bleachers, still watching the current fight. "The bleachers... third row up. That's where I'm heading. Go find a corner somewhere, out of the middle of all of this, please." She didn't need to worry about him while trying to steal from a manticore. Well, lull the manticore to sleep, then steal from her afterward.

"I'm not leaving you to fend for yourself in a den of highly poisonous and highly aggressive chimeras and manticores—no matter how capable either of us believes you to be." He grabbed her by the arm without warning. He didn't give her much of a chance to argue. With his advanced speed and a touch of magic, he easily placed them within range of the manticore's location. Not too close, but close enough that she could work her own magic without them being detected. He promptly released her and stepped back, returning her desired distance to her.

She narrowed her gaze at him and inhaled and exhaled a couple of deep breaths. Arrogant asshole. He had eight-hundred years on her, of course she was incapable of handling this herself. Ha! As if she hadn't done so in the past. Thalasia took another deep breath. If she didn't calm herself down, she wouldn't be able to use any of her abilities to lull another to sleep. It would be like a lion trying to calm down a mouse. Looking at their location and their distance to the manticore. No way she'd be able to use her abilities—some of them anyway—from here. Too much noise.

Seru stood stubbornly in his place, leaning against the wall.

Smiling, she did what any Atlis in her position would do. She walked forward and climbed up onto the bleachers, opting for the empty seat next to the female manticore. There was only one way to get the female's attention. Although she could clearly see what she sought hanging around the woman's neck. Sort of. It was a shell, but she knew it was more than met the eye. She shifted her attention to the fight. "Oh, come on. Really? Where did they get these guys? Do they know nothing of strategy?"

The female smirked.

Crossing her arms, Thalasia leaned back and shook her head. "Right hook, idiot!" she yelled at the ring. Really, it was pointless. Even if the two males inside the ring heard her, they'd fight in the way they knew how. Most judged her because of her slight build.

Few saw it as an advantage. Thalasia glanced over at the female. "It's a good thing I don't have any money on this. Unless they want me to bet on which one of them fights worse."

The female chuckled. "If you really want a bet, I'd wait until one of the later lineups."

"Oh yeah? You mean it gets better than this? At this rate, I feel like I need to go down there and coach them." She didn't plan to be there for longer than another ten minutes. Maybe fifteen. It all depended on how cooperative this manticore became.

"You'd be lucky if they listened." The female snorted.

Thalasia snickered. While she couldn't spare any of her attention for Seru, she didn't miss it when he moved to the top of the bleacher. "You're probably right. I'd be better off getting in the cage myself to teach them a thing or two about strategy." She held her hand out to the manticore. "I'm Lana."

Offering a small nod, the female took her hand. "Addie."

Smiling, Thalasia gave Addie a firm handshake while gently stroking her thumb along the top of the female's hand. Most overlooked something so minor in a handshake. It was the first step in soothing the manticore. "Good to meet you."

"You, too," Addie said as their hands parted. Her eyebrows knitted together as she stared at Thalasia for a moment. "You know, if you're serious about getting in the ring, there are a few slots still open."

"Yeah? How would it work exactly? I mean, would I get to size my opponent up ahead of time and decide who I wanted to fight?" While she didn't soften her voice, she controlled the fluctuation and lilt. The first time Seru had ever seen her use one of her powers, he'd been in awe. Of course, she was using the same power for a different purpose, which meant she wanted a bit more melodic and a little less song.

Addie paused for another moment before she said anything. "Uh, yes and no. You don't get to see them beforehand, but you get a glance at their stats."

"Hmm, so basic information. Kind of hard to determine the difficulty of the fight based on that alone. Stats can be misleading." This was one of those times when she had to take it slow. Word by word. Sentence by sentence, she maintained her control perfectly. The lull in Addie's eyes hadn't gone unnoticed.

"What makes you say that?"

"Take those two manticores in the ring, for example. The blonde-headed one is smaller in build, so you wouldn't think he could pack a punch. For his stats, they'd give his height and weight?" Thalasia paused for a second, taking in the way Addie's body had relaxed. The female's eyes were drooping. It wouldn't be long now. Phase two was almost complete. "However, if you actually pay attention to the distribution of his muscle, you'd notice his legs are impressive, as are his biceps. That means not only can he punch, but he has the power in his legs and arms to follow-through appropriately. One might think he'll lose compared to the dark-headed guy who has more weight, but I'd say otherwise."

"You've got a good eye," Addie said as the blond-haired male knocked out his opponent with a well-placed uppercut. Half of the crowd cheered. "I'd bet anything you could take out any opponent on that list."

Maybe, but that wasn't the point. She'd drawn the manticore in. Now she just had to give one little extra nudge, and the female would be right where she wanted her. And the timing was perfect. People would begin moving off to collect their winnings while the cage was reset for the next match. "Really? Anything?"

"Definitely. In fact, I'll make you a deal. I'll sign up if you do. We can even pick each other's opponents to make it fair."

Thalasia grinned widely. Although it would be nice to blow off a little steam, and she was going to agree to Addie's suggestion, no way it would get that far. Catching sight of the third part of her plan coming their way, she sat up and extended her hand. "Deal."

"Deal." The female shook her hand and stood. "Let's not waste any time."

With a nod of her head, Thalasia got to her feet and descended the bleachers alongside Addie. They'd just hit the floor when the third part of her plan bumped into her and knocked her back into the rows of bleachers. She fell back, hitting her right shoulder against the metal stands, and dropping her jacket.

"Watch where you're going, asshole!" Addie called out and then turned back to Thalasia. She held her hand out to help Thalasia up. "You okay, Lana?"

"Yeah. I think so."

"Here. Let's go around to the side where you can check everything." Addie nodded to the back of the bleachers, where it was less crowded. Once they ducked underneath the bleachers and were out of sight, Addie turned and faced Thalasia. "What do you want?"

Oh, this wasn't good. "Excuse me?"

"You've got a righteous act, I'll give you that, but I can tell you sought me out for something."

Alright. Plan B, it was. Dropping the dumb act, she smirked. The manticore was smarter than she looked, but she was still more relaxed than she probably was normally. "That." She pointed to the shell around her neck. Before the female had time to react, she grabbed Addie's arm and sent jolts of electricity coursing through her body. It took very little for the manticore to fall to the floor. Once she was out cold, Thalasia kneeled down beside the female. "I was really hoping we could've done this the easy way, but you had to be too smart for your own good."

"Easy?" Seru glowered down at her through a gap in the bleachers. "Paralyzing her and taking it from the start would've been easy." He shoved a hand through his mane, disheveling it further. "May we go now, or is there something else you need to get out of your system?"

"Easy would've been her handing it over to me without issue. But no, she had to be stubborn and pig-headed, like you, and make things difficult." She removed the necklace from over the female's head, opened her bag and tucked it in there for safekeeping. Oh, if he kept talking like that, she was going to find another way to piss him off. Instead, Thalasia bit her tongue and patted the female down to make sure she'd collected the right item. The manticore had nothing else on her.

Rising to her feet, she allowed a new glamour to fall over her and made herself appear as the female manticore on the ground. It didn't take long for her hair to grow longer and take on a raven-colored appearance with the horns atop her head. Her wings disappeared, and her clothes altered, changing into a simple pair of pants and something resembling a tank-top, along with a pair of moccasins. Her new look even included the shell necklace the female had worn around her neck. Thalasia collected her bag and pulled the strings tight. "Let's go."

Without another word, she stepped out from beneath the bleachers and made her way to the door.

Seru snorted at her. He hopped down from the bleachers with little effort, landing smoothly. He sidled up behind her. "Perhaps she didn't find you nearly as charming as you find yourself." His face gave away too much of what he thought of her new appearance. "They'll notice the bag," he commented. "And I'm definitely not sleeping with you like *that.*"

"Right now, you can sleep alone as far as I'm concerned." Arrogant ass! She quickly disappeared the bag, so it blended in with her guise.

He paused before they came too near another crowd or any of the bouncers. "She came alone. Leave alone and I'll meet you at the fountain in the center of town."

Thalasia stormed off, shoving anyone who got in her way. As if she planned to make this a permanent change. No. Instead of him asking why she bothered to use her glamour to look like Addie, he just made an assumption. Her reasoning was rather sound. Good gods, she really needed more space. As much as she cared about him, as attracted as she was to him, he really knew how to piss her off.

As she left, she took several deep breaths to calm herself. It wouldn't do either of them any good if they believed Addie stormed off instead of kicking someone's ass. Something she was sure the manticore would've done. She didn't know how, but she calmed down enough so that she didn't draw any unwanted attention on her way out the door.

Once she was in the alleyway around the corner, away from wandering eyes, she dropped the glamour she'd put up of the female manticore and made her way to the fountain. Now she could mentally cuss Seru out like he deserved. Gods, he was giving her a headache.

Chapter Sixteen

Thalasia rubbed her shoulder with a slight wince. The damn guy had shoved her out of the way harder than she expected. But it would heal. In no way did she plan on pulling on Seru's healing abilities. Hers may not be as fast, but sure as shit, she refused to use it. Arrogant ass. Reaching the fountain, she settled onto the edge, feeling the smooth, cold stone against her skin as she took out some coins. Tossing a piece of gold into the sweet scent of the water, she thought of another term to describe Seru: dickhead. For each new word that popped into her head, she threw another coin.

It wasn't long before he caught up with her. He crossed the cobble to where she sat tossing coins into the basin. "Making wishes?" Reaching into his pocket, he retrieved a pair of fruits, a peach and a plum, and held them out toward her.

Her gaze flicked from the coins to him. Each one had made her feel a little less aggressive. No reason to wish when every word she'd come up with already fit his personality. "No. Coming up with new words to describe you. 'Arrogant ass' has become repetitive."

She dropped what remained of the coins in her palm into the fountain and stared at the two pieces of fruit he held in his hands. Exhaling a deep breath, she took both the peach and plum from him. "Thank you." Biting into the plum, she winced and turned to face the fountain again. Really, she'd hoped it would hold some answers. Not that it did. It had calmed her down some, though.

Seru smiled, slipping his hands into his pockets. "I wish I could blame it all on my time amid the mighty dragon nobles high in the Clouds." He ventured to take a seat next to her, reclining against the wide lip on which they sat. Their shared reflection in the rippling water stared back at them.

"Here, I thought it was just your charming personality." She bit into the plum. Her gaze flicked to the central part of the fountain. Beneath the twinkling stars, the beauty of the scene was undeniable. Even romantic. Closing her eyes, she tilted her head back, enjoying the soft caress of the breeze that gently played with her hair and feathers.

Gods, she'd met no one who infuriated her the way he did. At least she was really calming down. And despite everything, they'd gotten what they needed. So, what if the reason was still unclear? She just had to crack open the shell to get to the green crystal. Another piece of the chaotic puzzle.

"One facet of it, I suppose." He paused. "Why *do* you like plums so much?"

Taking another bite, she chewed and swallowed the bite, and glanced at him. "They're sweet and juicy." It wasn't the only reason, but the primary reason. "I can also find them rather easily." There weren't many things that remained consistent in her life, but plums, for some strange reason—nearly every realm she ever visited had a version of plums. It comforted her in a small way.

His finger gently brushed the sweet juice that lingered on her lips. "Hmm..."

Her tongue swept across her bottom lip, where his finger had just been. If she were to be completely honest with him and herself, while she'd spoken the truth, it went deeper than even she wanted to admit. She lowered the hand that held the plum, and her gaze followed, falling to the water and its subtle, shifting reflections. "They were my dad's favorite fruit. After... his death, I don't know; I guess they offer some kind of... stability. Something I don't really have in any other part of my life."

He brushed a gentle touch over her cheek, tucking a few stray strands behind her ear. "A comfort object," Seru reiterated. He grasped her chin, lifting her fallen face. His blue eyes bore into her silver. "I did not ask to make you sad."

"You didn't." Thalasia paused. She couldn't remember where they'd been staying, but it had been the two of them in the kitchen. Her father had taken a huge bite from the plum, making a mess. Juice had gotten all over his face. It had made her laugh, and then she'd done the same thing. Her mother had been so angry over the disaster they'd created. Staring into his eyes, she offered Seru a smile that felt as warm as the sun. "The first time I ever had a plum with my father... it's one of the best memories I have of him."

"Best hold on to that one," Seru murmured, keeping her gaze a moment longer.

"I hold on to as many of the good ones as I can." But she did that with all of them. They even had a few. Not that they certainly hadn't argued a lot today, but they'd created a few wonderful memories. Part of which included making up names for Mac and Aurelia. Thalasia's smile brightened a little more.

Glancing back at the water lapping along the fountain's edge, his gaze focused on the coins. Some sparkled like tiny stars, but most shone tarnished. He dipped his hand in, retrieving the closest coin. Holding it up to the light, he turned it over; the rusted and discolored surface hid the denomination. He tossed it back. His nose wrinkled. Seru swung his legs over into the crisp water. He scrubbed at his face and neck, working his fingers through his mane until he was drenched.

Finishing the last of the plum, Thalasia stifled a chuckle. "The fountain isn't really made for bathing."

"If I didn't reek of a beast's belly, I'd agree with you," Seru replied. A faint grin flashed across his face. "Besides, where do you think those children who Aurelia was playing with last time we were here bathed? If it's clean enough for them, it's more than clean enough for me."

"Considering I was chasing after you, I didn't really pay them much mind." Actually, she hadn't really done much of that with this isle. Taken in any part of it. Strolled through the marketplace. She smirked. "We could've just gone back to the inn for you to shower." She shook her head. "Just... whatever you do... don't shake."

"I'm not a wolf or a cat shifter. You'll have to go back to Santos if that's what you're after." He palmed a handful of the cool water and flung it Thalasia's way.

She gasped. He didn't! Oh, he was going to get it now. Her eyes sparkled ever so slightly as she scooped some of the water in her own hand and flung it back at him. "Everyone shakes."

"You realize I can just drench you with another downpour," Seru mused. "The only way you win this is if I let you."

He could also just pull her into the fountain with him if he wanted to get her wet so badly. She snickered. "That depends on exactly what you think I'm trying to win."

Seru raised his eyebrows at her. "A wet siren contest?"

"As I'm the only siren in the immediate vicinity, that would be easy." If it's what she was trying to win. Not that it was a game between them. Though she loved his candor. Thalasia chuckled.

He wrung out his mane and clothes, and with a final splash, Seru stepped back onto the rough cobbles. He pulled his boots off, emptying them of water. "Maybe... or maybe not."

"What makes you say that?" She picked up the peach he'd given her and bit into it, licking the juice from her lips.

"You could be disqualified on a technicality." He readjusted the wet clothing around his collar. "Though I suppose the same goes for me."

It wasn't hard to see where he was going with this. She wasn't technically a siren; she was an Atlis. Designed completely differently from sirens, but created in their image all the same. Plus, her abilities went well beyond those of a normal siren. And he wasn't a siren at all. "Point made." She took another bite of the peach.

He retook his seat beside her. "You should save the pits. That way, you can plant your own trees."

"Plant them where?" It wasn't as if she stayed put in one place long enough to see trees grow. Or even to tend them the way they required. And except for the one realm she intended to return to, she'd never gone back to a place she'd already been.

"Wherever you decide."

She didn't know how to respond to that. While the idea seemed nice, it wasn't her reality. But they'd been getting along for a bit. And she certainly didn't want to sour that, yet the fact remained... their lives were completely different. Thalasia took another bite of the peach. "I wish it was that easy."

"It can be... if you want it badly enough."

She set the fruit down and turned her attention to the fountain, where the water moved in mesmerizing ripples. One drop of a coin would change their direction. Alter them to a different path. Her gaze flipped back to him. "What makes you think it's that simple, Seru? Do you think it's that simple for you?"

"Without this?" He looped his finger through the collar, putting it on stark display alongside the glinting coins. He looked at her then... really looked at her. "Sure. Until that happens, I stay the course I'm on."

"That's part of what makes us different." She bit her bottom lip. "We can find a way to remove your tether, but mine... there is no getting rid of it." Thalasia half-shrugged, her face twisting slightly as she winced and rubbed her aching shoulder. "It dictates... a lot of my life." She wouldn't have been on Prisma Isle if it hadn't led her here.

"What if you refuse? Pass the torch to someone else?" Seru asked, placing a hand on her shoulder. "I really wish you'd take of your own accord rather than make me force it on you." With a sigh, he pushed power into her, the energy flowing like a warm current, and eased the ache in her shoulder.

"I didn't think I'd hit it that hard." No, that wasn't it at all. She just hadn't wanted to depend on him. Not after their multiple fights earlier. No matter what, she'd thought he was to her... too many thoughts that went with that. Things she hadn't shared with him yet. She shook her head. The only Atlis she'd known before her had been her mother. Not every Atlis had visions like she did. They skipped a generation. It had always been like that. Even if she could choose someone... she didn't know how that would work. "Who would I pass it on to? There is no one left. It's just me."

"Someone who wants it?" His brows knitted together as he tended her wound. "I know that sounds overly simple..." He paused. "A person you identify as worthy and able based on a predetermined set of criteria. You cannot be the first to reject or desire to pass on your calling."

It did sound simple. He made it sound... easy. For once in her life, she wouldn't mind doing what she wanted. Staying somewhere because it was what she wanted to do. And she couldn't deny that she wanted to be with him. *That* was the simplest truth of all. "I've read the Atlis journal backward and forward since I was a child. If one has rejected it in the past... no one has written about it."

"In that book," Seru offered. "If you were her, would you have placed such... misgivings, where they were plain to see?" He settled back, resting his hands on his knees. "There are always more books, notes, scrolls, and there are often multiple spectrums and ways to truly *see* what's hidden."

If an Atlis had rejected their position, they would've never received the book. It was passed down, the same as the Allimos journal. Even if she found out they had done before it... It didn't mean she'd lose her visions. Though he was right about one thing... there were always other books, notes, scrolls... there was a book they still had to find. One she hoped held the answers she was looking for; ones that had everything to do with why she was here. Thalasia lifted her gaze to his. "And if I could? What then?"

"You choose."

"And what choice do you have?"

"What do you mean?" He narrowed midnight-blue eyes at her, allowing his dripping mane to fall to one side.

"It's not a tough question, Seru." She paused and stared at him for a long moment. They could debate their abilities to make their own choices, live their own lives for hours on end, but where would it get them? Thalasia pushed off the stone that had warmed beneath her body and stood. "Although maybe it is."

"It's an open-ended question that could be answered in several ways," he responded. "What is it you *truly* wish me to answer, Thalasia?"

She didn't know. No, that wasn't true. She knew exactly what she wanted him to answer. She just wasn't sure she wanted the answer. Though if she had one... she bit her bottom lip and regarded him. "What if my choice included you? What choice would you have?" No matter how he answered, she'd still do whatever it took to get that collar off of him. He deserved that.

Seru's mouth quirked up at the corners. His hand came up to his mouth to cover his smirk. "Are you—" An edge of laughter coated his words. An incredulous smile remained in place. "Is the mighty Thalasia, lone non-siren and valiant warrior for the greater good, asking me if I love her?" The question came out teasing.

'Love?' Where the fuck had he gotten *love* out of that question? She crossed her arms, a frown etched on her face as she glared at him. Was she attracted to him, yes? Did it seem as if he was attracted to her? Yes. Did she fully understand everything that meant? No. Did it make her curious? Yes. "You know what... I'm sorry I asked." The rhythmic grinding of her teeth punctuated her hasty turn away from the fountain. She was entirely done with this conversation. Completely done. Screw him. If he'd thought he'd share a bed with her now, he was sorely mistaken.

He stepped in front of her with lightning-fast speed, cupped her chin, and kissed her, his lips pressing firmly against hers.

Her body responded of its own accord. She reached up into the wet strands of his mane and gently plied his mouth open with her tongue. Gods, she couldn't seem to stop herself. A shiver ran down her spine. As she deepened the kiss, her grip tightened in his mane, and she could feel the heat of his breath. His other hand slipped around her waist. She threaded their fingers together and leaned into him, closing as much of the gap between them as she could.

His talons raked along the back of her hand. Aggression rose to ride their shared passion. The tips of his fangs cut the inside of her mouth. The coppery taste mingled with the warmth of her mouth.

He caressed her chin, sliding his hand to her throat, locking her mouth on his.

It all just spurred her on and sent a jolt of electricity through her veins. With their lips fused together, her tongue battling with his, she moaned into the kiss. Her fingers skimmed along the back of his head and dug into the nape of his neck as she attempted to draw him closer. There wasn't much space between them at all, and it still wasn't enough. Nor did she try stopping it as her body got a little hotter beneath his touch.

Breaking the kiss, Seru let out a ferocious snarl. In a flash, his hand constricted around her wrist. "Not there." The glow from his eyes reflected on her face, dancing within her silver. He drew back, breathless. "That's..." He shook his head, forcing himself to step around her. "I can't give you that," he said over his shoulder, concealing his features from her.

Her chest heaving as she sought to catch her breath, Thalasia folded her arms across her chest. It was the only way to cover the way her nipples pebbled in this top. It would've been great if she'd remembered to grab her jacket. Her first kiss. She had lost all conscious thought in the moment with Seru. Despite his teasing comment, her body betrayed her and easily responded. In the last few minutes, it was like they'd taken two steps forward, only to take three steps back. And there was a distance between them again. Every part of her wanted him. Every part of her wanted to succumb to his touch. She wanted to take him in ways she had no other. One of several things she hadn't lied about. It was almost ironic. His earlier words to help with her pheromones when he'd been the one to trigger them. Exactly how many times would they do this dance? How many times would she let him in for him to shut her out? She glanced at his back. She had no words.

Seru took a few steadying breaths before shrugging out of his shirt. He held it out to her. For a moment, she almost declined it. Not that it was really necessary. She could dig another jacket out of her bag. Losing one wasn't really a loss at all. But she didn't want to. It would smell like him. Reluctantly, she accepted it and tugged it over shoulders.

Several moments passed before he said anything. "The back of the neck..." he allowed his fingers to play over the area, the crescent moons her nails left behind beginning to heal. He cleared his throat, strengthening his voice from a low rasp to something firmer. He tried again. "The panther shifter in the half-breed village... He explained 'mate' means something different for their species, yours, and mine. I've told you before... I'm Verie's shadow. One of seven. I'm not a complete dragon. The base of the neck..." his hands touched the place she'd dug her nails into. "Is a vulnerable spot. When the more dominant of the species—the female—lays claim to a male for mating, *breeding*," he rephrased. "Here is where she leaves her mark." He didn't meet her eyes. "I can't give you that."

Although she despised the term *breeding*, she thought over his explanation. By that thought process alone, she'd never be able to claim him as an Allimos. Except her heart already had. How was that possible? Thalasia bit her bottom lip and walked around to look at him. "How do you know? I mean, just because it's never been done before, doesn't make it impossible."

Seru's jaw clenched in response. "During the war, Mother let us take our fill of what remained and do with it as we pleased. My brothers... most of them... took their... frustrations." His jaw clenched and unclenched as he continued. "Out on females of various species. They were indiscriminate. They could have anything, even the land dragons, that remained." He grew silent for a moment. His fingers idly stroked the cool metal of the collar. "Even before my betrayal... Before I positioned Marius to overcome Mother, she—" his words cut off. He remained quiet for a second. "We were her strongest creations, magically and physically. The saint beasts can't be matched, even by the highest members of her court. You don't see them with collars around their necks. In her vanity, I suppose, she thought mating with us would give her something stronger still. The Matriarch and the saint beasts. A destruction so powerful it could conquer worlds..." His hand stilled on the collar. "Sometimes I wonder if she'd have expanded her ambitions if I hadn't suggested it." Closing his eyes, he took a slow breath. "If in all that time, not a single—" Seru recoiled his lips in a snarl. "*Abomination* was born, don't you think that speaks for itself?" He finished softly, still unable to look her way. The question hung heavily in the surrounding air, unanswered.

Chewing on the inside of her cheek, she thought over what he said to wrap her mind around it. The world wasn't black and white. It was gray. Sometimes that applied to biology, too. Things that didn't seem possible could be made possible. Their powers had intertwined. *That* shouldn't have been possible. So many things by his logic shouldn't be able to happen, and still they had. Inhaling a deep breath, she gazed at him and kept her voice steady and low. "No. All it says is that *something* prevented reproduction. It doesn't make it impossible, Seru. Nor does it automatically fall to the fault of the saint beasts."

He ventured to look at her, then. "Even *if* it were possible... Biologically speaking, I'm several hundred times your size. Dragons mate in their true form, not—" he gestured to himself. "...these human guises." His eyes found hers. "Do you really think anything good could come of..." He left the rest unsaid. "You deserve a family, Thalasia. One you can love and hold. I'm not attempting to discourage you from that." He pinched the bridge of his nose as he spoke. "I'm simply saying *I* can't give that to you."

She could hear the unspoken apology in his voice. Although it wasn't a dragon or saint beast's nature, she'd seen it with him. Thalasia folded her arms across her chest again. Despite the information about how dragons mated, something she didn't know, that he couldn't give her a family, one he believed she deserved, changed little. It also meant she'd reveal something... a decision she'd made a long time ago. Even before her parents' death. "And if I don't want one? If I don't want to subject children—any that I could have—to my life... or their children..." She shook her head. "No one in my line has ever died of natural causes. With everything I know, everything my family has gone through, everything I've endured, everything I've seen—I don't want them. The line will end with me, whether it's in a matter of days, hundreds of years from now, or even a century. I will be the last."

He reached out to her, uncrossing her arms one at a time, drawing her in close, and held her there a moment before lifting her chin. "Aren't you allowing the magic to overrule your choice again?" His eyes met hers, concern softening his tone. "Giving that up because you feel you can't create a better future, or because of me, would be a terrible waste. It's whatever *you* want," he affirmed, holding and pressing both her hands to his chest.

"What I *want* is a future with you." If it were truly about what she wanted, then all she wanted was him. Her desire not to have children had nothing to do with him. Although she had happy moments with her parents, children deserved more than she could offer. They deserved a steady life. Not one that was constantly moving. They deserved to make friends. They deserved not to have every action they took about or for someone else.

She was already responsible for so many. It wasn't something she wanted to pass on to children. That's what would happen. She didn't want that. At all. She just wanted him. That was enough.

"That's what I want, Seru. A future with you. Can you give me that?"

He gave a resigned sigh, planting a kiss on her brow. Wrapping a single blue ringlet around his finger, he smiled down at her. "That, or I can die trying."

"I'm good with the first part of that." A small smile crossed her face. She definitely didn't prefer the latter. Although she'd read somewhere that a phoenix could bring someone back to life. She didn't think it was best to share that thought with Seru. Her smile broadened. Her body had already cooled down, which at least meant they could continue in the direction she'd initially started. "Now, should we go pay a visit to a certain jewelry store?"

He nodded.

"Would you like your shirt back?" she asked as they started back on their path. "I have another jacket in my bag." It might make him feel better if she covered up, just a little. The outfit had served dual purposes. Males couldn't resist cleavage. Most of them, anyway. Worked with females sometimes, too.

"It's up to you."

She stopped and took off his shirt, handed it back to him, and dug into her purse for another denim jacket. It didn't exactly match the skirt, but it worked well enough. "I have clothes in here that might fit you, too, if you ever want something different." She'd never known if they'd be needed, but she'd taken them all the same.

He accepted the shirt, slipping it back on and fastening the ties. "The clothes are more for your and their comfort than mine." His eyes darted to the various creatures milling around the market. They seemed uninterested in his scars, which benefited them.

"You'd be surprised how easily they go overlooked." She took his hand in hers as they continued on. "I am stealing your shirt later, though." It had way more room than the button-up she had on earlier.

"Your cleavage or my scars?" he teased. "Consider it a gift."

She chuckled. "My cleavage is never overlooked." Thalasia snickered. "Thank you."

"You don't say," Seru replied.

Usually, it depended on the attire she wore. The clothes emphasized it more, so it definitely didn't go unnoticed. Not that she thought the obvious had to be stated. The shop they needed wasn't too far from their current location. As they headed toward it, she thought about the material his shirt was made from. It was among the softest she'd ever felt, plus it practically swallowed her because of his broader shoulders. "Do you always wear clothing that's a bit more elegant?"

Seru turned her way with a smirk playing on his lips. "If you think that's elegant, see some of Aurelia's dresses. My clothes are simple compared to the ornate attire worn by the nobility. Even the priests have precious metals and gems woven into and adorning their robes. Highly intricate, delicate jewelry and hair ornaments are among the artisans' works in the Clouds. It will be interesting to see how the craftsmanship at the Four Muses measures up. If you're asking about the fabric, I prefer silk to the more sheer options."

"You mean they're more ornate than the dress she gave me a few days ago?" She raised an eyebrow. Not that she hadn't seen them; she just thought they were... over the top. "I have a full-length silk dress... and a nightgown." Thalasia shrugged. Okay, she had a few others. Some that appeared over-the-top, but she never knew if they'd come in handy one day. "I thought they were simple, but pretty."

"Mm-hmm. Layers upon layers of fine fabrics, silk ribbon and belts. So many tiny baubles I don't know how they keep track of them all." He smiled at her wardrobe choice. A look of mischief crept over his face. "I know how to simplify your current attire. Simple is practical. Some of us don't have several hours to waste everyday finding our way into our clothes. Which doesn't even touch the makeup and the jewelry. No thanks. I'll take my armor over all that nonsense any day."

Gods, that sounded... restricting. The idea of having to wear multiple layers sent a shudder through her body. What was there to simplify about her current clothes? Aside from the socks and boots, she had on four articles of clothing. Panties, skirt, halter top, and jacket. Her eyebrows knitted together as they approached the plum-colored door that led to Four Muses. "Exactly how would you simplify it?"

He opened the door for her. With a daring sparkle in his eyes as he let her pass, a challenge. "You keep wondering. And if you figure it out by the time we get back to the inn, I'll give you a reward."

"Thank you." As she stepped into the building, she placed a hand on his chest and winked. "Oh, I'm certain I have an idea. I just don't think I would recommend it in the market." With a teasing grin, she continued the rest of the way into the jewelry shop.

Chapter Seventeen

A slow grin pulled at the corners of Cipriana's mouth. She couldn't help it. This male siren, something she hadn't seen in years, had the most beautiful green eyes she'd ever seen. She didn't know who he was, but she couldn't stop staring.

Of the two of them, he was the first to move. He gripped the back of his neck. "Are you sure you're okay? These guys can get pretty nasty with their elements."

"Um, yes." Her gaze left his as she sought the remnants of the creatures they'd all killed together. It had taken all four of them. Certain that the things were gone, she shifted her gaze to her sister and Gavin. "How about you guys?"

Parthenia nodded. "A few injuries otherwise we're good."

"Good. That's good." It would've been better if there'd been no injuries, but she didn't know what they'd faced at all. Wait a second, the male siren. Cipriana peered back at him. "Do you know what these are?"

"We call them dark guilers. They've come across from the other isle."

Other isle? Right. Parthenia and Gavin and that female shape shifter had mentioned another isle. Not that she knew its location. That would be good to know for the future. Cipriana bit the inside of her cheek. "Well, thank you for your help."

"Of course." The male siren paused. "I'm Mac, by the way."

"Gavin." He nodded his head to the male. "This is my mate, Parthenia, and her sister, Cipriana."

Mac dipped his chin to the shifter. "Good to meet you all. Mind if I ask what you're doing in this part of the forest this time of night?"

"We're trying to find a path to a nearby village, but we got lost along the way," Parthenia answered.

Oh, good. Someone else took it upon themselves to introduce everyone. For crying out loud, why couldn't she stop staring? One might think she'd forgotten all about the concept of being polite, even simple conversation. *Get yourself together*, Cipriana thought to herself. Focus. She needed to focus. What had he said these things were?

Dark guilers. That's right. Not that it explained anything. Thankfully, her sister hadn't gone into details of what they were doing here because she had a lot of questions. "You said these were dark guilers. Can you explain that a little?"

"They're soulless creatures that have control over one of four elements: earth, fire, water, or air. Not all guilers are like that. You can tell the difference by the excessive deformities. Like this one with the spiky protrusions all over his body or this one with the scales." Mac gestured to the two creatures he'd referenced and pointed to the other two. "These two, it's a little less noticeable unless you've spent any kind of real time around guilers."

Both Gavin and Parthenia watched as Mac addressed the predators. "And they came from the other isle? The one on the other side of the bridge?" Parthenia asked.

"Correct."

"You mentioned this part of the forest. Is there a problem with it?" Nothing on the map they'd followed had indicated there'd be any issue for them. Then again, the news about the so-called invaders Mac had just told them about had only been received earlier that day. Cipriana raked her fingers through her thick mahogany hair, feeling the strands between her fingertips.

Yes, someone had referenced the possibility of enemies, but nothing to this degree. She walked over to the tree where both she and her sister had stashed their knapsacks. Collecting both of them, Cipriana returned to where Gavin and Parthenia stood. She offered her sister the knapsack, the soft leather cool against her fingers. Without question, Parthenia accepted it, not that she pulled it back over her shoulders.

"You've come into Iridescent Forest," Mac said.

"And?" Parthenia asked.

It was a good thing her sister posed the question. Cipriana shrugged her knapsack over her shoulders, feeling its weight, and crossed her arms. She may not have been as polite in her response.

The male siren smirked. "Regardless of what you've read or been taught, not all the fae are nice. Some, well, they like to play tricks. Now, how about you guys answer one of my questions?"

"What might those be?" Gavin took the leather bag from Parthenia and pulled it over one shoulder.

"You said you were looking for a path, but you didn't state what path or where you were trying to get to. Seeing as I'd like to help you move along, how about you tell me where you're going?" Mac snickered. "Really? It's not a complicated question."

What an arrogant ass Cipriana thought. She was grateful that he'd helped them out in the fight, but they didn't need him as their guide. Nor did he need to know which direction they headed. Male sirens hadn't been seen in eleven years, and he had the nerve to act like he didn't just appear out of nowhere.

Parthenia rested her head against Gavin's shoulder as her gaze flicked from Cipriana to Mac and back again. "Chicane Village. That's where we're headed."

Cipriana's brown eyes narrowed, her focus fixed on her sister. Really? She had to open her mouth. Why not just tell him why while she was at it?

"So, you were looking for Crow Skull Trail," Mac uttered as a statement, not a question. With a heavy sigh, he scrubbed a hand down his face. "Chicane is my village. I can take you there."

"We would appreciate it. Forgive our hesitation; traveling the isle is quite dangerous for us." Gavin looked down at Parthenia. "Would you like to ride there, love?"

"I'm okay to walk." Her sister smiled up at him. "Thank you though, my love."

Raising an eyebrow, Mac eyed Parthenia. "Did your wing get injured?"

"I believe it may have, yes."

Mac gave her a brief nod. "The village isn't far from here. Maybe an hour's walk. You guys kind of passed the path. We'll just cut through the forest until we hit it."

"I thought you said fae like to play tricks out here." This male seemed to go back and forth over the forest. Cipriana frowned. It was like watching children play with a ball.

"Normally they do, but most of them know me, so I'm pretty sure they'll leave you alone since you're traveling with me." Grinning, Mac started walking.

Typically, she wouldn't have bothered to move next to Mac, but she was curious about him. In a lot of ways. Cipriana glanced over her shoulder at Gavin and Parthenia. She just wanted to make sure they were doing okay before she questioned the male siren next to her. "You said this village, the one we've been looking for, is your village. How long have you lived there?"

"About eighteen *solaris*. The previous Elder took me in after my parents were killed."

"Alright, my love." Gavin kissed Parthenia's cheek, then her neck. He stared after the male for a moment, then laced his fingers with her fingers and followed him.

"I think I have some ointment in my knapsack, my love. Something to help with the slight burn," Parthenia said.

"I'm sorry to hear about your parents. I imagine that must've been difficult at such a young age." Although she couldn't be certain of his age, he appeared to be in his early-to-mid-twenties. It would make sense based on the timeframe. Did that mean his family had originally come from Pteryrina? She supposed it was possible.

"Thank you," Mac said. "It was a long time ago."

Cipriana glanced back, keeping Gavin and her sister within view, while her other eye focused on the alluring male siren.

Gavin frowned a bit. He smiled down at his mate, stroking the back of her hand with his thumb. "Thank you, love. I am sure it feels worse than it is, though. It will heal. Is there anything I can do for your wing?"

"I'll have you check it when we get to the village. I don't think it's broken, but it'll need to be looked over to be sure," Parthenia said.

Oh, gods. Cipriana rolled her eyes at the loving nature of the two of them. Yeah, better, she just looked forward. "Can you tell us a little about the village? We know little." None of them had told her anything about Chicane. They hadn't gotten that far. Or she hadn't bothered to ask. A bit of both. Not that she had any idea what her sister knew of the isle.

"Well, we're in the process of repairs. We got attacked by dark guilers a couple of *umbras* ago." Mac eyed Cipriana first and then the two behind them. "What do you know about the village?"

"We know guilers live there and that its Elder is Felix," her sister said.

"What? Guilers?" Cipriana's eyes widened. Why would it be okay to take them to a village like that? "Like the ones we just faced?"

"No. These are definitely not like them. If they were, dark guilers wouldn't have attacked us." Mac raised an eyebrow, and his gaze lingered on Parthenia and Gavin. "Felix is no longer the Elder."

Gavin nodded. "A friend of ours traveled there a few *cycles* ago. She did not tell us much about the village itself."

"A friend, huh?" The male siren muttered as they hit what appeared to be an unmarked path. He said nothing further about their *friend*.

"Yes. A friend of ours," Parthenia concurred. "If Felix is no longer the Elder, then who has taken his place?"

"For the time being, I have."

"Wait. You're the current Elder of the village?" Cipriana asked. How was that possible? One, he was young. Okay, he looked older than her, but she'd been appointed the next Elder of the sirens, so she couldn't really use that as a comparison. Two, he wasn't even the same species as those who lived in this village. Then again, if he'd lived there for nearly two decades, he knew the ins and outs of the place and from what she'd seen, he could definitely defend it.

A smirk played on Mac's lips as his exquisite green eyes met hers. "At least for now, yes. That may change in the coming *umbras*, but until it does, I'm in charge. Why do you seem so surprised by this?"

"I just... the logic isn't all there." Although she had worked some of it out for herself, she was quite curious about how he would explain it. Especially with the way he was looking at her right then; as if she amused him.

"Felix is the one who took me in and raised me, but even if he hadn't and I'd still grown up in the village, I believe he would've groomed me to take his place."

Well, okay, then. If he was the one they had to approach regarding a peace treaty, then so be it. Before she even broached the subject, she needed to ascertain how much he knew about Pteryrina and how it currently suffered. Cipriana rubbed her thumb above her eyebrow. It would also be nice to know if he came from there, which would make the most sense. Maybe she had known his parents. Who could they have been? Cipriana shook the thought away. That was something she could learn later. First, she had to determine what kind of link he had to the current home of the sirens. "Do you know of Pteryrina?"

"That's a rather broad question," Mac said.

"How?" Cipriana raised an eyebrow. It was direct without being straightforward. At least as direct as she intended to be. They didn't know one another, even though he had stopped to help them out.

"Well, you could ask if I know of its existence. Or the issues within the village. You may even ask if I'm from there."

Parthenia whispered to her mate, "I think that one goes to him."

Gavin gave a slight chuckle. "I think you are right, love."

Cipriana glowered, her narrowed eyes filled with an unmistakable glare. Arrogant ass. It hadn't been as broad as he interpreted, but at least he'd given her an answer without actually answering it. She folded her hands at the small of her back and grinned. He thought he had her with his cockiness, but that was his error. "Actually, that you questioned the question at all puts the first possibility out. If you didn't know of its existence, you wouldn't have even suggested it was a broad question. That would only leave the other two as possibilities, except for one tiny issue. I didn't ask how much you knew about it. I asked only if you knew it."

Mac stopped in his tracks, his eyes locked on her, and the others followed suit. "Valid point. I'll give you that one." He started walking again. "But I doubt that was what you really wanted to know."

"Oh, it wasn't, but that you pushed back on the question. That tells me everything I need to know." The male wouldn't have objected or asked for clarification if he wasn't from there. Not that she would ask who his parents were. He still looked older, and no one had ever mentioned a missing male child over the years. If a male child had gone missing, it would've been top priority in Pteryrina.

"It is like watching a game," Gavin whispered to Parthenia.

"I know, and I just can't stop watching, even when I try." Parthenia giggled softly.

Did they think she couldn't hear them? Cipriana glanced over her shoulder at her sister and her sister's mate, her expression darkening with a scowl. Really, she could deal without the commentary.

"What exactly did it tell you?" Mac asked.

Turning her attention back to the male siren, she considered how honestly to answer his question. There was no reason to hide anything; something she loathed doing. "That you were born in Pteryrina, likely escaped with your parents, but something happened and that's how you ended up in Chicane. I also get the sense you're aware of the issues, or at least that there are some."

"Pretty fair assessment."

"Which part?" Cipriana frowned. What kind of half-assed answer was that? Narrowing her eyes, she pushed forward, the scent of the sea thick in the air, seeking a tangible truth from the siren. "That you know of the issues or that you know issues exist?"

Mac raised an eyebrow. "Do you really need to ask?"

"No. With that look, I'd say you know *exactly* what's going on in Pteryrina. While I really don't need to know how, I am curious how. Yet, I'm willing to bet you only know because someone in your village does. Not because you have first-hand knowledge." That would really be impossible. She knew every siren who lived in Pteryrina, and he certainly wasn't among them.

With a slight smirk, he shrugged.

Cipriana had been on the verge of asking another question she already knew the answer to when they entered a large clearing. It was obvious the village was half-destroyed, given the sight of the collapsed buildings. Creatures, alike yet distinct, shuffled about, their movements echoing through the space. Several surrounded an enormous bonfire in the middle of the clearing, chattering away as they ate. Others worked on repairing several huts in both directions from where they stood. She heard children giggling not far off in the distance from the fire. Definitely not what she expected, but maybe that was a good thing.

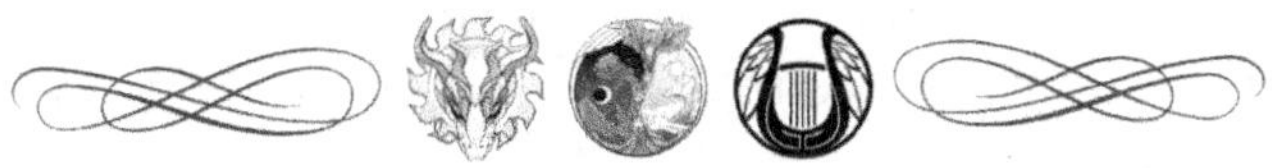

Thalasia looked around the store. In the center, two enormous glass cases gleamed, filled with glittering rings. The right wall displayed multiple shelves, each holding a different necklace. On the opposite wall, earrings and bracelets sparkled in the light. At least one thing stood true of what the onocentaur had told them: no piece repeated. They were made of a variety of precious jewels and sturdy metals. A few she'd never seen before.

"Is that so?" Seru followed her in, pulling the door shut and turning over the lock to prevent any undesired intruders from happening in behind them. He scanned the shop for the owner.

"Oh, yeah." Sure, it would be easy to glamour clothes, but she hated using power unnecessarily, even if no one would be the wiser to her nakedness. Besides, she enjoyed stealing clothes. Not to mention, glamour didn't protect her from the outside elements. Of all the beautiful pieces she saw, she didn't see—

The owner, a half-donkey, half-human on two legs, stepped out from behind a curtain near the oak counter on the other side of the room. "Welcome, welcome. Has a particular piece caught your fancy?"

"We're interested in something a little more... unique. Sharp. One of a kind," Seru replied.

"Hmm, perhaps something that was well wrapped and to be hidden. Ah, yes. I know what you seek," the owner said.

Thalasia wandered around the store a bit, monitoring Seru as she walked in no particular direction. She didn't intend to take anything. Nothing here really caught her eye. Jewelry wasn't really much of her thing. Although there were some extremely gorgeous and unique pieces. And she'd likely find nothing here anywhere else.

"I suppose," Seru replied.

"You do not know? Curious. Everything here is one of a kind. Perhaps you seek a trinket for your lady instead," the female said.

Was the woman talking about her? Thalasia glanced over her shoulder. "You have exquisite pieces." She could at least say that. Slowly, she made her way to the other side of the store. The rings were a bit much. And definitely a pass on the earrings. If she had to select anything, it would be something simple, maybe a small stone or charm on a silver strand.

"No. The lady is an irreplaceable gem all by herself," he assured the owner. "The piece we're searching for is like none on these shelves."

Thalasia couldn't help but smile. She strode over and stopped beside him.

The onocentaur nodded. "Then you are as I thought. Come with me." She gestured for them to follow her around the counter and beyond the curtain.

"Diamonds first." Seru ushered Thalasia forward. He took one more sweep of the shop and of what he could see outside the windows. They remained alone. He followed Thalasia through the curtain, ensuring it slid into place behind them.

The shop owner led them past work tables covered in scattered pieces. Some works in progress, some completed, and some not even started. Not a single one alike. Her hooves clicked against the wooden floor as she made her way toward the very back of the building. It was the only part where no table existed. Hanging on the left wall was a black and white sketch of a female siren that looked almost exactly like Thalasia.

It made Thalasia stop and focus on the drawing for a moment.

"Who's that sketch of?" Seru asked.

Peering over her shoulder, Thalasia's fingers grazed the parchment. The onocentaur kneeled down on the floor and pried two pieces of wooden panes free. She knew the answer, but she wanted to see what the onocentaur would say. It might help her understand at least one of her great-great grandmother's journal entries.

"The female who told my father to hide the piece you seek," the shop owner said. The female set the boards off to the side and picked up a small handheld shovel from the wall behind her. She dug up the dirt beneath the boards.

Thalasia opened her mouth and snapped it shut. A torrent of questions surged through her mind. Of all the things she wanted an answer to, she suspected Seru couldn't offer them. Marius had distracted him when she was speaking to Ambrosia. That made the most sense, considering when he'd spotted the onocentaur, he'd dragged her away from her conversation with the half-breed. The passage—the last entry she'd read. It might hold the information she needed.

"Who were they? That woman. Your father. How did they come across the piece?"

"My father? His name was Doran. He told me a strange male had placed it in his care. Though he could never quite remember the circumstances. Just that the female... hmm... her name... I do not recall it. I believe it began with an 'A.' Aya or Aurora..." the shop owner trailed off as she continued to dig. "She took him to hide it when he was but a mere boy."

Good gods, Thalasia thought. For once, she wished she had her telepathy so she could tell the female her great-great grandmother's name. She chewed on the inside of her cheek and eyed the way they'd hung the drawing. How easy would it be to steal?

Thalasia peered over her shoulder again. She caught a momentary glimpse of Seru digging his talons into his palms, and red spots bloomed on his flesh. Her gaze dropped to the shop owner. The female was quite busy digging away. Now would be the time to take it and test Seru's theory on her glamour. It didn't need to last very long. And the drawing wasn't tacked up all that well. Her eyes flipped back to the sketch. It wouldn't take much. With a gentle tug, it detached from the wall, making barely a whisper of sound. With a quick wave of her hand, it appeared as if she'd never removed the sketch. Holding it close to her body, she slowly opened up her purse and tucked it inside.

The onocentaur didn't appear to notice. That, or she was so engrossed in her task that it didn't even occur to her that either of them could do just about anything while her back was turned. Thalasia made her way back to where Seru stood. Tension rolled off of him in a small wave. She slid her hand around his arm. He needed to settle, just a little. The journal entry hadn't mentioned Seru by name, but it had spoken of a meeting and the boy. Not that the boy's species or name had been disclosed. Setting her other hand on his biceps, she leaned in close and whispered, "Relax."

"It should not be too much deeper," the shop owner said.

He took a deep breath in through his nose. He laid his hand atop hers, squeezing a little harder than he should have. His brows knitted together as he watched the woman delve into the earth for the item. Although he said nothing, it wasn't difficult to tell that a lot of the worst-case scenarios played in his mind. The worry practically vibrated off of him.

With her free hand, Thalasia cupped his cheek and readjusted so he was looking at her. "Focus on me," she whispered. They needed to calm down while the shop owner dug. She knew they were in the right place logically. The journal entry confirmed that.

His eyes darted between her and the woman's back. Seru squeezed her hand again. His teeth sinking into his lower lip.

A momentary distraction had been all she'd hoped to offer. Especially knowing her great-great-grandmother. Along with the one symbol in that entire entry that she'd nearly missed. And the *thunk* she heard from the shovel told her the chest had been located. A second *thunk* had her cringing as she turned and faced the female.

"I believe this is it," the onocentaur said.

Which was good because if she hit the chest one more time with that shovel, she was going to smack her with her wing. Ha! *Guess Parthenia was right*, Thalasia thought to herself. "May...we?" She gestured to where the onocentaur had brushed dirt away inch by inch, revealing the dull-colored chest they'd likely buried the dagger inside of.

"Yes, yes, of course."

Seru kept an eye trained on the strange onocentaur. His hands hovered above the grimy, wooden box. It seemed sturdy enough. "Is the chest hexed?"

"I do not know," the shop owner responded.

No, but he probably didn't notice the tiny inscription of lettering that matched the Atlese she'd shown him in her journal. Thalasia glanced at the onocentaur. "You think we could have a minute?"

The female smiled. "Oh, of course. I shall be up front when you have finished." The brown-haired onocentaur turned and paused for a moment. Her finger rested on her chin as she gestured toward the sketch with a sweeping motion. "She looks like you." Saying nothing more, the female continued on her way, her hooves clicking against the floor.

With the owner out of earshot, Thalasia brushed away the dirt, exposing the chest's gleaming silver plating. "It's not hexed, just needs a certain touch." With a pulse of light, she pressed her glowing hand directly over the well-hidden locking mechanism. Two clicks, and with a gentle hiss, the top sprung open.

"Why did you take that drawing? Can't you just replicate it in one of your journals?"

"Because I can't leave any trace of my family line here." She lifted the top of the chest. Inside was an unseen artifact wrapped in silk. "Do you want all the answers to your questions or to take your dagger?" Thalasia nodded to the item in the chest.

"Both," he said. "But I'm willing to wait for answers until we're on our way back." He removed the dagger and tucked it safely into his waistband, out of sight beneath his shirt. "It's also not my dagger. It belonged to my older brother."

"Semantics." Although a good choice on the answers. Closing the chest with a final thud, she tapped the silver, and the chest visibly shrank. Thalasia picked it up and tossed it in her purse before tying it off. She rose to her feet. "Come on, let's get out of here."

"Where does all of that... go?" he asked, incredulous.

"It has an extension and concealment charm. One makes it endless, and the other helps hide the magic of the items inside it." He'd be shocked if he knew how much she had in there. Books, all kinds of camping gear, a lock pick kit, lots of clothes—she'd taken to collecting them. Plus, a multitude of chests and all kinds of other oddities. "Basically, like a never-ending closet."

"That sounds overly complex. I'll never understand why women need so many... things."

She shrugged as they walked back toward the front. "I just constantly pick things up along the way. I never know when I might need something."

"Klepto," he teased.

Thalasia laughed. "You have no idea."

"That's probably for the best."

The shop owner glanced over at them as they stepped out from behind the curtain. "You both find everything?"

"Yes, thank you."

Seru nodded in agreement. "Yes, I think so."

"Very good." The onocentaur smiled as they passed by her.

Seru reached in front of Thalasia to unlock the door, keeping the onocentaur in his sights until they were out in the streets. "How about we head back? Get you something to eat."

"Heading back sounds good." She had a lot of questions. Though food sounded good, too.

Seru draped his arm across Thalasia's shoulders as they walked. He hadn't remembered her eating earlier and wanted to be sure she took care of herself while amid their chaotic and never-ending mission schedule. "You never guessed."

Thalasia smirked. "I just never told you my guess."

"Reading minds isn't really a saint beast thing," Seru said, returning her smile.

A soft laugh left her mouth. "I don't have that yet." She grinned. "If I had to hazard a guess, I'd go with fewer clothes and more glamour."

"Not quite what I was thinking, but it's a thought."

"Well, not really. It offers no protection." Thalasia raised an eyebrow. "What was your thought?"

"If your glamour slips, you'd also be in trouble."

"You don't say," she said, her words dripping with sarcasm. "That still doesn't tell me your idea. Unless it's a mixed combination or just different clothes altogether."

He grinned. "Keep guessing."

"There's only one option left, which would be me in your clothes. Or did I miss something?" She scrunched her nose. "Actually, I lied. There would be another option. Never change clothes."

"Mmm... No, I'll show you after you've eaten," he promised, kissing her temple.

The corners of her lips upturned. "We can hit the fruit stand on the way back."

"If that's what you're in the mood for."

"It's mostly what I eat. Fish occasionally, though I prefer it cooked, not raw. Some bread sounds good, too. I think I saw a bakery around here."

"Sure," he agreed, sounding somewhat distracted as they veered off toward the fruit stand.

"We could always just go to a restaurant or a bar, get drunk, and forget everything else." She paused. "I lose you somewhere?" Her eyes scanned across the crowd.

"My metabolism won't allow me to get drunk," he replied with a shake of his head. "No, it's nothing. Don't worry about it." He kissed the top of her head, hugging her close.

She wrapped an arm around his waist. "Right."

"You don't believe me."

"I just think it may be something you can't tell me right now... given what happened the last time you got distracted. Either that or you saw something I didn't pick up."

He shook his head. "Just thinking too much."

"That could be dangerous."

Seru glanced over at her. "When your life is constantly in jeopardy, it's more of an asset than a hindrance. But when you're trying to be... normal... it's definitely overwhelming."

"Unless you overthink the situation."

"Or person."

"Touché."

"Especially for those of us who aren't accustomed to having others in our lives on more than a superficial basis."

"Or having people in their lives, period."

"That is true." He nodded in agreement.

"One issue at a time, though, right?"

"Tell that to our increasingly complicated lifestyle," Seru offered with a smile.

"I'd say it may get less complicated, but there's no way to tell that." She cracked a laugh as they approached the fruit stand. Thalasia stood there for a moment and took in the different options. "Let me get four plums, three apples, and a handful of... what are these?" She pointed to some small, round, burgundy-colored berries.

"Rosenberry. It's what I have left."

"Okay. A handful of those." Thalasia dug around in her purse for a few coins while the female half-breed put her order together.

Seru extended his hand to the female's place on the stand, leaving a stack of coins before Thalasia finished digging out her own.

"Thank you," he said, taking the order for her, too. He held out a plum to her. The purplish fruit seemed easiest to eat as they walked. The apples brought back the argument from the hybrid village. Not a subject or series of behaviors on his part that he cared to dredge up or reflect on.

Taking the plum, she tightened the ties of her purse. "Thank you. Bakery? Or back to the inn?"

"Bakery. Then back to the inn."

She nodded and started toward the bakery. "You know, I can't remember the last time I had bread."

"Oh? Seems like a staple for most non-carnivorous species."

"Not every place has it, though. Fruit is the most common. All kinds of fresh fruit. At least it makes it easy to stay in shape. Probably why I eat so much of it at a time."

"How do you know each realm's fruit won't make you ill or worse?" he wondered. "What's edible for one species may not be for another." The bell chimed as Seru opened the bakery door, the sound echoing slightly in the otherwise quiet corridor, as he let Thalasia pass.

"The smell. If it's something that my stomach won't tolerate, it has a sour smell. Plus, we keep information in the journal if I go anywhere others have been." As they walked around the bakery, Thalasia examined the various loaves of bread behind the glass, their warm scent filling the air. She bent over and stared at one particular loaf. Taking a deep breath, she nodded her head. She pointed the loaf out to the female behind the case. It didn't take her long to find a couple of coins this time around.

Chapter Eighteen

Parthenia watched as Mac glanced over at Cipriana. Her sister had remained quiet as they walked.

"You said you're an ambassador. Does this mean you're going around to all the different species?" Mac posed.

"Yes. That is our goal—to reach out to all except the shape shifters, dragon-shifters, and those of the sea. We do not expect their cooperation." She paused. "Though you said you expected assistance from the dragon-shifters. Is that true?"

"It is." He gripped the back of his neck. "Maybe I can accompany you to these other places. Make sure you don't get lost."

Parthenia suppressed a giggle. Mac's offer to join them couldn't have gone better if she had prayed for it. "We could always split up. Cover more ground that way," she suggested.

Cipriana's glare burned as she glanced over her shoulder at her.

"She has a point," Mac said.

Gavin smirked. "I agree."

Scowling, Cipriana glowered daggers at the two of them. "Fine," she said through gritted teeth.

"That's great. We can cover the Seelie, fairies, and the chimera. You can take the dwarves, trolls, and manticores." Parthenia smiled. She'd given this some thought all during their walk here, and even more as Mac showed them to the huts they'd be staying in for the night.

Grinding her jaw, Cipriana narrowed her eyes at her. "You sure you don't want to do it the other way around?"

"I am just tagging along, so I am good with whatever you want to do, love." Gavin smiled down at her.

With a playful grin, Parthenia met his gaze before shifting her focus to Cipriana. "No. My suggestion is the best way to go." She winked at her sister.

"Great. Sounds like we have a plan in place." Mac snickered and gestured to the two huts they stopped in front of. He looked at Parthenia and Gavin. "You two can take this one on the right, and Cipriana, why don't you take the one on the left. I'll work on getting some dinner going. A *lacuna* sound good?"

"I think so. We'll just meet back up at the bonfire?"

"Yes." He nodded to the three of them. "I'll see you again soon then." With that, he strode off and made his way back toward the clearing.

Cipriana waited until Mac was far enough away that his footsteps faded before she spoke again. "What is wrong with the two of you? Sticking me with him?"

Gavin shrugged. "I thought it was a good plan. Splitting up will allow us to finish our travels sooner." He paused. "You know, he smirks a little when he speaks your name. And he seems to enjoy looking at you." He let out a soft chuckle and gently tugged Parthenia toward the doorway the male had indicated. "I am going to inspect your sister's wing."

"His opinion of me doesn't matter to me. I can't believe you stuck me with that arrogant piece of shit." She groaned, her annoyance evident as she directed her ire at both of them. Cipriana stomped over to the door of the hut that Mac had pointed out for her.

Parthenia giggled. "I think a little male company will do you good, sis."

"I hate you both," Cipriana snarled as she stormed off into the hut.

Gavin laughed out loud as they got inside. He sat down on the cool floor, then slowly, with a tenderness that made her heart skip a beat, he pulled her into his lap. He began checking her wing over again. "See if you can spread your wings, love." Her mate gently parted her feathers, checking out the wound she'd received. "I do not think she realizes it yet, but if she truly did not want to be stuck alone with him, she could have said no and demanded we continue to travel together."

"You may be right, but she will. She may be more upset with us when she does." Parthenia chuckled softly as she spread both wings. One went out its full five-foot span, but the other didn't. It extended about three-quarters of the way, and she grimaced, the pain in her shoulder blade a sharp, unwelcome stab. "That hurts a little."

"Easy, love." Her mate pressed a tender kiss to her shoulder and then searched over her wing. "Do not extend it any more. It really does not feel broken, but you are the first person I have ever met with wings. I hate to say I do not know for sure, but I think you may just have a bad sprain. You should rest it until morning, and I can check it again then. You can sleep on my chest tonight, so it does not get aggravated." He gently kissed her shoulder, his lips lingering for a moment. "Would wrapping it help, or should we just leave it?"

"We should be okay just to leave it. If it's a sprain, then it'll heal by morning. That's fairly minor." And she was pretty certain he was right. She'd probably landed on it wrong when she'd gotten thrown back both times. Though she liked the idea of lying on his chest. It was one of her favorite places to sleep. Parthenia tucked both wings back.

"Alright, love. I want to check it when we wake, all the same. Just to make sure." He nuzzled her neck, breathing in deep. A low rumble rose in his chest. "Mmm." He stroked her neck with his tongue. "I love you very much, Parthenia."

A shiver ran down her spine. She shifted slightly on his lap so she could look into his eyes. At least this way she could properly assess the injury to his mouth. "I love you, too, Gavin." Parthenia stroked his cheek. "Why don't we dig that ointment out for you?"

He caressed her cheek and pressed his forehead to hers for a moment. "Alright, love." He pulled the knapsack into her lap, and as she looked through it, she felt the warmth of his hand on her thigh.

It didn't take her long at all to find the small tin of ointment. It had been among the necessities... as a just in case. With a satisfying pop, Parthenia opened the container to reveal a light-yellow balm. "Do you want me to put it on or do you?"

He feigned a thoughtful expression. "Hmm. Put it on myself, or have my mate touch me?" Gavin smirked. "I can do it, but I certainly would not mind you doing it, either." He pressed his forehead to hers. "What is it made of? It has an interesting smell to it."

"It's a combination of aloe vera, beeswax, and a couple of different oils." Smiling, she kissed his cheek and then brushed her lips tenderly under his jaw. Gesturing for him to straighten up a little, she collected a small glob on her forefinger. Since it should treat burns, she kept the ingredients very basic. The last thing she wanted was something that would irritate the skin versus aid in healing.

Gavin kept his lips parted as she carefully spread the cool, soothing ointment. He stayed still while she tended to him, his eyes on her. "Thank you, love," he said when she'd finished. "It feels much better already."

"You're quite welcome. I'm glad it's helping." Parthenia put the cap back on the small tin and returned it to her knapsack. Her fingers gently traced the contours of his cheek. "Thank you for earlier. I mean, helping me with that one guiler." There was no doubt in her mind he would've been good in the fight, but she knew how much he disliked the idea of taking a life. Any life. They'd worked together and destroyed the one she'd been fighting.

He leaned into her touch, caressed her cheek, and intertwined the fingers of their other hands together. It was a moment before he spoke. "You do not have to thank me, my love. I would do anything and everything within my power to ensure your safety. It is upsetting that you got injured, even if it is just a sprain."

"I know, but I never want you to feel unappreciated." Neither of them liked the other getting hurt, but they had to face the fact that they might end up crossing paths with those things again. It was good that they could so easily work together. Not everyone had that luxury.

"I could never feel unappreciated with you. The words do not need to be said for me to know, but thank you." He brushed his thumb across her bottom lip. "You were magnificent. Not that you are ever anything less."

Her eyes shut briefly. She couldn't stop herself from pressing a gentle kiss to his thumb and opened her eyes. "I didn't quite feel like it. My quills weren't as protective as I thought they might be." He had to break the creature's scales for her quills to even cause any damage.

"They pierced its heart. I was just being overcautious. My teeth and claws could not pierce them, either. I had to rip them off." He pressed a soft kiss on her forehead before gently kissing her cheek. "You are always magnificent, my love." He grazed his nose down her jaw, then her neck, a shudder passing through him. "I am trying to be good, but it is not going very well."

Readjusting, she turned around to really face him. Setting the knapsack aside, Parthenia straddled his legs and wrapped her arms around his neck. "We could always be good now and enjoy some much-needed time later." She understood his need. It was there in her, too. And by maneuvering herself this way, she didn't help him in his efforts to be good. She gently kissed his cheek, then trailed kisses up his jaw, while stroking the soft fur along the back of his head. "Of course, we have a little time before last meal."

His low growl vibrated through the air before he nuzzled her neck and gave it a soft lick. His emerald-green eyes emitted a soft, ethereal light. "Mmm..." A low rumble sounded in his chest. As his hands traced a path up her thighs to her hips, a gentle squeeze escaped, and she gasped softly. "We are guests in someone else's home. It would feel..." He stroked her neck with his tongue.

She couldn't contain the moan that escaped her. Parthenia arched her neck and opened up more for him. Her fingers gently traced down the nape of his neck, the soft fur yielding to her touch as she moved to his shoulders. "If it concerned them so much, they wouldn't have given us one room together."

"That is true," he said. His breaths hitched. "Gods, you smell so good, love. I love the sounds you make for me." The gentle graze of his tongue along her neck sent shivers down her spine as he carefully untied the straps of her dress, allowing it to pool at her waist. "I want you," he growled. He nipped her neck, then placed soft kisses along her collarbone.

"Oh, gods." Parthenia groaned. "I want you, too." She dug her nails into his shoulders, feeling the tension in his muscles, and raked her fingers down the length of his arms, through his silky fur. The texture beneath her palms was something she loved to feel. She ran her hand over his shoulder blade, her fingers whisking across his shoulder and then following the line of his collarbone.

Gripping her hips just a little tighter, he took his kisses lower. He flicked his tongue over her nipple, the warmth of his mouth sending shivers as he growled and teased with gentle bites.

Another moan left her mouth as she ground against him ever so slightly. With the hand over his collarbone, her fingers danced lower, creating a path over each muscle. She began by tracing the lines of his pectorals, and then her fingers danced down to his abs. Using her other hand, Parthenia dragged the pads of her fingers up and down the length of his spine.

"Oh, gods," he groaned. Each breath left him in a hard rush. He moved to her other breast to give it the same attention as he laid back on the floor, pulling her on top of him. With his mouth still on her breast, he shoved her dress down.

She undid the belt around her waist, holding the dress in place. With it loosened, it would come off a little easier. At least it would if she weren't straddling him. It took a bit more effort as she caressed his thigh with one of her legs. Parthenia moaned as she attempted to help him get her dress off, which didn't work all that well from this angle. Part of her wanted him to just rip the damn thing. The other part, not so much, even though she had more.

Gavin parted his mouth from her just long enough to sweep the dress carefully down her legs. He growled. "Gods, you are perfect," he whispered. His fingertips danced from her belly, across her hips, down her sides, and then they returned to linger on her hips. He tugged her up his chest, inch by inch, the sound of a growl rumbling from deep within. As her sex hovered over his face, his glowing gaze locked onto hers. With slow, deliberate movements, he stroked his tongue upward along her slit.

Another blast of heat went through her body and lit her eyes up. "Oh, gods!"

He drove his tongue inside her and gently gripped her thighs as he devoured her, hard and slow. A guttural groan escaped his throat as she rode his tongue, the motion a gentle rocking.

Parthenia gripped his forearms, her nails biting into his skin as their motions drove her to the edge of ecstasy. Her talons curled as her thighs tensed up. She was close to an orgasm, the feeling building with each passing moment.

Licking up her slit, he latched onto her swollen bud, sucking hard, flicking his tongue repeatedly. He growled against her, vibrating her, and practically roared as she exploded. He held her against him and drove his tongue back into her to get every bit of her release.

She cried out again in pleasure as a second orgasm slammed through her body. Digging into his arms, she rode the waves of pleasure as he devoured her. Gods, she couldn't wait until she could properly taste his lips. Together, the two likely offered a symphony of incredible flavors. With labored breaths, she concentrated on regaining control of her breathing. All she could think about was crawling down his body and taking his cock in her mouth. She moaned at the image in her head.

"Please," he groaned. His tongue caressed her thighs tenderly, then explored her slit once again. Their gazes locked onto one another. "Yours is the best taste in the entire world."

Spreading her thighs wider, Parthenia slowly crawled down his body, feeling the warmth of his fur beneath her hands. She brushed a kiss across his forehead, pressed one to his nose, and licked down his jawline. "I can't wait until we can taste them together."

He growled at her words. "Gods, me, too."

She continued her path down his chest, his abdomen, and hips. With a slow drag across his pectorals, her fingers danced over his abdominal muscles, mapping the contours down to his hips. Parthenia licked up the inside of his left thigh, savoring the taste, and then moved on to the other.

He hissed. "That feels so good, love." Gavin propped himself up on his elbows.

And she was just getting started. She ran her tongue along the length of his shaft and traced her nails around to his ass, giving it a soft squeeze. Parthenia moaned softly as she took his cock into her mouth. She gently sucked just the head, swirling her tongue around the tip while her fingers traced soft circles along his thighs.

With a sudden movement, he cocked one leg up, his head jerking back, eyes wide. He opened his mouth, and all that came out was a long, drawn-out groan. Tilting his head back up, he gazed down at her. "Gods... Parthenia..."

She teased the tip of his cock with her tongue, then took in his shaft, before softly wrapping her mouth around one of his balls and starting the cycle again with a gentle pace.

His moans trailed off into a growl. The glow of his eyes pierced the room, swirling with the glow of her own, brighter than the midday sun. His hips rose and fell, pushing his cock in and out of her mouth, slowly at first, then faster. Another groan escaped him as she stroked the length of his cock with her tongue, her sucking growing more fervent. "Gods, do not stop."

She had no intention of stopping. Nothing could make her stop. Not until she'd had her fill of her mate and he'd given her everything he offered. Parthenia's grip tightened, her nails digging into his thighs and ass as she drew him deeper, her fierce intensity igniting a fierce fire between them. With a gentle touch, she stroked his balls, the sensation building until he erupted in her mouth. A moan escaped her as she swallowed every bit of his orgasm, the sound reverberating around them.

He fell back fully onto the floor. His cock gave one last jerk, the last of his release leaving him. As her tongue danced along his length, she lifted her mouth, savoring the final touch with another lick, which coaxed a growl from him. She laid her head on his chest, listening to the sound of his breathing while she caught her breath. His taste got better and better each time. While she eagerly anticipated their future endeavors, she found complete joy in their present moments. She pressed a tender kiss to his chest, over where his heart pounded beneath her ear. "I love you so much."

Gavin smiled as he slid his hands to her lower back, caressing her skin. A gentle purr rose from within him. "I love you, too, so very much, my beloved."

Gods, she could just fall asleep against him. If only they could hide away here forever.

Chapter Nineteen

"**I**'ve tasted things that smell sweet and aren't." Seru couldn't help but smile as he watched Thalasia make her selection. She seemed eager to enjoy the scents and flavors offered in this realm and those more familiar to her. "Your bottomless sack not good for storing food?"

"Oh, I have a few snacks in there, but food has to be prepared a certain way to be stored. I prefer fresh food to stored food." She nodded a small thank you to the female as she accepted her purchase and raised an eyebrow. "Really?"

"Yes," he said. "Though I suspect sweet to me isn't sweet to you."

"That's true. Plums smell sweet to me, for instance," she said as they made their way back toward the inn. She took a bite of the fruit he'd handed her a little while ago.

"I'd never have guessed."

"You smell sweet, too. A little like vanilla with a hint of orange." She grinned and took another bite of the plum.

"If you say so." He sounded curious and unconvinced. Comparing his scent to fruits and spices felt strange.

"You don't think I have a scent? I mean, it doesn't have to be fruit or spices. Could be like clean air. Or cotton... just for example."

He pulled her close, giving her an exaggerated sniff. "You smell like..." he gave a dramatic pause before settling on an answer. "Home." He thought back to their previous conversation. That seemed the best answer. At least better than his initial choice of *mine*.

Smiling brightly, she brushed a soft kiss across his lips. "I like that answer."

Seru pressed his lips to hers, deepening the kiss a bit more intensely than he would have liked to admit. He definitely needed to carve out time to curb the increase in aggression and the resulting frustration that threatened to overwhelm him every time they were too near to one another. He cleared his throat, smudging her kiss from his lips as the inn came into view. "Would you prefer to do downstairs or up in the room?"

"Up in the room. I'd like to eat and research at the same time." She licked the plum and the remnants of his kiss from the edges of her lips.

"Alright," Seru agreed, opening doors for her along the way. They bypassed the tavern and dining area downstairs near the lobby and went straight up. A bare nod of acknowledgement to the staff and little more.

Thalasia finished the last of her plum as they got to their room. He allowed her to enter first, securing the door behind them before passing off her parcels of fruit and bread. The room looked brighter, better lit than the last time they'd been inside. Perhaps a little sunshine wasn't such a bad thing. He settled on the edge of the bed, sure to keep a close eye on Thal.

As the glamour fell away from her legs, she set the bags on the nightstand on her side of the bed. She sat down and removed her boots and socks. She tucked the socks in the boots, set them aside, and untied the purple pouch from her skirt. Leaving it on the bed, she dug another plum out.

Somehow, the magic concealing her legs still fascinated him. "How long does that hold once you stop concentrating on it?" The real question: Worst case, how long before the half-donkey female realized they'd stolen from her? He watched her take up a post by the window. "What are you thinking about?"

Thalasia bit into the plum. "It holds as long as I'm conscious." Swallowing the bite in her mouth, she cast a glance his way. "Doing nothing, being selfish... maybe... a bit of both."

He tilted his head at her increasingly cryptic responses to his questions. The first impressed him. Her glamour proved more powerful than he initially suspected. Maybe even more powerful than dragon magic. Severing a mental connection that was interwoven into a magical illusion or spell was nearly impossible. Their worries, at least in that regard, could safely melt away. Thalasia wasn't likely to be down and out soon. Certainly not while they remained together. "I've not known you to be terribly selfish in the time we've known one another." Physically, that hadn't really been very long, but he felt like he'd known her for eons. Their souls connected on a much higher wavelength. At least in the moments they weren't fighting.

"Doesn't mean I can't be. You just may not have seen it... or our opinions of those moments differ." Thalasia shrugged. "I guess I just thought that maybe for one night... we could be as normal as we get."

His heart ached for her. Seru reached out for her before realizing the gesture was foolish. "Come sit?" He repositioned himself on the bed to make room for her to join him.

Finishing the last of the plum, she dropped it in a trash can on her way over to the bed and sat down next to him.

He pulled her in as close as he could, holding her tight. "What flavor of 'normal' are you craving, glory?"

"I don't know. Normal isn't exactly a part of my life."

"In all your travels, surely you've seen things you wish to try?"

"Mostly when I people watch, I see couples in bars or men and women attempting to flirt... some more successful than others. Dancing... not something I've done. Well, with another person anyway."

The corners of his mouth upturned as he spoke, "I'm not sure I'd consider bars the best place for romance. They're a breeding ground for one-night stands and poor decisions." Not unlike their lives. "But I think we can work with flirtation and dancing. It can't be much harder than training, right?"

Lifting her gaze to his, she grinned widely and winked. "I think I've got the flirtation part down." She tilted her head. "One-night stand?"

That stopped him. Right. He forgot she'd admitted to having limited relationship experience. If that even counted as a relationship. "Ah..." He did his best to explain. "It's basically spending the night with a stranger, where one or both of you are intoxicated. By 'spending the night,' I mean sex. Not slumber parties."

Thalasia frowned and shook her head. "That's considered normal? So, normal people don't think of their bodies like temples?"

Seru couldn't help but laugh. "I suppose it depends on the culture and their role within it. I'm inclined to say 'no.' Unless they're of a higher station or a religious cult." Not unlike Santos. Somehow, that intrusive, impulsive thought made him smile just a little broader. "Those relations are often sought by individuals searching to fill voids in themselves through unhealthy means. Some do so knowingly... others are led astray by poor decisions. Still more are simply arrogant... See others as a good time or a possession to be used and discarded at will." He shrugged, doing his very best not to let it show exactly which of those categories he felt he fit into. He offered her his hand.

Placing her hand within his, she studied his face for a long while. "Some Atlis wait hundreds of years." The corners of her lips tugged into a grin. "I like that there is only one person I'll share any of that with."

His eyes widened a touch at her admission. "Hundreds of years? That's..." A sentence better left unfinished. He helped her off the bed and into an open space in the middle of the floor. No music. But maybe they could make do? Her level of dedication made him waver. The perfect composure giving way to a shameful fumbling—a loss for words, completely forgetting how to fall into step with even the most basic of actions. Could he let her believe that? Just for tonight, without damning himself to a fate worse than his current existence? He wagered he'd soon find out. "You clearly have more experience in the musical arts than I do... how do we start?"

Thalasia reached for his hand, and he felt it land warmly on her waist. She placed her other hand on his shoulder, and with a subtle squeeze, clasped his hand. "We can try without music, or I can hum a melody."

He blinked for a moment. The realization that he was letting her lead settled in awkwardly. "I'm content with whichever you decide."

With a small nod, she hummed a gentle note, which didn't last very long. "My parents used to dance like this."

"You think of them often, don't you?" he murmured into her hair as he rested his chin atop her head.

"Sometimes. My father handled a lot of my training. At least regarding combat and my powers. My mother... knowledge." Thalasia closed a bit of the gap between them as they swayed to the nonexistent music.

"In most societies, family is more than mentorship," he said. He felt her pain but wasn't entirely sure how best to comfort her, given his relationship with his "mother" seemed entirely unnatural. Add on the extraordinary cultural restrictions of Draconic society and... He really truly couldn't relate no matter how hard he tried. The natural care and compassion between most species' parents and their young didn't apply to dragons or anything he'd known. Even his experience with his brothers seemed abnormally violent and tumultuous. "I'm sure they're glad you're thinking fondly of them and the precious memories you shared. Though, I'm not sure they'd wish you the weight of the sadness you carry with you."

"My father would call it a distraction," she murmured.

"Sadness is not a distraction. It's another form of expressing your love. You can't feel sad for someone you never cared for." That much, he knew. He didn't dare try to count the number of lives he and his brothers had carelessly snuffed out. A sea of extinguished candles. Their phantoms rose to haunt him. A mild shudder ran through him. He wasn't sure if it was having her so close or his own unkind memories floating too near the surface.

"There are several ways to express affection, I suppose."

He agreed. Ripping her out of that annoying little outfit sounded like a very satisfying expression of affection. He hugged her closer, doing his best to swallow the involuntary reaction. She needed comfort, not... Whatever that was. He tried to brighten her spirits. Seizing her by the waist, he hoisted her into the air, spinning her in a slow circle.

A small chuckle escaped her mouth. He gently set her back on her feet. He'd be content to bask in the joy of her smile forever. However, while he felt confident in holding her aloft, he didn't want to risk making her dizzy. Turning her sadness into illness didn't go with the plan. As he set her back down on her feet, her hands came down through his mane and settled on his shoulders. Thalasia smiled up at him as her eyes met his.

"Still with those diamond eyes," he said, unable to tear his gaze from hers.

"Only with you." Her fingers reached up and caressed the ends of his dark locks.

"I guess that makes me one lucky saint beast, then... Doesn't it?"

Still playing with the ends of his mane, her eyes focused on his, she smiled. "Maybe it makes us both lucky... or maybe... we're just finding something in each other... we each needed."

A discussion of 'needs' didn't seem agreeable to the war of instinct and his affection for Thalasia. The two couldn't have been more out of alignment at that moment. He cleared his throat. "Maybe, though I won't pretend I fully understand what that is." He paused. "What's next on our list of things to try...?"

"I don't know," she whispered.

"If that's the best we can do, we're definitely not normal," Seru offered with a bitter laugh.

She caressed his cheek. "Normal enough for us."

He couldn't argue with that. "So long as you're content, that's all that matters."

"Mostly."

"'Mostly?' I thought our first dance went well," Seru said. "I didn't crush your 'talons' and you didn't slap me, so... what more can I do to make you happy?"

"Oh, it did. I was more afraid I'd step on your feet than anything." Her eyebrows knitted together. "Isn't it possible for us to just make each other happy?" She stepped a little closer to him. Not that there was much space between them as it was.

"Is it? Yes," he mumbled thoughtfully. "For a short while, at least."

"So, then maybe instead of normal... We go for what would make us happy." Thalasia bit her bottom lip.

"Mmm... Only once in a while," he gave her a sideline glance before hoisting her into his arms with a smile.

Her grin was so wide it almost split her face as she wrapped her arm around his shoulder, her other hand resting against his chest, and her legs wrapped around his waist. "Then I think we should make this one of those times."

"I think," he replied, kissing her between words, "You may be right."

She gripped his mane and pressed her lips to his.

Seru growled into her mouth as his desire met hers. The sharp points of his talons traced along her thigh. Up until they found the hem of her irritatingly short skirt. He didn't think twice about tearing it from her form. The rough material made a satisfying ripping sound.

She moaned against his mouth as their tongues entangled, the kiss deepening. The hold on his dark locks tightened.

His sharp talons easily found the strings of her top. Slicing through the strands, he let the top fall to their feet with the shredded skirt. "If you wish to save that jacket, you'd better take it off," he growled, deep and sultry. His lips reclaimed hers. His desperate hunger for her burned through him like a fiery inferno.

Moaning loudly into the kiss, she shifted one arm from his shoulder and attempted to get the jacket off. "Fuck... the... jacket..." she said against his lips, and she began undoing his shirt.

He laughed into her mouth. Carefully, he dragged his talons along the back of the jacket, ensuring he steered clear of her wings. After a short while, he let the pieces of fabric fall to the floor one at a time.

Seru nestled into her neck behind a veil of blue waves. He kissed and nibbled from behind her ear, down her throat. Finally, he took pity on her and struggled free from the silk shirt, which he then threw to the side.

She traced her fingers over his shoulders, across his biceps, and to his back. The pads of her fingers danced across his skin as she slowly made a path down his spine all the way to his hips.

The sweet sounds she made were pure bliss. Music he yearned to hear for decades to come. He knitted his brow in confusion as she unwound herself from him, setting her feet gently back on the floor. He pulled back from the intoxicating veil of her hair. "Just where do you think you're going?"

"Nowhere." She smiled at him. Standing on her tiptoes, she pressed a kiss to his jaw, and then nipped his ear. "But how can I explore you if my feet are not on the ground?" She lowered her mouth and licked up his neck, back to his ear. "Unless... you'd like to lie down."

A soft rumble escaped him as her tongue trailed along his neck. He turned into her, luxuriating in her scent, and stilled at her words. He ran a finger under her chin. His electric-blue eyes narrowed at her, focused. "You're my Glory. This is for *your* pleasure. Not the other way around."

Staring into his eyes, she caressed his arms. "Your pleasure *is* my pleasure."

He squinted at her, trying to discern her meaning. The words were simple enough, but they were far from transparent. She spoke as if they were on equal terms, standing eye to eye. But they weren't. Not even close. He shook his head ever so slightly. The beads in his mane created their own musical tune as he raked his hand through his disheveled hair. He licked his dry lips, struggling to articulate his perspective without angering her as he had in the past or adding to the confusion. "That can't be. I bowed to *you*. And since you aren't a dragon, you're not able to escalate the marks... or grant me higher status. You're..." he gestured overhead. "Above me. This," he motioned from her to him and back. "Remains about you. Always."

"Even if I never see it that way? Even if to me it's always about us? Not one or the other."

"Yes." His reply didn't sound all that convincing, even to him. "There's... Women and men are not equal, Thalasia. We each have a role. Our strengths and weaknesses. It's not just about the rules of the crowning ritual. It's... It's just the way it is."

"I don't see it that way. I have never seen it that way. You will *always* be my equal. In every way. Whether it's here in private between the two of us or out there. I don't see a difference." She stepped into him and speared her fingers into his mane. "Here... there are no rules. No roles. It's just you and me, and the pleasure between us is what we decide. It's not for anyone else."

"In your explanation earlier this morning, you stated an Allimos supports the Atlis, did you not?" He tilted his head as best he could manage with her fingers snared in his mane. The luminescence in his eyes faded, returning them to darker pools of blue. "Even where pleasure is concerned, there's a purpose. No matter how we might try to fool ourselves. Is it really such a bad thing just to let me please you?"

"Yes. Pleasure. It's more than just a physical connection. It's emotional... spiritual... I want more than just for you to please me. I want to please you, too."

"Explain," he commanded, the confusion more evident in his features than before. "I understand your words, but not what you mean."

Thalasia lifted her gaze to his. "When I look into your eyes, I see the world. Pressed up against you like this, I can feel your heartbeat, the blood pumping through your veins. When we kiss, I feel your hunger for me... your desire." She brushed her thumb across his mouth. "The physical." She moved her hand to his heart. "The emotional." She caressed his brow just above his left eye. "The spiritual. By pleasuring each other, we strengthen all three... the bond we created with each other... every time we come together."

He lifted her back into his arms, sitting on the bed with her in his lap. He did his best to absorb her words and their meaning. His expression softened. "We see so many things differently."

"Yes, but that's how we complement each other. Balance each other. Even when we argue." She smiled as she gently twirled his hair around her fingers.

He wrapped his arms around her, holding her close. His chin found its home in the curve of her neck. He sat there for a long while, just holding her, feeling her warmth, as he mulled over everything she'd said. Trying with all his might to understand her perspective, even though it clashed with his own.

Her wings came around him as she ran her fingers through his locks. She pressed a kiss to his shoulder as she gingerly trailed her other hand up and down his spine.

He squeezed just a little tighter. A small shiver ran down his spine as he took an unsteady breath. Scales rose to meet her touch, retreating in its wake. Leave it to the beast to respond, even when he couldn't. He closed his eyes, quelling the slightly erratic jumps in his heart. He mimicked her gesture in reverse. A slow climb and descent along the slopes of her back. He enjoyed the soothing rhythm for a moment, settling into it before daring to speak again. "I'll make you a deal," he offered, relieved his voice came out steady.

"I'm listening."

He loosened his grip on her, just enough to caress from between her shoulder blades along her wing. "You can explore as much of me as you've already undressed to your heart's content. When you're through, it's my turn to do the same to you."

She closed her eyes for a moment and buried her face in the crook of his neck. She pressed a soft kiss to the side of his neck, and then she brushed another along the underside of his jaw. "One condition. My panties stay on."

"You mean these?" he asked, curling a finger under the delicate fabric. His eyes twinkled, amused by her request. He'd intended to leave them on, anyway. "Alright, deal."

A small smile crossed her face. "Deal."

"Where do you want me?"

"Just lie back." Thalasia uncurled her wings from around him.

He reclined back, stretching his muscles on the fresh linens. Not nearly as nice as what the Clouds spoiled him to, but refreshing. A nice contrast to the heat they both generated.

She leaned down and pressed a soft kiss to the spot just above the waistband of his pants. She followed this with a gentle lick of her tongue as she extended her wings once again, bringing them back into a slight cocoon over them. With tantalizing slowness, her mouth and tongue explored his body, while her nails traced a path over his belly button, down his abdomen, and across his chest.

Seru sunk his teeth into his lip. His eyes watched her every move. His gaze never wavered in its intensity.

As her silver eyes met his, her tongue moved slowly across the nuances of his abdomen, exploring every curve and muscle with tender precision. With a low arch in her back, her breasts met his lower belly as she followed a line up his abs. Her nails raked over his shoulders and across his biceps.

A static charge arose between them. Watching helped. Keeping his eyes on her while she traversed his body ensured he kept his reactions, at least mostly, in check. He knew in his heart, in his soul, that it wasn't in Thalasia to do him harm. But even all these years after Verie's demise, his body still remembered her cruel games of pain and pleasure.

The memories ran too deep to ignore. But he hoped that if they took it slow, and he gave her boundaries, he'd be able to work through it. Re-condition his response by creating positive associations and experiences.

He focused on keeping his breathing steady and his heart rate slow. It helped keep the rush of adrenaline from evoking his beast's more visceral reaction to the feminine touch. What aggression he could take out on Cyon, he almost certainly couldn't with Thalasia. Even a minor slip might have devastating consequences.

Her nails skating across his skin raised the beast's armor to the surface. His body reacted, muscles tensing. He curled his fists into the bed. The subtle tearing of linen gave him a diversion as his fingers brushed the gentle softness of the down.

His body eased enough that he dared to brush a stray ringlet from her cheek, tucking it behind her ear. But not before tickling the tip of his talon along the line of her cheekbone. A strained laugh escaped him as he whispered to her, "Such a little seductress."

Teasing her helped. Appreciating her softer beauty and delicate features helped. Her wings aligned with the touch of feathers. The burning desire roared in her eyes, even if they were silver.

She caressed the tops of his shoulders and down the length of his arms with the tips of her wings, allowing her feathers to brush along his skin until they folded back in. With her breasts against his chest, the pads of her fingers danced along his collarbone. She smiled up at him. "I may be a virgin, but theoretical knowledge goes a long way."

"Do I want to know what you've been doing with your precious little spare time to develop such 'theoretical knowledge'?" he asked, allowing his fingers to play in her hair, along her wings. The tension in his body eased as they spoke.

She continued to learn the contours of his chest as they spoke. "I read mostly. I learned the parts of my body."

He smiled at her. Books. One interest they shared. However, his inclinations—his obsessions—veered more towards magic. How it worked. How it could be restructured. Broken. Reforged. A lot of that he'd derived from delving into history. It hadn't taken him long to figure out the idiosyncrasies in the texts didn't add up. The Draconic histories in the Clouds had been altered, changed to suit the rule of one. He closed his eyes, stealing a breath of Thalasia's sweetness. Gods, why couldn't She stay out of his head? She was the *last* thing he wanted invading his mind like a phantom creeping down every darkened hall. "Resourceful. I bet you had a million questions."

And no one to answer them. The realization made him... Sad? Not in the same way missing Marius consumed his heart and permeated his person. More like... heavy clouds blanketing them.

While one hand danced across his chest, over his collarbone, along his shoulder and down his arm, her other cupped his jaw and stroked his cheek. "I almost always have questions, but I do my best to let them go. Otherwise, I'd get nothing done." She shifted a little and moved a little further up on his chest, her bare breasts against his collarbone, and her face inches from his. Her eyes brightened as she stared into the depths of his blue pools. Thalasia brushed the back of her fingers along his cheek until they reached his hair. Leaning up, she pressed a soft kiss to his lips.

He smirked in response. He knew that feeling all too well. Except he indulged his curiosity. Even when they got him into trouble. He roamed the curves of her body with his hands, compelling her painfully close, and returned her kiss with a wave of hunger he'd subdued. It sounded in his chest, a deep reverberation echoing through him into her where their mouths touched.

She moaned into the kiss as she drank in his desire. With the kiss deepening, her tongue danced intimately with his. Amazing heat rolled off her, infused with a silvery glow. He basked in the warmth, relaxing into it. She tasted divine, an intoxicating flavor of vanilla with earthy tones. He longed to delve deeper than their human forms allowed. He craved the scorching spice of her passionate fire.

The beast snarled its frustration. The fire was there. Right there. In sight. Just out of reach. The beast coiled around itself, bringing all its energy to bear. It struck through his mouth. The tunnel promised a decadent flame.

She moaned louder. The passion between them brightened her glow. She broke the kiss for just a second to gather her breath. She opened her eyes and stared down at him. Their normal silver had changed. Bright white, they glowed, sparkling like a thousand tiny diamonds in the vast sky. She speared her fingers in his mane and crushed her lips to his once again.

"You keep pressing him like that, darling, and he's going to snap those pretty wings," Cyon called from the doorway. "Along with the majority of your fragile little bones." In her hand spun a shell on its cord. The cylindrical shape let out a piercing whine.

Seru tore his lips from Thalasia's long enough to snarl at Cyon before the sound made him cringe. His ears rang, the frequency rebounding inside his skull.

The sea queen clasped the seashell in her hand. She was dripping in salt-worn burlap, a nautical net. Underneath, he spotted the faintest glint of armor. No, his vision refocused, a spear.

Through heavy breaths, Thalasia slowly sat up and tucked her wings back. "What can we do for you, Cyon?"

She grinned. "Now, now, little bird. That won't be necessary." Cyon wrung the leather cord in her palm, drawing it taut. "This"—she flashed the decorative spear—"isn't for you."

Seru swayed, head in his hands. The whistle's vibrations disoriented him up close.

"Since when do you get off ignoring the call?" Cyon asked him, stepping into the room. She draped herself over the edge of the bed. She laid a gentle hand on his shoulder, a less than comforting squeeze as her talons bit into his shoulder. "We summon. You show. Don't allow our new friend in her imaginary leather playsuit—" her eyes slipped to Thalasia "to distract you. Not when we're so close."

He bared fangs and gave her an unfriendly, unfocused glare. "Not distracted," he grumbled, shaking his head to clear it. The pinprick jabs of her nails on his shoulder helped.

A flash of silver crackled in the room.

"Is she borrowing your power already?" Cyon sounded more amused than threatened. "Is that wise? Especially since she's so inexperienced."

His hand closed around Cyon's, extracting her talons from his shoulder with a crushing pressure. Clarity returned to him in pieces. "It's not my power," his voice came out more gravelly than he expected.

Surprise registered on Cyon's face. Her grin broadened. "Truly?" She looked at Thalasia with fresh respect. "Perhaps your choices aren't as poor as you allow us to believe." Cyon stood, brushing the cloth back in place, affixing the rough sack to her form and tightening the rope at her waist.

Seru used the opportunity to gesture to Thalasia. *Calm down.* Cyon hadn't hurt him. She'd manipulated the mild discomfort to sharpen his focus. The sea dragon hated drawing things out. Almost as much as she hated being his proxy.

"You have a visitor," Cyon prompted him as she adjusted her clothing.

That got his attention. His eyes jerked to her, zeroing in on her lips as if to better discern her words.

Thalasia climbed off him.

He got to his feet, stumbling out into the hall.

Chapter Twenty

Thalasia glanced over her shoulder. It didn't surprise her in the least that Cyon followed behind her as she strode after Seru. As much as he'd told her about the Sea King, it definitely seemed the time she met the male himself. It wasn't hard to determine the direction he'd gone. Although she didn't know what was being said, she could hear the heated discourse from down the hall between the two males. Seru's harsh barking contrasted starkly with Marius's much more subdued hush. Entering one of the other rooms of the inn, she walked in to see Seru's hand closed tight around a male's throat.

The guy held a hand out to stop Cyon's advance. He looked far from well with the saint beast so close. His sharp talons pressed into the soft place just beneath the ears. Buckets had gotten overturned. The briny water soaked into the floorboards. His eyes flicked from Cyon to her.

Looking back, Thalasia noted the female had frozen. Interesting. Hadn't the female said she was *one* of Marius's wives? Unless this wasn't Marius. Except it had to be. Okay. Different culture. Got it. She had no clue what Seru and Marius had uttered. The one time she doesn't study the language when they appear in her book. She totally should've. It would've been highly useful. Thalasia grinned and wiggled her fingers in a hello. "Or am I technically supposed to bow? I mean, he isn't my king," she mused aloud. Really, she didn't expect an answer.

The Sea King shot the female behind her another look. "Downstairs, if you please." It wasn't really a question. "Thalasia is our guest," he offered with a warm smile her way, as if Seru's imposing form didn't overshadow him. "We mean her no harm." He offered a slight nod to her. "It's an honor to meet you, Thalasia." His eyes left Thalasia for Seru. "We'll be alright."

Saying nothing, nor objecting, Cyon left and shut the door behind her.

"Seru, are you intending to let him go?" Thalasia stepped forward and moved a little closer to the two males. As much as she hated it, the fact was Seru had made an earlier point about what they needed. She hadn't yet told him everything that she'd foreseen. One of which she had to ensure occurred before she put the barrier back up. "Or would you prefer we converse in this manner?"

His grip on Marius wavered, but didn't loosen. He tore the shining metal and pearls that hung from Marius's hair, neck, wrists, clothes, and ankles. One pretty piece at a time chimed as it struck the floor.

"It's okay," Marius told her, offering her a reassuring smile. "They're gifts from my wives. Trinkets I could do with a few less of."

She had a couple of choices here. This wasn't on her agenda. The male had interrupted—have mercy. This was either stupid or insane. Perhaps a little of both. She stepped forward a little closer, close enough to touch Seru. With the soft glow of her hand, she rested a gentle hand on his shoulder. "Seru," she called his name.

He spun around to her and met her with a snarl. More beast than man. The tension let up after a moment. The power electrifying his eyes diminished. Seru turned back to the other male and pressed into his touch and into him. Stooping to his knees, he nestled into Marius's chest and belly, rubbing into the smell of the ocean.

"Don't worry," Marius assured her. "He won't hurt you. He's just marking his territory." Another soft smile. He lowered his gaze to Seru, unperturbed by the man's aggression. The hand not tangled in Seru's mane grasped Thalasia's outstretched hand, placing it back on Seru's shoulder beneath his own.

Seru offered a soft growl, but didn't move against her as he had before. Instead, he settled back into his task, calming beneath their shared touch.

Not once did she flinch or move. "I know he won't," Thalasia said. "He's already laid claim to me, but you know that." It irritated her just a little at how he responded to Marius, but she didn't let it show. It wouldn't always be that way. Her only intention at this point was to get Seru to calm down.

"More intimately than you might imagine," Marius replied. "I'd always suspected he would mark the fledgling matriarch, another dragon. You were an unexpected surprise." He slipped his hand from Seru's mane, hushing the frenzied saint beast. He exposed the inside of his wrist, presenting it to Seru. Seru's lips recoiled, exposing his fangs as he followed the other man's wrist. The magic pulsating in Marius's blood didn't go unnoticed.

Interesting. She'd seen a blood exchange with others, and experienced it twice herself, but she certainly didn't expect it here. Not that she let her shock show. "I seem to surprise many people." She smirked. "But I doubt that's why he was called to you."

"Seru feasts on magic, the raw essence present in blood. But it's not enough." He stroked Seru's mane and spoke gently to Seru in his native tongue, waiting until the man's instincts overrode any hesitation. He winced at the pain of Seru's fangs penetrating his wrist. "The sky. This isle. They were never meant to sustain him. Or his brothers. For a while, I believed the sea might provide enough. But, I'm afraid, that's no longer an option. Even with the magic of the Matriarch in the Sky and the free rein of my seas, he's not thriving. He's dangling over a precipice with this... around his neck. He can't remain here," he finished, a soft whisper that had likely gone unheard by the man in his arms. "Your surprise arrival is a gift. Imperfect, but a gift nonetheless."

At least they agreed on something. She'd seen it the moment she saw that collar around his neck. An inkling had presented itself during the conversation they'd had on the bridge, but she hadn't figured it out. She hoped the hidden book would provide her with the last missing piece. "He has agreed to go with me." With her hand still on Seru's shoulder, she gingerly stroked it with her thumb. Her gaze shifted from Marius to Seru for a moment. "I'm certain you know what I am, even if Cyon didn't recognize it. I don't imagine my great-great-grandmother's presence on this isle went entirely unnoticed."

"One with a striking resemblance to you visited him many times. He spoke of her and her book only a few times. He seemed taken with her promises. I didn't ask for more than he told. Seru shares on his terms. I trusted him to know what he was doing, even where the risks reigned supreme. She disappeared, along with his memories of her. Though I would not be surprised if that wasn't the intention all along." Marius continued smoothing his hand through Seru's mane. He touched the base of Seru's neck. An audible pucker sounded as he freed his mouth from Marius's bloody wrist. Seru's head lolled them both into the dresser behind him with a thud.

Thalasia jumped to attention, helping Seru. It was just her instinct to help him to his feet, not to fall into furniture. If he shrugged her off, so be it. But she couldn't help herself. From the moment they met, he'd become her concern. That he fed... that there was a blood exchange... it told her she needed to know more. She needed to ask the questions she hadn't, and she needed to give him the information he didn't want to accept. The things he didn't want to hear. She knew what Adina had done. And that there was a way to retrieve the memory in full. She didn't think it had yet to occur, but he needed to be some place quiet when it did. Though she suspected Adina had broken the process into parts for a reason.

Slowly, Seru took the hand back that he'd used to secure Marius's wrist. It was another moment before he uttered a word. "You need water." Seru shot to his feet too quickly, knocking slightly into Thalasia. "The bathtub," he mumbled, steadying himself on the wall.

She kept upright on her feet. "Let me help." She didn't expect he was the one that needed water, but Marius. She moved to aid him without giving it much thought. The last time she and Seru had been in the forest, she hadn't dared show her strength. It was easier for those around her to assume she was weak, when she was much stronger than she appeared, both physically and magically.

Thalasia hooked an arm underneath Marius's to help him to his feet and to the bathtub. If it became too difficult or he didn't have as much strength to move his feet, she could always carry him. That remained to be seen. "Lean on me as much as you need. I'm stronger than I look."

"Unless you want him to—I don't think—" Marius objected, startled by her uninvited contact.

"I'm just helping you to the bathtub. As he said." The male needed help, and Seru wasn't in a direct position to do it. And she still needed Marius, something she hated to admit, even to herself.

A dissatisfied rumble came out of Seru. "He knows that. He just doesn't want me to attack you," Seru said, jagged and extremely unfriendly. But he stayed by the wall, watching from the corner of his vision as he wiped the blood from his lips.

"Point taken. However, without me, you don't get off this isle." If it wouldn't kill her to leave Seru behind, she thought some part of her might. But she had already gotten attached to him in more than just his way. Even if a ritual on her end hadn't occurred yet.

There were some things she'd have to figure out because she didn't know how it would impact his connection to Marius. She knew what it was supposed to do, but would it override that connection?

Marius allowed her to help him into the bath the rest of the way. "You have my gratitude, Thalasia. Please be more careful in the future. You can still love him without turning a blind eye to the threat." He lowered himself into the bathtub, just in time for Seru to conjure a rainstorm above him.

Seru untied his trousers, letting them fall as he crossed to the bath. He perched on the edge, dipping his feet in as the water rose. He watched the drops cascade down through Marius's hair, down his body. "Too hard for you?" he asked harshly as the other man squinted as the drops pelted down on him.

"Do you really care about my answer? You're still punishing me for pushing you away."

"I seem to be good at not seeing the threats," she muttered as she walked away from the bath and found a spot to sit. She could dig out clothes while Marius restored himself, but found it pointless. Instead, she tossed around his words regarding her feelings for Seru. Thalasia tucked her knees up against her chest, placed her hands on her knees, and set her chin on her hands. He was difficult to love, but she couldn't change how she felt. Was this something all Atlis had dealt with? Her parents had fought; she knew that much. None of the other Atlis spoke much about their relationships. Just their duties. What about the Allimos? She hadn't ever read the journal. It wasn't her place. Maybe she should.

Seru shifted his icy stare from Marius to Thalasia. "What are you doing? Come here." He held out his hand to her, expectant. The storm subsided in a swirl.

"Spending too much time in here," Marius said, pushing his mane aside before tapping his temple. "The same thing you do."

Seru kicked up a violent splash of water in the man's direction. "I wasn't asking you," he growled.

She nearly smirked. It wasn't her head that was the problem. Or maybe it was only part of the problem. She could control her emotions to a degree. It didn't make them any less present. She got to her feet and strode over to them, placing her hand in Seru's.

He warmed at her touch, guiding her in close enough that he could reach her. He undid the knots on her borrowed shirt, slipping it off her shoulders, and then removed her underwear. Her purse fell to the floor before he lifted her into the bath, settling her in his lap, opposite Marius.

"If I really wanted to punish you," he spat venom at Marius, "I could electrocute you."

She crossed her arms across her chest and draped one leg over the other, covering herself as much as possible. While she didn't care about being naked in front of Seru, she didn't really appreciate being undressed in front of Marius. "Not that he would do that. Whether either of us likes it, you're needed."

Marius managed a small smile in her direction. "Thank you for saying so."

Seru grumbled, busying himself snuggling into her. He nestled between her wings, burying his face in her neck—by now that had become his favorite spot.

"You and I both know it wasn't necessary. Otherwise, you wouldn't let the guilers cross into Prisma Isle. So, please don't placate me. It just irritates me." Something she tired of seeing Seru do with Aurelia. Although there were many things that bothered her, she tried not to focus on all of them. Her wings took to caressing Seru's arms. Something they did of their own volition.

"Why wouldn't I let the guilers cross into Prisma Isle?" Marius asked, genuinely confused. "Have you led her to believe they're under my control?"

The second part directed at Seru had an immediate and obvious answer. "No, I simply told her you'd allied with them, which is true."

"The ones from Candescent Isle are under no one's control. Not even their own." She'd been there long enough to see the truth, and she understood why the battle had to happen. One of the many things she had yet to share with Seru.

"They're enslaved to the corrupt magic in the heart of the isle they come from," Marius confirmed. "I'm not fighting against the isle, if that's what you think. I wouldn't even be fighting against the Sky if I saw any other way. My people are peaceful, and I pray that way of life is what we all return to after this is done."

"I didn't expect you were. I need them to cross onto the isle. It's the only way to eradicate as many of them as possible." She knew it would come to a battle. But she only had a piece of the puzzle. One that she felt she was gathering more of the pieces. And that despite Seru's earlier statement about there being no prophecy that included him...

"The guilers from that... black island, they're the only others that can stand against Her. That's why they were created. You can't blame them for succumbing to..." His words trailed off.

Seru gave a bitter laugh. "Bleeding your silly sentiments all over them will not change them into good guilers, Marius. You know that, don't you? You can't save every living thing you come into contact with. They're better off dead than they are living their tormented existence."

"No. Not everything can be saved. They have bled the magic from Candescent Isle. There is a battle coming to the shores of Prisma Isle, and it needs to happen. It's the only way to rid the plague they've created." Created to stand against the previous Matriarch? Curious. How had that impacted Aurelia and Mac? She didn't know if they'd even returned to Prisma Isle yet. Or succeeded in their quest to rescue Felix.

"*They* weren't given a choice," Marius argued. "Unlike all of us." He looked at Seru. "Please stop doing that."

"If that were truly the case, they would've found a balance like the ones in Chicane Village." She raised an eyebrow at the last comment. Did the attention Seru showed her bother him? If that was the case, then maybe Marius cared more than she originally believed. But obviously, Seru cared about him in return... which meant there was more that she hadn't considered in his becoming her Allimos. Seru pressed a kiss to her shoulder. His grip around her midsection tightened.

"You misunderstand—" Marius shifted across from them, unable to sit still as he failed to keep the pain from his face. "They cannot control any of it. They're born of the same, yet different, magic than the guilers residing on this isle."

While Marius's discomfort hadn't gone unnoticed, she couldn't really give it attention. It would make her question too much of Seru at her back. Something she wasn't prepared to do. "You don't think I just arrived here by happy accident? Or that I didn't watch the guilers across the way. They may have a few that have... usurped the dark desires that live within the older ones, and they may find a way beyond it, but only if they are given the chance to thrive. That can't happen in their current state. *They* do not differ from any other creature. We all have light and dark inside of us, but the choice is always there on which we feed, *even* when we are surrounded by nothing but darkness. Or nothing but light." Didn't she have this same conversation with Seru in the last hours? Or was it earlier that morning? The time was running together. So were the conversations.

"They're dead either way. It makes little difference," Seru said. "The decision is already made. Use them to your benefit until then, and go back to burying your head in the sand, if that's what you wish to do."

"Why do you get to choose that for them? For *any* of them? I'm not using them for my benefit. None of this has been for my benefit. It's been for yours! Because you're unable or unwilling to temper your impulses. If I hadn't pushed back through your reckless pursuits, she would have discovered the truth and killed you! Don't you understand that? Why do you insist on choosing the path that continues this... this... endless cycle of killing? It costs you everything. Any chance you have at happiness, joy... love." Marius's voice finally broke on the last. Tears shimmered in his eyes.

Thalasia inhaled a deep breath at the two males arguing. There were parts she didn't completely understand. Though she believed part of it was Marius protecting Seru... at least if she gathered it correctly between what Seru had told her and the words that Marius spat back at him. She readjusted the way she covered herself to one arm and rested the other hand on the hands wrapped tightly around her waist. "Would you sacrifice the species on Prisma Isle to ensure the guilers from Candescent Isle survive? Because that is what would happen. Prisma Isle can be saved. Its inhabitants can be protected. Not all the guilers from Candescent Isle can. If they could even inhabit this isle—you've seen what they have done to their own. Are you prepared for the consequences? Truly prepared to see all those here suffer and die."

"Of course not," Marius said with a shake of his mane. "But if there's a chance to restore and cleanse their isle, shouldn't she at least try before condemning them all to death?" His eyes flicked to Seru. "You assured me this new queen would not be like the last. Now is her time to prove that."

Aurelia. Yeah, they could bank a lot on Aurelia. Her personal feelings toward the female aside, she had seen little except for someone that reminded her of her earlier years. Or moments when she lost control of her emotions regarding Seru. Thalasia sighed heavily. "Every decision has a price. At this rate, there's no telling who will be left behind on that isle when she returns. I can only tell you a battle is coming between those that have crossed and those we haven't yet seen." The barrier would go back up afterward, but she didn't think it was necessary to tell him that.

"You forget. Aurelia's still coming into her powers. Until her Ascension, she won't have the capability of purifying an entire isle and its people—which Thalasia has indicated are sizable. If it were already possible, don't you think we'd have healed this land first and reinstated the natural balance you're so concerned with achieving between the sea, land, and sky? That aside, a significant population of guilers poses a potential threat to the dragons. She's young, not stupid. She'd never agree to their existence under their own rule. I doubt they are amenable to being ruled by the sky or the sea. We have little to no viable allies with enough strength and magic to keep them in check once they're purified—assuming that this is even possible and agreed upon. You can thank the Silver Queen for that. She saw to it they were all wiped out or diminished to the brink of extinction."

Purify? Why did the idea of that seem familiar? She shook the question away for now. The crystal in her bag was still a piece she hadn't figured out. There was definitely something she could agree with in Seru's assessment. Aurelia had made her dislike of other species well known. "Although we know the sirens have sent some of their people to visit with other species, and they seem to know that the barrier is down. That may be to our advantage."

"The sirens are much like the Sky, are they not?" Marius asked. "They've been closed off from the outside world for centuries. I commend their initiative and effort to change, but you're our only link to them. And with respect, you are an outsider. We cannot guarantee an alliance with them unless you know something we do not. I, for one, am not closed to the possibility, but we need a closer assessment of them before we jump into..."

"Bed with them. Yes, I agree," Seru finished, where the other man left off, turning more to Thalasia as he did so.

"Well, Parthenia, one siren we came across asked for me to take her, her mate and two others off the isle when I leave. I've given my word I'd do so. There may be something there in that. Though I'm sure we could conduct a proper assessment in other ways." Not that she knew how much she and Seru could blend in, as he seemed quite against using that potion Parthenia had given them. And she wasn't prepared to share her entire knowledge of the species.

"Didn't you eat the last siren you came across?" Marius asked.

"Half siren. Somehow, I doubt they'd mind." Seru gave a low, drawn-out growl at the mention of Santos.

Thalasia glanced over her shoulder at Seru. "Let it go." The fact remained that he was part phoenix. He'd never be able to truly kill him. Although it amused her, almost as much as the fact that she was in the bathtub with a saint beast and a sea dragon. Yeah. This was what she imagined happening when she hit the jump point. "We don't mention him," she said to Marius.

"Only once he's truly dead," Seru griped. "Or she... stupid fire bird changes with each lifecycle." Marius stifled a chuckle, drawing another unfriendly sound from Seru. "It's not funny."

Thalasia stifled a giggle. She reached back with the hand that was atop his and stroked his cheek. "I hate to be the bearer of bad news, but there's no way to permanently kill a phoenix." Not that she knew the rest about Santos, but she'd told him the truth.

"He's only *half* Phoenix. Everything dies somehow."

"As far as you know, anyway." She shrugged. How did they get to talking about Santos? Right. Marius had brought him up. Gods, they'd get nowhere at this rate. She redirected her attention to Marius. "Exactly what kind of assessment do you need to make to decide to work with the sirens?"

Marius sobered, giving onc last sideways glance to Seru as he turned to address her question. "You tell me. You're the expert. I've never met a siren before you."

"I'm definitely not an expert on sirens." Regardless of everything she knew, she hadn't lived among them. Her knowledge didn't go far enough to include those who inhabited the skies of Prisma Isle. "I can tell you some things, but some of it could be only what I've learned or heard since I arrived here."

Marius sighed, twisting around at the sound of boisterous drunks outside in the alley. "What of your personal experiences?"

"I have three. A child I rescued in the realm of Bahalah about four years ago, a male I met here two days ago, and the one we spoke with yesterday. The child... she was the most innocent of all of them. And scared..." She still remembered how the rescue had gone. That girl would likely come into her powers soon; something else she had to figure out, but that was for another day. "Parthenia, the female we met yesterday. She's true to what I know. They're keepers of knowledge. Hers is extensive. As for the male... he's the only one I've come across... in some years."

"He's not asking after the ones you've saved. He wants to know about the ones capable of turning on us."

"By what you know now, they're just as deadly and informed as our saint beast," Marius murmured in response, leaning out of the tub toward the sounds. He climbed out of the tub and wandered to the window.

With a heavy sigh, Seru lifted himself out of the tub.

"Just because onc has knowledge doesn't mean they all do. As for their being a threat—not likely. Don't use me as a comparison. I'm not like them."

Seru ripped a sheet from the bed, dousing it in the tub before draping it around Marius.

"Precisely," Marius responded. "You're friendly and, by all appearances, have sound judgment and good intentions. Yet, even you will ultimately end up on whichever side gives you and your... compatriots a way off this isle. What is wrong with those... those..." His words trailed off.

Thalasia pulled her knees up once again and laid her head on them. He misunderstood a lot. Not that she explained many things. She felt hardly like getting out of the tub. She was tired of talking to all these different people. Repeating the same things endlessly. "I have tasks to complete. I am responsible for ensuring that happens. Responsible for... all of them."

"They're drunk," Seru barked, steering Marius back toward the tub and only making it to the bed.

Marius clasped the sheet, still craning his neck to see the oddities unfolding down below. After a moment, he returned his attention to her. He frowned, utterly perplexed. "Don't you mean both of you? What you're responsible for, Seru, is too. You're bound."

Seru rolled his eyes at the other man with a derisive snort. He took him by the shoulders, forcing him to sit on the bed's edge.

Inhaling and exhaling a deep breath, she climbed out of the tub, not bothering to immediately cover herself. She was growing tired of covering her body out of respect for him. Why should she continue to follow her own rules when they only seemed to bind her hands? She snagged a towel, extended her wings and focused on drying and preening her feathers. For a few minutes, she considered replying with what she felt was true. She knew she loved him, and their situation was complicated. She'd accepted the ritual he performed, but there was still her own ritual to perform. In order for that to happen, he had to accept his role as her Allimos. "Yes. *Our* responsibility."

"What is 'drunk?'" Marius persisted.

"We'd just completed a few of those tasks prior to your arrival," Seru said.

She considered draining the tub for a moment but decided against it in case Marius needed it again as she hung the towel up. Thalasia picked up her purple pouch, panties, and Seru's top before she tucked her wings back and stepped into the bedroom. Hmm, a drink sounded good. The shot that she had back at Belly of the Beast had done little. And she could use a few good stiff drinks. Not to the point of getting drunk, but some of the night... she'd be better off not thinking about. "It just means they've had one too many spirits." Thalasia walked over to a chair in the corner, hung Seru's shirt and her panties over the arm, and opened her purse to dig out some clothes and shoes.

"It's like..." Seru paused. "Tossing a spiny balloon fish. They're intoxicated to a state of levity."

Although she could feel his eyes on her, she didn't look up. It wasn't something she could do at the moment. "Sorry. Poor choice of words." Yeah. Intoxicated. She glanced over her shoulder and half shrugged an apology. Spirits was the common word she'd seen in the brief scan she'd done of the languages across the isle. If she'd been smart, she would've studied a little more. She paused with her hand on a fresh pair of panties—a thong. It had been over a month since she'd worn anything like them. Not something she quite understood. The other option was nothing at all underneath.

As she stood there with her backside to both males, her wings tucked loosely back, she eyed the dress she'd been thinking of pulling on. It was like what Aurelia had given her the other night, except it was black silk and dipped to the small of her back. Why was she so intent on pulling on clothes she knew would irritate Seru? What was she trying to prove? Shaking the questions away, she tossed the thong back in the pouch and grabbed the dress.

It wasn't something she could answer. Or maybe she wasn't prepared for the answer. Thalasia stepped into the dress and slid it up the length of her legs.

The shake of Seru's mane didn't slip past her notice. Then again, given the beads in it, it would be hard to miss.

"You want her," Marius spoke up.

"Stop scenting me," Seru grumbled.

Gods, what she'd give *not* to hear the two males, but she hadn't been able to block them out. It had seemed like he wanted her, but he didn't want *only* her. She brushed her hands down the soft material clinging to her curves. Her emotions had become a bit too much to handle. It had been a long time since she'd been flooded with so much conflict. A drink would help her deal with some of them... at least as best she could. Jealousy was entirely new to her. Although she could identify the emotion, it wasn't something she'd ever felt before... well, Seru.

Thalasia dug out a pair of high heels. She could glamour the talons as she had been, but honestly, she was beyond tired of hiding... of blending in. It was damn time she stopped trying to be something other than herself. She reached over, collected her panties, and tossed them back in her pouch. Her hand hovered over Seru's shirt.

"Are we celebrating?" Marius asked.

She straightened at Marius's question. Something that had penetrated the swirl of emotions inside of her. In a snap decision, she left Seru's shirt right where she'd laid it and tightened the ties of the pouch. With the heels in one hand, she slid the pouch over and sat in the chair so she could slip the high heels onto her feet.

Question. Right. Marius had asked a question. Thalasia knitted her eyebrows together. "Um, no, no celebration. I just... I need to get out of the room for a bit." She only had one dress in her pouch for a... ritual... ceremony... whatever... and it wouldn't go into use for at least a few days if she remembered correctly. None of the other dresses she had would be used for a celebration of any kind.

"Alone." Her gaze flipped to Seru for a moment. She didn't care how pissed off he was or that the dress irritated him. She knew he had a past, and every time she thought she'd reconciled with it... she didn't like feeling jealous. And she didn't know how to deal with it.

Just as Marius opened his mouth, Seru dug his talons into his shoulder, stopping him mid-motion. Not that it completely stopped Marius from saying anything. "But she needs you."

Seru gave a bitter laugh. "No, if there's one thing you learn about her, it'll be that she doesn't need me. Or anyone else."

She clenched her jaw, her anger flaring at the necessity of relying on others. That was part of the problem. She needed him. In ways she wasn't accustomed to needing anyone. Not since... she shook the memory away before it got too far. She couldn't allow it to regurgitate. She would break in ways she hadn't in a long time. Thalasia stood. She grabbed her pouch, brushed the dress down one last time and left the room, only partially slamming the door on her way out.

Chapter Twenty-One

C ipriana rose to her feet. "I think I'll head that way myself." It had been a long day, and having to deal with her sister and Gavin flirting and being all-loving all day long had grated on her nerves.

"Really? I was hoping we could talk some more," Mac said.

Her eyebrows drew together, a sign of her inner turmoil. It took everything in her not to cross her arms. His having flirted with her had been bad enough. "What is there for us to discuss?"

"The peace treaty, of course."

Damn. He had her there. They'd both been put in certain leadership roles, and she was here to negotiate a peace treaty. Reluctantly, she sat back down on the log. "Okay."

"You won't put up a fight?" He raised an eyebrow.

Narrowing her eyes, she glowered slightly at him. "Would you prefer I did?" She'd be all too happy to argue with him. Even if he'd made a valid point. As far as she was concerned, she could spend as little time around him as possible.

"Not really." He rested his hands on the log, stretched out his legs, crossing one ankle over the other. "Can we be straight with each other?"

That could be dangerous, she thought to herself. If she were brutally honest, she'd tell him he had a one-track mind, and she didn't think he'd be good as a leader. Not that it was her place to judge him. Wasn't that part of negotiating a peace treaty? Then again, maybe not. It had been rather easy with Santos, but she wasn't so sure it would be simple and easy with Mac. Of course, she hadn't judged him, either. Or spoken with him prior to their negotiations.

Maybe this would give her the edge she needed. "Of course, we can."

"I kind of fell into this role. I think Maggie would be the better choice. My job since I was a teenager has been border-patrol." He paused as his eyes drifted to the crackling fire. "A few hundred *solaris* ago, after the war, these guilers came here and worked with the fae for protection. They've hidden here as much as possible because most people don't understand them. What I mean is... it's difficult for people to distinguish between these guilers and the dark guilers we fought earlier. So, for however long I *am* in the role of Elder, I'll do whatever I can to help keep these guys stay safe."

Wow, that really wasn't what she expected. She figured he'd say something about her looks, that this had been a ploy the whole time. Or that he'd reference his fighting skills again. But this, he actually cared for his people. That she could respect. Cipriana nodded. "People don't always respond well to what they don't understand."

"You're right. And guilers, they're about as different as they can get."

Well, he was right. Although everything she had learned about the different species across Prisma Isle came from books, guilers were the one thing that was never addressed. How would other sirens react to them? Or even to him? He'd lived among them since he was a child. "How old were you when you left Pteryrina?"

Bringing his legs back up, he leaned forward on his knees and glanced at her. "Not even a few *umbras* old."

Certainly, made sense why she didn't remember him. Or that no one had ever mentioned the existence of a male siren after her father had passed. As far as she knew, her father had been the last. It was part of why she and Parthenia were going around to the different territories. "Then how do you know of the issues we're currently facing?"

"Felix. I don't know how he knew, but he taught me everything he could about Pteryrina. The location of the main gates, plus I learned about the Poppy Fields and the Reflection Pools, along with the purpose of each."

Her gaze flicked to him. That made little sense. How could a non-siren know *anything* about Pteryrina? Their gates had been closed for nearly three hundred years. As far as she knew, no one had sneaked out before her sister, and no one had certainly gotten in. That would've been one of those many things... Cipriana shook her head. Who was she kidding? Nothing had been mentioned about Mac; why would anyone have shared information about the two most divine places in Pteryrina?

The problem was… she couldn't argue with even just the bit of information he provided. No one outside the sirens knew of their existence or what they were called. The only way he could've been aware of that was if someone had told him. Though she supposed it was possible, he learned of them from his parents. He'd admitted that he'd been taken from Pteryrina when he was just a babe, but that didn't mean he had learned nothing from his parents before they died. Or…his previous Elder taught him… as he said. Which made more sense than the former.

None of that mattered. It wasn't any more important than her finding out anything about him. The entire point of her staying had been to discuss the peace treaty. Cipriana rubbed her eyes and scanned their surroundings. A lot of his village needed to be rebuilt. As her people suffered, there wasn't much she could offer him. "You said the dark guilers attacked your village… your people here. Did you guys… was there any kind of… illness that had set in before that happened?"

"We've lost a few crops, and there's… something has infected the trees along the forest edge, but what does that have to do with the dark guilers?"

"I don't know." She sighed. But it sounded like Parthenia had been right all along. There was a problem on Prisma Isle that had developed. And they had to figure out how to fix it. "I'm not positive it does. I just… we've had our own issues arise in Pteryrina. My sister has a theory that the isle is… sick… so to speak."

"Is that why you're going around trying to negotiate a peace treaty?"

No reason to lie to him now. She'd already divulged more than she expected to share with him. "Part of it, yes."

"And what's the other part?"

She could just outright ask him what he knew of how bad things had gotten in Pteryrina, but it seemed kind of pointless. He'd been hiding out here this whole time. And it appeared Felix had educated him rather well. But there was a political way to put the information. "We opened our gates to give the inhabitants of Pteryrina the possibility of a better future. Otherwise, current circumstances would limit the potential for any further growth within our boundaries."

Apparently, their Elder's faith in her ability as the rising Elder wasn't unfounded. Although she'd successfully negotiated one treaty, Santos hadn't really asked for much. She didn't know how she had found the right words to describe their current situation, at least without revealing too much. Even though she'd been completely honest.

Mac's eyebrows knitted together as he stared at her. "So... the possibility for those who reside there to reproduce is... nonexistent."

That wasn't quite how she put it, but he obviously got the idea. "We accept our laws are antiquated and are doing more harm than good."

"Pretty much what I said." He smirked. "It's good to know your Elder can admit when things aren't working out, though. Shows strong leadership. With that said... and the fact that we're rebuilding, I'm not sure what we could offer you."

A slow smile tugged at the corners of Cipriana's mouth. "That's the good thing about a treaty. We can agree on terms that could apply in the near future. Seeing as you immediately need assistance with repairs, once I return to Pteryrina, I can certainly send a couple of our sirens with a variety of metal to help rebuild lost homes." And she already knew who she'd volunteer, along with one of their warriors, to protect them on their journey.

"And what would you ask of us in return?"

It hadn't been something she'd given much thought to on their way to Chicane. While she knew the names of leaders, her knowledge of each territory and the species was limited. One of the first things she'd done when she'd gotten here, she'd checked the place out. There were some things they didn't have access to rather easily. "Your people have access to a pier, and from what I gathered; they fish regularly. Correct?"

"Yes, that's accurate."

"For our aid in your rebuild, once everything is operational, I'd barter that a portion of the fish your people get is set aside for my people." It didn't seem like much of a payment, but seeing as they ate a lot of grain, fruit, and vegetables, fish would be a welcome change for sirens.

Mac shifted on the log, turning to face her, and stared at her for a minute. "You're great at this."

"I'm observant." It seemed the best way to explain how she'd decided on what he could offer her in return for the little help she could provide. They didn't really have many people, but that didn't mean there wasn't anyone to spare for a short time. Her idea was a great way to make connections as well.

Smirking, he set his hand near her leg and leaned in. "How observant?"

"Very. Why?" She didn't like where this was going. Nevermind that he was a little too close for her comfort, not that she was trying to push him back. Or at least part of her wanted to put some space between them. The other part wanted him closer, which was completely insane.

"I'm wondering what else you've noticed." He caressed her cheek, cupping her jaw in his hand.

"A lot." Maybe a part of her deep down had even noticed him. Something had passed between them when they first met, but she hadn't figured it out just yet. There was something happening between them now. Some kind of twinkle in that green gaze as he touched her, their faces inching closer together. Her eyes widened ever so slightly. Holy poppies! Was he going to... His lips pressed against hers.

Hesitantly, Cipriana knocked him back and jumped to her feet, taking several steps back. It took every ounce of willpower not to pace. She needed to put *space* between them. And a lot. Damn her sister for leaving her alone with him. "Why would you do that?"

"I thought you wanted me to," Mac said. "I mean, I know I wanted to as well, but the look in your eyes..."

"What look? There wasn't any look." The nerve. Thinking he could just plant his soft lips on hers without actually asking if she wanted him to kiss her. So what if she did? No, she didn't. That was absolutely *not* what she wanted. All she wanted was to negotiate these peace treaties and then return home without issue.

"There was—" His words cut off as he stood. Mac stepped away from the log and stopped between Cipriana and whatever approached. Green flames licked up his arms.

She rolled her eyes. Maybe she didn't know what was entering the clearing, but the last thing she needed was some chauvinistic male standing in front of her like she couldn't protect herself. Cipriana crossed her arms. As she looked at his hands, she furrowed her brow. What in the world? Wait, did he have that when they were fighting earlier? How had she not noticed it?

"Down, bird boy," a female commanded as she stepped through the brush, revealing herself to the pair. Her voice bubbled with laughter. "Besides, I think you're pointing your night lights in the wrong direction." Her fangs sparkled as she spoke. Hand on hip, she gestured from her and her people. "*We're* helping." The female nodded to Cipriana. "*She's* about to lay you out like a proper offering—that's saying, very dead, plucked, and roasted."

Dropping the flames from his hands, Mac smirked. "I don't think she would flambé me. Slap me, maybe, but not flambé me."

'Bird boy?' Lay him out like a 'proper offering?' Good gods. She didn't know who the female was standing there... wait. Her gaze narrowed. Hadn't he said something about dragon-shifters coming to his aid? And she'd just said they were helping. Flambé sounded like an idea. Slapping him did, too. Cipriana stepped around him, so they stood side by side. "Mac, you have some interesting friends."

A male hanging in the back snorted, muttering something in their native tongue to the female beside him, which earned him a swift elbow.

The female Cipriana assumed was Aurelia, Matriarch to the dragons, ignored the pair, and planted one foot on a nearby log. "*Friends* is a relative term." She gestured with a taloned hand from side to side. The chains decorating it tinkled, catching the moonlight filtering down from the canopies above. "Get what you came for, *ambassador*?" Her violet eyes narrowed.

"Ah, yes, of course. The sky people have little to do with land-dwellers." It hadn't slipped her mind what she'd been taught dragon-shifters thought of, well, everyone. Just because her people shared the sky with them, it didn't mean they all got along. Cipriana clasped her hands at the small of her back. "Of course, I did, Matriarch. Aurelia, if my information is correct, yes? That's what I thought. I'm quite good at negotiating terms that are agreeable to both parties."

Mac raised an eyebrow. "I'm sorry. Have you two met?"

"No, but it is my responsibility to know who all the leaders of each species are," Cipriana said. He didn't need to know how she knew Aurelia's name. While she didn't see him as beneath her, she also didn't quite see him as a true sky person, either.

The corner of Aurelia's mouth twitched upward ever so slightly. Another male with her strode forward, the blade on its way out of its sheath. Aurelia barred his way forward, raising her hand, catching him in the chest. He halted, with something between offense and confusion playing over his face. The question stayed locked behind his lips as his eyes zeroed in on Cipriana.

"I'm sure the mighty Elder's guest merely forgot her manners," Aurelia offered casually.

The male's blade returned to its sheath, but his hand remained firmly on the pommel. A warning served.

Aurelia eased back off the log and gestured the other two forward, ignoring Mac's question. The female bowed her head, while the male bared teeth at the two of them, dipping his chin, but refusing to allow his gaze to fall from the pair. "Aeriel is one of the Red Clan's brightest and budding strategists. Her inclination towards nature and knowledge of the defensive arts should aid in bolstering your defenses."

Aeriel stepped forward for her introduction and returned to her place once Aurelia finished speaking.

"Reaver is... uniquely suited to protecting your village," Aurelia continued. "They'll follow whatever command you give them. Within reason."

There was no sound as the two Seelie that had been left to offer aid landed on the ground from the trees above. With a crescent moon inked above his nose, the six-foot-tall man strode forward, his hand resting on the sword at his back. His golden eyes took in Mac and the surrounding others.

The other was a blonde-haired female with dark-gray eyes. While she hadn't reached for any of her weapons, she looked at the one currently in charge. "Maceron?"

Mac bit back a groan. "Things are fine." He glanced from Aurelia to Cipriana. "This is Geneen and Keir. They were also left to aid in protecting Chicane. And I'll be leaving in the morning to accompany Cipriana on her journey. Maggie is being left in charge in my absence."

Yeah, she hadn't forgotten about that. She noticed the way Mac watched the male who'd moved to attack her. Not that it would stop her from standing her ground. Although she hadn't intended to be disrespectful, it had irritated her the way the Matriarch waltzed in and treated Mac. Ugh. Really, this wasn't on her agenda. Maybe there was a way she could work this to her advantage. Cipriana smiled. "Yes, he'll be serving as a bodyguard to the Rising Elder of the Sirens of Pteryrina."

"If the Rising Elder of the Sirens needs a bodyguard it sounds like she's unfit for her role," Aurelia said, and then turned her attention to Mac. "Is it really wise to leave your people surrounded by strangers while they're still in so vulnerable a state, while you chase feathers?" Skepticism crept into her tone.

The more she listened to the Matriarch speak, the more she understood why they split the skies. Although bringing dragon-shifters out here seemed to contradict the female's consistent dismissiveness and derisive attitude. Maybe Aurelia had simply done so to placate Mac, or to make others see her as willing to work with other species. Either way, it was failing on an epic scale. And she sure as hell didn't need a bodyguard. Not that it had stopped him from inviting himself on her journey or suggesting that the two of them head in one direction while her sister and Gavin went another. Even though it was pretty sound, she didn't like it. No more than she cared for the female standing by the log. Or her snap judgment that she was unfit for the role of Elder. Though she couldn't very well not respond. Cipriana opened her mouth—

"She doesn't need a bodyguard. I've seen her fight, and she's quite capable of taking care of herself. Not that my decision to go with her is really any of your business, princess. But you know, something has come to my attention." His green eyes flashed. "I may have needed your help on the other isle, but I don't have to accept it now," Mac smirked. "And considering that I've seen you throw a tantrum because one shifter uttered a word you didn't really care for, I'm really beginning to understand a few things." Crossing his arms, he shook his head. "While I appreciate you returning and keeping true to your word, you're right about one thing: my people don't need to be surrounded by strangers. Thank you, Aurelia, for your insight. Feel free to leave and take your soldiers with you."

Aurelia shrugged. "Suit yourself."

The two dragons behind her exchanged a series of confused and uncertain expressions. Aeriel rested a hand on Reaver's arm when he unconsciously moved forward.

"The Emerald King rejects us?" he sounded confused.

"Seems so," Aurelia replied, eyes narrowed at him as Aeriel attempted to shush and usher him away.

"We will go," Aeriel interjected as Reaver opened his mouth to offer further protest. "May the Sun light your way, Mother. Elders."

With that, the two stepped back, transformed, and took to the skies. Their pink and black colors swirled around one another, intermingling until two dragons emerged, rocketing into the low-hanging clouds.

While she didn't openly question Mac, Cipriana did at least acknowledge the two dragons before their departure. Two that had better manners than their leader. She wasn't sure that was the wisest decision, but this was his village, and it wasn't her place to tell him how to run it. Although maybe he intended to ask Milla for more assistance when she returned in the morning. She glanced over at the two Seelie still standing by, but neither of their faces gave anything away. Both of them stood there with their hands clasped in front of their bodies. Interesting. It was a different pose from what her own warriors took.

"You know, Aurelia, after working with you last night and our return this afternoon, I had hoped that things might go more pleasantly should you come back. Especially with everything we learned along the way. That maybe you'd stop looking down the end of your nose at everyone. But I guess that was too much to expect," Mac said.

"Yeah, well, we can't all be foot soldiers pretending to be gods," Aurelia sighed. "I may not be prophesied like you or bluebird, but I'm doing the best I can with what's been left to me. If I ruled as you see fit, the other dragons would plunder the isle before saving us the trouble of fending off the dark guilers. Just don't go losing the orange stone between now and the next time we meet."

Mac pinched the bridge of his nose. "I won't lose it." He shook his head. "I understand the need to control chaos, but if you keep looking down at every species, they'll be less inclined to work with you. And as you and I both saw; we may have more than dark guilers—"

"I'm sorry. Did you say the blue *siren* was prophesied?" It had taken everything inside her to keep her mouth shut, but the more information she discovered, the harder it had become. As for the mention of the orange stone, yeah, that would be addressed. She got that there was way more going on than Mac had let on. So what if their eyes glowed earlier? And she liked the idea of his traveling with her. Obviously, there were still a few things he clearly forgot to mention.

"She's talking about Thalasia's arrival being prophesied."

Narrowing her gaze at Mac, Cipriana crossed her arms. "Just her arrival. Nothing more?"

"Maybe."

That wasn't an answer she liked. But it couldn't be what she was thinking. They weren't supposed to exist. Or they were all dead. The books in their restricted section hadn't entirely been clear on that. Her gaze flicked between Mac and Aurelia. "What else do you know about her?"

"What did you do with Fido, anyway?" Aurelia asked. Her eyes slid to Cipriana. "And here I thought you'd just finished swearing we were mortal enemies. What do you care about what I know or think of her? Besides, if you really are an ambassador... Elder-in-training, you'd know I'm not just going to give you information for free, so why bother asking? Does it make you feel all warm and fuzzy inside or something?"

"We both know you don't care what I did with Nomad." Mac snickered. "So, why bother asking?" It was posed as a statement, not a question. He glanced at Cipriana. "We can discuss Thalasia later."

Okay. Good. Plus, they'd talk about the orange stone, too. She had a lot of questions. This unexpected meeting with the Matriarch had certainly provided her with some much-needed information. Good to know the notes regarding the leader were accurate. Which was really too bad. She had hoped that it was wrong, but a pretty dress didn't mean you were a pretty person. Nor could it cover the female's insecurities. "I don't recall saying that. Although this little interaction has left a bit of a sour taste in my mouth, it has proven fruitful."

Really, she didn't need to say anything else. It was obvious the female had no clue or had forgotten what the sirens did hundreds of years ago. Before the war, during the war, and even after the war. And considering how cozy she'd seen the blue siren with the other dragon earlier that day, it kind of amused her to say nothing else. Cipriana smiled.

"Honestly, as much as I enjoy seeing the two of you duke it out verbally... why are you still here, Aurelia?" Mac questioned.

"I could have sworn your new girlfriend asked me a question." She shot an angry glare at the one male dragon who remained by her.

"Did we not come here as allies?" he blurted. His outrage was cool, like his constraint. "Are we actually entertaining peace for the sake of this isle, or is this all just a colossal joke?"

Still standing there to observe, Geneen snickered. She stepped forward. "If you are to make an allegiance, my Prime Warrior has granted me permission to speak on her behalf." Her gray eyes flicked to Mac. "Know that she is aware of all the interactions that take place here."

Cipriana sighed. Goddess, she'd almost forgotten the two Seelie were there. They'd been so quiet and hadn't moved a muscle. Or if they had, they hadn't made a sound. But the male was right. Maybe the meeting had been unexpected, but there was far more to concern themselves with than their attitudes. Not that she'd acted any better. Unfolding her arms, she clasped her hands behind her again. "You're right. There is a war waging at our feet, and by fighting amongst ourselves, we only aid them in their quest."

"And none of us can take the darkness on by ourselves." Mac gripped the back of his neck. "Nor can we remove the taint from all of those infected."

Aurelia remained quiet; arms folded across her chest. Her eyes churned as she stared at the male dragon. Her displeasure—however subdued—lingered over them like lukewarm bathwater.

The male kept his warrior stance, meeting her gaze head-on and unflinching. At the ready. "Go ahead," he pronounced when no further response came from her. "I spoke out of turn. I accept my punishment."

"Not that he was wrong," Mac said and shrugged. "Almost sounds like something the boyfriend would've said, were he around."

The situation seemed all too familiar. Her sister had been publicly punished for the way she'd addressed Fagonia. Not that Fagonia had a high-ranking position at all, but they were all supposed to show respect to one another. Regardless of personal feelings. Cipriana glanced back toward the huts, where she knew her sister and Gavin were together. All these months, she worried over what would happen if his king caught the two of them. And she hadn't been kind when she'd discovered them. Had she been acting any better now? Her gaze flicked back to Aurelia. "We're supposed to be better than our predecessors."

It wasn't her place to tell the female how to control her people, but she could agree with Mac. The male hadn't been wrong. They were being selfish. And not thinking of the damage that could fall upon their isle. She walked over and sat on another log.

Scrubbing his face with a heavy sigh, Mac followed Cipriana and sat down next to her. "Ball's in your court, prin... Aurelia."

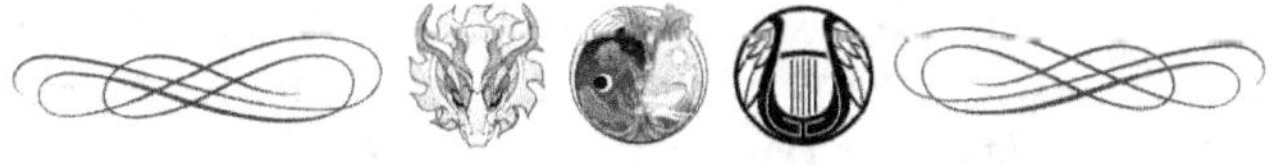

Thalasia had changed clothes into something more her, more comfortable before she left the inn. She much preferred the skin-tight jeans, white tank top, and black combat boots over anything else, especially the dress and heels she'd worn to the tavern. She didn't know how long she'd been walking along the road, but she was certain it had been a while. The buzz she'd had when she left the inn was long gone. She'd left the marketplace with no proper direction, at least initially.

At some point, she traveled down the road they'd taken. Gods, how many days ago... six? Seven? No, four days earlier. She'd landed on Prisma Isle six days ago. The full moon still wouldn't occur for a little over four more days. It wasn't her primary objective, but it was one of her major objectives, provided she actually remembered the details of the ritual between now and then.

Not that it mattered too much until she got more information on these marks. Even more so to the reference Cyon had made to the base of the skull, which she mistook as a reference to the brand on her neck. Unless she was asking about the mark a female placed on a dragon? That's what Seru had told her about his neck. Right? Thalasia scrubbed her face. Cyon probably thought she was stupid for trusting Seru so recklessly. Maybe she was idiotic about it, but as she thought back to how things had been before their fighting... she wouldn't have changed it. Nor would she change her desire for him. Or her choice of him as her Allimos.

All of this walking had solidified one thought for her: they needed to fix this. Until they did, she wouldn't draw on his power for anything.

She had a lot of questions about their power exchange. Something Cyon said had bounced around in her head the entire trek toward the hidden staircase. *'Dragons use magic to bind their true partners.'* She probably shouldn't have come here alone, but the walk had allowed her to rinse and repeat, so to speak. She kept thinking about how they should be able to pull on each other's powers. Although she hadn't gained all of her power, she'd hidden a lot from both Seru and Aurelia.

Self-preservation. It was taught early on, along with her ability to glamour. But for him to even do that, they had to feed their connection. Something she still didn't understand the full meaning of... did it mean he had to go down on her again? Sex? A feeding on magic through blood... something she hadn't done in years. Or was there more to it? Was that part of the problem?

His problem? She knew his desire for her just as surely as she knew her own need for him. She just didn't like feeling that way. If she were truly honest... it scared her to need him.

A lot.

Seru didn't scare her.

It scared her to need him.

It scared her to love him.

But she did.

The soft clicking of talons against stone caught her attention and broke through her haze of thoughts. Her gaze snapped from the ground she'd been staring at toward the noise. Long willow leaves. Was that—the clicking came closer toward the road.

Without a second thought, she plunged into the forest, landing softly and seeking shelter behind a sturdy tree trunk. She could climb the tree with ease if she had to, but now that she'd found the staircase, she was keen to discover who was stealthily exiting. Nothing she'd seen that afternoon indicated that would be necessary. Then why would someone feel they had to?

The siren who stepped from behind the curtain of willow leaves appeared like any other. Same brown wings, albeit the darkest brown she'd ever seen before. Her hair was neatly pinned back, not a strand astray, and her muddy-brown eyes held a look of determination. Aside from the difference in the wings, the female's shoulders were broader, her nose a tad longer, almost beak-like. Thalasia frowned. Something about the female seemed familiar, but she couldn't say for sure. Nevermind the female also appeared more bird-like than most sirens. Strange.

Whoever the female was, she didn't stand around long. The female quickly took to the sky. Nothing about what she'd seen explained why the siren had snuck down the staircase. It seemed opportune for her to—the sound of rustling tickled her ear. Thalasia's fingers brushed the cold steel of the blade tucked into the waist of her jeans as she turned, her eyes narrowed toward the commotion. She wasn't alone.

The canine snuck closer. "Whatever you plan to do with that blade, my fangs are longer."

That was cute. He thought she couldn't see him. The question was, why was he coming after her? No matter. With everything that had been going through her head, she could use a good fight. It was in her power to kill him quickly, but that wouldn't be enough. Not today. "You don't know what you're in for. That's okay. Let's dance, wolf-boy."

He licked his lips, then smirked. "I do not know how to dance, but I do like to play." He lurched forward, swiping his claws at her, and dodged the blade that came at his side. It at least nicked him, blood trickling down his skin through his fur. With a lunge, his claws found her thigh, and he quickly dodged her blade. He got up off the ground and jumped back when her dagger came across his face. Blood slid down his cheek, and he growled. It was then that he became visible.

Leaping into the air, she kicked him in the muzzle and used her wings to help her flip over and land on his back. She moved to stab him between the shoulder blades and stopped short. The symbol on his shoulder. It almost matched hers, except his was larger and more raised against his fur. How was that possible? No, it couldn't be. There was no way she got out of that realm. No way. He bucked and threw her into a tree. With a grimace, she slammed into it, a searing pain lancing down her spine as her blade clattered to the ground.

The male shifted to his humanoid form and gripped her arm.

"You are such an idiot," another shifter called down loudly above them.

Dropping his hold on her arm, the wolf whipped around with a growl, his eyes scanning the trees. "What did you just say to me?"

A feline shape shifter removed his camouflage and rested comfortably on the branch, just out of reach. "I said you are an idiot." He snorted. "Does your mental capacity shrink a little more each time you get hit or stabbed or somethin'? I swear, your brain must be about the size of a rat turd by now." The male growled and started heading in his direction. The feline broke a random twig off the branch with his teeth and tossed it down to the ground. "What, puppy? Feel like playin' fetch?"

There was no time to focus on the second shape shifter that had come up. Soon enough, she'd make time for the feline. Nothing like what she was used to seeing, but that didn't matter. It was time to stop playing. With silver crackling around her fingertips, she called a bolt to her hand, her eyes shining with power. Thalasia jumped into the air, landed on the wolf's back, and slammed the bolt right through the nape of his neck, killing him in one swift movement. Blood gushed from the wound, splattering across her clothes and matting her wings. Not that she cared. With one knee sinking into the soft, damp grass, she landed on the ground. Her hair flipped over her shoulders as she rose to her feet and lifted her gaze to the feline. She studied his appearance for a moment.

His blue-and-white fur with black stripes stood out as he towered over her in animal form, unlike any other shape shifter she'd encountered. Except for *them*. She shook those memories away for the time being. She needed to focus. The feline seemed uninterested in attacking her. Almost too bad. The fight ended quicker than she would've liked. Not that she needed to give Seru more of a reason to be upset with her.

He raised his eyebrows and blinked a few times. The feline stayed where he was on the branch, one paw dangling down, his tail twitching. "Nice. Though you should probably be more careful than you are. You are bein' hunted." His gaze lingered on the dead wolf for a moment, then went back to her. "Obviously. You okay?"

That was nothing new, but something about this felt different. She walked over to where her blade had landed and collected it. With the tip of the blade, she pointed to the mark on the dead wolf's shoulder. If this male planned on talking, then she planned on asking questions. The glow in her eyes didn't fizzle. "What is that?"

"Mark of the shape shifter king's Informants. His royal laziness's muscle, so to speak." He tilted his right shoulder a bit to show her better and then got comfortable again. "Some are willing," he nodded down at the dead male, "some are not." He shrugged a bit.

Not seeing the feline as a threat, she kneeled down next to the body and took the blade to the dead shape shifter's shoulder. Thalasia sliced the mark off his body, the blade gleaming in the dim light. "Tell me about this so-called king."

"Sure. Long as you can keep this whole," he gestured between them with his paw, "to yourself. That kinda reputation would get me killed. What do you wanna know?"

"I'm very good at keeping secrets." At least nothing that would get back to his so-called king. Some of this she wouldn't be able to hide from Seru. The damn wolf had gotten her twice, but those would heal within a few hours. Back to his question. What did she want to know? That was a good question. This was one of those moments she wished Seru were here. Damn that saint beast. "What is he? What does he look like?"

It wasn't hard to gather the male he was if he'd sent his muscle, as the feline had called them, to hunt her. That left her with other questions. Things she needed to know. Thalasia cut the last of the piece from the wolf's shoulder and wiped the blood from the blade across her jeans. She tucked the blade back into her waistband and stood. "Did he say what he wanted me for? Dead or alive?"

"First question. His name is Markham. Black bear, about my size, but I think he weighs more than me. White crescent moon shape on his chest. You cannot miss him, though. He is the only bear on the isle. He wears a crown, a circle with a skull in it, and he has magic. You would be much better off facing a bunch of them," he nodded down at the male again, "alone, then goin' anywhere near him. He prefers to use his magic over physical contact. Second question, no idea what he wants you for, but he definitely wants you alive. Cannot say with any certainty it would stay that way, though. So, yeah, be careful. Most who wear this mark are not like me, and every one of us knows exactly what you look like."

Bear? But that wasn't what caught her attention. It was the last thing he said. She hadn't come across any bear shape shifters in eight years. The first shape shifter she'd run into on this isle had been earlier in the day. Even if they'd shared what she looked like, it would be based on the feet. No one had seen her true self since Klaus had helped her escape. "How exact are we talking? Like the other sirens here with the bird feet or just as you see me now?"

"I have met no other sirens, but as exact as you can get. Like you are now. He put pictures in our heads, but…" His forehead creased for a moment. "It was like third-party images; not like they came from his memory. If that makes sense. You looked younger in them, but your colorin' certainly gives you away. He wants to get ahold of you pretty badly."

Thalasia blinked. It couldn't. There was no way. She stood there, the patch of skin cool and clammy in her hand, and shook her head in disbelief. As she gripped the tense muscles in her neck, she winced. Damn. Must've hit her head just a little when she got thrown into the tree. Great. She walked over to another tree and leaned against it. There was only one way to know for sure; the only way she'd been able to tell those five had been related. Her gaze lifted back to him. "Eyes? What color are his eyes?"

He frowned a bit. "Well, when they are not black when he's mad, or flash red when he uses his magic, they are dark gray. Not a normal shape shifter color." He paused. "Somethin' you mind sharin'?"

"Dark-gray eyes." She pushed off the tree. "If I'm right, I've met his family." It had always been possible. She believed Mistress had spoken to someone, but she could never be sure. No voice had ever been heard. Once or twice, she thought one of them had uttered the word *father*, but it made no sense. A bright-silver glow emanated from her hand as she summoned a silver ball. "I'd recommend moving from that tree."

He hesitated. "Yeah, sure." Standing up on the branch, he leaped down to the ground and moved away a couple of steps, staying clear of the body. "So, you are tellin' me you think fucker has a *family*? There are *more* of him?"

Taking a few steps back, she threw the ball, and with a deafening crack, it turned the body and surrounding trees to ash. She refocused on the feline. "How good are you at keeping your thoughts, images to yourself?"

"Markham can read thoughts, and I am not dead yet." He smirked a bit. "So, pretty good, I guess. I do not follow orders very well." He shrugged. "I was young when I mastered it."

This male was a stranger to her, but he offered her information that she needed. There was only one way she could prove that the so-called king he'd spoken of had family. Not in this realm, thankfully. No more hiding, right? Yeah, she was done. Inhaling and exhaling a deep breath, she pulled her hair aside and revealed the mark on the left side of her neck. "Yes. There are more."

He just stared at her mark for a minute, a replica of the one on his shoulder only smaller, then cursed. He paced for a minute and then sat down on the ground. "Well, that is just fuckin' wonderful." He paused. "They are not here though, on the isle, right? One of him is more than enough."

Her hair fell back into place. "No. They are not here. Five of them in total." It just meant that one day she might have to go back to where she had left them and ensure they were still there. There'd be no way she could face that alone. She scrubbed her face. Yeah. With the discovery of this, she and Seru had to fix things. There was no way around that.

He said nothing for a minute. "So, someone actually *bred* with that thing?" The feline shivered and shook his head. He looked back at her, but she'd covered the mark again. "I have never seen it on a female. Some females in my village have other brands, but not that one."

"I wasn't a member of her village. I was captured, likely for the same reason he wants me. They all had the same color eyes. It didn't change with any of them." She never understood all the reasons for the mark, but she had figured at least one out. Mistress had gone to great lengths to suppress her ever-growing power. "I suspect I was marked because I'm different, as you've seen."

"We are given this to make us stand out. It is supposed to be an honored position within the village." He rolled his eyes. "We are chosen only for our size and strength. There is no sayin' no to it. And we were not told why he wants you. Just that if we found you, we were to bring you back alive. If they are not here... You are not from here?"

"No, I'm not. Once my purpose is done, I'll leave." That was the plan. She just had a lot of things to complete between now and then. Which really meant she and Seru had to get their shit together. "Exactly how many of you are hunting me?"

"I am not the greatest with numbers. Several dozen at least. Maybe a hundred? It could be more." He shrugged a little. "Sorry. I try not to pay attention to them as much as possible. I really care only about two of them. Not all of us are bad, but it is best to just steer clear of any you might encounter. None of us has magical powers that I know of. A few have extra abilities, but nothin' like Markham does. He leaves the village often enough, but, as far as I know, he always sends us out to do most of his dirty work. A lot of retrieval, not that I take part in that."

Yeah, they'd just have to deal with that. But it was good to know exactly how many they might have to deal with along the way. She'd been gone long enough. She needed to get back. "Thank you. You've given me some useful information."

"Welcome. And thank you; that guy was a dick." He smirked. "You never saw me," he said as he pulled his camouflage back on and headed to the nearest tree.

"As long as you never saw me, feline." They had a deal. She didn't need to know his name. It wasn't important. He asked nothing of her. She'd been gone longer than two hours. She needed to get back. Pteryrina, they could do that in the morning.

"Saw who?" He went up the trunk and disappeared into the leaves.

Smiling, Thalasia soared into the sky, the wind whipping through her hair, and remained below the treeline. It was the quickest way back to the inn.

Chapter Twenty-Two

F agonia sat in the same tree she'd occupied the night before, but there was a minor difference. It didn't matter that she was waiting for the bear again. She'd discovered exactly what she'd hoped for, and it couldn't have made her happier.

Now, not only would she get the pleasure of torturing Parthenia, but she would get the enjoyment of watching Markham cause pain for her niece's mate as well. Hmm, maybe he'd let her watch. Oh, that would be wonderful. Knowing full well what little they could do to save one another. While she didn't care how long he took, she was eager to get things in motion. She'd been patient for years, and now everything was coming to fruition.

Markham approached in his robed form. He stepped through the trees and didn't bother to raise his eyes, his anger almost a physical crackling in the surrounding air. "You look awfully amused. I take it you have good news."

"Oh, I am quite pleased." A bird and a feline—the irony amused her. Two creatures that naturally didn't belong, and those two had gone completely against the odds. Not to mention, they would break off from their little group. Oh yes, she was in an excellent mood. Even Markham's emotional state couldn't break her joy. "I found your pussy."

"Did you now? Accomplished in mere *umbras* what my Informants have failed to deliver in two *cycles*? Where exactly did you find him?"

"He is traveling with the siren ambassadors. It would seem he has taken one of them as a mate." Her upper lip lifted in disgust. Not that she should've expected any differently. Parthenia had always been weak and pathetic. The female never understood their ways. "I have eyes in more places than you can imagine. I even know the bluebird and her dragon did not stay in the half-breed village."

"So, our suspicions were confirmed then. What path shall they take? I am eager to get a hold of at least one who has so far eluded me."

"The two ambassadors will part ways in the morning. The one your pussy is traveling with are heading further into Iridescent Forest to meet the Seelie and other fairies. I believe our best bet to grab them will be once they have left the Chimera village." Fagonia grinned. She'd given this a great deal of thought all night long, imagining just how she would torture her niece. Leaning forward on the trunk of the tree, her grin broadened and darkened at the same time. "We will even make it fair. You get your pussy and I get my niece. It will be quite enjoyable to see the looks on their faces as we separate them."

"I think that will work out nicely." A slow smirk spread over his face. "That will be very enjoyable indeed. I could certainly use some enjoyment. What they see as their strength, we will reveal as their greatest weakness. I do hope you plan to make it very painful for her. I certainly did when I rid this isle of the repulsive members of my bloodline. Is this the first you have known of her... particular tastes?"

"No. I knew something was going on. Her smell over the last few *cycles* has been... tainted. I just did not know the cause until today." She thought over some of what she had planned for Parthenia. Hmm, she'd added several guilers to her force. It would be interesting to see what powers they could unleash on her. "Oh yes, I have some excellent plans for her. I will certainly... draw it out this time. Before I ultimately claim her wings."

"I knew what he was doing. I just did not know who nor of what species they were. His ability to shield his mind kept the information from me, and he has cleverly eluded my Informants as well as myself. Until this point." He sneered. "My plan in allowing his escape from the village, apparently, just needed a bit of a nudge from... outside sources." He nodded once to her. "Claiming her wings will claim her life, yes? Hmm. I wonder... should that occur in front of him? Force him to watch as the last of her life leaves her? I have learned over the *solaris* how much pain it causes when one's mate is slaughtered in front of them. It could bring both of us a multitude of enjoyment."

"Oh, yes. I think that would be rather delicious. I have been looking forward to causing her great pain for *solaris*. Her previous punishments have not been enough." A little further, Fagonia leaned forward, her eyes growing wide with excitement. No, the pain her sister had delivered on Parthenia hadn't been enough in her mind. It should've been more painful and a lot bloodier. "My cave is within Kenos Ridge."

"His punishments have not been enough, either. Obviously. Once his form is nothing more than a broken, empty vessel, I think I will leave it on display longer than I normally do. It has been some time since I could do so. I think my subjects could use a reminder of what occurs when my most sacred law is broken. Mine is between the manticore territory and my own. Protected well against intruders. No one can enter unless I allow it."

"Then it should be easy for us to work together to truly make them understand the consequences of their actions." When they'd first agreed months ago to work together, she hadn't expected to get this much pleasure. Not that she hadn't done everything in her power to make sure everything benefited her. Regardless of what they agreed upon.

"Yes, I believe it shall. How long do you anticipate it will take them to reach the chimera territory?"

Fagonia sat there a moment. There were several fairy leaders for them to meet with. She tumbled the information around in her head. "Four or five *umbras*. It depends on how long they spend in the chimera village. It will take a few *umbras* to get through the gaggle of fairies."

"I will meet you back here in four *umbras* then. Same time, as always. We will finalize plans for their capture then."

"I look forward to it." Fagonia grinned. Four days was more than enough time to accomplish her own tasks. Certainly enough to see if she could resolve the issue with the bluebird without his aid. Without a sound, she stood on the branch, feeling the wind in her feathers, and flew off into the air.

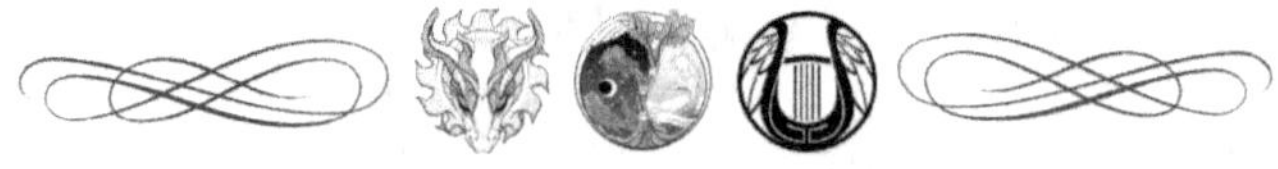

Cipriana blinked. Well, she certainly hadn't expected that. They each had their own laws and rules to follow. Yeah, the male had spoken when it wasn't his place, but he hadn't been wrong, either.

She shook her head, staring at the empty space, feeling the gentle breeze dance over her talons and the fire's warmth embrace her. Her opinion of the Matriarch hadn't improved. The female's tone had only changed when the other two soldiers had left. Now, instead of addressing the issue, both in the soldier who remained and in the war waging ahead—she runs away. Cipriana turned her attention to Mac. "The shape shifter she spoke of earlier, was that the one that was here before?"

"Yes. We crossed paths with him on Candescent Isle. I used the stone she spoke of removing the taint of the isle from him, and we brought him back here when we left." He looked over at the remaining dragon, and then back to Cipriana. "The stone has to be purified in the Reflection Pools of Pteryrina."

Good Demeter, he would say that. Okay. They'd be okay. There was still one full pool and three quarters of another. Plenty to do what he said. Her gaze flicked to the dragon. "Mind if I ask your name? I'm Cipriana."

The male didn't immediately respond. He looked to her, his hand dropping from his blade to hang by his side, all tension leaving him with that one exhale. "Oriel."

"Good to meet you." Before she uttered another word, she weighed all the information she'd collected regarding the dark guilers. As well as the stone that Mac carried and had to purify. What if it was one of the crystals referenced in the Elder's journal? It would make sense. Although there were so many questions brewing in her head; many she refused to ask with the dragon present.

Not that she wanted to know about them at the moment. What she really wanted to know—and would've gladly discussed with the Matriarch had she been able to control her snark better—was this barrier. And the invasion right on their heels. Still, she had to construct her question in a certain manner. "Have plans been made beyond the current patrol to defend against the invaders?"

"I am not a politician. You needn't phrase your questions, hoping to lighten the blow." He settled across from the pair but remained standing. "I won't pretend I know your customs or what's appropriate. I know you don't structure your hierarchy or military in the same way we do. As I don't wish to offend you, if it's all the same to you, I'd much rather speak plainly. The common tongue isn't so... common where I'm from."

Simple, she could work with that. She'd heard the other two speaking in a language she didn't know. Most of the sirens used the common tongue rather than their own. They'd grown accustomed to it. "I take no offense. Usually, I don't offend easily." Even with her sister. "I'm certain we don't structure everything the same, though, I believe that's for different cultural reasons than anything else."

Mac smirked. "That's putting it lightly."

Yep, she could see it now. She was going to slap him before the night was out. Cipriana glanced over at the two Seelie. "Did you still want to be a part of this conversation?"

"Yes, we absolutely do." With swift movements, Geneen made her way to a log to the right of where Cipriana and Mac sat. Keir simply leaned against a tree just along the edge of the forest.

Resting her hands on the log, she sat in silence for a moment. "Are the dragons only guarding the area surrounding the bridge? We ran into four dark guilers earlier, so I know they've found another way across."

"There are scouts dispatched along our borders, over the marshlands and the water," Oriel said. "They watch for movement and report in regularly, but without opening a discourse with the sea king, we are limited in our ability to monitor the seas beyond surface level."

"The wolf you left with Milla, Maceron, did you not say that it came from the other isle?" Geneen asked.

"Yes, it did, but his language skills are minimal. There's no telling how long he had carried the darkness within him. Maybe Milla can get more information about the dark guilers' movements." Mac shrugged.

"If she could, it would certainly be helpful." Cipriana turned her gaze to Geneen. "Are the fae monitoring the shores along here?" She'd discussed some of this with Santos, but as his warriors protected the inhabitants of Migas, there wasn't much he could do to scout. Spreading their forces wasn't wise, either. They needed to force the guilers to converge in a certain direction. So, they controlled the location of the fight.

"We have some, yes, but we handle the entire forest and all the species residing in Verdant Grove."

She leaned forward, her elbows digging into her knees as she thought. She'd speak with her sister in the morning. This wasn't information they could keep to themselves. Her gaze flicked back to Oriel. "Are there plans in motion or preparations in case they are planning a single point of attack to invade the isle?"

"We intend to funnel them to the beach. Their bridge may be more than symbolic. We also possess a greater natural advantage—the sheer cliff face and the vast underground cavern system. The Red Clan's favored Primoire has dominion over the volcanoes to the south. It may block further attempts of attack from the southern seas."

Geneen looked from the dragon to Cipriana. "We can protect the western side of the isle to ensure no others slip past our borders; however, that will still leave the northern and eastern sides vulnerable."

"Actually, some warriors from the hybrid village were dispatched to cover the northwestern part of the isle. The Elder there couldn't spare very many, but he agreed to touch base with his villagers and gain interest for those willing to aid in battle." It was the rest of the isle they had to worry about. Part of which she could help with. "Mac and I are heading to speak with the dwarves, trolls, and manticores over the coming *umbras*. I'll be able to provide them with the information to get their help. My sister and her mate can do the same with the chimera. The biggest problem is going to be the eastern shore beyond the shape shifter territory. Their leader won't work with anyone."

Mac turned toward her, opened his mouth and snapped it shut. He hooked a thumb over his shoulder. "Right. They have to hide their relationship."

"We can spread forces in that direction if we must," Oriel spoke up. "The shifter king is of minor threat to us."

Without disturbing her sister and Gavin, she didn't really have confirmation of how far out his territory went. Although the treehouse that she'd followed Parthenia to had been outside of the borders. "I think as long as your people keep to the shores, you should be able to avoid his territory."

"My Prime Warrior is redirecting warriors as we speak. The western shore from just past the marshlands to as close to the mountains as she can, until you can speak with King Kihrig," Geneen said. "They should arrive within the hour."

"Wow. You guys work fast." How was that even remotely possible? Yeah, she could fly, and so could Mac, but they couldn't pass information that quickly. Unless, interesting. Sirens couldn't speak mentally. It wasn't something she even knew the fae could do. Still, this was good. She didn't know why they couldn't accomplish this with the Matriarch there, but it was neither here nor there. Something to worry over at a later time.

"We do not believe in wasting time or resources." Geneen offered a cockeyed smile.

"With guilers roaming the isle, are we certain total avoidance is best?" Oriel asked. "If we can broker alliances within our isle, so could our enemy within and from beyond our borders. We don't know that the barrier contained their isle as it did ours."

"Normally I'd agree with you; however, with what I've learned of the shape shifter *king*, he doesn't work with any other species. His laws strictly forbid interaction with them of any kind. If a dark guiler gets past his borders, I'm pretty sure he'll kill it on sight. As for the limitations of the barrier, it was... as far as our knowledge goes, only surrounding our isle." Though his line of questioning posed another. Was it possible that another barrier surrounded the other isle? None of that was known. Except if it had existed, then there wasn't any way that Thalasia would've gotten across, theoretically. She hadn't asked many questions when they'd run into that other shape shifter friend of her sister's.

Mac reached across and squeezed Cipriana's shoulder. "The barrier only went around our isle. I can confirm that. As for the shape shifter king, I think there is a coup rising amongst his own people."

"According to my Prime Warrior," Geneen turned her focus on Oriel. "The shape shifter king even kills his own people if they disobey his laws. He is a true purist."

"Yeah, what she said." A true purist. With a heavy sigh, Cipriana sat up. Demeter, please don't let her sister get killed on this mission.

"Seeing as there aren't many bears in existence, his being a true purist seems... counterintuitive," Oriel replied softly.

It was kind of ironic. They'd been along the same lines, or so she believed, until just yesterday when their Elder agreed it was time to open their gates. Yet, no children had been born in eleven years. Fifteen sirens remained. Cipriana glanced at Mac—sixteen, if she included him. The only two that were even of mating age were she and Parthenia. Fantasia, Epiphany, and Enigma wouldn't hit mating age until next spring. How had they let it get this far?

Poppies, her sister had been right. They were slowly allowing themselves to die off by sticking with outdated laws. Had they changed things too late? Goddess, she couldn't think about any of this now. She smirked. "He's the only bear, and I don't think he cares. Or so I've been told."

"My apologies, Elder Cipriana. I hope this does not offend. However, my Prime Warrior would like to know if your warriors require any training," Geneen said.

The few they had still trained regularly, so she didn't think it would be necessary. While she didn't want to go into too many details, she could offer some information. "I'm certain they're okay. They train every day with swords, staffs, and in hand-to-hand combat. Plus, we each have our own unique abilities, beyond what we're trained to do with our siren song, which is good for more than just manipulation."

Oriel watched the two of them speak, but said nothing.

"That hardly seems enough," Geneen said. Her shoulders tensed, and the grip in her hands tightened. "My apologies."

Cipriana shook her head. "It's fine. Although our strengths are mental rather than physical, we aren't deterred. Our warriors may not go through the same rigorous training that you do, but don't count out the sirens. Our training is refined so that a lot of focus is on our song, which is our most powerful weapon. The right note can cause a storm, make the air frigid and difficult to breathe, move through... just as examples." She offered the female a small smile.

"I understand, however, you have mentioned nothing of strategy. Learning to consider all access points. Identifying strengths and weaknesses in an opponent. Training to push your agility, speed, and strength to their breaking point. Working to think five moves ahead consistently, so you can always anticipate the next step."

Glancing at Cipriana, Mac sat up a little straighter and scooted a little closer to her. "Cultural differences, Geneen. I know what Milla puts you through, but for centuries, sirens trained their females to their strengths and the males to theirs. Albeit for different reasons, but all the same, the genders were trained accordingly."

Which was something that needed to change. Maybe she could learn a few things about altering how her warriors were trained. Their song was still their most powerful weapon. That much was true, but having more physicality, it couldn't hurt. She had to find a way for her species to survive and thrive at the same time. "You make some good points, Geneen. I'll talk with your Prime Warrior in the morning when she returns."

Geneen offered a slight bow of her head to Cipriana. "She agrees to that."

"Your concern is well placed," Oriel said, his eyes shifting to the Seelie. "But our species also has several hundred to several thousand years on them. You can't expect the same standard in a fraction of the time." He looked at Cipriana. "If your strengths are mental, perhaps improving physicality isn't your best option. Defense, especially in close quarters with an enemy that can outmaneuver and overpower you, is more essential. We know we face the elements and high magical proficiency in the average guiler. A few have displayed the ability to use multiple elements and the reports from the Matriarch and the male Elder of the sirens—" he paused. "We might as well expect every species on this isle and some we've not yet seen to be joining the fight."

"You make a valid point." Geneen nodded. "Our lifetimes may span differently, but that does not mean they can be taught nothing in whatever time we have until this battle occurs."

"After my meeting with the Elder in Migas Village, I quickly realized it would be necessary to mention the invaders with every Elder I met with. It's the only advantage that we have." Cipriana glanced at Mac. "You said nothing about them having access to multiple elements. The ones we fought weren't like that."

"No. Those we crossed seemed to be in the middle. Two of them had stronger hides than I've ever seen before. Nothing like what Aurelia and I faced on the other isle, where at least one had access to multiple elements." He paused for a moment. "We need to make sure we have as little fire as possible at the convergence point. They depend on the element being nearby in order to use whatever their element is. While we can't do anything about water, air, or earth... we can control one facet."

These advantages seemed so minimal. No fire. Pulling all the species together. Even with the two warriors she had, herself, her sister, and Mac... that was five sirens. Six if she counted Thalasia, who she was pretty sure wasn't quite a full-fledged siren, but something else altogether. If she was what she thought, though, she'd be a great asset. Cipriana leaned forward again, digging her elbows into her knees. Demeter, what made Vasilia think she was fit for this role? All she could feel was the weight of every decision and how it affected her people. "It's imperative that we get every species to join in. The shape shifter king may not be up for helping, but that may not apply to all of his people."

"Planning our attack patterns in mixed waves, partnering in smaller groups to offset any... limitations in individual capability might also prove effective," Oriel said. "Now isn't a time for doubt." He directed his gaze at Cipriana. "Keep affirmative action at the forefront of your mind. Focus on what you *can* do. The rest... often has a way of working out. All hands..." he glanced down between them all, "Paws, talons... are welcome. We need all the able bodies we can muster. And safeguard those that aren't. The shifters may need to respond to other commands, if that's the case. Do you think them capable of doing such? In the heat of battle, there's no time for second guessing and discussing orders relayed."

What she could do. A small smile tugged at the corners of her mouth. That almost sounded like the pep talk her mother gave her last night. And the support that her sisters continued to reference she would have as she came into her own and filled the role she'd been chosen for. Slowly, Cipriana sat up. He was right. She had to focus on what she could do. Getting the various species to come together to protect their isle—that was something she *could* do. "The female I met earlier... Devin. She has... I don't know, I can't explain it. An air about her. If we could work around their current king, I believe they'd listen to her."

"My Prime Warrior says that she may have a way to touch base with the female you speak of," Geneen said, her eyebrows knitted together.

"What does she look like?" Oriel asked. His fingers brushed nervously over the hilt of his blade.

Goddess, she had to think. Cipriana closed her eyes for a moment and pulled up the discussion she had in that office with the female. Calling the image up had helped. She opened her eyes. "Canine shape shifter, she's taller... well, than Mac, in her humanoid form. Teal eyes. Light-brown-and-blonde-swirled fur."

"Did you just call her to your mind's eye?" Geneen asked.

"You mean in my head, from my memory, yes." That was a strange question. Not something she expected, either.

"With your permission, if my companion can access your memory, we may help provide a clear picture of the female."

Access her memory. She glanced over her shoulder at the male leaning against the tree. He had said nothing throughout everything they'd discussed. The female Seelie was asking her to trust him to only access a certain part of her mind. Although if she focused solely on the image of Devin, then it should be alright. She didn't know either of them, but Mac did. And he'd known their Prime Warrior, seemed to fully trust them. But she needed to help. Devin was the only one she could think of that might lead the shape shifters in battle. Cipriana looked back at Geneen. "Um, okay."

Keir nodded slightly, pushed off the tree, and rapidly covered the ground, coming to a halt directly behind Cipriana. His golden eyes flicked to Mac. "This will not cause her harm."

"Good. I'd hate to hurt you if it did."

Keir gave one last nod to the male and laid his fingers upon her head. "Think only of the female shape shifter you spoke of."

Cipriana frowned. She'd address the whole thing with Mac later. She did as she had planned and was told. Once again, she recalled what Devin looked like in her head. Everyone could see the image of the female projected over the fire.

Oriel stiffened at the appearance of the astral projection. He crouched by the fire and reached forward, passing his hand through the image.

Uh, yeah, that was kind of weird. She could feel the slight invasion in her head, although it was certainly limited and did not poke and prod any other parts of her mind. A faint halo of white light surrounded the figure, near to perfection as she remembered the shape shifter. A shimmering likeness of Devin continued to float above the fire, flames crackling and licking at the bottom of the image. Cipriana blinked. So... strange. How was that even possible?

"Thank you, Keir," Geneen said.

With a brief dip of his chin, the projection ended, and he removed his fingers from Cipriana's head, and then he returned to the spot he'd taken up against the tree.

Well, that was certainly different. While she'd definitely seen nothing like that, the tingles in her head were new, too. It was something close to how she felt after a good meditation in the Reflection Pools, but stronger, more focused. She shook the distressing thoughts away. "Okay then, we all know what she looks like."

Frowning, Mac still stared across the fire. He glanced over at Cipriana. "That's Devin?"

"Yes. We had a brief conversation earlier." It didn't seem important to go into the details of what they'd discussed. Or what she'd left with the female to be stowed away in secret. What she remembered from her predecessors had been mildly useful. Still, there was something about the look on his face that irked her. "Why?"

"She was here a couple of *cycles* back with another female. A hybrid, I think. They both spoke to Felix. He didn't share with me everything about their conversation, but one thing she asked about..." He paused, seemingly unsure if he should share what he'd been told. "...dark magic."

"Dark magic?" Oriel raised a brow skeptically at the male Elder. "There's no dark magic. Just dark intent."

"From what I was told, he has a power that he uses for his malicious purposes." Mac's eyebrows squished together, and his nose scrunched. "Ergo, dark magic. I mean, there's dark and light to magic. While you're right, magic itself isn't one or the other.

The way she saw it... it was dark magic. And Felix didn't bother correcting her on it."

Why? Not that she knew much about the Elder he'd lost. She didn't imagine he was the kind not to correct Devin on the truth of magic. Curious. From their conversation earlier, she imagined the other thing the female asked about... the barrier. "That makes sense with what I was told about their territory. That it all feels dark... like that part of the isle... is sick."

"While most fae do not leave Verdant Grove, those who do... will trek nowhere near that part of the isle," Geneen said.

"The Matriarch said the taint from Candescent is spreading to our isle through the invaders." Oriel's eyes changed to resemble the color orange. He let out a ragged breath. "It's not dark magic," Oriel interjected. "It's an accumulation of malice, toxic emotion, and sins over time. In drawing the poison from the individuals and the tainted sites across the isle, you're not curing the malady, only temporarily negating the effects at the cost of the wielder and the integrity of the stone."

Mac frowned. "It is spreading through the invaders. Same as what they did to their own isle. What does that have to do with the stone? My intention is to purify it as I was instructed."

How had the conversation steered toward the stone that had been brought up earlier? She didn't know. But since it had, who was she not to take advantage of it? "What are you supposed to do with it after you purify it in the Reflection Pools?"

"Felix didn't tell me. All he said before I took him to the gardens was where to find it, how to purify it and that afterward..." Mac shrugged. "... well... I would know what to do with it once my task was complete."

"That's... cryptic." And not very helpful. It almost sounded like talking to Santos. Goddess, she'd thought that meeting would never end. Then they'd been stuck there longer because of a storm.

"The old ones like their riddles." Oriel admitted, rubbing at his aching eyes. "The stones need to be brought together once they're in their purest state, or else their true power can't be realized."

"Stones? Like crystals?" Shit. Shit. Shit. Cipriana dragged a hand down her face and stood. Behind the log, she paced back and forth, her hands clasped behind her back, the scent of damp earth filling her senses. She'd read about the crystals. Even when she'd met with Devin this afternoon in the marketplace, a crystal had been mentioned. It was in Markham's crown. That's what they had said. According to the Elder's journal, there was supposed to be one for each species. But they had lost the one for the sirens some time ago. How? Where could it have gone?

"Cipriana," Mac said.

A radiant warmth spread through her body as her name left his lips, a soothing balm that erased all her worries. Goddess, how was that possible? Her gaze met his, and she stared into those gorgeous, green orbs of his. It took a moment for her to look away. "I... uh... that's what they think gives Markham... the shape shifter king... most of his power. He wears it in a crown on his head." Her gaze momentarily flicked back to Mac. "If Devin was trying to find out about magic, then she might've been trying to retrieve the crystal." She sighed heavily. "From what I know, the crystals you speak of were spread across the isle, left with each species."

"The Matriarch means to retrieve them. Combine them," Oriel stated. "How is it you rule the sirens, and he rules the guilers? Are you not? Do you not belong to one another?"

Her gaze snapped to Oriel. How in Demeter had he come to that conclusion? Narrowing her eyes, Cipriana crossed her arms. "Excuse me? What in the gods would make you think that? No! We're not together."

Mac stifled a chuckle. "We just met today." He stroked his chin to hide his amusement.

"I'm so glad you think it's funny." She rolled her eyes. Arrogant ass. Her species may die off, but nothing in the universe could make her copulate and procreate with the likes of him. Together. Ha! The notion was laughable. "He's lucky I haven't slapped him yet," she muttered.

"You were playing off one another's points rather seamlessly..." Oriel cleared his throat. "Conferring. It was not a criticism. Merely an observation."

Replaying his words in her head, Cipriana offered him nothing more than a blank stare. She had absolutely no words. No response to his *observation*. Had she been too friendly with Mac? Really played off of his suggestions? His comments? Good goddess, was Oriel right? No, that couldn't be the case. Even if they had come to some agreeable terms, and she'd been defensive when Aurelia called him things she didn't like... oh, fuck. He was right. Cipriana, trying to hide her exasperation, dragged a hand down her face.

Covering his mouth, Mac chortled. "That's some observation."

A small smile tugged at the corners of Geneen's mouth. "If the important issues of the meeting have been addressed, and we have reached our conclusion, I will execute a patrol of the grounds as Keir returns to his guard duty."

"If anything more comes up, I'll pass it on to you, Geneen," Mac said.

Oh yeah, 'anything more.' What else did they have to talk about? The way she shoved Mac off of her when he kissed her. Damn it. Cipriana glared at Oriel. "I'll have you know. He invited himself on my journey. Not the other way around. I was supposed to be traveling with my sister and her mate." The only good thing was she didn't have to deal with their lovey-dovey shit. She really didn't want to watch the two of them constantly making googly-eyes at each other.

Oriel downcast his eyes and bowed his head to her. "My mistake." He waited until the proxy got to her feet and went with her partner to resume their duties. He pulled up his sleeve, unclasped the device on his right wrist, and presented Cipriana with it.

Yeah, it was his mistake. Not that she should've gotten upset with him about it. It wasn't his fault. It was Mac's fault. Or the gods and goddesses... she really wasn't sure. Shaking the thoughts from her head, Cipriana eyed the device for a moment before she accepted it, inspecting it. Five shiny, slender pieces of metal tipped with crystals, all intricately designed with suns, moons, and stars. "What's this?"

"For your defense," Oriel said. "The transparent tips can be imbued with minor spells or poison. The other is a whistling dart. You can use it to signal when you wish to speak again, or as a standard dart, if you must."

She stared at it for a minute. Despite her rudeness in the beginning and the way she'd snapped at him for his assumptions, he'd been kind. Minus, maybe in one instance. Still, she had learned a lot in the exchange. Information that she needed. "Thank you."

Not that she'd have any spells to imbue the tips with. The poison she wasn't sure about. But the whistling dart... that would probably come in handy once they'd gotten the stone Mac had to the Reflection Pools. As she secured it around her wrist, her eyes lifted back to Oriel. "I apologize for snapping at you. It was unnecessary." And bitchy. And rude. She rubbed her forehead and smirked. "I'd blame it on the fact that I'm more accustomed to addressing females, but I handled nothing really well when you all first got here, either."

"You weren't the only one," Mac said. "We're all figuring out how to work together when we've kept to ourselves for centuries."

"It's easier to fight when it's all you've known." Oriel sighed heavily. "I will do my best to convey our discussion to the Matriarch and the Clan Commanders, but I cannot guarantee they'll act on, or even entertain, the suggestions seriously."

He'd been honest with her; she could be honest with him. Although it was something she rather preferred to keep to herself, it wasn't something she could change. Besides, there were likely rumors abound how much the sirens had fallen. "I'll be truthful with you. I have little to offer in the way of warriors. Our numbers have dwindled. Our own decisions and actions have served as a hindrance. But we will do our part to ensure the safety of the isle. It's time we all stopped hiding and keeping our knowledge and treasures to ourselves. Maybe if we all come together, we just might save this place."

Mac rose to his feet. "Aurelia may just surprise us. I mean, she kept her word and returned here with reinforcements."

"Well... then, Oriel, luck might be on your side." All of theirs if everything went according to plan. Though unexpected problems were always bound to arise, they'd deal with them the best they could.

"The Matriarch is... unpredictable and forceful," Oriel conceded. "But in Her own way, I believe She means well. Dragons aren't taught or trained to be kind and cooperative, even with other dragons. They're encouraged to accumulate as much wealth and status as they can by whatever means necessary. Be it violence, theft, deceit... or worse."

Cipriana shook her head a little. It went along with some notes and things they'd learned about dragons over the years. Of course, some of their ways were no longer used. Mostly because it wasn't taught anymore. "We've been taught to keep our multiple collections of knowledge and prophecies to ourselves. My sister was the one who convinced our Elder it was time we opened our gates. That we were just hurting ourselves with our outdated laws."

"Probably why there are nothing but females left." Mac draped an arm across her shoulders.

Narrowing her gaze, she shrugged his arm off. "Touch me again and I'm going to shove your flames up your ass."

"My bad." He took a step back.

Oriel kept his expression neutral. "Does that not make the males' decision making worse since there are none left?"

"Are you referring to males or my actions? Or my presence and leadership here?" Mac raised an eyebrow.

A small smile tugged at the corners of her mouth. Cipriana crossed her arms. She was kind of curious about how this would get answered. Their cultures were completely different. The females were warriors, and the males were revered, but they were held to a higher standard. They were forced to be as appealing as possible and to engage with multiple females. Not that she had to worry about that. As he was the *only* male, and her sister was the only other female currently at mating age, aside from herself, it left her as the one option. Since her sister had found a mate of another species. Unless she took a mate from another species. Cipriana rubbed her chest, feeling a dull ache. Why did that bother her so much?

"The males," Oriel replied, his brows drawing together in confusion.

Glancing over at Cipriana, Mac shrugged. "I left Pteryrina when I was a child. I don't know what has happened to all the males."

"The number of males that were born has dwindled every *solaris* for the last two millennia. This altered a lot in how they got treated. They became more revered and had to procreate with multiple females." She snickered. A nice brief history lesson. It sounded far simpler than it actually was. "Then we had our war a few hundred *solaris* ago with the hybrids that lived in Pteryrina. That caused... a further split, and many... left."

Yeah, that was a really simplified version. Watered down to the absolute basics. "Those of us who remain have different mothers, but the same father. He was the last male... that was known about. Currently, only two of us are of mating age. My sister, who is here with her mate, and me. Does that clarify a few things?"

"That is... unfortunate." Oriel worked the brief history over in his mind. "So, you," he tried, "are to be... given to him? And the blue siren, as well?"

While she didn't blame him for the assessment, it certainly made it clear she'd left off a few key points. "I may be of mating age, but I have a choice in who I take as a mate." Regardless of what destiny seemed to have planned. "As for the blue siren... she's not from here, nor do I expect her to stay." If she was what she thought, the sooner the female left, the better off they'd be. She'd read enough about those of the female's station to know that things weren't always in one piece when they left.

"Yeah, I have no interest in Thalasia," Mac said. "Though she seemed quite fond of one of yours."

"Male dragons do not choose. They are offered and chosen, bought, sold, traded." Oriel paused. "One of ours?"

Cipriana's eyes widened. She had to bite her tongue because it sounded horrible. The idea of sharing a male with another female irritated her. It wasn't something she had ever planned. If she took a male, he would be hers alone. But to be treated like property. Demeter, she didn't understand that.

"Um, yeah. Seru." Mac shrugged. "I've been calling him boyfriend. The two were attached at the hip when they were here yesterday."

"We saw them at the hybrid village, and they were... well, holding hands. They looked like they were together, according to what my sister said." She had paid little attention to them. Her purpose had been the treaty. They spoke to her sister and Gavin while she worked with Santos.

"The beast is not one of ours." Oriel swallowed. "Nor is he whatever prize the newcomer thinks him to be."

"Oh?" Her arms unfolded as her eyebrows knitted together. Well, wasn't that interesting? Cipriana glanced at Mac and then back to Oriel. "Thalasia isn't one of ours."

"She kind of broke the barrier." Mac chuckled. "To be fair, her arrival was prophesied."

"And you know this, how?"

"Felix made me memorize several prophecies as I was growing up."

"What *is* her purpose here?" Oriel directed his question at the male.

Mac looked between Oriel and Cipriana, both giving him the same look. He rolled his eyes. "Fine." His eyes flicked to Cipriana. "I'm guessing you weren't taught the accuracy of our history and *why* fewer males were born every *solaris*. We *used* to work well with other species. However, someone might've pissed someone else off, and they cursed the sirens. If what I've been taught is correct... she's here to break the curse."

"How is she supposed to do that?" This was the first she'd ever heard of a curse. If that was the case, then how was her sister... something she did and didn't want to know. Cipriana rubbed her forehead. Gods, she might actually have to ask.

"I don't know, and I'm not looking forward to finding out." He groaned. "Especially since I think it involves me," Mac muttered.

"Is that why you're... different?" Oriel lifted a hand towards the male's wings. "Green and blue."

"It's a strong possibility."

"That's one theory," she mumbled. Shit. She didn't mean to say that aloud. Although it had already been pointed out that the female wasn't from Prisma Isle. Let alone Pteryrina. Either way, she didn't belong. "What? I said *she* isn't one of ours." Cipriana sighed. "We have a myth amongst our people of so-called sirens that differ from us. They only half look like us, but can blend in and look like... anyone, and they have powers... well, we could only dream of. They don't follow our laws... aren't subject to our issues... they're supposed to be problem-fixers. From what I read growing up, they may fix things, but they also leave new ones in their wake."

Mac turned toward her and brushed a hand through his dark locks. "What kind of problem could she leave?"

"A supernatural disaster..." Oriel growled.

"Alright... didn't think about that." Mac sighed heavily.

"So, we need to find her... break this curse and get her to move on her way." Something else that sounded like a nice and simple plan. Why did it feel like it was too simple? And that there were things she wasn't considering.

"Yeah, about that. I'm not confirming this, but since she's the one that brought the barrier down, she's probably the only one that can put it back up."

"Are you fucking kidding me?" Cipriana pinched the bridge of her nose. Damn Atlis. They were *nothing* but trouble.

Oriel closed his eyes. "Why would she tear it down just to re-erect it?"

"I don't know. I can't answer everything. It isn't like Felix told me much of anything before he died. You now know as much as I do." Mac groaned.

Think. Think. The female had to leave. Her sister... at dinner. They'd mentioned they planned to leave the isle. Was that how? Parthenia and Gavin had spoken with the female when they'd crossed paths earlier. It wasn't like they knew why the barrier had been erected in the first place or who had done it. "Some information he shared."

"Yeah, well, he was as protective of it as we are."

"You're content to let her go? If she means to destroy our home, is she not another enemy?" Oriel asked.

"First off..." Mac crossed his arms. "I'm fairly certain she doesn't intend to destroy our home. Both she and the boyfriend took issue with my interrogation techniques when we had a dark guiler that we captured. Plus, she healed several of my people who'd gotten injured in the attack on our village."

Healing capabilities? The female could heal? Cipriana dragged a hand down her face. This so-called siren had to be *exactly* what she suspected. With a heavy sigh, her gaze flicked to Oriel. "From what

I know of those of her stature, their purpose isn't to cause harm or wreak havoc. But we have very little information about them at all. They're supposed to be a myth... nonexistent."

"Her companionship with 'the boyfriend,' as you call him, is exactly what takes your 'additional problems in her wake' to another disaster. Do you intend to accept her help, no matter the cost?"

"With breaking the curse, I don't think we have a choice." Mac shifted his gaze to Cipriana. "You're the one who knows how bad it is in Pteryrina. Not me."

Fifteen people. Three who wouldn't reach mating age for seven years. Four that were beyond their final reproductive cycle. That took half of them out already. If there were a curse... would it allow her sister and Gavin to reproduce? A conversation about their sex life wasn't something she really wanted to do. "You're right. We may not have a choice."

Oriel grimaced. "If you encounter them, do not trust Seru or anything he may have fed your newcomer."

Not that she expected to encounter them again, but she'd keep it in mind just in case. She'd have to find out exactly what her sister talked about with them. "I'd say the same thing about her. As protective as we are about the knowledge we've obtained over the years, her kind... they're worse."

"You keep saying 'her kind' or that she's not like us. I thought she was a siren. Just looked different."

"To a degree. If I'm right... she's what's called an Atlis, but I can't confirm that. And we have very little information about them." If that. Stories. That's what they had. Stories. Maybe the journal had more, but there hadn't been time for her to go through it.

"Worse? What do you know of Atlis?" Oriel asked before amending. "What do you know that you're permitted to share?"

"Not much," Cipriana said. "They have more power, more abilities than us. They can look like anything or anyone. Chameleons, so to speak. And they aren't held down to one place." Demeter, she wished she knew more than that, but that was all she had ever learned.

"So, she may not even be a blue siren at all." Oriel visibly swallowed. He nodded resolutely, his hand tightening around the pommel of his sword once more. "Thank you, Elders. You've been most helpful."

"You're welcome. And thank you for the information you've provided." Cipriana held up her arm. "And this." She didn't intend to use it until they handled the stone. Despite what she'd said earlier, the fact remained that she and Mac made a good team. They'd worked well together when they fought the dark guilers earlier. And had come to agreeable terms for a peace treaty.

"Yes, thank you. This has been productive," Mac said.

"I will be in touch if I don't hear from you first," Oriel said with a bow of his head. He stepped back, giving himself plenty of room to transform. He took a moment to assess the two of them, and then he effortlessly shifted into his true form of white scales with gilded features. From mane to talons, he shimmered. Without a moment's thought, he rose into the clouds, gaining height before he veered off toward the center of the isle.

Mac half glanced over his shoulder at her. "You held something back from him."

"He asked only for what I *could* tell him." With what had come up in conversation with Devin, that so-called blue siren might be her sister and Gavin's only way off the isle. And those two were determined. She just needed to confirm everything they spoke of with Thalasia back in Migas.

"So, what didn't you tell him?"

Folding her arms across her chest, she dragged a talon through the dirt beneath her feet and sighed. "A couple of things, really. Parthenia and Gavin spoke with Thalasia and Seru while we were in Migas. While I'm uncertain, I think part of that conversation might have included their desire to leave the isle."

He held up his hand. "Wait a second. You're telling me they might have made a deal with her to get off the isle?"

"Yes." Knowing what she knew now, it was an excellent possibility. Cipriana dragged a hand down her face. "Look, I don't know any of this for sure. I need to talk to Parthenia and Gavin in the morning. Find out what they talked about with those two. And see if my assumptions about Thalasia are correct."

"Okay." Mac nodded and gripped the back of his neck. "Do you think we can trust everything Oriel said?"

"Yes. He seemed to be honest with us about everything. It wouldn't do any of us any good for him to lie." With everything running through her head at the moment, she really needed sleep. If she hadn't been tired before, she definitely was now. Inhaling and exhaling a deep breath, she dropped her arms to her side. "I'm gonna turn in for the night. You should, too. We have a long journey ahead of us."

Chapter Twenty-Three

Thalasia's feet hit the ground at the front door of the inn. She stumbled, nearly falling, and caught herself with a hand against the rough wall. At least she'd made it through the flight without incident. Unfortunately, talking so much about Mistress in the last several hours opened the box she'd desperately attempted to keep closed.

The memory of when she had met Mistress flooded her mind.

Taking to the air, Thalasia soared back toward the hut she had stayed in with her parents. Maybe if she was lucky, she'd spot them on the way and then the three of them could just leave together. What if she didn't find them? What would she do then?

There may not be another choice but to leave. Alone. Tears pricked at the corners of her eyes. No, that couldn't be possible. It wouldn't happen. They were there. She knew it. Deep in her heart, she knew they were still here. That she'd find them and they would leave together.

This hadn't been the first time they'd asked her to hide for a short period. It had happened on at least two other occasions. Except they'd come looking for her afterward. After the fight was done. She swallowed. Maybe she'd flown too far this time. But they didn't tell her just to fly and hide; they'd told her to leave. To leave the realm.

No, she couldn't think like this. They were okay. Her parents were okay.

To quiet her racing mind, she looked up, seeking solace in the inky blackness of the night sky. She always preferred the night to the day. It was absolutely exquisite the way the stars sparkled against the velvety, dark-blue hues. The unblemished crescent-shape of the moon as it took its place amongst the ethereal night. It was quite peaceful.

Her favorite time to watch the sky was when the sun set, leaving an iridescent glow in its wake as the moon rose in all its glory.

Her gaze flicked back and forth between the stars as they danced across the sky and the ground below, constantly keeping an eye out for her parents. Mostly all she saw were animals frolicking, a few unknown creatures running about, but nothing of her parents. At one point, she'd slowed and hovered for a minute as she approached the jump-point. In the back of her mind, something nagged at her, telling her she needed to heed her parents' words. Listen to their warning that had been intoned, but she couldn't make herself go.

She didn't know how she'd survive without them.

With a slight hesitation, Thalasia continued on. She didn't stop or slow down as she sailed across the sky. The hut was still far away, and as she kept going, she saw no sign of her parents down below. Nor above or anywhere around the upper atmosphere. They were nowhere to be seen, but it didn't prevent her from—

Not far in the distance, she spotted a thin wisp of black smoke in the air. Its tendrils licked at the cloudless sky. As she got closer, she easily noted the pungent smell. The thin fabric of smoke billowed into the night as its sickly scent filled her nostrils. Her eyes widened, and she dove toward the remnants of the place she'd briefly called home.

The smell of copper sent her racing toward the ground. She had just passed the treeline when the evidence of the fight came into sight. Two sets of light brown wings, still and silent, were staked to the ground around a pile of contorted figures. The charred remains all looked the same, indistinguishable from each other. It stopped her heart in her chest as she landed, her feet hitting the grass with a subtle thud as she ran across the clearing.

No, no, no, no, no, she thought. It couldn't be her parents. Anyone but her parents. Tears welled in the corners of her eyes as she pleaded with the goddess for this to be anything but her reality. Thalasia skidded to a halt within the outer circle of the scorched ground. She could feel the wetness on her face, but she didn't want to believe it. Not as she stared at the clothing melted into blackened flesh.

Hesitantly, she reached out to the closest wing and ran her fingers across just one silky feather. She recognized the various hues of brown. It wasn't necessary to look at the other pair of wings. Or to scrutinize the burned bodies any longer. No matter how hard she prayed, how much she hoped, her parents... her loving parents were dead. Thalasia's knees buckled, and she crumbled, tasting the gritty earth as silent tears streamed down her face. Clenching the dirt in her palms, she rocked back onto her feet, the world spinning slightly.

It was not her parents.

It wasn't them.

Not her parents.

"NOOO!!" Thalasia screamed as a blast of silver light erupted from her, turning her family, home, and a few trees to ash, leaving only the smell of burning wood. Wrapping her arms tightly around her slight frame, she hung her head as she wept. *This wasn't supposed to happen. They were supposed to be safe. She was supposed to keep them safe. Why didn't they let her stay? She could've protected them.*

It wasn't their fault. They had trained her to fight. Hadn't they? Not that it mattered. She hadn't stayed. Instead, she fled like a coward. She let them die. She let them suffer. Her chest tightened as her breathing hitched. Letting the dirt fall from her hands, she clutched at the ache in her heart, the pain so visceral. *It was all her fault. For flying so far. Not fighting harder to stay by their side. These visions... these monstrosities in her head. Of all the people she'd saved, she failed when it counted the most.*

Her body shook as the tears streamed relentlessly down her face. *She'd allowed them to be slaughtered, to be burned, to be stolen from her.* Shakily, Thalasia reached for the newly formed pile of ash where their charred bodies had once been. *They had lost their lives... for her. She was to blame for this.*

It was her fault.

All her fault.

Agony washed through her as she gripped a small amount of dust in her palm. "I'm so sorry," Thalasia whispered. *Demeter, please bring them back. Bring them back.* She'd do anything. *Trade her life for theirs. Keep the visions for the rest of her life. Save whomever the goddess requested. Whatever it took, she didn't care. Even if she had to claim another's life to give them theirs. As long as they came back.*

They were all that mattered. They were all she cared about. "Please," she begged. "Please... please... bring them back." Tears streamed down her face as she silently begged the goddess, her voice barely a whisper, to bring her parents back. *Somehow, it had to be possible. If she could travel between realms, between planes, then she could get her parents back. Right?* "Oh, please..." Thalasia croaked.

It just had to be because she couldn't live without them.

She just couldn't.

"Oh child. Nothing will bring them back," a female voice said nearby. "They fought valiantly, though in the end, they were no match for me."

Her gaze slowly lifted to the voice and narrowed at the black bear's massive form in front of her. It had to be a shape shifter. Bears didn't speak, and she hadn't gained telepathy yet as an ability.

"Hmm, such power in such a young child. You will do nicely."

"What?" Her fingers, stained with earth, clung to the soil as she pushed herself up, each movement a laborious echo of sorrow. With the anguish in her heart, her mind hadn't fully grasped what the woman meant or what she had missed in her surroundings when she landed. Did she... did she say... "NO!!" Thalasia screamed as she lunged at the bear.

"Take her."

She didn't get far before a cloth with a sweet odor covered her mouth and nose and a pair of arms yanked her back. No! She couldn't let this happen. All the training she'd spent years enduring kicked in. Thalasia kicked her assailant in the knee. The snap was deafening, and she felt the tension break as the person fell backward, their grip on the cloth giving way.

Thalasia went to move, but she wasn't fast enough. Another pair of arms came around both her wings and arms to keep her from going anywhere. It didn't prevent her from struggling or kicking at the person who held her. She head-butted her new captor, but it didn't seem to faze them. Or if it did, it wasn't enough to loosen their hold. Without her hands, she couldn't pull on some parts of her power, not that the shape shifter needed to see everything she could do. She opened her mouth as a second option, but didn't get far. A sharp prick in her neck made her reel with fury.

But that didn't last. Within a matter of moments, her body went limp, and an overwhelming darkness pulled her into a deep abyss.

With a heavy gasp, she shut her eyes tightly to keep the tears at bay. The last time she'd seen her mother on this plane had been two days before that, with the promise that they'd see one another again. It had simply been a lie to get an eleven-year-old to leave without them. Inhaling and exhaling a deep breath, Thalasia wiped at the corners of her eyes and collected herself. She needed to be ready for the storm that likely awaited her, not thinking about the past.

Cyon stopped in her tracks, the blue cylinder in her hand faltering. "What in all the seas happened to you?" she asked. "He's going to—"

Thalasia opened her mouth to answer, but a loud boom sounded from above, cutting off both their speeches. The inn shook, the blast singing through the structure to the foundation beneath their feet. This wasn't good. Her fingers tightened around the patch of furry skin still in her hand. It wasn't like she could help the blood all over her. At least most of it wasn't hers. "I got into a fight. He lost," she muttered.

Obviously, it really didn't need to be said, but saying something helped her stop the emotions already bubbling to the surface. One memory... it wouldn't end there. It would continue, each memory further encouraging the agony clawing at her insides. Thalasia shook her head to step away from the edge of the box that had popped open. "I just want to shower and clean up."

Cyon's grip tightened around the spear, her fangs grinding. "You do that. With that. After. Every. Time," she growled out, indicating the canister. "Don't let him know." The female shoved the canister into Thalasia's chest before stomping to the stairs, taking them two or three at a time.

Great. Just great. Her head and emotions were already all over the place. Untying the purse at her waist, she shoved the canister in there before tying it back up. As if things weren't bad enough already. Heaving a sigh, she flew over to the staircase. They were wide and tall enough she could fly right after Cyon as the female raced up the third flight toward the explosion. She didn't know what she was coming back to, but her inability to control her emotions right now didn't help matters.

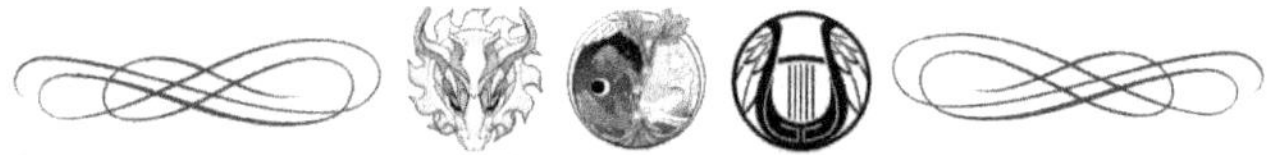

The touch of Thalasia's silvery power clashing with his own only riled the saint beast further. Seru snarled at her approach, not bothering to release Marius from his clutches. His fury surged. The blue warred with the silver, drawing on his magic to supercharge and ride the silver bolts to their source. The push of power carried a warning and a promise. *Stay out of this, and I'll deal with you later.* The collar emitted a soft silver light in response.

The glow that started with Thalasia's eyes quickly covered her entire body. "I am not a fucking child!" With her words, a blast of white light emitted from her. The doors of every room on the floor burst off their hinges with a loud bang, and the windows exploded into shards of glass. As the storm clouds gathered over the isle, a torrent of shattered glass fell onto the marketplace below.

A cool calm in the color of teal and blue bathed over her and the saint beast until it filled the space. The mingling magic overflowed, trickling down through the inn and surrounding streets.

Seru's incomplete marks faltered in the face of Cyon and Marius's complete bond. His power fought, growing before fizzling under their combined force. The collar's glow intensified to a blinding light. It went out like a candle in a strong breeze as the saint beast's strength was stolen from him. He ended on his knees, succumbing to the collar and the Sea King's command.

Marius's eyes betrayed his conflict in so forcefully subduing the pair. As he reclaimed his composure, readjusting the robes, he pled with them, his voice thick with sorrow, "This has to stop."

A low growl came from Seru as Cyon approached. The rain from the storm soaked the floor through the massive hole the saint beast had blown in the ceiling. Disgust and displeasure colored her features. As she reached out to lay hands on the saint beast, the low rumble grew. His power found his eyes, but so did hers. And she wasn't about to give him a second chance at Marius.

All it took was a slight flinch on her part and he'd seized the spear and knocked her back just enough to break the physical contact. In a flash, almost too quick to see, he'd outmaneuvered her, demonstrating how thoroughly he'd held back all these years—in strength, skill, and speed.

She barely had time to react; a swift attempt to dodge failed as the tip of the spear thrust upward and sliced through her neck as it burrowed into the wall behind her. The shared spell broke, falling away until all that remained was the downpour of rain and the dance of electricity concealed in the clouds above.

"We're no better than Her," Thalasia said.

Seru's gaze slid from Cyon to his female, covered in blood and soaked through. His lip recoiled at her statement. He almost asked her to repeat herself, unsure he'd heard her correctly. Despite his rage and resolve, when he glanced back at Cyon, he faltered.

Blood trickled down her long neck, pooling in the cloth before dripping steadily onto the floor. Her wide eyes had returned to disdain. She knew better than to make any sudden movements, ruled by her superior intellect and training, or fear. He wasn't sure which he preferred.

He still sensed Marius standing nearby, watching them with the same pained sadness that colored Thalasia's tone. The disapproval, the weakness. All of it aggravated and annoyed him. None more than the selection of Marius's first from another species. A decision made without him.

It took a moment, but he eased off Cyon and threw down the spear. It clattered, the sound amplified by the rain, amid the groan of the structure. "Leave. Both of you," his voice sounded calm but still held an edge.

Marius moved to aid Cyon.

Seru never let the pair out of his sight, even as he treaded over broken glass and splintered wood to reach Thalasia.

Her gaze had fallen from him to the surrounding destruction. Stepping further into the room, Thalasia pressed a hand to the wall. Once again, her entire body lit up. Except this time, instead of wood splintering and glass shattering, it all came back together. With the roof above them rebuilt, the doors reattached, and the window panes repaired as if the blow out had never happened. The tears didn't ebb as she focused on healing what they'd broken.

"Stop." He didn't understand why she was crying. The injury she suffered didn't appear all that severe. Most of the blood wasn't her own. "I said stop." Seru grabbed her wrist, yanking her away from the wall. He embraced her, pulling her against his chest as his chin rested gently atop her head. Her soft-silver halo enveloped them both. "Leave it."

He whispered soothing words into her hair. The remnants of the reconstruction tumbled down around them. The sea dragons remained blessedly silent as Marius tended to Cyon's wound.

"I have to fix it," she whispered, tears pouring down her face.

"Fixing it changes nothing." He couldn't explain why, but her tears bothered him. Her hurt raised a different turmoil in him. Something quieter than his rage. Softer. He just wanted to make it better for her. His brows knit together as he rubbed soothing circles along her back. Restoring it to how it had been before, rewinding time and spending energy senselessly, wasn't better.

Seru's knuckles caressed the lengths of her arms, up and down. Eventually, he took her by the chin, forcing those mirror eyes to his. His other hand found hers. His gaze shifted as his fingers brushed the wet piece of... flesh? "What *is* that?" he asked. *Some kind of trophy from her kill?* He'd read of a few dragons who'd been notorious for collecting trophies of their kills. The keepsake seemed misplaced in her hand. Then again, so did he.

He lifted the scrap of freshly carved meat from her hand, turning it over—a large 'M' stood in stark relief; a burn, a branding. "A shape shifter from Métamorphe." He sniffed the artifact. "Canine."

He looked at her quizzically, hoping she offered answers. He'd grown tired of being in the dark. Even more so of the people surrounding him making choices for him. Verie. His elder brother. The court officials. Marius. Aurelia. Seru squeezed her hand. "Do you want to tell me about it?"

As her tears eased, Thalasia nodded slowly. "They're hunting me," she whispered as she swept the hair away from the left side of her neck.

His fingers reached out to brush the mark on her neck. Identical to the brand on the piece of stolen flesh. The raised skin was smooth to the touch. Seru turned back to the sea dragons, tossing the scrap of flesh at their feet. Marius jumped, recoiling. Cyon didn't. Her hate-filled stare was the only betrayal of true indifference.

"Add them to your list," he demanded more than asked. It was the least Marius could do. The shape shifters bearing that brand and their pompous king would be an excellent test for their allies. He turned back to Thalasia, taking her by the shoulders. "Anyone who hunts you answers to us." That's right. Marius might be a fucking moron, but he needed them. The saint beast and the siren. Otherwise, his precious kingdom stood little chance. So, he'd comply. "No one's going to hurt you." He'd rip them apart.

Thalasia wiped at her face. "They've been ordered to take me alive." She swallowed. "He wants to free *her*."

"I don't care what their orders are," Seru insisted. "They won't have you." The certainty in his words resonated through his grip on her shoulders. Echoed in the depths of his eyes. He'd keep her safe. But he couldn't protect her if she kept leaving him behind. Insisted on doing everything alone. What had she been trying to prove? That she didn't need him? He already knew that. He shook his head. His mane clung to his face. "Who? Why?"

"Mistress," Thalasia said the one word as if it answered it all. "The one who killed my parents, captured me, held me captive for months. The one who tortured me." Her gaze shifted from Marius for a moment back to him. "The only reason anyone wants me. My ability to jump realms."

Seru gave a derisive snort. By the name... or was it a title? Either way, the woman sounded as pretentious and self-important as the Silver Queen. Another high and mighty female hiding behind fancy titles and dirty tricks, using puppets to commit her treachery. Every time Thalasia named her deeds, he vowed to inflict the same cruelties or worse on the cowardly woman who called herself 'Mistress.'

"I want you." He just wasn't sure it was the best idea. For her. Was that why he'd left the marks incomplete despite his initial intentions? Sure, he could protect her. But what about all the rest? His eyes fell from hers to wander the remnants of the room, beyond to the heavy downpour and the dark-gray world. He knew so much and yet so little about the proper bounds of a healthy relationship. A claim wasn't a relationship. The marks weren't a relationship. They were ownership. She didn't want that. Even if she thought she did. He didn't want that for her.

His dragon blood wouldn't allow them anything else. Not that his collar even allowed that much. His frown deepened. He wanted her to believe him. Needed her to. But was he offering her the truth? Or just another cleverly concealed lie? "Just..."

Frustrated and unable to find words, Seru barked at Marius and Cyon. "You two. Get out." Seru waited until the pair did as they were bid. A warning glare in Marius's direction kept him from asking questions or making unwanted suggestions as they left. Cyon refused the King's offer of assistance, collecting her discarded weapon from the rubble before proudly and briskly marching into the hall and down the stairs. Marius lingered, but heeded the saint beast's warning. He bowed his head in defeat, offering a small nod to Thalasia, and left.

Seru returned his gaze to the siren. She was a mess of blue, drenched in crimson, with her clothes torn and her hair disheveled. Still, a beautiful, beautiful mess. An electric blue emanated from his eyes as he stepped into her. "Let's get you out of those clothes." Without waiting for her reply, he reached for her top, yanking the waterlogged fabric up, exposing her midriff, and over her head.

Staring at him in utter confusion, Thalasia's body automatically complied with his request. She shook her head. "My clothes should be destroyed."

"Agreed." The response was automatic. His hands trailed lightly down her body, enjoying the softness. A low hum of electricity raised tiny bumps along her flesh. "The tiny, black dress, too?" The skin around his eyes tightened as he forced himself to work on undoing the button of her jeans. She'd clearly changed clothes before going out. Still, it bothered him. Burning the dress might be easier than burning the building pile of wet and tattered clothing.

As he kneeled to help her out of the boots, his hand inspected the slash along her thigh. "Heal your leg." Again, not a question. Seru met her eyes, his eyes aglow and hers as silver as ever. He forced his fingers back to work on the laces before moving to removing the leather shoes and sopping wet socks, peeling them down her legs. He added them to the pile one by one—nuzzling his cheek along her untouched thigh as he switched to her other foot, scenting along her skin.

"If it will make you feel better, the dress, too," she conceded. Her eyes lit up as she pulled on his energy, as she'd done twice before, and healed her thigh.

He ran his thumb over the newly healed flesh, a grateful sigh escaping him in a fog. The impending dampness and chill in the air barely registered with him. "Are you cold?" He left the tiny undergarments in place as they'd been her only request in their activities from before the sea dragon's intrusion. He longed to go back there. Maybe in the same way she'd attempted to pull the building back together. His beast found the prospect easy enough. He remained uncertain. Though the desire had been tempered, it still flickered to life. Ready. Waiting.

Seru rose to his feet, smoothing his thumb beneath each of her eyes, careful with his talons. He preferred the small smile to the tears. He leaned down, resting his forehead against hers. The tiny water droplets accumulating in their hair trickled down, making a game of racing toward the ground.

Softly, she caressed the ends of his mane, her arm lying gently against his shoulder. "I wouldn't say no to a hot shower."

"'A hot shower.'" An unnecessary repetition. Seru studied her a while longer before stooping to take her in his arms, capturing her behind the knees and using his other arm to support her back. He carried her over the wreckage in the room, down the hall toward a less damaged room, hoping it housed a shower. He was careful to let her tuck her wings through the narrow entryways.

As he paused in the center of the room, he noted that the cozier accommodations offered a fresh bed, a dry place to warm up, and a bit more privacy. He wandered in the direction he presumed housed the bath and shower, as if the rooms were set up similarly.

Thalasia buried her face in his neck and clutched her purse to her chest. When they got into the bathroom, it had the vanity on the left, the toilet in the middle, and the bathtub to the right. No shower. She sighed. "A bath will suffice."

He sat on the edge, keeping her nestled in his lap as he turned on the water, letting the steamy water fill the tub. While they waited, he brushed along her arm as he held her close. She felt fragile.

Because of their emotions battling, the weight of her role as an Atlis, the shape shifters hunting her, the conflict between his marks and inability to commit to that course added to those struggles.

"I never completed the mark. The one I placed on you the night I crowned you," he softly confessed into her hair. "In time, Marius says its magic will fade if it's not brought full circle."

Maybe that was for the best. The idle stroking ceased. Then why did it sadden him? Where did they go from here? Having her for the sake, to quell his own internal storms, after everything she'd been through since she'd arrived on Prisma Isle seemed cruel, even to him. He shut his eyes, inhaling a breath of her scent. He wondered if the darkness he found there would offer any answers.

"Why didn't you?"

Seru stilled beneath her. Why hadn't he closed the marks? "I don't know..." he murmured. "I meant to... I just... couldn't."

"Do you think... maybe... it somehow had something to do with this?" Thalasia asked. "I mean... I know you didn't know about it."

"No," he opened his eyes, watching her fingers play over the 'M' behind her ear. "You cut the mark off that dog. Why haven't you tried removing this one?" He placed his fingers alongside hers. "You're more than capable of healing a flesh wound."

She lifted her gaze to his. "I have. I have tried." Thalasia dropped her eyes in utter defeat over the mark. "Nothing worked. Mistress... she didn't mark me just to claim me as property... she did it to subdue my powers." She paused. "He was already dead when I removed his."

"Mmm," Seru reached over to turn off the faucet before the bath overflowed. "Your powers are still growing. Maybe in time, her brand will lose its potency."

He lifted her chin again. He knew what it meant not to belong to yourself. Eight-hundred years in chains. Verie's magic seeped away with each passing day since her demise. Aurelia's grew, promising to overtake it.

Focusing on the brand offered a pretty distraction. One he didn't feel he deserved. "I couldn't bring myself to enslave you. As much as I want you, you're not a piece of jewelry to hoard away under lock and key or a book to add to my collection. You'd be trapped here because I'm trapped here. My brothers took those women on the battlefield against their will. Just as Mother forced us to lie with her before she suspected us." The mental and emotional toll of those acts was high. The magical bindings came at an even steeper price. "I won't do that to you. Besides... You kinda fell asleep on me."

Thalasia narrowed her eyes at him, a crack of a smile on her face. "You wore me out."

He warmed at her smile, finding a new rhythm along her thigh. "Well, it was that or drug you. The former seemed the more enjoyable and kinder option."

"Yes. I don't really like being drugged." She shook her head. "The full moon is in four days. I don't yet have access to my full power. There's a ritual I'm supposed to perform to do that." She paused. "If I have an Allimos... I'm to perform it with them. As I gain my full power... we bind ourselves to one another, forsaking all others."

"Four days isn't a lot of time," Seru conceded, growing quiet behind her. "Guess we'll have to hope Aurelia hasn't killed our new green friend." He hadn't meant to growl out that statement so harshly. Mac didn't like him. Fine. But he also seemed like a self-absorbed child despite resembling Thalasia so closely in age. Even with his many failings, wouldn't the natural option be for her to complete the ritual with a siren? Yes, she'd told him she could choose. But he wasn't certain any truly viable options existed for her on the isle. No one he'd trust or recommend, anyway.

He'd already been tasked with being a matchmaker for Aurelia. The thought of doing the same for Thalasia brought on a whole new level of migraine. He barely acknowledged the groan that surfaced at the thought. Two headstrong young women. One set on marrying herself to a metal chair over selecting a suitable male counterpart. The other set on choosing a beast. Neither option sounded appealing to him.

Thalasia got to her feet and dug the Allimos journal out of her purse. She set it on the counter and tied the bag closed. "I don't know why you keep trying to push me off on Mac... or even any-one else." Shaking her head, she set the purse aside, stripped her underwear from her body and faced him. "My heart made a choice days ago. You turned it away last time, but by all rights, the journal belongs to you. Take the journal, Seru. No one would force you to read it. That choice belongs to you and only to you. As much as I deny it, I need you. I just don't know how to show that."

"A woman like you doesn't need any man," Seru responded, staring a little longer than even he felt comfortable with as she closed the distance between them. Thalasia pressed a gentle kiss on his forehead, catching him off guard. As she climbed into the bath, the sound of the water sloshing in the tub, his eyes shifted to the journal as he sank to the floor, the rough wood of the floor biting into his skin, sure to keep his back to her while he did his best to ignore the rising desire stirring within him. "Hearts make poor decisions."

He resorted to chewing on the talon of his thumb as a distraction. Did he reward her brutal honesty with his own brutal truth? Just staring at the book on the counter and gnawing at his finger seemed enough for now. His stubborn refusal to leave her side rooted him to the spot.

Every time she moved, disturbing the water, the sound of it lapping against the tub pulled his thoughts back to her naked form. Gentle rivaled what he wanted in that moment. He squeezed his eyes shut. Fuck.

"I would've let you close the mark," she said, her voice soft.

"I know. And you still would. Even after I've lied and deceived you, manipulated you, betrayed your secrets, and twisted you into someone you're not."

"You think you've twisted me into something I'm not? No, maybe pushed me to a rage I haven't felt in a long time, but you haven't twisted me into anything."

"You're the Saint. I'm the Destroyer." He'd allowed the damage she'd caused in the forest to be a warning sign that passed him by. The destruction of the inn and the sea dragon had been his doing. His power fed any reaction from her. She could deny that, too. But it wouldn't change it. "Though you are hot when you're pissed." The smile shone in his voice, even as he forced down another wave of heat.

A soft chuckle left her mouth. "Hot, huh? I don't think I've ever been described quite like that." She reached up to his mane and started gingerly running her fingers through it. "Yin and yang. Complementary forces."

"No? Guys your age have notoriously limited vocabularies." Seru leaned into her touch, knowing that it was a bad idea. He craved that touch. Her fingers tangled in his mane, rewarding her with the beads excitedly tinkling. "You're making this very difficult."

Keeping her fingers right where they were, she leaned on the edge of the tub a little closer to him. "Making what difficult?"

He looked at her out of the corner of his eye, not turning to avoid the view and all that went with it. "You might be new to this, but you're not as naïve as you want me to believe."

She sensed a stirring within him. The marks, however incomplete, only amplified her ability to feel what he felt. That'd been a huge part of their problem. Those feelings generated frustration, and the frustration translated to their moods and words, which triggered their magic. All that pent-up energy was determined to find an outlet.

The journal taunted him from across the room. It offered an increasingly welcome distraction to all that. Reading might give him something else to focus on. Then again, what if he couldn't even focus on that?

"No, but I am being nice enough to repress my pheromones." She sat back in the tub, removing her fingers from his locks. "It would be a lot worse for you if I released them. I mean, it's already hard on me. The only one stopping you, Seru—is you."

"You're wrong," and right at the same time. Yes, he was holding back. But with good reason. His marking her was one thing. Her performing her own ritual with him added another problem to their docket. "Even *if* I agree to being your Allimos and Aurelia senses whatever bond your ritual creates, or worse, if it breaks my link to her entirely, we won't have a way around that. Besides facing her wrath, I'd have to answer to the Cloud Court. With my elevated status within the Court, it's a direct conflict of interest with the duties I'm expected to perform. A relationship with another species is forbidden."

"Right. And your status means everything to you." Her words came out sarcastic, even slightly bitter. She sat up in the tub and leaned back so she could fully wet her hair and clean it out. Once she seemed satisfied, Thalasia got to her feet and climbed out of the tub. She snagged a towel from the rack and dried herself off.

"Without it, we're both fair game to any dragon who wishes it. Is that what you want?" An edge of anger crept back into his voice.

Thalasia glanced over her shoulder at him. "What I want is to get off this isle with you." She took the towel to dry her hair.

"And you're convinced your ritual will accomplish that?"

"I wish I could tell you yes with absolute certainty. I know it's a powerful ritual and that, unlike any other Atlis, I can only perform it in The Reflection Pools in Pteryrina." She looked back at him again. "What I know, I'm willing to talk to anyone that can give me the answers to get you off this isle and do whatever it takes to break your link."

He didn't like the idea of talking to anyone. Especially about their plans. It was information better kept to themselves. The more people that knew, the more likely one of them would end up spilling their guts, and the darker and bloodier their days would grow. He sighed heavily with a shake of his mane, snatching the journal from the counter. He pushed to his feet, brushing past her to return to the bedroom.

Seru didn't open the book. He ran a finger over its smooth, well-worn cover before tossing it onto the nightstand while he stripped off his wet clothes. Peeling the wet silk away, he let it fall to the floor piece by piece. He sat on the edge of the bed, thoughts swirling as he wrung the water from his mane.

Chapter Twenty-Four

"I don't know the specifics of the ritual. I think my mother repressed the memory of most of it," Thalasia said from the bathroom. "The onocentaur... do you remember everything about the day you gave him the dagger? Or is part of that memory missing?"

"Why would your mother repress your memories?" Seru asked the empty room. He lay back, stretching his arms, neck, and shoulders. He stayed silent for a while. "Why, do you think the woman who looks like you stole my memory, too?" The thought unsettled him, creasing his brow and pulling his face down into a deep frown. What was with sirens and messing with peoples' heads?

"Protection. In case..." Her words trailed off as she joined him in the bedroom. "You can't tell someone something you don't know. She wrote about it in the journal. It's an ability that I'll get. When we do... triggers are put in place so the memory can be retrieved at the right moment. I think I know how to retrieve the last of yours."

"No," he answered. "But they also wouldn't be torturing you if they didn't think you knew. For them to know, someone else had remembered and made a mistake. One you paid the price for. It's not protection. Knowing and being able to act accordingly allows you to protect yourself and prevent such things. Not to be taken by surprise by them, taken advantage of because of them. Stealing memories for your own comfort is cowardice and foolishness," he finished. He loathed the thought of someone playing around in his mind. He cared little that the woman in question was undeniably her ancestor. "And I suppose it's all up to her, at her discretion when that moment will be." His words dripped with disdain. "I have the blade. Why should I care about the memory now? It no longer serves me."

"How do you know there isn't anything important in that memory? How can you judge what you don't remember?" Thalasia sighed. "Yes, I suffered, but if I'd been able to tell Mistress how to leave the realm, how the jump points work... then how would Prisma Isle have suffered? Because here... here is where she would've come. She and her children. Markham, the shape shifter... king... leader... he's using her memories of me."

Thalasia rubbed her fingers over the mark. Tears pricked at the corners of her eyes. "I may have been tortured, but I'm still alive. I'm still here. That may not have been the case if I'd told her how it all worked. You're the one who told me that even with my visions, I can't see everything." She turned back around and glanced at him. "Neither can you."

"Your repression is slipping." With a sly show of teeth and a mischievous sparkle in his eye, Seru enjoyed watching her reaction more than he'd ever admit. The shift in her mood and the return of her tears abruptly stalled their game of devil's advocate.

He remained relaxed on the bed, lifting his hand for her to join him. Even if it fumbled their jumbled attempts at self-control—well, more his than hers—she deserved some comfort after the day she'd had. "You can't be certain if you were robbed of the opportunity to make different choices."

She couldn't have known how her Mistress would have fared on the isle any more than they knew what awaited them at the end of this journey they'd started on the day they'd convinced Aurelia and Mac to leave them behind.

Thalasia strode across the bedroom and lay down next to him. "I blame you for my repression faltering. You're the one that broke my damn walls and then set off my sexual awakening." Her words came out in a matter-of-fact tone.

"Whoops." A healthy dose of sarcasm betrayed by a smile as he laid his head back against the bed. His arm snaked around her. His fingers stroked her bare hip. A raise of his eyebrows. "You forgot your..."

"I've been walking around for the last twenty minutes without them, and you just noticed this?"

"No," he said. "You weren't pressed up against me earlier. Made it easier to ignore."

"Are you complaining?"

His eyes remained closed as he took a breath in. His eyebrows, the only show of expression, arched upward as he replied, "No." He focused on the dark, staving off the brief appearance of red at her unconscious shiver of pleasure. He licked his suddenly dry lips.

Thalasia half buried her face against his chest, brushing a soft kiss across his skin. "Why did they say we aren't feeding the mark?"

Seru stilled beneath her, even his breathing ceasing. Why did he insist on keeping the sea dragons around? Neither one could keep his or her mouth shut or his or her snout in their own business. "Because we aren't." As if her own body's response wasn't enough of a testament to that.

"Then why do you insist I use the link if we aren't feeding it? What do you think it'll accomplish?"

"It'll keep you alive." The rest was just details. Minor obstacles. The cost of the incomplete marks paled compared to their discomfort. That they could endure. "It serves its purpose, even like this." His fingers drummed lightly over her hip.

"And what does it cost you? Not feeding the marks. What does that cost you?"

The beginnings of a bitter laugh escaped him. "How—after all you've been through—do you remain so *good*?" Her genuine concern for his well-being should have touched him. At least, he thought it should have. He paused a moment, his fingers playing higher up her thigh towards the inside. Towards the warmth. "Nothing I'm not used to. Stop worrying and focus on what matters. Those silly little... missions of yours, or whatever you call them. Your calling to help people."

"Because I made a choice. I cared when others didn't." Her fingers curled into a ball, clenching against his chest. "You matter to me. That deserves attention."

"Why?" He felt a shiver run down her spine as he held her close, feeling the warmth of her body against his.

"Why does that deserve attention? Or why do you matter?"

"Mmm. Both." He let his touch wander south. Slowly, he trailed back up.

"I saw something in you when we first met. I didn't know what it was... at least not immediately. Not until you tried to comfort me the first time. Then chased after me when I shared my own scars. In those brief moments... I saw... someone who understood. Someone... like me. At first, I thought I just wanted to help you... set you free... but then you got upset when you failed to comfort me. It bothered me to see you upset. I didn't like it. When my wings came around you, I was surprised. I didn't even realize it was happening. You were stealing little pieces of my heart. Every opportunity you defended me, never once asking me for anything in return. Maybe you thought you were using me for your own gain, or maybe in those small moments... I got to see you. I've seen you happy. Felt your warmth. I *love* seeing that. Seeing your smile or the way your eyes sparkle when you look at me. Those things matter to me. You matter. Your happiness matters. And that deserves attention because I want to see that happen."

Seru sighed heavily into her hair. "You've only known one, maybe two, versions of me for days. How can you be so invested so quickly and hope to meet a lifelong partner?" Many searched a lifetime for such a partner and never found it. What made her so sure this was what that was?

"And yet you'd known me maybe an hour, and you'd already protected me." Slowly, she stroked her fingers along his chest. "It doesn't matter that I've known you for less than a week. Some people know the second they meet that they've met 'the one.' It's something in their eyes, in the way they look at one another. Wings don't just come around anyone. And for me..." She readjusted a little and draped one wing across his body. "Feel along the bottom, around the middle."

His eyes slid her way. He'd wondered which parts of her were more sensitive—the wings or the sweet place between her thighs. Shaking the thought from his mind, he obliged her request. Watching for expression as he played hide-and-seek in her wing for the second time. The first time, she'd revealed the lyre. The second... a bite wound? "Do you hide everything in there?" he asked, cocking an eyebrow at her.

"No." She bit her bottom lip. "I rarely hide anything under my wings. The lyre was a last-minute decision. This... the length of the feathers... that's just how they grew back. Like my body went into protective mode." Thalasia sighed heavily. "I didn't think I'd find my other half ever. For a long time, I wasn't even sure I deserved one. Some days..."

"Are you certain?" he asked, drawing out the sound of the pronoun. He stroked along the rest of her wing, traversing the scars and exploring her feathers and what lay beneath. "You're far too young to be thinking that way." He knew she'd disagree. The same way she had before. Experience equaled more years or something of the sort.

Her fingers curled a little against him. Thalasia swallowed as she squeezed her thighs together a little tighter. "Um... experiences and knowledge impact that. They age beyond physical years." A soft smile crossed her lips. "I'm not the first Atlis to question it. To be fair, most of them were well beyond me in years. Even Apollonia didn't meet her other half until she was over 400."

"Is this why they cut up your wings?" Seru played along the places that drew the most reaction from her, memorizing the path. He knew how easily pleasure twisted into pain. He closed his eyes against the sight of her. The other sensations were more than satisfying enough—the shuddering of her body pressing closer as she did her best to withstand his touch, the unevenness in her voice as she fought to speak through what she was experiencing, the press of her fingers into his chest. He enjoyed teasing her. "You're still a fledgling. A baby bird with soft fluff for feathers. Aurelia will be most eager to learn you've got none where she'd hoped."

Thalasia sat up a little and lightly scratched his chest with her fingernails. "Say one word to Aurelia about that and you'll see a side of me you never saw coming."

Seru couldn't help but smile at the rise he'd gotten out of her. "You realize... It was a joke." There was no reason he could fathom truly sharing that information with Aurelia.

With a slight snarl, she laid back down and got comfortable by draping her leg over one of his. She curled up a tad closer. Silence filled the room, but she didn't dare move. A single tear rolled down her cheek. "They went for my wings because watching them torture and kill people I was supposed to save... even that..." Thalasia wiped at her face. "I still refused to tell her how to leave the realm."

"If it brings back your pain, why do you share it with me?" He'd not shared any intimate details about himself or the origins of his scars with her. He may have given her general details, but nothing that elicited such a reaction. The memories were vivid for her, cutting into her like so many shards of glass.

"I don't want to hide from you anymore."

"If you were any good at hiding, you wouldn't be you," he said, looking down at her for the first time in a while. His eyes slid to the unopened journal on the nightstand. He inclined his head. "Of all the prior Atlis, whom do you admire the most? Feel the most connection to."

"I don't know." She frowned. "I mean, I look like Adina, but it annoys me how little information she really provides. Cressida didn't have a very long life, but she mastered her powers really early on. Kaja... she lived the longest. Her entries have always been useful. The only thing I've never been able to find is anything about her Allimos. If I had to pick one, it would probably be her."

Seru narrowed his eyes at her before indicating the journal she'd forced on him with his chin. "Does that one not offer you details about her Allimos?" He found it unsurprising she measured the women by the usefulness of their entries. She had placed the books in such high regard. They were likely among her most valuable tools and learning materials.

"I'm sure it does, but it's not mine to read. Twenty-two Allimos have written in that journal. It's typically passed from one to the next. Obviously, my circumstances didn't exactly allow for that."

He wrinkled his nose at that. "You really are a good girl." If he'd been given instructions not to open or read a book placed in his possession, no matter the contents, he'd have disregarded the rule at the earliest opportunity. Instead, she lived by a set of rules set out by a group of people she'd never truly met. It puzzled him. He scrubbed a hand over his face. If she hadn't entrusted her fate to him almost as easily, he'd have questioned it further.

"And I suppose all of them were accepting of this... transient lifestyle? Relying blindly on and following their female from place to place without questioning her destiny." One reason the role of Allimos made him turn up his nose. His life experiences left him suspicious—that, and curiosity and self-preservation led him to refuse vehemently to entrust anyone with anything of any importance. Especially his life. Being an Allimos involved leaning into a lifestyle that relied on believing in something greater than himself. No matter how great or revered the design, he simply couldn't enter into such a contract. Even with her at the forefront. Giving over that measure of control... was it really any better than being enslaved to the Clouds? He'd trade one master for another. One set of chains for another. Sure, he might gain a few gems along the way, but wouldn't they lose their luster over time? The excitement would wane. He'd grow bored, and there'd be no moving on until either or both of them met their end.

Just as she wouldn't rebel against her pre-destined role... assuming she even could. Thalasia's past seemed rife with events that only pushed her deeper into the role and the mindset her parents and predecessors undoubtedly drilled into her from a young age. Not unlike the priests and priestesses and the divine will of the gods and their musty old temples.

Thalasia stifled a chuckle and shook her head. "No. Not even close." She paused. "An Atlis and an Allimos are partners. In everything. They work side by side in various ways. On some occasions, that requires one or the other to stand off to the side while the other works. Most of the time, they work toward a common goal. I mean, you and I have been working together on things. Yeah, some of it has been based on my visions, but not all of it." She paused. "It's a relationship. No one person has full control over the other. I won't say that every one of those past relationships has been like that. Some entries have indicated the Allimos was the more dominant, some where they were the more submissive, and others where they were equals. I think that's why I admire Kaja so much. The way she spoke of her Allimos... she respected him."

"I remember this entry by Kaja. It had been a few days since she'd had a vision, so she and her Allimos looked at the map and decided on where to go next. From what I read; they spent a couple of days exploring the realm when they came across these farmers who just needed help with a shape shifter they'd been having problems with. The two of them worked together to... deal with the shape shifter. I remember because she commented that some days, she wished life could always be that easy. You know how the mark has allowed me to pull on your ability to heal, right? My ritual... it would give you the power to go through a jump point. Like I can."

"What's the catch?" The question was simple. The implications were not. There'd always be those undercurrents of mistrust and the questions that followed.

"The catch? With the ritual? I mean, it's binding. Deal with the onslaught of feeling what the other feels... all the time." Thalasia frowned. "Aside from its only being performed once... I can't think of anything else that could be construed as a catch." She sighed heavily. "One chance. That's the catch. We get one shot at doing the ritual. I've told you from the beginning, I'm not like any other. That's always been true. For me, I have to do the ritual in Pteryrina. Once it's done, there is no going back."

"And what if you miss your window? What then?"

"Then I spend the rest of my life alone." She uncurled her wing from him and rolled over to her side.

Seru sighed, a gruff, irritated sound as he cursed himself for allowing that to bother him. He heaved himself up enough to reach over her to the nightstand to retrieve the journal.

Thalasia laid there for a minute before climbing out of the bed and disappearing into the bathroom.

"What are you doing?" His eyes followed her.

With the shirt mostly buttoned up, she stepped into the doorway of the bathroom. She blinked. "My body is on fire. It's a distraction, especially when all I want to do is crawl up your body, take your cock in my mouth first and then, when you're on the brink, ride you until the sun rises. Since I don't think you're on board for that, regardless of what you say, your actions say otherwise, then I'm going to another room where I can at least get a couple of releases in."

He stared at her for a long moment. If that wasn't a shift from white to black, he wasn't sure what was. He didn't know how to respond to the sudden, extreme change. He flipped the journal open. Glanced between her and the pages. Closed it. Tossed it on the bed. Then, hopped off and made for the door. "The room's yours." He slammed it shut behind him.

Out in the hall, his grip on the handle tightened. He squeezed shut his eyes and blew out a breath. He pressed his back against the frame before sliding to the floor. Much as she flustered and irritated him, he couldn't leave her alone. Not with the shape shifters—and who knew who else—after her. He thrust his talons through his mane before slamming his fist into the floor. It responded with a satisfying crack. Not nearly as satisfying as the thunk the back of his head made as he sat back against the door.

Would this sloppy, ungraceful misstep dance of theirs ever end?

Chapter Twenty-Five

T ears started down her cheeks again. Good Demeter, she was so over crying. If it wasn't her past digging into her heart, then it was her present. With a loud thud, she put the blue canister on the counter and headed to the tub. Checking the heat of the water, she paused—when had her body lit up? Fuck. This damn glow on top of everything else. She thrust the plug into the drain and stood there as it filled.

Part of her wanted to slam her fist through something. It wouldn't make her feel better, but at least she wouldn't feel like her body was a freaking inferno. They weren't getting half the things they needed to do done. Nevermind the one thing she hadn't told Marius or Cyon about. Or Seru. She didn't trust Aurelia and Mac enough to have told them to deal with it while they were on Candescent Isle. Maybe Mac, but definitely not Aurelia. Not to mention the stupid strings.

A small part of her just wanted to leave them all to their fates. She didn't need the lyre to leave through the jump point. Although she'd never be able to go through another barrier again. But she couldn't do that. She was just frustrated. Thalasia swallowed the lump in the back of her throat.

"Rough time of it?" Cyon lingered in the doorway. "Be careful with that. I won't likely be able to get you more. Once we go, it'll be some time before we return to the isle. The King has a wedding to plan."

Thalasia half looked over her shoulder. When had the door opened? When had Cyon even come into the suite? The bath-room? And Seru had even let her by. Crikey, she should've heard all of that. See. Distraction. Her body was a distraction. Dragging a hand across her face, she sat on the closed toilet seat as the bathtub continued to fill. "Your directions were shit."

Marius was getting married again, huh? Well, that might've explained Seru's mood when she arrived back at the inn earlier. With a heavy sigh, Thalasia wiped the salty tears that streamed down her face. "What exactly is it?"

"Yes, well... Your 'alligator' was blasting his lightning bolts dangerously close to my husband." Cyon leaned against the opening, crossing her arms. She gave a huff, her mouth contorting. "It's sea salt. The harshest kind from the depths of the sea." She squinted. "Why give him the satisfaction?" She pointed to her own eyes with a pointed talon, painted a pearly iridescent shade of white. Her hair fell over one shoulder. "Are you usually this..." she cleared her throat, "Emotional?"

Sea salt? That explained... well, nothing. She didn't know enough about sea creatures to understand the purpose of the salt. From her education, it was supposed to be great at cleansing, but that couldn't be the only reason for it. Question. Two actually. "No. I'm not usually this emotional. At least I haven't been in a while."

She'd shut down to one emotion after Klaus died. Anger. It was months before she put walls in place, so she no longer felt anything. "I'm not trying to give him any satisfaction. He kind of... my walls have crumbled, and I can't seem to control my emotions. At the moment, I feel like a walking bomb." Thalasia stood and shut the water off. "What's the point of the sea salt? And exactly what am I supposed to do with it?"

"All your training and you never learned how to..." Cyon motioned upwards with her palm, "Shield. Protect yourself from metaphysical attacks?" Her expression dropped away. Her eyes hardened. "You use it to cleanse yourself afterwards. It stings. A lot, but it beats the alternative."

"My parents were killed when I was eleven. We'd only just started that part. Most of my training regarded controlling my power by controlling my emotions." She shook her head ever so slightly. She had only the information from her books to guide her. "Keeping myself together isn't normally this difficult, but between my body feeling like an inferno, my past coming back to haunt me, amongst other things, I feel out of control at the moment." She thought over what the female said about the purpose behind the canister. Yeah. Surely, she didn't need that. Thalasia stood and climbed into the bathtub as she extended her wings, so they were out of the way. "Alternative?"

"It's definitely a skill you must master, preferably before taking a partner. Especially if you still intend to share marks with him," she nodded toward the other room. "Yes," Cyon frowned a little. "The not-too-subtle movement of beasts swimming around inside your belly."

Now that she was sitting in this hot-as-sin water, she gained a little semblance of control over her body. Okay. So, holding back the pheromones had helped little, if at all. But between that one release and the sweat that trickled down her back, she felt semi-normal. At least closer to herself. Cyon had a point about mental protection. Thalasia raised an eyebrow at the female's latter comment. "He said he couldn't get me pregnant."

The kiss by the fountain, where she'd dug her nails into his neck. The two of them had talked about it then. Not that she hadn't spoken about the whole pregnancy with someone before. That was one conversation her mother ensured they had. Ten and her mother thought it would be the best time to have it. Then again, Seru had been the first male she'd even looked at with any kind of desire.

"And you're willing to bet your life on that?" Cyon asked incredulously. "He's a man. What in all the seas does he know... about any of that?"

"His gender aside, since I'd never heard of a saint beast before meeting him, then I can safely presume he knows his limitations better than I do. Nevermind the fact that we aren't having sex anyway, which I *thought* you were originally aware of considering you're the one that pointed out we weren't feeding the mark, to begin with." Not once did she say it didn't matter to her if she did. Yes, she didn't want to pass the life she'd led onto children. But *if* that happened, it wasn't like she didn't believe she and Seru couldn't figure it out. They were both stubborn. Probably part of the issues they were having currently.

Still, it didn't matter. They weren't having sex, anyway. After his reaction to her very blunt admission, gods, that was stupid. What had she been thinking? Oh, right? She wasn't. Her body had been screaming at her, which was why she rolled away from his extremely naked body. But it hadn't been far enough. Physical space. They just needed physical space, and she'd have to take some extremely hot baths. It had to pass at some point. Right?

"Yes, well, I'd assumed you were more determined and underestimated his ability to be devious—yet again," the female sighed, scratching into the door frame with her talon. "You can't hope to captivate his attention while he's so... Inside his own head. Problems are like a blowfish to a porpoise. They're his addiction, his high. So long as he can chew on a problem, he'll use it to avoid what makes him uncomfortable. Right now, that seems to be you... or having sex with you." She glanced over at Thalasia. "He doesn't seem to mind getting you riled up, though. You're so hot and bothered I could practically taste it out in the hall."

Thalasia tapped her chin as she listened and stared at Cyon for a minute. An idea popped into her head. There'd been a couple of things she hadn't shared with Seru. One of which would've taken them across to the other isle after they finished everything here. On the counter, she pointed at the purple purse, its color a stark contrast to the wood. "Can you hand me that bag?"

Then again, based on what Cyon had just told her and what she'd learned about Seru, he could probably pull a problem out of thin air? But she had no intention of letting him rile her up anymore. Clearing her head helped. No hand holding. Lying next to each other. No kisses. No touching his hair. And she sure as hell wouldn't use the link between them. Nope.

Cyon eyed the purple pouch, gathering it in her fist before tossing it Thalasia's way.

She caught it with ease. Although she nearly frowned at the female for throwing it. Then again, she was naked in a bathtub full of hot water. Cyon probably didn't want to get too close to it. Thalasia untied the bag and dug out a rock. It looked like nothing more than a simple piece of gradient stone, but it had a magical quality to it. She held it out to Cyon. "When I was talking to Marius earlier, I didn't tell him about the group of guilers I hid on Candescent Isle. There's about fifty of them, and their food supply will run short by this point. This will lead you to the cave they're hiding in. If you guys can get them, then it's one less thing for Seru to puzzle out."

Cyon looked at her quizzically before cautiously extending her hand. She gingerly took the stone, turning it over in her palm. "And you want me to... bludgeon them to death with this?" she asked. "If you've hidden them, they're the opposite of the guilers My King made a pact with. You think us your best option to retrieve them? They've got every reason not to trust us."

"No, I don't want you to bludgeon them. I want you to retrieve them and get them out safely. Good gods!" Thalasia shook her head. She tied the bag up and set it down on the toilet. What was wrong with this female? Was death all she ever thought about?

"Then you go. You said he has a wedding to plan anyway, right? And if you tell them I sent you, yes. They trust me and know I wouldn't put them in harm's way. All you have to do is get them to Chicane Village. Talk to Mac, Felix, or Maggie." She'd spent two weeks gathering them all in that cave. It had taken a lot of sneaking around to accomplish it, too.

Cyon rewarded her with a sly smirk. "You didn't specify, so I assumed you realized I'm not just Marius's wife. I'm the commander of his armies." Her eyes narrowed. "I may be more sensible, even friendlier than either of them. More of a warrior than my husband... but less of a true sorcerer. Violence is still my go-to with no parameters. My kingdom is at war, in case you'd forgotten." Confusion painted her face. "I'll gather a map, and you may mark this 'Chicane Village' you speak of. The names I can remember. I'll see this favor done for you, but I cannot promise it will be by myself... by a hand I command, if not."

"While I didn't know the commander part, the spear for fighting kind of gave the warrior part away. And the whole isle is at war. They just don't realize it yet." She did. She knew part of what was coming. The one thing that previously bothered her about that vision still bothered her. It was too small of a piece along the bigger whole for her to see. Like nothing in the skyline. Why?

Shaking the thoughts from her head, Thalasia nodded. "I can do that. I know that rock may not seem like much, but once you get it outside, you'll see the line it'll create leading you to the other one I buried in the cave those guilers hide in. Women and children. They don't deserve to get caught up in this. Mostly women and children. There are a few males there, but the same applies to them, too."

"You think they're safer here? On this isle than they are there? Their enemies are invading *this* isle, abandoning their homeland to its fate. Are they not safer behind the enemy's front rather than in its path?"

"Chicane Village has already been attacked. If what I've seen is true, then we'll be able to keep them from invading the isle. If they aren't taken to Chicane Village before the barrier is restored, then they'll be right back where they started. Possibly even suffering more. Chicane is the safest place for them." That she was sure of. Chicane Village wouldn't be attacked again. Not even by small factions of the darker guilers. No. If they were going to come again to the isle, then they'd bide their time for when Aurelia pulled her guards. She knew that would happen. She'd almost bet Aurelia temporarily put them in place based on a suggestion from Seru.

"As you wish," Cyon said, giving the rock one last look before shoving it into the folds of her makeshift garments. "I'll ensure they make it there and be sure to secure them proper protection and supplies for the journey."

"Thank you." It was one less thing she had to worry about. Especially as she'd been on Prisma Isle longer than she expected. They had maybe another day of provisions. She finally got full control of herself. Although part of her scent still lingered, she no longer felt like a bonfire had taken root between her thighs. Thalasia paused for a moment. She still had to figure out how to deal with the collar. "Do you know anyone who might have any information about the saint beasts?"

Cyon nodded, with a sharp downturn of her head. Very militant. The question turned her head back in Thalasia's direction. She shifted uncertainly from one foot and the next.

Thalasia folded her arms across her chest. "How badly do you want me to get him off this isle?" The female made no sense. She talked to her about the fact that they weren't feeding the mark, gave her sea salt to scrub down with for sex they weren't having, but she seemed to have an issue with this one question. Really?

"It isn't that," Cyon sighed. "No need to make idle threats." Cyon crossed the distance between them, crouching down next to her in one fluid, graceful movement. "I think your bath needs a refresh." She directed her eyes from Thalasia's to the faucet.

Right. She could easily take a hint. Which meant it would be highly intriguing information. And possibly dangerous. Yeah, that was gonna be fun. Thalasia reached over and drained the water a bit before stopping the drain and turning the water back on. "Spill."

Cyon glanced down at her feet. Her fangs sank into her lip. Her eyes flicked back to Thalasia's. Before she prompted her further, Cyon leaned in and clutched the edge of the porcelain bucket as she replied. "If you make it to the Clouds, find a yellow dragon that smells heavily of spices and incense. She won't be easy to locate, but she'll likely be under guard by the gilded warriors his queen holds so dear. I don't advise you to let her know why you're asking... and she might require some... Persuading."

"Are we talking, persuading beyond my normal?" She half-remembered how to get there, but she had a map of the isle that would aid her in at least finding the entrance. Gaining entrance... hmm... "Any thoughts on getting in?"

"She's a former priestess. You may not utilize your usual tactics to endear her to aiding you in your search for information." Cyon combed a strand of her wavy ombre hair behind her ear. "The Temple requires strict obedience of a certain kind. They forsake their magic for a chance at divinity. If she's attained it, she's more like you than you might expect. She'll know your tricks—better than you do. She's outlived you by at least a thousand years... probably more."

Thalasia dragged a hand across her face. "Yeah, many people have outlived me." She was so sick and tired of hearing how young she was. "Okay. But I might have something I can offer her from my bag. A lot has been collected over the years." And maybe if she was lucky, something by a dragon-shifter had been left in there or maybe there was something from a warlock, enchantress... there were all kinds of things in there. Most of it she didn't even know what it did. "Provided I can even get in. Aurelia hates me."

"Something... from your bag?" Cyon gave her a heavy dose of side-eye for that one. Her long finger directed at the purple pouch from which the rock had come. "An offering... isn't a bad idea," she conceded, sounding a little less uncertain. "Though, I can't offer you any information on her... tastes. I'm sure the war effort and fear of a true battle, one not weighted in her favor, might give the new Matriarch a... different perspective." Cyon offered a strained smile and a raise of her beautifully arched eyebrows. "Your saint beast has her favor and knows all-too-well how to manipulate it; use him as he does you. What harm could it do?"

Cyon pushed off from the tub, leaning over to the plug. The disappearance of the water—and its proffered cover—signaled an end to their conversation. Cyon slid across the room, lingering in the space in between. Her talon idly tapped the wooden recess she'd carved into the opening. She turned back one last time. "Do take care, Thalasia. Don't die. And enjoy your tiny... puddle." Without waiting for a response, she nodded, as if deciding on something before retreating out to the waiting thunderstorm in the hallway.

Chapter Twenty-Six

S eru leaned against the adjacent wall, eyes on the stairs. "Enjoy your little chat?" he asked, with no small amount of irritation in his tone. Maybe even a hint of malice.

"It was informative." Thalasia tossed a pair of silk pants at him. "Here." Standing to the side, she widened the door a little. "Will you please come back in here?" She gestured to their room. Her gaze left him as something else in the bedroom caught her attention. With the door still wide open, she stepped back into the suite, the silence of the room a stark contrast.

His tongue flicked over his fangs before he bent to retrieve the pants she'd tossed at him. He snatched them up and strode into the room at her behest, the pants bunched up in his fist. "Well?" Seru prompted her with a growl, pulling the door shut behind them.

Completely ignoring him, she tossed a piece of parchment aside, grabbed the Allimos journal that had been left on the bed, and opened it. "No, no, no..." she muttered as she flipped through the journal in chunks before stopping. Slowly, she sank down onto the bed. "He was an Allimos."

Seru offered a snort in response. In that moment, the conflict was undeniable. As attracted as he was to her, holding out any hope that she could give up her role and lifestyle as an Atlis for him was foolish. That was her choice, her calling. So, why did admitting that feel like a dagger to the chest?

Because he'd been stupid enough to allow himself to believe he might persuade her to some alternative? Or because he'd surrendered the responsibility of dealing with Candescent Isle so easily to remain by her side? Knowing that despite all those years of conditioning and training, Aurelia might still do less than what was expected?

He cursed himself for straying from the plan, for indulging in this foolish distraction. This fantasy. He dug his talons into his mane. None of this would have happened if he hadn't followed his idiotic emotions.

"Yeah. That's what I thought." She stood up and started for the door that he was still blocking. "Put on the bottoms. I'm going to the other room to get the food we bought earlier."

Truthfully, her barking orders at him only furthered his frustration. Yes, he required clothes to leave the inn unless he wanted to draw attention. But it still got a rise out of him. Seru swallowed it down, stepping aside to let her pass so he could step into the pants before following. Be a good guardian. See her to safety. Let her have her little missions. Deal with the shifters and whoever else was hunting her. Kill them. Get to Pteryrina and infiltrate the siren library. Return to Lake Lucent. Retrieve the lyre strings... *Then we can backtrack and deal with the rest.*

Hadn't the lyre strings initially been toward the top of their list? Seru gave a heavy sigh as he walked his way into the hall behind her. The list of things-to-do had settled the fire in his belly enough for him to regain his composure. He welcomed the refreshing calm the objectives offered, echoed by the cool breeze still billowing in from the hole he'd torn in the roof. The scent of rain helped plant his feet firmly on the ground and reinforced the calmness.

Thalasia stopped with her hand on the doorknob of the other room. She glanced over her shoulder at him. "Do you even *want* to go with me? Or do you *want* to stay here on Prisma Isle?"

He gave her a blank face. All but the eyes, which he was certain she'd feel boring into her. "I haven't decided... there are too many other variables in the mix to determine which course leads to the desired result." There, that was honest, wasn't it? Tit for tat. She'd made a show of brutal honesty for him. Now, he simply returned the favor and did nothing to give away that it bothered him. "I know where I stand in the power structure of the isle... I don't have a clue where I fit into the scheme in the many realms you visit. But whatever the case, you're intent on leaving. So, my answer shouldn't really matter. You love the job more." Honor and duty. Enough to bind the dragons to their posts. It didn't surprise him that Atlis lorded similar values over all else. Following the rules was easy. It meant never fully claiming the responsibility because you did exactly as was expected. Did what you were told. A life no better than living in the Silver Queen's chains in her icy dungeon. Seru blinked to stave off the sudden chill. His features remained carefully neutral at the memory. He refocused on Thalasia, so expectant as she stood there waiting for his answer.

By now, he should be used to this. He was. But he'd grown tired of it. A tiredness that radiated from his soul to touch every fiber of his being. How he'd survived eight-hundred-years of this shit he didn't know, but he knew he wouldn't stand for much more.

Thalasia frowned. "You're wrong. The job would never come before you." Shaking her head, she opened the door. "I'm just atoning for my sins."

"How's that working out for you?" The words tasted bitter as they left his mouth. He regretted them almost as soon as they left his mouth. His frustration left him in a huff. He didn't want to be like this with her. He really didn't. So, why was it what they kept returning to?

She stopped in the doorway and scrubbed a hand across her face. "Not any better than it is for you." She shook her head, a heavy sigh escaping her lips, as she walked across the room, only to stop again at the pile of shredded clothes. "Where did we go wrong?"

Maybe they needed to re-evaluate the way they were approaching this. "Let's just take it a step at a time. See where the pieces lead us instead of over-focusing on the larger picture we can't quite make out yet. Losing the trees for the forest." At least what they thought was a forest.

Walking over to the table, she collected the food and gripped the back of her neck. "One step at a time. I'm so used to focusing on the bigger picture... but I'll... I'll do my best."

"Eat your food. Rest. Recover. We'll start over in the morning." He sucked back his pride. "If it means that much to you, I'll read that stupid journal while you sleep." If nothing else, maybe it would offer some insight into her lifestyle and the choices she insisted on making. Maybe it would even better define the roles and expectations of an Atlis and her Allimos. Just maybe.

"I'm going to update my journal and map while I snack. Then rest."

"How will a future Allimos feel about someone like me rooting around in the private entries of his predecessors?"

"Isn't that wondering too much about the bigger picture?" There wasn't any sarcasm in her voice. It was a rather serious question. With a shrug of her shoulders, she left the room and headed down the hall back toward their new room.

"Not really... I find most people don't notice you've gone through their things unless you make a show of it, or are clumsy enough to leave traces behind," he said thoughtfully.

He followed her back down the hall. He noted Marius and a shadow he presumed to be Cyon lingering at the bottom of the stairs. Marius wanted to talk. He could tell from the pained expression on the man's face. A plea for apology. An 'I don't like leaving things this way.'

Seru stayed with Thalasia. They could talk once she was asleep. Marius seemed to understand his intent and returned his focus to his companion. He wondered if Cyon had shared her conversation with Thalasia with Marius. Small picture. Direct. "What did she say to you?"

"Yeah, well... it's meant to be shared." She opened the door to their room with a momentary pause of her hand on the knob. "She suggested I learn how to shield myself."

"Then, read it with me," he said, noticing her pause. He took her by the arm. "I'll go first, if that's alright with you." It wasn't really a request. Seru bypassed her to survey the room and the bathroom. "Shield yourself?" That wasn't really a question, either. More a repetition. Curse Cyon and her meddling.

Thalasia stepped into the room all the way and shut the door. "Okay. I can set the map out, and it can update while we do that."

"That will do," Seru mumbled, eyes scanning the rooms while keeping her in his sights, if not in reach.

With a small nod, she set the journal and letter aside. Thalasia collected her purse from the bathroom. Placing it on the nightstand, she untied it and dug out a rolled-up parchment. She went to the desk, and with a swift flick of her wrist, the parchment unrolled with a quiet rustle. Her fingers danced across the map in a set of unique taps.

"Topography your favorite subject?" Seru asked, catching her smile as she tended the map. He watched each gesture, committing them to memory.

Lifting her gaze to him, she tilted her head for a moment. "No. I just saw something I liked." Picking up the letter and journal, she sat down on the bed. "You coming?"

He forced a breath out through his nose. Crossing the distance in a matter of moments, he eased down next to her, still mindful of his distance. He reclined back, propping up on his arms, and closed his eyes. "Go ahead. Read."

Shaking her head, she smirked and readjusted on the bed. It was big enough they could each get semi-comfortable, even with space between them. She reached for the letter first and read it, pausing after several sentences.

"Continue," Seru instructed. Of course, the rescuer had secretly been an Allimos of a former Atlis. And for reasons as yet unknown to them, he'd kept that information from her. Didn't that just smell of trustworthiness? He resisted the exaggerated sigh by blowing out a shallow breath from between his lips. *Let's see what he offered regarding her brand.*

Emotional. A core element of most females he'd encountered. Those in power often mastered and controlled those tendencies. He momentarily wondered how they trained future Atlis to control those emotions at critical junctures, times when emotional responses became undeniable. When they couldn't hide their emotions. In the same thought, false vulnerability offered a nifty trick, an artful manipulation.

"Grand. So, by his prediction, we're to be stuck teasing one another into infinity." Did he say that aloud? He resisted the urge to smack himself for that. Instead, he resettled against the bed, attempting to ease the tension in his muscles. "Why doesn't he wish us to read the siren entries? Read Doru next, followed by the siren entries."

He hoped she didn't tear up at the mention of her father or at Klaus's care for her. Just as he hoped to progress over the endearment of Klaus's promise of rewards beyond measure.

"He knows I'd never choose a siren as my Allimos." The words came out matter-of-fact. Thalasia folded the letter back up and set it aside on the nightstand. She opened the journal and flipped through thousands of pages.

"Somehow that doesn't seem like enough," he pressed. "Doesn't it make you the least bit curious? You may be 'special' but you're still inherently a siren, right? Raised differently than the rest because of your 'special' status. Won't a siren's entries clear up missing information for us—for you—more than anyone else? So, why wouldn't he want us to read those particular entries?"

The tone of his voice carried the same stern force it had when he'd trained and instructed Aurelia, set on driving home a lesson or point. It pointed her in a direction, told her where to search, but without giving away precisely what she was searching for. That would come on its own. Usually. His eyes opened, watchful, waiting to see how she'd continue.

Thalasia shrugged. "Not likely. My breeding differs from that of a siren in several ways. Sirens currently have four reproductive cycles, something that I suspect will change when I break the curse. They don't have pheromones as an Atlis does. Sirens don't require their sexual awakening to be triggered. We have some shared abilities, but not very many. They can use their quills, both males and females, plus water manipulation, increased healing, and the siren song. Other than that, we're completely different." She reached for the bag of food, pulled out the rosenberries, their sweet scent filling the air, and popped one into her mouth. "Aegeus might be the only one that would be useful, since he's the only siren that was here on Prisma Isle."

"Then, read Doru," Seru amended, "followed by Acgcus." Resting atop his arms, and thus, his hands, definitely helped subdue the unconscious desire to touch her. It didn't, however, help with the way his eyes wandered over her as she ate and worked.

Thalasia popped another rosenberry in her mouth, chewed and swallowed it before she read the first entry.

Seru tried to contain the laughter that sprang forth. He commended her effort and resolve to read the entry in its entirety. After biting his lip failed to silence the sound, he chuckled into the back of his hand, a small, forced sound, and crossed his legs to gain better control.

Thalasia raised an eyebrow at him as she popped another rosenberry into her mouth. "What's so funny? I miss something?"

Sitting up, Seru cleared his throat as he did so. He sensed Marius outside the door but ignored him for now. Reaching over Thalasia's shoulder, he pointed to the page. "I thought only you Atlis got visions of the future. The dragon Allimos says our remedy is sex. Who knew?" he marveled, leaning back with a mild chuckle. "You have to admire the humor. Or at least the timing."

"Only every other Atlis gets visions." From the page, Thalasia glanced at him and gave a small shrug, her eyes still holding a hint of confusion. "There might be some irony in it, but I don't really see the humor." She paused for a moment and popped another rosenberry into her mouth. "To be fair though, you only asked to have his entries read after Klaus pointed out what would happen if the window on the sexual awakening closed." Chewing on another rosenberry, she swallowed it. "Are they planning to be out there all night?"

"It's a rough, short timeline," Seru replied, sobering. "If it's true, time is running out. If it's an exaggeration... Well, he neglected to mention the details relating correlation to causation." He glanced toward the door, left slightly ajar. "You mean Marius and Cyon?" Marius at least seemed to have retreated downstairs over the course of their brief conversation.

"The sexual awakening reaches its peak under the birth moon of the Atlis. He's not wrong about the timeframe. Maybe there's more in the next couple of entries." She eyed the door and then looked back to Seru. "Yes. Why don't you go talk to him while I update my journal, and we can come back to this afterward?"

"I'd rather resolve this, make him wait, and talk after," Seru insisted. "If you think the next entries will help solve our problem or provide us with answers, keep reading."

A small flicker of something appeared behind her silver eyes. "Klaus said the first few entries were the ones to read. I may have only spent a month with him, but everything he did was to protect me. I don't imagine this is any different."

"I'm sorry he isn't here to be your Allimos and continue that trend." Their gazes locked onto one another. She trusted Klaus. Trusted him at his word. Felt protective of him, or his memory. He nodded toward the journal. "Read."

"Klaus? My Allimos?" She burst out laughing, the sound filling the air. She doubled over, laughing so hard that she had to grip her side.

"You value him. Clearly, with the lifespan difference in partners, there's been an opportunity for an Allimos to serve more than one Atlis." He paused. "Though that ignores your pattern of ones."

"Like... a... father..." she said between chuckles. "And... he... was... older..."

Seru shrugged. "It's good to know you can still smile."

It took her several moments to collect herself. Her laughter was so unrestrained that tears sprang to her eyes. She wiped at her face. "What would make you think I couldn't?"

He shrugged again. "We seem to have our share of hot and cold. When it works, it works. When it doesn't..."

"Maybe we just haven't found our balance."

"Oh, I feel like I've been teetering on the edge of the cliff-side amid the worst storm in history," Seru mused, resting on his side as he watched her.

Thalasia cocked an eyebrow at him. "Whose storm? Yours or mine?"

"I'm no longer sure," he admitted. "I used to think it belonged to Verie. Now, I don't know." He glanced down at the journal in her hand. "I don't like not knowing. I like having choices stripped from me more than I like not knowing."

"That has never been my intent—for you to feel you didn't have a choice in this. That's why I tried to give this to you before, so you could make an educated decision. For you."

Seru shook his head. "Looking at you... at being your Allimos seriously means choosing my losses as well."

"No choice comes without sacrifices. Even if I stayed... there'd still be something we'd each sacrifice."

"Precisely. My life here isn't exactly desirable. But it's known. And while I'm not afraid of the unknown, there are certain losses I'm reluctant to commit to at this moment. I do care for you, Thalasia. So, do not misunderstand. But we have only known each other for days. To sacrifice a lifetime's worth of work for the promises of a few days is..."

"I never expected us to figure anything out right away. It's why I said nothing about the ritual before. Actually, that's why I kept a lot of things to myself. I didn't want to say anything too soon, but I also didn't want to wait too long. There is no straightforward decision in this. We just have to do what's right for us."

"If I'm understanding him correctly, it doesn't sound like we are deciding," he argued. "The world doesn't need another ice queen."

"No. Just not to let it go too far." Thalasia flipped the page. "Let's just go to the next entry."

Seru settled into silence, allowing her to pick up where she'd left off.

"Gods... Do you expect me to write entries like this? Fully detailed play-by-plays of our intimacy for future generations—that may or may not be our relations?" Seru pressed the pads of his thumb and forefinger into his eyes, massaging them in slow circles.

Thalasia chuckled. "Negative. I really don't want play-by-plays of our intimacy in *any* journal." Turning the page, she eyed the next passage and gestured to it. "Look. This one is way shorter and doesn't look like it details anything more. Shall I read it?" She stifled another bout of laughter. "Besides, he could've been *way* more detailed. With some of the poetry I've read... yeah, this is nothing."

"Is it actually helpful or just more unfiltered sharing?" He sounded doubtful. He cocked an eyebrow at her. "Who writes erotic poetry?"

"Poets lamenting about the female form." Thalasia read over Doru's third entry. "It's actually relationship advice."

"Oh, joy..." Seru uttered sarcastically. "Go on, then."

Thalasia covered her mouth, snickering, and read the next entry.

> *Summer 1204.*
> *I hope I have not oversimplified the relationship of an Atlis and an Allimos. Of all the things I have learned is that it is like any other relationship.*
> *It requires open communication.*
> *Not being afraid to reach out to one another.*
> *To seek advice from one another. Depend on one another.*
> *Protect one another.*
> *These things are ways to show you love each other.*
> *I don't think I can stress enough how much fear can hurt you. Both of you. Do not be afraid to argue. It'll keep you both on your toes. And making up, nothing compares to it.*
> *Just make sure you never stop respecting one another. That and trust are the hardest to earn back once you've lost them. If you do these things through the awakening, the ritual, and beyond, you'll both prosper together.*
> *You both will have to make many decisions. Don't use your head to make them. Use your heart. Decide what is best for you both as a couple and never let that go.*
> *This includes the sexual awakening. Following your hearts will keep you from going wrong. Just remember... pleasure brings you closer together. It doesn't tear you apart.*
> *An Atlis's sexual awakening does just that.*
> *Brings you closer together.*
> *Doru*

"He'd best thank his lucky stars his glorious Atlis granted him the ability to hop realms," Seru offered with a snort. "The man isn't a dragon. He's a fairy."

Thalasia chuckled. She shook her head. "I can't imagine the rest of his entries are like that. Though we could've always read Baro's entries. He was a dragon-shifter, too. Plus, the first Allimos. Or would you prefer to go to Aegeus now?"

"Anything that might be remotely useful and isn't soaked in some poor bastard's heart blood."

"I know little about Baro, but I know Apollonia was a take-no-shit kind of female. As for my great-great grandmother, well, she had no fear. Of anything."

"Fear—in moderation—is healthy. Keeps you alive," Seru replied. "Deciding with your heart is foolhardy. Only idiots let their emotions guide their path. So far, these Allimos have not impressed me. It's a wonder they lived as long as they did."

"Baro is the one who created the journals. Both of them, actually. Still, I believe Klaus is the one who lived the longest. He and his Atlis... I believe they parted ways. She was killed nearly a thousand years before he was."

"Is that unusual? Do you think he wrote about what happened?"

"Very unusual. Every other Atlis and Allimos have been killed at the same time." Thalasia shrugged. "I don't know. His access to the journal didn't die when Kaja was killed. That's how he slipped the letter in. I was severely weak when he rescued me. He took the journal out, likely while I rested. I don't know if he just talked about my recovery or if he mentioned what happened."

"Do you think that's a coincidence, or are they being targeted?" he asked more to himself than to her. "Read on."

"Um, go on with Doru or jump to Aegeus?"

"Switch. Doru signed his death warrant pages ago."

Thalasia smiled with a shake of her head as she flipped through the many entries from the Allimos between Doru and Aegeus. Her eyes widened. "That is a lot of exclamation points."

"Great... a drama king—just what we need!" Seru flopped an arm over his eyes, craning his neck over the edge of the bed.

Another chuckle left her mouth. "He's bitching. Oh, my gods, this is so freaking funny." She giggled again. "You might get a kick out of this. Or not. At least it's short." Without giving him the chance to decline her reading it, she started.

Spring 1708
This woman is crazy! Absolutely insane! Off her rocker!
It's a great idea, Aegeus. Come on, Aegeus, it'll be fine.
I feel like I have sky-burn. Why did I agree to something so asinine, you ask? Because I'm an idiot who fell in love. Granted, I could've said no, but she gave me those eyes. I've never been able to say no to those damn eyes!
I'm weak. So weak.
Adina can talk me into almost anything, even if it's the most ridiculous thing in the entire universe. And now she's laughing at me. She's not the one who has a burn across her wing. I'm going to remember this.
Aegeus

"'Weak. Weak. Idiot.'" Seru paraphrased, a small smile touching the corner of his lips. "Yes, I concur." The smile quickly wilted.

Did she say 'Adina'...? Why did that name sound so... familiar? His brows knit together in contemplation. "Continue."

"Yeah, well, Adina was definitely known for her crazy," Thalasia muttered. She flipped through a few pages and located another passage to read.

"History dictates they failed," Seru mumbled. His thoughts raced with images of the willful female, her swollen belly, the ono-centaur foal, his brother... the gilded dagger with the ruby in its hilt.

A frown crossed her face. "Failed at peace? Maybe they only partially accomplished it."

"Partially? They erected a barrier and split, leaving the inhabitants to find peace or destruction on their own. Which do you think they chose? Do we seem at peace to you?"

"And how much worse would it have been without the barrier? Do you even know what it's like over there? How much they've destroyed that isle?"

He glanced at her out of the corner of his eye. Of course, he did. "You'll defend their efforts regardless of the outcome," Seru replied, hoisting himself up and swinging his legs over the side of the bed. He stood to stretch. "And regardless of the outcome, here you are. Sent to clean up the remnants of their efforts. Or do you argue this is an entirely new problem?"

"You think I'm defending them? Hardly. I hate having to clean up their mess. The position I've been put in. I've been cleaning up other people's messes for years. I was over it a long time ago." Thalasia leaned back against the pillows and scrubbed her face with a heavy sigh. "I'd love to do something for myself for once. Not have to fix someone else's fuck-up."

"Now's your chance," Seru offered with a shrug of his broad shoulders. A sparkle of mischief lit up his eyes. "You've said it before; you don't have to accept these powers or keep pursuing these prophecies. Why not use this as an opportunity to make a different choice? Play by your own rules. Follow your own desires."

"And do what? Go where? Stay here? And then what?"

"Does the prospect of making that choice and all subsequent choices terrify you?"

"Partially. Mostly... it makes me feel alone."

"More alone than jumping from place to place at the behest of your visions? The possibility of finally seeing how everything turns out without having to lift a finger or wondering if you'll ever go back? To be in one place long enough to actually solidly forge those things for yourself. Assuming those are what you choose."

"You know what I thought when I started toward Prisma Isle? Maybe it could be some place I could settle down. A place where I could make a life for myself." Thalasia lifted her eyes to him. "You know what I think now? Maybe I could stay. Then I think about how much Aurelia hates me and if I take you from her, even if I stayed here... she'd just hate me more. Then what kind of life is that?"

"So, that's it then? Even the Atlis fear the Matriarch. Her hatred burns brighter than a thousand suns, and you choose to wither before Her." He shook his head, angling for the door. "Do you ever consider she might not hate you if you were no longer an outsider? If she saw you as someone who was more than a threat. Someone she could learn to respect and work alongside toward a common end? She hates what you stand for. Disrespect of her culture, lack of regard for everything she holds dear. A rogue with no allegiance to anything she's familiar with. An undetermined power with the potential and the will to rise against her. Would you not react similarly if a stranger of that sort infiltrated your home and presumed to know more about the state of affairs and imbalance of your world than you did? Then, telling you she's here for a purpose, she's unaware of the details of... and, oh, let me introduce another land overflowing with death, whose inhabitants wish to kill me and all of you, too." He cringed inwardly at how much he sounded like her at that moment. Yes, they'd spent far too many hours together.

"I didn't mean to cause an issue with the barrier. That was the last thing I expected. I figured it would return to its normal state like all the others I'd gone through had. Having to fix the lyre wasn't on my agenda. None of this was. All I figured I had to do was find out how to break the siren curse, and that was it. Meeting Aurelia... you... none of that was in my plan." She sighed. "Though I feel like I should've known better. There's a war coming... I just didn't know when. Or even how it happened... I couldn't share the details. The first thing we're taught... never tell the truth. It's the only way to protect ourselves. Which has... failed gloriously." She shook her head. "I don't fear her. I worry about her."

"I'm not blaming you. Emphasizing her perspective. You both seem eager to misunderstand one another. Don't get me wrong, I know firsthand exactly how difficult and stubborn she can be once she's set her mind or heart on something." He put up a hand. "But if we don't put a stop to this infighting, Marius's forces combined with the guilers from Candescent—with the potential addition of the merfolk courtesy of his new wife—" The acutely sour flavor to admitting that aloud gave him pause. He shook it off. "They'll overrun the isle. The land will again pay the price, with heavy casualties for both Sea and Sky. There won't be anything left to save."

"That's what I've been trying to tell you. There's already more in motion than just that. The land species banding together. I'm here until the battle is done. Until it's finished." She set the journal aside, swung her legs around and dug out her own journal from her purse. "Aegeus and Adina were here for twelve years. She spoke to you. The sirens, who've been closed off, have two sirens in formal attire in the hybrid village. The knowledge they have of the barrier being down. And the prophecy with the manticore."

As she spoke, she got her journal set up and opened it to a specific page. She set it on the bed and pointed to the image. The combined species of the land clashed with the guilers on the beaches of Prisma Isle, while she worked tirelessly to rebuild the barrier from the shore. Everything was cut off below the horizon. "You want to know what I see when I get a vision? This is what I see. I got this two years ago. The only thing I don't know is what's happening in the sky."

"That's a pretty *massive* blind spot." Seru stepped closer to better inspect the image. His eyes scanned the page, studying it. He meant to discern every detail, even the tiniest ones. Yes, Adina had spoken to him. She foretold to him Thalasia's arrival and what she'd mean to him, that their futures were closely tied. Something he hadn't wanted to hear back then and didn't much wish to hear or own up to now.

He'd spoken to her—and let's not forget her weakling of an Allimos, too. He risked a great deal to help those two. It seemed at least Adina kept her end by safeguarding the onocentaur and the dagger. He sighed. How much longer would he deny ultimately coming together? Until he had extinguished absolutely every other available option—that's when. And they weren't even close to that yet.

"No shit." Thalasia folded her arms across her chest. She stepped to the other side of the nightstand and leaned against the wall. "Every step, every piece of information answers one thing and leads me to more questions. Why did Aegeus and Adina spend twelve years here? Who did they meet with? Why hide the map in the ancient texts in Pteryrina? Why not add it to the purse? Leave it in the hands of the Atlis. Unless there was a purpose for it all. Even

Adina meeting with you... considering her opinion of you wasn't very high, why do it at all? Whose purpose did it serve? Yours? Hers? Both?"

Seru remained silent in the face of her questions. He brushed his fingers over the incomplete picture. Beyond a few faint shadows in the clouds and a potential reflection of scales in the waves, he saw nothing to indicate which way the war would go based on the depiction.

How annoying. If it wasn't one thing, it was another. The incomplete visions, the missing memories... The lack of complete information was more than a little irksome. So far, he'd purposefully avoided intimacy with her—since as both journals seemed to confirm, emotions were critical to that aspect of her powers—and avoided committing to a course in the unlikely event he still triggered a more revealing version of the vision. Frankly, it was wearing on him.

He knew he couldn't share the whole truth with Thalasia, but he had to give her... Something. He let out a low growl, pushing away from the bed and the picture. There was precious little to be learned from that clue.

"I take it you see no more than I have," Thalasia said. It wasn't a question, but a statement. "You've remembered the meeting with her."

"No," Seru announced, eyeing her as she crossed the room and seated herself. Her words hung in the air, and he locked eyes with her, the silence amplifying the moment. How much did she know? How much had she guessed? Either way, it made little difference. "I do... and it's nothing that helps us with our current predicament. She was an arrogant, reckless little harpy, who thought her sight gave her all the answers."

"You're probably right." With a shrug, she got back to her feet and crossed to the desk where she'd left the map. She flicked her wrist, and it rolled back up. "It's been a long day, and if I'm right, finding the book won't be easy since Aegeus and Adina are involved. She may have been arrogant, but she was also good at hiding things."

"Was she?" he asked, only half interested in the answer. The other half didn't really expect an answer. "I need to speak with the two traitors downstairs," he said, returning to rubbing his eyes. "You should get some rest."

"Aegeus was the one who signed the letter Parthenia gave us. Didn't I tell you that?" Thalasia shrugged as she collected the map and returned it to her purse. With a brief nod, she half-glanced at him. "We'll take turns. We both need the rest."

"It is your turn," he reminded, coming to sit on the edge of the bed. "But I will sit with you, if you like."

"That's unnecessary." She picked up the Allimos journal, shoved the letter from Klaus back in there, and leaned across the bed to place it on the nightstand closest to the window. Then she climbed into the bed, hefted her journal onto her lap, and flipped to a blank page.

He watched her for a moment. The controlled distance and lack of desire to be touched had remained intact. She hadn't believed him. Or he'd given her enough of something to reinstate her emotional wall. He should have moved to leave. Instead, he stayed rooted to that spot.

Thalasia placed her hand on the blank page. Her gaze lifted to his. She opened her mouth and snapped it shut. She turned her attention back to the blank page. Magic swirled around her hand, sparking and crackling, as words materialized on the parchment.

"Do you always 'write' that way?" he asked, nodding toward the page.

Lifting her gaze to Seru once again, Thalasia blinked. "Yes. Both journals were created that way. It allows for a simple transition and ensures every word and image is legible. You can even do the same in the Allimos journal until you decline it."

The muscles in his face reflexively tightened, giving her a glimpse of fang. Even if only for a moment. "I much prefer quill and ink, thank you. Magic has its place. And it isn't for translating one's thoughts to a page."

Her lips tugged in a faint smile in amusement. "The journals are also meant to be read by others. If you were keeping a journal just for yourself and intended no one else to read it, then quill and ink are the way to go."

His eyes jerked back to hers. They held there for a moment, observing the mirthful light twinkle in the silver. "Doesn't that defeat the purpose of a journal?" he asked, more than a little perturbed.

"Only if we never intended to learn anything. No one's perfect. It's usually best if we don't make the same mistake twice."

"Journals typically have a more personal quality to them... as I'm sure our earlier read-through showed. Why would anyone feel compelled to share their innermost thoughts and feelings with someone else, especially one they've never—nor will ever—meet?"

Her gaze lowered for a moment. She looked at the entry she'd just inputted and glanced at the Allimos journal. "That's not how it's been in the past. The Allimos journal is usually passed from one to the next. Same with the Atlis journal." She refocused on him. "We learn from those who have come before us. They can teach us about the different realms they've visited, the creatures they've seen... and so on. Keeps us from wandering blind. Sometimes, it even keeps us from making the wrong choices."

"Wrong choices can't be avoided. If you don't make your own mistakes, arguably, you never truly learn from them."

She tilted her head. "Do you think what's coming at us could've been avoided?"

Shadows played behind his eyes like laughter had in hers. "Yes, but that was a very long time ago."

"If different decisions were made," Thalasia said. "Different choices. The question that usually follows is who would've had to have made those decisions differently. What if the path began the same, but the person who came in after altered their choices? The result would change. Mistakes are inevitable. The fact remains, we can learn from those who made mistakes before us just to make all new ones."

"Maybe there is no wrong choice... just different ones." He glanced back toward the door.

"We'll just have to disagree on that one." Thalasia laid her hand on the book once again and paused. "Maybe you're right. Different choices yield different results."

"Exactly." He turned back toward her and approached the bed. He climbed in next to her, plucking the journal from her hands and placing it with the others.

"What are you doing? I wasn't done."

"Making a different choice," he said, looping his arm around her and tucking her into his side. "You can finish that some other time."

She blinked, staring at him without uttering a single word.

"You seem like you're at a loss," Seru told her. "Would you rather I went downstairs?"

"No. I like you here."

"Good," he whispered, kissing the top of her head. "I enjoy being near you, too."

The corners of her lips upturned as her body relaxed a little more. With a contented sigh, she snuggled closer, her hand on his chest, and drifted off to sleep.

Chapter Twenty-Seven

Soft fingers caressed her wings, beneath the feathers, over the scars. A pair of lips pressed a tender kiss to the back of her neck, sending chills down her spine. Thalasia rolled over to her other side and stroked Seru's cheek. Their lips crashed against one another as he unbuttoned the shirt she had on. Trailing kisses along her throat and over her collarbone, he pushed the shirt from her shoulders. His fingers danced across her skin.

"He does not want you," a voice whispered.

Releasing the kiss, Thalasia glanced over her shoulder. But it didn't last long. Whatever she had heard disappeared as Seru pulled her face back toward his, their mouths once again claiming one another. His hand found her breast as his thumb brushed across her nipple. She moaned into the deep kiss.

"You will never be good enough for him," the voice whispered again.

Thalasia broke the kiss off and searched the dimly lit room for the voice. How could he not hear this? See this? His mouth on her breast distracted her once more. Her back arched as she gently dragged her hands across his shoulders.

"He will never claim you as his own," the voice said. "He could not even finish what he had started."

"No! You're wrong!" Thalasia hollered. But the voice wasn't wrong. Seru hadn't finished it. They hadn't fed it. She shoved at the warm body, only to push at air. What the... Where'd he go?

"He disappeared. You were unworthy of him."

"What? No! That's not true." Where was that voice coming from? Why did it sound familiar? Like someone she knew. Thalasia went *to cover her breast and found her clothes in place, as if they'd never gotten removed. What was happening?*

"Of course, it is. There is only one you will ever belong to."

No, it couldn't be. Mistress? She wasn't here. She was in another realm. Far away. Thalasia frowned. Her arms were bound, cuffed tightly to her sides, and her head was held in an unyielding grip. No, this couldn't be happening. Not again. "Seru! Seru!" Thalasia struggled against the binding.

"Do you really think he will save you? He does not even want you."

"Yes, he does! He told me he cares! I know he does!" She believed him. She believed his words. Thalasia strained against the binding around her wrists, ankles, her head. She'd freed herself twice... before the mark... before all the injuries. And she was stronger now. She could do it again. All she had to do was focus. Closing her eyes, Thalasia turned her attention inward. Toward her power. The connection she shared with Seru. Toward her feelings... her feelings... where were they?

"They were just words. How can he love someone so weak? Someone marked by another," Mistress said. "He will never love you. You will always belong to us."

As the mark seared into her skin, the word 'always' echoed in her thoughts, a haunting refrain. Her neck throbbed as the burning sensation lanced down her neck, across her collarbone, and pierced her heart. The bright red combatting the interlinked silver and blue lines within.

"No!" Thalasia cried out as she jerked upright. Her heart hammered in her chest, a frantic drumbeat that echoed in her ears. Ragged breaths escaped her mouth as her lungs tightened painfully. It felt like she couldn't breathe. Her eyes bounced all over the room, flicking from the window to the desk. Where was she? The inn. She was at the inn... in the room... in the bed... with Seru.

"Are you okay?" Seru asked quietly.

Pulling her knees up to her chest, the words evaded her, and she didn't know how to answer. "Just a bad dream..." she muttered, more to herself than to him. If it was just a dream, then why did her neck throb? Thalasia swallowed. She hated to ask him, but she had to know. It wasn't in a place she could see without getting up to look in the mirror. It worried her. "The mark... my mark... can you..." she requested softly, unable to finish the question.

"Sure," he replied, sweeping her sweat-drenched hair aside from her neck. A few blue strands clung to her skin. "What am I looking for?"

"I don't know," she whispered. Thalasia swallowed. "My neck is just..." It felt like it was on fire. But that was ridiculous.

"It's a little red..." He brushed a finger over the site. "Does it hurt?"

She nodded. How was that possible? It was just a dream. That female had never got into her head. Even when she was at her weakest.

Seru reached over to the nightstand, retrieving a shallow dish filled with cool water. He tore a fresh corner from the sheet with his teeth, doused it in the liquid, and squeezed out the excess before pressing it to her brand. He eased her back against him, cradling her against his chest.

Thalasia remained quiet, gently chewing on her bottom lip and the inside of her cheek. Yes, the mark had irritated, but it just had to be in her own head. That female hadn't broken her in six months. She wasn't as strong back then as she was now. No way she'd found a way in. Not that she believed that. If that were the case, she'd easily fall back asleep. That wasn't happening. "You should rest. I don't think I'm going to fall back asleep soon."

He hummed in her hair. "What would you say to taking your mind off your nightmares instead?"

"Depends. What do you have in mind?" She didn't have the energy to read any more entries in the Allimos journal. Or to discuss the entries, especially since she was still mildly curious about what else Aegeus had written, even more so of what Klaus had written.

"You still owe me from earlier," he ventured, sounding more than a little amused.

She opened her mouth to ask what he was talking about when it hit her. The wager they'd made on their way to Four Muses. Shifting her head, Thalasia's eyebrows knitted together and smirked. "You never actually told me your idea."

"Mmm... What fun would it have been to tell you? It was easier to show you," Seru replied. "I enjoyed destroying that awful outfit and exposing the beauty that resides underneath."

Although she tried, she couldn't help smiling. "So, your idea was to rip apart my clothes?" Why did he have a thing about destroying her clothes? One was her idea, but the other two... all him. "Please don't tell me you want to burn more of my short skirts and dresses."

"You shouldn't have told me there are more," he growled playfully in her ear.

Thalasia chuckled and sat up just a little. "You're not destroying more of my clothes." She could barely contain the giggle. She covered her mouth with her hand, suppressing her laughter at the sight of his comical expression. "You said I *owe* you. What do I owe you?"

"We shall see about that," he challenged. "I might destroy all of them, if we can find a suitable place away from all this—where it's just the two of us." He kissed along the back of her neck, following the path of her spine. "Hmm..." he smiled faintly. "I suppose that depends on what all you feel up to."

Just the two of them. She almost asked if he intended for her to wear them before he did, but the words never left her mouth. His kisses along her neck warmed her just a little. Not that it helped her from thinking about her nightmare. It was a little too close to how it started. But there was no voice. No sound in her head. It had just been a bad dream. One that played on her own insecurities. There was no one else in the room but them. Thalasia shifted her gaze to his and bit her bottom lip. Hesitantly, she reached up and caressed his cheek. "I honestly don't know."

He took hold of her hand, turning to press his lips to her fingers. "Not knowing is reasonable."

"It is?" His response didn't confuse her, but she wanted him to explain a little more. To understand his perspective. Earlier, they'd just been them or so she'd thought. No implications of anything. No fretting over decisions that had to be made.

"It's easy to lose yourself in the dark," he clarified. "Even when you're awake, your mind still wanders to your dreamscape, searching. You can't really know much when your thoughts have you elsewhere. Reality becomes the dream."

She'd lost herself in the dark once before. It lasted for months. Not something she wanted to deal with again. It had happened because she hadn't dealt with her emotions. The memories of what had happened, they'd spoken about them. He was the first person she ever talked to about them at all.

He'd told her earlier he'd stopped with the mark because he didn't want to enslave her. It had stopped her from asking about them more. All they had talked about was that she would allow him, even though she didn't know everything about them. Thalasia bit her bottom lip. "Will you tell me about all the marks? What do they entail?"

His jaw set at the question. A shallow breath escaped him. "You don't give up, do you?"

"I just want to understand them." She sat up and readjusted her position so she was sitting next to him. "You don't have to answer. I just... I want nothing between us."

He narrowed his eyes at her, studying her facial expression and body language. He found only sincerity. "'Nothing between us,'" he repeated, looking around the room to escape her gaze. He picked at the loose threads on the sheet where he'd ripped the corner, allowing silence to flood their senses. "The first set of marks joins the flesh."

For a moment, she didn't expect him to answer. She was glad he did. Thalasia nodded. "Okay."

"The second set links the mind," he continued, closing his eyes and retreating into himself as he spoke. "The third pools magical ability. The fourth set aligns the spirit. The fifth is... something to do with the divine. Becoming one with the universe," he muttered.

She sat there quietly. It made sense that Cyon gave her a look like she was crazy. And even more so why he stopped himself. They each had their own secrets. Things she wasn't ready to tell him, and he probably felt the same. Thalasia bit her bottom lip again and glanced toward the window. "It didn't start as a nightmare. I was... dreaming about us... just... us... then out of nowhere... I heard a voice. Echoing my own... concerns, but it was like you couldn't hear it."

He turned back to her, running his hand up her arm, a firm caress. He listened intently, but didn't speak.

"You just started kissing me again. Then I heard it again. The third time... you just disappeared, and I was bound. I couldn't move my arms, my legs... my head... that's when the pain started... like she was marking me all over again. Reminding me I would forever be hers." A single tear rolled down her cheek. Thalasia wiped at her face as she looked back at Seru. "I know you care about me. Just like I care about you." She swallowed. It was hard to admit everything, but she needed to do it. "It scares me to care about you. I've lost the only people I've ever cared about before. I don't think I'm strong enough to handle losing anyone else."

"You won't lose me," he started. "I know your scent, and I'm far too large for you ever to miss me." He rubbed along her arm, a half-smile appearing briefly before he returned to a somber thoughtfulness.

Sitting up on her knees, she scooted a little closer to him. His slight joke about being unable to lose him brought a small smile to her face. Thalasia reached up, more confidently this time, and caressed his cheek again. "I think I'd just like to be us for the next few days and not worry about what's waiting on the other side. I'll even let you rip a few more dresses." She grinned.

"I'm not sure what that means," he admitted, genuinely perplexed. He pulled her closer. His hands found her hips and the soft fabric that clothed them. "What about these?"

"We do things because we want to. Not for any other reason." She glanced down at the full-length yoga pants and half-chuckled. "You want to rip my pants off?"

"That... or you can take them off. If I shred all your clothes, we'll both be in trouble."

Stroking his cheek, she snickered. "Then maybe it's a good thing I'm a klepto who has a pretty big closet."

"Your bottomless sack has a closet?" he asked, glancing around for the thing.

She threw her head back in laughter. "No. Not litcrally, but it has a lot of clothes."

"Maybe you and Aurelia can trade," he said. "I don't think I've ever seen her wear the same thing twice."

"Only if I don't change clothes for a couple of days." Thalasia grinned. "I believe in not wasting everything I've taken. I think I have four or five more pairs of these. Maybe six more short skirts and seven short dresses. Two or three long ones. Lots of jeans and tank tops. And combat boots. Those are my favorite."

"Too many clothes," Seru confirmed, nuzzling into her neck.

Thalasia ran her fingers through his hair. "Enough clothes."

"Maybe without the short skirts and dresses," he said with a kiss.

"At least I didn't wear lingerie out." Thalasia continued running her fingers through his mane. Something she rather enjoyed. "There are so many clothes that are much worse."

He cocked an eyebrow at her. "Always strive for 'better,' not worse."

"I prefer comfortable." It didn't mean she hadn't been curious. Or that some of them hadn't been useful. "Trust me, women have the strangest clothes. Some... I really don't understand the point."

"That, I can certainly believe."

"Which part?" Thalasia grinned, her fingers gingerly making their way from his mane to his shoulders.

"Women hoarding bizarre clothing for reasons no one can comprehend."

Although she fell into that category, she nodded. "At least I know I'll always have enough clothes to ensure I have something to wear."

"I'm not sure if I should feel comforted or frustrated by that," Seru said, in-taking a whiff of her scent.

"Mmm... what if I told you most of my clothes comprise jeans, tank tops, and boots?" Tingles crawled along the length of her spine, her skin warming beneath his fingers.

"That might be more... acceptable." He smiled into her hair. "You get flushed when I touch you."

"It happens when you bury your face in the crook of my neck, too." Though she was fairly certain he knew that. "Even when you kiss me. And sometimes with just a look."

"I didn't think an Atlis born under a full moon could turn into a sun."

She leaned in close and whispered in his ear. "I also glow."

"Really?" he teased, feigning surprise. "I hadn't noticed!"

"Right," she said, drawing the single word out. "Because that's so hard to miss."

"Nothing about you is difficult to miss."

Thalasia beamed. "Depends on who's looking." While one hand went back to playing with his mane, the other stroked lightly over his shoulder and over his collarbone.

"I think that list is longer than you might imagine."

"Maybe, but you're the first I've really paid attention to."

"Is that right?"

"You don't believe me? Yet, you're the only person I've ever kissed. The only one to have touched me intimately. To have seen me naked..." If any men had ever noticed her looks, she didn't pay them any mind. She used her charm to get information or accomplish tasks. Nothing more. Same with the short dresses he hated so much.

He shook his head. "I prefer not to live in fairytales. When you live as long as I do, you're disillusioned about love at first sight, a one and only, and happily ever after. If they still exist for you, by all means... Enjoy them," he said, kissing her hair.

"I don't believe in fairytales. Nor do I believe in happily ever after. But that doesn't mean I don't believe in love. Or hard work. Any relationship worth having, takes work. And love is definitely worth it."

"And how do you see your perfect love story working out?"

Thalasia raised an eyebrow at him. "What love story is perfect?" She shook her head. Even the relationships she'd watched over the years—none of them were perfect. "If a love story is perfect, then it's going to be boring. I don't want boring. I want love from someone who makes me feel alive."

Seru grew quiet.

"Nothing about my life has been easy, even simple. I never expected that to change. Constantly being hunted, many fights... it takes a toll. Sometimes, you forget how to live amidst all that." She'd never expected to find anyone at all, but if she had, it would be someone who could remind her regularly that she was alive. Someone who reminded her that life was worth living.

"Life is never simple or easy. Just varying levels of challenging."

"I suppose so." She continued stroking the ends of his mane. "Doesn't make me believe in a perfect love story. I don't even think my parents had a perfect love story, but they had perfect moments." Thalasia smiled. Didn't they have a few of them?

"What are you thinking?"

"Our perfect moments." Her smile brightened just a little as she bit her bottom lip. "The first time we hugged. You seemed surprised, but you hugged me back, and then my wings shocked me by coming around you. When we got to the marketplace, you pulled me tighter against you. I don't care for crowds, but I can deal with them. Our kiss at the fountain earlier. The dance we shared in the middle of the room. We could've just gone around in circles, but you lifted me in the air... just out of nowhere."

He leaned into her. Just listening, taking it all in. Watching her facial expressions shift. Her smile brightened. Her eyes lit up. The warmth coming off her intensified as she spoke, fondly recalling each memory. "Those are the moments that remind me I'm alive. That despite everything we see, there is beauty in the universe... something worth fighting for."

"What about before you met me? What moments did you live for?"

Running her fingers through his mane helped her confront the truth. Those moments had been fewer and fewer after she pulled herself back together. "After Klaus died, I wasn't. I was angry. My visions dried up while I was in captivity. For months, I just jumped from realm to realm, causing destruction. I didn't care who got in my way. It was after my twelfth birthday that things changed. I was rescuing a young Seelie girl. It was the way she looked at me, the way she cowered behind the body parts... after that... there would be moments I'd see joy on the faces of those I saved. I needed them more and more until they just became a part of the job."

"So, you allowed the business of saving weaker creatures to be your... salvation? Your way back toward the way things used to be?"

"Yes." Thalasia swallowed. She'd made it clear a few days ago that she wanted to end it all. "When I landed on Candescent Isle...

gods... three weeks ago... the darkness there... it knocked me on my ass. That... that made me realize... it would never be enough."

"You don't go back. You can't. Not after you've seen and experienced the truth. You adapt, you evolve. Or, you die."

Her gaze shifted to his. She placed a soft kiss on his cheek. "Then I guess that means I have to figure out how to adapt or evolve."

"Yes."

"Although I think we've been thoroughly distracted..." She bit her bottom lip with a twinkle in her eye.

"Have we?"

"Mmm, I don't know. I think I'm feeling less distracted by the second." She continued running her fingers through his mane, letting her other hand caress over his shoulder and along his arm.

"You seem to find adequate distraction in stroking my mane and hide." He observed her.

"I rather enjoy it. It's both calming and warming at the same time." Almost as warm as his hands on her hips. Or his sniffing her neck. A shiver traveled the length of her spine.

"Only when I'm like this."

Thalasia raised an eyebrow. "What are you talking about?"

"Like your talons, this form is just a magical illusion. I can't promise you calm or offer you any warmth when I'm... in my true form."

That's what she thought he was talking about, but she wanted to confirm. "The calm comes no matter what form you're in. It's still you. As for the warmth... that's my own body heat. It's generated just from being close to you. Again, it doesn't matter what form you're in. Either way, all I see is you."

"Yes, right until I decide to eat you," he retorted.

"Why do you automatically assume that's what would happen?"

He gave her a short bark of a laugh and a roll of his eyes. "I devour magic. Even if I spared you the feast of unicorns, you saw how my beast responded to yours during the ritual. You saw what happened when Marius offered me his blood... Your magic is growing, and the ritual you must perform will only strengthen your magic exponentially. Our bond has moved up the time between my feedings and agitated that delicate balance of control—for both of us. I use the mark to pull calm from you. You become agitated. Forcing calm on the other isn't nearly as effective... I tried while you were sleeping. It didn't help. The decision to avoid feeding the marks is causing them to fade. We feed the marks... That has its own... drawbacks. Where do you actually see this all working out, okay?"

She listened to everything before she bothered responding. "What drawbacks?"

He rubbed his temples. "Feeding the marks might strengthen the marks, close them, and seal the deal."

"Something you're not sure you want."

"Something I'm not sure either of us *should* want."

"Why? Because of our age difference? The difference between our species? Because together when we're both pissed, we're volatile? Or is it something else?"

"It's a lot of things," Seru grumbled. Frowning, his hand swept over his face as he untangled himself from her. "No more questions," he said, his exit from the room quick but deliberate.

She almost let him go. It took her but a second to jump to her feet and follow him out of the room. "There are several explanations for half of what you said. I won't apologize for asking questions because I'm trying to understand your perspective. Because you flip-flop so much, I don't know which way is up and which way is down with you. You complain to Aurelia about how you thought things would change, but you don't seem to want them to. You fight any feelings you have for me because we shouldn't feel something for one another, but good gods, you explain why. Yet you want me to stay, but you don't want me to stay."

Thalasia shook her head. "I'm sorry that my arrival has deterred your plans and impacted everything you've spent your life working for. Exactly how far has that gotten you? In a position where you complain about the court? Constantly trying to feed? Aurelia playing with the collar you desperately want off? You want to know how I could see this working out... a lot of different ways. There are thousands of realms out there that could offer possibilities. But you're too busy pushing me away... especially any time my feelings show themselves. You seem to think that everything that has happened in the last day is because of this bond you created between us instead of considering there's something else going on. Don't worry, Seru, I won't ask you any more questions." She spun around, walked back into the room, and slammed the door shut. She stormed over to the bed, crawled back under the covers, and let the tears fall. No more questions. No more pulling on the bond. Nothing. She was done. Done trying to reach out. Trying to offer him possibilities. Done... with him.

Chapter Twenty-Eight

Milla had led them away from the Seelie kingdom. They'd been walking through the forest, along the river. Making their way through the maze of Verdant Grove, climbing over large roots among the varying hues of the leaves. This was a sure sign that fall was just around the corner. Her steps slowed; the soles of her sandals were quiet as they approached the entrance to the dryad territory. "When we come to The Three Sisters, you must agree with everything I say. Is that understood?"

Raising an eyebrow, Parthenia glanced at Gavin. That seemed like a strange request, but the dryads obviously trusted the female and had informed Parthenia and Gavin of the Seelie Elder. "Yes, of course."

Gavin nodded slowly. "Of course."

"Good." She paused mid-turn. "One last thing. Keep your mind clear at all times while you are in their presence. Ivora can read minds."

"So, we should focus on something in our minds, then?" Parthenia asked.

"As long as it is not something you wish her to know."

Her mate had done that because of Markham. It wasn't an ability she'd known anyone to have, but she could certainly focus an image in her mind. "I'm certain we can do that."

"Can she still do so with those who can shield their minds?" Gavin asked.

"I cannot say. I would think not, though I recommend precaution, just in case."

"Duly noted." Parthenia gave Gavin's hand a squeeze. Although he was adept at shielding his mind, they were in completely uncharted territory. And she had no clue how to shield her mind, so it was definitely best to find an image she could focus on. Maybe the springs. They held little value, and she had powerful memories there.

Gavin brought Parthenia's hand to his and kissed the back of it. "I can certainly manage that as well."

"Excellent. We will reach their border momentarily and then make our descent." She started walking again. They had two rivers that ran through Verdant Grove. One dipped below the treeline, over a small waterfall, through a set of jagged rocks and became a minor stream. This was the way they traveled as they took an unmarked path behind the rocks and continued their trek past trees with spiral markings. In this part of the forest, the trees were less dense. As the sun streamed through the leaves, the surrounding air sparkled, producing a vivid display of colors.

Her eyes widened ever so slightly as she followed Milla. She'd seen nothing like this...it wasn't just the short waterfall, but the height of the trees. The trees grew so tall their tops were lost in the clouds, making it hard to tell where the forest ended and the sky started. Before she could fully appreciate the scene, the sun cast a prismatic light. "This is absolutely stunning."

It took Gavin a minute to answer her as he stared around at everything. "It really is."

Beaming, Parthenia looked back at Gavin. Would the new place they'd be living in look like this? If not, what differences would there be? She didn't know anything on Prisma Isle like this existed. Would the rest of the places they had to go to in Verdant Grove be like this? Or would they all look different? Fitting to each individual species. "Does everything look like this?"

"Only within the dryad boundaries. The swirls in the trees are a design of their own making. They also purposely choose to put more space between the trees."

Her mate smiled down at her as his thumb stroked the back of her hand. His tail raised up to caress the tips of her wings. Gavin looked back over at Milla. "What is the purpose of that?"

"Nearly every tree is linked to a dryad. The swirls represent the lifespan of that dryad. The longer the tree and dryad have been alive, the more swirls that are present. Dryads will often return to their trees, so it is necessary for there to be more space between them."

Parthenia looked over the swirls of the trees as they passed. Most of them had lots of swirls. "How long do dryads live?"

"That depends on their tree. Like us, they can live for hundreds of *solaris*."

"Wow... so they are connected in every way? If something happens to the tree?" Gavin asked.

"Then something happens to the dryad," Milla finished for him.

"So, if the trees were burned? Then the dryad linked to that tree would be hurt?" Or was she thinking too simply?

"Technically yes; however, there are precautions set in place to prevent things like that from happening. You have only been allowed to pass into the dryad boundaries because you are with me. Otherwise, they would have stopped you as you reached the border."

"That makes sense. Of course, you would want to protect not only the territory, but the individual trees as well. Damage to one means damage to a person."

"Yes. It is my job to ensure that they are protected."

There had to be a lot of safeguards in place to keep the dryads safe then, especially if harm could come so easily. It didn't seem as any harm had recently come to this part of the forest. At least it looked intact. Not that it truly meant all the dryads were safe. "So, you're responsible for the soldiers over all the fairies, then?"

"We prefer the term fae, and yes."

"My apologies." That was something she needed to remember in the future.

"That must be such a tremendous responsibility. Do you at least enjoy your position, though?"

Milla didn't look their way as she continued to lead them forward. "I have been training for it my whole life; however, that does not detract from my enjoyment of it. While it elevates me to a higher status, I get to meet many new people, watch the stars, and communicate with the animals as I see fit."

"Sounds like you handle everything well." She didn't think she could do that. Then again, she still wasn't certain how to handle the ambassador position her people had given her. Some days, she wasn't even sure how she'd gotten it.

Gavin wrapped an arm around Parthenia and pressed a kiss to the top of her head. "It sounds like quite an exciting existence, though. I have not met very many new people over the course of my life." He chuckled slightly. "Probably why I put my tail in my mouth more often than I would like to admit."

With a slight turn of her head, Milla offered a small, tentative smile. "My sister would say you have met the most important person in your life and that is enough."

While she disagreed with her mate about him putting his tail in his mouth too much, she could absolutely agree with Milla's words. They had both met the most important person. "If you don't mind my asking, do you have a mate?"

"I do not."

"It is certainly more than enough." Gavin beamed at Parthenia. He contented himself, stroking her arm as they walked, taking in more of the scenery.

"I'm certain you will find one. When I was a child, my father used to tell me we find love when we're least expecting it." Parthenia's face lit up.

Milla entered the small clearing, the first to step through the tree-line, and was greeted by three thrones in a semicircle, each crafted from a tree trunk and set amongst fragrant roses. A different female sat upon each throne, their individual styles and personalities on full display. She had previously described The Three Sisters and given their names to Parthenia.

To the left was Ivora, her sky-blue hair tucked neatly behind her pointed ears. A warm grin spread across her face as she brushed down the sheer gold dress she wore. It sparkled against her ash-blue skin and the crown of white flowers atop her head.

In the middle seat sat Eira, her skin somewhat dark brown and appearing slightly brittle. Her eyes, the color of fiery amber, shifted and swirled like the leaves of autumn. Her hands, blackened and marked with jagged designs, stood out against the glorious sun-light. The leaves adorning her bark boasted varying hues of red, orange, and yellow, flaunting the barest hints of browning decay at their edges.

To the right sat Abella. Like Eria, she looked a lot like a cross between a tree and a person. Her long, light-brown hair was braided back, away from her pointed ears. She wore an ivory-colored dress that stood out against her tan skin and clearly revealed her green veins. Her bright-green eyes assessed Milla, Parthenia, and Gavin equally.

"Welcome, Prime Warrior," Ivora said. "I see you have brought company."

Milla waited until they both joined her before she spoke. She offered each female a small bow of her head. "Yes, my ladies. I present to you Parthenia, ambassador to the sirens of Pteryrina, and her mate, Gavin. They come to discuss business."

Parthenia bowed her head when introduced, but did little else. Something told her it was best she remained quiet until the three females in front of her gave her the okay they would speak with her. Neither she nor Gavin had spoken with the Elder of Migas. And they'd kind of left her sister to technically speak with the Elder of Chicane Village. Deep breath. Demeter, she prayed these three females gave her a chance.

Gavin bowed his head to each of the sisters, then kept it lowered.

"Have you spoken with Aragar first? Is he aware of their presence?" Ivora asked.

"Yes. He declined to meet with them, but opted to allow them to meet with others."

"What say you, sisters? Shall we hear them out? Or send them on their way?"

"I, for one, wish to hear the ambassador—" Eira stated, "and her *mate* speak their truth."

Gavin gave Parthenia's hand another encouraging squeeze.

"I concur with Eira," Abella declared.

"Very well," Ivora uttered.

Parthenia lifted her gaze to the dryad council. "I am here on behalf of *my* people to seek a peace treaty. We've recognized that the time has passed for us to open our doors and work with other species on the isle."

"To what end?" Eira asked.

Crikey. She was horrible at this. Why had they sent her again? Cipriana was next in line. She should handle it. A quick glance at her mate reminded her what all of this was for. "There is much that we have access to that we believe some species do not and that they may have access to that we don't. I know that seems like quite a simple answer; however, it is true. We have spent centuries accumulating information regarding the isle itself, and what we've been able to of the species that inhabit Prisma Isle. In the last few *solaris*, we've discovered that much of the isle is failing. My mate and I, along with another ambassador, my sister, who has gone on with... her mate..." Parthenia stifled a smirk. "...to speak with other species for the same purpose. Along the way, we've found that many issues are arising on the isle, such as crops that won't grow and difficulties with pregnancies. We believe the way to resolve these problems is by coming together as we once did."

"What are the sirens prepared to offer for our aid?" Abella asked.

"Knowledge, access to potions to begin with. We could even offer access to our warriors. I know Milla here handles the protection of your territory, but we have a significant advantage with our extensive eyesight and ability of flight." She didn't know where the idea had come from, but it made sense.

"For someone entrusted with such a critical mission, you seem rather... under-prepared and inexperienced," Eira spoke plainly. "You bring with you another, yet he seems content to allow only a siren's offer. What of his kind? Do they not agree to this pact of yours? What is to say we don't already possess that which you propose to offer? Or can't forge a more powerful alliance with another species? One who might find themselves less fond of you and your kin."

"My sister has handled negotiations that have been successful. She has established a line with Santos, the Elder of Migas Village, and Mac, the current Elder of Chicane Village. As for my mate's kin, while there might be individuals in his village who would be alright with other species, his elder has outlawed it. He can confirm that if you require." She squeezed Gavin's hand. "So, then you're aware of the barrier? And the dark guilers that have made their way onto Prisma Isle?"

"How did you learn of this?" Ivora asked.

"My sister, Mac, my mate, and I fought against a group of four of them last night."

Gavin gave Parthenia's hand another squeeze. Keeping his head lowered, he raised his eyes and spoke to the female who'd referenced him. "My mate is correct. The peace treaty has not, and unfortunately cannot, be brought before the shape shifter king. He would not be receptive in any manner. Besides that, I no longer reside in that village. There are many of my species who would wish for such a thing, but it is unattainable and not something I could offer to anyone. Not that I would have nothing to offer... I just cannot offer peace or aid from my species."

He paused a moment and gave Parthenia's hand another squeeze. "While my mate may seem under-prepared and inexperienced to you... her Elder entrusted her and her sister with this mission because they had faith in the both of them to see it through. As do I. While the words may not flow as smoothly to your ears as you might like, everything she spoke is the truth. Whether you believe you already possess what is offered, or even if you forged a more powerful alliance with another species... the fact of the matter remains that the isle is failing. Maybe slowly, bit by bit, but it is occurring. If the isle fails completely, what will remain of the place that all the species, not just our own, call home? The two of us are far from the only ones that believe that the only way to fix it, the only way for every species to truly thrive once more, is for everyone to come together in order to make that happen."

Eira inclined her head towards her sisters. Her eyes focused on Gavin. "What *do* you propose to offer, Gavin the Wanderer?"

"Not as much as I wish I could offer to anyone. But I could offer knowledge, both of my species, and their current leader. Though I cannot say if any of what I could tell you is knowledge you already possess, I know others have been unaware."

"Then if you have nothing to offer, as it sounds between both of you, why exactly would we consider a peace treaty?" Ivora stated.

"Perhaps there is something you haven't considered. The three of you seem quite confident I've given you everything that my species could offer." Parthenia nodded. Her mate had stood by her side and given what little he could. If he could be that confident, maybe she could find her own. "It has been our job to protect the information we've gathered over the *solaris*. The gods and goddesses entrusted us with this duty. It isn't something I would give out lightly. Maybe instead of questioning what we offer, you could provide the same. My intention is to give my people a chance at a better future. Can you say the same thing? Or do you intend to remain hiding here behind your people for the next several hundred *solaris*?"

"You make quite a valid point, young siren," Abella said. "There is much we can offer one another, though it would certainly require trust on both ends. Allow us to discuss this for a moment."

Silence stretched between them as it appeared the three females mentally conversed with one another. Then Ivora clasped her hands together. "My sisters and I agree that there is little you can offer us. We have heard your request, and we deny it."

"Thank you for your time." Parthenia bowed her head to the three of them.

Gavin bowed his head once more to the three.

"I will escort them out, my ladies." Milla bowed her head and slowly turned Parthenia and Gavin back through the treeline they'd come out before.

She completely agreed with Gavin, but there were things she refused to share with them. Not without knowing they were truly willing to hear them out. Even as they left, she kept the vision of the springs in her head. She refused to say anything as they followed

Milla. Parthenia squeezed Gavin's hand, her emotions swirling as they headed through the trees.

Gavin stroked the tips of her wings with his tail. He said nothing further either, as Milla led them out.

Once they were back in the unclaimed portion of Verdant Grove, Milla sighed heavily. "That did not quite go as I expected. Though perhaps I should not have been surprised."

"You thought they would've been more receptive?" She'd hoped they would've been more receptive, but there were just certain things she couldn't reveal. Like the healing power of the Reflection Pools, even if they were slowly dying, somehow, they would revive them. No way she dared to mention a powerful relic like that. Or the Poppy Fields.

Milla opened her mouth and snapped it shut. "Yes, I did."

Gavin tucked Parthenia into his side as they walked. "We did the best we could. I hope I did not overstep my bounds in anything I said. I had meant to keep quiet unless they addressed me." He paused for a moment. "Things might change and get better here and there, but nothing is going to, not unless everyone can come together. I do not see how that is going to happen. I do not believe Markham would ever seek to align himself with anyone, and now that Aragar and the dryads have refused as well..." He paused again. "Who knows for sure what the future will bring for the isle, but people rarely forget who extended a hand, so to speak."

"You're certainly right, love. People don't forget." Some traditions of her people had ceased over the years, but with all the texts they had in their library, sirens never forgot. Parthenia leaned against Gavin as they walked. "I don't think you overstepped at all." She hadn't imagined they would question him about what contributions shape shifters would make. She was the ambassador, the one seeking the peace treaty. Not him. If nothing else, it gave her a chance to be better prepared the next time.

"We have a bit of a journey ahead. Dyeera... she is more receptive to outsiders. You may have better luck with her," Milla said.

As Parthenia leaned against Gavin, he stroked her hip. "We will hope for that." He smiled down at her. "We will just have to continue to do the best that we can. I know how important this is to your people."

It mattered a lot to her people. Once she returned to Pteryrina and gave her report, she'd leave for good. It was important she left them in good standing; that they had a fighting chance at a better future. She beamed at Gavin. She couldn't have done this without him. Maybe if she knew more of the female they were going to see, then she could prepare something that would pull the female to their side. "What else can you tell us of the Nymph Queen?"

"Many things. Is there something in particular you wish to know?"

"You said she's welcoming of outsiders. How often does she help them?"

"Often. They usually seek her out for her power to grant... Well, she prefers to refer to them as 'desires,' though it seems to me to be a wish. Either way, she makes deals regularly."

Gavin brushed the back of his knuckles across her cheek. He glanced back over at Milla. "So, you think she will listen better than the dryads, then? That she may agree to the peace treaty? Or is granting wishes the only deal she makes?"

"I believe she will listen better than the dryads. It does not mean she will tell you all she seeks in negotiations for a peace treaty, but she is likely to be... more receptive." Milla paused. "If she offers to grant a wish... that is something she will offer for the two of you. It will have nothing to do with your peace treaty."

Grant a wish? Nothing with the peace treaty? That made little sense. "What if she offered us something we don't want?"

"She is quite apt at reading people. I have never seen her offer something a couple did not desire."

Gazing back down at his mate, he pressed another kiss to the top of her head. "Why would she offer something like that? Something that had nothing to do with the treaty?"

Milla smiled. "Entirely for her own reasons."

"You mean you can't explain it?" She was curious, too. Why would someone just offer something like that?

"It simply means that nothing is free. If she offers to grant you a wish, then there is something she wants in return, and she is not afraid to be vague."

Gavin's brow creased a little in a slight frown. "That sounds strange."

"That simply depends on your perspective. Many might think your ways in Métamorphe are strange. We do not restrict ourselves in such ways. With that said, I do not believe you do, either." Milla offered them both a warm grin. "I do not need to understand Dyeera's purposes to respect her."

It wasn't likely that the woman would offer them anything. They had little of any value, even if she could give them what they wanted the most. Something they were both certain wouldn't happen until after the curse was broken. Still, she was curious. Parthenia chewed on the inside of her cheek. "Do you remember any of the deals she's made?"

"'Strange' is not the word I would use for the ways of my old village." Her mate smiled softly, though it didn't quite meet his eyes. His tail raised again, stroking over the tips of Parthenia's wings. He tilted his head a bit at Parthenia's question.

"I remember a few," Milla said. "One in particular that I recall... a young couple came before her, asking for her aid. No matter how they had tried, they could not produce a child. It was what they desired most. Dyeera agreed to grant their wish for one of their... faculties. She chooses her words carefully. While the couple believed this would be one of their five senses, they didn't consider that she meant it would be one of their powers."

Parthenia blinked. How was that even possible? It had to be something particular to nymphs, or maybe just the nymph Queen. That might make sense. Milla hadn't once mentioned another nymph granting wishes, just the one. But who would think of their powers as part of their faculties? Then again, shape shifters had two forms. She could do more with her voice than just sing. These were all things that were inherent in their species. Things that made them who they were. It made perfect sense. "So... they lost one of their powers and could make a child in exchange."

"Yes. They had their only child five months later."

Gavin's eyes widened. "Did it make them happy?" he asked. "Despite what they lost?"

"After some time, yes. They were quite happy."

She didn't know how to respond to that. They'd given something to gain something. Sacrificed one for the other. She imagined the couple had had a bit of an adjustment without the one power, but if they were happy, then it had been worth it. Her gaze flicked back to her mate. Just like them. Although they'd both suffered punishments and had to endure a lot of time apart, their time together... it made it all worth it. "They probably considered it a small price to pay for what they wanted most."

"I am certain they did."

Her mate's gaze met hers once more. "It sounds like it was very worthwhile then."

"The nymphs live closer to the center of Verdant Grove."

"How long do you think it'll take us to get there?"

"Could take a few *lacunas*."

The smile was still on Gavin's face as he spoke. "At least the scenery is enjoyable. It is quite beautiful here."

"There are many parts of Verdant Grove that are exquisite. Queen Dyeera's kingdom is second only to the Seelie kingdom."

"I'm sure they're all quite stunning." Parthenia beamed at her mate.

He stroked her cheek. "Me, too. The village I come from pales compared to... well... everything I have seen since leaving it. So, it all seems beautiful to me."

Chapter Twenty-Nine

Thalasia knew exactly where she was going as she headed down the stairs and left the inn. She didn't bother taking in any of the remnants of the destruction they were leaving behind. At least this time of morning, it wasn't busy in the marketplace. She liked the quiet as she made her way toward the road that would lead them to the entrance she'd found the night before.

Despite the rest, she was exhausted but focused. It had been some time since she had felt like this, but it was a welcome respite from how she'd been feeling. Tired and confused. If nothing else, the little sleep she had gotten had given her clarity. Seru was a coward. He laughed at the males who had spoken about their feelings because it was easier to mock than face his own. No, with that, he ran. For all his power, he couldn't deal with his emotions. Something she understood all too well.

Continuing on in silence, she thought it best she moved forward as if he wasn't there. He had made all the decisions, including this one. As much as he didn't like others deciding for him, and yet he'd done it for her. Clarity.

It would be a long trip to the entrance, but she could manage it. It helped that she snacked on the purchases from the day before as they walked.

Seru broke their silent march. "Tell me about the 'First Prophecy.'"

Thalasia stopped dead in her tracks. How in Demeter did he find out about that? She'd purposely avoided telling him a single thing—motherfucker, she'd left the Allimos journal out. It was on the floor this morning. Grumbling beneath her breath, she started walking again. The one time she didn't expect him to do something, he did.

Fucking walking contradiction. That's what he was. A self-absorbed asshole. She finally understood why Adina thought the way she did. Still, he could be more than what he'd become. She popped a piece of the bread into her mouth and chewed.

"Or... don't," Seru said. "Yell at me if you want to, but doing this angry and distracted is only going to get you cut up worse than when you snuck out of the inn. Markham's shape shifters will use that against us if we allow them to."

She spun around on her feet. "I didn't sneak out of the inn. I left. Regardless of what *you* think, I don't need a babysitter. Please don't misjudge the wounds. I could've taken him with my eyes closed." But she wouldn't have burned any of her frustrations off. It hadn't lasted nearly long enough to her liking. The only reason he had even thrown her off his back was because his mark had distracted her. "And yelling at you doesn't do a damn bit of good. It's just wasted words." With that, she turned back around and started walking again.

"Yes, just like you almost didn't get mangled at the fight ring when that chimera knocked you into the bleachers." Seru sighed. "We're both stubborn in our own ways, Thalasia. Both are so used to relying on no one but themselves that we take up arms when things aren't going our way instead of coming together. Fighting feels good, burns off pent-up energy, and temporarily beats back the demons, but they'll always come back. You asked what Adina had discussed with me. I elected to keep it from you out of spite. For her, for you, and for these meddlesome visions you both have. I don't enjoy being confined or constrained. Having some woman I met once, whose husband was nothing but an obedient fool... Following her instructions blindly only to be rewarded with promises several hundred years in the future I might have never seen, frustrated me endlessly. It still does."

He thrust his hand through his mane. "Even though you're right here in front of me... Offering me everything you have... I don't know what to do with it, what I should do with it. Part of me regrets sending Aurelia with Mac to investigate Candescent Isle. I don't think she'll have the stomach for it... but she's proved me wrong before. So have you. I won't apologize for my nature... it wouldn't do either of us any good. And I don't expect you to keep trusting me. You'd be foolish to... You want me to... *love* you, when I don't know what that means. Is it enjoying those moments that makes you feel alive when I know, eventually, they'll kill you?"

She stopped walking again with a piece of bread halfway to her mouth. Damn it. Damn him. Thalasia swallowed the lump in the back of her throat. He wanted to know the first prophecy like he wanted to know everything else. It was knowledge, but he wouldn't like the knowledge. It was exactly why she had said nothing about it. Slowly, she turned around to face him.

"I wouldn't expect you to apologize. And you're right, I don't trust you. You've burned that. You don't enjoy being constrained... I saw that when we walked across the bridge, when I asked you about your collar. My visions offered me the ability to understand that tether. As for loving me, you already do. You just can't recognize it. If you hadn't, you wouldn't struggle so much with the consequences. They wouldn't matter. The problem is the back-and-forth hurts me. Especially when *you* decide to pull me close and then push me away. Yes, you. You marked me. You asked me to trust you, and I did. But then you decided not to close the mark. You decided not to feed the mark. You made those decisions, not me. And we've both had to live with those consequences and how good they seem to make everything." Thalasia shook her head.

She might regret this, but the words left her mouth before she could stop them. "The first prophecy says, 'She will be the change, bringing forth the right direction; A new way they will pave, and it all starts with his protection.' Over the last several hundred years, the conclusion was drawn: it was about me."

"You're right. I made half-assed decisions because I second-guessed my judgement. Following through and just doing the unspeakable act, committing to the consequences, no matter how awful, like it should have all fallen on me. I don't deny that." He did his best to subdue the growl in his voice, but failed. "I altered the marks... so, even if I'd closed them, the magic may still have been volatile. More destructive than leaving them incomplete. The original goal had nothing to do with these shit emotions, these feelings." Seru blew out a breath. "I know it may not seem like it, Thalasia... but I am trying to level with you as best I can. I realize it's not enough, and it may just be making things worse. What do *you* interpret that to mean?"

If they were going to hash it out, then they needed to hash it out. Maybe they'd accomplish more than they had all day yesterday. "Everything that's happened... I'm not blameless for this. You keep thinking my agitation was because of your pulling calm from me.

Did it ever occur to you that I was having difficulty dealing with these emotions myself? You think I put on short skirts or dresses just because I wanted to piss you off? I was jealous and angry. Pissing you off made me feel better... even just slightly. Instead of talking to me about it, you just made assumptions."

With a heavy sigh, Thalasia dragged a hand across her face. Her interpretation of the first prophecy. The one that had been ingrained in her since she could understand words. "That I can make changes, but they come about with the right partner; that *we* make them together."

"I think you do it because acting out is your way to escape for a while—however temporary. You want me to notice you—I've already told you I see you—in so many ways. But you seem intent on not believing it. I'm not asking you to take any blame, nor would I... I don't..." He let out an exasperated sigh before starting again. "Talking about this... what do you expect it to change? No matter my actions or words... even what I'm sure others have warned you of... you won't even consider that I may not be the 'right' partner? There are many individuals out there better suited, better equipped to give you those 'alive' moments not just sometimes but every time. Because I know that's what you deserve, and I also know I'm the wrong person to give it to you—and not because I don't want to, I just can't—"

"Because every time I believe you, I even give you a fraction. You do something that says otherwise." She shook her head. Yeah, of course not. According to him, she was a fucking saint. She wasn't perfect, and she really wished he wouldn't act like it. "I think you have more potential than you seem to believe you have. I think you deserve better than the life you have planned for yourself, but until *you* see it... until *you* realize that no matter what or who you push on me, it won't change my heart, then *nothing* will change between us."

That was the bottom line. Thalasia turned in their original direction, but stopped. "You keep talking about *can't* instead of thinking about what you *can* do. If I thought like that, I'd never have figured out half of my abilities. Nor would you have come as far as you have. Think about that." She began walking once more. Their conversation was over as far as she was concerned.

"I'm not like you... I'm not still coming into my powers. I know what the Silver Queen created me to do. Know what I am. My purpose. It's not a matter of potential," he said, lengthening his strides to come up beside her. "I know what I'm capable of. With—and likely without—this damned collar. What I didn't know was the severity of the mark you already possessed. The hold your 'Mistress' has on you... and what it might take to undo her magic."

"Just because you were created for one purpose doesn't mean you can't alter that course. Or have you already accepted *that* as your fate?" Thalasia munched on the day-old bread. Would've been better fresh. She didn't stop walking, even as he mentioned her mark or the power behind it. Maybe she didn't fully understand it, but she knew what everyone had told her, what happened every time she tried to remove it. The last priestess she spoke with refused to even attempt the feat. It was 'old magic' as she described it.

"I'm not arrogant enough to think I can break the cycle completely. It's not a matter of acceptance or denial. Magic created me. You can't just rewrite it after-the-fact without breaking something or splitting and crossing channels. It's highly complex, intricate and sensitive. One wrong move, one misstep and the entire system fails. Writing over marks isn't easy, either. Not even for those naturally inclined towards magic with a lifetime's worth of experience in the art."

"Which is where knowledge of anything regarding your existence, your collar, would come in handy, don't you think? Or should I no longer concern myself with keeping my promise to you?" Whether he left with her, she'd *never* gone back on her word. Sure as shit, she wouldn't start with him.

Thalasia continued to yank pieces from the bread. But what was he talking about with writing over marks? He talked about her speaking in riddles. "Whatever you are going on about with the mark on my neck, spit it out. I spent six months with that monstrosity and her children. I don't want to think about her anymore."

"You are the type to make your word your bond, aren't you?" he huffed. He reached up to massage his neck. He couldn't help the bitter sound he made at her admission. "Your bond to her wasn't willing; her skills lacked."

"Yes, I am." She had nothing without it. Her anger slipped just a little. Yeah, six months probably meant nothing to him, but she fought daily to maintain her control over the mark. For the last several years, she'd succeeded. His constant pointing out of their age difference was irritating as fuck.

Thalasia inhaled and exhaled a deep breath. "That isn't telling me something I don't know. Let's simplify this a little. Like I told you before, she used it to subdue me. I know she used old magic to make the mark. She drugged me beforehand because I'd already nearly escaped her grounds twice. Every attempt to have it removed over the years backfired. I usually ended up injured, and it always took longer to recover than it should've. The last priestess I went to wouldn't even touch it. Hopefully, that clears a few things up."

"I'm not talking about removing it. I'm saying to supersede it."

"Which I've been able to do for years."

"Not permanently."

"I gave up on there being a way some time ago."

"Yeah, well... you don't sound like you've crossed paths with too many stronger than yourself."

"No, but I've sought many thoughts from a variety of species. Most didn't recognize it, not that it stopped them from having the supposed answer." She scoffed.

"The shape shifters recognize it. As do many others on the isle. Markham, your 'Mistress's' male counterpart, is far from the strongest or most knowledgeable magic user here."

"They recognize it because he used something similar to mark them, except theirs is on their shoulder. According to the one Informant I spoke with; some are more willing than others. He wasn't willing. Otherwise, I wouldn't have even discovered Markham had sent them out to hunt me or had an old image of me, likely from Mistress, that he'd shared with his Informants." She paused, recalling some of what the feline had said between pieces of bread. Yanking on it made her feel a little better. "According to the Informant, I'm the first female he's ever seen with the mark."

"I'm sure there's a reason for that."

"Well, if those two are anything alike, which, given what I know, I'd say they are, they're both purists. Females are property, nothing more."

"The dragon believes similarly. Though, the balance is shifted towards females being revered. Women create life. We men just... contribute and serve."

"Obviously, I don't. Women and men contribute in different ways, but that doesn't make one more valuable than the other." She finished the last of the bread and turned to the remainder of the fruit.

"I'm not attempting to dislodge your opinion about the matter."

"I didn't say you were."

"Feeling calmer, focused?" he asked.

"Yeah. Pulling on bread will do that." She smirked.

He gave her the confused, concerned look the comment deserved.

"I'm calmed down. I'm more focused. It doesn't change my being upset with you." No way he believed that. It didn't mean they couldn't have a conversation.

"Be upset. Just don't let it get you killed."

"I won't let it get me killed. I have people to get off the isle, and I wouldn't do them much good dead, now would I?" Gods, she was tired. Tired of talking about this. Of going around in circles with him. Tired of it all.

"No, but emotions make you vulnerable when you otherwise wouldn't be." He ran his fingers over one bead in his mane. "You really need to stop living for other people."

"They can also strengthen you." She finished the last of the fruit, almost wishing she had more. Not that she was eating because she was hungry. It was just a way to occupy her hands. "It's all I have to live for—helping others. If nothing else, what I do matters to them."

"Until they move on and find something or someone else to invest their energy in."

"There's always someone who needs help. That will never change. There is always darkness and light fighting for control." If this was all she had, then it was all she had.

"I'm understanding why you wanted to end it all on the beach," Seru muttered, glancing down at her hands. "Do you need to grab anything before we leave?"

Or find something for herself. A home. A place to stop and settle. To stop moving. She scrunched up the empty bag, untied her purse, and placed it in there. She had no intention of just leaving it. Once her purse was tied up and locked back through one of her belt loops, she shoved her hands in the pockets of her jeans as they continued walking. "No."

He nodded. "Okay."

And they were back in silence. She preferred the original silence. At least she could keep her hands to herself and stop encouraging something he believed he couldn't do. Not that it made her feel better. Nothing made her feel better.

This was going to be their quietest trek yet. It had taken over a couple of hours to make it last night, but she'd walked and flown. Though this time they'd get the rest of their tasks. Thalasia frowned. They'd spent so much time fighting and having the same conversation repeatedly. Not once had they discussed the strings. She sighed. "Where are we supposed to find the strings?"

"For your lyre?" Seru asked.

That really was a silly question. Part of her wanted to respond with sarcasm. She chose the straightforward option. Less likely, another argument would ensue. "Yes, for the lyre. It may be my power that rebuilds the barrier, but I still need the lyre to make it permanent."

"Lake Lucent," Seru said. "It's the same lake that darling boutique is on, the one we visited the first time we passed through. It's rumored to contain an abandoned hoard brimming with riches. Particularly those of a magical gold variety." He sounded as excited as he had the first time she'd asked about seeking the place.

"Even if I agree to make the dive for you, the magic surrounding the lake will strip away my human form."

There was a slight bit of humor behind her eyes. Not that she found it amusing. Not in the least. Things just had to be complicated. "Explains why you weren't thrilled when Aurelia mentioned it."

"That close to the epicenter of trade and commerce for the isle?" he replied. "I risk revealing myself. That can't be undone. You can't charm the entire isle, even with my magic to aid your efforts."

"I understand that. That's definitely not something I want." She dragged a hand across her face. "Maybe if we're lucky, Adina or Aegeus hid some with the book." It was highly probable, given the one chest that they had already found here. "Or I can try to sneak into the armory while we're in Pteryrina... see if I can find anything there."

"You're grasping at straws. Let's just focus on getting into their archives. We'll come back for the strings. If Mac and Aurelia have returned by then, maybe we can convince Aurelia to make the dive. We just have to find something she wants more than the strings between now and then."

"I'm offering possibilities. Atlis have hidden treasures across a plethora of realms. Hmm..." Her words trailed off for a moment. "I know there's none in my bag, but I could always look for something to trade. You said it yourself, I'm a bit of a klepto." A smirk crossed her face.

"Just don't steal from any of the dragons while you're here," Seru groaned. "You don't know the meaning of being hunted."

"I wouldn't dream of it."

"Uh huh..."

She chuckled ever so slightly. "Seriously. Worst I've ever stolen from was an Unseelie."

"Dark fae are pretty unforgiving."

"Yeah, well, it's a good thing he's in another realm." And he shouldn't have pissed her off.

"You shouldn't rely so heavily on anyone remaining in another realm," Seru cautioned. "You might have an extremely rare gift, but you shouldn't underestimate the will of others to replicate it or uncover their own way to accomplish the same feat."

Thalasia opened her mouth to object and snapped it shut. He had a point. There were ways. She didn't imagine Mistress had given up after she escaped. She didn't even know how long that female had been there. Just that she'd been desperate to leave. Damn. Thalasia chewed on the inside of her cheek. There'd be no choice. One day, she'd have to go back. Ensure the female never left.

Seru's eyes shifted to her. "Don't do that."

"Do what?" She raised an eyebrow at him.

"Over-focus on your problems. Especially the ones you can't actively do anything about. Focus."

She frowned. How did he... stupid mark; that's how. "It was just something that hit me. *That* is not over-focusing." No, she couldn't do anything about it now. Now, there were other things at hand.

"You keep fearing her, and you're granting her control of not just your past, but your present and your future."

"I don't fear her. I fear the chaos she would bring with her." She wasn't the little girl she'd been back then. The one who'd lost her parents. The one who was still figuring out her powers and gaining control. "They stole magic to increase their power. All five of them. She was the worst, but her kids... she encouraged it."

"Stole magic?"

"Yes. She tried stealing mine, but it... backfired... it was part of what allowed me to nearly escape the first time. When that didn't work, she tried other ways. Used my visions to find people whose power she could consume. It was never enough."

"Interesting."

"The second time... I don't think I've ever flown so fast." That hadn't stopped them from catching her. She shook the memories away as she caught sight of the spot where she'd incinerated the shape shifter and a few trees beyond. "We're almost to the staircase."

"Put your 'Mistress' and her children back in their box. We can talk more about them later. Right now, I need you here. In the moment. With me. Think you can manage that?" He glanced her way briefly out of the corner of his eye as they stepped into the space. He wrinkled his nose at the stench, scanning the area for activity.

She'd thought she was done talking about them. Back in the box. Yeah. Thalasia nodded her head. There were other things that required her attention. She turned toward the road and eyed the hidden staircase. She pointed out the long willow leaves over the entrance. "There. That's the bottom of the staircase."

"After you," Seru said, turning to ensure he brought up the rear and trusting her to handle the front.

While she didn't expect any shape shifters on the road, she scanned both directions before crossing the dirt path. Pulling the leaves aside, she ascended the stairs.

Seru backed into the passageway, ensuring the willowy curtain remained intact and in place before following her up the steps.

She gently ran her fingers along the stone walls of the passage as she made her way up to the top of the staircase, which no one could see from the bottom. The condition of the walls amazed her. It had at least been in place when Adina and Aegeus lived here. There were no markings of any kind embedded in the stone. Nothing but naturally rough edges. Thalasia glanced over her shoulder once at Seru before focusing her attention on the stone door ahead.

When she got to the top, she paused on the third step from the door. Of all the things Parthenia had told her, she'd forgotten to mention how to open the door. Good thing Adina had told her. "You have the choice to plug your ears."

Seru reached into his shirt and retrieved two pieces of sea sponge, which he swiftly fit into his ears after a bit of grumbling. He gave her a nod once they were in place.

Thalasia cracked a smile. She'd warned him this time. Thankfully, it took little effort. She opened her mouth and belted out the precise notes the door required. The stone door slid open, giving them direct access to the library. She climbed the last few stairs and stepped through the entrance. Her eyes widened a bit as she drank in the sight before her. Row upon row of books. So many aisles.

Seru crested the top of the stair not long after, removing the sponge from his ears. He leaned in close, his breath heating her neck. "Let's find what we need and get out of here."

She balled up her fists to control the shiver down her spine. Shaking it off, Thalasia walked forward and rounded the corner as Parthenia had instructed. Her eyes flicked to the siren labels along each aisle. The path led her to the last row of ancient texts, where the air hung heavy with the scent of aged paper and leather. "The bottom shelf. This is the one we need. Can I leave you here for sixty seconds to go through the books for the map while I hit the family archives?"

"Yes," he crouched down to begin his search. "Sixty seconds. I'll be counting."

She rolled her eyes and turned in the direction they'd come from. Wasting no time, she hit the glassed area where the family archives resided. Before digging out her lock picks, she checked the door. It was surprisingly unlocked. Not something she expected. Worked in her favor. Again, she followed the signs for the row she was looking for. Thalasia crouched down, collected the book she wanted, and paused. *What in Demeter?* Her eyes fell to the title of the book behind it, written in Altese: Seru.

This made little sense. Not only was the title in Altese, but it also had the same type of binding on nearly all the books belonging to the Atlis. Setting her family's tome aside, she picked up the tome with Seru's name. There wasn't time to read it now, but she might scan through some entries. Just enough to understand it. It wouldn't be long before Seru came looking for her.

She opened the book to the first page and scanned through the scribblings. What in the gods? Flipping through the remaining pages as quickly as she could until the very last. They'd been watching him. His entire life. Well, almost. The last entries were from... Adina. Grumbling, she opened her purse and tucked both books inside it.

"Got what you need?" Seru asked, extracting the rolled map and extending it her way.

"Yeah." *And then some*, she thought to herself. Thalasia accepted the map and unfurled it for a moment. She pinched the bridge of her nose as she read over it, rolled it back up, ensured it was tied, and placed it inside her purse. She shut the bag up tight, rose to her feet, and attached it to her belt loop again. "No one ever said anything of value would be easy to obtain." She dropped her hands to her hips. Some days, she really, really hated her family.

"Usually, it isn't. We're used to having to fight for what we want, jump through hoops. We'll be fine."

Thalasia tapped his shoulder with a small smile as she walked by him. "See if you're still saying that after we go through Adina's booby-traps."

"I think we'll wipe the floor with your great-great's booby-traps," Seru shot back.

"Maybe." She shrugged. "I'm sure that despite your visit with her, she didn't expect you to help me. Or really even considered how strong I'd be." Either way, they had no further need to stay in the library. She headed for the same hidden staircase they'd entered through.

"Exactly," he said. "We have our own edge."

"At least we do when we're not trying to piss each other off or kill each other." She smirked. Once they got to the closed door, she knocked on it, and it opened once more for them.

"I don't remember trying to kill you," Seru offered, trailing behind as he scanned the library one last time. "Is the only way to get in to belt out those notes you used earlier?"

Not that he realized it, but he was; slowly, one action at a time. He was breaking her in half, and he couldn't even see it. She shook the thought away. There were people here who needed her. That's what she had to focus on. "Yes. We use musical keys to open a lot of different things." She began descending the staircase.

He glanced back at the door, maybe longer than he should have, before following her down. "You didn't answer me."

"I answered the only question you asked." The notes she belted out were the only way in through that door. As she continued the descent, her hands traced the rough stone walls, and she heard the echo of the door sliding shut.

"It wasn't a question. You said we tried to kill each other. When do you perceive that to be the case?"

Normally, he wouldn't press such a statement. But she'd said it. And it mattered. It mattered a lot. He was right. She should've just said he was killing her. He'd be fine once she was gone. His world would be exactly as it had been before she arrived. Unchanged. Unmoving. "If you have to ask, then maybe that mark is weaker than I give it credit for. Either that or you pay attention to what you want, refusing to see what's right in front of you."

His eyes narrowed at her. "I am not actively trying to kill you," he said clearly. "If I were, you'd never have made it to this isle... and perhaps, you'd be better off for it."

"I wish more and more I hadn't come, but then I think about the lives that wouldn't be saved because the gods know you wouldn't do it. Nor would anyone else on this isle." Not that some wouldn't try, but how many would lose their lives in the process?

"What else do you wish? That you'd never met us? That some other species received you on the beach?"

She wished she had said nothing, but she opened her mouth and the words had rolled out. Thalasia stopped in the middle of the unlit staircase and looked at him. "I wish you could be less indecisive. I wish you could see how much your contradicting actions are slowly killing me. I wish you'd stop trying to push me off onto someone else because you *think* somehow, magically, they will redirect my emotions. I don't give two shits about what other people think about what we have or don't have. The only opinions that matter are yours and mine. No one else."

Seru snatched her up by her tank top and forced her back against the wall. "You want me to take you right here? Now. Seal the marks, sink my teeth into your neck, and call it done. Is that what you want?" he whispered harshly through gritted teeth, glowering at her.

There was no point in trying to escape from his grip. Only a small part of her wanted to. The other part... her eyes brightened. "I want you to decide what you want. I want you to face your emotions. Yes, emotions can be fucked up and scary, but they can be beautiful, too. If you let them."

"Gods..." he replied, raking a hand through his mane before slamming his fist into the wall a little too near her skull. "Do you hear yourself?! Do you think listening to one of my hearts is going to magically make this all better?! My emotions are not my friend! They're not on my side. They'll get me—and you—killed. What about that do you not understand? You see what following my heart has done to Marius, to his kingdom? What happens when I follow my heart and the Sky turns on us?! We don't have an army at our backs. They'll kill me—like they've always wanted. Capture you. You think 'Mistress' is the worst the realms offer... You're wrong."

His emotions shone in his blue gaze, playing in the shadows lurking there. He squeezed his eyes shut, still looming over her, as he visibly swallowed. "What do you need me to do? I choose you. I've kept choosing you all along." His voice broke, the back of his free hand pressed to his mouth more than a little unsteady. Reluctantly, he forced himself to release his grip on her. He took a step back, rising to his full height. The shadows obscured his face, casting it into darkness.

Nothing would make it all magically better, but with some of the information she'd gathered, she felt like they had a shot. More and more, she grew confident, but she had to hear the sincerity. For every moment he'd been sincere, he turned it around with doubt. "There is always someone bigger, someone stronger. That's just a fact of life."

Marius... she didn't have words for that. She knew what Marius was trying to accomplish. She also knew he was trying to let Seru go. Thalasia swallowed. "I just need you to stop waffling. We have three days to formulate a plan. And we may have just—"

The sliding of the door cut off her words. Without a second thought, she grabbed his hand and raced down the stairs. They had only the sound of the door opening to cover the sound of their steps.

Seru stumbled as she dragged him down the first few steps, quickly reclaiming his balance. "Why are we running?" he hissed.

She didn't answer him as they made their way down the rest of the staircase, back across the road, and into the forest. It wasn't until it safely covered them that she turned to watch the hidden entrance. "I saw a siren leave last night," she whispered. "I know her somehow, but I haven't figured out how."

"Is she a friend?" he implored, eyes flirting between her and the entrance.

"Yes, because I had them before I arrived here." She smirked. "The only siren, so to speak, like that, is somewhere on the isle. The last thing we need is to kill unnecessarily."

"Killing one to avoid killing many seems like a more than fair trade," Seru returned. "More so if she's not a friend."

"And until I can remember how I know her..." Her words trailed off as the woman stepped out from the willow leaves. She watched as the siren looked around for only a moment before taking off into the air. "... we don't know which she is."

"Hiding still makes no sense," he growled, getting to his feet.

She faced him. "Fight first, ask questions later doesn't always give us information."

"We have what we came for in your bag," Seru said with a calming sigh. "What more could that siren offer us?"

"You never know. You didn't think Parthenia would be useful. And she was *very* useful."

"Let's just find this hiding place of Adina's and find this stupid book before *I* off *myself* to escape this bullshit," he grumbled, shaking his mane, head in hand.

She closed the distance between them, rested a hand on his chest, and chuckled ever so slightly. "If a few days of riddles has you frustrated, you have seen nothing yet."

He grasped her wrist. Thought better of it. And let go. "I'd much prefer the booby-traps," Seru relinquished.

"Well, getting there should be easy." She stepped back and began the trek through the forest. "We're going to a cave behind Mosina Falls."

"Great," Seru drew out the word.

And he preferred the booby-traps. She chuckled. "Ah… I love my family." Her words dripped with sarcasm. They were her family. She could be annoyed with them. Nevermind the book that she was going to have to read. If only so, it would help them, well, figure out how to break a little magic.

"I don't." The comment was biting.

"I don't blame you," she muttered. And that was without him knowing how much they'd watched him over the years. Wait, how was that possible? Without his knowledge. That seemed impossible. Unless… the bowls? Her mother had told her about them but said they were antiquated. They were no longer used. It would make sense.

"Sure, you do," he replied. "Just not for that."

"Mostly, but not completely. Whether you agree, I don't think I've handled everything as well as I could have." No, she knew she hadn't. There were so many things she could've done differently. A lot, actually.

"Does it really matter? The result is the same."

"It does if we learn from it."

"And what do you think we should learn? Commitment. What else?"

"Better communication. We're pretty much alike in that arena. We don't reveal things until absolutely necessary, and even then, we don't lay everything out." She glanced at him. "I know the two of us haven't told each other everything."

"Do you ever stop to think there are things you're safer not knowing?" he asked.

She considered his question for a moment. "No."

"Why?"

"Aside from the fact that I enjoy knowing things, it allows me to make smarter decisions." There were things she'd wished she'd done before she'd come across the bridge, but it had all spun out of control once she'd been shot with an arrow.

Seru grit his teeth, set his jaw. "What do you want to know?"

That was a good question. Sensing his annoyance, she shook her head. "Not like this." She shoved her hands in the pockets of her jeans.

"For fuck's sake!" Seru threw up his hands before seizing her arm and spinning her around. "If not now, when? You say you want all these things... Demand them. I try to give them to you, and you refuse. No matter what I do, I can't seem to appease you. It's just one argument to the next, one fight to the next."

Wow, didn't those feelings sound familiar? "The annoyance in your tone. I thought I was avoiding another fight by not asking while you're annoyed."

"I'm not *annoyed*," Seru emphasized.

There wouldn't be a good time, but she wanted to know without having to read someone else's account of him. Multiple times over. "How involved were you in the first war?"

"Which war are you considering 'the first'?"

"The one that led to Candescent Isle. Is there one before that?"

"There's always a war before a war into infinity," Seru said. He rolled his tongue over his fangs as he sorted out his thoughts before replying to the question. "The Silver Queen created us to ensure her dominance in the war that followed her breaking from the land. The saint beasts were—and remain—the Clouds' primary offensive."

"But you're the only one left. Why?"

"A key term of the treatise required the destruction of the saint beasts. What purpose could creatures bred for war serve in times of peace? None. They ordered She destroy us. She resisted for a time. They forced Her hand. I destroyed my brothers, consumed their flesh and all evidence of them. She let me live."

"Is that when she put the collar on you, or was it before that?"

"Before."

"Have you always had it?" She tilted her head.

"It wasn't always..." he reached up to touch the metal. "Physical." His hand fell away.

Good gods. He didn't have to say more for her to figure out what kind of binding he could've had before. Thalasia swallowed the lump in the back of her throat. "The uh, the stone that Aurelia left? Do you know where she got it?"

"No."

"With the many... issues over the last day or so, would having it back benefit you?"

"I'd rather not rely on it unless I absolutely have no other choice."

She could understand that. Some of her questions had come up unexpectedly, while others had been brewing through their arguments and discussions. "Thank you."

He didn't reply. Just stood there, waiting.

There wasn't anything more that immediately sprang to her mind. Well, one. She reached up to stroke his cheek. "Can I kiss you?"

Seru stiffened at the unexpected touch, uncertain of how to reply. "If you must."

They had both done this. His reaction. The two of them pushed and pulled in their own ways. For a moment, she just stared at him. They were both trying to take steps toward each other, unsteady. But they were steps. She stood on her tiptoes and brushed a soft kiss across his lips.

He flinched only slightly. Made no move toward kissing her back or pulling away. Frozen.

Dropping back down, she stared at him a moment longer. "I'm sorry."

He blinked at her a few times, like he couldn't comprehend what she was saying. He'd heard her. Finally, after a few moments, his muscles relaxed. His stance softened, his voice coming out a bit strained. "Don't be. I'm not."

They couldn't change the actions they'd both taken. Things they said. The number of times they'd pushed each other's buttons. Maybe he wasn't wrong, but she wasn't, either. A soft smile played on her lips. "Why?"

He cocked an eyebrow at her. A few expressions warred on his face. He cleared his throat. "Because if I hadn't been through the experiences I have and forewent all the horrors, I wouldn't be here today."

Pretty much what she thought he'd say. Her smile brightened a little more. She stood on her tiptoes once again, pressed another tender kiss to his lips, as her wings wrapped around him.

"Why are you smiling?"

"Because I feel like the tides have turned and the stars are aligning in our favor." It was the simplest explanation.

"Is that right?" Seru asked, starting off again.

"Yes," she said as they walked. "I found something that might be of use to us in the archives. Maybe something we can read together." She stifled a slight chuckle. "Not another journal, but recordings."

"What sort of recordings?" Seru ventured, sounding less than excited by the prospect.

"Yeah. Hold on to that feeling." There was no easy way to tell him. Best she just got it all out at once. "It would seem the Atlis have been watching you since your creation. Until Adina left Prisma Isle."

He drew to a halt. "Why?"

"I don't know. I glanced through it briefly. Believe it or not, they actually left opinions out of the few entries I scanned." Though she could gather a few theories, that would mean the Atlis had known for longer than she believed she would fulfill the first prophecy. Her eyebrows knitted together. "Unless they had suspicions, you would help fulfill the first prophecy, even if they didn't know the Atlis."

"They were recording factual information... Data?" he asked, his brow creasing. "Just me? Not my brothers?"

"Yes. It was your name on the front. Of the few passages I skimmed, all were facts. Nothing more." The last entry from what she ascertained had been a meeting Seru had with a few other creatures and Aegeus.

He gave a short, bitter laugh under his breath with a shake of his mane. "We have to keep going."

"I wasn't suggesting we read it now. I was just telling you." It would give them answers. Things they needed to know to break his binding. It was that simple. And it was that complicated. No, she wanted to get these last couple of tasks finished. At least closer to finishing. Then she could focus on everything else.

"Let's just find this booby-trapped hiding place."

"Right." Two steps forward and five steps backward. She sighed as they walked in silence toward their destination.

Chapter Thirty

Mac ran his fingers through his dark hair. They'd made most of their trip in silence. He didn't think it was possible to trek through the forest and into the mountains for hours on end without uttering one word. Somehow, he and Cipriana had done just that. They hadn't spoken once. In fact, the last time they had talked had been the night before... and it had been about Thalasia. And he'd left out information about the female. He glanced at Cipriana. "You're thinking too much again."

"Maybe," she muttered.

While he could ask what she was thinking about, he was fairly certain he knew. Hours had passed since they left Chicane, but before they departed, Cipriana had spoken to Parthenia. Although he hadn't heard what the two females said, he could guess. "Does it have something to do with your conversation with Parthenia?"

Sighing heavily, Cipriana pinched the bridge of her nose and crossed her arms. "Yes." Her gaze flicked to him. "Am I that easy to read?"

"Well, you get this little crease in your forehead when something with substantial weight is on your mind." Maybe he hadn't eaves-dropped on the two of them, but he had watched Cipriana from afar. He hadn't been able to stop himself. There was something about her that just called to him. Just like he'd gotten defensive the night before when Oriel had put his hand on the hilt of his weapon. It bothered him. A lot.

She raised an eyebrow at him and then shook her head. "Whatever." With another sigh, she uncrossed her arms. "This morning, my sister confirmed what I suspected last night. I don't know...

I guess... it just leaves me wondering if I misjudged Thalasia. I mean... it wasn't like I talked to her, so I don't know what kind of person she is, but according to my sister... she seemed willing to help them."

"You're being protective of your people. That means you have to use the information available to you to make a judgment call that serves their best interests." It was how he planned to rule, at least for as long as he remained in the position of Elder. That was something they could reassess after everything was over. After all, he would do what was right for his people. "But I don't imagine that has gotten you all twisted in your head."

"Are you sure you're not telepathic or something?"

"Not an ability of mine. Now... stop dodging and talk." He didn't know how he knew, but something in his gut told him that while he suspected their lack of conversation was in part due to what she learned from Parthenia this morning, it had more to do with something else. The question was... what?

"Okay, fine." Cipriana frowned. "I keep thinking about what Oriel said... about you and me."

Now, didn't that just put a little pep in his step? Mac smirked. The male had incorrectly assumed they were together. Yes, he hoped by the end of their journey together that would in fact be the case; it hadn't happened yet. "Oh, really?"

She rolled her eyes. "You can wipe that smirk off your face. I thought about it only because he had a point about us making a good team."

"So, you haven't thought about me kissing you again?" Because he sure as hell had. Not that he intended to tell her that. He was trying to take heed of what Parthenia and Gavin had recommended to him last night before they went to bed. Talk about something else besides war stories. He had other things that interested him. And Felix had been pretty good about allowing him to explore what he wanted, as long as it didn't take away from his studies.

"I didn't really enjoy it the first time. Why would I think about it?"

He gripped his heart with a snicker. "Must you always be so mean to me?" Oh, yeah. She'd definitely thought about kissing him again. Not that she'd ever admit it. Well, maybe not right now. By the end of the night... she'd be begging him to give her another smooch.

"Is it really mean, though, if it's true?" Cipriana snorted. "After all, my mother raised me to be honest."

"But do you think it's always right to say exactly what's on your mind?" He grinned. Honesty was a good policy, but sometimes a little white lie never hurt. Plus, there was always a way to say something without being mean about it. Well, unless they *really* deserved it.

"That isn't what I said. I just said I was raised to be honest."

Okay. She wanted to play it like that, huh? Two could play that game. And he bet he'd play it ten times better. "So, if Parthenia came to you with a new hairdo asking for your opinion and you thought it looked ugly, you'd tell her?"

Cipriana frowned. "Well, no. I'd tell her... it was alright, but maybe it could look better."

"So, you'd lie to her?"

"No... I..." She groaned. "That isn't what I meant, and you know it!"

Oh yes, it was; she just didn't want to admit it. Honesty was great. And yeah, he was honestly sarcastic ninety percent of the time, but sometimes you had to know when to fabricate or stretch the truth and when to be completely truthful. He certainly enjoyed teasing her about her so-called honesty. While he could absolutely let it go with what he'd accomplished, he had one more point to make. It hadn't slipped past his attention that Cipriana wasn't all that thrilled by Parthenia's choice of mate. "Okay, okay. So... when Parthenia introduced you to her shape shifter mate, you congratulated her and wished them nothing but happiness?"

Her eyes narrowed as another frown settled on her face. "No," she muttered.

Mac stifled a chuckle. He didn't know how she reacted, but based on that look, he'd bet anything it wasn't kindly. "Oh? Care to share what you said? Or do I have to guess?"

Grumbling under her breath, Cipriana folded her arms across her chest and glowered at him. It didn't look as though she intended to answer.

"Alright. I can take a couple of guesses. Hmm... let me think." He tapped his chin as he considered all the options. Her lack of response solidified his stance that it wasn't kind, or even polite. Plus, the two had stated the night before that they'd hidden their relationship from both sides for quite some time. And Parthenia *had* admitted to sneaking Gavin into Pteryrina multiple times. Something that seemed to shock Cipriana.

She threw her hands up in the air. "Fine! I interrogated him. To be fair, I would've done that if any of my sisters had brought home... a mate."

This time, he couldn't hold back a chuckle. He hadn't even guessed, and she blurted out the truth. Damn, he was good. None of which had been the point. It had simply been to push her into talking about something that wasn't weighing her down. "Any of your sisters, huh? How many do you have?"

"Including Parthenia... six in total."

His eyes widened. The guilers never had over three children in total. For one couple to have *that* many... could sirens even have that many? Well, she hadn't said it was one pregnancy. Maybe they hadn't all been born at the same time. That seemed plausible. "Wow. That's, uh... a lot. I imagine your house is... always noisy."

"Sometimes... but we don't all share the same mother. Like I said last night, males have been... procreating with more than one female for centuries. We... haven't really had... true mates. Not in a long time."

No true mates. It followed exactly what Felix had taught him over the years. That procreation had become more important... more valued than a valid emotional connection. "I think that's why my parents left. Well... one reason, anyway."

"You mean because you were the last male siren born? Or because of their relationship?"

"Little of both. From what I remember of them... they truly loved one another. I think they hoped I might find that one day, but it wasn't something they believed would happen if we stayed in Pteryrina." His parents hadn't ever told him that he'd been born in Pteryrina. That information had come from Felix... several years after his parents' death. He supposed there had been a purpose behind that. This allowed him to cherish the five years of happy memories he shared with them before someone killed them.

Cipriana nodded. "With the law changed... I'm certain it's more possible now than it was back then. I mean... look at Parthenia. She found her mate, and I'm pretty sure she wasn't even trying."

"Have they not told you how they met?" He raised an eyebrow. It was curious, given how close she seemed to her sister. Then again, she had been shocked earlier when they'd mentioned their desire to leave the isle in its entirety. Given what little he'd learned from them at dinner... it made sense.

"I know she's been sneaking down to land for years. I just... I never gave much thought to... any of us finding a mate. Or at least not with an outside species."

"But you support them, right?" From what he saw, Parthenia and Gavin were happy. Though he was curious about how they worked around the curse, he also had no desire to ask, either.

Her gaze flicked to him, and it was a moment before she answered. "I want my sister to be happy. She deserves that."

If he hadn't known any better, he'd swear she had dodged the question. Cipriana hadn't actually stated whether she supported her sister's relationship. Mac smirked. There was a way to lead Cipriana back around to the question at hand. "And he makes her happy. So... you support their relationship then," he said, more as a statement than a question.

"I worry about them." She sighed. "While our laws have changed... the laws of his species still haven't. What happens if his leader catches them? Before Thalasia gets them off the isle safely."

Mac rubbed the back of his head. It was a valid concern. He didn't know how long Thalasia planned to stay on the isle. Though with the questions about the barrier, he suspected it would at least be until that could be replaced... rebuilt. Stopping their trek, he gripped Cipriana's shoulder. "*If* that happens, then we'll stop at nothing to find them. However, they are traveling with one of the finest warriors I know. And shape shifters rarely go into Verdant Grove." He'd heard the stories of how many didn't leave unscathed. He hadn't been kidding when he said some fae liked to play tricks. "To that end... you know that at least for the next few days, they'll be safe."

The corners of her mouth upturned slightly. "You're right."

That wasn't the response he expected. Instead of being sarcastic about it, he smiled in return. Taking her hand in his, Mac nodded over his shoulder. "There's a cave up ahead. We can make shelter there for the night."

"Um, that's probably a good idea. It is getting late."

Yeah, the sun had set about an hour ago. Pleasantly surprising, she didn't remove her hand from his as he led her on farther through the jagged path they'd traveled for a good bit. His gaze shifted toward the deep, pear-shaped entrance. The subterranean appeared rocky, but they both had wings, so they should be able to navigate it easily. While it looked rather extensive from his current position, it wouldn't be necessary for them to slip too far inside it. They just needed to be out of sight.

With no further conversation, they successfully crossed the terrain to the dark cavern. He squeezed Cipriana's hand. "Stay here, and I'll go check it out really quickly. Okay?"

"Um, yeah. Okay."

Releasing her hand, he flew up to the den's vast opening and landed just inside of it. Mac pounded his fists together, allowing green flames to lick up his arms as he ventured a little deeper. It was utterly silent, dank, and dim. Although he had excellent eyesight and could see well in the dark, the faint light from his power helped a great deal. Nothing appeared out of the ordinary. It looked like nothing more than an extensive, but empty cavern. It would suffice for the night. Tomorrow they'd be with the dwarves and, hopefully, not seeking shelter in another place like this.

He ambled back to the entrance and stopped a few feet from the ledge. Mac glanced down at Cipriana. "It's safe to come up."

With a small nod, she shot into the air. Her talons touched the ground right beside him. "Thank you... for checking it out first."

"Of course." He offered her another lopsided grin as their eyes met. It felt eerily similar to the night before. Except the air between them was slightly different. It seemed... strangely charged. She hadn't pulled her hand away from his moments ago. Maybe... if he... taking a chance, Mac caressed Cipriana's cheek. Unlike last night, she leaned into his touch. That... that was a sign.

But he needed a little more encouragement before he kissed her again. He closed the little space there was between them, and with his other hand, laced their fingers together. Still, she didn't back away. Or slap him. Mac slanted his head, his mouth hovering over hers as he gave her one last opportunity to stop what was about to happen. To tell him 'No.'

She pressed her lips to his.

Talk about the best kind of answer to an unspoken question. He licked across the seam of her lips. They parted with a slight gasp. He swept his tongue along the inside of her mouth and her tongue entangled with his as the kiss deepened. Good stones. He didn't realize it could be like this. That a person could even taste so... wonderful. She was like the sweetest ocean breeze he'd ever sampled. And he certainly planned to savor it.

At that moment, he was positive that he'd never desire another. Cipriana was the only female he would ever want to enjoy in this manner. There would be no other. Not for him.

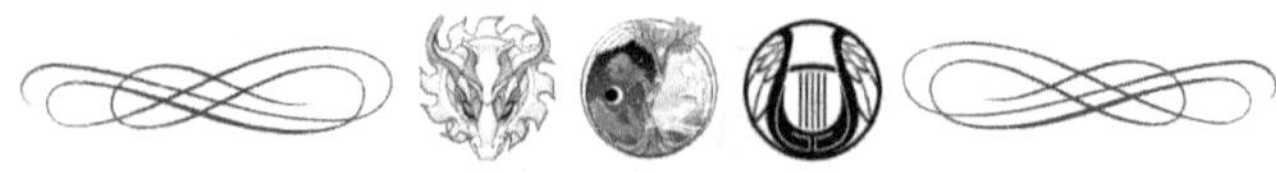

"We are entering the heart of Jade Gardens, and the Queen's palace," Milla said, her voice low.

Parthenia's eyes widened as she, her mate, and Milla stepped onto a stone path completely covered in red rose petals. It was the sweetest scent. Between that and the lavender trees, she could easily believe they'd entered paradise. Ahead stood a semicircle of columns, the scent of damp bark rising from the branches twisted to form the arches. The pale light of the moon shone down, its silvery light beaming between the breaks in the awning of lavender. At the center of the marquee was a throne made of entwining vines illuminated in teal.

A voluptuous female with pale-green skin, hunter-green hair, and bright-green eyes sat upon the throne. A crown of cherry blossoms and baby's breath rested upon her head. Her long, shimmering dress flowed around her, the fabric whispering as it pooled softly at her feet. "Welcome, Prime Warrior." The female's voice sounded like wind chimes blowing in the breeze.

"Thank you, Queen Dyeera." Milla curtsied, tucking one foot behind the other as she bent her knees and bowed her head.

There had been little time to really take in the exquisite beauty that surrounded them. Parthenia followed suit. She bent at the knees, tucked one foot behind the other, and lowered her head until her chin touched her chest. Her only addition—she released her hold of Gavin's hand and politely gripped the sides of her dress as she curtsied.

Keeping both arms at his sides, his head in line with his back, Gavin bent at the waist as he bowed.

"Rise, so I may see your hearts," Queen Dyeera said.

Slowly, Parthenia straightened, lifting from the curtsey. Not that she understood the rest of what the nymph Queen wanted. How was she supposed to see their hearts? Out of the corner of her eye, Parthenia noticed Gavin had straightened, as had Milla.

Queen Dyeera brightened as her gaze fell upon them. "Who accompanies you today, Prime Warrior?"

"This is Parthenia. She is an ambassador sent on behalf of the sirens. And this is Gavin, her mate."

Gavin kept his eyes lowered, but his hand gravitated back to Parthenia's.

The nymph queen rose to her feet, crossed the stone platform, and descended the staircase. Rose petals bloomed beneath her feet with each step she took. "A siren and a shape shifter. How you must hide your relationship."

Well, that answered one thing. The female apparently knew about the issues they'd faced. She squeezed Gavin's hand. "We do, but to us, every second we have together is worth it."

"Yes. I can see your desire for one another. Perhaps something I can aid with; though that does not seem to be the reason you have come. I see another purpose."

"That's correct, Your Majesty. I'm here representing my people to negotiate a peace treaty." She was certain at least part of the female's words intrigued her mate. They certainly piqued her curiosity. As far as she believed, Thalasia was their only hope of overcoming the curse. At least that's what she thought the Queen was talking about.

Gavin sent her a smile as his thumb stroked the back of her hand.

"I am certainly amenable to a deal. Though in order to properly ascertain what we could offer one another, it is imperative I learn more about you and your species." She walked over to where Gavin stood. "For example, shape shifter, if I were to ask you to release your hold on your siren, would you?"

"I can, Your Majesty, if that is something that would be necessary. I just prefer not to. We have spent much time apart. It comforts me to be touching her."

"It is unnecessary." The queen turned her attention back to Parthenia. "Sirens, the keepers of secrets and charmers of information."

"That is what we've been known for in the past." Why did that bother her a little? She didn't have any intention of doing anything like that for the Queen. Nor did she think Cipriana would be okay with any of their people doing that for her, either.

"With a magnificent library, if I am correct."

"You are." How did she know that? Had she met sirens in the past? Milla had said she was someone who granted wishes.

Gavin's tail brushed over the tips of her wing.

The queen watched the two of them closely. She grinned widely. "I believe I know a way we may work together to negotiate terms we are both agreeable to. However, before we discuss that, I would like you to spend the evening with my people. Is that satisfactory to you both?"

"I'm perfectly fine with that." They'd hoped she would allow them to spend the evening here to begin with.

"I am as well. Thank you, Your Majesty."

"Excellent. Now, allow us to address your other issue. Are you both willing to discuss those details in front of the Prime Warrior?"

"That is your choice," Milla said. "If you wish me to step outside, I can certainly do that."

Her gaze flicked to Gavin. They didn't tell anyone about their problem. Not even their own family members. It had been something they'd kept to themselves until they ran into Thalasia. But what did he think? If Milla was okay with stepping outside, then that could be done. "Outside?"

"Um... if that would be alright?"

Milla curtsied with a bow of her head. "Queen Dyeera." She turned and left the three of them alone.

The queen waited until the female left before she spoke. She clasped her hands at the small of her back and offered them both a warm smile. "I am aware there is a curse placed upon the sirens. While I cannot offer you a way to a permanent resolution, I can give you... a reprieve from it for one night."

What the nymph queen offered was something they'd both wanted for quite some time. It didn't really seem all that important how she found out about it, but she was curious. More so to see if the female would answer the question. "How do you know about the curse?"

"You do not believe you are the first siren to seek me out, do you?"

To be honest, she hadn't really thought about it. Given what she'd seen in the hybrid village, it would make sense. How many times had they come to her, though? She said only for the night.

"What might you ask for in return for such a gift?"

Her attention turned to Parthenia. "Two feathers from your wings. Nothing more."

Two feathers? That's it? It wouldn't be permanent, but they both had enough patience to wait for that to happen. For it to be as simple as that, it almost seemed too good to be true. Parthenia looked at Gavin. She didn't know what to say.

Her mate smiled down at her. "It is your choice, my love. The feathers are yours. If it is not something you wish to do, I am okay with waiting until the curse is broken."

It was just a couple of feathers. She'd removed one the first time they'd been physically intimate. Maybe she should really give it some more thought, but it was just feathers. They would grow back. And it wasn't like they held any power. Parthenia turned her attention back to the Queen. "One night for two feathers. That's acceptable."

"Excellent." The Queen beamed. "Our meal should be served shortly. Allow us to eat, and then we will take the steps for the exchange. So, you know I will hold up my end of the bargain. Will you raise your joined hands?"

Gavin, still grinning, brought their connected hands up into the air.

With one hand above and the other below, the Queen's palms completely enveloped their joined hands. "This is to signify the agreement you are entering for one evening, free from the curse that has restricted your intimacy. Two feathers from Parthenia's wing will be provided." As her hands lit up, a soft, green glow illuminated their hands.

A wave of warmth blossomed from their intertwined hands, and Parthenia gasped. It almost felt like basking in the sun.

Gavin's eyes widened.

The warmth and the green light dissipated, and then the female removed her hands from theirs. "Excellent. Come, let us feast, and then we will fulfill the contract." Queen Dyeera turned to the right and headed for a short staircase beyond the circle of columns. As she strode forward, rose petals bloomed beneath each step she took, leaving a trail of them in her wake.

Chapter Thirty-One

Thalasia bit back a yawn. It had been a long, somewhat uncomfortable, quiet walk. Something she could've dealt without. Whatever. She was too tired to think much about it. As they followed the dry riverbed uphill, the climb became increasingly steep. Rocks and pebbles skittered downslope with every step. Their pace slowed to accommodate the shift in terrain.

Despite the slight height difference between them, she'd kept pace, but stayed far enough back to keep some distance. It was easier to focus on the hike that way. Certainly, made her grateful she'd opted not to waste more energy on glamour. She was tired as it was. No need to make it worse.

"The river is up ahead. The falls shouldn't be too far off," Seru called back, offering a hand down to help her up a ledge.

She was too tired to fight him on the proffered hand. Accepting it, she pushed up with his aid onto the ledge, but said nothing. Seemed pointless, really. What more was there to talk about? She released his palm once she was over the ledge. It hadn't been necessary as they continued their trek toward the falls. With the direction they were going, uneven land beneath their feet, they'd have to hike to the top of the waterfall to climb down into the cave.

Then why did she have this inkling to head toward the east side of the basin? She shook it off. It didn't make any sense. Not if she'd read the map right. Her brow furrowed as she took in the towering trees, the branches she sidestepped, and the untouched undergrowth.

With as close as they were now, she heard the water as it pounded against the basin. It created a beautiful tinkling sound, almost the same as Seru's beads made. Thalasia let the thought go.

"Can you please make some effort to shield?" he grumbled.

A frown creased her forehead as she brushed off his comment. He was always muttering about something. *He will never love you.* The voice disappeared as quickly as it had appeared. It had her stopping for a moment. Mistress wasn't here. It had just been a nightmare. Shaking it off, she pushed forward over the terrain and focused on the surrounding sounds. Her eyes drank in the unfamiliar sights. The streaming sun across the forest. The rush of the falls... the rain... no... what rain... it wasn't raining. Thalasia rubbed her temples. She was getting a headache. Gods, she was tired. Mentally, physically, and emotionally exhausted. The sooner she got away from this isle, the better.

Seru stopped, turning back to her. "Do you need to stop and rest?"

She looked at him for only a second. "No. I'm fine. Just keep going."

"You don't seem fine," he said. "You don't *feel* fine."

She stared at him incredulously. How was she supposed to feel? Like a war wasn't waging inside of her? Even without the stress of the impending war on the isle. Thalasia sighed. "Can we please just keep going?"

"Take a few moments," Seru encouraged, taking a seat on a boulder and motioning her over to sit next to him.

This wasn't what she had expected. And it sucked because she'd never been able to tell him no. Despite the small part of her that wanted to, she strode over and sat down on the boulder next to him.

He massaged her shoulders, working away the tightness in her neck. "There's no shame in needing to rest," he murmured in her ear.

"I don't need rest," she mumbled as her feathers ruffled. She needed the conflict between her head and her heart to stop. At least some of the tension in her body was easing. She'd pulled her hair back before they left. There'd been no point in hiding the mark any longer. Seru had seen it. She'd shown it to Cyon. Even to the feline who'd offered information.

Seru's hands stilled on her shoulders, trailing down her back to encircle her waist. "You should eat something." He pressed his forehead to the back of her head, just resting there for a bit. He inhaled deeply, swept aside her hair, and pressed a firm kiss to the back of her neck.

Leaning into him a little, her feathers ruffled again as a soft breeze blew past. Food? But she wasn't hungry. She'd eaten all the leftovers from the day before. She didn't carry fruit in her bag. It'd never keep. Her eyebrows furrowed. She had jerky in there. Something she'd picked up a tasting for the last time she was in the human world. It had always kept pretty well. Maybe he was right. Maybe some food would help.

Thalasia untied the bag from her belt loop, dug out a piece of plastic-wrapped jerky, and reattached her purse before addressing the food. With his arms around her waist, leaning against him, she found it easy to believe his earlier words. *He is just placating you, like he does her.* Thalasia shook the words away. With her grip tightening around the jerky, the plastic bit into her palm. Mistress wasn't here. She wasn't in her head. It just had to be her mind playing tricks on her.

"You can hear her in your head, can't you? How long has she been there?" Seru growled, securing her hair out of the way. "And I changed my mind about the crystal. Give it to me. Now."

Loosening her grip on the jerky, Thalasia frowned. She didn't have to ask him who he was talking about. She dug into her bag again for the crystal he asked for and almost pulled out the wrong one. "That's not possible. She's never been able to get inside my head before."

Maybe she couldn't shield everything, but she'd always been able to block her head from Mistress and her children. As far as she could remember. She paused momentarily as she switched the crystals out. What if he was right? The nightmare. Over her shoulder, she handed him the crystal, its smooth surface cool against her fingers. "Last night."

"Yeah, well... Markham's not realms away. You're no longer outside her reach. Their reach," he amended, snatching the crystal from her. He lifted the golden dagger from his belt and jumped off the boulder. He placed the purple crystal into the indenture. The light sent a wall of purple reflections scattering across the rock wall. Seru quickly shielded the crystal with his palm, using the other to bring the hilt of the dagger down on the crystal.

A few blows returned the desired crack as the stone fractured. Soon, the crystal broke into pieces. He didn't stop until the slivers of stone turned to a fine luminous dust. He scooped up as much of the powder as he could, spinning Thalasia to ensure he had the best access to her mark and the back of her neck. "Need to borrow your knife," he said, shoving the useless golden trinket back into his belt.

Her brow furrowed with concentration as she drew the blade, flipped it in a graceful arc, and presented the hilt to him. Between his manhandling and his words, she was utterly confused. "That makes little sense. I know they have kids together, but they'd have to be connected in order to do that. Even if that's the case, why would it have changed between now and...." Her words trailed off. There was only one thing that was different.

Seru retrieved the knife, positioning the blade in his free hand. "Try not to move," he instructed. As he carefully carved symbols over the mark, the air filled with the coppery smell of blood as the steel sliced into her neck. Her blood blossomed in red beads that eventually ran together as the cuts came together.

Once he finished the symbols, he swiftly buried the tip of the blade in his palm, holding the dust. He hissed as the weapon found its purchase. He swiped the blade clean on his pants before passing it back to her. His dark blood soaked into the crystal particles, turning their bright purple into a darker color.

Using their blood as a catalyst, he placed it over the mark, infusing the symbols with the magic. The light emitted from the crystal shone brightly as it integrated with her skin, resealing the wounds with its magic. When he removed his hand, the symbols remained glowing the same color as the crystal.

He seized Thalasia by the hand, yanking her to her feet. The black blood trickled between their fingers despite the wound having closed almost instantly. "A mark over a mark. It's not the same as the other marks... it's old magic. It'll force her back and buy us a window. A few hours or a few days. It's hard to say."

They were scrambling for a better position. With the wall at their backs was an advantage, but not enough of one. "I gave away our position when I crushed the crystal. We have to find somewhere to make a stand. I don't imagine Minerva or Markham will be gladdened by the metaphysical pushback. Whatever reasons they had for holding back their attack just disappeared." He bounded over a weak point in the rock, but just barely. "Can you fly?"

The throbbing in her head gradually diminished. The ache in her body dissipated. Her mind and her heart reconnecting, realigning together to the path she'd chosen. For the first time in the last couple of days, she felt like herself. It took her a moment to register everything he'd said, even more so than what had just happened.

Mark over a mark. A window. Her ears pricked. There wasn't time for her to piece all of it together. She climbed over the boulder with ease; her gaze flicked in the direction she heard the gentle pounding of paws against the ground. As her feathers ruffled, she quickly replayed his last question in her mind. "Yes." She could fly, but this wasn't the time to run. The only time she ever did that was when she questioned what she was seeing or hearing. Or out of fear. Her father had taught her to be brave.

A feline and four canines left their hiding places and raced across the ground in their direction, still coated in their camouflage.

Another voice sounded in her head. This one was softer, gentler, loving. One she'd nearly forgotten. *You have always been brave, Thalasia. It's time you became the warrior you were always meant to be. Show them who you are!* Her gaze flicked to Seru. She looked back toward the shape shifters that came into her line of sight. Silver light crackled across her hands. "If we can get to the cave, we can use Adina's booby-traps for protection. We may just have to get a little wet."

"That was the thought," Seru called back. He tugged on her hand to get her attention. "Good, then get there. Behind the falls. I'll catch up." Letting go of her hand, he turned to face the incoming assault. He called down a blue bolt, large and potent enough to split the path behind them. Surely, the shifters would think twice before attempting to jump the distance. Though claws offered a way around the rift, it might take them a few extra seconds to figure that out.

If he thought for one second she was leaving his side; he was seriously delusional. Although the air would give her a better vantage point. Thalasia darted into the air, but she remained above Seru... from here... she could certainly play whack-a-shifter.

The feline in the trees, as he was, used the height of a branch to launch himself over the void. The canines picked up their speed and did the same, one after another. They hadn't yet made it across when Thalasia called a bolt to each hand. Finding the right position as she hovered in the air, she aimed and threw both down at two of the wolves running in their direction. They hit two of the canines in their chests, knocking them into the void that had separated the ground. The other two canines made it across, though barely.

While that still left three continuing toward her and Seru, it was the two in the tree that had both shifted to their larger form that drew her attention. The way they curled in on their bodies, clung to their heads... she understood that pain. Knowing the hold the

Informant mark likely had on them, she'd been able to cut the mark off from the dead wolf the day before. She didn't know if she could do it while they were alive. Or if it would help. Still, she couldn't kill them. They needed freedom, not death. "The two in the trees... we might aid." But the other three. She dipped her chin toward the two wolves and the feline chasing after them. "Think you can handle them?"

Another bolt struck the rock face, several smaller bolts leaping off to deliver a harrowing jolt to the pursuing shifters. Seru summoned a charge in his free hand, still backing toward the falls. With a shake of his mane, he called up to her, "Make it quick!"

Eh, he was pissed at her. What was new? Thalasia grinned, a flash of teeth, as she dove through the air toward the pair sprawled on the ground. The wind beneath her wings felt good. As she made her way to the felines fighting against their markings, she formulated a plan. One that wouldn't take long. She didn't imagine Mistress was happy with what Seru had done. If Seru was right and Mistress had used a connection to Markham, then they could likely expect more shifters coming their way.

The newest bolts knocked the canines off their feet. Her gaze flicked from Seru to the feline right below her. The male shook his head as his eyes flicked to black, his claws extending. "Get... away... from... me," he growled out through gritted teeth. "I... do not... want to... harm you."

"I'm going to help you." Well, this ought to be fun. She knew exactly where the marks were from her experience the day before. She hadn't landed yet, which was probably a good thing. Seru would be even more pissed if she got hurt. Before the feline could react, she landed on his back, her hand sparking with a searing silver glow, channeling her healing powers through his marked body.

Rivulets of blood slid down the left side of his cheek as his claws retracted of their own accord. He fell forward, barely holding himself up on his palms. The male's chest heaved. He barely pushed himself up as the other feline lunged off the ground, knocking her down. He grabbed onto the first part of the other feline he reached, which was his throat, and slammed him into the grass, holding him there as he fought. The feline's claws swiped at him, catching his forearm. He flipped the other feline over onto his stomach, using his forearm and knees to press him into the dirt. Although the one she'd helped appeared to struggle just a little, he was the larger of the two. He looked over his shoulder at her as she picked herself back up. "What did you just do to me? I do not... The voice... It is gone."

Thank fuck! It worked! No time to celebrate. She had one other to deal with. The one he was holding down. "Released you." Thalasia didn't waste time brushing herself off. As she dropped to her knees, her silver hand, already bright with power, met the mark on the second feline's shoulder. Her healing power pulsed, and the air around the feline crackled with energy.

While she'd fought to get the other one released, they seemed less inclined to let this one go. The power holding onto this feline seemed all too familiar. She gritted her teeth and fought harder, as she refused to cave. Her whole body lit up as the truth of her power revealed itself. "Not this time, you bitch."

Finally, the male's snarls and growls trailed off. The black in his eyes changed back to a normal color, and he stopped fighting under the other feline's hold. Slight trembles went through him and he just lay there for a minute, huffing. As she withdrew her palm, the one holding him down sat back. The place where the Informant brand had once been was completely bare. No fur, no anything. Though the spot was slightly warped, as though she'd burned him.

The one on the ground slowly sat up, reaching up a hand to feel the spot where the mark had once existed. "What?" He looked down, then shook his head a little, raising his other hand to his face to wipe the blood away his claws had drawn. His gaze flicked from the other male to her, and then back again. He looked back at her. "My apologies. For almost... attacking you. What..." He paused, his hand still over the spot on his shoulder. "How is this possible? What did you do?"

Thalasia sat back on her feet, swallowing a few deep breaths with each heave of her chest. She glanced back in the direction she'd left Seru to see he'd made it all the way to the waterfall. It would've given the two males the only chance to see the mark on her neck, now covered by whatever Draconic symbol Seru had etched.

Her gaze flicked back to the two male felines as she rose to her feet. Shit, that had taken more out of her than she thought possible. She needed to get back, and these two needed to leave. "There's no time to explain all that. All you need to know is that you've been released from Markham's hold. There's a village about forty miles east of here. It's the safest place for you. It'll look like a wall of trees. The entrance is hidden. Don't waste time. Look for apple trees and follow those around."

Without another word, she shot into the air, feeling the pull of gravity and stumbling a bit as she flew toward Seru. It took a second for her to steady. It really took a lot out of her. They needed to get into the cave so they could rest for a minute.

Thalasia glanced back one time to ensure the two felines heeded her words. They had. Good. It felt indescribable, a mix of triumph and exhaustion, to fight back like that. A surge of warmth coursed through her veins, the taste of victory a sweet balm to her battered spirit. The corners of her mouth upturned slightly. She hadn't let them win. It was about damn time.

Chapter Thirty-Two

"It is my responsibility to take care of my people. Every action, every deal, every negotiation, every allegiance is all toward that one goal," the Queen said.

"That's what we believe," Parthenia replied. At least it had slowly changed to that. "Everything we do, it's all to make sure my people have a good life." It's what she wanted for all of them. For her sisters to have the same happiness she'd found with Gavin. She was fairly certain that Cipriana was on her way to it.

"I think it is what every leader should believe. Otherwise, why be a leader? If one's goals are only to benefit themselves, they do not deserve the title," her mate said.

"I concur." Queen Dyeera offered Milla a small smile, the corners of her eyes crinkling, and then turned her attention to Gavin and Parthenia. "It has been a delight having you both here this evening."

"Thank you. We've enjoyed ourselves as well." Everything they'd talked about had given her hope that they could reach a peace treaty. That they actually had common goals and something to offer one another.

"Yes, thank you. We truly have. Your hospitality has been wonderful." Her mate gave her hand a gentle squeeze.

"I am certainly glad you have enjoyed it."

"Queen Dyeera, if it would not offend, I believe I am ready to turn in for the evening," Milla stated.

"Of course not. I will have an attendant show you to your quarters."

"Thank you." Milla stood with a small nod to Gavin and Parthenia. "I will see you both in the morning."

"Have a good night." Parthenia offered Milla a brief nod in return, bidding the woman goodnight, and watched as a female nymph escorted her from the room.

Gavin finished the rest of what was on his plate, as well as his water, then ensured he hadn't made a mess anywhere. His arm slid around Parthenia, stroking her hip. "I hope I do not sound like I am repeating myself too much, but the meal really was excellent, Your Majesty."

"Not at all." The queen grinned, then focused on Parthenia as a servant entered and quickly cleared the remnants of their meal. "I believe I have come up with something that will benefit us both. It would certainly be a way to solidify our... allegiance. As you are an alchemist, are there not certain herbs that you do not have access to?"

"That's right. A few I've had picked up for me in the market-place, but even still they don't get everything." And there were some things she'd never been able to grow. They typically required better soil than what they had in Pteryrina.

"If we provide those herbs to you, then in exchange, I would ask for access to your library."

It sounded like a good idea, but then she remembered Milla had told them earlier. The Queen was very precise in her wording. If she agreed to those terms, then it would be open access to every part of the library. Nor was there a specified timeframe for how long they'd be given the herbs. "I would grant you and your people access to the main part of the library as long as whatever herbs we asked for were provided. The restricted section would *not* be accessible to you or your people. Agreed?"

"Agreed."

Gavin gave her hip a gentle, encouraging squeeze. "I have been there twice myself, unbeknownst to most everyone. As someone who grew up with books being such a rarity, I feel like I could spend several lifetimes there and still not have time to read all the books." He paused and gave a soft chuckle. "Not that I know how long my species lives. But the sentiment remains."

"That is good to know. Many do not understand the treasure of knowledge that can be found in books. We have a small library, though not as much as I desire."

"Well, I'm certain the main part of our library can provide great wealth to you." And she'd protected the most important section of the library by making it inaccessible. This would be enough to open them up to working together in the future. She didn't mention the invaders, as the dark guilers had been dubbed, as that was something her sister negotiated with Milla.

"It will," the female responded. "Now. I believe we have one other deal to see through. If you both are ready?"

Her mate turned in his chair to face her and reached up to cup her cheek. "Are you ready, my love?"

She leaned into his touch and beamed up at him. Goddess, she loved him so much. Even if this didn't work for them, she wouldn't change her decision. Two feathers seemed a small price to pay. They'd been ready for this moment for a while. "I'm very ready."

"As am I." His forehead met hers, then soft kisses landed on either side of her mouth, and he squeezed her hand before turning away. "Yes, Your Majesty, we are ready."

"Excellent." The female stood and gestured for them to follow.

Parthenia got to her feet at the same time as her mate. As they followed the Queen toward the throne room, she slid an arm around his waist, the scent of roses filling the air. Except they passed the staircase that would lead to it by just a little and took the steps on the other side of it. A soft tinkling reached her ears before the cause even came into sight.

At the heart of the room stood a vast, circular, stone fountain, adorned with countless finely carved roses on every stone. In the center of the fountain, an eight-pointed shining star sprayed water with a gentle hissing sound. Steam rose from the water, filling the reservoir. It was quite stunning.

"The two feathers, please. And you must pluck them yourself."

"Okay." She removed her arm from around Gavin's waist, extended her right wing, felt the sting as she yanked out one feather with a small wince, and then another. Once they were out, she handed them over to the nymph Queen.

As the Queen accepted the feathers, a smile graced her face. "Thank you. Now, if you will both take the stairs into the fountain. Once inside, you will need to go together beneath the star. It will light up and warm under your feet. After it has returned to its natural color, as you see it now, then you may step out."

Gavin beamed as he stared down at her. One step closer. He laced his fingers with hers. Together, they ascended the stairs to the fountain. Underneath the radiant star, he gazed at her, and clasped her other hand gently.

The water was quite warm, which certainly explained the steam. Not that she noticed it much. As they stood beneath the star, their hands linked, all she could see was her mate. Her wonderful mate.

A male who had her whole heart. The opalescent star lit up beside them, and she barely registered it or its light as it completely bathed them, or the water swirling under their feet. All she saw was Gavin.

At least until the feel of the stone under her talons changed. Wait, those weren't talons. She dropped her gaze from Gavin's beautiful emerald green eyes to the clear water. Parthenia swallowed to wet her parched throat and stared at the lower half of her legs. The skin of her calves had smoothed out and meshed to match her natural coloring. In place of talons, she had toes and feet, much like Gavin did, just without the fur. It felt... strange.

"Why did that happen?" her mate asked.

"I don't know." The light that had bathed them dissipated, and the natural opalescence of the star returned. Wiggling her toes, Parthenia blinked. Was it supposed to do that? Her eyes lifted back to Gavin, and then to the star. Was that it? Was it done?

"Perhaps, seal the evening's change with a true first kiss," the Queen said.

With the queen's words, her gaze flicked back to Gavin. As she gazed up into his eyes, she was reminded of the countless times she had done so in the past six months. A smile tugged at her lips as she watched his cheeks flush with warmth. Maybe she couldn't physically see the blush through his fur, but she could feel it. And understood it as well. Their first actual kiss, and they had an audience. Not that she gave it much thought. When she was in his arms like this, everything around them disappeared. It was just the two of them in their own little bubble.

He cupped her jaw, stroking her cheek with his thumb. Everything she loved about him sent shivers down her spine. Goddess, that musky scent of his filled her nostrils, even more so as he leaned closer to her. Their lips were barely an inch apart. The first time they'd attempted this, it hadn't gone so well. She grinned at the image that she saw flash through his mind. They'd grown so much since then. Not just in themselves, but they'd grown together... as a mated couple, as well.

His lips pressed to hers, and nothing blasted them apart. A soft moan left them both at the same time. Poppies, his lips were so plump and soft. And he tasted... oh, gods, the taste of him was an intoxicating blend of flavors. As his other hand slid into her hair and his tongue stroked along the seam of her lips, she groaned and slowly opened up for him. He tasted so sweet; she yearned for more. Parthenia slipped her tongue into his mouth and hesitantly licked over his fangs.

Her mate let out a growl as he deepened the kiss even more. Trembles shook him as their tongues slid together... touching for the first time, as their lips just had.

Oh, goddess. A blast of heat shot straight to her core. His hand found her hip, and he tugged her close, the sudden contact of her hardened nipples against his chest. A groan left her mouth as she trailed her fingers up his arms and gripped his shoulders. His tail wrapped around her waist and sent another blast of heat right through her. With the kiss deepening, she couldn't stop from tugging him closer, not that there was any space between them. Goddess, she never wanted this to stop. His moans and his growls heated her up like they'd done before, but with all new sensations combined. The way his tongue slid against hers, the taste of him in her mouth... she didn't think she'd ever get enough.

The Queen cleared her throat.

Somehow, they broke the kiss. Her mate pressed his forehead to hers, attempting to catch his breath. "I am going to go with... it worked... and rather well," he whispered, chuckling a bit.

Poppies, she didn't want the kiss to end. Both of them had ragged breaths. She bit her bottom lip and offered him the faintest smile. "Yes, it did." Definitely made two feathers worth it. If they only had one night, they could make it count until the curse was completely broken.

"I will have an attendant show you to your quarters. Should you both wish?"

Without moving her head or looking over to the Queen, Parthenia beamed. "Yes, we'd definitely like that."

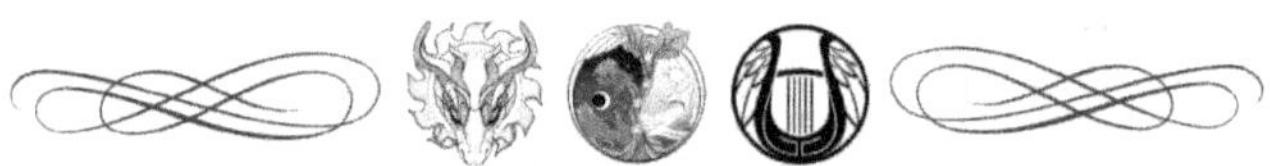

"What happened? Are you okay?" Seru demanded.

"A little worn out, but I'm okay. Markham fought with me a little more to hold on to the second feline than he did the first."

"Likely because he didn't expect it the first time." His eyes fell over her, head to toe and back again. The visual assessment didn't betray her words. She appeared uninjured. Still, he didn't seem convinced.

"Likely." She raised an eyebrow at him. "I can strip once we're in the cave and out of sight if necessary to convince you I'm uninjured."

His facial muscles twitched in response. "Unnecessary." He reached out his hand to her, fully prepared for her to refuse it and brush past him.

Thalasia took the offered hand. "Shall we see what Adina has in store for us?"

"If we must." He rolled his eyes as his fingers curled around hers.

"Either that or we see how long we last against more shifters I'm sure Markham has sent our way."

"We'll get inside and see if we can navigate our way to a safe resting spot before you collapse."

"That sounds like a better plan. I'm certain that saving two felines is my quota for the day."

"Leave it to you, Atlis, to set the bar exceptionally high for the rest of us."

"Shit. This is nothing. I stowed away fifty guilers in a cave on Candescent Isle." She lifted her free hand, shielding against the spray as they slipped into the cave behind the curtain of water, the air thick with the smell of the falls. "Only good ones, I promise."

"Why is it you're so fond of the guilers?" He wrinkled up his nose at the revelation.

"I don't prefer one species to another. I simply recognize those who aren't inherently dark."

"Light or dark," he replied, with a slight squeeze of her hand. "They're unnatural."

"So, they should be killed because of that?"

"They never should have existed."

"That same sentiment can apply to a lot of different creatures. Just because they shouldn't exist doesn't mean they can't make the world better." She flicked her gaze from him to the extensive cavern in front of them.

"Right." As they paused at the cave mouth, eyeing the tunnel before them, Seru reluctantly dropped her hand. He returned the dagger to his hip before venturing forward, lowering his shields just enough to extend his senses. "I go first, unless the clever bitch implemented two-man traps," which would be much more intricate and time consuming than he cared to imagine. "Even if I spring one, it shouldn't kill me."

"Depends on how long ago she hid the book. If memory serves, she would've been pregnant around the time she met with you, maybe three or four months along."

As they trekked forward, it wasn't too far before they saw the first. The overgrown veil of green, thorn-covered vines. It made her giggle. Thalasia crossed her arms and stared at it for a minute. "Horam's Snare. From the looks of it, I'd say there might be some bones in there."

"She was, but her trusty tool wasn't," Seru muttered, unwilling to doubt the Atlis's forceful insistence on their coupling. "We'll leave those for the puppies and kitties... C'mon."

"There's only one way through this. We hack it, it'll get worse." A hint of amusement lit her eyes, and she grinned.

"Then what do you want us to do with it?" Seru asked, losing his patience for these silly games.

"Cover your ears." She smirked, giving him mere seconds before she opened her mouth and began singing a soft lullaby about the ocean and sky. With a slithering motion, the vines unfolded, coiling back toward the jagged walls. Cracking resounded around them as the bones broke and released from the snare's hold.

Seru cringed. The ringing in his ears was high and shrill. "Isn't that charming?" he grumbled, stepping over the bones. Of course, the traps only released for siren tricks. He should've figured as much.

Shaking her head, she trailed after him. "I highly doubt she set up the same the entire way. That would be redundant and highly irresponsible."

"Isn't the purpose of all this redundancy? She created backup plans for her backup plans. Leaving the barrier to be *your* problem was highly irresponsible," he said. "I'm sure Adina covered *all* her bases."

"That depends on the purpose behind the barrier. If it should protect the magic within Prisma Isle, then it only became my problem because the lyre broke when I landed. If it was never meant to be permanent, well, it would've still been my problem since I was brought here for other reasons."

Seru shook his head. "I'd call her paranoid, but..."

"But?" she asked.

"It pays to be paranoid."

"Yes, it does." A tripwire strung across the cave appeared several feet ahead of them. Connected above was a big, old slab of stone that looked ancient. "How do we set that off?"

"I'm sure it's simple enough once we're on the other side. It'll serve as an extra blockade for our furry friends in the event they get past your vines."

"You reading my mind? I was just thinking that."

"No, even with marks, I'm not sure saint beasts can read minds or share thoughts without—" Seru paused. "We can't read minds."

"Without?" As they stepped over the tripwire, Thalasia's gaze lifted momentarily to the slab above them.

"Vibrations."

"Kind of like sound waves? Or something?" She paused for a moment as they made it beyond the slab.

"I suppose."

"Maybe we were just on the same wavelength." She shrugged. The deeper they'd gotten into the cave, the danker it became. Although there was still no light, it didn't seem to bother either of them. It had even gotten cooler.

They'd probably gone thirty feet since the last booby-trap before they came upon the next one. The stone floor's pattern changed a little in the distance. It had only been semi-rough before. Pebbled flooring, the pattern reminiscent of a honeycomb, with an array of colorful stones, now covered the floor.

"Thalasia! Stop rooting around in there and watch where you're going," Seru demanded, reaching back to steady her.

He caught her just in time. She stopped, her gaze no longer focused on the multitude of items in her purse, but on the indentations around the stone she almost stepped on. Thalasia scanned the stone floor and noted the change. Her eyes lifted to the ceiling and then flicked to the walls. "Thanks," she muttered.

"I don't want your thanks. I want you to pay attention. You need to stop—for anything—speak up," he said, his eyes boring into her own.

"The jerky can wait." With a sigh, she yanked the ties on her bag tight.

"We can stop once we're through," he promised, returning his attention to the trap before them.

Thalasia offered him a quiet nod. She rubbed her eyes and focused on the flooring.

"What do you see?" Seru called back, sensing her attention dropping.

"No discernible pattern." She frowned, then lowered herself, her knees hitting the damp earth as she examined the stone. There was a faint sparkle of silver reflecting in the glow of her eyes. "I wonder..." Thalasia brought a gentle shine to her hand and held it over the floor.

Seru watched her in silence. The glow from her hand revealed the intricate patterns on some tiles, while others remained hidden in shadow. "What does the glow mean?"

"The one in front of me is indented. Means those are the ones we avoid." She rose back to her feet and offered him her hand. "Take this one together?"

He let out a reluctant sigh, then took her hand, his palm meeting hers. Her hand pulsed with light, revealing the marked stones and the path through the trap, which resembled a checkerboard as they walked safely. "This feels like a tedious, senseless game like those the nobles play when not at Court."

"Yeah, it does. And irritating as fuck." She smirked.

"I've never understood the pleasure people find in such games."

"Makes two of us."

He focused on following the path her light provided. His steps were sure but careful. He silently vowed to find Adina in the afterlife—assuming there was one and it wasn't just some endless void—and kill her all over again. He hated her, hated the hoops she designed for them to jump through, and hated that so much of this felt like fate molded by her hand, regardless of their will. They didn't get a choice. Not really. They were just expected to go through the motions. He was tired of that game.

Taking the last steps necessary for them to get through the third trap, she eyed the last of the path. Her silver eyes lit up with mirth. "One more down."

"This amuses you?" Seru shook his head, releasing her hand. "Get your jerky or whatever it was you were hunting for earlier. We can rest a moment." He turned his attention back toward the direction they'd come. It had been eerily quiet since they had entered. No shape shifter. No second wave. The silence worried him. The idleness agitated that, causing him to pace in small circles.

"Uh, no. I'm amused because, as much as I'd like to strangle my great-great grandmother... I can at least say that everything I've ever heard is accurate. She was crazy, but brilliant and usually right." Thalasia dug back into her bag and quickly found another piece of jerky. She tightened the ties, unwrapped the casing from the single piece of meat and bit into it with a soft moan.

"Don't go stroking her ego," Seru grumbled, eyeing her as she ate. His pacing intensified. "Are you *that* hungry?"

"You'd moan, too, if you ate jerky. It's just that good." She watched him pace back and forth as she found a spot to lean against the cool stone comfortably. "Why are you moving around like a caged animal?"

"Magic doesn't keep in dried... meats." Seru wrinkled his nose, uncomprehending.

"It's from the human realm. They use a thing called preservatives."

"It looks like leather. Would you eat your armor?"

She chuckled. "It's not leather. And no, I wouldn't."

He shook his head again. "We should have heard something by now."

"Maybe they couldn't find our scent."

"There's nothing here pungent enough to mask our scents," he said, giving her the look the comment deserved. "It's more likely they're lying in wait." If by happy accident the bones at the entrance were shifter, they might have already discovered the danger of the booby-trapped tunnel. If that was the case, lying in wait made the most sense. Being up against a stronger opponent didn't mean as much if that opponent was exhausted and worn down. Patience could reward them with added rest and strength while further diminishing their own.

"The only way they'd be successful in their endeavor is if they separated us. They know that. But they also know that we're more powerful than they expected." Her lips twitched. "You said the mark would buy us time. What if they just intend to wait that out?"

"It's possible. But Markham and Minerva don't exactly seem like the patient type. If they rely on your sympathetic nature, the weakness is their own numbers." He shrugged. "I prefer all my enemies very dead. A threat from the inside could provoke an uprising. Two escapees, however well intended your efforts, and a severance of their connection to the pack with ties as intimate as the shape shifters' demands an answer. If a leader can't keep their house in order, he or she has lost before he or she has even begun. They won't just kill the deserters; they'll root out any they can use to send a message. Weak links. They don't have to be actively revolting; just the suspicion is enough to slaughter them."

"There's a reason I sent them to Migas Village. It seemed to be the safest place for them. I don't think the refusal of the orders they'd been given impacts all of them the same. The feline I spoke with last night didn't appear to be in any pain at all, and he had no intention of attacking me. He actually taunted the wolf I killed."

Chewing on the last of the jerky, she pocketed the casing in one of the front pockets of her jeans. "Unless their attention is split." She tilted her head. "There have been plenty of times I've been alone. When I first arrived, after Aurelia left me to consult Enoch. Even after she showed up with her entire force, after you and I first met, I spent the night in a tree. The marketplace after Aurelia stole the pipe, when you were feeding. What if there are some places even the Informants won't go?"

"That only gives our adversaries more reason to lock down their ranks." He tried to settle against the wall, the cool stone at his back. "I'm not saying they don't have blind spots; I'm saying we just put the weaker members of their village in harm's way. If I were Markham, I'd want to enforce my rule, motivate my strong and expose the weak and questioning. He's not been kind to his people over the years. They lack the obvious... progress... the rest of the species enjoy. They'll be ever more cautious and on the look-out for such spots. The only spot they won't likely venture is the Swallows, the volcanoes—because they can't safely reach them, and maybe this cave." He swept his hand to gesture to the surrounding space. "Of those places, only one has enough magic to combat the likes of Markham, enough distance. Maybe a natural threat... They'd seek to prevent us from entering those places. Unless they think we might meet a more suitable end. But they have no way of confirming that. They'd be relying on faith, and somehow, I don't think that would sit well with a woman reaching across realms to get you."

"While all that's true, we also don't know if there are any within his village that are already working against him." Thalasia bit her bottom lip. "How did you figure out her name?"

"There's always someone." Seru crossed his arms. "I resisted using the crystal Aurelia lent to us because that type of magic comes at a steep cost." They were already paying out so much for the incomplete marks. The crystal-infused mark only increased their cost of energy, magic, and time. He'd avoided that as long as he could. His talon found its way between his teeth.

"How do you think? Klaus wrote about her in the journal." He shifted. "We need to close the marks. Restore our strength. We can no longer afford to be burdened with my indecision."

"I guess that would make sense. He was a part of her..." Her gaze lifted to him, and she stared at him wide-eyed. Thalasia reached up to the mark on her neck. Her fingers traced over the pattern he'd cut into her skin with her blade.

He hadn't really expected her to comment on the rest. After all, what could she say that she hadn't said already a thousand times? He pushed away from the wall. "If you're finished eating, we should keep going."

Thalasia lifted her gaze to him again. "I've always believed you. I think that's what made it so hard. Impossible even... to just lock it up... and forget."

"What?" He turned back to her, not quite understanding what she meant.

"The constant conflict I saw in your eyes with me. I thought if I could lock my feelings up, that I could make it easy on you and just walk away." She pushed off the stone wall. "That I could let you go. Then you would do something or say something to make me believe you all over again." Thalasia gripped the back of her neck. "Makes it impossible to let you go."

"It's not your burden... To resolve my conflict."

"Doesn't mean I wouldn't try."

"Your energy belongs to other matters," he replied. "I'm not like the dragons. I gain nothing from arguments or debates. Verie gave us free rein. Surrendering my decisions to the will of another isn't...."

"Something I want." She paused. "I feel you haven't been given any choices, and I hate that."

"I've made do with less, Thalasia. That's survival. I do not want your pity."

She shook her head. "It's not pity to want better for you. To believe you deserve better."

"Wanting it also doesn't make it so."

"No, but it won't stop me from trying to give it to you, either." She closed the distance between them and cupped his cheek. "Even if it didn't include me."

"I don't need you to fight for me. I can make my own choices. Similarly, I won't promise you a future I can't deliver on. Nor do I expect you to give up... Your role, this thing you do for the Atlis. Closing the marks is necessary for us both to survive just a little longer." Or so he hoped.

Removing her hand, she quietly nodded.

"If you feel Minerva again, say something," he said before shifting his attention back to the booby-trapped hallway. "How much farther do you think we have to go?"

She offered one last dip of her chin. "The map didn't indicate how deep the cavern ran or the number of traps we'd have to face. If I had to hazard a guess from the stories I've been told, I'd say one or two more traps and we should reach the deepest part of the cave."

"Let's get there," Seru said. "Then we'll see if she left us a way out or if we have to trek our way back through the tunnel. If possible, we'll rest for the night. If not, it'll at least give us a chance to figure out the next steps."

"Here, I thought I'd never have a need for that tent or sleeping bag." She chuckled.

"You and your fancy trinkets."

"There's nothing fancy about it. Neither of them."

"You're almost as spoiled as Aurelia." He laughed. "What would you do without your bottomless sack?"

Her eyes widened. "Don't even make such jokes. Without my bag... no... nope... that couldn't happen."

"That sounds like agreement to me." Seru gave her a small up-turn of his mouth.

"I will have you know they have passed this bag down for the last thousand years." A small grin bloomed on her face, a silent acknowledgment. "It's like a family heirloom containing more... family heirlooms." Thalasia snickered. The sight ten feet ahead of them silenced her amusement. "I'm calling it. She really was crazy."

"Sounds like a bag of burdens and excuses, you blue-feathered thief." Seru paused long enough to follow her gaze. "That's one word for it." Several others came to mind.

"Hey, being a klepto has its perks." She smirked. "Bat-shit in-sane?"

"Well prepared," he granted. "For those far less than us. Though I wouldn't be so sure this was her handiwork."

"Maybe it was her idea, but you're probably right." Thalasia rubbed the back of her neck. If it had just been the hollowed-out bottom full of spikes and the illusion of the bridge, it would have been easy enough for both of them. The back-and-forth movement of the logs created a whooshing sound that posed a challenge.

"They're swinging to a rhythm. If we remember the beat, we should be able to pass with ease." He'd explained as best he could on her terms. "Just don't sing to it," he offered, less than thrilled by the prospect.

"Oh, yeah, cuz that would do any good. I'm more concerned about the nonexistent bridge. Or are you going to surprise me and slip through another way?"

"I'll manage," he conceded. "You're better suited to this obstacle. Makes more sense for you to scout ahead. Just be careful. No more jerky hunts."

She untied the bag from her waist and held it out to him, then removed her boots. "The lighter, the better right now."

"Ignoring the fact that you're asking me to be your bag boy." He extended both hands to accept her gear. He set the bag at his feet and tied the shoes together, using the laces to sling them over his shoulder. "See if you can shut it down once you're across. Call if you need anything. Draw on the marks if you have to."

Taking a couple of steps back, Thalasia extended her wings and, with one good flap, hefted herself into the air. "I'm sure it could be worse." A grin spread across her face as she studied the logs, timing the swings by counting the seconds between each of the seven.

"Better not to tempt fate with thoughts like that." He stepped back, giving her room to work and focus.

She said nothing in response. With her attention on the task, she took a deep breath and started toward the first, her resolve firm. Slipping past that one with ease, she paused between the two and waited once again. Counting the timing, she slipped past the second, then the third... and the fourth. It wasn't until she'd gotten beyond the fifth that she faltered a little and pulled energy from the mark to stay in flight.

Seru did his best not to give in to the nagging in his gut. It pulled sharply when she faltered. His body moved to aid her before his mind stilled the impulse.

"I'm okay," she called out over her shoulder. Inhaling and exhaling a couple of deep breaths, she repeated her words. "I'm okay."

He cringed inwardly. She may have thought she was okay, but her repetitive reassurance did anything but convince him of that fact. She seemed to say it more for her own benefit.

Thalasia refocused on the timing of the swinging logs and made it past the last two. "I'm okay," she said one last time through heavy breaths as she sat.

He breathed a shallow sigh of relief once she landed safely on the other side. The feat appeared to have taken a lot more out of her than either of them expected, even with her ability to draw on his agility and stamina to help her through.

Sitting on the dirt-covered floor of the cave for another minute, Thalasia glanced from one stone wall to the other. A lever. Torches on each wall lit up. She pushed to her feet, strode over to the lever, and pulled it down.

The swinging of the logs slowed as a hidden grate slid out over the spiked hole in the ground and locked into place on the other side, providing Seru a safe way across.

Seru took a few wary steps onto the grate, testing the structure with his boot. When it held, he proceeded the rest of the way across toward where Thalasia stood, offering her shoes and bag. "Put it back." He nodded toward the still logs. "We'll sleep together."

With a half nod, Thalasia pushed the lever back to its original position. She accepted her boots first, shoved her sock-covered feet back in them, and did up the laces before collecting her purse from him. At least this way, they'd be protected.

Chapter Thirty-Three

Parthenia cupped Gavin's jaw and stroked his cheek, which her mate leaned into. "I'm perfectly okay with taking our time because I want to really explore every beautiful inch of you." They had several hours before the sun would rise. Until the curse was broken, things might go back to how they were, but they would still make every second count. She slipped her knapsack from her shoulder, and slowly backing up, she set it on the coffee table.

A soft growl left him, his eyes flashing a brilliant green. "As I wish to truly explore *every* single perfect inch of you, my beloved." He followed her, his eyes never leaving hers, his steps just as slow. "Do you know what I think, my love?"

She bit her bottom lip as another shiver shot down her spine. Her eyes shimmered, casting a soft glow across the room. Parthenia reached up to the hooks of her dress, just over her shoulders, as her ass hit the bed. "That this dress is an unnecessary confinement?"

"Absolutely," he growled. His eyes never left hers as he continued across the floor. He met her on the bed, wrapped an arm around her waist, and the soft mattress dipped as he scooted her up, climbed on, and leaned her back. As he hovered over her, his free hand, with a featherlight touch, began a slow trail of caresses, beginning at her mahogany hair and cheek. His touch sent shivers down her neck and collarbone, and her body curved into his embrace. His fingers brushed against the soft fabric, then danced against the side of her breast. "Gods... please, take it off." His plea was lost as his mouth descended once again, and their lips met in a frenzied kiss. His thumb moved over her nipple, now hardened against the thin dress.

Yes, she really *needed* to take it off. She swallowed his deep moan like it was air to her lungs. As their lips met, she shrugged her shoulders, freeing the dress and belt. Goddess, she'd yank the damn thing off if she thought it would come off faster that way. Caressing the nape of his neck, she lowered the front straps, feeling the soft material slide against her skin, and then the back straps down to her shoulders. She moaned against him. Gods, it was so much more than just a simple kiss. Her desires and emotions surged, mingled with the feel of the dress, as she arched her back with another groan, tugging it down to her waist.

A purr rose out of him. He slowly slid his hands down her body, the fabric of the dress rustling as he pulled it down, until it fell to the floor. As the kiss deepened, a low growl rumbled from his chest. Beside her on the bed, he pulled her close, his arm a secure band around her waist, their tongues still intertwined in a passionate kiss. He palmed her breast, groaning as he massaged and kneaded it.

Her body was already on fire. And it wasn't like the fire he'd always built in her before. He could touch her in ways he normally couldn't. But the sensations were all still pure bliss. She shivered with delight as his fingers danced across her, a symphony of pleasure erupting in every nerve ending. With a fluid motion, she draped a leg over his hip. With a soft touch, she traced the lines of his shoulders, then his shoulder blades, her hand gliding up and down his spine, before her hand inched lower.

His hand, after leaving her breast, continued its journey, lingering on her hip before coming to rest on her ass. He squeezed her rear and then took his fingers back up, starting all over again until he reached between her thighs. A deep moan escaped Gavin as his fingers first brushed against her sex. "Oh, gods."

"Please, don't stop," she whispered in a haughty breath.

"I am not planning on stopping for the entire night, my beloved," he rumbled. Gavin drove his tongue into her mouth as he found her center. He slid a finger inside her, and his thumb began a slow, sensual massage of her nub. "You feel so good."

"So do you." Beyond amazing. It felt wonderful. Like her body was sparking from the inside. Then she got an image of what had popped into his head. With a moan, she squeezed his hip, her leg tightening as her hips moved against his finger. Carefully, she ran her hands over the warmth of his back, sides, and chest. Grabbing the back of his head, she sealed their lips once more, her tongue gliding inside his mouth as she moved her body against his finger.

As he slid another finger into her sex, his strokes grew more forceful, matching the fervor of their kissing that filled the air with breathless sounds. Tightening his hold around her waist, he gripped her rear end.

Parthenia deepened the kiss, her hips moving faster as his fingers slid in and out. Her grip on his ass grew firmer as the pulsing sensation inside her intensified. A shiver of pure ecstasy danced along her skin, and she gasped, her muscles relaxing in blissful surrender. She cried out his name as she came hard, the heat of the moment making her toes curl and press into his ass.

Her mate pressed his face into her neck, inhaling deeply, and ran his tongue along the skin where her pulse thrummed. He growled softly in her ear, the sound raw and urgent as he helped her through her release. Even when it ended, his fingers and thumb still moved, though slower, as if reluctant to stop entirely. "There is something about my species I have not told you, my beloved." Gavin licked over her pulse point again, the warmth of his breath mingling with the softness of his fingers as they gently eased in and out of her sex. "When we make love to our true mate... we like to mark them. Canines here." He kissed her shoulder. "Felines here." He grazed his fangs gently over her neck. "I want to mark you as I make love to you," he growled. "I want everyone to know that you belong to me and that I belong to you."

Goddess, she loved how that felt. Wait. What had he said? Mark her? "Oh, gods..." She exposed her neck more for him, tilting her head back slightly. A mark from him—something that would show everyone they belonged to one another. "Gods, yes... yes... I would..." A groan passed her lips as her hips gently ground against his fingers. "I would... love that."

A low rumble resonated in his chest. His emerald eyes lit the room, a warm glow mixing with hers, reminiscent of brown agate catching the sunlight. He stroked the inner walls of her sex more firmly as their eyes locked. "My mouth will be here... many, *many* times, before this evening is over... but, right now... I want to make love to you." His lips met hers in a tender kiss, and he slowly removed his fingers from her. As he brought them to his mouth, his growl echoed in the space as he savored every drop before rolling her beneath him. She wrapped her legs around his waist, her heels sinking slightly into his flesh.

His breath hitched with a loud moan when his thick erection pressed against her warmth. "Oh, gods. I need you, Parthenia."

"I need you, too." His lips crashed against hers in another deep kiss. She arched her back, making his entry smoother. With a gentle motion, his cock slipped just a little more inside her, heightening their shared intimacy. Each time he moved deeper inside her, her nails found purchase in his shoulders.

Continuous growls and moans left him as he inched further and further into her sex. He fisted the blanket beneath her. "Tell me if I need to stop." His voice sounded a bit strangled, as his cock nudged up against some kind of barrier within her.

Oh, gods. His girth felt so huge. It wasn't painful. Not at all. Instead, it was like she was flying high above the clouds beneath the glowing moon. A rush of euphoria lifted her, the world swirling in a delightful dance of pure, blissful sensation. She'd been told that losing one's virginity... at least on the female side... it could be both painful and beautiful at the same time. That the two went hand in hand. She sensed his reluctance to cause her any pain, a feeling that resonated in the air between them. But the last thing she wanted was for him to stop. With her fingers still tracing the contours of his back, she tilted his head and kissed him softly. "Don't stop," she whispered, her voice husky. Maybe they only had this one night for right now, but soon they'd have forever. "Never stop."

A tear pricked one corner of his eye. Removing his hand from the blanket, he reached up to cup her jaw, his thumb caressing her cheek. A thousand words and more passed between them in that moment. The words he'd spoken to her, so very long ago—but felt like just moments before—left his mouth as he gazed into her eyes. "You are my beloved, my fate, and my destiny," he whispered against her lips, and then he thrust fully inside her. As his orgasm exploded out of him, he cried out her name, the sound echoing in the room.

Despite the sharp pinch, the searing orgasm that erupted from him instantly soothed the pain. With a loud moan escaping her lips, she arched her back, the friction of their bodies intensifying, and her hand moved from his face to his shoulder.

The hand that had been on her cheek retreated to grasp the blanket, and his arms wrapped tighter around her. He drew back gently and then drove back inside her. "Oh, gods, Parthenia..."

Holy Demeter. Mother of all gods. Her sex felt alive, every nerve ending ignited like the vibrant sparks flying from a crackling fire. As their lips fused together again, his growls pouring into the kiss with each slow thrust, the fire building inside of her was palpable. Gods, this was more than she ever could've imagined... more than she dared dream. Each thrust caused her hips to lift, as sounds of pleasure and need spilled from her. She squeezed his ass with her legs while her fingers smoothly slid down his back, sensing every muscle flex with every movement.

His hand, having left her waist, found its place again, gripping her ass. Continuous growls rolled out of him as he thrust harder inside her, his pace increasing.

With each joining of their hips, the heat inside her built, each movement fanning the flames of an inferno within her. A rush of warmth surged through her, amplifying the familiar pleasure tenfold. Her face flushed, and she let out a delighted gasp as the slight touch intensified. Gods, she didn't want him to stop. This was the moment. Without a second thought, Parthenia tilted her head, exposing the curve of her neck. "Oh, gods!"

Gavin's grip on her ass tightened, his fingers digging into her as he cradled the back of her head. As the glow of his green eyes intensified, he bared his fangs, and the air filled with the sharp sound of his hiss. His thrusts came harder, faster. "Come for me, beloved," he growled, and then sank his fangs into her neck, right over where her pulse pounded. It wasn't hard enough to puncture her skin, but there would definitely be indents. Indents that everyone would see—his mark—showing the world that every bit of her was his, and every bit of him was hers. He sucked on her skin, his tongue gliding over her neck, and he let out a deep roar as he came fiercely.

Her body tensed, every cell exploding with a searing, furious heat that left her breathless. Her thighs tensed as the warmth of their connection deepened, and the inner walls of her sex clenched tightly around his cock, sending them both over in a mighty wave. She cried out his name and dug her nails into his shoulders.

It was difficult to tell how much time passed before their mutual release ended. Even as the last wave trickled away, Gavin didn't stop the movements of his hips, though they slowed down. His hold on her ass and the back of her head remained as he took slow, deep strokes in and out of her. Separating his teeth from her neck, he stroked his tongue over his mark, a deep purr rising out of him. Sweeping his lips up her neck and jaw, he brushed a soft kiss over her lips as their gazes met. "I love you so much, Parthenia."

Her hips kept lifting to meet his. She just couldn't stop. As she ran her fingers up his spine, she felt the warmth of his fur, and stroked the nape of his neck, then tightened her legs around his hips. "I love you, too, Gavin. So much."

His cock slid deeper inside her as he moved up onto his knees, altering their position. "Gods, I cannot stop," he moaned out against her lips. "You feel so... so good."

"I don't want you to stop. You feel... incredible." It didn't really cover it. There was so much she could feel from him. A vibrant energy surged through her, each touch, every scent, magnified a thousandfold. As if their connection had grown stronger in the last couple of days or even the last hour. She couldn't say for sure. "Gods... don't stop... ever."

"Never, my love..." he groaned. "Never..." Gavin fused their lips together in a hard, deep kiss. He rolled over, bringing her with him, and suddenly she was on top, her legs wrapped around his waist. "Oh, gods, Parthenia..." Gripping her hips, he thrust into her with a growl, the air thick with desire.

"Oh, gods... Gavin..." How was it possible that she felt him *so* much deeper? She curled her feet under his ass, feeling the heat, and pressed her hands into his chest, her fingers flexing as she rocked against him. Her back arched as she moaned, the sound echoing in the silent room, her neck bent back, her breasts prominently visible.

"Oh, gods..." he cried out. "Do not stop!" He growled, then lowered his head to her breast, sucking and licking as he teased her with gentle bites. With each hard thrust, Gavin's hand massaged and kneaded her other breast, the pressure intensifying against her sensitive flesh.

She had no intention of stopping. Not that she could even if she wanted to, which she didn't. She shifted her hands to his biceps, and they sank slightly into his firm muscles. With a deep moan, her pace against him quickened, the sensation of his harder thrusts pushing her over the edge. "Oh, gods... come with me, love..." Her toes curled into his ass more. A gasp of pure, unadulterated pleasure escaped her lips as light exploded behind her eyes. Parthenia cried out his name, feeling the warmth and tightness of her inner walls gripping his cock.

He roared, the sound echoing through the room as pleasure overwhelmed him. His hand left her breast, gripping her ass tighter as it slid up to the nape of her neck, where soft strands of hair brushed against his fingers. Drawing her against him, he kissed her deeply, a growl rumbling as they found release together.

Gods, she had no words for how that had all felt. Nothing. With her arms around his neck, she deepened the kiss, savoring the moment as their bodies slowly stilled. A symphony of joyous pants bounced through the air, their happy breaths filling the room. Her forehead met his, and her fingers playfully explored the back of his neck.

Purring, his hand moved to caress her cheek as the other traced a path up and down her spine, across her wings. Neither of them uttered a word. Staring into those beautiful green orbs of his, nothing had to be said. Everything they desired... everything they felt... she could see it all. Sunlight bloomed in her chest, a warmth spreading through her veins at his nearness. These months, all the pain they'd endured... the time they had spent apart...it had all led to this moment. Tonight. Although it might be days before they had it again, for now, this would be enough.

Gavin wasn't sure how long it was before they finally made it into the bathroom. He carried Parthenia through the small dwelling until they'd found it, then carefully set her down on the floor. Nope, he didn't have a clue how to use anything in here, either. But they could figure it out together.

There was a smaller basin-type thing attached to the wall, opulent in coloring, and a silver oval-shaped contraption on the floor, against the other wall. Parthenia ran her fingers across it and then turned her attention to the glass door. There was a silver top with holes in the ceiling. "I think the water comes from there... but..." Her words trailed off.

"I honestly have *no* idea." He laughed softly. "We can figure this out, though." Smiling, he took her hand and led her inside, the scent of the place inviting. There weren't any handles or anything, but there were small, round silver things on the wall. "Those maybe?" Gavin let out a short chuckle. "Perhaps we should have asked for instructions earlier." It wasn't hilarious, per se. This was certainly much different from bathing in the river, or the springs in Pteryrina, though.

"Probably." She glanced between the two round silver things on the wall. Neither of them was clearly delineated. "Guess we'll just try one and see?" She shrugged. Hesitantly, her finger hovered over one. Glancing up at her mate, she depressed the button. The silver thing above poured down cold water that splashed and echoed around.

He couldn't stop the hiss that came out of him as the icy spray rained over them, and stepped out of it.

Parthenia shrieked and pushed it again, shutting it off. "Oh, gods, that's freezing."

"Really, *really* cold!" He shook off his fur. "That felt like the river in the middle of winter." He laughed. "Um, well, the other one?" He cocked an eyebrow. "Or maybe both at the same time? We do not want to burn ourselves with straight hot water."

"Yeah, both." She pushed the other silver disc first and then the one she'd depressed the first time.

"Oh, yes, that feels much better." He let out a soft chuckle as he shut the glass door, closing them in together. He stared up at the silver thing with holes in it that the water was coming out of. "Ingenious. This would certainly make things easier, especially in the colder months." He ran his hand under the spray, feeling the droplets on his skin before embracing her tightly. Smiling down at her, he stroked her cheek. He loved everything about her. She took his breath away each time he laid eyes on her. "You are so beautiful."

Sliding her arms around his waist, she grinned and leaned into his touch. "Thank you." She stroked his biceps. "You're stunning."

He purred. Gods, what just that small touch from her could always do to him. He'd never thought of himself as stunning, but she always made him feel that way. What he felt from her, how she was toward him, the way she looked at him. He leaned in, his touch lingering on her cheek before their lips met in a slow, passionate kiss. His hands found their way down her body, finally cupping her rear as he hoisted her. His tail encircled her waist as she brought her legs around his. "Gods, I will never get enough of you," he whispered against her lips. It was true. No matter how many times they met, whether for one night or in their usual manner, it always felt insufficient. "I love you so much."

"I love you, too. More than I ever thought possible."

One hand stayed on her ass. The other slid over her hip, his touch like a feather, his fingers trailing up and down her side. As he leaned her back against the vine-covered wall, water cascading over them, he savored another kiss, his lips lingering on hers. Every moment they'd ever spent together had been perfectly wonderful, beyond special. Even though they were dealing with tough times, that they were together made all of it beautiful. He wouldn't change a single moment of it. This fresh experience, one they were sharing, would be etched in their hearts forever. Gavin brushed his lips over hers again, then pressed his forehead to hers. "You saved my life when I met you."

Caressing the nape of his neck, she kissed him tenderly. "I believe we saved each other, my love."

He couldn't imagine not having her in his life. What she'd done for him since the day they'd met. She'd changed everything for him. Shown him a love such as he'd never known. Given him hope and helped him to realize dreams. Supported him and comforted him. Given him an undying happiness. Smiling, he brushed a soft kiss over her lips. "I am glad I could do that for you, my love. You have given me everything I never could have imagined I deserved. I cannot wait to spend the rest of my life with you." He kissed her, the sound of his growl rumbling in his chest as the kiss became more intense.

As the kiss deepened, she tangled her fingers in his fur, moaning softly, while her wings wrapped around them.

One hand found its way to her ass, while the other began a slow journey down her form. "Hades, I need you again." He slipped his tongue back into her mouth, and their tongues met and entwined. How was that even possible? They'd already been together so many times this evening. A surge of warmth enveloped him, the vibrant flames of passion igniting within him, mirroring the blazing fire within her.

A groan escaped her lips as she swept her tongue across his fangs. She stroked his arms with her wings, then planted her feet firmly on his ass.

He let out a growl, a sound that reverberated all around them at the desire in her head. She wanted him to bite her again. Oh yes, he could *definitely* do that again. Hades, the heat that radiated from her was so intense, it felt like standing in an inferno, fueling the fiery blaze within him. His cock was begging to be inside of her once more. It was a desire he had no intention of denying. His hand slid down to her hip, guiding her with a gentle touch, and he moaned with pleasure as he slid deep inside her, the rhythm of their movement filling the air. Oh, gods, it felt like he was *so much deeper* inside her at this angle. Slowly, he thrust in and out of her. She felt so incredible, so amazingly perfect. No words could accurately describe what all of this had felt like. Being with her in this way. A radiant warmth spread through him, igniting a symphony of sensation beyond touch, connecting their souls. "Oh, gods... Parthenia..."

As she spread her thighs, the scent of their bodies mixed as their hips swung to meet. Her wings brushed against his arms with each up-and-down sweep. "Gavin..."

Shivers shot through him. Her moans made his cock even harder. Not that he knew how that was possible. "Oh, gods, you feel so good, my love." Skating his lips down her jaw, then her neck, he brushed her skin and rumbled against her pulse point. He'd marked her other side. She craved another bite, but he hesitated, not wanting to deepen the marks already visible on her skin. His thrusts became more insistent, his tongue tracing her neck before a playful bite on her ear. "I am going to mark you again," he growled. "When I do, I want you to come all over me."

As a moan slipped from her mouth, Parthenia tilted her head, offering her neck to him. Her nails dug into his shoulders while her wings, with their soft feathers, moved across his back. "Oh, gods, yes, Gavin..."

Another rumble deep in his chest rolled out of him. Grazing his fangs down her neck, he let out a groan that echoed as his thrusts became more intense. He could feel her body tense—on the very precipice—as the moment drew near. "Come for me, beloved." A massive growl escaped him as he sank his fangs into the soft flesh of her neck.

With the heels of her feet digging into his ass, she tightened the grip on his shoulders and pressed her wings into the backs of his arms. "Oh, gods! Gavin!"

Oh, Hades, yes. A momentary puncture of his skin intensified the pleasure, bringing his climax nearer. The sound of her crying out his name electrified every synapse in his body. She came all over him, her wetness covering his cock as the muscles of her sex clenched tightly around him. With each harder thrust, Gavin clenched her ass and hip, the rhythm of their bodies syncing in the heated moment. With a powerful roar, his eyes shone brightly, their green light bouncing off the glass shower walls as he erupted within her. He sucked hard at her skin; his teeth still connected with a tight hold. His roar echoed as their mutual release ended, the scent of exertion still thick in the air. Trembles swept through him. His teeth parted as he kept his face hidden against her neck, purring and licking at the fresh mark. Gods, what it felt like to mark her. He could never have imagined how it would feel. Just as powerful the second time as it had been the first. Somehow, he knew it would always feel that way.

Her breath came out in heavy pants. "I have... no words..." she uttered between exhales.

Gavin kept his face right where it was, his grip, too, his breaths coming out in ragged patterns. He continued to purr, inhaling the scent of her body, which was still imbued with her arousal. So much stronger, so much more intoxicating. "Mmm..." He stroked his tongue over his mark again and gave a soft growl. "Me, either."

Chapter Thirty-Four

S eru watched the floor fall away and the timber resume an increasingly steady swing like a pendulum. Back and forth, back and forth.

"Come on. That was likely the last one, but I'd prefer to be a little deeper before setting up the tent and stuff," Thalasia said. It wasn't like the bed they'd slept in yesterday, but it was better than the tree they'd been in the other night. Certainly more comfortable.

A second passed before Seru responded. "Yeah. Okay."

Her eyes shifted toward the torches lining the rest of the cave. There wasn't much farther for them to go. From where they both stood, she could see the enclosure in the back. It would be the best place to set up. The farthest back they could go. She suspected he could see it as well. She didn't immediately see a way out, but that meant nothing.

"Good job with the logs and pit." Seru gave her a small smile as he swung his arm across her shoulders.

There were several responses on the tip of her tongue. A few included how it could've been handled with better finesse, but she'd gotten through with a little help from their connection. Reminded her they did, in fact, make a good team. "Thank you."

"What else do you have in that bag of yours?"

"There's way too much in here to even begin listing everything. Are you looking for something in particular?" Lots and lots of stuff. She slipped an arm around his waist and laid her head on his shoulder as they continued forward.

"No," he said. "Just curious."

"Say that I have enough to cover almost any circumstance." She half shrugged. "I like to be prepared for anything."

"You can't be prepared for everything all the time."

"I didn't say I was, but it doesn't mean I can't make the attempt. There's no way to always know what's coming ahead." Even her visions were only a small part of the story.

"For all the good it does."

Thalasia's eyebrows knitted together with a small sigh. "We'll have something a little more comfortable to sleep on than the cold stone, with some protection around us." She paused for a moment. It was minor in the reality of things, but it helped. "No one can be prepared for every circumstance."

"No, we just roll with the punches."

"I asked my father once why we bothered training if we tried to avoid fights as much as possible. He told me, 'It's better to be prepared in case the need ever arises than to be in the heat of the moment without a way out.' It's always kind of stuck with me." A grin spread across her face as one memory came to mind, prompting her to stifle a chuckle. "Of course, he was quickly reminded that sometimes, even when we are prepared, the unexpected happens."

"Why is that funny.?"

"I kicked him in the balls." She attempted to suppress the giggle, but it burst forth anyway. Pulling herself together, Thalasia cleared her throat. "To be fair, not only did he tell me to do it, but he also said he'd block it."

"Your family is really," Seru scrunched up his face, "weird."

"He was teaching me different ways to force a man to his knees." Of course, the idea always was so she could run away afterward. Something she wasn't all that great at doing.

"Wager he got that technique from your glorious grandmother, Adina."

"No." She didn't bother correcting him on Adina's relationship. He'd missed a couple of generations, but it wasn't important. "Adina was dead before my parents even met."

"Isn't that the value of shared blood?" he asked. "They needn't always be alive to be there. Certain traits and instincts gifted to the future."

"My father didn't share any blood with her. That came through my mother."

"Legacy allows them to live on, even after death. Maybe it's your mother who taught it to him. She chose him, didn't she?"

"Yes, she chose him. As for where he got his fighting techniques... I don't know. He never told me." She knew nothing about his family. His parents. If he had any siblings. Was it possible?

"Why?"

"Maybe because I never asked. Maybe he thought he was protecting..." Her words trailed off. "Or are you asking why she chose him?"

"Why did she choose him?" he repeated back.

Thalasia lifted her head from his shoulder. The answer was there in her head. She knew it was. This was something she'd discussed with her mother. She rubbed her temple and blinked as the words found their way into her memory. "She found someone she couldn't live without."

"Cryptic nonsense definitely runs in your family."

"I don't think it's nonsense. I think it makes perfect sense." The corner of her mouth tugged into a faint smile as she laid her head back on his shoulder.

"You sure that's not Adina talking?"

She chuckled. "I'm certain."

"How can you be sure?"

"Adina died about ten years before my mother was born. If that doesn't convince you, who do you think told me all the stories about what Adina did?" She snickered. "My mother used to gripe a lot about Adina's passages. 'Why couldn't she be more forthcoming?' 'Just what was she trying to hide?' 'Even dead, that woman is a pain in my ass.' Not to mention, Adina irritates me as much as she did my mother. Besides, I saw how much my parents loved each other. I believe she spoke the truth." Thalasia paused again. "Sometimes they drove each other insane, but then I'd catch moments where they just looked at each other and a silent conversation passed between them. In the way they held each other, almost always wanting the other person close... the stolen kisses...." Back then, she thought it was disgusting.

"Certain people complement certain parts of you. I don't think I've ever seen everything concentrated on just one person. It's natural to have moments of friction and affection, depending on what is compatible and what isn't."

She thought about what she'd heard about her parents when they first met. And what she saw during the short time she had with them. It was still hard to believe she'd lost them over eight years ago. "That's pretty accurate. I think that's why you learn to compromise."

"When you must," Seru agreed.

"You know, the more I think about it, the more I'm convinced my mother handled that whole kicking incident." Thalasia grinned. "She is the one who punched him once and slapped him twice within a week of them meeting."

"I'm sure he deserved it."

"According to her, he did when she decked him. That's how they met." She chuckled.

Seru didn't respond to that. They were making quick work of the trek to the end of the tunnel.

Her head lifted from his shoulder as more of the back of the rounded wall came into sight. The marking embedded in the stone wasn't hard to miss. Like so many things she'd seen, it was in Altese. And it noted a secret door. There were probably fissures somewhere. That also meant the book had to be buried beneath the floor nearby. "We should be good to set up anywhere here." She pointed out the symbol. "We have a back exit."

"What do you need from me?" Seru asked.

Unwinding her arm from his waist, she untied her bag and dug out this large circular-looking zipped-up black case. "Just unzip that. It has Velcro or something around it. Undo that, and it pretty much pops up."

Seru hesitated, if only for a moment, but he followed her directions, pulling the zipper along its track. More of the fabric unfurled, showcasing a vibrant array of colors. The fuzzy pieces separated with a skritching sound.

While he got the tent set up, she dug out the two-person sleeping bag and tossed it over her shoulder. It took her a minute longer to find the blanket. "It just unfolds from there. Really easy set-up."

"Doesn't this draw attention?"

"If we were in the middle of the forest, yes. We're in the back of a cave with like four different booby-traps between us and them."

"I was speaking generally. Most days, I don't imagine you've got the cover and added protection we do in this cave."

"Most days, it's either a tree or an inn. So... you're right. I don't have this kind of protection. This is my first time using the tent."

"So, why carry it around for a onetime use?"

"It's just in case. It may be used again. I never know."

"Excessive baggage."

She shook her head and smirked. "Just finish getting it set up so I can pull out the pillows."

"As you wish, Atlis," Seru teased sarcastically.

"That's more like it," she replied, her own words dripping with sarcasm. She grinned widely, highly amused.

"Shall I plow your fields next?" he offered. "Plant a few plum trees in your honor?"

"My fields don't really need to be plowed," she said with a glint in her eyes. "But if you really think the plum tree will grow, by all means, plow away."

"I don't think any tree grows in a cave... except maybe a magical one."

She covered her face part of the way with the blanket as she bit her bottom lip hard. It was the only way to keep a semi-straight face; even that was failing. Thalasia stood there for a minute as he finished with the tent. It really just unfolded and popped into place. She walked over and unzipped the entrance... when had her mind gone into the gutter? Gods, she must really be tired.

He eyed her as she inspected the structure. He shook his head. "Where would you live if you had the option to stay?"

Nearly dropping everything in her hands, Thalasia glanced over her shoulder at him. No one had ever asked her that before. She pursed her lips as she thought it over. "I don't know. I mean... you're the closest I have to a person... someplace I even belong." As she gave his question more thought, she kneeled down, set her bag aside and laid out the sleeping bag. She paused for a moment with her hand on the corner. "Realistically, I'd want to stay with you." She unzipped the corner and opened the sleeping bag up, spreading it out further before she laid out the blanket and pillows. "If we're speaking generally... somewhere by the ocean, where I could watch the sunrise and sunset. Someplace quiet, so I could spread my wings in the morning and again at night."

"Another island?"

"It wouldn't have to be. Just someplace away from people... away from the consistency of loud noises. I enjoy being able to walk along the beach, feel the sand between my toes, even run my fingers through the water as I fly across it... where I can feel the wind... fly between the clouds." Thalasia continued straightening out the blanket. Not that it really needed it. "Somewhere... I could feel... free."

"A realm without people might be nice. Can you go to places like that? Or only those that are inhabited by the weak and needy?"

She chuckled. "I can go anywhere. Even realms that don't have a lot of inhabitants or none." Finally satisfied with how it all looked, she readjusted to a sitting position. "You can come in now."

Seru ducked down, taking her announcement as an invitation. A pop-up bedroom. He crouched down near the entry, careful not to step on her bed. "But the visions force you to move on. Doesn't mean you can't go back."

"Eventually, yes. I don't exactly know when I'm going to have them or even how often. I mean, I've had three or four here in the last week alone." She untied her boots and slipped off her socks to get comfortable. "But you're right. There's nothing preventing me from going back."

"So, why haven't you?"

"A few places I've been told not to come back." Her lips curled into a small, amused smile. "What? I've caused trouble once or twice." Thalasia stretched out her legs. "Some places, they hold memories I'd like to forget. Others, there hasn't been a need or the desire." She sighed. "I don't trust easily. I don't make friends easily."

"Is that by choice or an inability to do so?"

"Probably a bit of both." She leaned back on her arms and crossed her ankles. "I've been raised to be mindful of what I tell people. That it's safer to keep secrets than it is to be... honest. Makes it difficult to make friends when people never get the chance to know the real you."

"Being convincing and being able to determine what they need is more important than making friends," he replied. "For someone to really be your friend, they have to equal you—and that's rarely possible."

"I don't know that I agree with that." She lowered her back to the ground. It wasn't perfect, but it was better than the alternative. "Everyone brings something different to the table."

"Codependence means reliance. It's not wise to rely on anyone fully."

"You're right. It's dangerous to rely on someone, except we can't do it all alone." No matter how hard they tried. Or even how hard she tried. No one could do it all by themselves. "Sometimes, you have to depend on someone and trust that they have your best interests at heart."

"No, you trust they have their best interests at heart. You ally with those with similar interests, all while you plan an exit strategy that ends in your favor once those interests are met."

She didn't bother looking at him as she thought about his words. Instead, she stared at the multicolored material of the tent above her. "Sounds like a great way to always be alone."

"You don't get stabbed in the back when you're alone. I've never minded solitude. Then again, I've never been one who relied on the opinions of others to validate my worth or existence."

Thalasia propped up on her elbow. "I don't believe solitude doesn't get to you. Because if that was the case, you wouldn't need to pull anyone close to you. You wouldn't seek comfort because it wouldn't matter."

"I have my books."

"Ha!" She smirked. "You sleep with your arms around your books? Do they hug you back? Offer you warmth... without being lit on fire? Talk back to you? Push you outside of your comfort zone?" Thalasia sat up a bit more with each question. She had books, too, but they had their limits.

"The books are a more secure option than most people," he tilted his head. "I have no use for warmth or conversation with lesser minds. I'm able to push myself when necessary."

"Yet you not only made the choice to consistently protect me, but to tie yourself to me." Pulling a leg close to her chest, she laid her chin on her knee and stared at him for a long moment. "You know what Klaus told me the day before he was killed? He said, 'Everyone needs someone, Thalasia. When the time comes and you find that someone, don't let it pass you by. Let yourself need them.'" She paused. "If all of that were completely true, no one would matter to you except you. Regardless of your involvement, the war coming to the isle wouldn't matter to you. You wouldn't have second-guessed yourself when you started the mark. You would've just gone through with it no matter the consequences because it would've brought you closer to your goal."

"Didn't it, anyway?" He stared at her for a long moment.

"I don't know. Did it?"

He glanced down at his feet and shrugged. "Guess we'll play it out and see."

A small smile tugged at the corners of her mouth. He could fool himself, but he couldn't fool her. "We should get some rest."

He nodded.

"There's enough room here for both of us. You can sleep under the blanket if you want or on top. However, you're comfortable."

"Yeah..." he mumbled, reluctantly climbing in next to her.

As she lowered herself, her back finally met the blanket, and she sank her head into the pillow. Seru did his best to settle next to her, closing his eyes. Slow, shallow breaths. Though exhaustion weighed heavily on her, she pushed through, needing to see him drift off. Last time he'd ended up with a nightmare, and she hoped they could prevent it.

"Watching me sleep won't offer you any rest," Seru said, eyes still closed, with his hands resting atop his chest.

"No, but trying to prevent a nightmare might."

"You can't prevent them. Go to sleep, Thalasia."

"You sure about that? You calmed down a little." And then it resurfaced, and his claws ended up in her thigh.

"Yes, I'm sure. And, no. I don't want to talk about them." He cracked open an eye, glowering at her. "Close your eyes and go to sleep."

"Oh, I didn't think you would." She rolled over onto her side, adjusting just a little for her wings before she got comfortable. "Curl up to me if you desire."

"Don't need warmth, remember? You might." He opened one arm to her.

It wasn't the reason she suggested it. Still, she curled up to him, one of her wings draped across him.

"You don't care if I spear you with my talons again?" he asked.

"Eh... you're less likely to do it this way, but if it happens... it happens." The only way to stop the nightmares was to talk about them. Give them less power.

"Could you be any more stubborn?" he smiled, if only slightly.

"Yes. Yes, I could." She half-smirked and snuggled a little closer.

He mumbled an imperceptible sound.

"You know you like it," she muttered with a hint of sarcasm. Her voice lacked the sarcastic edge it deserved; she was too tired.

"No, I don't," he said. "It's that kinda stubborn resolve that'll get you killed."

"It's the kind of resolve that has kept me alive." Not that he was wrong, but she wasn't, either.

"Not your training, just your stubborn resolve."

"Just as stubborn as I am," she yawned. "Both of us... stubborn and pig-headed." Her eyes drifted shut. She was too tired to argue.

"If you say so..."

"Yep... now stop talking. My pillows..." she yawned again. "...don't talk."

"I'm not a pillow," Seru grumbled.

"You are for now... now shush... or I'm going to fluff you." A small grin played on her lips as she leaned into him, her body melting into his embrace.

"Don't even think about it," Seru cautioned.

"I amend my earlier assessment. Stubborn, bossy, and somewhat grumpy." Her mouth stretched wide as she yawned once more. Although he had it in him to be kind. She snickered in amusement.

"I can force you to go to sleep, if you prefer," Seru's voice contained a gravelly edge to it.

"See... bossy."

"Yes, now... Go. To. Sleep."

"Bossy... kind... lov..." She mumbled, the last word cutting off as sleep finally claimed her.

Chapter Thirty-Five

With a gasp, Thalasia bolted upright, her eyes snapping open. She rapidly scanned the area, trying to absorb everything around her. The burning torches on the stone wall. The bright colors of the tent. Right. Right. She and Seru were in the cave. With a ragged exhale, she looked over her shoulder, her heart pounding.

Next to her, Seru let out a low rumble, settled into a deep slumber. A small book lay open in his outstretched right hand. A faint glow emanated from between its pages. The blue-violet light strobed on the dimly lit cave, a slow steady thrum—like a heartbeat.

What in the world? If the small book hadn't caught her attention, she might've focused on the nightmare that had stirred her from her repose. Or made note of the fact that Seru had actually fallen asleep. Instead, she scooted back as quietly as she could, positioning herself to inspect the book in his hand, the pages rustling softly.

An eerie, otherworldly light bathed the pages as they fanned open. Nestled between the folds, a small cluster of seeds rooted into the parchment as if feasting on the empty folio. A pair of buds grew from the seeds, the larger very near blooming. The tips of white petals just barely emerged from the indigo sprout.

Well, that definitely wasn't what she expected. But what in the gods was it? White petals. Something about it looked familiar, though. She couldn't quite pin it down. A persistent thought was scratching at the back of her mind. Thalasia stared, her brow furrowed, at the budding petals, as if scrutinizing them for a hidden message.

On closer inspection, the plant's roots connected not only to the pages but to Seru. The dainty branches entangled themselves around his thumb, down the palm of his hand, straight into the veins at his wrist. They brightened and dimmed, darkened and paused, before brightening and dimming again. Some form of energy flowed through them.

What the fuck? Her eyes flicked from the book to him, then quickly returned to the page. *Holy fuck!* Damn poppy flowers. She'd been told about the red fields in Pteryrina. Except these weren't red, which could only mean... "Son of a bitch," she muttered. Was he out of his fucking mind?

Without giving it much thought, Thalasia climbed over Seru to the other side. She shoved a hand through her hair, then gently traced a finger along the coarse branches that had rooted themselves into the veins at his wrist. She had to figure out how deep they'd gotten before she tried to separate it. The last thing either of them needed was for things to get worse.

Her touch brought a nearly imperceptible spasm of the muscles in his arm. In an instant, his free hand constricted around her wrist. The movement was so quick she hadn't felt or seen it. "What are you doing?" Seru asked, voice thick with sleep. His eyes, intensely blue, bore into her.

Inhaling and exhaling a deep breath, she calmed the pounding in her heart. It wouldn't do any good to get upset with him at the moment. "I'd ask you the same thing. What is this, Seru?"

He sat up, pulling her onto his lap. The strength of his arms captured her around the waist, securing her close and pressing her sweat-slick form against the front of his body. "What is what?" he asked, closing his eyes and nuzzling along her shoulder. In the same motion, the book quickly disappeared. He inhaled a slowly drawn out-breath of her scent. Whispering a warm rush over her neck, he cracked open his eyes—no longer alight with power—like a lazy cat to find himself face to face with the marks on her neck. The barest brush of fingers tickled along the outside rim of the brand. "Does it still hurt?"

For a split second, she almost got distracted. Except her pheromones were well under control. Even the remnants of the nightmare running around in her head couldn't deter her from what she'd seen. Nor could his questions. Or the book that she'd lost sight of. Thalasia pressed her hand on his chest and pushed him back ever so slightly. "If you think you're going to nuzzle me and focus my attention elsewhere, you have another thing coming. I saw the flowers, and I know *what* they are. Why?"

"They help me sleep," he replied simply, sounding drowsy and disappointed. He buried his face in her neck. "You smell really nice."

It was the answer she had expected. His nightmares. The things he refused to talk about. Letting out a soft breath, she couldn't stop her hand from coming up to play with the ends of his mane. "Once we get off the isle, maybe even before, we'll have to find another way for you to sleep."

She hadn't noticed the gentle throbbing in her neck when she'd startled awake. The damn female had gotten in her head again. Though she snapped herself out of it. Now, it was more like a dull ache.

Seru let out a deep breath, ruffling her hair. "Mmmm. So, you're not angry..." he mused, daring to run his tongue along her neck.

"Not as angry as I should be." She should be furious, but it wasn't as if she'd told him about her experience with being drugged. Nor could she blame him for trying to find a way, one he had likely used before, to rest. She was all too familiar with nightmares. Still, there were other answers out there. Something else they could do that would help him sleep.

He rested his chin on her shoulder. "Do you want to talk about it?" His grip tightened around her waist.

Although she hadn't fully registered it, the feel of his tongue along her neck had sparked something faint inside of her. Something that still lingered. She continued to play with the end of his mane, slowly twirling it around her finger. "Minerva... trying to find a new way to use... my fears and my..." No, that wasn't entirely right. It hadn't just been her desire, but it had been his, too. "Our desires... using them against me. Though it felt damn good to knock her out this time."

Damn good. Thalasia smiled. Actually, it almost made her feel like herself. Something more at the same time. Seeing Seru without the collar around his neck in her nightmare, it had almost done the job. Truly thrown her off. To see that they'd succeeded only to be captured by Minerva and Markham. To watch Minerva cut Seru, see his blood pool, but something had snapped. Like a rubber band falling back into place. She couldn't say what had made her see the truth, but once she'd accepted it as just a nightmare—everything had fallen away.

"Our desires?" he questioned, nuzzling her again. This time all the way up her neck until they were ear to ear, cheek to cheek. His hand wove its way up her arm. Interlacing his fingers with hers, he pressed her hand deeper into his mane.

Her fingers played more with those silky locks, something she rather enjoyed. The faint spark lit up a little more. Her eyelids lowered ever so slightly. "Yes," she whispered. "Your collar... it was gone."

Not that it had been the only thing they'd desired. But Minerva had already tried playing on her insecurities with that. The tension in her muscles eased. She'd taken full control of her mind. Just as she'd done with her powers and her body.

Seru was the only one who had ever drawn a more sexual response out of her. One... that after their earlier failed kiss... she wasn't sure would return. But something was igniting. It was a little stronger, but still nothing more than a small flame.

That drew a derisive sound from him. "If only she were as powerful as she fancies herself... she sounds delusional." A slight smile graced his lips as he settled in against her, dropping a soft kiss atop her shoulder, where his lips seemed content to linger.

A slight shiver rolled down her spine. "I don't know about delusional... Maybe. Insane. Crazy. I suppose any of the above would work." She chuckled. "Though I agree with you about her power."

The female she'd feared as a child hadn't changed. But she was no longer a child. She'd grown into a woman. Her power was gaining strength more and more each day, especially the closer she got to the full moon, her birth moon. "I think she was trying to use it to make me feel like a failure. That even though we'd been successful in our endeavor, they'd still been able to capture both of us."

Something she hadn't really thought much about. If they had been so focused on nabbing her, then why would she have shown Seru in chains, too? Huh. Was it possible—they wanted both of them?

"You are far from a failure," Seru mumbled. "You're stronger and braver than that foolish woman could ever hope to be." His fingers played over her exposed skin. He blew a warm breath over her feathers. "If they ever capture us, it's because we allowed it to happen."

It was something like what she'd remembered. At least part of it. Although she might categorize his comment as brave with stupid, brazen maybe. Despite her attempts not to run into anything half-assed, sometimes it happened. Goosebumps trailed across her flesh.

"For a moment, I felt like it, but then she did something, something I knew wasn't possible. That snapped me out of it. And in the dream, once I accepted it wasn't true, I broke my chains." It seemed quite metaphorical, even if it had felt real in her mind. That's what she was trying to do—break her chains.

"Villains often over-glorify themselves to the point of creating a false image. Their egos surpass reality. I'm glad the spell worked and you're feeling more... yourself."

A conversation about Minerva and her ego was unnecessary. She'd spent months chained up in that cabin. Tortured by that female's hand. "Mostly." Part of her still felt out of sync, but she could pinpoint why. That wasn't true. There had been a difference when he'd first started touching her, nuzzling against her. It would've normally affected her more. Though some responses seemed to peek through.

"At least more so than in the last few days." And the rollercoaster of emotions that she'd gone through. She was still trying to figure out how to truly navigate them. Not that it stopped her from playing more with his mane. She quite enjoyed it.

"Is there a part we should be worried about?" he prompted.

Despite the trials of her emotions, and the one time she'd truly been angry... a small smirk crossed her face. According to him, she'd looked hot when she was pissed, but it wasn't helpful. Though was that worse than how little she'd felt as they made their way toward the cave? "Maybe... but I'm not entirely sure yet."

Thalasia bit her bottom lip and sighed heavily. "My emotions are at the epicenter of my power. I may be more like myself, but I can't be like I was when I first got here. On the verge of a complete shutdown. That could be damaging."

"You'll figure it out," he reassured. "Balance. Just like in training."

She just hoped she figured it out in time. They may have been in a cave, but she could still sense the pull of the moon, which meant it was nighttime. The two of them had slept for hours. But they'd both needed it. She pressed a soft kiss on his forehead. "I'm sure you're right."

For now, they had other obstacles to address. A book and strings. One was a little easier to get to than the other. "I'm gonna get my shoes on and we can get all of this cleaned up, then find the book."

"What about the book you took from the sirens?"

There was only one book she'd taken from Antekilio. Well, no, that wasn't true. But the other was just supposed to be family history. Would that have an answer? Hmm, she supposed it was possible. "I didn't really look at it, but I suspect it's just a bunch of information on the family line. No. The book that should have the most information is *Celestimo*. Which, according to the map, is supposed to be buried here."

"So, you want us to dig up the entire cavern floor?" he asked dryly.

Thalasia chuckled. "No. There are markings on the cavern wall. I should be able to open it fairly easily. What?" She grinned. "I saw it as we were setting up earlier."

"Very well..." Seru sighed.

"Gee, don't sound so excited." Finding the book had been one of many goals they'd made. "I thought you wanted the book for your collection. Or are you disappointed for another reason?"

He reclined back on his elbows. "Except for you, I think I preferred the everlasting darkness behind my eyelids."

Readjusting her position, she straddled him. Another shiver trickled down her spine. It had been about the mission for so long. Something she'd simply grown accustomed to over the years. But things had slowly changed with him. There would always be something to do. What was it Cyon had said she needed to learn how to do? Smell the roses? "I've never been very good at slowing down."

He watched her, smoothing his hands up her thighs. "The way you barreled across that bridge onto the beach, I never would have guessed."

Her body warmed a bit at his touch. Something she hadn't expected after the earlier disaster. Yeah, so he'd pointed out that they needed to close the marks. She swallowed to wet her parched throat. "I... uh... that was only partially my fault. I was trying to get to the other side before more guilers came after me... the barrier decided I wasn't moving fast enough."

"Ah..." Seru replied. A faint smile touched his lips.

"I don't *always* come tumbling out like that. My entrance... normally, it's a bit more graceful." So, to speak. She had, as he so eloquently put it, barreled into a few other places. The corners of her mouth tugged into a grin with a small chuckle. "Okay. So, some of them have been pretty bad."

Were they really sitting there talking about her lack of finesse when she crossed into a new place? Or was there something else going on in that head of his? His hands had been on her since she'd woken him up. Her eyes met his. She had a slight sense of déjà vu as her scent thickened. Except instead of a cave, they'd been in the fae forest. "We seem to have a thing about me sitting on you like this." Not that she minded. In fact, she rather enjoyed it, especially now that he knew more than she'd ever meant to share with him.

His nostrils flared. "Do we now?" Seru teased with a slight raise of his brow. "Your scent is so strong I can taste it."

Her body warmed a little more as her scent intensified; slowly rolling off of her in waves, almost to where it filled the tent. Not that she hadn't noticed the way her body was responding to him. She could feel the flush as it spread out from her core. Placing her hands on his belly, they inched higher to his chest.

They very much had this as a thing. She bit her bottom lip. "The forest... the inn... here..." It was only a few times, but it also felt like the most natural thing ever. In the forest, she'd done it to clarify that she thought he was stunning. Gorgeous no matter his form. The inn... where they'd sufficiently made out... and then... now.

"Guess we're becoming too predictable," Seru replied, only half teasing. "Please stop that." He reached up, gently stroking his knuckles over her cheek. His thumb traced the skin beneath her teeth, coaxing her to release her lip.

With a soft, heated breath, she released her lip. Not that she could really help herself. It had become second nature around him. Especially when her body was reacting this way. When her sexual awakening had first been mentioned, she'd acted as if she didn't understand the reference. But she had. At least enough.

Her scent was so thick in the tent, though nowhere near what it could be. With only a few days before the full moon... if everything she'd ever learned was accurate, her scent should go beyond the tent and seep into the cave. She leaned into his touch, nuzzling her cheek ever so slightly against his palm. "Would you prefer me to do something else?"

"Come back to bed... and forget the book?"

Eventually, they'd have to look for the book, but with the way she felt at the moment, spending a bit more time in bed sounded heavenly. Take some time for them. Not like it could hurt. The corners of her mouth tugged into a smile. "We haven't actually left."

"Weren't you just about to go hunting for shoes?"

"Yes, but I'm not looking for them now. Am I?" She leaned forward just a little.

"No..." Seru replied hesitantly. "I suppose you're not."

"Then it would seem we're staying in bed a little longer, wouldn't it?" Was he unsure of the simplicity of the question? Or was he back to questioning his desires? Either way, she wasn't moving, but she also wouldn't keep putting herself out there. Well, her heart anyway. Not that any of that seemed, at the moment, to deter the heat in her body or the way her scent rolled out in small waves.

After a moment, Seru grasped her wrist and pulled her forward. He nestled her against his chest, kissing her hair. "I'm not second-guessing my offer."

As her scent intensified, her wings shifted, brushing softly against his arms. "Good." The nightmare had reminded her of something else. Her worth and her value. For the male she chose, he had to equal that worth and value. She certainly didn't expect to find that in a saint beast 800 years her senior. Listening to the steady beat of his heart, Thalasia traced slow circles on his chest. "Comfortable?"

"More than. You love birds and your fancy... tents." The last sounded more like a question.

She chuckled. "Does the color bother you that badly?"

"No, I'm just still not used to such extravagance," he teased. "The dragons bathe themselves in luxury and cherish their brilliant gemstone hues, so it's not that unfamiliar. It's just strange being here."

"Oh yeah, this is *really* extravagant. This nice tent, large sleeping bag, and fluffy pillows." She chuckled and continued tracing slow circles. Strange could be comforting. And normal. She preferred trees when she could, but a pleasant inn was good, too. This was better than a tree, but not as good as an inn. Usually. She was actually comfortable lying on top of him like this.

"It's more extravagant—and more crowded—than I'm accustomed to," Seru admitted. "Books don't typically talk back or blast me with pheromones or pounce on me."

Definitely more crowded than she was used to. She propped her head up, resting it on top of her hand, and smirked. "The pheromones are your fault, and I didn't pounce on you. However, I'll concede the first." Books didn't talk back. Though the spacing, they'd get used to that. Or so she supposed.

"Is that right? At least you come with more books."

Slightly amused at his latter comment, she shook her head with a faint smile on her face. Especially considering he hadn't wanted to even read one book in her possession when it had first been presented. Hard to believe that hadn't been that long ago. A day or two at most. "Oh yeah, the pheromones are completely your fault. If it hadn't been for you, they wouldn't have been triggered, nor would they have continued to intensify. Drawing you in more and more, until there's no choice but to respond."

Her scent flared. Yes. He hadn't been able to allow her to go through with her original plan. Maybe he'd been right. While it hadn't really been the beginning of everything, it had certainly been a small part of what led them to where they were in that tent. The decisions they'd made. The fact remained, whether she stayed here on Prisma Isle or they left together, she'd do whatever it took to help him get the collar off.

"If you want me to leave, all you have to do is say so." He closed his eyes, stroking her hair as he breathed in her scent.

"The last thing I want is for you to leave." She bit her bottom lip again. Second nature, especially with him stroking her hair. As she closed her eyes, she exhaled a sigh of contentment, and her captivating aroma became more potent. "I never want you to leave," she whispered.

"It's not like I could go, but so far, you've already seen most of what this dreadful chunk of rock and its surrounding waters offer," Seru replied.

That wasn't really the point. Maybe she needed to explain herself. Opening her eyes, she started tracing circles on his chest again. "I don't blame you for triggering them. Maybe it sounded like it, but I don't. I know we've had our back and forth and difficulties over the last couple of days. Though it feels longer. Like we've been doing this dance for months." A small smile crept onto her face. "And maybe... it was unexpected, but... I'm glad you're the one that triggered them."

"I don't pretend to understand your logic, but I appreciate your faith in me."

That was the thing. It wasn't logical. It was emotional. Maybe she needed to come clean about that. That she'd understood what Mac was talking about; although she had been curious about how he knew about them. "Sirens don't have pheromones. Only Atlis do." She wasn't sure if that really cleared it all up, but maybe it would.

"Yes, well... I doubt your average siren faces the same..." he paused, "complications in passing on their... legacy."

"No. They don't." Which was why pheromones would only be triggered by someone suitable and worthy of her. Hmm, that made her curious, though. If that was the case for all Atlis, how had her great-great grandmother and mother found sirens as suitable? Not something she was truly going to question at the moment.

"If only one child becomes the next Atlis, is it always the firstborn? How is that decided?"

"It's always the firstborn female." She knew her great-great grandmother had more than one child. It wasn't until her lastborn that the woman had the next Atlis.

"Because males can't be trusted." It wasn't really a question.

She wasn't so sure about that. She'd kept a lot from him. Even now, she still had secrets. It wouldn't surprise her in the least bit if he did, too. "I think it has more to do with the female psyche."

"The female psyche?"

"Yes. Our ability to find a balance between the mental and emotional." She didn't think she had explained it very well. Hmm, maybe there was another way. "We have to be passionate, but maintain control and consider all outcomes with every decision we make. And usually, it has to be done in a matter of seconds, so we have to be quick-thinking, too."

"And men can't accomplish those same qualities?"

She lifted her gaze to his. "I think they can. I've seen males accomplish impressive feats." Maybe that was one way they were supposed to change the role. The way they fulfilled the prophecy.

"Hmm," Seru's gaze locked on hers. "Do your thoughts directly alter the rules guiding the position of Atlis?"

"I don't think it has for others, but... if everything I've learned is accurate." She paused. They'd discussed some of it, but not everything. But this... it was a beginning. "With my Allimos at my side, we'll be able to change it all."

"That's a tall order," he said.

Yeah, well, she'd been given the power for it. But it was more than that. "Is it? Or is it just a way to ensure that the Atlis grow stronger, survive longer, and help other realms thrive?"

He shrugged at that. "I don't know. What do you think? You have infinitely more experience in being an Atlis than I do in being an Allimos."

Her thoughts? She'd been prepared to die on this mission. But nearly everyone in her line had been killed as they were discovered. If she were honest... "I think I'm tired of having to hide in fear that I'll follow in my parents' path. It's one thing to blend in... but it's entirely different to hide everything about who you are."

"If the Atlis are as powerful as they claim, you wouldn't need to hide," Seru continued. "What did they do wrong that you can do right? Do better?"

"I don't think they've been as strong as I am. Or had the same powers that I do." Many of them had surprised her parents when she was younger. What had they done wrong? She couldn't think of any one thing, but she wasn't her parents, either. "Just do better."

"Powers you were born with, however strong, aren't equivalent to 'better.'" He exhaled a pained breath, throwing his arm over his eyes. "Can we just change the subject?"

"No, it doesn't." She conceded. It meant she had more responsibility. More to learn. More to be in control over. It wasn't something she particularly cared for, but it wasn't something she could change, either. Shifting her position on top of him just a little, Thalasia reached up over his arm and stroked her thumb across the top of his brow. "We can do that."

"Can we?"

Thalasia sighed. "Inevitably, we'll have to make our decisions. I can feel how close the full moon is... like a clock neither of us can ignore. Whether we table it for now, the decision will still be waiting."

Had they been going about this all the wrong way? She'd told him she wouldn't have done anything differently. But that wasn't entirely true. She might've asked more questions, handled the situation with Cyon initially better. Her own jealousy had caused that, but would he?

"Let me ask you something. It's okay if you don't have an answer. Given everything you know now about me... would you still have marked me?"

"It's not that simple," he replied, peeking out from behind his arm. His tongue flicked across his lips. "The beast's part of the mark would have without question. But the beast doesn't rely on thoughts or decisions; it's purely fueled by instinct." Seru paused. "My answer—as more than just bestial instinct—is more... complex. Not because of you. As a man viewing a woman, I'd have made the same choice. But, because of the weight of the collective burdens we've, individually and collectively, chosen to bring about... I fear they may be more than any of us has any right to ask the other to bear."

"But did we actually ask the other... or have we consistently made an active choice to choose the other? Regardless of the consequences." As many times as he had pushed her back, or she had attempted to shut him out, they had still continued to choose one another. It had been that way since they had met. That was something the nightmare had made clear. They had chosen one another. "When I said I didn't want you to leave... I didn't just mean here. Whether we've wanted to accept it or recognize it... I don't think that has altered any since the bridge. We worked together to fight the guilers, then you carried me and lied to Aurelia about my passing out. Even when I flew off after Aurelia's... comments on sex... you came after me. Every moment, every opportunity, we could have done something different. Gone a different path." She half shrugged. "But we didn't. We each saw something in the other, and that has been leading us this entire time. Yes... it included some arguments along the way..." A small smile crossed her face. "Just means we've easily figured out each other's buttons."

"We both saw—see and seize—opportunity in one another for our own ends. Is that really the same thing?" Seru asked, skeptical.

"You really think you're an opportunity?" She pushed up to a sitting position. That wasn't how she'd seen him. It hadn't changed. "Do you really think you *still* see me that way? Do you really still think you're prepared to dump me in someone else's lap? Because I don't." If so, he wouldn't have given two cents about her going in search of the book. Keeping her here in bed would've been the last thing he cared about doing. Nor would he have nuzzled her to bury himself in her scent or cover her in his smell. None of that would have mattered. Not one bit. "You've never been just someone else to help. Someone whose tether I could figure out how to break when I can't do a thing about my own. Is that how it started? Yes. Somewhere along the way... it changed."

"I'd have more difficulty doing so, but if I believed it truly to be in your better interest in terms of survival... If I didn't believe I could loosen this noose around my neck... Yes, I would. Even if it meant you resented me for the rest of your life."

"That's what you don't seem to get. I wouldn't resent you. Nor would I accept another person. I refuse to tie myself to someone I don't care about. I'd rather spend however many years I have... alone... than be with someone... simply for survival." Whether he liked it or not. That part... it wasn't his decision. It was hers and hers alone.

"My robbing you of choice would be the spark that ignited your resentment." He sighed. "Atlis are granted free will. Dragons submit to those more powerful. It might even work out so we can see each other regularly."

"You still don't get it." Shaking her head, she climbed off of him. "It's you or nothing. *That* is my choice."

"So, you'd do whatever it took to remain with me? No matter what it cost you?"

"Yes," she said without hesitation. It had been a decision she'd made days before. Even with everything she knew now, it didn't change her mind about that.

"You haven't even seen with your own eyes what that could mean," Seru replied, watching after her, eyes narrowed.

"And you somehow think that will alter my decision..." She glanced over her shoulder at him. "If that's the case, then you don't know me as well as you think you do."

Once she decided on something, she stayed the course. Maybe she didn't know how this would impact everything else, but honestly, she didn't care. For the first time in her life, she wasn't bowing to someone else. Doing what others thought she should do.

Thalasia tugged her knees up to her chest. Wrapping her arms around her knees, she rested her head on them, her hair falling to the side as she did. This time, she was choosing for herself.

"You're a strange bird," he whispered.

"Guess that puts us on equal ground because you're strange, too," she said without bothering to look at him. Not that she'd ever crossed paths with a saint beast before. A dragon, yes, but the ones she'd dealt with hadn't been as... snarky as Aurelia. They hadn't exactly been agreeable, either.

"How do you figure?"

"While I have little to compare you to... at least, saint beast wise... but in another capacity..." She had her interactions with others and people watching. "You have a tendency to act like a jealous boyfriend, but then act put off by the notion. You find more comfort in books than people... granted... I don't fault you for that. People are crazy." And difficult to tolerate ninety percent of the time. "When you get close to people, you push them away if they care too much, but then get upset when they do the same thing to you." Yeah. She'd gotten more from their time with Marius than she bargained for. Or maybe she was just finally piecing more of the puzzle together. After all, Marius had said Seru was hard to love. Not impossible, just hard.

"I am not typical of my brothers, either," Seru said. "I'm not sure what a 'boyfriend' is, and I am *not* envious. The only people other than yourself I've ever cared for—even remotely—are alive because they're not closer to me. Keeping terms in place allows them to stay that way."

Lifting her head, she peered over her shoulder at him. The first part, she believed. The second... bullshit... minus the term 'boyfriend.' She'd spent *way* too much time around humans, picking up on their vernacular. "Oh? So, you didn't care that I was flirting with the bartender at Belly of the Beast? Muttering for me to call him 'hot stuff' one more time, it was just for laughs?" The third... he seemed to offer an explanation, but was it really one? Or was it only half of the answer? "If they're alive because of it, then why do you care if they pushed you away? Why would it matter?"

"Finding issue in your sullying your dignity hardly qualifies as envy," Seru reasoned. "Especially over some glitzy ponce, who succumbed to your charms. That bartender had nothing for me to be envious of. You degraded yourself more than you aided any objective—yours or mine. Should I have simply remained silent and allowed you your—" He placed his head in his hand. "Control... I suppose," Seru offered weakly through gritted teeth. "Both the comfort in having it and the lack of it... I don't..." His tongue flicked over the points of his fangs. "Marius is mine. Not the Sea's, or its peoples. Just because we painted the illusion into reality doesn't change the facts."

Was he really that delusional? That blind? Dropping her legs, she reached for her boots and socks. "Believe it or not, seducing that bartender to get passes to the VIP section was the goal. I got exactly what I wanted from the manticore. Whether I had to expose a few of my assets to him or the bouncer... it wouldn't have made a difference. The outcome would've been the same."

Yeah. She could feel the pain in her heart, but she was trying her damnedest to look past it. Now, they'd come full circle. Without looking back at him, she pulled on her socks. "Marius is trying to let you go. Trying to do what he believes is best for your safety." Hugging her knees to her chest again, she pressed the heels of her hands against her eyes and dragged her palms across the top of her head. "It amazes me how brilliant and idiotic you can be at the same time."

"Just because that *method* is tried and true doesn't mean alternatives—like using your substantial wit to outsmart them—without the show of flesh, aren't just as effective." He sighed heavily. "Can you stop with that? You wanted answers. Now, you're eager to storm back to the mission because that's easier?" He pushed his mane back. "Marius is trying to please everyone else instead of himself. He's a sorcerer and a powerful one. But his underlying desire for acceptance and peace is clouding his judgment. He never wanted to be king. He only did it because I pushed him to. I pushed him so we might raise a force capable of combating Verie and the Clouds. I didn't expect his softness would undermine the effort. He remained obstinate throughout the time I sheltered him in those caves. I wrongly assumed that... fire would remain intact, even underwater."

Yes, it had been effective. It worked... mostly with males. She used different tactics with females. Like she'd done with the manticore. Which hadn't worked the way she'd hoped... at least not entirely. Thalasia sighed heavily and looked back at him. "We keep going in circles. Repeating the same cycle over and over." She was tired of saying the same thing differently. That's what it felt like. Shifting her gaze back to the bright colors of the tent, she laced her fingers together at the nape of her neck. Accepting that he had a past, which included prior relationships, was a lot different from hearing how someone *still* belonged to him. "Have you bothered to consider that maybe... just maybe... your path doesn't include him? That *maybe* there are others that will help him get where he could be? That you're so busy trying to keep yourself in his world... that you can't see what is right in front of you? Or are you determined to continue to stand in your own way?"

"My path?" Seru wrinkled his nose. "The way you say it sounds like his path and mine aren't the same." Seru shook his head. "Loving Marius doesn't lessen what I feel for you. You believe in a single life partner, but your kind also lives much shorter lives. Hundreds to thousands of years facilitate multiple life partners for most, at varying stages. While it's possible to outgrow a partner as one passes from one stage into another, the connection is never completely severed. The same is true if another partner is added." He looked at her then. "I cannot see how that leads you to believe I'm standing in my way."

No, she didn't believe his path and Marius's were the same. Somehow, he couldn't see that. As for her kind... she shook her head. She turned to face him. "If you leave this isle as Marius wants... then no, your paths... do not align. As for my lifespan, no one knows exactly how long an Atlis will actually live. The oldest was 710 years of age when she was killed. Like *every* Atlis before and after her, she was killed. Seeing as you already have 800 years on me... I could outlive you."

Unless she got killed somewhere along the way, too. But that wasn't the point. "I know you'll always have a connection with him. I get that; I do. But the way you're talking... it's like... that's the connection you want. I'm sorry if the idea of sharing you with someone... if it just utterly pisses me off and breaks me in two. But *that* is how I feel. And *that* hasn't changed. Not when you pulled me into the bathtub naked with you and Marius, where I was highly uncomfortable..." Not that he seemed to notice. "Because... I belong to you. No one else. And *no one* may see me like that. Yet, you got highly pissed off both times I threw on something skimpy. Are you seeing a picture here?"

"So, you're comfortable flashing a stranger but sitting in a bath with... I realize Marius is little more than an acquaintance to you... Especially at the time..." He rubbed his temples. "The completed marks bridges that... unexpected... disconnect."

Thalasia pinched the bridge of her nose. There had to be a better way to explain herself. "Let me see if I can clear this up. Cleavage versus naked. Big difference." And if that didn't help, well, she could always go the extra mile. Not that she was really in the mood to give him a demonstration.

Seriously, would they ever get past all of this? Okay. She gripped her shoulders, giving them both a tight squeeze. "The marks that we haven't completed... once that's done, they're supposed to bridge... what... this disconnect between us?"

"Where I'm from, one promises the next." He gazed directly into her silver eyes at that last question. Blew out a breath. "They're supposed to do a lot of things."

"Where I'm from... it doesn't." She sighed again. The idea of being shared... no, she couldn't fathom it. At all. "The only one who is ever supposed to see you naked... taste your flesh... is the one you intend to give yourself to. Until that point..." Heaving another deep breath, she rubbed her brow. "It had only been you. I may have withheld and lied about a lot of things, but not that." His response to her question regarding the marks... it seemed half-assed. Incomplete. And they couldn't keep tiptoeing around this. They just couldn't. "Like what? What are they supposed to do?"

"Give yourself to?"

Had he not understood? Or had she been unclear? In talking about this... her giving herself... the soul and the flesh... she thought more about what she'd learned from Cyon about the marks. Maybe if she lined things up according to how their two cultures worked, it would make more sense. To both of them. "Think of it like this..."

She gripped her shoulders with another tight squeeze again. "In your culture, there are different levels of marks. Right?" That's what both he and Cyon had told her. "The first marks... are the equivalent of an Atlis choosing her Allimos. The person she's decided to share herself with in their entirety, soul and body. That's when the pheromones are triggered. Like intimacy feeds that first mark in your culture... intimacy... both physical and emotional feeds that connection in mine. It's why the pheromones intensify and thicken, especially the closer one gets to the ritual... the one I've told you about... like completing the marks in your culture... it solidifies the connection in mine... and it's usually concluded by a full day of... well... sex."

Seru gave a low growl. "That's highly improbable. Let me rephrase, impossible given our species differences before cultural conflict even becomes a part of the issue."

"Right. The difference in our species." A shiver ran down her spine as his growl echoed in the tent. She crossed her arms to cover her nipples and tilted her head. Yeah, she wasn't entirely sure she believed that. Although something had popped into her mind as a probability... she wasn't certain she could pull it off currently. Nor did she intend to try while she was on this rock. Oh no. If she was going to attempt that... it would be somewhere completely remote. In case it didn't work. "Yet, you could start the marks knowing that they'd never be able to be closed."

"Pleasure," he gestured at his current state, head to toe. "Like this is... fine. But sealing the deal or mating doesn't happen in this form. This is just a magical guise."

"Yeah, we've covered that before. But it leaves me wondering whether you ever intended to close them. Because you *knew* that when you placed them."

"Yes, clearly, I overlooked that minor complication." His words dripped with sarcasm. A shiver of scales passed over him. The iridescent dark scales shone like dark rainbows in the night. "I had no intention of mating with you when I marked you."

Well, that certainly explained—actually... no, it didn't. If he didn't intend to mate with her, then why had he kissed her? Why had they made out? Slept in the same bed? Traversed the market... like they were on a... she couldn't remember what the humans called it. Thalasia swallowed as her arms slowly unfolded, dropping to her sides. She no longer cared if he saw how he affected her. Because, sure as shit, she didn't know what to say. That wasn't true, either. "And now?"

"Now, we're both vibrating with so much pent-up energy..." he trailed.

"That doesn't answer the question, Seru. And you know it." There wasn't any point in their beating around the bush. Not any longer. Yes, they were both driving each other physically crazy. It was part of why she'd tried to... just completely shut down.

Like so many of the conversations before, this caused her pain. But it was entirely different this time. The two of them were being honest with each other. It made her want to cry with how it broke her heart.

"And now, I want you to stay, but I don't know what that would be... I don't think you'd ever belong here. Maybe among the sirens. Not in the Clouds."

It was something she'd considered when she first arrived... even until the marks were made. But the more and more she learned... the more she realized... it was an impossibility, one he seemed intent on remaining delusional about. Especially regarding their mutual desire to break the magic in his collar. That was the key. They'd both long concluded that one of them would have to make the sacrifice. But she needed to slap some sense into him.

"Then why are we trying to break your collar? You've already pointed out that Aurelia is going to have a shit-fit when we cross paths again, and she senses the mark. Do you honestly believe that if we find a way..." Her words trailed off. That was it, wasn't it? "You don't think we'll be successful?" As much as no one seemed to believe they should be together, no one appeared to doubt that she'd be the only one who could get him off the isle. Which, as he'd pointed out, would require breaking the collar. Something he obviously doubted they could do.

He looped his thumb through the metal ring. "It isn't any looser than it was the day we met. Or from the time it went on. There are reasons for that. Ones, no matter how hard I might try, I cannot seem to fully wrap my head around." He let the collar fall back into place. "Whether it remains intact or we take it off," he shrugged, no longer looking at her. "Does it matter if the consequences are equally disastrous?"

Did he seriously think she'd pick one or the other based on the possibility of a disastrous outcome? Or refrain from her decision to help him get it off because *that* might be the worse of the two options? "My position to help get it off... it still stands. That will *never* change."

Regardless of what could happen afterward. And maybe it wasn't looser. But it wasn't exactly like they'd really been trying, either. Or had they? She couldn't really be sure, since she didn't understand the intricate design of the band. The Clouds. They'd have to go. She needed to find the female Cyon told her about.

"You witnessed the unbridled destruction that a fraction of our true power unleashed on the inn," he mumbled. "Do you truly wish to discover what such power would do uninhibited?"

"Yes, I know that our combined powers can be... volatile. Just like we can each be that way individually, too." She ran her fingers through her hair, gripping the back of her neck. If she didn't know any better, she'd almost swear he was trying to talk her out of it. Not that it would make any sense if he were; either way, this conversation had certainly caused her pain.

Not to mention, she hadn't been at her full power, either. If something like that happened again, it would be ten times worse. The destruction she'd left in her wake as a child... it would pale in comparison. "Yes, it would mean we'd have to learn how to keep ourselves, each other, in check. Learn to control our powers on our own. Or do you think we're incapable of that?"

"Do you *really* believe that?" Seru asked in utter disbelief.

"Yes, Seru. I can keep my emotions in check. Unless you think we'd be hell-bent on running rampant through the realms and destroying anything that got in our way."

Did it mean they wouldn't likely cause some destruction if they got into an argument... no... were they incapable of arguing... nope, she didn't believe that, either. "Though to point out it seems like we're having a conversation we've had before, to a degree, and neither of us has had a flare up."

"A flare is sudden and brief," Seru explained. "There's nothing brief about an ascent of power. Power doesn't just awaken when you need it and slip back into its hiding place when its job is done, Thalasia."

"No. It constantly sits there beneath the surface, waiting to take you over." She sighed heavily and rubbed her forehead. This wasn't getting them anywhere. Or maybe it was; she couldn't be sure any longer. "We can have a conversation without... blowing up at each other. But that doesn't matter, does it? At this point..." Her words trailed off because she just didn't know. She knew little of anything anymore.

"Yes, we can. We can also avoid sex to a point. We can suppress our abilities and follow someone else's design to a point," he emphasized. "But we also need to acknowledge that our desires—beyond staying together—aren't exactly linear."

No shit. She'd figured that much out for herself. Not that she believed he still wasn't delusional. Then again, she'd always focused more on the bigger picture. And the pieces were all coming together. Whether it had been destined, she didn't know. Either way, she didn't know what else there was to say. Thalasia turned back around for her boots, hesitating a moment.

Seru brushed past her out of the tent.

Yeah. Space was good right now. They'd clearly hit an impasse. Both of them... as stubborn as ever. Each believing they were right. As she tugged on her boots, the sobs she had stifled transformed into tears. It was better this way. They couldn't control each other, and how much control they had over what was to come... that yet remained to be seen. With her boots back in place, she gathered her purse and shoved the pillows in first.

As she packed everything up, mostly shoving it in her purse, she didn't bother repressing her emotions. It didn't do anyone any good. What she felt was what she felt. If nothing else, she had tasks to complete in the meantime. She needed the book for more than one reason. It offered answers... or so she hoped. There would only be one other way to get some of what she needed regarding the impending ritual.

But nowhere on this isle would be an ideal place for that. Not that she wanted Seru to know everything she was up to. So, how did she—Thalasia paused. Oh, that made sense.

Wiping the tears from her face, she inhaled and exhaled a deep breath. Thalasia finished packing the last of everything and then climbed out of the tent. She quickly dismantled it. "Once we've finished here, I'd like to head to the lake. See if I can get the strings. I feel like I need to try. Then... we can head to the Clouds."

"Unless you have another magic trick hidden in that bottomless bag of yours, you'll never make it anywhere close to the bottom," Seru said. "If I go in for you, we risk exposing the beast to the entire isle."

"If I don't, then I don't. It doesn't stop me from trying."

He crossed his arms over his chest.

From what he told her; she'd be lucky to get past the surface. Her feathers were buoyant. Still, she had to try. Packing the tent in her purse, she removed a small brush so she could clean the dirt off the symbol she'd spotted earlier.

Thalasia strolled toward the wall, her footsteps echoing in the cavern, close to where he stood. With each grain she dislodged, the path forward became more apparent. Tossing the implement back in her bag, she pressed her hand against the collection of symbols, a derivative of her language.

Seru shifted out of her way.

She paid little mind to his eyes on her. Not that she hadn't felt them boring into her back, watching exactly what she did. It wasn't the first time, and certainly wouldn't be the last.

Her hand glowed, and the magic, silver like liquid mercury, filled the crevices, like individual pieces forming the bigger picture. With the symbols based on her own tongue, she followed the direction of the words represented by the various markings. One intricately detailed carving lit up, and then another, and so forth, until each had followed the specified order. Upon completion, a small slab in the floor a few feet away clicked, sliding open with a low groan to reveal another chest. It looked just like the one that had held the dagger they'd retrieved from Four Muses.

"Gods, I bet you want to murder your ancestors a little more with each passing day... their treasure hunts have gotten tiresome in just the short time we've been together."

"You have no idea." With a half-hearted smirk, she took her hand away and moved the short distance, the chest now visible in the open space. Reaching down, she lifted the cold, heavy crate, set it on the ground with a thud, and watched as the slab slid back into place. "I've found twenty others across the realms I've traveled, and I believe there are probably a good hundred more or so hidden."

To say she wanted to murder her ancestors... it was a bit of an understatement. Although they were all dead. Not like she could really do anything, but cuss them out strenuously each time she had to deal with yet another puzzle. Her gaze fell across the trunk. Huh, this one had a tumbling mechanism to open. A bit more on the simple side.

She quickly got it open and stared at its near emptiness. It was large enough to contain a book, at least the size she expected *Celestimo* to be. Instead, all that lingered along the bottom was a single silver ring with the eight moon phases in a circle, along with two scraps of parchment. Thalasia picked up the ring and both notes. "That's it?"

"Why? What's the purpose behind playing hide-and-seek with a bunch of artifacts that end up in your bottomless sack, anyway?" Seru inhaled a breath and growled. "So, help me if either of those contains another riddle."

His first question was obviously rhetorical. Like she'd understand exactly what her ancestors had been thinking when they had hidden all the artifacts. At least some of them were magical. She knew only what one of them did, and that had been by happy accident. Not something she had practiced much of, either. Hmm… maybe The Clouds would have a suitable spot for her to use. Might help her see the unseen in the Atlis journal.

Shaking the thought off, Thalasia focused her attention on the ring and the note. "I'd love to tell you it doesn't. While I can figure most of them out, I have no clue what this means. 'The answer lies with him.' As for the other one… it simply says to step into my power."

She held them both out for his inspection. While she really didn't know what the first note meant, the second… easy enough. And the writing belonged to her great-great grandmother. Not that she was going to tell him that. He cared little for Adina. Truthfully, the female had really grated on her nerves, too.

"Why would anyone put on a potentially magical artifact through faith alone?" He shook his head.

Really? Did he *really* want her to answer that? Yeah, she'd called him an idiot, but she had a few idiotic moments of her own. "Well, curiosity is a perfectly plausible excuse. Another… the person in question recognizes the handwriting."

Standing there for a moment, she stared at him. Like he had any better ideas. Was it likely stupid to trust Adina? Sure. What other choice did she have? With a shrug, she slipped the ring onto the second finger of her right hand. A sharp, throbbing pain suddenly erupted at the back of her skull. "Oh, shit… not again," Thalasia muttered.

Chapter Thirty-Six

"Not again?" Seru asked, pushing away from the wall as he awaited some cue from her about what was going on. "Thalasia!" He called to her, but to no avail. She'd become lost in another of her visions. He cursed her meddlesome ancestors and their insistence on tormenting her. He focused on keeping her steady, her sweet scent filling his senses. Placing his hand over hers, where she gripped his arm, he rubbed soothing circles over the back of her hand, the movement slow and calming. He wasn't sure she could hear or feel him in that moment, but he had to try something, anything, to help her through the painful experience.

Several minutes passed before her breathing steadied. Another slow breath. "Eight moon phases... sixteen objects... six magical..." Thalasia muttered. Her silver eyes snapped open, a flash of surprise in them. "I know what to do."

"What?" Her gibberish meant little to him in her current state.

Letting go of his arm, she pressed the heels of her palms against her eyes. "The ritual. I remember how to perform the ritual. There are eight moon phases. Sixteen artifacts. Six of them are magical." Her gaze fell on the note in her hand, and then on the empty chest. Her eyes flicked back to him.

"Are you alright?" Seru asked, stowing away the information she'd given him for another time. Right now, ensuring she remained on her feet became a priority.

"I'm fine. The pain is going away." Thalasia crossed her arms. "How'd you know the book was called '*Celestimo*?'"

"What?" he repeated, ensuring she was steady before releasing his grip on her. Of course, back to business as usual. With a huff, he tangled his fist in his dark mane. "I've been on this isle eight hundred years and some change, Thalasia. In my search for a way to remove the collar, I've come across a lot of magical texts and references to them."

Her lips pursed. "The answer lies with him. Aegeus attended the meeting you held with other Elders of the species."

"Yes, he was a part of the resistance that opposed Verie's dominion over the earth," Seru answered. "As were the enchantress's pets—the guilers and the bird Aurelia is so fond of, the dryads, the centaurs, that blasted phoenix, the shifters, and even Cyon—appeared in Marius's stead."

"This is Aegeus's handwriting. The note that led to the map, also his. Even the map itself and the note scribbled on it—his. The ring... brought back a memory of time with my mother... repeating the steps of the ritual I'm supposed to perform in two nights, and you're telling me that *you* have nothing to do with any of it... except some cockamamie meeting. That it was all just some big coincidence?"

Seru tilted his head at her. "If that's your only question, you seem to have drawn your own conclusions." Meaning she didn't really require any answers from him. She had it all figured out.

She pinched the bridge of her nose. "If you have the book... I don't care that we went through all of this..." With a heavy sigh, she crouched down on the back of her haunches, closed the trunk, and as she'd done with the other, shrunk it down. "I would've done the same thing," she muttered. "But confirmation would be nice." Placing the tiny chest in her bag, Thalasia tied the purse off and walked over to the closest torch. She used it to burn both pieces of parchment.

"We had to go through all of this," Seru said sternly. "And you should care." He watched as she set fire to the riddles, the fire greedily consuming the scraps until they were nothing but ash. Which one of them would be the parchment? And which one was the flame?

"I expect you had your reasons for us to go through all of this." With a small sigh, Thalasia turned and faced him. "Why should I care you kept this from me? There are a lot of things I'm sure we haven't told each other."

"Because you've been trying so hard not to care all this time... and where has it gotten you?" He could see the strain, the tightness around her eyes, the slump of her shoulders, and hear the endless sighing. It drained her. Being with him.

"You want to know what caring too much gets you..." Tears welled in the corners of her eyes. "Grief... heartache... pain..." Her gaze dropped to the floor.

"Me," Seru clarified. "Let's go get you those strings." He reached out his hand to her, only to realize the tears there. His hand faltered. His face fell, brows drawing together. What exactly did normal men do with this sort of thing? Drowning in Lake Lucent was going to be so much easier than this.

Her gaze lifted to his. "She killed you. In my dream. Right in front of me."

"Even with this, she stands little chance against me." He moved closer, drawing Thalasia against him.

Naturally, and without hesitation, her arms wrapped around him. "I did... eventually see that... but not before I thought I'd lost you." She choked back a sob. "I can't lose you."

"You won't," he reassured her. At least not to her captor from another realm. That much, he could promise with certainty. Promising she wouldn't lose him at all might prove challenging.

Wiping the tears from her eyes, she inhaled and exhaled a few deep breaths. "I'm sorry for all the crying."

"You needn't apologize." He unwound his arms from her, giving her enough space to settle herself.

"Are you sure? I feel like a bit of a disaster at the moment." She got the rest of her face cleaned up. Thalasia reached up and threaded her fingers through his mane. "Thank you."

"We're not in the Clouds, so don't worry yourself over appearances. Cry as much as you like." He wasn't sure it was an act that required a reply or thanks, but he responded anyway. "You're welcome."

"Is that your way of saying I'll have to be more mindful of how I look when we're in the Clouds?"

"I'll ensure you have suitable attire. Though being mindful of your manners and conduct, who you address and how—those are things to be mindful of, yes." He'd really hoped that all went without saying. But based on her question, it clearly hadn't. He wondered if she'd ever even been to a place as extravagant and regal as the Clouds. She seemed almost as accustomed to roughing it as he was... did that leave room for her to have attended court or encountered royalty?

Thalasia smiled. "I can do that."

He really hoped so... of course, he didn't say that out loud. "Most of the lower castes don't speak unless given permission from their betters. You're more likely to find speakers of the common tongue among the higher-ranking females, a few Primoires, and the Primoras. Though, just because they know and understand, doesn't mean they'll choose to acknowledge or address you. Anyone who isn't considered a dragon in the sky, even earthbound dragons and sea dragons... Or you as my Glory... are beneath them and they're able to interact with you at their discretion unless ordered to do so by someone who outranks them."

She took a step back, and with a flourish, she executed a perfect curtsy; the imaginary dress seemed to swish with the movement. Without saying as much as a single word.

Seru tilted his head in question. "Is that how you present yourself in other realms?"

"It's what my mother taught me, but I don't usually... present myself in most realms. Or if I do, it's a bit more laid back."

Interesting... Seru blinked a few moments, then gave a nod. "Let's get your strings before I change my mind." He held out his hand to her one more time. Thalasia was an astute observer, much like himself. He trusted her to mimic others should she encounter anyone of consequence during their time in the Clouds. The higher the rank, the larger the envoy, typically speaking. The exception would be in private quarters and the Regal Crescent, and she had no reason to venture into either of the two places. So, it wouldn't be an issue.

Taking his hand, she laced their fingers together. Together, they made their way toward the exit, leaving the cave behind and onto their next task.

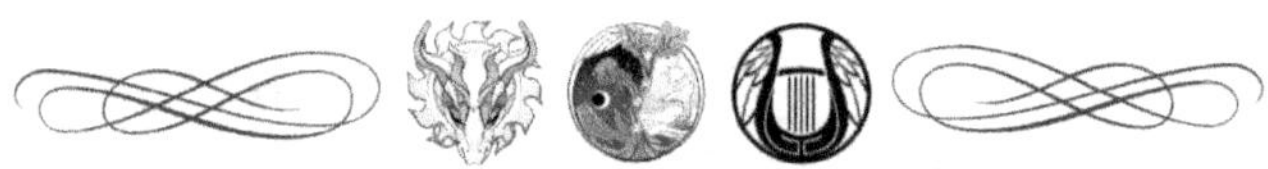

"You won't make it," Seru insisted, not moving to take her purse and shoes. "The hoard belonged to a lesser god. Only one worthy may traverse his domain," Seru said. "Besides, it seems Aurelia has already beaten us here." Her radiant energy sparkled atop the waves and shimmered along the shore. Between the trees, he saw a familiar glint of armor, and the figure came into view. Seru stiffened beside Thalasia. He hadn't expected Aurelia to find a new escort, especially *this* one. With a short, suppressed growl, he gripped Thalasia's arm firmly.

"Friend of yours?" A little sarcasm tinged the term *friend.*

"Hardly," Seru whispered harshly. "He's one of the Ascendant, a sect of the Matriarch's elite guard with a very... specific set of powers and knowledge."

Her eyebrows furrowed as she clutched the purse and boots. "What powers are we talking about?"

"I'm not entirely sure," Seru admitted, a tint of embarrassment in his voice. "There's a secret order of guardians rumored to be hidden among the Matriarch's guard. They're supposed to have access to many lost arts and information from the time the gods roamed the land. They're superb fighters. I've believed him to be among their initiates for a while... but, no proof."

Oriel had clearly noticed them by now, but he'd elected to stand his post. He eyed them briefly, his focus fixed on the shimmering surface. The lotus flower mist had dispersed in the night, but the power of the scent lingered.

"Guess there's no sense in having my glamour up then. Maybe I should put my boots back on."

Seru grunted a reply, leaving her to her task while he sought a better vantage point.

The driftwood planks creaked underfoot as Seru tread gingerly out onto the maze of walkways. The pathways weakened in places and became submerged at night.

Oriel glanced his way long enough to catch a flash of fang. The guard let out an amused snort.

Seru navigated his way farther out, one slow, calculated step at a time. The rickety bridges caused him to grit his teeth each time a board shifted underfoot. He inhaled a deep breath to steady his nerves, catching the barest scent of the lotus perfume. The fragrance generated the opposite effect. His scales bristled to a stand, slicing through his skin. He let out a hiss.

With concentration and patience, he got the wobbling under control. A shallow puddle lapped against his boots. Accursed water. He forced his gaze to the water beyond, a stretch of deepening blues. Aurelia remained somewhere beneath the surface, so far down. Even straining his eyes, he still couldn't locate her or gauge her position well enough to anticipate where she'd surface.

He scanned the shoreline, finding both Thalasia and the smug Ascendant watching him. If he was going to drown the man, now would be the time. Blame his beast and its reckless abandon. Somehow, he doubted Thalasia desired her lyre strings delivered blood soaked and smelling eternally of death and lotus blossoms.

Seru snorted at the thought before redirecting his attention to the too-blue waters.

Why had he agreed to this?

He didn't have a suitable answer. Waiting until he agitated his beast by standing around, dreading the plunge wouldn't serve anyone, either. Steeling himself, more against the transformation and the lake's power to strip away his disguise than the chill waters, Seru dove into the water. His only parting gift was the faintest hint of pleasure at the glimmer of movement, a startled tension he caught from the armored dragon by the shore.

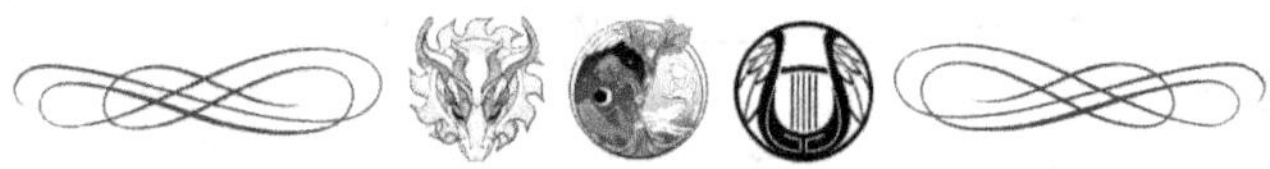

Her eyes widened at the sight of Seru diving in. Wait a second. Was *that* what they'd agreed to? She hadn't actually clarified, but obviously he'd seen her determination to try. Still protecting her. That was the only semi-logical conclusion. Except he'd said, Aurelia had already beaten them to the punch. What was he hoping to accomplish? Thalasia rubbed her temple. No point in getting upset now.

Out of nowhere, a gilded blade, sure and sharp, hovered just shy of her skin. "Hello, Thalasia. I'm not sure what you and the saint beast did to the purple crystal, but I'm going to need you to reverse it. All crystals in your possession. Not only the one in your neck. Now. Please."

That he knew her name didn't really shock her. The blade against her throat... that shouldn't have caught her off guard, either. Her own calm demeanor surprised her. Either way, she had no intention of parting with the two crystals she had in her purse. Especially since she had yet to discover the purpose behind them. The one in her neck, since she didn't execute the magic—that was what she could focus on. "I don't know how to reverse the magic on the purple crystal."

The edge of his blade pressed into her neck. "Do not make me repeat myself, Atlis," he warned. "And don't even consider using your voice to work your way out of my grasp. If you choose to make this simple objective difficult, make no mistake, I will kill you."

And here she'd thought for a minute she could get away without having to use any of her powers. That her birth moon was closer... best to see if she could delay. Still, she couldn't chance it too much.

There were some things even she couldn't come back from. She dug into the connection that Seru had created between them. After all, he had some abilities that she didn't. Like speed. Just as she had abilities, he didn't.

Not that she could let the guard's use of 'Atlis' go unacknowledged. There was only one way he knew that. "I see you've been talking to the sirens. Though it's a shame they provided you with such little information." Lightning crackled across her hand, danced in her eyes, and struck the ground inches from where he stood.

The likelihood that he would assume it belonged to Seru stood a good chance. It was something Cyon had done. "I wouldn't suggest that, Ascendant." It wasn't much, but it was all she had. "Not only would you ensure the death of a species, but you would also bring the wrath of the beast upon your head, and surely the rest of the isle." It wasn't an empty threat. She preferred to stall without revealing many of her powers. "Not to mention, the magic in my neck... came from *him*."

He growled through his teeth. "It is not my wish to kill the sirens. I merely require the stones. As for Seru, I know of his affinity for lightning. I'm not as under-prepared or surprised by your ability to draw on him. He gives you a little so it won't sting so badly when he rips it all from you later on. You're a fool for allowing yourself to be bound to such a wretched creature."

She hadn't expected him to be, but that hadn't been the point. And he assumed, just as she expected. Good. Especially since that wasn't the ability she'd pulled on. She just hadn't used it yet. "Whom I bind myself to really isn't your concern. But as I told you, I can't reverse magic I didn't use. Means I can't really give it to you, can I?" Thalasia exhaled a slow breath. "The blade at my throat won't change that. And seeing as you don't wish to have the blood of a species on your hands, really, don't you think it would be in everyone's best interest if you figured out a better way to work *with* me?"

The last thing she wanted was to initiate a fight. Her father had always taught her to discern her opponent's weakness and exploit that. In a controlled manner, she discreetly called her lightning. It wouldn't do anyone any good if they fought. Not to mention the further issues it would cause as she and Seru planned to go to the Clouds. Plus, she didn't have eyes in the back of her head.

"I'm less worried about you and more worried about what he intends to use you for. He's a destroyer. He'll make you one, too.

You're a liar or a fool," the guard said. "Maybe both. I'm not sure which is worse—for you, that is. Working with you and him isn't an option. Not if the isle is to survive." He unsheathed another blade and pressed it just beneath her wings. "You may fool the Matriarch and those you're going to assume you save, but you do not fool me."

"I love how much trust you have in your Matriarch. I'm curious if she told you that I'm the only one who can put the barrier back up. And you know, I've been really nice about all of this so far. But I'm really tired of you thinking you know everything and have every single fucking detail." She balled her hands into fists. Really, she was trying hard to keep her cool and not to blast him, but a blade at her spine... no... she wouldn't deal with that. The lightning she'd built up, she released, throwing him back, not as far as she would've liked, and knocking the blade at her throat from his hand. With the speed she borrowed from Seru, she spun on her heel to face him, grabbing the blade before it fell to the ground and retrieving the dagger from the waistband of her pants. Thalasia pointed both blades in his direction. "Now... shall we—" A shrill screech suddenly pierced the air, startling them both.

Fuck. She should've expected those damn things. Her resistance to the noise wouldn't last forever. Blood trickled from her ears. Thalasia swallowed and attempted to pull on her lightning... but didn't get far. It merely sparked along her fingers. She glanced at the blade she'd taken from the dragon... it had to be the problem... all she had to do was let it go. Damn it.

Fine. Before they started dive-bombing, she took to the air and charged straight at the two large-ass birds that were causing issues. Gods, the more time that passed, the more she wanted off this damn isle. A separate pair flew toward the guard.

There didn't seem to be a need to monitor the male. She was certain he could take care of himself. Since her flight didn't require magic... like theirs did... killing these two wouldn't wear her out. Though seeing the small flock of seitadi certainly clarified things a bit.

With his blade, she beheaded one dark siren and dispatched the other one by piercing the creature in the heart. As both fell to the ground, she continued to hover in the air. Her gaze flicked back to the male and the dismantled bodies of the seitadi that had attacked him. Interesting.

"Ready to negotiate yet, Atlis?" he called from the ground.

"Let's see if I can dumb this down for you. Symbol... Draconic language... Not. My. Magic. You want it reversed... you'll have to talk to Seru." Have mercy. She couldn't be any clearer about it. He seemed to expect her to have all the answers. Crikey. She preferred the dragon-shifter in that one realm. Of course, he'd been young, too.

He seemed really eager to have the crystals. Maybe she could figure out their purpose this way. She had asked Seru where Aurelia had obtained the one in her neck, but he either lied or didn't have an answer. "Why do you want them, anyway?"

"That might be true if I believed you didn't possess more than just the one stone," the male returned. "The longer you hold the blade, the weaker you become. The stones need to be protected and kept out of the wrong hands."

Good to know. Not that he answered the question and why he wanted them. "And you seem to think I have the wrong hands. Knowing nothing about me. Or that my purpose here is to protect the isle—just like you think you know what's on the other isle. You seem to think the barrier shouldn't go back up, yet your Leader is down there trying to get the strings needed to restore it." She lowered herself. "You want me to trust you, but you can't seem to offer the same. So, you want to negotiate... let's start with you taking this blade back and keeping it from my throat. Because *that* will get you nowhere."

"I trust your and your companion's lust for power," he shot back, sheathing his sword. "As for the Matriarch, in this instance, She merely ensures She has the upper hand. She places the interests of the Clouds first and foremost. Even as new as She is, She can tell when She's being set up to be stabbed in the back."

"Lust for power?" She flew down to the ground, landing with finesse. Yeah. This happened when you got just a little knowledge. "I don't know what the sirens told you, but *no* Atlis wants power. All I want is to ensure the safety of the isle. That includes putting the barrier up to prevent the magic of the isle from being corrupted."

"Locking all its inhabitants off from the rest of the world so the infighting may continue? What gives you, Atlis, the right to make that call? For all of us? Do your lies and short-sightedness end? You claim you don't desire power, yet you tie yourself to the single most powerful being our isle offers. You operate on your terms, not ours. If you were the great ally you claim, you'd not be off with the saint beast doing gods knows what... deception, thievery..." His words trailed off. "Helpful. For the good of the isle, I'm sure."

Yeah. This one needed some education. Things she knew because information had been available to her from others. "Maybe you need to consider the destruction that the dragons left in their wake on the other isle before you pass judgment. Infighting only continues if species are unwilling to work together. No action I take impacts that. I can *prevent* the darkness that has practically swallowed Candescent Isle from happening here."

Good gods, why did everyone think so poorly of Seru? The realization that he was among the most powerful hadn't really occurred to her. "Whether you believe it or not, I care about him. That is the *only* reason I have tied myself to him. As for what we've been doing, he's been helping me find what I need to break the siren curse. Given that they've come down to meet with other species... *Yes,* that helps them."

Why did every dragon-shifter have to be so damn stubborn?

"Your assistance is not required," the male said. "We can work out our differences and overcome our problems ourselves. Break the siren curse. If that's what you're here for, give back the stones, and be on your way." He smirked. "Then you're an even bigger fool. He loves no one, nothing."

"Oh, so then you guys were already working on fixing your problems with the other species before I arrived and the barrier went down. Really? Color me surprised considering it didn't seem like your Leader had met with any of the other leaders across the isle." The female had been too thrilled at the prospect of the marketplace. Though it looked like many others that Thalasia had seen over the years. Well, except in the human places.

Honestly, there was no point in defending what she and Seru felt for each other. She didn't think this male or anyone else would ever get it. This male wanted to negotiate, huh? Okay. Aurelia had gotten to the strings first. Although Seru had gone down there, she needed to prepare for the possibility that she returned with them. "You want the crystal? I want the strings your Matriarch has gone down for. Seems like an equal trade to me."

"Sure. You first. *All* the crystals in your possession, starting with those in your bag. The one in your neck can wait until your companion resurfaces."

"Yeah, you must think I was born yesterday. See, you have to convince Aurelia first to part with the strings." And she didn't think the female would do it. Seeing as the female had yet to surface, she sure as shit wasn't giving him the crystals. He *still* hadn't told her what he wanted them for. Like she was going to part with something she had that he wanted. Not that she was going to confirm what she did or didn't have. The bag would prevent him from locating them, even if he got it from her. It would only appear to be filled with random items. None of the magical artifacts she had in her possession. "Then we can talk about the crystal."

"She will part with the golden strings for the crystals."

"You still must think I was born yesterday. I'll believe that when it comes from her mouth." He really had to think she was a fool. Just because he said it, that didn't mean it was accurate. Yes, she'd been prepared to leave the isle, but she had to keep an open mind with the Clouds. That had been what she'd told herself. More and more, she had nothing but a sour taste in her mouth.

"Very well." He swept an arm towards the lake.

Cute. He still thought she was born yesterday. "In the meantime, take this back. No telling how long those two could take." They both had a tendency to take their sweet-ass time with things. The last thing she needed was to pass out, leaving it up to chance that he killed her. The bag would be protected regardless, since she hadn't been the one to spell it. Still, best not to take any chances. "And I don't trust you any more than you trust me."

"I think I've granted you enough on *your* terms." The male resumed his position, a tireless guardian's stance. His eyes slid back to her and immediately away. "No one trusts you. Not even the saint beast."

Yeah, he just had to keep telling himself that. She was fairly certain they'd gotten past their trust issues. Not that she intended to share that information. She had offered enough. Wiping the blood from her own dagger on her pants, she re-sheathed it. Waiting wasn't really her strong suit. Maybe that was a good thing. Something she needed to work on. Though she really hoped they emerged soon.

Not once did she bother to take her eyes off the male. She didn't trust him. At all. Really, she'd seen why the sea dragons had such issues with them. Of course, she didn't know half of the problems they'd faced over the years.

A few small dragon-like creatures, woken by the commotion, peeked out from hiding spots around the water's edge. Some found their homes in bark niches or between roots; others were nestled among the smooth, cool pebbles near the lake. They warily inspected their new guests. They scampered around their feet, inching closer for a sniff or a scratch against their boots. A few of them even dared to admire themselves in the male's golden armor once it became apparent he wouldn't hurt them. One overexcited fellow rammed his tiny skull against the entrancing reflector of his breastplate, stunning itself. The male shook his head. He gave the dizzy beast a perch atop his hand.

A small smile pulled at the corners of her mouth as she watched the creatures. They must be one thing that Seru had told her about. Amongst their conversations. And they were wary of her. Yeah, in her current condition, she'd be wary, too. Then again, she was normally wary of everything. She'd crouch down, but if she did that, she'd have to sit. With a heavy sigh, she wiped the slight sheen of sweat from her forehead and then wiped her hand on her pants.

Thalasia held out her hand to allow them to sniff and paw at her. Of the various creatures she'd met throughout her travels, this was pretty common with them. At least the lesser ones. And maybe some of the higher. Despite the way she could weaponize her power, most of them rarely feared her.

The tiny creatures perked up, suddenly alert. A faint light near the docks with a slightly pink -and-purple hue mounted, shifting and swelling into a shallow dome. The animals spooked, screeching warnings before tucking tail to flee and hide.

Finally. She rubbed her forehead. She was beyond ready for this male to take back his damn blade. At least she had a better understanding of things and knew what to avoid in the future. For however long she was here. There was still a good possibility that she stayed, though it seemed further and further away as each day passed.

Thalasia wiped the sweat from her brow once more. This damn thing was really draining her. But she was still standing. For the moment. She didn't know how much longer that would last. Good thing she had that egg in her bag. They could just use it to get to the Clouds. She'd have to depend on Seru's mind, though.

The bubble burst, showering the surrounding area. A very displeased band of black scales coiled itself over the docks, splintering the wood. Seru, in his saint beast form, emerged first.

"Seru! If you don't get your giant scaly hide off me—" Aurelia grumbled, heaving herself in her human form onto one of the still intact walkways.

The saint beast responded with a deafening roar of his own. His head rose to a better vantage as he shook out his scales, snorting and sneezing at the fragrant-rich water.

Okay. Her body was giving out a bit. She dropped back onto her ass. Though the coolness from the water that came up felt good against her skin. Yep. She needed a good, cool bath, food, and sleep. It would be the only way to fully recover from this thing. Thank the gods for small things like the fact that none of them had access to the magical artifacts in her purse. Yeah. Dumbass thought it was a good idea to leave this thing in her hand. Thalasia smirked.

"I wouldn't try putting that dagger in your bag if I were you," the guard informed her, moving to intercept the pair on the docks.

Embroiled in an argument of their own, Aurelia and Seru traded words, some in the Draconic tongue, most in Seru's bestial growls and snarls. After a moment, Aurelia strode over to the guard and Thalasia, wringing water from her golden mane.

"What's wrong with you? And what are those?" She growled at Thalasia while shooting the guard a quick look of annoyance. Her eyes darted to the felled, feathery bodies.

"Seitadi... also known as dark sirens." She let the first question go because, honestly, she didn't think it needed to be answered. Not if she looked at the blade in her hand. And oh yeah, stuffing it in her bag was exactly what she planned to do. No, she wanted the damn thing out of her hand. Had even offered for him to take it back.

It would be good to know who controlled the seitadi. If everything she knew was accurate, that person didn't have to be anywhere nearby. Also explained how the shape shifters had found her and Seru the way they did.

"Great—" Aurelia forced a smile, drawing out the word, and placed her hands firmly on her hips. "Seru, get out of that godforsaken lake before your girlfriend's new friends decide to send in reinforcements."

The saint beast grumbled, struggling to untangle itself from the floating docks.

Aurelia rolled her eyes and attempted something to aid Seru. When he remained in his beast form, she frowned, throwing her aggravation at the guard. "Whatever you did to her that's keeping him like *that,* will you just cut it out?!"

His gaze fell on Thalasia. "Not until she gives up the stones."

Keeping Seru from shifting back to his human form wasn't something she'd expected. Must have something to do with the connection between them. Would it have affected him, too, if she hadn't tapped into it? Damn it. Something she couldn't answer. But sure as shit, she wouldn't hand over the stones without answers or without the strings. But she couldn't leave him like that, either. She was trapped, and the hard place felt as cold and unyielding as the rock. "Take the blade and I'll give you one." Thalasia looked at Seru apologetically before she turned her gaze back to the other male. "And if you're waiting for me to pass out, it won't do you any good. I'm the only one who can retrieve it."

"I'm not waiting for you to pass out. I'm waiting for you to come to your senses. If you'd rather pass out, you're more childish than I first thought," Oriel said. "Let's see them. Prove you have them, and I'll reclaim the dagger. The Regent may reclaim his other form, and you'll hand over the first stone."

"My senses? This coming from someone who had a blade to my throat and spine... that's rich." Passing out wasn't an option. She didn't trust the male. Nor did she trust Aurelia. Although she believed his assumption about her having more than one crystal was accurate. Provided that was what the shell necklace she'd taken from the manticore held inside of it. None of the other items in her sack contained the other crystal. So, the blue one and whatever was inside the necklace. Fine. She'd prove she had two others aside from the one that Seru had crushed up.

Thalasia untied the bag attached to her belt loop. First, she removed the blue crystal, ensured they saw that, and then returned it. Each magical artifact had its own individual compartment inside the purse. Parting with whatever the shell necklace contained didn't bother her. The magic in it had felt similar, yet strange, when she'd stolen it from the manticore. If she had to part with one of them, that was the one she chose. She retrieved the shell necklace, held one string of the bag against her knee, and yanked them tight before she held up the necklace. "There. You've seen them. Now... your turn."

"You cannot recognize your place and seem to think more of yourself and your abilities than what actually exists. You're not nearly as powerful or knowledgeable as you think." Once he got a brief nod from Aurelia, he stretched out his hand, playing his fingers. The pull on the blade was instant, as if invisible strings connected it to him. It slipped from Thalasia's grasp and into his hand, effortless. He tucked the dagger away out of sight and resumed his stance.

Seru remained blessedly silent at their backs, still in his beastly form.

Aurelia looked down her nose at Thalasia, her gaze cold. "Believe that's your cue."

This was one of those moments where it was best just to bite her tongue. If she were to get technical about it, she only had the siren hierarchy to go by, which didn't really compare to theirs. If she only went by the siren hierarchy, she was above the Elder. Regardless, offering any of this information was pointless. Not to mention, she didn't want to put Seru in a position where he went on the defensive.

Instead, she simply held out the shell necklace. "As requested," she said. Unless they wanted her to open it. Honestly, she wasn't sure how to go about that. Her original plan had been to just crack the shell, but she wasn't certain that was in everyone's best interest.

Aurelia snatched the shell necklace from her, lifting it to inspect the contents. She crushed the fragile casing in her hand, brushing away the shards to claim a green crystal. Holding it up in the moonlight, the shadows sluggishly drifted at the center, clouding and darkening the luster. She spirited it away to a safe location in a golden flash.

Thalasia just sat there, resting her arms on her knees. It didn't take a genius to discern that Aurelia wouldn't be any more forthcoming about the reason she desired the crystals so much. Nor did she intend to access the artifact in her possession that would restore her energy. At least not in front of Aurelia and her guard. No, they didn't need to know everything she had in her purse.

She had other ways of getting the answers she wanted. Some, even the book, might have. Something else she didn't intend to bring up. In fact, at the moment, she was comfortable sitting there quietly... patiently waiting. Preferably for Aurelia and her guard to leave. She didn't exactly want to pull out the egg in front of them, but she would if it came down to it.

Seru gave a low grumble. Another shake of his scales showered them in a fine mist.

Aurelia turned, speaking to him in their native tongue.

He gave another quick burst, ruffling her blond mane, before settling down on his haunches. His serpentine body sank beneath the water, mostly.

"How many strings do you need to repair your catalyst?" Aurelia asked, turning back to Thalasia sounding none too happy.

Simple question. Simple answer. "Two."

"Very well." Aurelia materialized a single golden strand. Luminous and bright, it glittered even under the chill moonlight. She tossed the strand into Thalasia's lap.

This wasn't exactly what they agreed on... although, now that she thought about it, she hadn't specified the number before now. But she didn't have the energy to fight it. Maybe she could figure out how to split it. Thalasia untied the strings of her purse, tucked the tough gold into its own pocket in the bag and retrieved the blue crystal. She pulled the strings tight. She'd reattach it to her belt loop when she was completely finished with it. Holding up her end of the bargain, she opened her palm, holding out the blue crystal.

Aurelia extended her hand, clasping the blue jewel between her talons. She inspected it briefly. Glancing at her guard, she disappeared it just as she had with the emerald. "You'll get the second string once you deliver the amethyst. In. Tact." In their Draconic language, she directed her terms to Seru.

His maw opened, revealing rows of sharp fangs, as he roared back at her. A long, drawn-out guttural sound echoed over the lake, amplified by the waters.

While she didn't understand what they said between the two of them, whatever response Seru gave, it was obviously one of displeasure. Not that she was certain why. Was he upset because Aurelia used the strings over them? Or was it something else? Yes, the strings... were necessary to repair the lyre, but was it really what she wanted?

Her gaze settled on Seru. As much as she'd tried not to care... she hadn't been able to help it. It made her want more out of her life. More than just a vessel to be shipped from realm to realm, picking up the pieces and fixing problems that others couldn't resolve themselves. More than just a messenger.

How did that affect... well, everything? She wasn't sure. Her eyes lifted to the moon. They had only days to figure it out.

"Since he's refusing to remove the enchantment from your master's mark, it seems our little tradeoff has concluded." Aurelia forced a smile. Then, she and the guard disappeared.

Once they were gone, Thalasia went back into her purse and dug out an amber-colored, sun-shaped pendant. As the warmth of the jewel enveloped her, she exhaled, rose, and clasped her purse shut. Good gods, that felt amazing. She closed some of the distance between them. "This will restore our energy. You want to stay like that while I use it?"

The beast bared its fangs at the object in a nasty snarl, spittle dripping between its fangs. The scales on its hide rose defensively, forming armor. Obviously, it didn't want any part of the magical artifact. From the water, the beast emerged, water streaming down its massive frame. Slinking its way past her into the forest, the trees groaning in its wake; the beast followed its keen sense of smell, where it quickly located the corpses of the dark feathered fiends. It gave a quick sniff before sinking its fangs into them with a sickening crunch. The sinews tore as the beast ripped the creatures to pieces, caking itself in tacky blood and feathers.

"Or you could go with that option." It was her second recommendation. Not that she'd expected any of what had happened with the guard's blade. She held onto the pendant until it fully restored her energy, and then she returned it to the pocket in her purse. That felt so much better. With the bag tied off, she reattached it to her belt loop. Rubbing her brow, she turned around, and Thalasia's quiet chuckle filled the air.

Really, the way he looked shouldn't amuse her. Yet it did. All she could think about was that he needed to wash his face. The feathers transformed him, giving the impression of a scaly bird.

He snorted as feathers found their way up his nostrils. As the beast snarled, the irritating fluff stuck to its wet muzzle, getting inside its mouth and clinging to the soft skin of its snout as it licked. Giving a final sneeze, the beast turned away, leaving nothing but the dirt it had rooted around in and smatterings of blood that had soaked in.

Covering her mouth with her hand, she snorted with laughter. Though she tried *hard* to keep it together, she just couldn't. Not at the sight of the feathers up his nose. It was too much. And he thought she'd be disturbed. With the corpses now gone... it left her curious... had any that hadn't been killed stuck around.

Thalasia walked to where Seru had been and lifted her gaze to the tops of the trees. The one thing about seitadi... the fuckers blended into the background well. Even if she spotted one amongst the branches and leaves, she might not tell it apart.

Flipping her gaze back to Seru, she snickered. Definitely not a sight she ever expected to see. The beast rolled over the scent, scales catching bark as it pushed the trunks to near breaking. The leaves rustled. Its tail flicked about, uprooting a few with resounding snaps as the roots broke free. He paid her little attention. "Are you planning to make a mess? Or are you trying to deter others from coming around here?"

The beast grunted, content to scratch and mark its space.

Stupid question. She shook her head in amusement. "Alright. If you're gonna spend the next few minutes doing that, then I'm going to fly up and make sure we have no more crunchies hiding out. Sound good?"

That must've sounded like an invitation. The beast rushed at her with all its might in a fit of excitement. The massive scaled creature knocked her off her feet and onto its back, taking off into the sky like a projectile.

She laughed out loud as she clung to him. "This wasn't what I meant." While it made travel a lot easier, how were they supposed to make sure there weren't any more seitadi hiding out like this? Not that she really thought that was the point. Still, it amused her.

The beast rocketed them into the sky with enough force that the trees fanned out in their wake, forming an almost floral pattern. As the trees spread out, she caught sight of two large, black-feathered birds, likely seitadi from what she could ascertain from this distance, fleeing. The beast shot up into the clouds, climbing at incredible speed, seemingly oblivious to the effects of the higher altitude. The blood and feathers shed from his muzzle as he sped up.

Really, she couldn't fault him for needing to fly. Not to mention, she'd kind of promised it a few days back. Besides, it would be nice to bathe in the moonlight for a bit. To the naked eye, it would look like a full moon, except it would be slivers away from that. "Just for a little while," Thalasia said, a smile in her voice. Snuggling close against him, she stroked his scales with one hand while she burrowed her other hand into his mane. Her gaze drifted upward, where stars twinkled against the inky canvas of the night. It was absolutely beautiful.

With him in this form, she cozied up more under his mane than anything else. Not that she was cold or even cool. Just the opposite. She was quite comfortable. Although it might have something to do with the way her skin shimmered beneath the moonlight. Interesting. She didn't realize it would do that. But it certainly kept her warm.

Sitting up just a little, she peered over him as best she could, still continuing to stroke his scales. She loved its silky smoothness underneath her hand. Hmm, the large birds hadn't flown off, but had perched in another set of trees, blending in a little less. "They're watching us."

The beast let out a low, barely discernible rumble.

And they probably had been, too. Which meant they knew about the crystals. If they'd been watching long enough, the two of them as well. While it would be nice to know who their master was, for the first time in her life, she didn't feel like she was in a hurry to do... anything. To find answers, to finish the mission... none of it. She was content just being up in the air with him. "Think anyone would miss us if we just stayed here?"

He turned back to her, at least enough to steal a glance. The beast flicked its tongue across its fangs.

Yeah, it wasn't logical, but it was fun to think about. Just staying up in the air. Except they'd each require their own nourishment. And rest at some point. A small chuckle left her. "I know... we can't stay up here forever."

It let out an irritated growl, vibrating through its fangs and along its sides.

Her grip tightened ever so slightly on his mane, and she raised an eyebrow. She followed the direction of his attention. Yeah, the seitadi were still watching them. Their beady, red eyes stared straight at them. Something she could see even from their current position. There weren't many clouds for him to hide behind tonight. "You thinking about going after some more crunchies?"

The beast's lips lifted to expose its gums as the ferocity of its growl intensified. The black birds reflected in its eyes, a deep and visceral bloodlust illuminated by the cold, silvery moonlight.

"I'll take that as a yes." She adjusted herself on his back, her fingers sinking into his thick mane as she leaned into him. At least this way, she had a good hold on him. Not that she couldn't stop herself from falling. She had wings. But he was larger, faster, and a bounce off of his hide. It might hurt.

Once she settled, it turned abruptly, whipping its body around into a rapid downward spiral. It utilized the darkness and its incredible speed to barrel toward its targets, waiting until it was upon the birds to open its maw wide. The beast captured its prey in its jaws, taking with it the splinters of trees and greenery, swallowing them whole.

Really, some part of this whole thing should've disturbed her. But it didn't. Nope. Not even close. It fascinated her that even *if* the three-foot-tall creatures had seen him coming, they couldn't have flown off quickly enough to survive. Certainly, gave her a whole new understanding of hunting. "Hopefully, that doesn't give you indigestion later."

After spitting out wood and foliage, the beast ascended, now weaving itself leisurely into the star-speckled sky.

A small chuckle left her mouth. She meant the bird-things, but that, too. Still lying against him, Thalasia stroked her fingers along his scales. They couldn't stay in the sky forever, but she hadn't really been able to get a lot of what he'd said earlier out of her head. Especially as she replayed everything in her mind since her arrival.

Eventually, they'd have to go to the clouds, but why did they have to run off tonight? Couldn't they just hide out somewhere... obviously not with him in this form, and worry about duties... the next day? They'd tried it once before, but had done little. Just danced. "What if we just went somewhere and forgot about the rest of the world tonight?"

The beast shivered, the scales losing their armored rigidity as it climbed to new heights, angling away from the lake. It sneezed, snorting in contempt.

She wasn't exactly sure how to take that. Aside from wanting to get away from the lake, a place it had been well-established that he wasn't fond of, it didn't actually answer her question. Not that they could really escape. Or go anywhere that wasn't on the isle. Not yet anyway.

As she continued stroking his scales, she watched as her skin glowed brighter the higher he climbed. Even her internal body temperature warmed to offset the coolness of the night sky. That was weird. It hadn't done that before. Maybe it had something to do with—her third eye opened, completely cutting off her train of thought. Just like it had done earlier.

As if the beast understood what was happening, she noted a low, deep hum emitting from him and his flight leveling out. Her grip on his mane tightened as an image of a gruesome-looking gigantic bear with fur as dark as the abyss exited a cave. A crown with a nearly blackened stone sat upon its head.

The image disappeared from her head, and her mind's eye closed as quickly as it had opened. She blinked, trying to pull pieces of what she'd seen, but there wasn't much to go on. A cave in the forest somewhere. Although with the information she had on the male... she may have just seen the leader of the shape shifters. But why?

Shaking the image and the thoughts off, Thalasia rolled her shoulders and took notice of the way her hand sparkled. It continued up her arm. She sat up and looked over the rest of her body. Even through her pants and tank, she shimmered, like a diamond. "Huh..." She didn't expect that.

The beast grunted at her as it lowered them until its belly dragged on the ground. Its body coiled around itself, forming a protective barrier around where she still clung atop its back. It pressed its massive snout in her direction, scenting her while trying not to crush or knock her off. Though blessedly briefer, its hot breath hit her with the force of a strong wind.

She giggled. His breath ruffled her feathers and blew her hair back from her shoulders. Reaching up, she stroked along the top of his snout, at least to where she could touch, which meant the side. It just made her entire body light up brighter.

The beast wrinkled up its snout.

"What? Don't like it?" Her eyebrows knitted together as she tilted her head, and the shimmer across her skin dimmed as her scent thickened in place of it. Well, wasn't that interesting?

The beast bobbed its head, bumping her hand with enough force to knock her back.

Her wings extended as she laughed, catching herself before she moved too far. Her body seemed to respond naturally to his request. The sparkle across her skin disappeared altogether, leaving behind only her thickened scent. "You have a unique effect on me."

His nostrils flared at the scent. Its pupils constricted and expanded from slivers to oval slits. It nuzzled her, rubbing across the scent.

Her fragrance intensified, becoming the dominant aroma, except for the lingering smell of him. The combination of the two filled her nostrils. It was the best scent in the world. Something she didn't think she'd ever tire of smelling. So much, she leaned into his nuzzle. Her feathers ruffled, and she beamed. The beast pushed her back until she found herself sandwiched between its nose and scaly hide. Its tongue flicked out, tasting and scenting the aroma emanating from her.

She chuckled and used her tank to wipe her face. Certainly not what she expected. On either part. "Do you feel better?"

The beast gusted a warm breath her way, settling its head.

Exhaling a soft breath, she leaned against him. Not that she had much of a choice. He'd kind of wrapped himself around her. While they had things to do, she was content just to lie there with him.

Chapter Thirty-Seven

Parthenia squeezed her mate's hand. Her feet registered a slight change in the earth. The air grew heavier, making each breath a struggle that caused a slight burning sensation in her lungs. The leaves on the trees themselves had turned a brittle brown. A heavy, chilling aura settled over the forest floor, as if something was slowly leaching the life out of it.

Frowning, Milla held up a hand. "Stay here." She didn't give them much of a chance to respond before she launched into the air and flew ahead of them, disappearing from sight.

Gavin shifted a bit where he stood before wrapping his arm around her. His tail swished nervously, and his fur bristled, making his arms look even bigger. The hold he had on her tightened as he dropped his head and pressed a kiss to her neck, against the one mark he'd given her. "Are you okay, love?"

"I don't know... this... it feels... strange." At least her voice still worked. Although her breaths came out a bit more ragged. *Stay here.* Sure, that sounded like a great idea. Goosebumps erupted on her skin as a chill snaked down her back. Gods, she'd felt nothing like this before.

"It does. Very. I dislike it. It reminds me too much of Métamorphe, only worse." He flicked his gaze over his shoulder.

She didn't like it, either. Her gaze followed his, but there was nothing there, though. No one was near them. And going forward was out of the question. Her lungs tightened, her breathing more rapid. "I know Milla said to stay here... but I feel like... we need to go back."

His forehead creased further, and he rubbed his hands up and down her arms. "Me, too. At least… until the atmosphere lightens… and you can breathe easier."

"Yes." It was the only word she could get out. Her breath hitched as she struggled to inhale, and a wave of dizziness washed over her. While she could still walk without tripping or falling over her own two feet, she didn't know how long that would last if they continued to stand there. With a slight dip of her chin, Parthenia turned, facing the direction they'd initially come from, and started forward.

He turned with her, but shifted to his animal form—which took him a moment—before following her. Her mate slid up next to her, bumping her gently as he walked by her side, the rustling of leaves underfoot. "We should not go too far. Just as far as necessary to get out of this."

"I agree." She rested an arm across his shoulders. They were much closer in height this way. Her steps were slow. She wasn't sure how much further she could go, but she hoped the pressure on her lungs would soon ease and allow her to breathe deeply. They trekked forward for several minutes.

"Do you feel better, love?" he asked, nuzzling against her before he scanned their surroundings. The leaves slowly regained their vitality, shedding their withered exteriors. "This is so strange. Do you think that was part of what was going on with the magic of the isle? Or something more?"

With a small nod, she stroked his head. "I feel better."

A soft purr rose out of him. "Good. I am glad." With his tail, he stroked the tips of her wings.

As for his other question, whether this had something to do with the magic of the isle, she had no answers. This wasn't like anything she'd ever seen. Parthenia sighed heavily and shook her head. There was no valid explanation. "I don't know. Everything I've heard or know about; it's just crops not growing or issues with pregnancies. This… it's different. I don't know what this is."

"Neither do I. The closest thing I have ever experienced is Métamorphe, but this is different. I do not know how to explain it. It is darker, denser. Whatever it is, perhaps when Milla returns, we can see about going around it instead of through it."

"I hope so. I don't think I could go through it." She enjoyed breathing too much. He remained unfazed, though her mate confessed it was more unsettling than his childhood village. She found it unimaginable to be in a situation her whole life that induced a constant, unnerving feeling of her skin crawling. Where air didn't exist around them. "I don't know how you survived in something even similar to that."

He nuzzled against her, his rough tongue gently stroking her neck. "I was born into it, grew up in it. Until I got older and left the boundaries for the first time, it was all I ever felt. I suppose my body was just used to it. The more I left, though, and the more I had to return, the more difficult it got to be there. I think I noticed it more and more after every reprieve."

The corners of her mouth curved upward in a gentle smile. She'd braided her hair back, revealing the marks Gavin had given her on each side of her throat. For a moment this morning, she'd thought it had all been a rather vivid dream, at least until she'd seen them in her reflection. Parthenia turned, her arms encircling his neck in a warm embrace. "I'm glad this is something our children won't ever have to worry about."

He burrowed his face into her neck and rested his head against her shoulder. His tongue swept over one mark. "I am glad as well, my beloved. The things that we have endured, our young will never know things like that. We will give them everything we never had, and so much more."

"Yes, we will." She didn't know when they would have them, or even how many days they still had before they would get to leave the isle, but they would give their children the best life possible. Parthenia leaned into him. She loved not only wearing his mark but having it out on full display. Lifting her head, she stroked her fingers along his muzzle. "Do you know how long the marks last? Are they permanent?"

A contented purr escaped him as his eyelids fluttered shut for a moment. "Not that I am aware of. I wish they were, though. I think they last probably just until they heal. But that just means I get to give them to you again and again." His smile widened as he softly pressed his forehead to hers, a silent acknowledgment passing between them. "I only ever saw them on a few people back in the village. Very few. It was such a rare thing to have a true mate there. Most never had a mating mark. A couple never went without them. It is not something I ever saw on my parents. I never saw one on Gabby either, but it is not something Derrick ever could have given her there."

"We have nothing like it." Although she'd heard that there used to be an exchange of gifts, that hadn't happened in many years. Then again, few mating ceremonies occurred. Especially since the males ended up impregnating multiple females. It kind of seemed like no one really wanted to acknowledge just how far they'd fallen. Her fingers gently brushed against the soft fur behind his ears. "I enjoy having them. I never want them to go away."

"I love seeing them on you. I do not want them to go away, either." His purr deepened. "We could make sure that does not happen. Just because they are something my species gives their mates during sex does not mean I cannot give them to you when we are just being intimate. At least until the curse is broken, anyway."

"I like that idea. I think it sounds like the best one I've ever heard." It wasn't something they could've done before last night. Just as she couldn't wear the necklace he'd given her months ago. She hadn't put it on until after they'd left Pteryrina. So many things that had to be hidden, and no longer had to be done. Almost.

"Then we will certainly do that." He beamed, his eyes crinkling, as he gently nuzzled the mark on the left side of her neck. "I will make sure you always wear at least one, from now until the end of our days on this earth. It fills my heart with joy to see them on you... that I could finally give you one." He stroked his tongue over the mark again. "Soon, my love."

She bit her bottom lip. If he kept doing that, well, it would certainly put them in a bit of a bind. A sudden warmth spread across her face as her smile brightened. Not that she minded a bit, either. "Yes. Soon."

"I take it you both sensed it?" Milla asked.

Gavin quickly positioned himself in front of Parthenia, almost completely obscuring her from sight. His fangs, sharp and gleaming, were exposed in a snarl that threatened to break free.

A tiny flinch rippled through Parthenia. "Holy Poppies!" Where had the female come from? As her breath settled, she glanced back at Milla. Question. Milla had asked them a question. "Um, yes, we noticed the darkness."

Her mate's body and jaw relaxed quickly. "Um, yes. Yes, we sensed it. Our apologies for moving. It just became too difficult to remain amid it."

"My apologies. I did not mean to frighten you both," Milla said.

Moving more toward Gavin's side, Parthenia stroked the top of his head. It would help calm them both. She offered the female a nod, accepting her apology. "Do you know what caused the path to become like that?"

"No. I cannot say that I do. However, it only seemed to get worse the deeper I traversed. I know the intent was to take you both to

Arcadia Meadows; however, I no longer feel that is possible. Instead, I am going to have one of our creatures lead you to Monarch Crescent. There you will meet Selene. She is the Queen of the sprites and responsible for the butterfly drakes as well."

Leaning into Parthenia, Gavin gently nudged his head deeper into her palm, a soft rumble emanating from him. He nodded to Milla. "Thank you. We were hoping it would not be necessary to travel through it. Is there anything we need to be aware of with meeting the queen of the sprites?"

"Just be respectful. Selene is really laid back. She doesn't even like being addressed by the normal monikers designated for her station."

Sounded a lot like her sister. She didn't expect Cipriana would enjoy being called Elder or even Rising Elder whenever she was addressed. "I'm certain we can handle that."

"Yes, I believe we can as well. Should I shift into my other form before meeting her, or will this one be alright?" Gavin asked.

Milla folded her arms across her chest. "I think that form is better. Given how small she is, it might make her more comfortable."

Small? Her eyebrows knitted together. Oh, right? Milla had said *sprite.* They weren't big at all. But she thought she'd read somewhere that they had that one ability. "Aren't they able to increase their size?"

"Some can, yes."

Her mate's forehead creased in a frown. "This one it is, then. Thank you, Milla, for everything you have done for us."

"You are quite welcome." The female turned and peered over her shoulder. "Ah, here she comes now."

Parthenia blinked, catching sight of a brown rabbit-like creature with delicate wings, quick ears, powerful hind legs, and a long tail as it soared toward them. What in the world was that thing? She'd encountered nothing like it or even seen anything in her books that resembled it. But it looked harmless. And it wasn't very large, only a foot or so.

Gavin tilted his head. He glanced back at Milla, then flicked his gaze back to the creature. "Is... she... going to escort us onward?"

"Yes. This is Dala." Milla beamed as the creature landed on her shoulder. She stroked its nose with her finger. "She's a lepoid."

"It's nice to meet you, Dala." Parthenia offered the creature a smile. Yep, she'd never heard of or seen anything like this flying bunny. It had short ears and a long torso, but couldn't weigh over five pounds.

The lepoid squeaked. "She says it's nice to meet you, too," Milla said.

"Lovely to meet you, Dala. This is my mate, Parthenia, and my name is Gavin."

Milla's eyes widened as the lepoid squeaked again. "Dala! That isn't very nice to say."

What could be so bad that the female would scold the creature like that? She didn't quite know, but it kind of amused her. "Dare I ask?"

"She said you both have funny names."

Covering her mouth, Parthenia stifled a giggle. "I suppose we do."

Gavin's amusement bubbled to the surface. "It is a shame we do not get to pick our own names, yes?"

Dala squeaked. Milla laughed. "She agrees."

It was a fascinating creature. Though she couldn't say what intrigued her more. The lepoid itself, or that Milla could speak to it so easily. "What names would she give us if she could pick them?"

The creature tilted its head, its big eyes darting from Parthenia to Gavin before emitting another high-pitched squeak.

"She would call you Cinnamon," Milla said, gesturing first to her and then to Gavin. "And she would call you Emerald."

"I like those names. They're quite... unique." Parthenia grinned. And very representative of their colors.

"That they are." Her mate's tail wrapped naturally around her waist. "What would you call yourself if you could choose your own name?"

The lepoid squeaked. Milla raised an eyebrow. "Squeak? What kind of name is that?" Dala let out another small squeak, prompting Milla to nod in understanding. "My apologies. She said she'd call herself Dove because it's pretty."

"It is beautiful," Parthenia said.

"Dove would be a pretty name." He glanced at Milla. "Will it be an issue that we cannot understand her speech?"

"No. She will make herself understood. Many do not speak with animals as I do." Milla looked back at Dala. "Be sure to take care of them, alright?"

The lepoid squeaked and leaped into the air.

Parthenia chuckled. "I feel like that's an agreement."

"You're quite right." Milla grinned. "You're both in excellent hands."

"I think we will be just fine. Thank you again, Milla." Gavin bowed his head to the female.

She inclined her head slightly in a small bow to each of them. "You're welcome. Now, I shall leave you in Dala's capable paws." With one last nod to them both, Milla took off into the air.

Once the female disappeared from sight, Parthenia turned her attention back to the lepoid. "Lead the way."

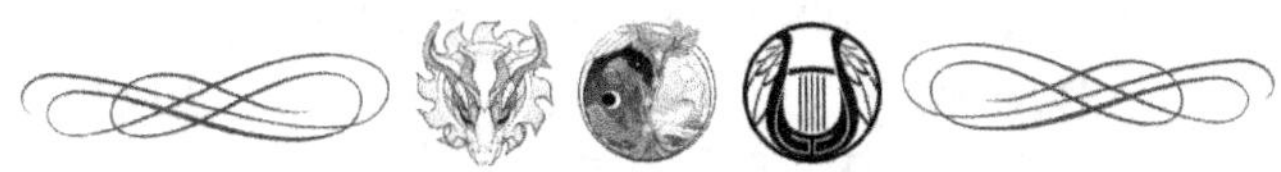

Seru hesitantly reached out to claim the large enameled egg from Thalasia. He turned it over, using both hands to counterbalance the weight. The swirling blues shone glossy in the light; tiny gems twinkled from their inlays in the gilded pattern. He scrutinized the pattern of the wingless dragons wrapped around it carefully. "And what exactly is this design supposed to depict?" His brows knit closer together as his skepticism grew with each new angle.

"Looks like two dragons moving toward one another. It isn't something I've used very often. We touch it together; you think about where you want us to go and it'll transport us there."

He leveled his gaze at her, doubt coloring his tone. "Even if it's somewhere beyond a barrier?" Several thousand-year-old wards accompanied the protective shield. But he saw little point in elaborating further. He doubted she knew the specifics, even if asked. A single use hardly produced the same results as infinite trial and error, accompanied by thorough research.

"On the isle." She smirked. "It'll get us closer to the Clouds. Otherwise, we'll waste time traveling."

Lovely. Seru suppressed the urge to roll his eyes and huff at the predictable answer. Why exactly had he bothered asking in the first place? With a slight shake of his head, he righted the egg-shaped device in one palm, extending it into the space between them. There was little point in arguing that the time to travel from their current position—or even the isle over—took little to no time at all for him. Instead, he resigned to her choice to use the questionable artifact.

If nothing else, maybe the use would reveal more precise information about the artifact and its mechanics. He hated to think of what very well could and likely would go wrong if he dared to misuse or tamper with it magically without further knowledge of its maker, previous owners, and the artifact's history. "Just out of curiosity—" and maybe a bit of distaste, "If I'm selecting the destination, does that mean you're to think of nothing at all?"

"Yes. It means I have to fully clear my mind. Trust me. It's not fun when both parties are thinking of a place." A slight frown crossed her face. "I really don't want to end up in the river again," she muttered. Inhaling and exhaling a deep breath, her eyes met his. "You ready?"

Trust her, right? Sure, it was that simple and easy in her mind. Just trust her. What could go wrong? Seru pushed the thoughts away, swallowing the sudden lump in his throat, as an image of what happened the last time he'd foolishly done such a thing flashed through his mind. "Not really," he turned the grimace into a grumble. He forced his eyes closed anyway, calling up the memory of... smooth, porous rock, worn by the caress of the briny surf. The scent of the shore intermingled with the spice of brimstone and the stench of sulfur from the volcanoes farther off, billowing smoke in the distance.

As he opened his eyes, he reclaimed the egg. The light reflected from the tide pools played off its metallic surface. The waves sucked at their ankles. As Seru stepped onto shore, he offered her a warning, "This is Red Clan territory. Their leader, Vera, is Aurelia's closest and most trusted... friend. Try not to do anything to rouse their interest in you."

He rather hoped the harsh fumes concealed her abundant scent, though, somehow, he doubted it. "Cynric, Vera's brother, holds dominion over these volcanoes. He's a potent infernal force and among the Clouds' best warriors. One of the few males permitted a title of his own. It's taken a lot of effort to win his allegiance—" Though that wasn't entirely true. Cynric had always possessed a fondness for the Matriarch, even before she'd risen to power. The red dragon had a particular grievance against him. "So, avoid him altogether." He surveyed the area as he spoke and absently held his hand toward Thalasia.

Thalasia slid her hand into his. "I don't try to draw attention... not that it ever makes much of a difference."

He offered a disgruntled reply, tucking the egg beneath one arm and leading her by the other. The crustacean creatures that made the small isle home scuttled into the waves, wary of the intruders. They'd rather face the enemies they knew—turtles, crabs, and salamanders—than those they didn't. He paid them little mind, his steps sure, and practiced as they navigated the rock.

"We can put the egg back in my purse."

He hazarded a glance her way and almost instantly regretted it. "Hatching mischief already?" His features darkened into stern disapproval. It wasn't really a question. Her expression said it all.

"I don't know what you're talking about." She grinned.

"Of course not." Just like Aurelia never knew, or tried to convince him otherwise. He resisted the urge to sigh and shake his head. These women and the trouble they brought with them would be the death of him. His hand reflexively constricted around hers before releasing. "No one is ever up to anything. I guess that makes me delusional."

Thalasia chuckled, a full, hearty laugh. "If you must know, it amused me that of all the artifacts I have in my possession, you're concerned with an egg just because of the image depicted on it. As far as I know, it's just a teleportation device."

"'As far as you know' after only one use," Seru paraphrased back to her. He sounded tired. Exactly how much sleep did being her Allimos require? The change in his usual patterns and the predictability of them were frustrating him in a whole new way. He dropped her hand as they neared the spell circle at the center of the isle, the markings nearly invisible to the naked eye while inactive.

"If I thought you'd give them to me, Thalasia," Seru said as he stooped to brush away stray sand that had accumulated in the creases. "I'd gladly take them off your hands." The tone and irritation crept into his voice, denoting exactly how forthcoming she'd be with that request.

That after everything, she'd trust any Draconic symbol or anyone in possession of such a thing ate away at him. With all she'd been through and their ongoing struggles, how did she still trust him—much less complete strangers and their array of miscellaneous magical artifacts?

Dragging a hand down her face, she crossed her arms. "Actually, I've used it a few times in different realms. Many of the artifacts in my bag are heirlooms from my ancestors. And you..." Her words faded away as she ran a hand through her hair, a heavy sigh escaping her lips. "I'm not fighting with you over this." She dropped her hands to her hips. "I won't tell you I'm perfect or that I have all the answers, but you don't, either."

Seru paused mid-motion to look at her. His eyes narrowed, his face blank. "No..." he said after a moment. "I don't, Thalasia. But I think you'd be surprised by exactly how much I *know*." Would it always feel like this between them? Her obstinate and determined to prove herself. With him equally resigned to feeling like... some horrific combination between... what? Lover and father?

The thought alone made him cringe. He rolled his shoulders to ease some of the tension before correcting his posture and gesturing to the center. "Can you just stand in the middle, please?" He rubbed his neck. What in all the hells had he been thinking? He forced his gaze back to hers. "Try not to get eaten in the few moments you're up there alone." Again, not a question. Still, he had his doubts.

"No, Seru. I wouldn't be surprised by how much you know. You have a lot of years on me, but that doesn't mean I constantly have to be schooled. I guess for that to happen, you have to stop seeing me as a child." She shook her head. "Maybe it's time I stop trying to prove to you that I'm enough. Because if you haven't seen it by now... I don't think you ever will," she said before she stepped where he gestured, following his instructions.

"You aren't a child," Seru said. "But, you're still..." Lost for words, he raked his fingers through his mane. Blowing out a slow breath, he returned his attention to the spell circle. As his magic flowed from him through the collar, illuminating its intricate pathways and into the circle, activating the dormant magic within it, the complex symbols shone an intense red-orange.

"Try not to be sick," he gave her a hint of a sympathetic look before adding, "You don't need to prove you're enough. I know you are—I just..." He pursed his lips, directing his gaze elsewhere. "Nevermind," he whispered, activating the spell and sending her skyward in a flash of red.

Once she'd disappeared, Seru took a moment to collect himself, gazing out over the white-capped expanse of the ocean. Thalasia posed so many problems that his other companions didn't. They'd been cautious, even resistant, at first. But eventually, they'd come together in mutual self-interest. Maybe, with a helpful dose of coaxing and manipulation, where Marius was concerned.

Neither approach worked with her. She wasn't one to submit to his will or to take his lead without question. Now seemed a choice time to realize how much that bothered him. Was his inability to cede control to her part of the reason they remained divided and distrusting?

With a sigh, he forced himself to his feet. The sorry state of his attire only gave him more reason to dread this visit. As he stepped into the center of the circle, he promised to remedy that first. Too much in the Clouds was at stake based solely on appearances.

Thalasia accompanying him would be difficult enough to explain. A state of poor dress half dipped in seawater promised disaster. He closed his eyes and prayed they'd slip quietly to the library without incident. The red glow encompassed him, ferrying him to the Clouds without need for transformation.

Thalasia hadn't gone far, only a few steps away from where he appeared. Resisting the urge to praise her, Seru strode down the hall, conscious of his posture and confident in his steps. As much as he disliked admitting it, he knew the Clouds' upper echelons well enough to navigate the halls blind. He ignored the bubbling of her attitude as it threatened to boil over, trusting the quickened pace to give her something else to focus on besides her new surroundings.

She followed him... silently.

Seru did his best to ignore Thalasia's lack of showmanship and pride. She wanted so badly for him to accept her, yet she clearly held the same disdain for the dragons and their customs as many of the earthbound did, electing what came easiest over constant effort and precise action.

A few servants and a gathering of concubines bypassed them. The servants kept their heads down. The concubines didn't, allowing their judgment to filter through their steely glares of disapproval. At least they had the decency to cover their smug faces with ornate fans crafted with silk and flowers. Though the predatory energy they allowed to coalesce in the corridor nearly smothered them in their desire to hunt, a clear and intentional threat—if only the opportunity arose. To them, Thalasia, no matter her spectacular colors, registered as prey.

Thalasia pushed stray strands of hair from her shoulders, lifted her chin, and relaxed her arms, a subtle Cheshire cat-like smile gracing her lips. Setting her pace, she walked beside Seru with her head held high and a glint in her silver eyes.

The dragons snickered.

The instinct to retaliate rose between Seru's shoulders. It took every ounce of practiced self-control not to turn on them. While on a basic level he—and his beast—read the same signals they did, the overwhelming urge to protect what was his overruled his baser instincts.

"A few steps behind my right flank... please." He hated using that word. Asking nicely wasn't really his forte. A hushed growl more than a polite command, but he was working on it.

She did as he asked and shifted to a few steps behind on his right.

Seru led them through the endless maze of hallways until everything opened up into a large circle of commerce, open to the sun and clouds overhead. He skirted around the market, weaving in and out of passersby too preoccupied to notice their approach and move out of the way. Most lesser dragons strayed away from him. The nobility and foreigners stood their ground, if for entirely different reasons. At the far end, he climbed the grand stair, out of the exchange toward the Regal Crescent.

Although she kept to her position, her eyes scanned all around as they walked. He waited until they reached the corridor leading to the library, where they found themselves alone, before confronting her. "What are you looking for, Thalasia?"

She bit her bottom lip before speaking. "A way to a yellow dragon under guard."

Her statement stopped him in his tracks—so abruptly that she nearly plowed into him. His outrage lashed at her like a white-hot whip. "I don't know who—" That wasn't true. The options were slim, a fifty-fifty shot in the dark. Confident Marius would never betray him, Seru seethed. "If you think you can conspire with Cyon to any avail, you're both extremely gullible and—"

Sucking in a breath before his vocal range elevated beyond his control, he bit down on his lip. His fingers massaged his temples. What did it matter? With a shake of his head, he gave one last venomous reply. "Stay away from *her*."

As he moved to enter the library through the double doors, he paused. The doors remained slightly ajar. Shifting his focus from Thalasia to the intruder, Seru braced himself before throwing open the doors.

Chapter Thirty-Eight

Thalasia narrowed her gaze, her eyes fixing on the expanse of Seru's back as he slowly surveyed the large room. Despite his anger at her admission, or his demand that she stay away from the female, it only made her want to find the dragon more. If the male had learned anything about her by now, he should've learned that she didn't respond to demands very well. The more people told her *not* to do something, the more she wanted to do the exact opposite.

Instead of allowing her annoyance with him to get the best of her, she bit her tongue. Arrogant. Dickhead. She was getting damn tired of this endless cycle with him. At this point... two tasks. Once she completed them both, she'd rather face the firing rang with the sirens than continue spending one more damn day with him. Damn it! Three. They had to remove the fucking crystal from her neck. Then... then she was done.

Her eyes followed Seru as he skillfully maneuvered his way around a massive desk, moving deliberately toward the far-off corner. What the fuck was he doing? Whatever. For the moment, it appeared they were truly alone, and it loosened her tongue. Though she didn't bother moving from the entryway of the double doors. It mattered little how much rest she got; he could drain her with just an influx of emotions. Which usually meant consistently defending herself and her choices. Thalasia folded her arms across her chest. "I wasn't conspiring with Cyon. She simply provided me with information. Because all I wanted was a way to understand you better. You've bitched countless times that I'm judgmental, so I thought for a second that maybe... I could make a better effort to comprehend your perspective, although you yourself have been just as judgmental. Not to mention the one thing I thought we agreed on." With a sigh, she shook her head, her hand sweeping down her face before settling on her hips. "Excuse me if I thought this female might offer some insight and maybe some answers that either you can't or won't provide. Some days I'm not really sure."

"Yes," Seru answered, his tone cutting like frozen blades. "And it never occurred to you, in your quest to understand me, that Cyon and I maintain a certain distance. If not for her status as Marius's wife and protector of his underwater realm, she'd be little more than another enemy."

"Of course, I did; usually every time she looked at me with pity." The female had given her a lot of those looks over the couple of conversations the two of them shared.

With no acknowledgement of Thalasia, Seru proceeded down aisle after aisle of book-laden shelves. "Perhaps you should meet his other wives so you may better understand what it means to be bound to a dragon. See how little attention he gives them while you permit your brain to absorb their gossip and folly like a sea sponge."

Seriously? What the fuck was he searching for? Thalasia's silver eyes narrowed, keenly watching him as he navigated the space. "Not that I really need to meet his other wives. Marius made it quite clear exactly how difficult you are; how much you work against yourself. And honestly, you've done a fine job of proving him right."

With a snarl, Seru thrust his arms into the dark. The room echoed with the sound of tiny, clawed feet skittering about. "Marius doesn't see the bigger picture," Seru emphasized as he ripped a young boy from his hiding place. "Unlike you, he's accepted he never will and fulfills his role without question."

If she didn't want to slap the ever-loving shit out of him before, she sure as hell did now. *Marius doesn't see the bigger picture...* yeah, that was a load of bullshit if she ever heard it. Her eyes narrowed at the child he dragged out into the open. One with alabaster skin, a flawless complexion despite his current disheveled state, and silver eyes. She'd never seen another with eyes so close to her color. It was strange. And obviously Seru was a bit displeased with him.

Thalasia shook her head. "You mean the role you delineated to me? If you expected me to be silent, look pretty, and keep my opinions to myself, then you linked yourself to the wrong damn woman. As for the bigger picture... if you're so certain Marius can't see it, then what exactly is it, Mr. Know-It-All? Because there are things I think he sees just fine and the one that's blind to them... is you."

A playful gleam lit the boy's eyes as they flickered between Seru and her. "Oh! Look! A pretty sapphire bird," he exclaimed, writhing in Seru's grasp. With a pointed finger, he indicated her, his breath catching as he tried to elevate himself for a better look. "Is she yours?"

"My assisting the Matriarch in her duties doesn't give you permission to enter this library unaccompanied. This isn't a playground!" Seru announced through clenched teeth.

Bird. Yeah. She gripped her hands together firmly behind her, the tension evident in her posture. There were few terms she despised in the common language. That was one of them. "I'm Thalasia and I belong to *no one.*" It hurt more than she expected to say that, but it needed to be put out there. He wanted her to care, but not too much. He wanted her, but he refused to do anything about it. Yeah, she could've kissed him again when they were back in the cave. While her body might have reacted to him, he had to put in a bit more effort to achieve that response. It wouldn't happen again unless he put in something more. Maybe even something completely out of character for him.

"Is that why your 'Thalasia' is not in a cage?!" the boy blurted. "Your Thalasia doesn't have a collar or proper bindings either." His grin broadened. "You're going to be in so much trouble!"

A brief frown creased Seru's face as his eyes briefly shifted to her.

Good gods. *Someone get me off this isle before I strangle someone.* Although at the moment she didn't know who she preferred. Collar. Bindings. She held back a grumble of irritation. Maybe she didn't know who the young boy was, which was probably a good thing. Someone else for Seru, the supposed biggest badass, to placate. "I'm sure he'll be able to escape that. Not like I'll be hanging around this place longer than necessary." Yep. As soon as Seru removed the crystal from her neck, she planned to leave. At least she knew what awaited her in Pteryrina, even if she'd avoided the place for days now.

"Master escape artist!" the child replied.

With a decisive stride, Seru returned to the desk, gently plopping the boy onto the raised area and freeing his own hands. "Where are your nestminders?"

The boy's attention remained fixed on her. With a lazy sway of his legs, he offered an indifferent shrug. "Somewhere. Not here." He shot a devilish grin at Seru, his eyes glinting with mischief. "What's 'necessary?'"

Neither of them immediately answered. Seru ran a hand through his thick mane, letting it settle at the nape of his neck. Obviously, he was growing more irritated by the second. Thalasia opened her mouth to explain the term, but a clicking sound stopped her short. Her eyes snapped toward the sound as rocks grated against each other, a hidden passage slowly emerging. Wasn't that interesting? Though it shouldn't have surprised her. Given that one entry she'd read in the book she had about him. Hmm, she'd forgotten about the book. If she spoke with the female, well, two sources were better than one.

"Enough!" Seru bellowed. Magic surged outward, a wave that swept dust from the room, rustled book pages, and scattered loose papers from his desk into the hall. Paper rained down around them.

Her gaze, a quick sweep, took in the dusk-hued leopard sprawled on the floor and then landed on her presumed Allimos. Absolutely, a bit of distance was exactly what they needed. And she needed to talk to someone... who wasn't a dragon or dragon-adjacent. One would think she would've learned after her last experience, but no... her heart had to get involved this time around.

Thalasia folded her arms across her chest. She'd ask if he felt better, but she doubted it. It had never made her feel better. While she could probably use the connection he created between them to calm him down, why should she? He was the one who had created his own mess. And he didn't seem to want her help. She leaned against the wall, casually crossing one ankle over the other.

The leopard rose unsteadily on trembling paws as the last piece of parchment fluttered down. A sheet fell precisely onto its head, and it swiftly swiped at it, snagging it with its sharp claws. As it tried to dislodge the object, it risked a look at Seru. With its ears tucked into its spotted fur, the creature adjusted its stance, sinking back onto its haunches. "Io–I mean, the First," his eyes darted between her and Seru, "requests an audience with... Your... ah... Excellency."

As if that didn't speak volumes about the difference between her and everyone else in his life. Gods, what had she been thinking? Atlis chose an Allimos who was her equal. Neither bowed done to the other. Yeah, she and Seru had certainly fucked all that up. If he wanted a female who'd defer to his every choice and decision, it definitely wasn't her.

All she could do was shake her head. Her decision to head to Pteryrina sooner rather than later was the right thing to do. It was time she figured everything else out on her own... at least the decisions she had to make. "Do whatever you need to, Seru. You and I... we need some time away from each other."

Taking a deep breath, Seru squared his shoulders and addressed the leopard. "Tell the First I'll be with her presently. In the meantime, retrieve a suitable set of attire for Thalasia." He pointed at her while he went behind the desk, grabbing a change of clothes and unbuttoning his shirt. "Be sure to come back with something that accommodates her wings and status as my *companion*."

The identifying term didn't bother her. It was how he'd introduced her thus far to anyone they'd come across. Only the female siren and her shifter mate had used other terms. Whatever the female *thought* she saw, it looked less and less like it every hour that passed. At least Seru didn't argue with her statement. Not that it was a demand, it was just the way things were in the present moment... and maybe more before that.

The leopard's lavender gaze flicked briefly in her direction. "Right away, Master," the creature purred, dipping his head and casting a last look her way before disappearing into the tunnel.

As Seru shrugged out of his attire, a heavy silence settled in the room, broken only by the soft click of his new shirt cuffs. He reached out an arm to the boy, who was still perched on the edge of the desk. "Swear to stay quiet, or I'll return you to your confinement with three times the guards."

The child pouted, his lower lip jutting forward, and extended his small arm in a gesture of acceptance. As blue markings pulsed with light beneath Seru's skin, they transferred onto the child's arm. "Fine," he whined. "But I want the pretty wisher you keep in your desk."

"What you hear doesn't leave this room." Seru gripped the boy's arm tightly; their pact sealed with the firm clasp. From an unlocked drawer, he retrieved an opal stone, its surface a milky white with an ethereal blue shimmer. He flicked it upward, and it flew through the air before landing squarely in the boy's hands. The gilded rune etched into the face shimmered, mirroring the sparkle in the child's eyes.

"I *need* you to stop undermining my decisions simply because it feels liberating," he called out as the double doors to her right slammed shut. "I *need* you to stay put and for once just do as you're told, Thalasia. You say you want to build trust and grow this bond between us, but your actions prove you're no more willing to make that sacrifice than I am. And, if you trust nothing else, you can trust that magic imbued into every inch of this room is going to see to it, you do just that until I see what pressing fresh hell, the First wishes to bestow on us."

She should've seen all of that coming. Not just the doors, but his demands. He seriously thought that little of her? Thalasia pushed off the wall, her eyes narrowing with intense focus. "First, I don't do something because 'it feels liberating.' Like you, I act and decide things for a reason. Second, you said yourself... you aren't willing to make that sacrifice, then *why* do you deem it necessary I make the first step? Give a little, get a little. Or feel free to get the thing out of my neck and figure it out on your own."

"You realize, while it's not verbatim outlined in your little journals, the expectation is that every Allimos sacrifice everything for their Atlis?" His voice grew increasingly unsettled and desperate with every word he uttered. "That's what you ultimately desire from me. I can't protect you *your* way. Only mine—and for reasons I cannot comprehend, you refuse to let me. I'm not a siren or anything else in your holy instruction manuals!"

"You don't think an Atlis sacrifices?" She dipped her head in a sharp, curt motion, the dismissive gesture cutting off further explanation. He'd made his fucking point. And she was tired of correcting him. "Fine. But something you should think about in all of this... if we were actually to succeed in our endeavors... do you really think they'd let you stay? Because regardless if they think you're the biggest badass on the isle... they'd turn on you the second they thought you couldn't be controlled any longer." This was the problem. She wasn't a siren. Or like anything in, as he put it, her 'holy instruction manuals.' "I'll stay put like a good little glory. But don't think you can keep me locked in here for as long as you fucking please."

"What's a 'glory?'" the child piped up, directing his question at Seru, per usual.

With a sharp intake of breath, Seru met the boy's scrutiny head-on. "Your responsibility until I return. Keep an eye on the 'pretty bird.'"

At that very instant, the leopard emerged once more, a tightly fastened bundle held firmly in its jaws. With a slow, deliberate movement, he maneuvered around Seru, depositing the parcel at her feet and then settling down, his gaze fixed on her expectantly.

Thalasia inhaled deeply, the fresh air doing little to quell her rising irritation with the word "bird," as she dug her nails into her palms. She'd take siren over that. At least she had sirens in her DNA. Among several other things, given her ancestry. Whatever.

Fighting with Seru beyond exhausted her. And if he was going to lock her up like a doll, she sure as shit was going to go through the books in his library.

Feeling the rough texture of the package the leopard had presented, Thalasia bent down and picked it up. It was rather hefty. She walked over to the desk where the kid still sat and removed a midnight-blue velvet dress. It sparkled. A lot. Although she appreciated the overall appearance of it, including the halter style she preferred, it was a lot. And there was a draping of some kind that connected to each side of the dress and hung down. Hmm, she might have something of her own that would work with it. She looked back at the shape shifter. "Thank you."

Her gaze flicked back to Seru and the kid. Hopefully, the leopard would leave, but just in case. "Either turn around or give me some space. I'm not changing in front of you."

Simultaneously, the kid and the leopard turned to Seru, who clearly didn't think she was talking to him as he finished dressing himself. He threw his head toward the passageway. The shape shifter rose from his seat and silently padded his way back through the opening.

The kid stared. "I can't keep an eye on her and turn around."

Really? Really? Just fucking really? Pinching the bridge of her nose, she groaned. "For the love of all things holy, Seru. Either he covers his eyes or turns around. Pick one." Yeah, she'd made it pretty damn clear how she felt about being naked in front of strangers. At this rate, it included him.

The boy frowned. "Why does your Thalasia address you that way?"

"There's a curtain in the far corner." Seru pointed out the reading nook to her. "Let her dress in peace," he said, angling the kid with an icy glare.

"Why does your Thalasia need a curtain? Is she disfigured?" he leaned forward, intrigued. "Does she have a tail like us?"

A tail? Seriously? She picked up the dress and hairpiece in a huff. "I do *not* have a tail! And I'm *not* disfigured!" Stomping over to where Seru pointed out, she muttered something about ill-educated children. Disappearing behind the curtain, she yanked it into place.

"I don't think she likes you very much," the boy proudly announced.

"Not at the moment," she called out from behind the curtain as she worked on getting her boots and clothes off. As well as putting her dagger in her bag. Not that it seemed to change very often. In fact, if they were counting, she'd probably disliked Seru six or seven times in the last couple of days alone. Maybe more.

While she could go without a bra, if she was going to put on this... gorgeous monstrosity, she wouldn't go without underwear. She dug around in her bag for a pair and paused in a pocket. She'd nearly forgotten they were in there. It wasn't the jewelry she originally thought of with the dress, but it actually complemented it well. Shaking her head, she collected a fresh pair of hi-cut panties and slipped them on before she turned her attention to the dress.

"It's okay," the kid said, poking his head through the curtain. "I don't think he likes himself, either. At least most of the time."

"Get out!" Thalasia screamed, yanking the dress to cover herself.

He cringed, but didn't retreat. "Why are you so loud and angry? You're not ugly like some others, so why do you need a curtain? Are you hiding?"

Deep breath. Deep breath. Don't kill the child. Don't set him on fire. At least she had underwear on. Small reassurance, but it was better than nothing. Turning around, she gave him her back and spread her wings enough to cover herself as she stepped into the dress and tugged it over her hips. "Because dragons don't seem to understand the term privacy."

"What's 'privacy?'" He swayed from the curtain.

"It means that someone is concealed from view." Zipping the back of the dress up, she hooked it where it rested at her mid-back. She pulled the halter part of the garment up around her neck, securing it with a click before lifting the shimmering train. It was split, so it hung on either side of her wings, but still connected to the dress.

"Why do you want to be concealed from view? Don't birds have pride? Do you not like belonging to the Regent? Is it because of your wings?"

Didn't they already establish she didn't belong to him? Good gods, he had to leave her with the child. She should've gone down the stairs when she had a chance. This was one of many reasons she didn't want kids. Had she been like this when she was young? No. Never. Not that she remembered. Shoving her clothes and boots in the bag, she dug around for a brush. Except she still had the beads in her hair. Thalasia rubbed her temple. She opened her mouth to respond to his multitude of questions when it occurred to her to turn the tables. "You have pride. Why do you wear clothes? Why do the females here cover themselves with fancy gowns and priceless jewels? Are they hiding something?"

"Because my hatchmaids make me," he answered matter-of-factly. "Most of them only cover themselves when they're outside their domains, or presenting at court. You're not outside your master's domain and you're not allowed at court, so you don't need clothes. Jewels are just shiny status symbols, tributes to their status and their clan. A lot of the nobles flaunt how many jewels they have because it makes them feel important." He dug around for something. "Like this wisher!" he proclaimed. "Isn't it pretty?" The kid paused. "Secrets are like riddles and puzzles! If you possess more secrets than the others, you know the most, and you win the game. Most of the nobles aren't that smart, though. They can't keep their secrets, so they rely on power to force their will on others. The Regent and Mother have the most secrets!"

Yeah, she bet he had the most secrets. She carefully maneuvered the beads, then gathered her hair into a carefree bun, using the comb to keep it in place. As she did, it made her conscious of the two symbols on her neck. The one that Minerva had embedded into her skin and the one that Seru had carved into it, using her blade and the crystal.

Her master's domain... was that what she had allowed? No. When Cyon had asked her all of those questions, she'd been very specific regarding their positioning. She shook the thoughts bubbling in her head away, returned her brush and dagger to her purse, and retrieved the jewelry that belonged to her grandmother. She glanced over her shoulder at the stone the kid had held up. "Yes, it's beautiful."

She put the teardrop diamond earrings on, along with the necklace, and found a pair of ballet flats that would work with the dress. "Where I'm from, I don't need to flaunt my attributes to feel important. And I cover myself because I respect my body, and my... *master*, as you put it." Good gods, she despised that word. Even more than she hated the word 'bird.'

"Respect your body? Isn't that what training and meditation are for?"

"They are part of it, but when other people, who aren't Seru, are around, am I being disrespectful to not only him, but myself, by walking around naked even if I'm in his domain?" Especially when she'd made a point of already telling Seru exactly how uncomfortable she was being put on display, which was exactly what he was doing. Despite her efforts not to pressure him into her traditions, he continually pushed his own upon her. Another issue they had. Thalasia slipped her feet into the shoes and yanked the strings of her purse, tying them together and sliding it over her wrist. Turning around, she pushed the curtain open. Seru had left without so much as a word. Perhaps she shouldn't have expected differently.

"You shouldn't call him that. You'll get in trouble!" The kid smirked. "No, that would be silly," he offered, backing away to allow her to come out into the open. "You're really weird."

"Tell me something I don't know," she mumbled. She'd been called weird her whole life. That wasn't new at all. As for getting in trouble... yeah, she completely overlooked that. Pissing him off happened even when she wasn't trying. Thalasia scanned the books lining the walls and paused for a moment. There was still paper and shreds of it all over the floor. Hmm... exactly how protected was this room? She whistled, altering it to use the air in the room for the sheets to lift and re-stack neatly on his desk.

"He doesn't like it when you mess with his things," the kid warned.

"He doesn't like half the things I do. And if cleaning up his mess pisses him off, well, that sounds like his problem." No way he didn't expect her to inspect or look through his books. Although he'd probably accuse her of looking for *Celestimo*, which would be idiotic. He wouldn't keep a book of such value out in the open like this. "Besides, I highly doubt these are the books he *really* treasures. Those would be hidden. Secret."

"He doesn't let anyone clean the library."

"He gets really mad when things are moved. It's not your duty to clean. Stop." His command was weak at best. "He has a room in Mother's den. With her harem. But I don't think he uses it."

She doubted he'd hide the book there. And if he didn't use it, then why even look there? Besides, she didn't plan to leave the library. *That* was what he demanded. "Then what do you *think* my duty to him is?"

"You don't know?"

"I'm just curious about what you think. You seem to know so much." Aside from him not having the same gusto as Seru, and he asked a thousand questions, the kid was like a miniature version of Seru. Not to mention, this was one of those things she and Seru didn't quite agree on.

"Most serve to keep their master company, use their skills to gain their master's favor and ensure their master's satisfaction." It sounded like a question. "You should try turning into a book. He likes those."

Thalasia chuckled. Except for his suggestion, everything else was pretty much what she expected he'd say. "Sounds more like a slave than a companion."

"What's a slave?"

"Someone who does whatever their master wants to stay in their good graces and to keep from being punished and who isn't allowed to decide for themselves." Would he see the difference? She didn't know. Her eyes moved along the rows of books, her mind open to anything that might spark her curiosity.

"That kinda depends on the preferences of the master."

"Still slavery. Something that is… outdated." And something she stood against. In some realms, it was outlawed. Just to test the limitations of his magic, she focused on a book. It didn't matter which one, and tried to pull it off the shelf.

"How do you know if you don't know?"

With the book in her hand, she glanced over her shoulder at him. "You mean if you don't know if someone has been enslaved?"

"If you don't know your duties, how do you know it's the same as being a slave?" His gaze fell from her face to the book in her hand. "You really shouldn't be touching those. He'll know."

She smirked. This coming from the person Seru yelled at for being in there. Thalasia opened her mouth to explain and reconsidered her words. Even as an Atlis, she had basic or sacred laws. But it wasn't exactly the same as being enslaved. Or expected to blindly follow. "Servants don't immediately know what's expected of them unless they're told. Right? But they have no say in how they're treated or boundaries that they aren't willing to cross. They are simply expected to do what they're told without question."

"Everyone contributes to a household. Your clan is your family—unless you're clanless. Would you prefer your clan suffer because you'd rather make the choices, even if you're ill-equipped to do so?"

"As a single decision affects everyone in the household, wouldn't it make more sense to talk through those choices and decide together what everyone can agree on?" She returned the book in her hand. Although every decision she'd made up to that point only impacted her, she'd tried frequently to talk to Seru about things and, more than once, it ended up in an argument.

"No one ever agrees on anything," he pointed out. "Discussions take time. If you discuss every option, you'll lose a lot. It's easier for each individual to fill their role and commit to the duties they're given. Do you expect a craftsman to decide how best to prepare a meal or how to train an army?"

"And when they're life-changing decisions, they should be discussed. Especially when some roles depend on one another." She paused in front of another book. "If that craftsman knows how to cook, then yes. And if that craftsman has insight that the training officer doesn't, yes. People aren't just one role. They can fill multiple roles." Turning toward him, Thalasia crossed her arms. "You called me a pretty bird. Does that mean you assume I can sing? Or that I have no *other* role?"

"Even if the craftsman can cook, he doesn't cook as well as the cook. Training officers can't craft; they fight. What you're saying doesn't make any sense," he lamented. "Just because you can sing doesn't mean you sing well or to expectations. If your master doesn't like your song, you wouldn't sing. If he prefers quiet, you don't sing. What can you do for the Regent that he would appreciate?"

It didn't make any sense. Yeah, she could say the same thing about him. "People have the possibility to fill multiple roles, to be good at a variety of things. Limiting them to one role, you stifle their potential for growth." She dragged a hand across her face, continuing to walk around because it was all she could do. Seru would prefer that she do nothing. That she sat there and did... nothing.

Gods, what had she been thinking? Him as her Allimos. He expected that he'd be making all the sacrifices. Would it be an enormous change? Yes. It meant he'd have to leave everything behind. But he'd get so much more. Yet he couldn't see that. Or he refused to... no. He'd become convinced they couldn't get the collar off. Not that they'd even—she stopped mid-step. Unless... she reached up to the mark on her neck and traced the outline of the symbol with her fingers.

She shook the thoughts away. If she was stuck in here, she had to do something. Anything that would quell the tightening in her chest, the urge to lash out at the unseen bars of her confinement. Because it was exactly how she felt. Thalasia inhaled and exhaled a deep breath. "Nothing seems to make him happy," she muttered.

"Can you even read those?" he asked, indicating the books she selected at random. "You wouldn't be here if there wasn't *something* about you that makes him happy," he insisted, tiny hands on his hips.

Opting to ignore his latter comment, she focused on his question instead. Because the truth was... half the time she and Seru fought. Yeah, she made him happy alright. Not in any way that she could see, or maybe it was the other way around. And that was why he'd become damn wishy-washy over his decisions. For a moment, she offered him a way out. What he wanted. Which had changed to something... she didn't think was possible. Even if she wanted to stay here, too. Just not like this. "I don't know if I can read them. It's probable. I speak seven languages." Although most of them weren't used in this realm.

"That's not very many," the kid said, disappointed. "Are you looking for a particular one? I don't think he keeps how-to books."

"Not very many?" She glanced over her shoulder at him. "How many do you speak?" Seru probably spoke more than that, but also had eight-hundred years on her. She didn't quite know how dragons aged. This topic had never surfaced in conversations with the two people she'd encountered before.

"Twenty-seven!" He beamed.

Either the kid spent a lot of time bored out of his mind, or he'd been forced into more education than even she had endured. Unless... "Twenty-seven different languages or twenty-seven different dialects of one language?"

"I know the difference between a language and a dialect!"

She smirked. "I didn't say you didn't. I just rarely include dialects since the language isn't always altered that much with the dialect. Or it can often include slang." She shook her head. Not that she needed to impress the kid. "To answer your other question, I am looking for a particular book. It's leather-bound, really old, will be locked, and has an embedded spot for a lyre with wings."

He flinched. "What's a lyre with wings?"

While she could pull out the item in question, she didn't really want to show another dragon something shiny. She walked over to Seru's desk, removed a piece of loose paper and a pen from her purse, drew the symbol, and then held it out to him. "Looks like this."

"A flat bird?"

"It's not a bird. The lyre and wings represent the sirens." She rolled her shoulders, reminding herself not to let the kid's ignorance get to her. Good gods, she was trying really hard not to find a way out. What had Seru been thinking? Oh, wait... he hadn't.

"More birds like you?" He took several steps back before turning to wander between the shelves. He ducked into one of the lower shelves, settling himself into the empty-space. "Maybe he meant to pick one of them and you were an accident. Be grateful he didn't eat you."

"There isn't another like me. I'm one of a kind." After returning the parchment and pen to her purse and tying its strings, she fastened it back onto her wrist and leaned against the desk. Which lasted for all of a second. Thalasia stood and paced around the library. Seru needed to come back. Not that she had any idea how long his meeting with... the First... was that what the shifter had said... would take. What part of her being chained up and locked up had he forgotten? The library wasn't much bigger than the cabin she'd been trapped in for months.

"If you don't know where the book is... well... it wouldn't surprise me." It was likely something Seru had kept close to the vest. It would make the most sense. She rolled her shoulders again, a sigh escaping her lips as the stiffness lessened. Walking around in circles, ducking through the aisles that were there, she needed something to occupy her mind. Her growing frustration wasn't helping her pent-up energy, especially as she replayed conversation after conversation in her head. "Tell me about yourself, kid."

"I'm not a kid!" he blurted, poking his head out just long enough to shout his reply.

"And I'm not a bird." She gripped her shoulder. This wasn't helping any. She had to do something to stop the endless repetition of words in her head. It didn't aid in her annoyance or energy at all. She had to expend it... carefully. She realized she could finally do something she'd put off for days. Returning to Seru's desk, she untied her purse and retrieved the dagger her father had given her years ago. A quick squeeze of the hilt, and the weapon elongated by several inches, transforming into a broadsword.

Thalasia inhaled deeply, the scent of old paper and dust filling her lungs, before exhaling slowly as she surveyed the room, letting her senses map its dimensions. With the image clear in her mind, she unleashed the sword in a graceful arc, each step deliberate as she continued her practice. At no point did the blade come into contact with a shelf, bookcase, or book. She even worked around the train of the dress with great precision.

"Your Thalasia, you aren't supposed to have weapons! It's against the law."

"Why?" she asked, her movements fluid and practiced, adapting seamlessly to the unfamiliar constraints of the dress and the library's cluttered surroundings. It wasn't an ideal place for practice, but it certainly worked well enough. And it helped her spend some of her pent-up energy.

"B-because..." Momentarily, he faltered. "You're not a dragon or a fighter. You're just a pretty bird that does nothing she's supposed to."

And the kid was back to sounding like Seru. She smirked, not that it stopped her movements. Nothing the boy muttered would do that. Unless he offered a location for the book, but she was positive he didn't know where it was located. "If I'm not a dragon, then why would your laws apply to me?"

Just a *pretty bird*. They'd come full circle. Just like she and Seru often did. Even that didn't make her alter her actions. Pent-up energy wasn't a good thing. "Are your laws more important than the laws of my people?"

"You belong to the Regent. You're in dragon territory by his extending you protection contingent on you following the rules!" He crossed his arms in a huff. "Stupid bird," he mumbled.

"He only gave me two rules. Stay here and touch nothing." As far as she could tell, she'd followed those requests thus far. Mostly. Yeah, she'd pulled out a few books, found one she could actually open... not that she saw anything in it. And there was that thing about protection. Not that she could say what exactly he was protecting her from.

In fact, the more she thought back on their conversations, there had been one where he'd pointed out that *he* had bowed down to her. Cyon had referenced the same thing. It made her wonder... exactly how far did that extend?

"See the aforementioned. 'You're in dragon territory.'"

"Then what other rules do you think I'm supposed to follow, 'oh-wise-one'?" The last words of her question dripped with sarcasm. Her irritation simmered, but she masked it as she continued to swing the blade.

Nothing. The kid said nothing.

That was about what she expected. It seemed to be the common response. Challenge how a dragon or saint beast thinks, argument. Question the so-called rules. Silence. She could be respectful, but they weren't asking for that. No, they wanted her to submit. Plain and simple. And that... that was something she couldn't do. It went against every fiber in her being. Maybe Seru had chosen wrong. Because she was beginning to believe she had done so herself.

With a final, whispering swish, she tightened her grip on the hilt, and the blade magically contracted to the size of a dagger.

She walked across the room to the desk, her hand brushing against the cool, smooth wood as she leaned there for a moment. Staying here... it wasn't an option. Not when she had no clue how long Seru would be gone. Running through the routine had released none of the energy she'd hoped it would. Instead, it just made things worse. Pushing her to the limit of exactly how closed in she'd allowed herself to become. Again.

A sharp knock resounded on the double doors.

Chapter Thirty-Nine

Thalasia took in their sparse surroundings, a detailed scan of the meager space as she followed the female dragon, who had freed her through the library's grand double doors about an hour prior. A simple knock that had been a much-welcomed reprieve. During that time, the female had taken her for a bath, which she hadn't expected. Still, it wasn't something she had denied. And it had been quite luxurious. The abundance of exfoliants, the fragrant aromas, and the steamy mineral water had made it a luxurious experience she could've quickly grown accustomed to, yet also grown bored with. She had also seized the chance to don her own comfortable clothes, shedding the borrowed garments.

Her blue hair was now better swept up into a chunky braid updo with added pins for accessories. Something that complemented the teardrop earrings and necklace she'd maintained, and the royal blue velvet, mermaid-style dress with a slight train and a low back that she'd changed into. Which was much more her style.

They'd taken a variety of staircases, skirting the marketplace she'd glimpsed earlier. The female held onto the young male's hand, her so-called babysitter... though she was certain Seru hadn't seen it that way. But this gave her an unexpected opportunity. The kid had gone into a rant earlier about the different clans and their clothing. She wore well-made, understated clothing, accented with white gold or silver. Gleaming silver cuffs encircled her neck, wrists, and ankles. Interesting. Not that she had a damn clue what it meant.

The kid would occasionally cast a look back at her as they moved past the vacant structures. The artwork, once vibrant, now crumbled into a state of decay, its renderings becoming completely unidentifiable. "You look like a peacock!" He turned back to the servant, repeating himself more quietly than he had the first time, though still loud enough to echo in the quiet hall. "She looks like a peacock, Yelena."

The servant shifted her gaze to him for only a moment, an acknowledgement without commentary.

Thalasia stifled a small chuckle. "Thank you." Many viewed peacocks as beautiful creatures. Although the kid probably didn't mean it as a compliment, she'd taken it as one.

"Are we almost there?" he asked, tugging at the servant's hand.

She had to stop herself from gripping her shoulder or the back of her neck. How many times had she heard that very question? Too many to count. Her last rescue alone had asked it, like every five seconds. Hmm, a kid who had annoyed her worse than this one. Almost amusing.

The nameless female did nothing more than nod. No... wait... the female wasn't nameless. The kid had called her... Yelena. Still, not talking sounded great for a second. She'd argued with Seru enough to last a lifetime of conversation. And he was probably going to be *really* upset with her by the time she returned to the library. Something she wasn't in any hurry for. After this, she might find her way somewhere that she could slip to another plane for a bit.

As they turned the next bend, the robust fragrance of spices invaded their senses. Oh, wow. Now, that was a wonderful scent. The scent was a bit too potent for her liking, yet it possessed a pleasant aroma. Her head tilted at the sight of the yellow drapes. This couldn't be the one that Cyon had told her about. Not with the lack of guards. Although she supposed it was possible. As well as a high coincidence.

The servant halted in her tracks. "You may take her the rest of the way."

Yeah, spending more time with the kid wasn't high on her priority list, either. But she didn't expect it would be any other way. Hopefully, it didn't last. Really, she wanted to escape his presence, too. Thalasia looked at the kid. "Shall we?"

A sneer twisted his lips before he spun around, marched forward a few paces, and burst through the shimmering curtain.

She gave a slight nod to the woman and then went after the child. She wouldn't run, even though the flats she had on again made it a futile endeavor.

In a room bursting with color, an aging woman sat poised at a table, enjoying the service of hot blooming tea and an assortment of delectable baked morsels decorated in a similar floral pattern. The woman and the kid exchanged a few words of greeting in their native tongue. The woman rose from her seat to greet the boy, but stopped to stare at Thalasia, her expression stern.

Without a second look at Thalasia, the kid darted to the cushioned chair opposite his fellow dragon, jumping up to hoist himself into position. He sat perfectly and well within reaching distance of lemon cakes.

If the woman's look was anything to judge by, the female already didn't like her. Usually, she had to open her mouth for that to happen. "Hello." Because what else did one say to a look like that?

"Who is this? And why is she here?" The woman demanded, equally confused and insulted. Her eyes scanned the room and then refocused on Thalasia. "Why are you here? What do you want?"

The female's questions brought on questions of her own. None of which she expected an answer. How had that other woman, Yelena, known to bring her here? Then again, maybe this was just some ploy by the female in front of her. Either way, she was getting a headache. Thalasia massaged her temple with a slow, circular stroke. "At the moment, escaping an arrogant know-it-all," she muttered.

Had she really said that? Yep. She had. Not that she meant to utter the words, even if they were true. Gods, she wanted to strangle that damn saint beast who'd somehow become a prominent feature in her plans. Dropping her hand, she looked at the female, fairly certain this was the one Cyon had told her about. "I'm Thalasia and I thought we could talk. Can I sit?"

The woman gave her guarded eyes that said she wasn't sure she bought into the cover story. "Is she yours?" the woman asked.

"No," the kid answered simply between bites. Popping a handful of gooey sugar into his mouth, he continued, "I'm just watching her."

Right. They didn't believe in manners or being polite. Fine. She walked around and sat down at the table, draping one leg across the other, the dress shifting as she moved. "I came with the Regent and he told me I wasn't allowed to talk to you. Actually, I think he forbade it, but I'm not very good at listening." She gestured to the child. "And that's why he's watching me."

The woman stiffened and all but spat at her. "What could you possibly want from me that your precious master can't provide? You shouldn't be here. Get out."

With her fingers clasped together, she placed them in her lap. Yeah, she shouldn't be in a lot of places. Not that it ever seemed to stop her. "I'm going to overlook the whole *master* thing because having the property discussion has been nothing but daunting. And there are a lot of things I can't seem to get from him. If we talked about all of them, we'd be here all day long."

"What makes you think I know any more or less than that repulsive serpent?"

Her lips curled as she tried not to laugh. It amused her how the female saw Seru. Yeah. He totally wasn't sacrificing himself around here. She settled her purse a little better in her lap. "A sea dragon thought we could come to an accord." Thalasia shrugged. "But maybe they were wrong, and what you know about *that* repulsive serpent isn't really worth anything."

"All talking to you is going to get me is a quicker death."

The kid flinched, his eyes widening. "But you can't die!"

"Besides, who's saying you're not here to kill me yourself? Your master's been trying for years," she responded, eyes silently assessing Thalasia.

Interesting. She hadn't expected that Seru had been trying to kill her. Nevermind that if she intended to kill her, she wouldn't have wasted time talking to her. She could point out the kid who'd been left to babysit her, but she wanted to know more about why Seru wanted to kill her. "I know why he tried to kill the Phoenix. Why would he try to kill you?"

The woman's face screwed up, irked by the question. "If you're that ill-informed, I hardly see why he brought you here. You're unusual. Don't know your place," she listed, studying her all the while, some of the hostility fading into the background. "Unless he wants you dead, too."

Her place... oh, she knew it... and it didn't fit into their... rules. "I don't like to make assumptions. I prefer facts. And while I can make a guess or two on why he'd want to kill you, it doesn't make it true." Nor did what information she had about the female coincide with a desire for her to be dead. It seemed to be contradictory to what she'd learned from Cyon. Thalasia tilted her head. "Unless it has something to do with Candescent Isle, but then I'd link that more toward the Matriarch than the Regent."

"I don't know anything about Candescent Isle," she admitted, turning an eye to the garden amassed on nearby shelves and drying herbs overhead. "If you were smart, you'd bite your tongue regarding either."

"In general, or just around here? I mean... around here... sure... I'll keep what's happening to myself. Not that anyone is eager to talk to me anyway. They see me as nothing more than a pebble in their shoe." And it wasn't a fair assessment. It was why she heard so much about her *place*. Which had made it clearer that staying here was less and less a viable option. "If you're talking in general, I can't exactly do that. The isle needs to be protected from what's coming."

"If you were merely a 'pebble in a shoe,' you wouldn't have made it past the gate." She gave a derisive snort. "So, either you think you're kidding me, or you're kidding yourself." The female leaned on her elbow. "Protected from what? Or perhaps, who is the better question?"

The female might've been partially right on that. Most just wouldn't give her the time of day. She was beneath them. Thalasia settled into the chair, her wings unfolding slightly as she found her comfortable position. "Answer for an answer. We've easily circumvented my question and, as I said, I hate making assumptions."

The woman sighed, maneuvering to accommodate a servant coming to refresh her cup. The male poured one for Thalasia and the kid, too. He removed the empty plates and retreated to fetch more. "Your Master doesn't enjoy when others hold his secrets. But I presume you've already figured that out. As I'm sure he's kept many from you as well." As she spoke, she dressed her tea with a dainty sprinkle of sugar and stirred with a stick of cinnamon. The colorful petals and florals spun in the clear glassware.

"Yeah, he excels at it." Yet the one thing she expected he would try to take and he hadn't. A book all about him. Where she suspected she might've gotten a lot of answers; then again, he'd probably taken into consideration it had come from her ancestors. They hadn't been all that forthcoming, either.

"'Yes,'" the woman corrected through gritted teeth. "Never 'yeah.' Always 'yes.' That's your answer, girl," she shrugged, sipping her tea. "I hold one of his secrets. For him, that's more than a reason for slaughter."

Good gods, at that moment, the female reminded her of her mother. Of course, it had been years since she'd practiced sitting down for tea and replying with 'yes' and 'no' versus 'yeah' and 'nah.' Her mother used to get quite testy with her.

Focusing back on the female, she considered what she'd said. She was definitely curious about which secret. There were a couple of things he'd told her, well, half-told her when they'd been making their trek toward the cavern. A few questions that he'd answered. Well, fair play. Thalasia offered her a small nod. "The creatures from the other side have made their way onto the isle."

"The magically inclined deformities, the children of that meddlesome enchantress," the woman amended, taking a small bite of the soft cake diamond.

Enchantress? Well, that was certainly something she hadn't heard before. It hadn't been recorded in any part of the Atlis journal she could recall. And Seru hadn't uttered a word about it. Interesting. "They've been increasing their forces; intent on launching an attack. I can't say when, but soon."

It had been a bit more than what she'd offered in an answer, but she hoped it would be enough to continue with what she ultimately wanted to know about Seru. It was too soon to lead in that direction. "The secret you hold... does it have something to do with his involvement in the Silver Queen's war?"

"Waste of magic, if you ask me. Hah!" she laughed bitterly. "No, not the war."

The female's reaction to the guilers attacking the isle surprised her. For a second, she considered offering information on some forces the guilers had gathered. But she kind of liked Marius... to a degree. And it was a secret she enjoyed having. Her response to the war... that didn't surprise her. It didn't seem like something Seru would want to kill over. And it was probably best she didn't play twenty questions, either. No telling when Seru would return to the library. And she'd been dumb enough to tell him what she wanted to do. No doubt, it was the reason he'd locked her in the library. "Does it have something to do with the magic that binds him to the isle?"

"In a way..."

That made little sense. Why wouldn't he want her to know more about the collar? Over the last few days, it seemed like he'd been hellbent on breaking the damn thing. Except... she hadn't specified the collar. What she had asked had been about the magic, which they'd have to break in order to free him from the collar. Except he'd told her that it used to be magic that bound him and not the collar. Why wouldn't he... No, it couldn't be that... but she had to ask. "Does it have something to do with what happens... if that magic is broken?"

The woman set aside her teacup. "No, when the magic *breaks*, the beasts unravel, cease to exist," she explained. "On this plane, anyway."

That had certainly caught her attention. Thalasia shifted, uncrossing her legs, and subtly straightened her posture in the chair. "But they would survive on another?" It had been some time since she had traveled to another plane of existence. It was something... she still wasn't very good at, except the spiritual plane, but that was only when she used the lotus blossom. Something she hadn't done very often in the last few years.

"Their essence. They're supposed to be sacred entities summoned only in a time of great need."

"Except they weren't used that way." None of this made any sense. Although maybe in some small part it did. "So... to exist on this plane... if the magic tying him to the isle... if it no longer bound him... then he'd require... another source. Something else... something strong enough..." Her words trailed off. She thought back to when they'd met with Marius and how he'd fed from the male. Something she'd done... only twice in her life... to re-trigger her own power.

"That's not the purpose they were given. That's correct." The female laughed at her question. "The beasts aren't bound to the land. They're bound to the one who summoned them. The price for summoning one is significant. The beasts aren't intended to remain in our world for extended periods. They're supposed to serve their purpose and return to the realm beyond." Her expression soured. "This one is taking his sweet fucking time. I'm not sure what kept it from returning. When the former Matriarch's time ended, it shouldn't have remained. Yet, somehow, the bond transferred—at least in part—to the newly risen."

The woman's attitude toward Seru amused her slightly. It took a lot of effort not to snicker. Yeah, with some things they'd gone through, she could understand it. However, it occurred to her this had nothing to do with the secret, but it was going in the direction she'd wanted. Part of her wondered if that had something to do with what he'd told her about his so-called brothers. As for why he hadn't left yet... yep, she could explain that. "Only in part?" His connection was more to Aurelia, which explained the control she had over the collar. But if only part of that bond had transferred to Aurelia, then what about the rest of it?

"From what I've heard, the new Matriarch struggles to overcome the former's mastery over the bond. Though that may yet fade with time or resolve itself once She is official."

Or if it was severed before then, but she couldn't say that. Cyon had warned her against stating her purpose. Not that she had. Would the female figure it out if she continued asking about this? From what she'd seen, it was definitely something Aurelia struggled with... maybe she could find out more... carefully. "She isn't official yet?"

"She's Matriarch in name. Her power hasn't yet reached its ultimate level of ascension." The woman's eyes narrowed. "Though that's a line of thought you should be advised against."

Interesting. Made two of them... so to speak. "Going against her isn't in my plans." She was more thinking that if they intended to sever Seru's bond with her, then it had to be done before Aurelia ascended. In theory. "How would one expect her ascension to affect the bond? Do you think it would strengthen it? Or cause a further disconnect?"

"I'm sure the hope is that the bond will right itself. Become complete. However, I'm only as knowledgeable as I was then." After a thoughtful pause, she continued, "I doubt she'll speak to you. She hardly takes visitors anymore."

Speak to someone else? Oh, fun. "Who are you talking about?"

"That foreign whore he sneaks off to every chance he gets—as if no one notices! She seems to enjoy odd creatures like yourself."

Her fingers curled around her purse. She had to remind herself he had a past. Besides, thus far, it had been made pretty clear he didn't belong to her. Regardless of the marks he'd placed on her. "You'll have to be more specific. I'm not exactly... from here."

"She's one of the nine divine." A harsh bark of laughter interrupted her words. "A Primora with a high seat at court—if you believe it! Be careful, though, Ione sees the beast as some holy savior, a creature deserving of sacrifice and reverence—worship even."

Ione? She tossed the name around in her head for a moment... Of course. The female who'd asked to see him while she was in the library. Lovely. Good gods, she was getting a headache. And he bitched about the various clues her ancestors left. Okay. She needed to rewind this conversation. The woman had said his secret had to do with what bound him to the isle, but he was bound to Aurelia, not the isle itself. Hmm... she opened her mouth to ask about it... really... Did she need to know? Her ancestors had devoted an entire book to him. If she wanted to know his secrets, she'd read that. "Thank you. Now, I believe I'll take my leave."

"As you should." The woman turned her attention to the kid, who lay, belly full, back in the chair. His eyes drifted lazily skyward, threatening to close. He'd eaten himself into a coma. "Do take that one with you."

Biting back a heavy sigh, she glanced over at the kid. What the fuck was she supposed to do with him? It hadn't been in her plan to take him with her when she left, but she couldn't leave him like that, either. Thalasia rose, tucked the chair beneath the table with a scrape, and then lingered by the chair the kid had claimed with a sprawl. "Are you going to fight me if I carry you?"

"Try... and find...out," he challenged groggily.

Crossing her arms, she eyed the kid for a second. A slow smile crossed her face. She could always go about this a little differently. Thalasia whistled, taking control of the surrounding air to lift him up. Not that she needed to whistle, but it worked to stay somewhat in the lines of how people viewed her. She looked like a siren. Best to make them think that.

"You waste magic, much like your master," the woman stated flatly. "Though I suppose that should come as no surprise."

It amused her to lift the kid in the air like that. And it didn't take much effort at all. She glanced back at the woman. "What makes you say he wastes magic?"

"You who have too much, use it, even when it isn't necessary. He's never not used it."

With a subtle shift of her energy, she gently eased the child back into the chair, then intently studied the woman. More and more, the woman sounded like her mother. She had no words, which rarely happened. But the female had a point. Seru had told her he'd been pulling on the link between them. How much had he done it without her even realizing it? Thalasia scooped the kid up in her arms, holding him tenderly as one would a beloved child. Looking back at the female once again, she nodded. "Thank you. You've given me a lot to think about."

Thalasia left without glancing back at the female. While everything she discovered offered her more information on freeing Seru, it didn't help with her decision to stay by his side. It only made her question her sanity a bit more. Her heart was set, but her head... it definitely wasn't on the same page. She found Yelena waiting out of sight, almost where she'd left her. For a moment, she thought she'd be able to slip away, but by the look on the female's face... Her conversations about Seru were far from over.

Chapter Forty

As Thalasia approached the estate, she took in its imposing façade. Yelena had left her moments ago to find the rest of the way on her own. The air was thick with the cloying sweetness of mint and cherry, underscored by a whisper of chocolate that tickled her nose. She blinked. More poppies? How was that possible? Unless it wasn't the same pedigree as those that they had led her to believe only grew in Pteryrina. Still, it made little sense of how others had even garnered another strain unless they had one to work from to begin with. Either that or the history she thought she knew—had been completely falsified.

Although that would only be one small part compared to the whole. While she continued looking forward, she also drank in as much of her surroundings as she could. It was in her nature to notice the insignificant details that were often overlooked. That even included the difference in obvious luxuries between Ione and the female she'd just left. One was cozy cottage while the other was fit for kings and queens.

She stared at the door in front of her. Despite the earlier correction in her choice of words, her mother had raised her with manners. It would be rude to even attempt to just walk in. The door creaked open less than two seconds after her knock, revealing a sliver of the interior for her to peer into.

Why did this suddenly feel like a dream? Except she wouldn't have fallen asleep around the kid, nor would she have meditated. Being locked in the library had agitated her too much. And she didn't have any of the tea back at the other dragon's place, so no drugs. Thalasia peered over her shoulder for a second before poking her head inside the door. "Hello?"

No one responded, and there wasn't anyone in sight. There was a lot of exquisite furniture. The room featured more upscale items, such as a couple of chaise lounges, finer chairs and couches, and remarkably clean end tables positioned strategically. What intrigued her more were the different pretty items set about sporadically. Though it probably looked like a semblance of order to the owner. Leaving her to explore was a little dangerous. Not as much recently. She hadn't caused problems since the drokar four years ago. She gave the door a slight push to see if it would move and let her inside.

The door opened without issue. Oh, that was dangerous. Not that she was planning to do anything stupid. She'd already met her quota on this trip. Slipping inside, Thalasia softly closed the door, the quiet click echoing as she ventured deeper into the space. She clasped her hands together, resting them just beneath the small of her back, and strolled around the foyer to really check it all out.

As she meandered, her gaze drifting over the varied objects, the nine-pointed star, encircled by cosmic glyphs on the marble floor, was the sole element that truly captivated her. Maybe the artwork. It had been some time since she'd meandered through a museum. Though they could be quite boring occasionally. The vases and flowers were okay, but they didn't look like anything special. She ambled towards the staircase, the blue-violet tapestry on the wall catching her eye.

Through all of her steps, she kept an eye out in case someone made an appearance. Nope. Still, just her. Okay. That was great, but if she wanted to hang out here by herself, then she could've done what she intended to do upon leaving the last female. Another thirty seconds and she started really exploring by heading up the stairs.

Nothing. Without further hesitation, she began her climb up the magnificent staircase. The top of the landing opened into a vast layout, including a kitchen where a human-type person worked on a meal as they chit-chatted with a tiny fae companion and another casually occupying the bar. Not far off, the leopard she'd met earlier lazed about on a plush couch. From her vantage point, as she carefully surveyed everything, she realized she had neglected to inquire about Ione's looks. Although if she had any doubts about where Yelena had taken her, they'd been dashed at that moment. This was certainly a strange place, at least compared to the rest of what she'd seen thus far. Not that it changed her mind on some things regarding what the rest of The Clouds was like and how much she'd never fit in. The drapes in the room swayed from an odd breeze, making her feathers flutter.

"Hello, Thalasia."

What in the... she blinked, turning toward the female voice. The woman had appeared out of nowhere. Before she said anything, she took a second to look over the female. Plum-colored hair with reddish undertones. Bright-purple eyes. Porcelain skin covered in a purple dress with white gold intricately woven into the design. Although she had no identifying details, this had to be the female she sought. She didn't suspect anyone else would know her name or even address her by it. "Ione, I presume?"

"Correct," the female chirped, a sugary smile gracing her lips. "I trust you found your journey here enlightening."

Enlightening. Not as much as she would've liked, but that's what happened when you dealt with someone who was ornery half the time. "As much as it could've been, I suspect."

"Yes, well," Ione started, her smile straining. "The dragons here are quite reserved, and their mistrust frequently tips into paranoia."

No shit. Not that she was going to say that. The female actually reminded her a little of another dragon she knew. Although she couldn't really say much about the paranoia. Until Seru, she had trusted no one in what felt like a long time. He, of course, would've seen it as a blip on the radar. "I'm sure some have their reasons. My ancestors have been no different, so I suppose I can't say much."

"That's incredibly kind of you," Ione said. "Please, make yourself comfortable and choose any seat in the room. I'm certain you'll find my friends more welcoming than the dragons."

It was just the truth. They'd all been secretive for centuries, so they stayed alive. "While I appreciate that, you're the one I'm here to speak with." And she preferred not to waste time.

"Oh? What do you think I can assist you with?"

How did she state this without stating it? Not to mention, they were in an open space, and some of the female's friends had excellent hearing. "Protection," Thalasia paused because she didn't want to get into too many details. Nor did she know how much the female knew about her or if Seru had shared any of his knowledge. "I'd prefer we speak privately before I say more."

Ione gestured behind herself, indicating an archway. "Of course. This way."

"Thank you." A quick nod was all she offered before she walked in the direction the woman pointed. She entered a bedroom, lingering just on the other side of the sheer curtains. Her eyes landed on two plush lavender loveseats, arranged like a gentle embrace around a sleek glass coffee table. Thalasia peered over her shoulder as Ione directed her toward the sitting area. As she settled into the seat, she reclined, crossing one leg over the other to find a more relaxed posture. Yeah, she had full-length dresses in her bag, but she rarely ever wore them. "How much do you know about... what I am?"

"I know you're special," Ione replied as she draped herself across the couch opposite her.

That was vague. Also sounded like what she'd told Seru when they first crossed paths. And if what the female from earlier had said was true, she knew Seru had spoken to Ione about her. He'd already spoken to Cyon a little about the lyre...at least what little he knew of it. She'd purposely kept things close, uncertain how much she could trust him. "Do you know any specifics?"

"I am aware of what Seru thinks you are and who he believes you to be. Although I trust his judgment, I don't allow the opinions of others to decide for me what is true and what isn't. I prefer to make my own assessments."

"I understand that. I like to check and recheck. You never know when or what people will lie about." Or what truths they'd keep to themselves. Although if she knew that, then she might know more than her. She knew only what she believed she could do for him. Thalasia untied the strings to her purse, removed the clamshell she'd tucked away in there, and plucked one of her own feathers. She paused, her eyes fixed on her wing for a beat, a faint shimmer emanating from it. Wow! She'd done that without a second thought. Not something she would've expected given her history and guard over her wings.

Refusing to give the action too much thought, she used the feather to tickle the clam the way Seru had shown her. As the shell opened, she drew out the lyre, its strings shimmering faintly in the light. "More special than you could probably imagine." She paused. "I know the last thing he told me he wanted, but staying here... it's not possible. I don't think it would work out the way he believes. Leaving is the only option."

The female's expression hardened a touch. "Regardless of his dreams for the future, in his heart, he's pragmatic. He deals with what exists and doesn't count his eggs before they hatch. However, he knows nothing beyond this isle, which has trapped him since he was called forth. I'm uncertain he sees your 'out' under the current circumstances."

Thalasia returned the lyre to the clam and, with a sigh, placed everything back into her purse. "I know he has his doubts." She lifted her eyes to Ione. "I don't. I'm positive that with some additional information I can sever his bonds. That's why I'm here."

"Is that why you seek my protection?"

"I'm not seeking protection for myself. I'm trying to protect... him." It probably sounded strange, given who and what Seru was, but she'd gone around in endless circles with him. That was all she'd wanted to do. Protect him. Maybe he hadn't realized it, then again, maybe she hadn't been ready to accept it either, but she'd been choosing him over and over. "But I need your help to do it. I need more information."

The female blinked, her eyes growing wide with astonishment. "My apologies," Ione stated. Silence stretched briefly between them. "What information do you think I have that might further you toward this goal?"

"I need to understand the former Matriarch's magic better. I know the control the current Matriarch has... that bond is... unstable. Not as strong as it could be. From what I've learned... if we're going to fully disconnect that bond...it would have to be done before her ascension." Although she hadn't looked into the book her great-great-grandmother left, she didn't think her ancestors would've been watching him all these years if she couldn't break the bond.

With a shake of her head, the female stared at her. "I'm sorry, your solution is to break the bond that tethers him to this existence?" Ione paused. "Vicious and cruel, her ambition, eager to obliterate any obstacle in her relentless pursuit of power, utterly consumed the Silver Queen. Even in your brief time here, you've no doubt seen the greed of the dragons inhabiting this isle." Ione inhaled sharply, wincing, and said, "I'm not from this place, Thalasia. I wasn't born in the Clouds or grow up here. All I can share is what I've witnessed since my arrival until now."

Thalasia's eyes flew open wider. She hadn't expected that last part. Slowly, she nodded. "Well, that makes two of us. And yes, I've noticed how different they are from other dragons I've crossed in my travels." She shifted her weight on the couch, finding a more comfortable position. She didn't think there was any other way. That if they pushed the magic, even overpowered it, it would end up breaking. "You have more information than I do. Or you can at least corroborate some of what I have. I understand the repercussions and that it would require something else that he could tether to, that would keep him on this plane, that would still allow him to depart the isle."

Inhaling and exhaling a deep breath, she eyed the woman. She hadn't meant to put it out there like that, but there was no taking it back now. And, obviously, he'd told the female something. "I know it probably sounds... insane, but if anyone could do this... I believe I could."

"You're the first siren of paradise I've seen on this isle," Ione admitted. "They don't seem very prevalent here, assuming they exist at all." With a soft sigh and a gaze that drifted, she inquired, "Thalasia, what knowledge do you possess regarding the saint beasts?"

Thalasia raised an eyebrow. *Siren of paradise?* Not a term she'd ever heard before. There were definitely other sirens. They'd already crossed paths with a few. Though she was a lot more than a regular siren. The blood of her ancestors made her that way. None of which mattered. The female had asked her a question. "Seru is the only saint beast I've ever come in contact with, so very little."

Ione made a thoughtful sound. "I'll make a deal with you, Thalasia," she offered, her tone dropping, becoming almost forlorn. "First, tell me what this bond you've struck with Seru will accomplish—from your end. Leave nothing out. Then, I'll tell you everything."

She could do that. "Deal." Now that she remembered more of everything, she could certainly disclose more than she'd been able to tell Seru. Not that it changed the basics. "Just so you know, I wasn't looking for him when I got here. But my parents always told me, 'You never know when you'll find an emotional connection.'"

He hadn't been a part of her plan at all. With a slight bite of her lower lip, she pondered the most evocative way to put the experience into words. While the female had asked what it would accomplish, the memories of their time together replayed in her mind. Not just the bad, including their arguments, but the good things, too. While she hadn't intended to recount it verbally, the words just poured out of her. "It's not a bid to gain power. I want nothing more than to set him free, but I guess that's not really what you asked," Thalasia concluded.

"And yet, it seems to grant you all manner of power, nonetheless."

"My power grows the closer I am to my birth moon. The way I'm built, our natural power continues to grow the more of our emotions we have to take control over. Especially once we meet the one we view as our other half. Because of how far we can travel and the way we can impact lives, even whole species, our emotions are so important. And our other half, they have a tendency to push us outside our current limitations."

She paused for a moment as she thought of what this really meant. What it really meant to have him in her life. "When the last person I cared about was killed, I never thought I'd care about another person again. Although we fight... argue... what I feel for him... it just gets stronger." Thalasia shrugged. "I don't care about gaining power. If I had, then I would've just done what I needed to when I got here and spent the last several days in Pteryrina. I wouldn't have gone on this journey with him. Done whatever I could to learn more about him, to stay by his side. I could've left multiple times." A gentle smile, like a whisper, touched her lips. "I don't want to leave here without him."

"So, the object is to meet one who challenges you," Ione said. "From your own admission, it sounds as though you've found that, at least."

Thalasia chuckled, which just made her eyes sparkle brighter. "In a lot of ways." Yes, he certainly challenged her on a variety of levels. Not just mentally, but emotionally, spiritually, even magically. "My mom used to tell me the goal was to find someone you couldn't live without."

Even though she'd told the woman all of this and talked about everything they'd shared, things that made them realize—or at least her—that a normal life existed, she hadn't actually said what she got out of this. "I care about him. I'm not the best at showing it, but I do. More than I thought possible. Despite how stubborn and arrogant he is, I care. Though I imagine I'm nothing like what he's used to dealing with."

"Finding someone who's equal parts difficult and irresistible sounds like a tall order. After all you've seen today, are you certain what he's used to is what's best for him? I'm sorry. There's no record in scripture or crystal that indicates a bond can be transferred. As for breaking the bond, it voids the contract and the saints return. Once they go back, they must rest for a long time—likely several lifetimes for your kind—before they're able to be called on again. If the bond is broken and the terms unfulfilled, there's a further penalty."

No, she didn't think his staying here was what was best for him. But she'd considered it for his sake. As for all the rest of it, her lips pinched together tightly. "I see why he's had doubts." She sighed heavily. "But there has to be a way to remove the collar, unless I'm misunderstanding that as the physical representation or even what contains the bond." She had to be missing something. Thalasia chewed on the inside of her cheek. Wait a second... "Seru told me that the former Matriarch she wiped out a lot of how she created the bond? You said you didn't come from here."

"The saints are children of Chaos tempered by the holy rituals. The bond you're referencing is the magical interlacing, a joining of the saint and his contracted partner. The one who calls upon the saint must offer his or her own magic in exchange for their desired blessing. If the saint finds the offering to their liking, a bond is forged. No one is supposed to call all the saints at once. It's said it will trigger a devastating chain reaction, one that cannot be undone." Ione paused. "Once we arrived on the isle hoping to conduct peaceful diplomacy, it horrified us to discover seven of the saints were already present in this world. Before the Silver Queen slaughtered our envoy and took our princess and myself prisoner, we attempted to get a missive to our countrymen, requesting they summon Aracel to break the chain. I do not know if that message ever made it."

There were a thousand questions running through her mind. All the other saint beasts were gone, not that she knew specifics on how. Although Seru had hidden the dagger of one of them for a purpose. And her great-great-grandmother had either knowingly or unknowingly helped. Thalasia chewed on the inside of her cheek as she processed what Ione had said. The female hadn't said where she came from. Just that they'd attempted to get a message out. Maybe that was where she began with her questions. "How would that chain have been impacted, as Seru is the only survivor? And how would Aracel have broken the chain? Where did you come from?"

She didn't know if it was some place she could go or maybe even had been. It was possible, given the number of realms she'd already traveled to in her life. "Is that bond part of the interlacing of the collar? I'm sorry if I'm asking a lot of questions, but my understanding was that they were integral parts of one another. And the more I think about what you've said, that there's no documentation that states the bond can be transferred, it then makes me wonder how even a part of that bond moved from one Matriarch to another.

However, if only part of that bond was transferred, does that mean that the part that isn't in her control lies with him? Which might then make it further possible to override that bond, pushing it to another or at least sever that which holds him to the isle."

Ione smoothed her hands over her skirt as she replied, "I'd hoped—due to the state of the saints on this isle—that properly summoning the next in line might sever the chain, preventing the Silver Queen from harnessing their full destructive power. There was no guarantee it would work. But we had to try *something*, especially once it was made clear none of us would leave the isle of our own free will." The female cleared her throat and poured herself a glass of water before continuing, "The mainland, to the north. I served as a diviner prior to being selected by the royal family to serve as the princess's escort. We'd grown up together. This was to be her first diplomatic mission alone. I tried to protect her," she offered. "I failed. If not for the eldest of the saints, the Silver Queen and her warriors might have slain us all. Instead, she opted to spare one to witness the price of our misstep. The dragons here believe a life of weakness is a fate worse than death."

Yeah, she'd kind of gathered what the dragons here believed. Every time she attempted to educate one. While she hoped that her conversation with the kid would've challenged him to really consider what he'd been raised to believe, she doubted it did any good. The mainland, though. Could Ione mean? "Are you talking about Candescent Isle?" At least that's what she'd heard it called. "Or is there another isle in this realm?" It was possible. Adina and Aegeus had lived here, but they hadn't been all that forthcoming with details.

Ione shook her head, setting her glass aside as she replied, "Prisma and Candescent Isle are two prominent isles among a larger chain. However, they've been..." she hesitated, "cordoned off for centuries. It's not surprising most of the species here retain little to no recollection of lands beyond their own. I'm from a much larger continent, a much larger, more diverse and collaborative place than this."

A chain of isles? Could that be what those little dots she'd seen on the map were? Candescent Isle was where the jump point had been, but she hadn't really looked too closely at it. "If I had a map, would you show me where?" The only person outside of her family that had ever seen the Atlis map had been Seru. But something about the female said she could trust her.

"I'd be willing to try. I'm not a navigator."

"Well, I'm certain this isn't like any other map you've ever seen before, either." She untied the strings of her pouch and paused a moment. Damn. How could she have possibly overlooked the way her body had illuminated? Thalasia raised her hand, bringing it to her nose to inhale its scent. And her natural aroma had intensified again, too. Her control was faltering. Not that she could stop this. Not that she wanted to, either. Shaking her thoughts away, she focused back on her bag. Quickly locating the ancient parchment, she retrieved the item and rose to her feet.

Hesitating a moment, she gave herself one last chance to question the direction her mind had taken. No turning back. Thalasia unfurled the map, allowing it to hover in the air as she located the coordinates for this realm. With a graceful sweep of her fingers, she magically enlarged the item until it perfectly spanned both couches. "From here you can see some details of Prisma Isle and Candescent Isle," she pointed them out. "Along with what looks like dots. Now that I look a little closer... the way they're spaced apart, I can see them as other isles. It doesn't appear that any of my ancestors have explored them."

"Only the parts they—and you—have visited?" Ione asked, leaning forward to survey the map more.

Obviously, Seru hadn't told the female as much as she suspected. She kept a watchful eye on Ione. Even with the realm expanded like this, the influential moments of her life weren't hidden. They still lingered around the edges. And she didn't have to look to know which ones were there. Her parents' death. The day she'd been captured. Flying again after her escape. The Minotaur village and the Seelie child. The lotus blossom. Along with several memories that comprised Seru and their time together up to that point. "Yes. The map can be instructed to extrapolate information from whatever realm an Atlis is in at that point. If I find myself somewhere that one of my ancestors has been, then I try to ensure the map is updated. Realms change as time passes."

Ione's chin rested in her palm as her eyes moved over the isles. She channeled a small amount of magic to her fingertip and traced a rough outline into Thalasia's map.

With her finger, Thalasia touched the dot, and the land that Ione identified easily enlarged. A silver Atlese symbol appeared. No one in her family had been there, but there was a jump point. While she still had to fulfill the arrangement she made with Parthenia and her crew, it wouldn't take much to get there. "I could travel there."

"I'm uncertain that's advisable," Ione said, withdrawing her finger apologetically. "While my compatriots may have welcomed your arrival centuries ago, my country was embroiled in a terrible war with chaos monsters from the rift. Without the aid we'd hoped an alliance with Prisma Isle might offer, I fear the centuries have not been kind to my people. Factor in the butchery by the Silver Queen..."

Except the female had said she wasn't certain a message had even made it back to her countrymen. With a flick of her wrist, Thalasia made the map curl and retract. Once it was back together, she took the map and returned it to its rightful place in her purse. "But that was a long time ago, right? You wouldn't have any idea what things would be like now. Unless I've misunderstood what you've told me thus far."

"It has been a long while, yes," Ione agreed. "I can only hope they've held out."

Maybe coming to the Clouds hadn't been entirely futile. Back in Seru's library, she'd thought it had been. In actuality, it may have served more than one purpose. Higher powers always worked in ways she never quite understood. Sometimes she even thought they had jokes about what they wanted her to accomplish. She didn't think this was one of those moments. "From what I could tell of the jump point, it isn't visible anywhere. Would certainly be worth a shot."

"I won't tell you about your business, Thalasia," Ione conceded.

That surprised her. All she'd heard for days was how much she didn't understand. How she couldn't possibly make any actual decisions. It was shocking. And they'd gotten off topic. Sometimes she couldn't help it. "Back to Seru." She paused again as she thought back to what she'd heard. Not just from Ione and the other female, but from what Cyon and Seru had told her as well. "The collar is designed to control his beast, but freeing him from the collar wouldn't break the bond he has to Aurelia? Especially if she only has a part of that bond, not all of it. Right?" That was what bothered her the most. And it wasn't something any of them could seem to explain. If only part of the bond had transferred to Aurelia, then what about the rest of it?

Thalasia let out a soft sigh and sank back into the plush cushions of the couch. How much did she tell this female? She'd already revealed more than she ever expected. Only one way to find out. "I'm guessing Seru has mentioned nothing about the ritual I've told him of... or the marks he's placed on me..." Although Ione probably saw the latter. It wasn't like the mark he'd done on her neck could be missed.

"They're entirely separate," Ione confirmed. Her mouth twitched into a small smile. "He's uh..." she cleared her throat, "mentioned something along those lines, yes."

Thalasia raised an eyebrow. "What exactly did he say?"

"I think you know better than to ask," Ione replied, looking slightly guilty. "I won't betray the faith and trust he's placed in me. While I may not be the one who summoned him here, or the one whose magic he's drawing on, I hold the utmost respect and regard for him. His presence here is a blessing—and should be treated as such. While that sacred spiritual and magical connection has undeniably been tampered with and defiled, we're fortunate."

She hadn't expected the female to tell her, but she'd also never been one to back down from asking, either. Not that she didn't have her reasons. "I learned a long time ago that to get to the truth... to get to the heart of an issue... sometimes you have to ask the questions that no one else is willing to." And she wasn't certain anyone else would've been so bold. "The reason I asked is because the Commitment Ritual is supposed to be one of the most powerful rituals, at least known to my people. This ritual, at least what I have to do, it's nothing like what my ancestors have done in the past. There are similarities."

Just like there were similarities to the Draconic marks Seru had told her about. "For me, I have a specific time, a specific location, and specific items that are required to perform it properly. This ritual... It only happens once in a lifetime and it bonds the two parties together until the end of their days. The power behind it bonds them physically, emotionally, and spiritually, forsaking all other bonds."

Ione nodded. "I can see the merit in utilizing such tactics. You said you couldn't imagine leaving here without him, so I know you care... but I can't help but wonder if you're certain of your decision regarding the ritual. Not just because it's only been a matter of days and the commitment sounds as if it's for a lifetime, more because you've seen the consequences and fallout of using powerful magic as a Band-Aid solution. Are you sure proceeding with yet another ritual is the wisest course for both of you?"

The only magic she could see as being used as a Band-Aid solution was the marks. Yeah, that hadn't been the wisest decision. But it wasn't as if either of them had been forthcoming with anything when that had been started, either. He hadn't known about the mark already on her person, nor had she really understood what kind of agreement she was entering. Although he'd explained the different degrees of them to her, there was a lot about them she still didn't understand. Even with her own ritual; compounding that on top of what he'd already begun... not something she was certain of, either. Despite the unanswered questions and the bit of doubt that lingered inside her, she intended to stay true to her course. "I will not tell you I don't have my doubts, because that would be a lie. What I can tell you is that I'd do anything to set him free. And I believe whole-heartedly that this... it'll get us there. And I'm prepared for whatever consequences follow."

"Do you know that he feels the same? If—and it might be a big if—your ritual forsakes all other bonds, you may be asking him to give up his sainthood, his ability to return to the other plane alongside his brothers where they rest and restore their life force. Have you truly considered the implications of asking him to be... Ordinary? Or, at least less of what he is and more of what you are."

Honestly, she wasn't sure he did. Yes, he cared, but if their last conversation was anything to go by, he had more doubts than she did. "That's the thing. Nothing about my life is ordinary. The life he has now, to me, that's ordinary. He sees the same thing day in and day out. Gives a little more of himself to every person demanding a piece. For what? So he can do it all over again?" She shook her head. "I've thought about what he's recently asked of me. To stay here. But I don't think he's thoroughly thought that through. Or even what it would truly mean."

"I think this existence may be the exception to the rule. As far as his 'wants' are concerned. They're ever-changing. What I mean is... depending on his state... His condition, his answer may change completely from one moment to the next. The longer the saints have lingered in this world, under the Silver Queen's contract, the more they seem to... Fracture... Or diverge from their true form. Like they're losing themselves to the shadows."

Okay. She could see the first part of the female's statement. It had seemed like Seru flip-flopped a lot. Part of what she thought led to some of their arguments. Amongst other things. Knitting her eyebrows together, Thalasia leaned forward, digging her elbows into her knees. She didn't like the last part of that. "Is it possible that this is part of the chain reaction you spoke of earlier? Or... that ultimately... there is a way to return him to his true form... I mean... his brothers are dead. Right?" Unless they still existed on another plane. Something she hadn't considered before this conversation and the last one.

"I don't know," Ione admitted. "I didn't have the chance to complete my studies prior to our voyage. What little we recovered from the ruins of the temple here wasn't nearly as informative as I'd hoped. A lot appeared to be missing or destroyed. I've temporarily reversed some of the damage, rewound to a certain point. But it doesn't last." The female shifted her weight to one hip. "There's something you need to see."

Ruins? She recalled seeing them on the map, but there hadn't really been enough detail to discern more than that. Given their location, she assumed they had something to do with the fae of the isle. "Okay? Um, go ahead." She wasn't certain what the woman intended to show her, but she'd offered a lot of information. And added more questions. It made her wonder... would the inscriptions of her ancestors in the book they left behind offer more insight? Or leave her more confused?

Ione glided across the room, stopping beside the archway leading to the balcony. She waited patiently as Thalasia made her approach and assessed the saint beast, lying amid a bed of night poppies. A garment of blue-violet and ivory silk clutched in his hand. His bare upper body shone a complex web of spell circles and runic symbols in many languages, even a few glyphs illuminated. The blue light emanated from the flora, pulsing in time to the same rhythmic beat as before. Seru appeared younger, less stressed, and almost peaceful. His features were softer, his hair less unruly. The scars were less prominent.

As Thalasia stared at Seru, she prayed her body remained subdued. The glow had lessened during their conversation. And she'd maintained control over her scent. Taking in the various markings across his chest, she chewed on the inside of her cheek. She was so ill-prepared for this. Not enough years in her studies. Not enough years in her training. Gods, she wished her parents had been around. If she visited her mother on the spiritual plane, would the woman be able to offer her any insight?

Her eyes followed a path from her hand down her arm. Damn it. A vibrant glow started radiating through her skin. And she was just looking at him. Before she uttered a word or caused him to wake, she backed up a few steps. "I've seen him rest a couple of times, but nothing like this." She paused for a moment. "You said that you studied before you left. Are you talking about the Saint Beasts as a whole?"

Ione dipped her chin. "Yes, my position permitted me to study them at length. However, at the Emperor's request, I was forced to cut my studies short to accompany the princess."

Of all the things she hadn't planned on doing, mentioning the book seemed like the least of her concerns. Nothing regarding Seru had been something she planned. "What if I had a book specific to Seru? Do you think that might help?"

"A book specific to Seru?" Ione parroted in disbelief. She shook her head to clear it. "I don't see where looking would hurt."

The female had a point. And if she was going to do it, then it was best to do so with someone who might actually understand what her ancestors saw. With a nod, Thalasia turned and walked with purpose back toward the couch. As she dug the book out of her purse, she flicked her gaze to Ione. "I don't suppose you have any plums lying around?"

"You didn't seem all that surprised by the night poppies," Ione noted absently. "Their effects seem to wane. Finding time to safely put him under is also becoming increasingly challenging as his duties demand more of him. They were never meant to be a permanent solution, but…" She paused. "Plums? Ah… Yes, you're hungry. Of course. Forgive me. If you give me a moment, I'll see what I can manage." Bowing her head slightly, she excused herself, stepping behind the curtain toward the kitchen.

Thalasia stood there quietly. She placed the book and her purse on the couch before returning to the archway. She couldn't seem to help herself. Not that she wanted Seru to realize she was here. Especially as she wasn't sure how he'd react. Angry she'd disobeyed him yet again. Upset that she was asking questions he didn't seem to want answered. He looked truly at peace. But if the poppies were only going so far… What would it take for him to rest if she got him off the isle? Would the dreamcatcher in her possession be enough? If it did, how long would it last? Would it wane, too, just like Ione said the poppies had done?

The saint beast slept peacefully. His dark lashes barely fluttered against his sun-darkened complexion as he dreamed. The hand clutching the silken garment held tight to the item, like a precious treasure. The night poppies steadily swayed and pulsed with the energy flowing through them. Butterflies, the same hue as the tapestry downstairs, flitted from flower to flower. A few even settled over the saint beast's markings, drawn by the blue light and magic circulating just beneath the surface.

Although she was curious about what he was clutching in his hand, she refused to move from her spot. He needed the rest. That much had been made clear over the last few days. Even more, seeing the change in him from what he'd gotten while there. Not that she knew how much time had passed since they parted ways in his library.

Her gaze flicked briefly to her arm, assessing the strength of the glimmer that had settled like a sheen of sweat. Maybe she had little control over that, but at least her scent wasn't compounded on top of it. She'd take partial command over her body versus none. Turning her eyes back to Seru, she continued to watch him as she waited for Ione's return.

The female stepped through the curtain and crossed the room to Thalasia and presented her with a tray of exotic fruits. "I'm afraid the dragons don't eat many plums or standard fruits as you're used to. They prefer to grow their own produce. Hopefully, you'll find at least some of it edible," she announced apologetically as she placed the tray on the floor between them. She retrieved a cushion, offering one to Thalasia, before kneeling next to her, hands clasped neatly in her lap.

Accepting the cushion, she offered a small grin to Ione. "It's okay. Every place is a little different. You'd be surprised at how fruit can vary between realms." Before she took a seat, she retrieved the book she'd left on the couch. At least from where they sat now, she could keep a small eye on Seru. Lifting the dress just a little, she eased her body down and settled on the cushion.

"You mentioned my lack of surprise at the poppies. A different strain of them grows in the fields in Pteryrina, home of the sirens. As part of my training, I had to learn how to tell the difference between herbs, flowers, spices and their various medicinal uses. Aside from that, he used them when we stopped to rest yesterday. Looked more peaceful than when he was clinging to me the day before." She hadn't meant for the last statement to come out, but it was too late to take it back now. Even if it were true. With the book settled on her lap, she lifted a piece of fruit from the tray, taking a delicate sniff, then reaching for a different one to inspect.

"I can imagine," Ione replied. "You must develop a robust stomach to effortlessly switch your diet to accommodate so many foreign delicacies. If you're uncomfortable, you're welcome to change," she spoke around the clip held between her teeth. "Apologies for not offering sooner. I wanted to be sure of your intentions before relaxing my guard." She combed the long plum mane high before securing it back and out of the way. "I surmised their origins. When he first presented them to me, they were red, likely similar if not identical to those you're referencing. They only took on this coloring, the dark blues and purple centers with outliers and speckling after several dozen generations—and a lot of trial and error."

"You're fine. I'm naturally suspicious, so if it had been offered too quickly, I would've declined. Regardless of how much Seru trusts you." Especially since she questioned his judgment sometimes. Then again, there had been times she questioned her own, too. "Uh, no, thank you. I'd just have to change again when I leave."

With a bit of readjustment of the skirting of the dress until the flowing portion of it was over her knees, she could sit comfortably. The time to get the right strain of poppies didn't surprise her. It worked the same with any DNA that was being altered. "Do you know what he's holding? In his hand?" She took a bite of the fruit; its vibrant color was a stark contrast to its semi-sweet aroma. It was a little bitter, but not as much as she expected, given the scent.

"Only if you're shy about taking the servants' corridors," she commented. "Stay somewhere long enough. You learn all the loopholes. Especially when not knowing them means endless hours spent dressing and undressing." Her question produced a long stretch of silence. Ione sat straight. The picture of refined elegance, even then. When it came, her reply was simple. "I believe it's the dress I died in."

The fruit in her hand slowly lowered from her mouth. What had the female just said? Everything up to that point convinced her Ione was alive. She swallowed the lump in the back of her throat. She didn't need to really ask. It was absolutely possible to converse with those who were no longer on this plane. While she'd told Seru otherwise, she had spoken with her parents several times since their death. Well, her father, at least. Her mother never came. "Uh, yeah... servant corridors can be... helpful." Her gaze flicked back to Ione. "I'm sorry... I didn't know." A lot of things were making sense. At least with her initial attraction to Seru. Aside from the fact that he challenged her. In a lot of different ways. Thalasia bit into the juicy fruit again, its sweetness bursting in her mouth as she picked up the book. She stared at it for a long moment before she called on it to translate to a common tongue.

"That was a surprisingly rapid recovery," Ione appraised, rewarding her with a smile. "You weren't supposed to. No one here is supposed to, though I fear keeping that secret is becoming increasingly taxing."

A secret she could certainly understand. "Both of my parents were killed when I was younger. It... hasn't stopped me... from communicating with them." It was easier to state that way rather than break it all down. She was positive the female would understand. Biting into the fruit again, she held the book out to Ione.

Graciously accepting the leather-bound tome, she offered Thalasia a dip of her chin. Her eyes fell to the pages fanned out before her, inspecting the contents. "Pardon my... being ill-informed, but is offering my sympathies appropriate? My people celebrate death—though differently than anything I've witnessed here—it's merely a step in a celestial recycling, so to speak. We don't mourn our dead or view their passing to the next stage as a loss the way most species do. They're gone in the way we knew them, but not gone entirely. They've progressed to an elevated existence."

"They are, yes." A celebration of death. She'd been to a few places that were like that. It had been the first time she considered the possibility of speaking to either of her parents again. A lot had happened during that time. "Not everyone has that... luxury. When I first lost them... I didn't know I'd even be able to speak to them again. Not that it lessened the pain."

She finished the fruit in her hand, all the way to its core, leaving behind mostly a large seed. Something Seru suggested a day or two ago resurfaced. Maybe she could find some place... nodding to herself, she set the seed aside.

"Then you have my sympathies, Thalasia." Ione lifted her gaze before bowing her head in the woman's direction. "I'm sure your parents are very proud of you and the strength you've mustered in the face of all that's come against you." Her gaze returned to the page as she traced the lines with a finger hovering over each sentence.

All she did was nod. The truth was there were some things they wouldn't be proud of—things she wished she'd done differently. Handled better. But she couldn't change the past. She couldn't change the decisions she'd made. Thalasia reached for another piece of fruit, giving it a good sniff before taking a bite. Her face contorted, her nose wrinkling at the acrid flavor that assaulted her tongue. Returning the fruit to the tray, she began trying different ones, seeking a satisfying choice. It took a few, but she finally succeeded.

"Your ancestors, though not your parents, spent much of their time and resources observing him," Ione murmured. "They were very careful and—or knew someone intimately involved with the dragons, who escaped suspicion... a feat during the Silver Queen's reign." Her face lit up briefly, her fangs making an appearance. "Whoever they were, they don't sound terribly pleased with their target or task."

"I only skimmed over a couple of entries, but from what I gathered, they watched him until about three-hundred years ago. And it constantly changed hands." Though, as she thought more of that, it may not be entirely true. It could very well have been one who transcribed everything related to him. A watcher, maybe. The last entry, though, had to be either Adina or Aegeus. That meeting was likely when her great-great-grandfather had given Seru *Celestimo*. She smirked. "My ancestors did... everything in their power to ensure he and I met." Even if the fog hadn't thrown her from the bridge, she would've had needed to find him.

"Multi-generational matchmaking... how unconventional," Ione returned, her amusement growing, tinted with the barest hint of sadness.

Yeah. Going all the way back to the first of the Atlis. Not that she thought that needed to be vocalized. She swallowed the piece of fruit in her mouth. "Is there anything that might help us understand the collar and the bond?"

"Not that I've encountered as yet." She flipped the page, continuing her line-by-line read-through. "It's curious your ancestors only appear interested in this iteration of his being."

"What do you mean? Are you referring to his beast form? Or another plane of existence? Or a different life cycle?" Any of them were possible. Though she didn't know what any of her ancestors knew of saint beasts. Aside from very little.

"His previous existences," Ione clarified. "Each time the saints bless this realm, they take on a different existence. Your ancestors only took an interest in his present existence. While the circumstances make it unique, it's far from the only time he's blessed us. Though their notes are thorough."

"I'm sure there was a reason." Probably because this was the only existence in which she crossed paths with him. Her gaze flicked to Seru as she munched on the fruit in her hand. Gods, she hoped this gave them something. That someone spying on Seru all this time proved... useful.

"Perhaps," Ione said. "But it's still an oversight. One that neglects his true purpose by observing only his current state, which we just clarified, is ever-changing. Though more so in recent years."

The book had been something she stumbled on by accident. She hadn't looked at the other books in the archives. It wasn't something she'd considered. "I presume that whatever name or guise he used in those other existences would've altered. Correct?"

"It's based on pure precepts and a stable, defined connection. His current life is based on those principles, even if most of them have been violated."

Thoughts tumbled around her head as she munched on the fruit until she reached its core. Even if she had information on his prior existences, using the seeing bowl… one of those things she'd never gotten the hang of; or a trip back to the library in Pteryrina… but she'd have to astral project and again… hmm… still, not something she was that great at doing. Gods, there were so many things she wished she'd done differently. If she got him off this isle, she was going to improve her studies. Not just physical training, but mentally, too. "Maybe my ancestors didn't know about them." After all, she'd never met a saint beast before Seru. Maybe they hadn't, either.

"Possible." Ione handed off the book to her. "Hold this, please." The female rose to her feet, lifting her skirt as she stepped off the cushion. She moved around their temporary spot of study to the far side of the room before disappearing behind another sheer curtain.

Wrapping her hand around the book, she dropped her gaze to it for a moment as she set the core of the last piece of fruit aside. She peeked over her shoulder, drinking in Seru's peacefulness. There was so much about him she didn't understand. And she knew him better than seemed possible in such a short time. Maybe he had his doubts, and there were a few she had, but she wouldn't stop until she set him free. As she'd told him in the beginning, she was stuck with her tether for the rest of her life, but his… that was a problem she could resolve.

Ione emerged with an armful of crystals. She retook her position beside Thalasia, gently setting the crystals into a pile. The long pieces sat nicely astride one another to form a small, self-sustaining pyramid.

"What are those?" The question popped out of her mouth before she could stop herself. The only crystals she'd seen with such odd shapes had been the ones that had previously been in her possession. And the one in her neck. All the magical artifacts she kept in her bag looked nothing like these.

Ione held up one crystal. "Long before we interacted with other species, before we had reason or access to parchment, this is how we kept our records. Without Draconic magic and proper lighting, they're just crystals, but with the knowledge of how they work and a little luck..." The crystal lifted to hover just above her palm, capturing the light pouring in through the balcony. It shone bright enough to blind before projecting its contents into the surrounding air.

She blinked at the light. It only threw her off for a second. Her eyes adjusted faster than she expected they would. Her gaze flicked to the various bits of information... things she didn't understand. The corners of her lips tugged into a faint smile. This was one of the coolest things she'd ever seen. Though it made her wonder. She had two dragons in her heritage. Had either of them hidden content like this in any of the artifacts that belonged to them?

"While you can magically safeguard crystals, it's not usually advised. The rebound is volatile at best. Which is why Seru prefers to collect books over crystals," Ione explained. "Though I'm sure he's got a few tucked away somewhere."

Yeah, at least one in her neck. She frowned a bit. The other two hadn't been in dragon possession... as far as she knew. The one she'd stolen from the manticore... and then the one that had been in her bag. But she didn't know how long it had even been in there. Her gaze flicked from her purse on the couch back to Ione. "Is this something... *all* dragons do?"

"What do you mean?" Ione asked, knitting her brows together.

How did she answer that question? While she'd told the female a lot about herself, the only one she'd shared *that* particular detail with... was Seru. Thalasia bit her bottom lip. "My bloodline... it's... rather extensive. Unique, if you will. Includes... all sorts."

"Traditionally, storing information in crystals is a strictly Draconic process. It's how we keep our most highly valued knowledge. If you're asking if someone born of a dragon directly—or indirectly—has access to the ability or information, I'm inclined to say no, but I'm not entirely certain. This is the only instance I know of the information being shared among another species—in part or in full."

"Okay." It simply meant that Doru or Baro could've stored information in some pieces of her treasure. She just may not be able to access it. Yeah, that sounded like the people in her bloodline. Hide everything. Jump through hoops to get stuff accomplished, or even to retrieve the damn things in the first place. "Did something in the book give you an idea? Is that why you pulled these out?"

"Nothing specific jumped out," Ione remarked. "But," she cycled through each crystal, briefly scanning the information. "Having a complete work for comparison never hurts. Though what resides in these crystals is hardly complete. If we pair what we know, in addition..."

"It might offer a better picture and lead to understanding something that seems menial in other circumstances." Yeah. That was something she understood all too well.

"My thoughts, precisely!"

She could see why Seru liked the female so much. And Ione had certainly been helpful. As had the other woman; just differently. Gods, she couldn't recall the last time she delved so much into information. Although it was quite similar to piecing a puzzle together. Thalasia picked up another piece of fruit. The two seeds from others she'd eaten still sat off to the side. She glanced over at Seru, letting her gaze settle on him for a moment. She couldn't seem to help herself. Without bothering to sniff the food in her hand, she took a bite. Oh my. Maybe it wasn't a plum, but it was just as sweet.

"He's not going anywhere," Ione commented softly. "One reason this method of cleansing and communing is becoming increasingly ineffective is because it essentially renders him immobile for extended periods. And while I can wake him, if needed, I prefer not to destroy the palace and risk hurting my friends."

"He definitely doesn't need to be awake. Nevermind how upset with me he'll be..." Her words trailed off as her gaze flicked back to Ione. "I just... I keep thinking about the few times he's rested around me. The first... I could keep the nightmares at bay... for a brief time. The second... poppies... and the third..." She smirked a little. "It was kind of like being in the middle of a Seru donut. He just... coiled around me." Thalasia sighed. "But none of that's the point. I keep... I guess I'm just wondering if I found another way... how long would it last? What would it take to find something... more permanent?" Yes, she was worried about it. With the access she had to so many realms, would she be able to find a permanent solution for him? No, that wasn't what concerned her. She was too stubborn to give up. She'd definitely find a way. Whatever it took. The question was... how long before she found it?

"Rest isn't really necessary. More an unintentional side effect of the poppies. At least, from my perspective." Ione swapped out crystals as she cross-referenced the book in Thalasia's lap. "He clings to my memory, calls my spirit. It's easier for him to reach me through a sleep state, through dreams." She paused. "That aspect is less about purifying his spirit. More that he refuses to let go."

There seemed to be a lot he had a hard time letting go of. Probably why he thought he could mold her to fit into his world. Perhaps, why he pushed so hard for her to... do as he said. The so-called role he tried to place her in... a role she'd never fit. "What happens to you if he does?"

"My spirit initially returned to serve as a guide," Ione confessed. "Soon, I imagine my purpose will be fulfilled and my time here will end. That said, my spirit won't truly rest until my remains are returned to my motherland."

Listening to Ione's response, she thought of her own family. Those she had cared for. Were her parents at rest? At peace? She visited with them... at least her father on the spiritual plane... and she'd never asked. Was it even something she could give them? Their bodies had been destroyed. At her hands. What about Klaus? He'd forced her to leave without him. The only reason she even knew of his death... the coin in her possession. The light had gone out. And she'd never gone back to the realm... where she lost so much. Her gaze flicked back to Ione. She didn't know if she could give it to her loved ones, but... she could make sure it was something she and Seru gave this female. "Everyone deserves to be at peace."

"In life as much as in death," Ione replied with a smile. "Yet, we find less and less of it with each passing day."

Yeah, she knew that feeling. Maybe it was time she started letting go of some parts of her past herself. While she intended to attempt a visit with her mother, it should probably be the last. Exhaling a deep breath, she finished the fruit in her hand and glanced back up at the symbols the crystals produced. Maybe it was time she changed a lot of things. "Thank you... for helping me."

"I'm uncertain I've done so," Ione replied. "But you're most welcome, Thalasia." Her eyes glittered in the cast-off light.

"You've given me more than I had before." Even if it led to more questions. It also helped her see some truths, too. Then again, some things Seru had said over the last few days had done so as well. She just hadn't been ready to hear them. "I know we may not find everything... but I won't stop until I free him."

"You mean free from the Silver Queen's collar?"

"Well, yes, but free to leave the isle, too. If that was something he wanted, I believe it's a choice he should have." While she wanted him to go with her, she'd respect his decision if it was something he chose not to do.

"Isn't it our nature to want the things we cannot have?" The female paused. "You're a kind soul, Thalasia," Ione amended.

Her gaze flicked once to Seru before turning back to the glyphs in the air. Yeah. She'd truly believed that. Despite what her ancestors thought or the first prophecy stated, maybe she wasn't truly meant to have Seru. Thalasia offered a small, polite smile, her lips curling slightly in a gesture of gratitude. What else was there to say?

"You realize, even if you give him his freedom, he won't find contentment. He'll just seek something else in a futile attempt to fill the void." She reached back for a previous crystal while simultaneously flipping back a page in Thalasia's book. "What is it *you* want from all this, Thalasia? I don't just mean Seru. All of it."

It seemed like such a simple, yet complicated, question. Was it really? Despite everything that had happened between them, it changed little of how she felt. Just made her see things more clearly. Nor did it change what she wanted... what she truly wanted. "A home. Someplace I belong." She watched Ione for a minute. "I've moved around my whole life. The longest I've ever stayed anywhere... maybe a month, but I never felt like I wasn't home, wherever we were... until the day my parents died." She paused, recalling what she told Seru her father had said about the feeling. "I never thought... I'd have that again. Even with all our arguments, that's how I feel about him. Like I'm home."

Ione gave a thoughtful hum. Her attention flickered between the written words and the displayed image until a firm hand clasped hers, causing her to gasp in shock.

"Do I even want to ask?" Seru rumbled, low and gravelly.

Damn it. She hoped to be out of here before he came around. Not that he appeared entirely with it. Still... she wasn't sure he wanted to know. He'd been pretty stubborn about her finding answers. Although he'd likely realized she was here, she wouldn't say anything. Not yet.

He ran his fingers over the back of Ione's hand. When no answer came, his eyes shifted towards Thalasia. The skin around his eyes tightened as he registered her presence. His hand stilled over Ione's. "Do you ever listen?" A hint of irritation crept into his tone.

"When I'm not treated like a prisoner." He should be grateful someone busted her out. She hadn't handled the locked doors as well as she thought she would.

He pushed up onto his elbows with a grunt, his hand closing around Ione's. "You clearly don't know what it means to be kept prisoner, or you wouldn't have disobeyed me."

"I sent Yelena to escort Thalasia here," Ione interjected, setting the crystal aside to rest her hand atop his. His eyes slipped to her, his expression softening a bit. "After our discussion, I enlisted her help. I thought her insight might prove useful given the gravity of our concerns."

He huffed, clearly unhappy but not willing to go against her.

Scooping up the seeds she set aside, Thalasia got to her feet. "Clearly, you've forgotten I was held captive. Unless you just thought I was being hunted purely by accident." She circled him, her footsteps silent on the carpet, and retrieved her purse from the couch. Her gaze shifted to Ione. "Is there somewhere I can wash these off?"

"He hasn't forgotten," Ione reassured, gripping his hand tightly before he reacted. "He's simply concerned that you're not treading as carefully as he believes you should."

Seru narrowed his gaze at Ione. "And was she?" he asked, moving to clarify when her answer wasn't immediate. "Helpful? Insightful? With any of our concerns."

"She's been nothing short of a pleasure. While she may not go about things your way, she's trying and doing her best to assist in any way she can. She's provided us with information and her desire to assist." He opened his mouth, but she interjected before he could say anything. "Again, perhaps not your way and not to your preferred standards. I understand. But do you ever stop to consider that from her perspective, she's offering you all that she can and has to offer? Be gracious and accept her help as offered, not as you feel it should be. She *is* on your side. Otherwise, we're nearly out of options. Out of time. What do you propose we do once you've burned every viable bridge and find us all trapped and encircled in flame?"

He faltered, his jaw going slack. He closed his mouth.

Ione turned her attention to Thalasia. "Yes, through there." She nodded towards the curtain. "In the kitchen."

"Thank you." Thalasia headed for the curtain and stopped before going through. She'd been as careful as she could be. If he'd taken time to give her any information on the layout of the Clouds or taken a second to trust her... she glanced back at Seru. "You shouldn't need someone else to tell you I'm on *your* side. Otherwise... everything I've said and done... has simply fallen on deaf ears and blind eyes." While she was certain her voice betrayed the hurt, she didn't care. She would not placate him. At all. With nothing further, she pushed through the curtains and made her way toward the kitchen she'd spotted when she first entered.

Thalasia easily found what she needed to clean off the seeds and dry them. Although she caught sight of the shifter she'd seen earlier waking up, she probably wasn't the best company. Somehow, she always felt on the defensive with Seru. Yes, she cared about him, but after constantly sticking by his side... how could he, for one second, doubt that she wasn't on his side? Why did he *have* to talk to everyone else about her behind her back? But it wasn't okay for her to even ask questions about him? When *all* she was trying to do was help him?

Her gaze drifted to the seeds. Really, she didn't know if keeping them was a good idea. It was nice to think that maybe somewhere there was an unoccupied realm where she could plant them. She drew in a long, deep breath, stowed them away in her bag, and let her gaze rest on the counter for a silent minute. She needed to collect herself before she went back in there.

The leopard pounced atop the marble counter, where he settled back onto his haunches. His tail flicked back and forth as he watched her.

She glanced at the shape shifter, somewhat surprised by his reaction. In some places, it wouldn't be considered sanitary. At least it brought a small smile to her face. "Sorry if I woke you."

He let out a yawn, watching her intently from his perch, saying nothing.

Right. She gave the shifter a small nod and stepped away from the counter, starting back toward the draping she'd come through before. There were other things she could do than stand there being stared at.

Pausing at the fabric, she turned her head back and gave a slight shake. That was the strangest thing she'd ever encountered. And she'd seen a few things. Okay. Thalasia stepped through the curtain, pausing just inside it. "If you needed nothing else from me, Ione, I believe I'll take my leave. You can give the book back to Seru when you're finished with it."

"Won't Seru be accompanying you?" Ione asked, shooting each of them a questioning look.

"Well..." The rest of her response trailed off. There were several ways to respond to that. They hadn't exactly been getting along lately. Even when they did, it lasted all of five seconds. If that wasn't enough of a reason, she'd taken no one with her to the spiritual plane. Then again, she wasn't even sure she could. Or how it would work.

Seru used the edge of the balcony to hoist himself to his feet. "I'm going with her, whether or not she agrees," he replied matter-of-factly. "If Thalasia doesn't want that silly piece of garbage, destroy it. I have no use for it."

Fine. He could do a lot of sitting and staring and sitting on his ass, doing nothing while she did what she needed. Silly piece of garbage. Seeing as she wasn't given any choice in the matter, as if that was something new, Thalasia walked over to where Ione still sat and held out her hand. It might still come of use. "If you're finished with it... please."

Ione closed the book, placing it carefully in Thalasia's grasp. "I'm sorry I wasn't of more help to you." She rose to her feet to stand beside Seru. "I'll continue to consult the crystals, see if I can't piece anything together." She turned to Seru, concern gracing her features. "Usually, a thorough cleanse improves your mood."

"I'm sure we can thank her for that, too." Seru said, rolling his shoulders. "Drawing on our connection creates a myriad of delightful little side effects."

"You gave me more information than I had before." Tucking the book into her purse, she narrowed her gaze at Seru. "Oh no! You do *not* get to blame that on me. I didn't tell you to do it. Nor have I had a say in our lack of feeding the damn thing. If you intend to talk about me, at least make sure you lay out all the facts. Since it would seem Marius's belief that the effects were fading is obviously a bunch of crap."

"Then go ahead," he said. "Have your say, Thalasia. Shout it from the rooftops if you must."

"Why? So you can ignore what I say some more? Blame me some more? Because I'm the only one that's difficult, right? You haven't played a single part in all of this?" She shook her head. Fine, he wanted her to have her say, then she would. "I could've fulfilled my duty days ago. Instead, I stayed with you. Could've left after fighting the Informant, but I didn't. I came back to the inn. I could've used the egg, and again... left. You talk about how much you've chosen me and you can't seem to see that I've been doing the same damn thing. I'm not entirely blameless for all of this, but neither are *you*. You can't expect me to bend to your will and do whatever you want because it's what everyone else does." Not once did her voice waver. She remained calm through every word that came out of her mouth.

"Because holding onto it isn't doing you any good," he replied.

Out of all the things she said, that was his response. With another shake of her head, she looked at Ione. "Thank you for your hospitality." Thalasia turned on her heel and stepped back through the curtain, heading for the staircase.

"Was that not liberating enough for you?" Seru asked, sidling up to her easily enough. He did a double take. "Your ever-revolving wardrobe never ceases to awe."

It definitely wasn't liberating. Slapping him might make her feel better, but why waste the energy? He'd just find something else to blame her for. It was all her fault, right? It didn't matter. She had finished talking to him. Not even in response to her change of clothing. It got them nowhere.

Thalasia continued her way down the stairs and out the door. Once she was on the other side of it, she went into her bag and retrieved what appeared to be nothing more than an antique compass. In truth, it was much more than that. One of the magical artifacts once owned by Doru... the astrolabe that would lead her to the best location for her to access the spiritual plane. Taking a deep breath in and out, she paused, letting the air fill her lungs as she centered herself. Her agitation would prevent it from working. She took another deep breath, then opened the compass and focused as its needle whirled wildly.

The hand settled, intently focused, pointing in one direction. She'd kept in her mind the servants' corridors, something that she and Ione had spoken of, and prayed the compass followed that link as it led her toward a suitable spot. One she expected would be quiet, less occupied, and the veil between planes would be thinner. She lifted part of her dress to make it easier as she walked, following the direction the compass continued to point in, and that it was blessedly quiet... point for Seru.

Chapter Forty-One

Thalasia paused as the hand on the compass spun counter-clockwise. She'd reached where she needed to go. And Seru had been quiet the entire time. It was a blessing that would hopefully last. Especially with what she was about to do. Her gaze lifted to what was in front of them.

Her nose wrinkled. The air was thick with dust and unbearably stale. It had been a minute since anyone had used this passage. She took that as a good sign. After stowing the compass, she closed her eyes for a moment, heightening her senses to map the place's contours in her mind. At least until she found an excellent open spot that would serve her purpose. Then she continued her trek forward. There were a lot of different questions running through her mind. Many of which no one here could answer. Not once since the first vision she had of the place four years ago had she expected things to get so complicated. Hoping Seru would stay hot on her heels, she wound her way through the maze of corridors, ignoring the way the dress felt against her skin. Or that the air was balmier than seemed possible.

"What are you looking for?" Seru asked.

"At the moment, someplace that's open and has cleaner air. And in the vicinity." She'd given him the perfect opportunity to stay with Ione, but no, he had to be insistent. Gods, would it annoy him to sit there and do nothing? So many questions. And they all began with her sanity.

"To what end? You're following a gadget—likely from one of your ancestors—that's hundreds or thousands of years old. If it were as simple as fresh air, the courtyard at the front of the manor would have sufficed, but you've opted for somewhere off the beaten path. In the dust-infested servants' quarters."

"If it was that simple, then that's where the compass would've led me. However, it led me to a place that would meet my needs. Based on the layout I've gotten, these stifled corridors lead somewhere that's out in the open, with a magnificent view of the sky." The explanation could've been more detailed, but she didn't feel like offering any information. Not when he refused to converse with her on things that mattered.

"You realize we could've simply walked to the outlook—the highest point in the city—through *normal* passageways." He shook off a web that clung to his mane and brushed the dust from his clothes.

Stopping mid-step, she glowered at him. "No. Because you don't feel the need to share *anything* with me." She continued in the direction she'd been going, inhaling and exhaling several deep breaths as she walked along.

"Not true," Seru replied. "I share information with you. Not all, but what I think you need to know. If you'd rather continue not to speak, I'm content to do my duty silently."

With a sigh of exasperation, she continued forward. If what she'd gotten was accurate, they should be approaching the outlook shortly. He was only partially correct. "Just not everything you *should* have shared."

"Based on whose criteria? It's a matter of opinion, not rule or law. You desire to be treated like my equal? Act the part and I'll gladly keep you up to speed. But until you've proven you can step back and not make every decision impulsively and emotionally, sharing everything you believe I should share isn't an option in my eyes. Not with everything that's at risk, under these critical conditions."

She half-glanced over her shoulder. "What impulsive decision do *you* believe I've made?" Because she could only come up with one.

"You've blindly trusted me only hours after we met—despite several indicators that you shouldn't. Yes, that includes allowing me to mark you. You've stormed off—or tried to—multiple times. When you did, you returned injured. You're lucky you escaped and returned at all. Whenever things don't go the way you like, you allow your emotions to guide your decisions. While that's part of your nature as an Atlis, it's a great way to get yourself killed. I'm provoking you intentionally. You take the bait almost every time or choose to suppress it so deeply you're as frigid as Verie. You're far from stupid and can be level-headed instead of hot-headed if you choose. If you're angry at me? Good, fine. Stab me. Poison my tea—whatever outlet you like, that will not put your life—our lives, in jeopardy. In case you hadn't noticed, there are enemies abound. Pick the one you know instead of the ones you don't." He raked his fingers through his mane in a huff.

The first wasn't impulsive. It had been emotional. Not that she suspected he saw the difference. Nor was it the one decision she'd thought of, surprisingly enough. "I trusted you because I saw something in you. As for the marks, I blame my emotions. And I haven't stormed off. I *have* gone on a long walk that, while yes, resulted in an injury, I knew I could take care of myself."

Should they talk about the number of times he'd left? Twice at least. Usually, she either said something that made him uncomfortable or asked questions he refused or couldn't answer. And yeah, they were great at provoking each other intentionally. She'd done it twice herself. There was something else in his statement, though. "Did it bother you when I suppressed it? That I became frigid, as you so eloquently put it. Because that is what it was like kissing you in the forest. And I'm not angry at you." No, she was angry at herself. She stopped just before they got to the overlook and faced him. "I'm frustrated with you. You run when I ask too many questions. Get annoyed with me when I'm pushed to do things you don't like. And then have the audacity to criticize me for doing the same thing you do."

"You saw the good in me—or, as she puts it, the pure part of my spirit. Undoubtedly the weakest parts of me. Electing to see only those parts is foolish. Expecting those parts to win out over the darkness even more so. I wasn't called here to do good things, Thalasia. I was called here to do unspeakable acts of violence, to inflict insurmountable pain and death on the people of this isle. Do you ever consider that the barrier your ancestors created wasn't just to keep the invaders out but to keep us in?! Contained, abruptly ending our conquest."

He paused for a moment. "I didn't mean to shout at you." He blew out a frustrated breath as he massaged his temples. "You may be capable of taking care of yourself—to a point—but you have limits, Thalasia. You don't have natural armor to protect you. Your childhood training and life experiences only offer so much in lieu of my 800-years of mastery. That's not me discounting your efforts. I know you do phenomenally well with what you've been given and the fate that's been dealt to you. But there's going to come a time when it's not enough. That woman, the bear shifter that's been hunting you and her brother. They're going to keep coming until they're stopped. Do you prefer to take the risk of getting recaptured—perhaps as a consequence of the injuries you've sustained—and subjected to those torturous games a second time? Or are you going to allow me to do what you've tasked me to as your Allimos?"

Another breath through his nose this time as he crossed his arms. He licked his dry lips, pursing them before continuing. "I don't enjoy being touched." He shifted his weight to one side. "And, it's not just by you... I don't..." His words trailed off. "Physical intimacy hasn't always been a choice for me. I realize you don't have hundreds of years to be patient with me *while I decide and sort through my own demons,* and we have only a matter of days to make some huge, life-altering choices."

While he yelled, at least she'd gotten confirmation of something she suspected. Thalasia exhaled a deep breath to keep herself collected. A screaming match would get them nowhere. Not to mention it would hinder her ability to leave this plane temporarily. "I'm aware there is darkness in you. Just like there is in me." She held up her hand. "Regardless of innocence, purity, kindness... it's there. I *know* what I'm capable of. And yes, I understand that there will come the point where what I've been taught won't be enough and that I'll have to depend on someone else." She sighed heavily. "I'm not trying to risk getting recaptured. Keeping that woman off this isle..." Her focus had been to put the past in the past. "It doesn't mean my protection is only *your* responsibility. Or even the only thing... as my Allimos. The touching I've kind of figured some of it out on my own." Their one make-out session came to mind. He'd been so still as she touched him. And it was something she'd been grateful for because he'd tried. It was one area where she counted herself lucky. Minerva's men hadn't been able to rape her, though they'd indeed attempted it once. And they'd been fearful of endeavoring it again after that.

"You're mistaking your capacity to do evil with the actual physical manifestation of darkness." He shook his head, pressing his fingers against closed eyes. "Do you intend to keep pushing until you've reached beyond the point of no return? Where I can't reach you? If you're not alive, none of the rest matters. It's not like I can—or care—I'm not invested enough, or as much as you are, to carry on the torch if something happens to you."

"I'm not trying to get myself killed, Seru, but I'm not built to stand on the sidelines, either. Yet that doesn't mean I can't work with you." Something he might see if he just trusted her a little. She pushed on the door into the open area she needed. That was something he had to accept. Some places he wouldn't be able to follow.

"I never said you were—but I need to know you've got multiple escape routes and contingencies. The skills to get yourself out of those situations if nothing else works."

"That's what training is for." Something else she needed to work on, too. Before she sought the central point, she glanced back at him. "I understand there are some things that we will need to do separately. Things you can do that I can't. Just like there are things I can do that you can't." She gripped the back of her neck. "We need to figure out how to find that balance."

"Yes, and you haven't nearly enough." He opened his eyes toward the end of her statement, unsure how to reply.

"I'll give you that." Her training and studies should technically still be happening. It was one of many reasons she didn't believe it would even be possible to meet her Allimos.

"And the lookout?" he asked, pushing off the wall to follow her to the top. "The air is thin up here. Doubt you're going flying."

"It's where the veil is thinnest. I can leave this plane from here." With a bit of help. "I have questions that need answering, and there's only one person who can do that."

"Just tell me it's not someone who's going to kill you and get it over with," Seru grumbled.

His response brought a smile to her face. "Not someone who wants me dead."

"You'd best be certain of that and not just hazarding a guess."

Such faith. She chuckled. No. Her mother definitely wouldn't want to kill her. "I'm not."

"Must you always laugh? This isn't a joke." He sighed before the wind descended upon them, swallowing all sound.

Her smile faded. No. Her parents' sacrifice wasn't a joke, even if it amused her that he might suggest it. Not that she'd said who she was going to talk to, just that it was someone who could answer questions. Thalasia found a suitable spot, then withdrew her dagger from her bag and slashed a cut through her dress, from her thigh all the way to the hem. Gods, that felt so much better. Then she sat down cross-legged. She set the dagger in her lap and removed an encased lotus blossom.

Seru dismissed the miserable gusts, giving her enough room to do as needed without further distraction or cause for delay. "Be quick."

"I make no promises. Time doesn't exactly pass the same way there as it does here." Something he should already know. Thalasia set the crystalline globe containing a lotus blossom down in front of her. The last time she'd used the lotus blossom, it had left her emotionally drained for days. But she already felt like that. Of course, she'd traveled to the spiritual plane and trained with her father. Maybe this time, no, there was no perhaps. She needed her mother. Thalasia lifted the blade from her lap, pricked her finger, and let a couple of droplets of blood stain the white flower through the opening at the top.

Setting the dagger to the side, she licked the blood from her finger and rested her hands on her knees. She'd cut the dress so she could sit cross-legged, which allowed more room and offered skin-to-skin contact. It was the best-suited position for what she was doing. With each slow, deliberate inhale and exhale, she let go of her worries until her mind was utterly clear.

She didn't have to see to know the lotus blossom had accepted the offering. Gusts of wind no longer played in the loose strands of her hair. Instead, lush waves of green enveloped her. Not far off in the distance, the sound of water thundering down a rocky hill caught her attention. That combined with the fact that she was already standing, blades of grass tickling her feet, she returned to the spiritual plane. Slowly, she turned and walked around the massive trees toward the waterfall.

A smile settled across her face as she truly drank in the sight of the forest. It had been a long time since she'd seen this place, but it had always been her mother's favorite. Most of her time in that realm, she'd spent training. But when she got to relax, her mother would take her to that waterfall, even for just a few hours. They'd stare at its Caribbean-blue color as the water spurted over the basalt rock and threw up bubbles of spray. Then they'd watched as the hues of the sky changed with the setting sun.

The ache in her heart eased the second she spotted her mother sitting on a nearby boulder, staring out as the funnel of water cascaded down the mountain, plummeting toward the ground in a whooshing vortex at the bottom. Her smile brightened, and she lifted the skirting of her mermaid-style, royal-blue dress and raced across the terrain, the dress's train trailing behind her. It appeared the new split in her dress remained behind. "Mom!"

Her mother jumped to her feet and quickly wrapped her arms around Thalasia. She hugged her tight and then pulled back a touch. "Let me look at you, my beautiful daughter." Her mother gently cupped her chin, her thumb tenderly wiping away the salty tears that traced paths down her cheeks. "Come now. No tears."

How could she not be expected to cry? It had been eight long years since her mother had been killed. This was the first time she'd seen her since then. Her previous visits to the spiritual plane had been with her father. And mostly educational. Thalasia wiped at her face. "It's beyond my control. I've just I've missed you so much."

"I've missed you, too, but we have this time together now."

"Yes, we do." Time wouldn't last forever.

"Goodness, look at how much you've grown. And this gown, your hair, the jewelry, your grandmother's earrings, and the necklace are all so unlike you. It suits you well."

"Does it?" It felt like droves of fabric that left her exposed and naked. That didn't even take into account the jewels. At least it was something she'd picked out for herself. And the low-back was much more comfortable than the dress previously selected for her. Though with everything she'd stolen over the years, she shook the thoughts from her head. Her thoughts had nothing to do with clothes and everything to do with Seru.

"What's going on? I can see the wheels in your head turning." With a soft tug on her hand, her mother coaxed her to take a seat on the rough, moss-covered boulder by her side.

"You know how we used to talk about my Allimos... and I always said it would be a long time before I met him?"

Her mother sighed and wrapped an arm around Thalasia's shoulders, hugging her close. "You've made it to Prisma Isle then I will take it?"

Thalasia sat upright. No. No. For the love of all things holy—no. She swallowed the lump in the back of her throat and stared at her mother. "Did you know?"

"Yes. We all have. Long before he was even called upon, it's been foretold for over a millennium. The two of you, you're supposed to be a force to be reckoned with. That—it has always been prophesied. We've just never been sure if it would be a good thing or not."

"And you didn't think to tell me *any* of this!" She sprang up from the boulder, her heart pounding, and paced restlessly. "How could you not tell me? He has his moments, but often he's an arrogant, self-centered, righteous asshole!" Way to describe the male she'd fallen in love with. Oh, gods. What did *that* say about her? That like she'd told him; she could see the good in him. She just set off a lot of the darkness.

"Honestly, sweetheart... I didn't think you'd be willing to listen."

She shot her mother an incredulous look, if only for a second. If she was honest with herself, her mother was probably right. Back then, she didn't think she'd meet her Allimos for quite some time. That was wrong. Way wrong. She let out a weary sigh and squeezed her shoulders, seeking comfort. "You don't know what he's like, Mom. Every time I think we've pushed past our issues; I swear all we do is end up falling five steps back. Even now, things have settled, but I don't know how long it'll last."

"No relationship is perfect. It's hard work, but you both have to compromise."

"I've tried. Every way I know how. In the end, we just piss each other off. Which doesn't help either of us." Sinking onto the boulder, she covered her face with her hands, the cool, hard rock a stark contrast to her flushed skin. "It's exhausting, Mom."

Her mother rubbed slow circles along her back. "Something to think about, whereas you've had less structure to work within, he hasn't. The life he has built for himself, he's had to do behind a lot of closed doors, working in the confines of not only his creation but of the surrounding hierarchy. You've had the privilege of not being limited by that."

"I get that we've led very different lives, but that doesn't mean everything about our relationship works one way. That's how it feels. I'm just expected to do what he wants when he wants without question." Granted, it probably would make things easier there in the Clouds, but that wouldn't fly everywhere else. Something she was desperately trying to make happen. Yes, she'd suggested he consider what would occur *if* they were successful in removing his collar. Did he ever think about that? Or was he so convinced that they'd readily accept him without that control?

"You're right, but have you asked him what *he* wants or expects from you?"

Thalasia opened her mouth and snapped it shut. She thought she had, but maybe she hadn't. He just kept asking her to do what he said, to learn her place. That was the problem... her place... it didn't jibe with what he believed it did. And here lately, he referred to the journals about how he'd have to sacrifice everything. Something she thought he was already doing, sacrificing himself to please everyone else. She sighed heavily. "No."

"Don't you think you should? That perhaps you should discuss what each wants from the other?"

"Maybe..." There was no maybe to it. Her mother was right. But was it something he'd ever agree to talk about? Or would he just fight her more or give her more excuses? "I just don't know how we do that. All we do is butt heads."

"You both have very dominant personalities. It's one of the many reasons we've questioned what kind of relationship the two of you would have."

Frowning, she looked over at her mother. "How could it be determined before I was even born what kind of personality I'd have?"

"We look at many things, Thalasia. The stars, the words of each prophecy, plus we listen to the gods and goddesses. Some of our ancestors even had visions of you both."

Visions? She didn't think that was possible. If there had been, wouldn't the vision have been jotted down? She shook her head. "There's never been a vision of us recorded in the journal, though."

"There are many pages in the journal that have been... hidden. If you open it here, then you'll see a lot of entries that would be considered lost."

Thalasia shot up ramrod straight again. "What?"

"Many of us are not proud of the things we've done. Some chose not to include anything, while others opted to record what happened and place it on a different plane."

Her eyes widened as she stared at her mother. It couldn't be true. It just couldn't, except for even her own experience. The months she'd been in captivity, and then the time that followed. None of which she recorded in the journal. Logically speaking, she couldn't have been the first Atlis to go through dark times. Maybe that applied to the Allimos journal, too. Some entries just couldn't be seen by the naked eye. "Is it the same thing with both books?"

"I wish I could tell you it wasn't, but many of us... we let our pride get in the way."

The irony of that statement wasn't lost on her. Over the years, she tried not to think too much of herself. To recognize her flaws, even if she didn't record them. As she thought back to some of the Allimos entries she'd read at Seru's behest and how he reacted to them, he would have looked at them differently if he read the pages her mother spoke about. Would it alter his view of the title? "He may not even agree to be my Allimos."

"If he doesn't... don't perform the ritual. Not without him."

"Really? After everything that I've been pushed toward? Stepping into my power?" That made little sense. It seemed like everyone in her family had wanted her to take it. Yeah, she'd questioned it a few times; even then, she wasn't positive that she desired everything that came with the ritual. But she thought she had no choice.

Her mother sighed. "Pull out the journal. You need to see it to understand."

Thalasia, absently gnawing on her cheek, reached into her purse for the Atlis journal as requested, a task that unexpectedly caught her off guard. She didn't think it would be accessible on the spiritual plane, but there it was. Wait, was it thicker? Shit. It was freaking massive. And it hadn't been small to begin with. She glanced at her mother. "How is this even possible?"

"I told you. We hid the things we didn't want others to know."

"Why are you telling me this?"

"Because it's time you saw the truth." Her mother hovered her hand over the book, and it opened, rapidly flipping through pages. A lot of pages until it finally stopped on one. "Here. This. You need to read this."

Her gaze fell to the wisp of a page in front of her. If they hadn't been on the spiritual plane, then she didn't think she'd be able to see it. Thalasia blinked at the name at the bottom of the entry. It wasn't the name of an Atlis. How had it gotten in there? This made little sense. "I don't understand. Who is Alcmene? And why does she have an entry here?"

"She was Klaus and Kaja's first child. An Atlis, like you."

"What? No, I know all of them. You made me memorize every Atlis that was ever born." It had been a part of her training, her education, to know those who had come before her.

"Alcmene isn't one we teach about." Her mother blew out a slight breath. "Like you, she had issues with the male she'd chosen as her Allimos. The day of the ritual, she met him where they'd decided, but he never showed. So, she opted to perform it without him." Her mother turned to a couple of pages ahead. "If her journal entry is accurate, she believed it would force their connection. Instead, it backfired. The ritual stripped her of her ability to feel all emotion. Without those things to hold her to her duties, she no longer cared about saving innocents."

No emotion. She couldn't even look at her mother as she listened to the words. Although she hadn't yet approached that, it reminded her of those months after she escaped from Minerva. Where she traveled to whatever realm she wanted. She stole things simply because she could. She even took lives if they got in her way.

Her mother slipped a finger beneath her chin and forced their eyes to meet. "I know what you're thinking, and it isn't the same thing."

"But... I killed so many...." Thalasia whispered.

"And you never took an innocent life. Alcmene did. One she'd been meant to rescue. Within a matter of days, she killed a child. Kaja discovered the body. Even with Klaus's help, she couldn't figure out how the girl had died. She utilized the Kota bowls to see what happened."

Kota bowls. An ancient tradition she'd never really been able to learn. It required patience, and she often got frustrated with them. Maybe something she could add to her list whenever she and Scru had downtime. There he went again! How did thoughts of him constantly invade her mind?

"Kaja didn't want to believe it," her mother continued. "She turned to the journal for information... guidance... hoping it would tell her that what she'd seen was false. Instead, it supported it." Her mother turned the page.

Just a sparse collection of jotted-down lines could be seen. Three floated in the center of the page. *I killed today. Because I could—pretty freeing. Something I look forward to doing again.* Thalasia's eyes widened, and her focus snapped to her mother. "There is no way she was an Atlis! We don't kill for pleasure."

"I know we don't, but Alcmene did." Her mother paused. "It forced Kaja and Klaus to make a decision... Neither of them ever thought they'd have to..." Her mother's words trailed off.

Her mother didn't have to say it. She knew what they'd done. They'd murdered their daughter. To be forced to make that kind of decision—Thalasia swallowed the lump in the back of her throat. While her mother had said they were different, she hadn't mentioned how they were alike except for difficult Allimos. "You said there were issues with her male. What issues?"

"They were both... willful. And similar to you and Seru, there was a vast age difference between them."

Many people were stubborn, but being a lot younger than one's other half, it wasn't all that common. Staring at her mother, Thalasia swallowed again. While she didn't want to know, she also felt like she had to ask. "How old was she?"

"Nineteen."

With a sudden jump to her feet, the book slid from her lap and made a gentle thud as it hit the ground. She retreated from the boulder, her footsteps echoing as she paced. "No. No. I'm nothing like her! Even *if* you hadn't told me not to do the ritual without him, I wouldn't have, anyway. I don't want the power! She had to—I don't care what she wrote in the journal. I guarantee it was nothing but utter bullshit! We are nothing alike!"

Yes, she *had* killed before. But she hadn't done so for pleasure. For months, it had been out of anger but not delight. Most of the lives she'd taken had occurred so she could save another. No matter how they painted it, she was *nothing* like that female.

Her mother stood, her grip firm on Thalasia's arms, halting her restless pacing. "Listen to me. I didn't say you were like her. Yes, there are similarities, but I *know* your heart. Plus, I can see how you feel about him." Her mother nodded down at her limbs. "Though I expected you'd be brighter."

Thalasia looked down at her arms. "Damn it," she muttered. Even on the spiritual plane, the glow of her skin followed. She frowned. Wait a second. Her mother had tacked something on at the end. "What do you mean 'brighter'?"

"Well... the way your sexual awakening works in conjunction with the commitment ritual, by the day of, you should be as radiant as a shining star in the night sky. It's an expression of the relationship you have with your Allimos."

Oh, this wasn't good. Not good at all. Pulling away from her mother's grasp, Thalasia lowered herself back onto the stone. Okay. Questions. She had questions—so many questions. Inhaling and exhaling a deep breath, she dragged a hand down her face. "What if I'm not?"

"Then you won't be strong enough to perform the ritual."

Son of a bitch. That wouldn't do either of them any good. Not that it was the only reason to figure things out. But she believed it would be part of what helped set him free. If she wasn't strong enough, shit, shit, shit. Was this what Doru had been talking about? "I need you to explain the ritual to me fully. This isn't training, Mom. I need to understand it."

"You know the three sides—the physical, spiritual, and emotional—right?" She sat back down next to Thalasia. "The reason yours has always been so different is because of The Reflection Pools in Pteryrina. You won't just use the magic of the water, but magical artifacts, too. Those will connect you both spiritually and magically. The emotional comes from the non-magical artifacts.

They strengthen and solidify that bond using a unique power. As for the physical... that's kind of in three parts. These last couple of days leading up to your birth moon, your pheromones will be impossible to control except with physical intimacy—part of what bolsters your luminescence. The second is the kiss you share during the ritual. And the third is the period of consummation that follows. They all build on each other, intensifying the lifelong bond between the two of you."

Thalasia groaned. Certainly, explained why the glow kept making an appearance, not to mention her scent earlier. Impossible to control without intimacy; this conversation just got better and better. They had to find a way past their differences. "So, the three sides interlink and build onto the inherent power of the water, deepening and cementing the bond between an Atlis and their Allimos."

"Yes, that's correct."

"Okay, and by physical intimacy, are we talking full-blown sex or just pleasures of the flesh?" Because one would be easier than the other. Especially with what he told her right before she took this happy trip.

A smile settled across her mother's face. "You've become much more brazen over the years."

"Mom, please..." The question was awkward enough, but she didn't have time to fret over that. She needed specific details. Thalasia's hand went to her forehead, pressing lightly as if to soothe a growing tension. Good gods, was it possible to get a headache here, too?

"Until the ritual itself, the simple pleasure of the flesh will suffice."

As much as she didn't want to ask for further clarification, she had no choice. Probably something she should've done when she first brought it up. "Does it matter if... you know... he's just... pleasing me?"

"I don't understand why it wouldn't go both ways, but no, it shouldn't."

Burying her face in her hands, she dragged her hands down to her lap. Great. At least that simplified some complexities that had been added. Especially if they had to address the situation with her awakening. Hopefully, it didn't worsen. "Okay. What about this re-triggering thing that Doru talked about?"

Her mother tilted her head. "You read the Allimos journal?"

"A little. Not that it was the point. Nor had Seru thought it particularly useful. He and I read some of it together."

"Good for you. I always thought it was stupid they were supposed to be kept secret from one another." Her mother shook her head. "I hate Doru used that word because it's... well, complete horseshit. Your sexual awakening cannot be re-triggered. It occurs once in a lifetime. You have one chance at the commitment ritual; that's it. Doru and Cressida figured out how to come together in all three manners befitting a couple. After she attempted suicide, but that's neither here nor there."

"What?" Thalasia's eyes flicked back to her mother. The woman had to be lying. Except for the look on her mother's face, said otherwise. Wait, wait—she reached down for the journal and scanned through until she found Cressida's pages. It took her a few minutes to confirm the accuracy of her mother's words. Clear as day; there was the suicide note, another one of those translucent pages that they could only see on this plane. She'd have to go through all these one day, but not right then.

"I'm sorry, Thalasia." Her mother tucked a loose strand of hair behind her ear. "I wish I could've taught you all of this a while ago, but you haven't been ready for it. And ten was too young to even truly comprehend the importance of everything."

It had been too young. Not just understanding the fundamentals of sex, but the importance of the ritual. Even beyond that. But it had nothing to do with her training and her education. She wished she had more time with them, period. Closing the book, she returned it to her bag and offered her mother a faint smile. "I'm sorry I couldn't save you and Dad so we could've had all of this together."

"That wasn't your fault. You need to stop blaming yourself for it. There was *nothing* you could've done to save us."

"But I feel like... like I was a coward... for running away." Yes, they'd told her to do it, and while she had, she'd been strong enough to fight by their side.

"Your mother's right, Thalasia," her father's voice came from behind her.

Peering over her shoulder, she jumped to her feet and ran toward her father. She wrapped her arms around him and squeezed him with all her might. Tears rolled down her cheeks. Gods, she didn't think she'd get to see both of them. While she hoped it would be the case, it didn't always work out that way.

"My brave warrior," her father said.

Yeah. More like the kind that ran away and let other people handle her problems. "I don't feel brave," Thalasia whispered. "I left you both to die."

"It was our job to ensure you lived." Her father's arms tightened their hold on her. "That is a parent's job, Thalasia. To make sure their child wants for nothing. To keep them safe and to teach them morals and values." He pressed a kiss to her forehead. "That's exactly what your mother and I did. So, no, you didn't leave us to die. We protected you. It's time you stopped blaming yourself."

Thalasia pulled back, her eyes now fixed on her father's face, a mixture of emotions playing out. Stop blaming herself. "I'm not sure I know how to do that."

"Yes, you do."

Was her father right? Did she know how to let go of the self-blame? Yes, she did. And it was something she could do. With a deep, ragged inhale and a shaky exhale, she reached up and brushed away the tears that blurred her vision. "I just always thought... I could've stopped her."

"Nothing could've changed what was meant to happen."

Meant to happen. It seemed illogical to think it had simply been her parents' time to go, but how many visions had she followed without question? How many people had said it was illogical for her to care about Seru? To love him in any way? Things didn't have to make sense to be true.

Her father brushed the tears from her cheek. "You've grown into a beautiful young woman. One I'm so proud of." He hugged her again and then grinned. "Now, let's talk about this male of yours. You need to tell this selfish shit to treat my daughter better."

"Oderon!" Her mother exclaimed. "We talked about this. The two of them need to work together. That is the *only* way they succeed."

Thalasia glanced at her father. "I appreciate your siding with me, Dad, but Mom's right. I haven't exactly helped the situation any." Her mother had made many valid points earlier—that along with the insight she'd given her about the ritual. And now she needed him as much as he needed her.

"I'm glad you see things my way, Thalasia." A wide grin crossed her mother's face. "There is one thing I should tell you... about the pheromones. If you don't handle them appropriately, you'll feel it. You'll be in physical pain, and it won't pass until the day after the full moon."

Yep, there it went. Things just got more complicated. With a deep, rumbling groan, she returned to the heavy boulder, a small chuckle escaping her lips as she shook her head. "I'm thinking that whoever decided Seru and I should be together had a sick sense of humor."

Her father's eyebrows knitted together. "Care to elaborate?"

"Aside from the fact that he's a saint beast, which comes with its own set of complexities regarding his existence and trying to free him of the collar and sever the tie he has to the isle." Honestly, she wasn't sure what she'd gotten herself into. They were both damaged in their way. Each was trying to get past their demons and trying to let the past go. Maybe that was the point. She'd consistently told him that she saw something in him, and she still did. And maybe he saw something in her, too. Because for the first time she was *trying* to face her past.

"Thalasia, sweetheart... I know right now you think this is an impossible feat, but I have faith if anyone can accomplish this, you can." Her mother sat beside her, gently brushing away the tears that streamed down her face. "Listen to me, when Ismene first started watching Seru, she didn't realize he'd be a saint beast. None of us did. It took her a few days. As she couldn't stop watching him, she had to attain help. There is a blank page amidst Doru's entries. Use your powers to call the writing forth. It isn't much, but it might offer some insight into his previous existence."

Some additional pages. More than what had been recorded in the book specific to Seru. Another reference. Minor, but another one. "Are you saying that Doru is the one who recorded it?"

"Yes. He used the Kota bowl and jotted down what he saw," her father answered. "I read it over not long after you were born. Despite what I said before, I know he'll be good to you. Just tell him not to try to fill the shoes of those who came before him. Forge a fresh path. One that isn't just for you, but for him, too."

With a slight nod, Thalasia's gaze shifted to her parents. Gods, she wanted more time with them. So much more time. There had been more than one purpose behind this trip. Even with everything she'd needed to know, she'd needed to see her parents more. Talk to them one last time. Say goodbye to them. Something she hadn't been able to do eight years ago. Staring at her parents, she swallowed to wet her parched throat. She wasn't ready to say goodbye, to let them go.

Why was this so much harder than she thought it would be? Gods, she couldn't do it. She couldn't walk away. There were so many more questions she had for them. So much more for them to teach her. She wanted more time with them, just to do simple things, like watching the waterfall. Or see the sunset. But if she didn't let them go, they'd never have peace. That wasn't something she could handle.

Thalasia glanced between the two of them. How could she fault Seru for not being able to let go when she hadn't been able to do it, either? This was the first step. One she was sure her parents knew had to happen. So, they could move forward, and so she could, too. Her arms encircled her mother in a tight hug, and the familiar sting of tears returned to her eyes. "Thank you for everything."

"I love you, Thalasia. I'd help you in any way I could." Her mother hugged her a little tighter before releasing the hold she had on her.

Offering her mother a smile, she stood and embraced her father. There was so much that she'd never get to share with them, but it wouldn't make her ungrateful for the years she'd received. Many people got less time than she had. "Thank you, Dad... for always believing in me."

"That isn't something that'll ever change, Thalasia." He pressed a kiss to her forehead and released the hug. "My strong, beautiful, brave warrior... I'll always love you."

"I love you both, too." The tears flowed freely down her face, and she didn't even try to wipe them away. Not that they were entirely sad tears, either. No, they were happy tears, too. She stood there as her parents wrapped their arms around each other.

"Don't forget the life lessons I taught you, Thalasia. They'll help get you through. As for Seru..." Her mother laced her and her father's fingers together. "Tell him you may be willful and obstinate, but your heart is pure. The love you'll give him is the greatest treasure he'll ever receive."

"He may be difficult, but trust him, Thalasia. He'll take care of you," her father said.

They both smiled at her, and like the seeds of a dandelion, they both fluttered away into silver flecks that danced along the breeze toward the waterfall and disappeared. It was a brilliant display; one she couldn't look away from. She knew Seru was there waiting, but she wasn't quite ready to leave, though she would soon.

Chapter Forty-Two

Thalasia's eyes opened. Tears stained her cheeks. It was a good thing she hadn't worn makeup. It certainly would've been ruined after that trip. Sniffling, she wiped the wetness from her face. Her scent filled the shimmering cocoon surrounding her body. She eyed the silver glow that appeared to radiate from her entire form. Her mother's words replayed in her mind. *Not bright enough.* Beneath her dress, her skin felt uncomfortably hot, a sensation that, combined with the ambient temperature, made her regret her clothing choice. She lifted her gaze—holy shit.

Her eyes flicked around to the golden-clad soldiers that surrounded her and Seru. Lots of dragons. As stealthily as she could muster, she slipped her dagger into her bag. The last words her father spoke to her replayed in her mind as her eyes found Seru's. *He may be difficult, but trust him, Thalasia. He'll take care of you.* Given their current situation, she could admit it; she was in over her head. Thalasia nodded at Seru. She'd follow his lead. The protective layer dissolved, releasing a sweet, musky cloud of pheromones into the air.

The dragons nearest her recoiled at the powerful scent washing over them. Some moved to cover their noses; others wrinkled up their noses in disgust. One man even curled his lip at the smell.

"What *is* that?" one of them asked.

"Hold your ground!" a male barked. "Hand over the weapon—and the pouch," he demanded. He stood near Seru, where two heavily armored guards held him with their halberds.

It kind of amused her that they thought she stunk. Or did they find it enticing and were unsure how to react to it? Given their desire to stick to their own species. Curious. Not that she asked or let her amusement show. It wasn't like she could control it. Thalasia hovered her hand over her bag as the one had demanded. Her blade had been close enough to it that she'd slipped it inside. Not that she was trying to hide it, more like put it away. Her eyes didn't stray from Seru as she continued to sit there.

"The bag and weapon—NOW!" the male insisted. "Don't make me ask again."

The blades slid in closer to Seru's throat. The spears surrounding Thalasia closed in. If one thing could be said about the dragons, it's that they weren't well-versed in patience.

Seru stayed his ground, looking more annoyed than anything.

Lifting her purse off the ground, she tied the strings tight and tossed it to him. It hadn't been her intention not to comply, she just hadn't heard him correctly. Since the blade was inside the bag, the two would be together. It only left the encased lotus blossom on the floor. Something she'd be fine without. Not like anyone else could use it.

Okay. So, if she hadn't screwed up before, she had this time. Damn dragons—pain in her ever-loving ass. Not that she expected they'd kill either of them. Aurelia still wanted the crystal in her neck. Something she and Seru hadn't discussed how he intended to remove. Gods, she hoped he had some kind of plan or figured something out. She didn't want to be stuck here in the Clouds beyond another twenty-four hours. Not with what she learned from her mother about her pheromones.

One of the female spear-wielders intercepted the bag. She quickly secured the item in a transparent, metal-enforced container.

"On your feet," a guard to her rear prodded her. "Keep your hands visible, and don't even so much as twitch those pretty blue wings of yours."

At a moment like this that she was grateful for the charms on the bag. It would protect the items inside it. Unfortunately, there was the problem of getting it back, but one issue at a time, right? Thalasia got to her feet with ease, her wings remaining tucked back. Where exactly did they think she was going to put her hands? Inside the tight dress that clung to her body?

The same female who'd secured the bag stepped forward. A pair of gilded bands in her palms. "Put out your hands."

Seru shifted as much as the predicament allowed, which wasn't much. One blade nicked his throat, causing him to grimace. The gesture revealed his fangs.

Her entire body tensed. Even the sheen of sweat at the base of her neck barely registered. Gods, she was trying. Saying goodbye to her parents had been one thing, but her past... the memories there in her head. Her eyes met Seru's. She stared into them because it was the only way she'd get through what had to be done. That and several deep breaths. It wasn't precisely like dragons gave a shit about her. Or what was coming at them? More and more, she understood Marius's stance against the sky.

The bands weren't the same. They didn't look the same. Though if the armor the male had on earlier was anything to go by and the fact that someone had forewarned him about her kind. She bit her bottom lip so hard that she tasted the metallic tang of blood as she hesitantly lifted her wrists.

Another dragon closed in from behind while the female secured the metal bands around her wrists and ankles. She could feel the dampening of the shackles. Nothing like that one blade, but it definitely would prevent her from using any magic.

"Open up," the dragon behind her instructed, looping another gilded securement over her head. Another female mirrored the gesture with Seru. The guards buckled the muzzles tightly to their faces, an internal piece slipping between their lips, compressing their tongues—no vocal casting or singing for them. The only difference was that the male behind her also had a length of golden rope for her wings.

All the air in her lungs vanished in an instant. Even focusing on Seru didn't help. Her wings fluttered and pressed closer to her body as she quickly shook her head. No. No. No. No. She couldn't do it. Not the wings. Not her wings. A silent sob wracked her frame, her chest collapsing with each mournful exhale, the ache a dull echo of her sorrow. *Tell me what I wish to know, and your pain will be swift.* Words from years ago replayed in her head.

No, she wasn't there. She wasn't there. Dragons, not bears. Dragons, not bears. No matter what she told herself, it didn't become easier to breathe. The salt stung her skin as she felt the dampness seep into her dress, a silent testament to her inner turmoil. Why couldn't she breathe? Where had all the air gone? Her breathing became more ragged. Her body shook.

Out of nowhere, her mind filled with tranquil recollections of her and Seru's flights. Freedom of the clouds, beneath a heavenly star scape. Her ragged breaths softened, and the frantic pounding in her chest subsided. A calm washed over her, allowing the dragons to secure her wings.

The guards corralled them into the center of the room. Seru bumped Thalasia, a comforting rub of his arm against hers. At least until the butt of a spear jolted him forward. "Single file, Saint Beast," a male sneered. The man ushered Seru forward and out of reach. Seru growled around the mouthpiece, falling silent as they guided him to the front of the procession.

Keeping the images of their flights together in the forefront of her mind, along with the minor bump, helped. More than his attempts in the past, despite the devices locked around them.

Head held high, Seru situated himself in the center of the circle, where he awaited the guards getting into place. Four of them took up posts, removing enough armor to cast from their point. The circle illuminated. The mana from each dragon joined in the center. In a flash of light, Seru disappeared. She was next.

A guard on each flank maneuvered her into position before retreating to the exterior of the circle. The four who'd cast Seru's transport swapped out with a fresh set.

She wouldn't go any other way than with her head up. As far as she was concerned, the *only* person she owed an apology to at the moment was Seru. The images of their flights, among a few others, played on repeat in her head. Their devices would have no impact on the glow of her skin, the sparkle of her eyes, nor her heady scent. That was all her body's natural response. It had nothing to do with magic, but it helped her remain calm in the situation.

The dragons pressed their palms to the circle, channeling their mana through the veins of the design. The circle illuminated once more, casting her into darkness. Soon after, the solid, polished marble beneath her feet transformed into loose, parched soil. The warmth of the palatial city turned to an empty stone cell. One she and Seru shared. He stood against the steep wall, where debris clouded the air.

Thalasia swallowed, her throat constricted by the metal bit. She couldn't focus on the differences. Although little light filtered in from above them, the glow from her body offered some. There hadn't been time for her to determine how much time had passed from the time she'd gone under to when she returned. Even while she'd been there, talking to her parents, the glimmer of her skin had been something that annoyed her. And her scent, gods, it was only going to get worse. Not just as her smell thickened, but in the next day, it would cause her physical pain without appropriately being addressed. That's what her mother told her. Remaining calm, she shot an apologetic look at Seru. She should've listened.

He stared back, a steady blue. His shoulders dropped as he slid to the floor, stirring up more dirt into the air.

She watched him for a moment. Gods, it would be great if she could still repress her pheromones. They likely weren't helping him any, but only serving as an agitation. At least she didn't have to worry about being cold. Her skin was hot and slick. She'd been ready to get out of the dress for a minute.

Closing her eyes, she shifted her focus to the bands around various parts of her body to determine any kind of weakness. Or a way out. A way to remove the piece in her mouth, and the bindings that held her wrists, ankles, and wings in place. Things that hadn't gone unnoticed—they hadn't bothered to remove the pins or comb from her hair. Depending on how the bonds were set, she might use any of these pieces to remove them.

Opening her eyes to an echo throughout the chamber, a diamond stare focused on Seru for a moment. She returned her attention to the locks, working to glean information about how they worked. Although she could follow his movements, the ropes around her wings restricted her. Alright. She went through slight shifts in her body to test the constriction of each bond, from wiggling her ankles to her wrists, minor adjustments in her wings, and then her jaw. It was all she could do to find a way out of the shackles. At least one to start with would be great.

The slight noise Seru made caught her attention. He was trying to say something. Maybe whatever she was doing wouldn't do any good. Okay. Then what would work? She needed out of these things. Something she was positive he understood. Of course, it appeared he was trying to free himself, too. She'd guarantee they agitated him just as much. Breathe. Her heart was racing, though not as intensely as it had before. How long would that last?

He made a show of breathing in and out, slow and deep.

The irony of getting captured a second time wasn't lost on her. It happened almost the same way it had the first time. Yeah, there were differences. No. She couldn't let the past push forward. Not even to look at the differences. It all boiled down to one thing. As her mother put it, her willful and obstinate nature. Fucking idiot was more accurate. Seru had every right to be upset with her, not there trying to keep her calm.

Talking to her parents, letting go was supposed to have been a good thing. Not *this*. Her father's last words replayed in her mind again. Her eyes met those beautiful blue pools of Seru's. *Trust him.* Peace suddenly washed over her. Her breathing eased and grew calm, while the wild thumping in her chest returned to a normal rhythm.

Thalasia blinked. Somehow, he'd used the marks between them to push calm to her. Not that she understood them enough, still to be sure she could do it as well. She thought back to a few nights ago when they nearly ripped the inn apart. As both of their magic had gotten restricted, was there a way they could combine them together? Or somehow use the crystal in her neck? Not that she had any clue how that could be done.

Seru eased back, settling with his back against the wall. He used the stone surface to push himself back to his feet. He walked the space, toe to heel. After a few moments, he located the center and began drawing a complex design with his foot. He took a few careful steps back.

Thalasia watched him. It reminded her of the circle that they'd used to get into the Clouds, along with how she accessed the jump points. Her gaze followed along until an image of Seru, distorted, wavering about, rippling, reached her mind. Her brow knitted together at the memory. It was like looking in a mirror, somewhat skewed, but a mirror nonetheless.

Her eyes lifted to his and then flicked back to the design. She gave him a slight nod, found where everything would line up to help with the composition, and used her foot to create a copy. Not something she'd ever done before, but yeah, she could do the same.

He drew slowly and deliberately, pausing at intervals to give her time to catch up. It wasn't something she'd ever attempted before. Most of the jump points she'd been through weren't this complex.

As they continued to work on such an intricate design, she stole the occasional glance, but not for long. Not that she had to look to feel the toll their slow progress had taken on him. Earlier, he'd used their connection to send calm to her, something that he'd done before but hadn't ever really worked until today.

Any other time she'd gone previously, she always returned feeling drained and slept for days—not this time. She came back more energized and more at peace than she'd ever felt in the past. This connection between them. He told her before that he pulled on her soothing ability, but he always believed it agitated her. She wondered if it had something to do with her trip. Hard to say. But he needed something because she needed—no, they needed each other to get out.

One thing she'd always been fairly decent at: multitasking. As much as she could against their bonds, she sent some energy and some of the soothing he usually pulled on. Since she was uncertain how much of it would help, she didn't want to overwhelm him, so she tried just a little—enough of a nudge that maybe he could pull on it on his own.

A vicious wind kicked up, sweeping their carefully made progress up into a cyclone funnel. The grit abraded their exposed skin. At the center of their former circle, a familiar golden mane caught their attention.

"Are you finished stewing in your new girlfriend's pheromones?" Aurelia asked, her anger and annoyance overshadowed by the self-satisfaction she'd garnered from getting the drop on them.

Although she was a little annoyed by all of their hard work gone, she was more curious *why* Aurelia made an appearance. Was it so she could keep them locked up? A way to trade for the crystal still in her neck? One thing she knew for sure: it wouldn't be to kill her. The tête-à-tête she'd gone through the night before with Aurelia's guards confirmed one thing—those two had made some kind of deal with the sirens. And she highly doubted it was Parthenia. Which meant it had to be the other one. Not that any of it had to do with Aurelia's appearance.

"I'm not sure if I'm more disappointed in *you* for trusting *her*." Aurelia hooked a thumb in Thalasia's direction. "Or if I'm more disappointed in her utter stupidity and lack of diplomatic tact when establishing new relations with species that are not her own." She gave a feigned pause. "Oh, wait... That last bit *was* predictable. So, I guess that just leaves me disappointed in you. You know, I can't figure it out." Aurelia postured. "Is my rise leaving you feeling unnecessary? Do you *need* to fill that vacancy? I thought you hated babysitting fledglings? So, why tie yourself to a baby bird? Is it because she doubles for lunch and needs your attention?"

Why the fuck did they all call her a damn bird? Stupid lizard needed some education in how the rest of the universe worked. Or an attitude adjustment. Maybe both. Wait, she forgot—they were like gods. Thalasia rolled her eyes. Gods that nobody revered. It was a good thing she had a cycle of memories going in the back of her head. It would only hurt her if she let the snob get a rise from her with all her goading.

"Tell you what," Aurelia continued, moving in her direction. "I'll relieve you of your troubles for a while. Give you time to clear your head, reconsider your options." She seized Thalasia by the arm, none too kindly. "If in that time she proves herself useful in some capacity, I'll consider returning her to you and letting you both continue about your silly little charade." A toothy smile graced her face. "If not..." She shrugged a bit theatrically. "Well, then, I guess we'll regroup and re-establish our objectives. Get you back to yourself."

Turning to her without offering either of them much chance to reply, Aurelia glanced down at her destroyed gown. "What a hideous dress. Did you dig that out of your grandmother's armoire?" The blatant disapproval resounded in her tone. In an instant, she'd transported them through space and time. A shimmering light guided them into an enchanted forest. Aurelia quickly reached behind Thalasia's head, undoing the clasp that held the muzzle in place before she could even orient herself. Tossing the binding aside, Aurelia's expression became sterner. "I'm uncuffing you, but don't think that means you can just fly off. I've got an offer to make, so pay attention."

Unwinding her jaw, Thalasia shifted her tongue, trying to dislodge the unpleasant flavor. She'd considered a snarky response telling Aurelia she'd pulled the dress out of Aurelia's closet, but decided against it. That they were now in the fae forest—a thousand questions popped into her head. An offer? Her eyebrows knitted together. "You want something." It could be to her benefit, depending on what Aurelia asked. That concerned her—a lot. While she wanted the ties and cuffs off, she watched Aurelia like a hawk. No, she didn't trust her. Even less than the first day they met.

"Obviously," Aurelia replied deadpan. "Your ability to... realm jump... Does it extend to other planes of existence?"

Oh, she didn't like where this was going. Although she was confident, the guards hadn't realized where she'd been when they showed up out of nowhere. Maybe Aurelia just made an automatic assumption. At least she could work this to her advantage, though. "Yes." Her gaze didn't leave Aurelia.

"Great," Aurelia granted her a too-bright smile. "You're going to reclaim a precious artifact for me. In return, I'll pardon your crimes," Aurelia stated. The metal bands sprang open with a loud *snap* and then tumbled noisily onto the grass. "Sound like a deal you can work with, bluey?"

Oh yeah, because going to another plane was just *so* damn simple. Good gods, the female didn't know shit, did she? Thalasia dismissed the matter of the crime, shaking out her limbs and preening her feathers. "I need some details. A *lot* of details. I'll also need my bag." It would be the only way to counteract the issues traveling to another plane often caused. "What plane? And then specifics of both the artifact and location would be necessary as well." That wasn't the only thing, but it was a beginning.

Aurelia blinked, as if caught off-guard by the strict business demeanor. "This bag?" The female held up the purse the guards had lifted from her earlier. She tossed it to her. "The rift between worlds," Aurelia offered. "A realm the reapers use to ferry souls, where their fates are judged before they're sent off to the celestial or abyssal plane. The artifact is a sacred flame stolen by the rainbow crow. Now, a dark horse bird. From our kingdom during the war."

Yeah, that bag, Thalasia thought to herself as she caught the bag. A rift between worlds. Joy.

The female produced a slender metal band, one like Seru's collar, and held it out to her. "Once you've obtained the flame and returned to the isle, use this to regain access to the Clouds—more specifically, a sacred chamber in the high temple, exclusively for this very artifact. Place the flame on the Brazier. The collar will allow you to walk about freely without further hindrance from my guard. Rest assured; they'll be watching you but won't retake you unless ordered to do so..." she trailed off. "I'll receive you in the throne room once you're finished. And before it crosses your mind to deceive me, the Brazier won't accept any flame but the one. Try anything funny and this," she lifted the band. "Will do so much worse to you than Seru's collar does to him. Your siren friends will have to find a new savior. Try not to incinerate yourself."

She didn't care too much about the idea of a collar. However, it could offer some insight into Seru's. Sort of. Not likely. Although the concept of a collar really, really annoyed her. She crossed her arms. "And the collar comes off when our deal is done." A slight smirk settled on her face. "Let me be very specific; it comes off when I get to the throne room. At *that* point, we're finished."

As she thought over the details provided, their current location made little sense. Unless... they were close to some place where she could easily cross over. She refused to take the collar until she had confirmation of when it would come off. It could go in her bag, since it definitely wouldn't be required until she made it back in one piece. Gods, there were issues she could see already.

"That's right," Aurelia assented, folding her arms across her chest. "*Your* collar comes off once I'm satisfied the service has been rendered. Unless, of course, you care to pay a few more visits to the people of my kingdom before you're through."

Oh, she expected that clarification. But considering where the female wanted her to go, negotiations were far from over. "While

I'm making this... trip... for you, Seru gets let out of the cell and the shackles removed, provided that hasn't already occurred." Thalasia held up a finger. "*That* is not negotiable. You're asking me to go someplace I could not only end up trapped, but you haven't uttered one word about what it would take to retrieve this artifact." Although the amulet she intended to put on would offer her aid, it wouldn't fully protect her from the in-between.

Aurelia settled back on her heels, hands shifting to her hips as she stood tongue in cheek. She eyed Thalasia suspiciously. "You realize he's my Regent. How do you think my imprisoning him looks to the dragons of my kingdom? Much less the other kingdoms? Besides," she sneered. "You only get trapped or maimed if you're incapable of your only redeeming quality—thief." She paced the grassy clearing a bit. "As for the retrieval, I don't know... I've never been to the rift between. *Obviously*. Seems rather witless to state the obvious: Avoid the scythes."

"You'll have to forgive me if I don't trust you. Or your judgment calls. Not like we're besties or anything." She bit back the groan. Nor did she believe Aurelia cared all that much about Seru, or at least not as much as others. Thalasia dragged a hand down her face, wiping sweat from her forehead. "You can know things about places you've never been." There were things she knew about realms, even Prisma Isle, and this was her first trip there. Gods, how was this female expected to ascend? And she was supposed to be older than her? By what? Five seconds?

"Why are we in this part of the forest, Aurelia?" The woman had to know something. More than what she'd given her, especially if she had to steal the damn thing with next to nothing to go by.

"Right... because I'm not over 200 years your senior—most of that time spent being groomed to rule," Aurelia brushed her off. "Because you believe simply being commands respect for you courtesy of your rather unique species. I could guess, but as much as I loathe you, I need you to return. However, many pieces you're in are really up to you." She bounced back on her heels, sweeping a hand behind her. "Because... This is where he crosses over. Are you truly this much of a bimbo? Or are you just assuming I can form a lesser opinion of you than I already have? I might also have avoided giving Seru the opportunity to draw on your..." she tapped the side of her neck. "It really shouldn't surprise you to learn he's completely duped you. You realize that, don't you?"

Thalasia grinned, kicked off her shoes, and felt the cool blades of grass tickle her bare toes. That felt great. "I don't give a shit *what* you think of me. Unlike you, I prefer not to make assumptions about a place, especially with as little as you've given me on this sacred flame." She removed the earrings, necklace, and hair comb and returned them to her purse. No, he hadn't duped her. Maybe she hadn't known everything she had gotten into, but with the crystal or symbol on her neck, that she expected. She retrieved the dress she'd gotten from that shop over a week ago. While it wasn't what she intended to use it for, it was the best option she had in her bag.

As much as she hated the idea of changing in front of Aurelia, or in the middle of a clearing, she didn't trust the female enough to turn her back. Slipping the dress straps down her shoulders, she attempted to use the connection to nudge Seru. She had no clue if it would work, but there wasn't any other way to check on him.

"You *believe* you're 'marked' and tied to him because... what? He conducted some... ritual? You really don't give him enough credit. He'll spoon-feed you lies till the drakes come home, if it gets him what he wants."

No. There was more to it than that. There had been a time or two that she'd questioned whether or not he truly felt something for her, but then she'd catch the way he looked at her. Nothing Aurelia could say would make her doubt that. With both the destroyed dress and underwear off, she tugged on the other dress and shoved them into the bag. Then she located the sun pendant and draped it over her neck, tucking it into the valley of her breasts. Thankfully, the chain was long enough that she could do so. "Come on, Aurelia. Let's not pretend this is anything more than what it is."

Aurelia shrugged. "Hey, I've done you favors on multiple occasions; if you wanna keep ignoring them—that's on you. Just try not to be surprised or devastated when his deceptions—not him—bite you on the tail feather." She eyed the sun charm until it disappeared. Aurelia's eyes found hers soon after. "For the record, dragons don't mark prey, which you definitely are. And there's no... elaborate ritual to bind two parties together in eternal mush. He's fucking with your head by fucking with your heart because he can read you well enough to know what you desire. It doesn't take a genius to realize someone like you is obviously lonely... bouncing from place to place doesn't really leave room for friends or tagalongs. Sharing yourself in any capacity with someone in any sort of meaningful way. So, he lets you buy into the fantasy that he'll be that unobtainable thing for you. Because then he's got you, right? You and all your powers. In case that wasn't clear enough, he's not interested in you. He wants your abilities at his disposal. He doesn't even like women."

Oh, yeah. He wasn't attracted to women. It took everything in her not to roll her eyes or let her face reveal her thoughts on that. Thalasia dug out a pair of simple sandals that tied up around her ankles. Still nothing from Seru, but it was a shot in the dark. She hoped he was okay. He hadn't looked well in the hole. Her gaze flicked to her skin. There was still a slight glow to it—nothing she could do to change that. Hopefully, it benefited her. She removed the dagger from her purse, pricked her finger while kneeling on her haunches, and let a few droplets hit the ground.

Aurelia could talk until she was blue in the face. The only thing she cared about was getting this damn flame and returning safely. She carved a symbol out into the dirt using her bloody finger and then pressed her hand over it to seal it. It wasn't the preferred anchor, but it would suffice under the circumstances. "Looks can deceive, Aurelia. Honestly, I figured you, of all people, would know that much."

"Flyboy wasn't lying about your..." she gestured to the musk in the air and the glow of Thalasia's skin. "Whatever you call your sensory mating call. His looks or yours?" Aurelia asked. "I'm still not convinced you're not a flock of colorful chickens. Seru, he's physically pleasing if you overlook the collar. Much more stimulating if you enjoy his infinite knowledge and lectures. Emotionally, he's the equivalent of a belly-up snake in the dirt baked by the sun."

"Both," Thalasia said simply. Yes, he was physically pleasing to look at, but she'd never really noticed males before. Not that she hadn't seen them. She just hadn't paid them much attention. And there were a lot of things he stimulated, challenged, amongst other things. With her scent, it was something Seru seemed to enjoy. Rising to her feet, she returned her dagger to her bag and found the compass. "In case you haven't figured it out, that's a rhetorical question. You believe what you believe." She held her hand out for the collar. "And it's fine by me. Just remember, you're asking prey to retrieve something you need."

"Yep," Aurelia replied, popping the P as she handed over the collar. "Once you're through, he's definitely free to eat you. You will *not* be missed."

"Yeah. I won't miss you either when I leave this rock." Thalasia tucked the collar into her bag and retrieved the compass. It would show her the exact spot to go. She opened it, her gaze flicking back and forth between the needle and Aurelia.

"Great," Aurelia forced a smile. "Once you do—for good, I mean—don't bother coming back."

"Wasn't planning on it." Like there would be a need. Nope. Once she got herself, Seru, and the crew off this rock, there definitely wouldn't be any coming back. At least not here. Her gaze dropped back to the compass, inhaling and exhaling a deep breath as she focused on the needle.

"Do be quick," Aurelia encouraged, using her magic to disappear. Back to the Clouds, no doubt.

Oh, yeah. That said *so* much about how little the female understood of other planes and the passing of time. She couldn't let that bitch get under her skin. There were a lot of things she wondered about this sacred flame. Information she wouldn't get. Her gaze dropped to the compass. The needle finally settled, directing her toward a shimmer. Thalasia returned it to her bag and tied it to the inside of her dress before she strode forward, making her way toward the in-between.

Chapter Forty-Three

"Are you ready to quit? You won't out-drink him," Cipriana said as she crossed her arms.

"Watch me." Her confident predictions of his downfall sparked a triumphant fire within him, a defiant grin spreading across Mac's face. Though, they were already several pints of ale deep and he was quite certain he'd tumble if he tried to stand.

"Come on, laddie. We're not there yet!" With a thunderous sound, King Kihrig placed two more overflowing tankards of ale upon the table. He turned his attention to Cipriana. "How do ya feel about partaking in a drink, lassie?"

Cipriana held up her hands. "Oh no. I'm good, just watching."

"Then what will ya do, lassie?"

That was a good question. Mac grinned wide as his eyes settled on her face. She had threatened to smack, slap, and elbow him several times in the last couple of days. Not that she'd followed through. After what he was about to suggest, she very well might. "She should sing."

"What? Oh no, I... I couldn't." Narrowing her hazel-brown eyes at him, Cipriana glowered. "I wouldn't even know what to sing."

"It's a celebration!" King Kihrig raised his glass, the clinking sound echoing in the hall. "Sing!"

The group of dwarves they'd hung around echoed his response. Kihrig had introduced many of them before they'd sat down, but he couldn't remember a single name at the moment. Mac joined in and hefted his mug up. "Sing!"

Reluctantly, Cipriana stood. She brought her face near his ear, her breath warm against his skin. "I'm *going* to kill you," she said through gritted teeth.

"I'd like to see you try, sweetheart." He took a large, satisfying drink of ale. She made it too easy to tease her sometimes. And he enjoyed it more than he thought possible. It was her snarky threats. Even the way she glared at him. Good gods, something was wrong with him.

Before he could react, she snatched the mug of ale from his grasp and drained the remaining contents in one go. She set the empty stein down, then opened her mouth and powerfully sang a tune completely new to his ears. She spoke of a male who had been wrongfully arrested on a winter's night for robbery.

Yeah, *that* sounded cheerful. Mac surveyed the room while Cipriana's fingers playfully traced patterns on his shoulders. A thrilling current coursed through his veins, a bubbling excitement that made his whole body buzz. His gaze flicked back to her. That had to be on purpose; no way she'd done it by accident. He listened as her voice bounced off the stone walls, continuing to sing of a male who'd been found guilty and sentenced to ten years in prison. Without an alibi tomorrow, he'd mourn the loss of his freedom.

Curious. He smiled as she clapped her hands, her rhythm matching the song's quickening tempo. She moved into the chorus, singing about how he'd count the days for the next ten years but return home one day. As the melody shifted and the chorus intensified, a rhythmic clamor of mugs striking rough wooden tables erupted from the dwarves. While he may not have known the song, it seemed they did because they all joined in. Mac glanced at Cipriana. Her entire face lit up as she continued with the song, slowly making her way around the room.

In the second verse, the man's alibi became clear. He'd been with his best friend's wife, but at the risk of losing everything, he remained silent. His eyes widened. Well, he didn't see that coming. The dwarves, unfazed, continued banging their mugs in rhythm with her renewed singing as she launched into the chorus. Mac collected his empty stein and accompanied the noise.

"Over the hills and," Cipriana sang repeatedly. The voices of those gathered mingled with hers four or five times. Then she belted out, "Over the hills and far away," before progressing into the next verse. Each day the man looked through the bars, reading the letters his love had written to him, holding out for when he'd get released and one day return to her.

Her voice rose in song, and the chorus swelled as he and the dwarves added their voices and steady beat. Their voices mixed with hers through the last line of the song. They all raised their mugs and cheered. Mac whistled and shouted, "Woo! Woo!" While he couldn't say for sure if she used her power at all, all of those there seemed to enjoy the performance she'd given.

Failing to hide the flush in her cheeks, Cipriana returned to her seat next to him.

"Another round!" Kihrig hollered.

Without a moment for them to object, three frothy steins of ale materialized in front of them. Mac hoisted his mug in the air. "To Cipriana!"

Everyone echoed his toast, and then someone else broke out in song.

It was nice to see her a little more carefree and less worried about what kind of Elder she would be. According to what he'd learned, she'd already successfully negotiated a peace treaty with three different leaders. Okay, one of them was him, but he was reasonably sure Maggie would find the terms agreeable. Grinning as she raised her glass in response, he downed half the ale in his mug. Mac set his drink on the table and held out his hand. "Come on. Let's dance."

"What? Oh no. You got me to sing. Isn't that enough for one night?"

"Not at all." He pushed himself up, his balance faltering for a moment, but he regained his footing before he could land ungracefully. "I'm good. I got it." Maybe this wasn't such a great idea. Damn. He hadn't drunk that much. How strong was this stuff? He slowly adjusted his stance, his muscles tensing as he straightened himself. Somehow, he missed a step or his talons caught, resulting in his face contacting the floor.

Cipriana giggled. "Are you sure?"

With a grunt, Mac propped himself up, rubbed his throbbing nose, and then flopped onto his back. Alright. He didn't have it. Afraid he might make a bigger fool of himself, he lay there on the ground for a minute.

"Are you planning—"

"Ya should quit drinkin', laddie." Kihrig cut off Cipriana's words as he hooked his hand beneath Mac's armpit and hefted him to his feet.

The world was a blur, spinning erratically. With a chuckle, he looked over at the king. "But we were doing so good."

"Ya think so? I'm already five ahead o'ya, laddie." Kihrig laughed.

"Here. Let me take him. If someone can just show us to our quarters, I'll make sure he gets to bed," Cipriana said as she slid a shoulder under his arm.

"You just want to be close to me," he whispered loudly to her. "But I like it."

"Aye."

He didn't completely recognize what was happening, but they started walking. And he had his arm draped around his mate's—did he just think that? No. No way he thought of Cipriana as his mate. Yeah, he liked her *a lot*, but that didn't make her his, did it? Mac buried his face in the crook of her neck, the soft skin yielding to his gentle sniff. "You smell excellent. Like the ocean breeze."

"That's good to know."

"You sing beautifully, too." Regardless of the song, she sounded like an angel. It had been a long time since he heard anyone with a voice so divine. "Just as exquisite as my mother when she sang."

"Thank you." She paused. "Do you miss her?"

"Yes... every day." It didn't lessen how he viewed Felix. The male had raised him, and he'd lost him, too. He felt a sting in his eyes and hastily brushed away the tears that threatened to fall. His gaze flicked back to the female currently keeping him upright. "I think she would've liked you."

"Oh?"

"Yeah." A wide grin spread across his face. "She was a bit of a spitfire, too." At least, that was the term his father often used to describe his mother. He always believed he took after her in a lot of ways. At least her personality. Physically, he looked like his father.

"I'm not sure if I should feel complimented or offended." Cipriana laughed with a slight shake of her head.

"Complimented definitely." Despite his slightly swaying steps, he pressed a kiss to the top of her head. Someone else said something, but he didn't quite catch the words. He was too busy focusing on Cipriana. The way her smile illuminated her features.

"Come on. In here." She ushered him into a small room with a bed, a couch, and, likely, a bathroom. "You can sleep on the bed, and I'll take the couch."

"No, no, no, no, no. I'll sleep on the bed, and you'll take the couch. No... wait. I meant you get the bed, and I'll use the couch." Yeah. That's precisely what he intended. In absolutely no way would he *ever* allow her to sleep on the couch. She deserved better than that. To prove his point, he removed his arm from around her shoulders and staggered toward the sofa. He went to sit, missed the cushion, and his ass hit the floor with a thud. Mac laughed.

With a slight chuckle, she closed the door and kneeled beside him. "Are you okay?"

"My ass hurts." He erupted in laughter once more, the sound echoing around him. Not that he could even explain why that was funny. It just was.

"I'm sure it does. Can we get you on the couch now?"

"Yes." he nodded his response but stopped. The way his head sloshed around; it didn't seem like a good idea.

"Okay." It took a bit of effort; however, they got him safely lounging. She stroked his cheek. "I'm not sure if it was just the alcohol or if you're this crazy, but thank you. I had a good night." Cipriana pressed her lips to his, a gentle, lingering touch. "Now go to sleep. We have another day of travel tomorrow."

Another smile tugged at the corners of his mouth. "Yes, ma'am." She didn't have to tell him twice. Not only had he gotten to hear her sing, but the laughter and the look on her face, along with the kiss... Maybe he had found his mate.

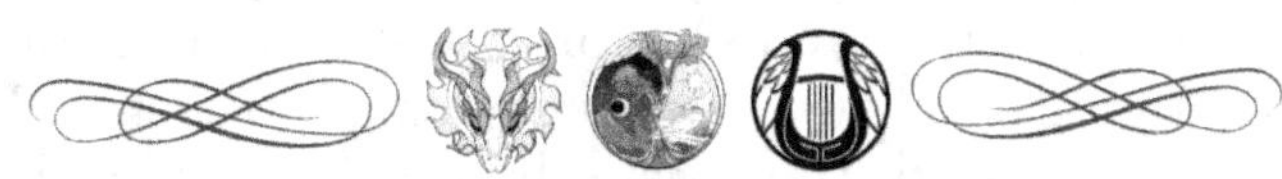

As the doors abruptly opened, the guards stepped aside. Seru's gaze settled on Thalasia as she entered the throne room, but he didn't move to go to her. He noted how all eyes fixated on her as she approached the throne, where Aurelia sat on the gilded chair, poised at the highest point in the room, and remained in discussion with him. The Saint Beast wore a fresh set of finely embellished silk in his trademark midnight blue with silver accents. He looked every part the royal advisor and regent he was expected to be, conveniently, with no visible weapons on his person.

Aurelia reclined back in her throne, tapping talons over the arm. A sly grin crept over her features. "Took your sweet time, bluebird," her voice echoed, bouncing off the marble. "I take it you completed your task?"

"Yes, it is done." The luminescence that had covered her skin had become lackluster. Even her scent had diminished a bit. Her gaze flicked to Seru briefly.

Aurelia uncrossed her legs and disappeared, leaving them alone in the throne room, surrounded by golden guards.

Seru gave it a moment before rising from his place and descending one platform at a time. The throne through three tiers of nobility to the floor, where orators aired their concerns before the court. With court out of session, it felt like a void, vast and empty. Every sound echoed, resounding off every surface, amplifying.

He handed off a scroll of parchment to the plain-clothed scribe. He proceeded toward Thalasia, each step intentionally paced. His eyes searched her from head to toe before settling on her face. Doubt and concern played in the shallow pools of his eyes. "What did you do?" he asked in a hoarse whisper.

"The sacred flame," she responded, her voice low, as she lifted her eyes to his. "I had no choice."

"Sacred flame?" Seru whispered. His eyes darted back and forth as he ran over potential answers in his mind. He was still assessing her condition as he thought it through. His hand reflexively took up hers, his thumb moving in soothing circles along the back. "Are you alright?"

"I'm just exhausted. I need to rest and eat." Her eyes focused on him, taking in as much as she could. "Are you okay?"

He nodded curtly. Completely alert, his eyes never stopped scanning the room, assessing each Draconic soldier and counting their weapons. Gauging strengths and likely attack patterns. Identifying escape routes. "With the mask off, I'm fine." Simple as that, whether or not it was a shadow of truth. He toyed with the idea of staying, allowing her to rest before they moved on. But somehow, he knew she wouldn't be able to until they'd left the Clouds. Even then, the repercussions from their brief captivity were likely to rear their ugly head.

Realizing he'd taken up her hand—her comforting squeeze barely registering—he promptly released it. The last thing they needed was attention garnered by ridiculous sentiments.

In a flash, Aurelia reappeared, seemingly satisfied with the result of Thalasia's task. "Sure you don't want to keep the matching collar?"

Seru stiffened, his eyes finally falling on the golden band secured around her neck. Surprise and alarm registered over his features before he could stop it. How had he missed that?! "Take it off her! Please..." his snarl forcibly softened by the end. But it remained enough to provoke the guards into readying their weapons.

Aurelia placed her hands on her hips, scrutinizing him. "I didn't even realize begging was in your skill set."

Seru shied back from the affront. Neither had he. Only the earth-bound asked, nicely requested politely, with any hope of eliciting action.

Keeping one eye on him, Thalasia looked at Aurelia. "No... Matriarch," the words came out perfectly polite and without her usual attitude. "I've held up my end of our agreement; it's time you held up yours."

"You say that like I've consistently done the opposite," Aurelia replied, narrowing her eyes. The violet of her irises sparkled, her magic manifesting as she projected just enough to penetrate the channels in Thalasia's collar. An audible click released the band, sending it clattering between her feet.

Seru bowed in gratitude. He nodded to Thalasia. "We'll be on our way. You'll have the violet crystal returned to you before the agreed-upon time." Without waiting for a response, he strode from the throne room. They both wanted out of here as quickly as possible, where they ended up meaning precious little so long as it wasn't the Clouds or another Draconic domain. Thalasia trailed behind him, sticking as tight to his heels as she could.

The enormous metal doors rumbled shut behind them. The mural of mythos left to stare at their retreating backs. He followed the curved hall around to the pathway that led them down from the Regal Crescent into the dispersing fray of the exchange. His steps slowed as soon as they hit the sales floor, permitting Thalasia to catch up to his long strides.

Seru rolled his shoulders ever so slightly. The perfect posture while at court, following their miserable prison sentence, had left him tense and stiff. The throbbing pain between his shoulder blades surged upward, reaching his neck and then settling at the base of his skull. He felt a soothing sensation come from Thalasia through their link.

His steps halted abruptly. "Did you not just admit you were exhausted?" he whispered harshly. "I'm fine. Reserve your strength. We still need to get back on land and begin making our way to your—*the* sirens in Pteryrina. You don't have the energy to spare, and I'd rather not carry you if it's all the same."

Thalasia nearly plowed into him. She raised an eyebrow. "Here, I thought you couldn't hear my thoughts." A faint smirk played on her lips.

He scrunched up his brow. "I can't hear your thoughts," he clarified. "But you've consistently attempted to run off there since you've arrived, and after meeting their ambassador in Migas, I think it's high time we visit them. If they're truly seeking new alliances and suing for peace, there should be no problem in our requesting an audience on behalf of the Atlis and the Clouds."

"I was talking about my exhaustion." Her forehead wrinkled. "Yeah, I'm pretty sure they already have some kind of deal in place with at least one of those." Before he could ask her to explain, she interjected, "Not here. Just keep going."

He frowned. "You don't even know where I'm going."

"Do I need to?"

Try as he might, he still couldn't bring himself to understand her level of blind trust. No matter what she got herself into, surviving by the skin of her teeth seemed to be enough for her. He brushed the back of his hand over his forehead, willing away the building frustration. Without another word and with a heavy sigh, he turned and resumed his trek through the palatial halls.

He led them back through to another obscure transport circle. He'd already taken time to tidy and lock up the library while Thalasia went on her mission for Aurelia. While it had been difficult with her hovering right over his shoulder, he'd also destroyed a few tidbits, information he didn't want her getting her talons into while he was away. She'd breached the library's security—though he didn't know how—and had been rifling through his things. She'd made that evident when confronting him upon her return. He wasn't taking further chances with the less secure items that might solidify what she already suspected.

Gesturing for Thalasia to take her place at the center of the circle, he stood back and waited patiently for her to comply. She stepped into the center of the circle without question or hesitation.

"Mind your wings," he instructed, placing his palm flush to the marble. His other hand came up to readjust the tightened collar with an irritated sigh. The circle flashed a brilliant blue, transporting Thalasia to the dank tunnels of caverns concealed within the cliff-side beneath the Clouds. The same caverns she'd hoped to camp out in hours after she had crash-landed on the beach.

Another blue flash and Seru entered the narrow underground tunnel. "This way," he said, turning to traverse the winding pathways. His eyes changed lenses to accommodate the pitch darkness, so it took him no time at all to get his bearings. The tunnels were old friends, passageways he knew better than any person. "Be careful; it gets slippery farther down. The tides flood the lower levels regularly."

"Got it." She followed him. Sandals probably weren't the best option in these tunnels, but she seemed to manage.

Left, left, right, left, right. Stop. Overhead, a cluster of unusual glow-worms marked the archway. He waited for Thalasia to step through before guiding her back underneath.

As they stepped back through, the tunnel morphed into a spacious room, illuminated by intricate designs etched into the walls. Seru left Thalasia by the entryway. He proceeded to the far wall, to a barren patch absent of the luminous designs. He glanced back at Thalasia, her weariness weighing her down to the point she seemed ready to collapse.

He shook his head, acknowledging that this might well be the worst sort of idea before opting to do it, anyway. He traced a predetermined pattern over the wall. The spell housed in the stone activated, sending ripples over the surface as if it had turned to water. He reached through the wall into the liquid space. His hand quickly located the desired object and removed it.

In his hand, a hefty leather-bound tome—the same one she'd searched for in the booby-trapped stretch behind the waterfall. *Celestimo.* He tucked the book under his arm, heading back in her direction to retrace his steps, guided more by the magic than the physical pathways.

She remained still, her eyes scanning the surroundings until they returned to him. Her gaze fell to the book. Thalasia opened her mouth and snapped it shut.

"Yes, I made a bargain for an item I already had in my possession. You can stop gawking now," he grumbled. "We'll unlock it later. For now, we need to return to the circle and use it to make our way back to the inn."

"That's not what I was thinking." Not that she further explained herself. "The inn, okay."

His eyes slid back to her. "Can you make it, or should I carry you, too?"

"I'm okay, as long as I have the pendant on. Just don't be surprised if I pass out the second it comes off."

Seru nodded, setting his jaw. Now was not the time to barrage her. Instead, he continued on their way in silence. She'd seemed to enjoy that earlier.

Thalasia rubbed her forehead as they walked along quietly.

He spared little time in transporting them to the secluded alleyways near the inn they'd continued to frequent time after time. Seru wandered his way back to the inn, paying for a room on the second floor. No need to force her up more stairs than necessary. Besides, if reconstruction had begun, the third level would likely be cordoned off and too exposed to the elements, too hazardous.

Seru unlocked the door to their assigned room, allowing her in first. His eyes followed her as he moved to shut the door, giving them privacy. The dress she wore hadn't escaped his notice. "Where'd you get that dress?"

Halfway to the bed, she stopped and glanced back at him. Her eyes narrowed at him in confusion. Slowly, she faced him. "That shop... here in the marketplace."

"I thought you'd abandoned it," he said, eyeing her curiously. He shook his head in dismay. "Forget it; it doesn't matter. Go to bed. Get some rest." Laying claim to the writing desk in the room, he set *Celestimo* atop it. He settled into the chair, determined to keep the book in his sight and possession until she opened it. He'd allow her to rest first. Keep watch over her, too.

"I did. It was in my room when I got to the inn." She strode over to the bed, removed the purse from the inside of the dress, along with her sandals. While she tossed the shoes aside, she set her bag on the nightstand. Dragging a hand down her face, her gaze flicked to the bathroom. She sat there on the edge of the bed for a moment before she pushed up to her feet.

"You didn't find that... odd?" he asked, tracking her movements. It didn't surprise him that she desired a bath, but with the way her pheromones had overwhelmed them both in the sky cell, he wasn't sure if he should follow or stay. He changed positions in lieu of his indecision. "Do you wish me to come in with you, or can you guarantee you won't drown?"

She paused in the bathroom doorway. "If you're asking whether or not I'll drown myself, the answer is no. As for you coming with me... honestly, I'm in no position to decide right now. So, the choice is yours." Saying nothing else, she disappeared into the bathroom.

His eyes stayed fixed on her, even as the roar of rushing water filled the air, then the rustle of fabric followed. His long, powerful strides quickly shortened the space separating him from the bathroom entrance. Despite his better judgment, he remained transfixed, unable to move from his position in the doorway. He placed his back against the jamb, facing away from her in some futile effort to prevent his body from acknowledging her. More specifically, her state of undress. He slid to the floor, his height and long legs making it nearly impossible to find a comfortable position. He settled for tucking one knee against his chest while stretching the other out into the bedroom. His spine rested against the wooden doorframe, granting some release of the built-up tension as he pressed back into it. A tired groan escaped him in a sigh.

The faucet shut off, and the water sloshed around as Thalasia climbed into the tub. "It's bad, isn't it?"

"Which part?" Seru inquired, briefly allowing his lids to drop to rest his eyes.

"I'd say all of it, except it all seems to have just compounded on each other."

Seru rumbled, scratching beneath his mane with the sharp tips of his talons. He said nothing in response to her assessment. Would granting her room to consider the consequences of the pursuit of certain lines of decision help her understand the gravity of it all? Would it improve future choices? So far, the answers were no and hell no.

"I fucked up," Thalasia whispered.

The salty scent of her tears permeated the air. "Crying about it won't help," he offered, barely audible. "Nor will indulging my rage," he tacked on, resettling. "Emotion clouds judgment and leads to poor decision-making. A luxury we cannot continue to afford."

"Yeah... I'm sure that was something she was counting on. My emotional attachment to you." He heard the gentle swish of water, the soft thud of feet on the floor, and the gurgle of water spiraling down the drain. A gentle rustle, like soft cloth whispering against skin, reached his ears. "Is she right? That the only thing you care about is my power?"

His brow knit together; he hazarded a glance over his shoulder. "You're referencing Aurelia?" He bit back a bitter laugh. "She's the least of our worries. We came to an agreement before she freed me. Similar to how she ferried you away to conduct her little heist." He saw little point in going into details at length. What was done was done, and they were both exhausted—drained seemed more accurate. Curse those dampening technologies crafted by the dragons. What an odd question. "Power breeds advantage. Especially in an environment as laden with it as the Clouds. Dragons possess the rawest magical and physical strength of any species on this isle. It's not the *only* asset of importance. But it's certainly up there. Why do you ask?"

"Because... regardless of what my father said, I'm not sure how much to trust myself anymore. Let alone you. Your choices affect mine." Thalasia partially shrugged. "For all I know... she could be right. That you're just waiting for... I believe, as she put it, 'the drakes to come home' and that you'll lie to me to get what you want. Play on my lonely heart because you just want access to my abilities. Yeah, she was wrong about one thing. And yeah, this connection I feel to you, I can't explain it even when it seems like I've known you for longer than I've been alive. But I just..." She shook her head. "I don't know. Forget I said anything." She turned back, her entire focus shifting to the meticulous task of drying her waterlogged feathers.

He heaved himself from the floor, using the jamb for support as he turned to face her. He glued his back to the opposing side. "No. Your father is dead," Seru pronounced after a thoughtful pause. "That's where you ventured with that..." he gestured absently in the air, searching for the words. "That lotus bauble you fed your blood."

"Yes. The lotus blossom allowed me to speak with my parents' spirits. There were things I needed to understand." Her fingers stilled. "The last thing he said to me... you might be difficult, but to trust you. That you would keep me safe."

"Just like those at the lake... used by that skinchanger. The one who undoubtedly gifted you that dress." His voice darkened with each passing accusation. "How do you know it's not just another illusion, a trick of your mind... playing off your memories?"

He shook his head, the pressure behind his eyes growing. A visible static crept along his skin. "Do you know what these artifacts are capable of *before* you play around with them? Or do you simply toy with them and hope for the best? You'll argue and protest that you make sound decisions. That your decisions are based on *my* decisions. But every time we encounter a problem, or a 'fuck up' as you so eloquently put it, it stems from recklessness, impulse, poor and... or uninformed choices, which then result in very predictable retaliation at our expense. Breaking the goddamned puzzle isn't working. Going behind my back—after I specifically instructed you not to—just so you could have the satisfaction of doing so to prove that you can take care of yourself, you don't need me or anyone—" He cut himself short as the pain in his skull intensified. He forced a slow breath through his mouth—calm, anything but collected.

"I can protect you until one or both of us dies... at which point, I'm not sure it really matters." He paced into the bedroom, turning on his heel about midway. "As far as trusting me, I've encouraged you not to. I don't trust myself. I can't. As I'm sure, Ione told you. Your ancestors also have a history of unreliability paired with ulterior motives. Despite that, you're relying on these images of your very dead parents to offer you insight and epiphany? I don't even know where to help you realize the depth of delusion and subsequent oversights." He stilled, both hands buried in his mane. Eyes squeezed shut until the red manifested in force. "None of this is *safe*. And it's a fool's errand ever to believe it will be."

Wrapped in a towel, Thalasia appeared in the doorway, her hair still slick with water. "That's what you think? That every decision I make is impulsive and uninformed?" She paused. "Let me clarify a few things. One, I researched the hell out of that lotus blossom when I received it four years ago. It isn't something I just use all willy-nilly. As for talking to the dragon, it wasn't to prove that I could take care of myself. No. I did that because anytime I ask you questions or try to get *some* kind of answer from you, you get pissed off and walk away."

Her words didn't have the same anger behind them as his had. "And, yes, my ancestors are just as great as the dragons at hiding their dirty laundry." She smirked. "And if it's such a fool's errand, then leave. I didn't ask you to decide you'd protect me. I didn't ask you to come back with me." Grabbing hold of the bathroom door, she turned to disappear back inside but paused. "Oh, and Ione... she didn't utter a single word about *not* trusting you. It never came up. The only things we talked about were that damn contraption around your neck and your bond to Aurelia." She spun around on the back of her heel and slammed the bathroom door shut.

"And did she provide you with adequate answers to your questions?" he asked. "Or did she tell you what you wanted to hear? Your actions did little more than invite additional trouble our way, but I suppose you know better than I. You're the great prophesied Atlis. Ione is naïve in her own way, but she's proven herself clever in more ways than one. Her information is useful in more instances than not."

Thalasia yanked the bathroom door open. "And I suppose you played no part in that, right? You're so busy blaming everyone else; don't you think it's time you owned up to your own decisions or indecisions as you're pretty good at doing both. I'm sorry, that's right, I forgot. The big, badass saint beast is never wrong." With a flick of her wrist, she sent the towel skittering across the floor and strode purposefully toward the waiting bed. She settled onto the bed, the soft mattress yielding beneath her, then untangled the sun pendant from her hair, its intricate design catching the light before she tucked it away in her bag. Then she lay down and rolled over, giving him her back.

He retreated to the desk, swiped up the book, and decided it was best to give her space. He was going to take a walk and get some much-needed fresh air.

Chapter Forty-Four

D espite her pheromones rearing their ugly head, Thalasia made it down the stairs and to a booth. After ordering her breakfast, her eyes landed on Seru at the bar, his nose buried in a peculiar-looking herb. Keeping a firm grip on the book, he pushed off the bar. The stool slid back, toppling over as he fled the bar. He discarded the herb. *Damn it.* She got to her feet and followed in the direction she'd seen his blurred form head off in.

Thalasia took to the air. It was the only way to see where he was going. They needed to figure everything out. Time was of the essence. While she recognized it, maybe he didn't. Or maybe he did. Either way, they couldn't afford to fight any longer. Which meant one of them had to bend. If last night was anything to go by, it wouldn't be him. Though she hoped that if she laid out the consequences of the direction they were going in, maybe something inside him would realize that they had to work together. Even if it meant they had to lay down some rules. Something they could both agree to because that was the only way they'd be able to accomplish anything.

Yeah, she'd come to some realizations yesterday, and that was before she'd even left his library. That all along, they'd only had two options. One kept them together, and the other, they each went their own ways. Provided they could undo some of the emotional damage that their constant arguing had caused, especially since every argument comprised of them pointing out each other's flaws. They had to stop that. As he'd indicated, they couldn't change what happened, but they could change how they continued to react to it. Maybe if she bent first, he'd follow. Or so she hoped.

Otherwise, any chance they'd have at being together would be gone. If she survived the upcoming battle, she'd leave with the four she promised to take with her and never return. Finally, she spotted him ducking into the apothecary. Crikey. Could he make this more difficult? Yes, yes, he could. She flew as close as possible and landed on the ground. A bell rang as she entered the shop.

Seru pushed a sizable pouch of gold across the counter at the girl operating the counter. He buried his nose in his sleeve. "Anything to cover—" he groaned. "That."

The female nymph tucked the pouch aside and pulled something from beneath the counter. "Try this."

Making sure she had locked the door, Thalasia dug out a pouch of coins she had set aside for this isle. Not that she'd spent any of it, and tossed it across the room to the woman. "Give us some privacy."

The female caught the bag in the air with a faint smile, gave them both a nod, and disappeared into the back.

"I'll give you a second to get your bearings," Thalasia said. His running away didn't exactly bode well, but she was going to do her best to overlook it.

"You realize I left to give you your space," Seru replied. "As for my bearings, I know precisely where I am and why I came here. There's nothing to get. Go eat your breakfast," he added, inspecting the odd item the woman had granted him.

Yeah, that's why he ran off like a bat out of hell. To give her space. Nope. Nope. This would not become an accusatory conversation or another argument. Facts. Stick to the facts. She took a moment, inhaling and exhaling a slow breath, before flipping the sign to officially declare the apothecary closed. It had only been luck that ensured it was empty when she chased him there. "I also realize the time we have to address our current situation is limited."

"Have another of your epiphanies, did you?" he asked, giving the plant a sniff while eyeing her.

"Didn't require an epiphany. The timeline for that hasn't changed. The only thing that has fluctuated is our attitude toward one another." And their ability to work together. In the beginning, it seemed to come so naturally. Their only issues then had been the difficulties they faced with Aurelia and Mac. Of course, all of that changed after he marked her, now that she thought about it. Although, it seemed sometimes they played the role of a couple; there were others where they just reached for each other automatically. Even when she'd come into the throne room, no, he hadn't come to her right away, but after Aurelia had left, he had descended the levels and reached for her hand. Not that she was sure he even realized it—any more than he'd noticed the collar around her neck.

He rubbed the strange plant against his nose and face—something like the beast would have done.

Gripping the back of her neck, she sighed heavily. They had moments where they didn't fight. One or both of them had tried a few times to balance the scales. Watching him practically bathe in the plant, it was almost like seeing him shove his nose into some herb he'd snatched from the bar. "The longer they go unaddressed, the worse they'll get, and that won't be good for either of us."

"You don't say." He narrowed his eyes at her.

She bit her tongue to keep from responding with her own snark. Fighting would get them nowhere. The pain that had lanced her body as she hit the top of the staircase was only the beginning. Facts. "Right now, our path ends one way. Me, at the inn, until the full moon passes, at which point the pheromones will end. Or if we make it to Pteryrina, me, not strong enough for the ritual, provided that's even something you believe will help. Either way, it still leaves you right where you've been."

With that damn slave band around his neck, unstable and stuck. "And me, provided I survive beyond that, I'll take the four with me as promised and leave without returning." Plus, alone, but she didn't mention that. She'd said it before, and the echo of her words settled like ashes in the quiet room, a familiar ache. And the mere mention of it still plunged her into a pit of despair, her world dimming to gray. "I have some solutions to a few of the problems at hand, but not all of them, especially the ones I don't know about yet." Like his agreement with Aurelia. And the result of the flame. "We can't go back and change what's been done. Either we move on, or we go our separate ways." That was the bottom line.

"I'm listening," Seru offered, no longer giving her direct eye contact as he replaced the plant in its pouch. He slipped the loop of the string around his wrist.

Progress. A small step, but it was progress. She rolled her shoulders, but the oppressive heat did little to ease the discomfort; her skin slick with sweat that ran down her back. Gods, she couldn't wait for this to pass. Okay. Focus. Where did she start? Not with the pheromones. Maybe in the middle. "I'll break down the components of the ritual so you understand exactly how it works. I believe this will offer a solution to one issue. It may even push the other in the right direction." If her assessment and understanding of everything was correct, then it might loosen his collar, but it should override his bond with Aurelia. It pulled on many ancient powers, along with that of the moon, to link them together. "It still leaves your instability. I have an artifact that can help with the nightmares. Before you ask, it came from one of my ancestors, is used in the ritual, and it's something I used myself after my captivity. Now, this is only a temporary solution and only offers aid in that instance. I believe the book in your hand may offer something else to help with your instability, too. Since these are temporary, that leaves us to find a more permanent answer, but I have an idea of finding that. And it isn't on this isle."

No answer. Nothing. Nada. She wasn't sure if this was a good thing or not. Well, she might as well address the solution to her pheromones. "As for my pheromones, I can't repress them any longer. However, if we rewind time a little and handle things more your way, then not only will they repress, it will strengthen me for the ritual at hand. If you want me to break it down, I'll do that, but in someplace a little more one-on-one." While she remained by the front door, she scanned the apothecary, taking in the varying herbs and items for sale—poppy seeds. Did they produce the same strain as the ones in the Clouds? Maybe. "It might even offer some aid in the backlash we seem to keep suffering through," she tacked on.

"You're proposing we utilize chronomancy?" he sounded skeptical. "You realize that takes a tremendous amount of energy and mana? In addition, it's ranked among the most advanced forms of magic, requiring skill and precision."

"No." Gods, wouldn't that be great? She wasn't confident that would be something she'd ever be able to do. Jump realms, sure. Jump time, yeah, not likely—in any lifetime. "All I'm saying is that we fall back to your initial desire to please me; it'll undo some of the damage that's been caused. And possibly address some of the backlash of the marks as well."

He visibly relaxed, leaning on the counter. "Okay."

Did he think she was an idiot? Not that she asked. Yeah, she didn't speak as eloquently as he did, but she was far from stupid. "Provided this is all amenable to you, then I have a few other suggestions. We set clear expectations and a few ground rules we can *both* agree on."

"Go ahead," he instructed.

The ground rules would be based on expectations. But she could lay out what she expected of him. They had to stop treating the other as an enemy. And get back to working together. "I expect we share ideas. That going forward, we decide things together. I expect that we'll stop being so secretive. Yes, I understand times may call for it, but we don't trust each other. And we need to get to a point where we do."

"Because you sincerely believe others can be trusted," Seru countered. He glanced away at that moment, finding something else to focus on. He let go of a breath through his nose. "I can share certain things with you and attempt to decide alongside you. But I'll never be an open book. I'll never be transparent—like you seem to crave."

"I don't expect you to be, but I don't expect you to get upset with me... when I'm not, either." There were a lot of things she hadn't told him. And that was part of their problem. They argued because she decided behind his back with the information she had at hand, but he could do the same? Fuck no. It was a two-way street.

Seru's tongue flicked across his lips. "You want me to refrain from commenting when I think you make poor choices," he sounded uncertain, questioning.

"Only if you can accept it when I point out the same." Theoretically, they avoided that if they worked together.

He grinned at that. "I treat you as I do because, despite your continued insistence on the matter, you are younger and significantly less experienced. Those qualities arise each time you make the aforementioned choices. Aurelia may make less than ideal choices, but she knows when she's making them. She also has a support system, a rather unique one, who somehow sees her succeed—even whilst indulging her choices. You do not. You make choices only based on your knowledge and experiences. Your ancestors and a bag of magic trinkets can hardly be considered a support system." He clasped his hands together. "They're invaluable tools, yes. But they're not the same as having active players on the board. Out of everyone we've encountered on this isle, who among them would come to your aid? Truly back you, even when the benefit to them is nil."

Okay. Her entire point had been to avoid this circle. She'd stated her expectations. Maybe it was his turn. And while dragons may not be on her side, at least not here, it didn't mean she had no one to back her. Thalasia folded her arms across her chest and leaned against the doorjamb, crossing one ankle over the other. "Then what expectations do *you* have of me, Seru?"

"I expected you'd dodge the question. Or refuse to answer," he returned. "Beyond that? I expect you to serve your own interests. You do your best to live up to being an Atlis. You revere your ancestors—no matter how annoying and untrustworthy they might be. Similar to the way you've trusted me, despite evidence to the contrary. I expect your next trip is to Pteryrina. Following that, I suspect you'll fulfill your prophesied ritual and receive your full power. I expect you'll see if they can't help release the spell—and subsequently the crystal—housed in your neck, temporarily holding your mistress at bay until you come into those powers. I expect you'll save the sirens as prophesied. Once that's done, you'll make your escape plan with your charges to leave this isle and this realm. You may or may not aid in restoring balance to the isle before executing that escape plan. How're those expectations?" he ventured; the distaste evident in his tone. "None of those plans have changed. You can pretend they have, add my unexpected presence around them, or even remove me entirely. Those series of events and the intent behind them remain the same."

Thalasia ground her jaw and narrowed her eyes at him. "I didn't answer the question because I'm sick and tired of going around in circles with you. You're so busy pointing out my flaws yet refuse to see your own. For five seconds, I thought I'd avoid an argument with you since we keep repeating the same mistakes over and over again. I have admitted as much as screwing up a couple of times, but that doesn't seem good enough for you. Instead, you continue to harp on it and avoid what we need to accomplish."

She pushed off the doorjamb and stepped further into the store. "In case you missed the earlier information regarding our current path... I can't perform the ritual without you, asshole, since you were so kind enough to, as you put it, whoops, trigger my sexual awakening. Not unless I want to have every possibility of feeling any kind of emotion stripped, which would put me on no one's side. Because *that* is what would happen, and since you put the crystal in, you get to figure out how to take it out. You know, again something *you* brought back into my life."

Yeah, because she was the only one who made idiotic choices. She inhaled and exhaled a deep breath. "Just because the dragons here wouldn't back me doesn't mean I'd stand alone." She shook her head. "I was talking about expectations going forward, though it seems you're doing what you always do."

"I believe I just agreed to assist you with your sexual frustrations," Seru replied calmly. "As for the crystal, I can remove it whenever I choose. I simply dislike your mistress coloring your judgment; it skews your perceptions and judgment—which is counteractive to both our objectives. I won't leave you an emotionless husk; I'll help you complete your ritual," he stated. "But I won't pretend I don't know how this works out. We can read the book." He lifted it. "Together. Maybe by some stroke, it'll provide something useful."

She would agree with him on that part. It gave the woman more control than she'd ever had in the past. Thalasia dragged a hand down her face. It hadn't kept her out of her head the other night. She'd bet anything the woman was biding her time. "Exactly how do you think this works out? You've asked me that question multiple times. Maybe it's time you answer it."

"You already *know* how I believe this works out. What I don't understand is why we need to keep reiterating. Nothing has changed for me." He shrugged, rolling his eyes and throwing his hands up. "Barring your little provocation of the yellow dragoness."

Yeah. That female hated him. Gee, she couldn't imagine why. She crossed her arms. There was something else she wanted to know, not that she expected he'd tell her. "What arrangement did you make with Aurelia?"

He sighed, rubbing his brow. "The return of the violet crystal. And my loyalty and allegiance for the coming battle."

That seemed too simple. Way too simple. She opened her mouth and snapped it shut. No, she'd only shown him a small portion of the vision. Although, obviously, he knew Marius was involved. And by extension, the merfolk. Maybe that's who the male was marrying. She hadn't asked for details when Cyon mentioned the wedding. "And the purpose behind the flame?"

"You stole the artifact with no idea as to its purpose?" He shook his head dismissively, putting up a hand. "Don't answer that. Or the myriad of implications it contains." He pushed his hand through his mane. "During the harsh winter war, the Matriarch used her power—*our* power—to blot out the sun. She plunged the earthbound into darkness. Famine plagued the land while we slaughtered their forces until they neared depletion. In a desperate act, they forged a small council—one that met in secret. Through discourse, they cooked up a plan to infiltrate the Clouds and return light to the isle."

Her eyes widened as she listened to everything he said—the Silver Queen who'd wanted nothing but power. And Aurelia had her take something that would offer the same. The crow's warning—it was so clear. She wanted to kick her own ass over it. "Do you honestly think if Aurelia had told me *any* of that, I would've stolen it?" She pinched the bridge of her nose. If she'd known any of that, she wouldn't have stolen it, let alone returned it to Aurelia's so-called temple. "There are some lines even *I* won't cross." Innocent lives could be lost. And she wouldn't care. "I'm understanding Marius's point-of-view more and more each passing day."

"Don't you realize that's precisely why she didn't?" Seru shook out his mane. "When are you going to realize the secrets you're in on aren't the danger? It's the ones you aren't." He paused. "At your core, you're a good person," he confessed. "It's what makes you easy to deceive. You strive to see the same goodness in others. You strive to help. That drew you here. What drew you to the beach. To me." He offered a low, bitter laugh. "Marius's point of view is what it was designed to be. Granted, he has veered slightly from the intended course; he's still on the main track." His eyes narrowed to an icy blue.

Of course, it was why she didn't. Aurelia knew she would've sacrificed herself before stealing something that would allow her to take innocent lives. Just as much as the woman banked on how much she cared for Seru. It tore her up inside. The crow was correct. This wasn't something that could be taken back. And he was right. That was something she'd accepted the day before—she was in over her head. Inhaling and exhaling a deep breath, she dug in her purse for another pouch of coins. "If you agree, we'll head back to the inn. Go through the book, strategize for after the ritual, and head to Pteryrina in the morning. Before today is over, will you please rest?"

"If you pay that woman again..." Seru warned. He breezed past her, flinging open the door. "We agree on all points except for the last one. I don't need rest. I need to work. Of which, I'm sure I'll have plenty once you open this book." Without awaiting a further response, he took off toward the inn.

Fine, she wouldn't pay the woman again. Instead, she'd just take what she wanted. Shaking her head, Thalasia returned the clinking coins to her purse and instead grabbed several small pouches brimming with poppy seeds. Just in case. Then she followed suit and left the apothecary, heading for the inn.

Chapter Forty-Five

Though not dawdling, Thalasia visited a fruit stand and acquired some provisions before returning to the inn. It wasn't really on her mind, but at some point, she needed to eat. After finding out the new room information from the front desk, she collected her thoughts before walking in and shutting the door behind her. "We really need to work on our communication skills." She strode over to the bed, the floorboards creaking beneath her feet, and took off her boots.

"What makes you think so?" Seru inquired. He'd claimed his place by the window, where he'd drawn the curtains.

"Because, while I appreciate the unnecessary workout, it would've been great if you mentioned changing rooms before you left." Barefooted, she headed back to the door, ensuring it was locked, and then made her way to where he stood. Her purse and purchase remained on the nightstand. Neither would be required to open the book. She paused in front of him and held out her hand.

He bothered to look back at her long enough to blink. "Between your scent and the fact that we're in possession of *Celestimo*, I trusted that if it wasn't common sense, you'd figure it out."

Which she did. For a moment, she almost pointed out that no one knew what she smelled like... except that wasn't true. Though she suspected she was the only one who knew he had it. "Point taken. The book, please."

He hesitated, but eventually extended the book her way.

As she took the book from his hand, her fingers grazed his, sending a jolt through them. She stood still for a moment, waiting for the chill to subside before moving to the desk and sitting down. Did he think she was going to take off with it? She wiped her hands across her skirt before she got to the task at hand. While she hadn't asked, part of her was curious how many times he'd attempted to open it. Given his response to her refusal to read the Allimos journal a couple of days ago, she'd wager a few. Thalasia ran her hand across the embellished material of the book. The sight was incredibly detailed and absolutely stunning, especially the intricately engraved lyre.

Positioning her fingers just right, she ran them across the unseen strings of the instrument. Just like opening the hidden staircase to Pteryrina, it involved the right chords in the right order. As the last note faded, the lyre-shaped indentation glowed, accompanied by a tiny click and a breathy exhalation that seemed to unlock the book.

Seru watched her intently. His neutral expression turned to a frown, and his talons bit into the wooden frame of the windowsill.

Thalasia opened the book, the binding creaking ever so slightly. Her eyes narrowed at the folded piece of parchment sitting clear as day in the very front of *Celestimo*. She rubbed her forehead and exhaled a deep breath. Did she even want to know? Rolling her neck, she retrieved the paper and read through it.

My dearest Thalasia,

I am certain by now you have many questions. I hope that your mother passed on everything you needed to know before you took this journey. Though I suspect that may not be the case.

Our line is unlike any other line. We are Atlis, protectors of the innocent and guardians to 'The Key.' The goddess Demeter herself created the golden lyre you hold in your possession. It is a skeleton key that not only allows the possessor to jump between realms, but will open any door. There is nowhere in the universe you cannot go.

It was given to our line many centuries ago to keep safe and ensure it did not fall into the wrong hands. We are warriors who are duty-bound to this task. This is the reason we were given visions. Not only to aid with threats, but to prevent them as much as possible. Often, this comes at a great sacrifice. Not only to ourselves, but to the ones we love.

Your birth, your arrival in Prisma Isle has been foretold for hundreds of years. Long ago, a curse was placed on the sirens. I do not know if you were ever educated on this, so I helped the best I could. Like you, I had visions. I had one of you. One that told me you would fall for a Saint Beast here on the isle. If everything has gone accordingly, he did not recognize you upon your landing.

Again, you are unlike any Atlis ever born. You will be the most powerful of us all. Many prophecies surround you, even more than are in *Celestimo*. I cannot answer all of your questions, but I can tell you it is not just your duty to protect the lyre, but you are one half of the pair to break the curse.

The sirens were designed to coexist and thrive with other species, which includes procreating. This can only begin again once the curse is broken.

Once you have fulfilled your destiny on Prisma Isle, you must leave with the lyre. The barrier protects the magic within the isle. It also means you must make a choice.

No one can make it but you.

Duty or love.

The choice is yours.

Your Great, Great Grandmother, Adina

A letter from her great-great-grandmother—addressed to her. Chewing on the inside of her cheek, she read through it once. Thalasia read the letter again. Duty. Responsibility. She had to protect the lyre. But it couldn't stay on the isle. Her gaze flicked to Seru and then back to her great-great-grandmother's words. She swallowed to wet her parched throat.

Her whole life had been about duty. She had followed every vision. Mostly. Helped nearly every creature the gods had led her to, and for a moment, she thought... just once, she could have what she wanted. That was the entire reason she stayed on the isle with him. Instead of running off with Mac—her duty. She tossed the letter aside. She'd burn it later.

Her fingers brushed the textured parchment as her gaze landed on the circular arrangement of the eight main moon phases. She had chosen Seru. Not that she had handled it very well at all. Would things have been different if she'd told him after Aurelia and Mac left why she stayed? Less strained than they were now. Yes, he'd agreed, but that didn't mean she couldn't sense the distance still between them.

First rule of an Atlis—never reveal the truth.

Second rule of an Atlis—protect the innocent.

Her eyes shifted back to him again. Some of her conversation with Ione about the saint beasts replayed in her head. Over eight-hundred years and there was a lot he'd been through. While he certainly hadn't shared all of it, and she hadn't read the book detailing his life in this existence, she understood enough. Followed by a lot of their arguments. And practically every decision she'd made since Aurelia and Mac left them alone.

Although she'd countered much of what he'd said over the last few days and defended her choices *a lot*, sitting there, she could see where better decisions could've been made. Not just in how she had revealed things, but in how she went about her quest to learn more about him. "You're right, Seru. My judgment has been pretty poor in a lot of instances. I can't change the decisions I've made, but I can do better. Nothing will ever make me think choosing you was a poor decision."

If she had to do it all over again, she'd always choose him. Yes, they hadn't known one another long. She had just found him, her one true home. Her one chance at happiness. Duty be damned. Nothing would come between them. No matter the consequences, she would always choose him. Even if it meant letting him go one day, so he could return to his brothers.

"More wondrous news from Adina?" Seru asked, a bitter growl escaping his lips.

"More like unwarranted advice." Advice that couldn't be more wrong. "Read it if you want. I plan to burn it." It hadn't just made her recognize her own mistakes; situations that she could've handled better; alternative decisions to some problems created between the two of them... but it also made her question how she'd interpreted her visions. She'd always believed that some she was meant to ensure happened, while others... she had to stop. What if that had been the case with all of them?

Thalasia pressed her fingers to her temples, trying to soothe the ache, then fanned her tank top to catch a breeze against her warm skin. Not only were the various questions giving her a slight headache, but she was already unbearably hot. Shaking her head, she turned her attention back to the book and skimmed through some of the beginning pages. All of them were prophecies. Good gods, how many were there? She stopped, her fingers lingering on a page.

Seru carefully accepted her invitation to read the letter. As he crossed the room and picked it up from the floor, he watched her. "If it's that bad, take a cold bath." His eyes shifted to the letter.

"I will soon," she said as she skipped past the prophecy she'd scanned. While it had certainly told her something she hadn't known, it made little difference. She'd choose Seru every time. She moved onto the next prophecy. At least it was short and sweet and told her exactly what she suspected. She smirked and lifted her gaze to him. "Joy. I get to kiss a toad to break a curse."

"Pardon?" Seru replied.

"The prophecy here." She gestured to the page she'd just read. It confirmed her suspicions. "In order to break the siren's curse... I have to kiss Mac." Thalasia shuddered. Gods, that was the last thing she wanted to do. The idea alone made her queasy.

He moved to peer over her shoulder, swiftly bringing the pouched plant to his nose. He straightened, backing away as he shook his mane in dismay. "Of course, you do."

"Yeah, I'm not thrilled by it, either," she muttered and returned to perusing the book. "Most of what's in the front here are prophecies. I won't go through them all. Reading them alone can cause migraines... and that's without trying to interpret them." No, what she wanted was something useful. She already knew it was what she'd have to do. Thalasia flipped page after page until she reached a sketch of what looked like several crystals connected in a prism.

"But you'll do it anyway," Seru said.

Leaning back in the chair for a moment, she glanced at him. "What right do I have to tell someone like Parthenia and her mate that they can't be together because the idea of kissing someone repulses me? Am I just supposed to let them suffer? All because some higher being wanted revenge?" It wasn't in her role to play goddess. "There may be some things about the Atlis lifestyle I don't agree with... things I want to change... but others... others I agree with. These are innocent people. They shouldn't have to pay the price because of someone else's... poor choice." Yes, that meant that if she could figure out a way to address her decision to steal the flame, she would.

"Doesn't sound like they've done much in the way of reparations or attempts at appeasing the god they provoked, either," Seru noted, laying back on the bed.

As much as she tried, she failed to stifle a slight chuckle. "While we could debate how the sirens could appease the goddess of revenge, I think that's a discussion for another time. This interests me more than that." Thalasia shifted in the chair, turning to face him slightly. "Did you know there are seven crystals and that they all connect into a prism? And if I'm reading this correctly, it looks like there's a spot for them to be placed into the isle—restore the balance."

"I'm aware why Aurelia and the Ascendant seek the crystals. I know they've already collected a majority and have their sights on those which remain. You won't beat her to the punch. And even if you did and stole the crystals in her possession, only a dragon can wield the power of the prism."

"I wasn't planning on trying. It just interests me." She tilted her head at him. His reaction regarding the sirens had partially amused her, but mostly because how could he even determine that? The sirens and dragons hadn't worked together in over three hundred years. Even she knew that much. "Does it bother you... what I have to do to save the sirens?"

Staring at the ceiling, Seru shrugged. "Not really. It's your choice. Your lips on his. Not mine."

"It's not a choice, Seru. You unconsciously reaching for my hand, that's a choice. Deciding to stay with you, that's a choice. Marking me, that was a choice. Doing everything I can to... set you free, that's a choice." She shifted a little more in the chair. "Whether or not I have to kiss him... I still choose you. And there are things you have that he'll never have." And they mattered more than having to kiss some smart-mouthed turd for a few seconds to break a curse.

"It is a choice. Just one that might stain your conscience," he countered, undoing the topmost ties on his shirt.

"But you don't know that for sure." Turning around, she faced the book again and went to the next page. "It's a risk I'm willing to take."

"You're too mindful of others for it not to." The sheets ruffled, indicating he readjusted his position. "Do as you like."

Most of the time, that was true. With him, it was different. Silently, she skimmed through a few more pages. More information about each crystal, referencing their origin, how each species had come by them, along with their strengths and weaknesses. Her fingers stopped as she moved to the next page—her family tree. Narrowing her eyes, she scanned over exactly how extensive it was, including every Atlis and Allimos. That wasn't all that caught her attention. Alcmene, the one her mother had told her of, who only lived for nineteen years. Along with the many family members that were still alive, which made absolutely no sense whatsoever. Thalasia stood, the chair scraping against the floor. "I'm going to go ahead and, uh, take that bath." She headed straight for the bathroom.

She just stood there in the bathroom doorway, unmoving. Really, she didn't know what to think. Family she didn't know existed.

How much more had her parents lied about? People she trusted. A searing jolt of energy, fiercer and more agonizing than the previous one, pierced her core. She instinctively reached out, her fingers desperately gripping the countertop as her knees buckled, and a sharp pain bloomed on her lower lip as she bit into it. The edge of the marble pressed into her palm. Not that either pain seemed to deter the agony that lanced her core.

It'll pass. It'll pass. Her grip on her lip intensified as she focused on breathing through her nose. She didn't know how much time elapsed, but it eventually ended. On an exhale, she collapsed against the floor. Ragged breaths left her as she lay there, embracing the feel of the cool tile against her skin. Good gods, a sexual awakening sucked. She swallowed to wet her parched throat. At least she only had to go through it once.

As she stayed there, sprawled out, she thought back to the fact that she had family. Why had her parents lied? Kept it all a secret? For what? If she couldn't trust they'd been truthful, then how was she supposed to trust anyone? Even Seru. He'd told her multiple times not to trust him. Maybe she didn't. But that didn't mean she had to play by those rules. She *had* intentions to change the way being an Atlis worked. And she *had* told him they'd decide together. That could be where she started. As soon as she could get off the floor.

"I hope you're not falling in there," Seru called from the other room.

That's not the term she'd use. It wasn't as if she had dived toward the floor. But it was kind of comfortable. Sort of. Thalasia licked her lip. The taste of copper hit the tip of her tongue. Lovely. Yeah. That wasn't the pain she wanted to go through again. And it was probably far from over. How did anyone survive this? "I'm okay," she responded, slightly muffled. Alright. Up. She needed to get up. Her palms pressed against the cool floor as she gradually lifted her body.

Thalasia shakily got to her feet, bracing herself against the cool counter to steady her wobble, then confidently walked to the bathroom doorway. Not that she exited. Instead, she propped up against the doorframe. "See. One piece." Although her hair likely appeared disheveled, amongst other things.

"Yet, still in disrepair," he commented, gazing down the length of his body at her.

"I haven't gotten into the bath yet. Not that it's a solution. It's a Band-Aid." That was how Ione had put it, right? Yeah. She shook

the thought from her head. "I'm getting in here in a second."
She paused. "Although you said you didn't care..." Something she
didn't quite believe. He'd reached out too many times without
realizing it not to care. "I told you we'd decide together. I figure
I need to stick to that. Not that it has to be decided right away."
There were several other things to handle beforehand. "I'm not
sure what makes you think the sirens don't deserve to be saved,
but something to consider... Why do any of the species on this
isle deserve to be saved? Not a single one of them has bothered to
reach out and attempt to work together until war lingered on their
doorstep. Each species has hoarded something; dragons with their
treasure, sirens with their knowledge... every single one of them has
remained in their own little world. Why save any of them?"

"They don't." He sat up. "And who says we are?" He reached
out a hand to her, not quite managing eye contact. But, making
the offer all the same.

She walked across the room, her fingers brushing against his as
she placed her hand in his. "Aurelia arranged with you for your loyalty. Something that shouldn't have been necessary. I ensured your
being released from that pit was part of my arrangement. That's
beside the point. Any part we play in this war, we're choosing a
side. Either fighting alongside those on land against the other isle,
or attempting to help them. Even putting the barrier back up..."
She shrugged. "Doesn't it do the same? Protect the inhabitants of
Prisma Isle from the inhabitants of Candescent Isle?"

"Yes, well... she's been trained to be suspicious. Add in my recent,
out of character activities and, well... you." He narrowed his eyes
at her, a hint of pride coloring his tone. "She's merely gauging
the situation as odd and reacting as any good leader should." The
corner of his mouth twitched up in response to her questions. He
raised his eyebrows. "I don't know... does it?" The smile formed, if
only just long enough to reveal the whites of his teeth.

A small smile tugged at the corners of her mouth. She missed his
smile. He had a really nice one. It was good to see, even if only for
a split second. Thalasia caressed his cheek. "Either that or it traps
them all here."

He shrugged. "Until it came down, most didn't know any better
anyway; those who did likely grew accustomed to it."

"Likely." It had been up for three hundred years, give or take.
"But maybe there's some kind of purpose behind all of this."

"There's always a purpose. Everything is by design. None of it accidental or left to chance—unless, as you've already stated, the result is the same."

Then the gods and goddesses had some crazy-ass sense of humor when they designed her line. "Some of which we'll just never understand."

He studied her, then. Opting to say nothing in response. He pulled her closer. "If I thought you'd be desperate enough to try fucking the floor, I would have conceded sooner." He smoothed her unruly hair back into place as best he could while not snagging her waves with his talons.

"I wasn't expecting the pain to drive me to my knees yet." She bit her bottom lip. At least not for another day. Apparently, she was wrong.

"Has any of this really been as you've expected?"

That was a good question. She bit her bottom lip again, tilting her head thoughtfully. "No. Books don't really prepare you for... anything like this."

"No, they don't," Seru confirmed. "Only experience can do that."

It was a good thing there wasn't any vocal response to that. Though she could've simply agreed. Instead, she had another option. For once, it didn't include words. Her fingers wove into his mane as she rapidly shortened the space separating them. She loved playing with it. Something she didn't think she'd ever tire of. Her gaze met his, and then she brushed a kiss across his lips.

"It really obstructs your focus, doesn't it?" he murmured.

"Yes. It's very distracting." More than just that. It was completely uncomfortable, but was it necessary for that to be pointed out? No, which meant he'd done it on purpose. Thalasia bit the inside of her cheek and sighed heavily. "What's going on in your head?" She still played with the ends of his mane. "There's more here than just the result of our usual fighting. I can feel the disconnect. I see the flickers come through..." She didn't know how long before another wave would hit her. Or how long it would last.

"Beyond the fact that you're a very sexual being—be it courtesy of your ancestry or your awakening—and I am not..." he inhaled a breath, looking away. "Many things. The war is nearly upon us. I'm weighing our options, considering which alliances are worthy and which will be severed. None of them are simple choices."

She'd go with her awakening. Not something she had any interest in before him, but that wasn't the point. Things were drawing to a close. There had been a shift... one of her reasons for being here. "I think there are things you don't give yourself credit for; things I can see, even if you can't." It was in the way he reached for her, especially when he didn't realize he'd done it. A small smile pulled at the corners of her mouth. "We know the sirens have been going around negotiating treaties with the different species. Don't you think we would be better equipped to assess alliances once we know what they've accomplished?" And maybe, just maybe, the Elder would see her line differently than the one ambassador that had been alongside Parthenia. That was the only one she could see as having shared information with that Ascendant.

"I care for you, but affection and sex are entirely different matters," he replied. He pulled her close, leaving only a sliver of space between them. "The sirens are but a piece of a very complex puzzle."

"I care about you, too." Possibly even loved him, but that wasn't something she was prepared to say. She slid her fingers a little further into his mane. They'd never been overly affectionate, and that was completely okay with her. "Affection and sex... maybe that's something we figure out together." Yeah, the sirens were definitely part of some bigger puzzle. Still things that they only had pieces to and not the entire picture. "The sirens have made some kind of arrangement with Aurelia. And I don't know about you, but I'd like to know what." Although he could very well know already, however, like both of them, Aurelia played things close to the vest.

"You say that... but there's precious little time left." His fingers played along her hips. "We already know what," Seru replied, his gaze returning to her. "If the green one or another possesses any of the crystals, she's likely arranged for their temporary use or safekeeping in exchange that they'll grant it to her when the time comes."

Time definitely wasn't on their side. Meant they had to be a little more forthcoming than they'd been in the past. Hard to believe it had only been days. "I know, but I have faith we can figure it out. We have a bit of a foundation. Small moments, yet they exist. That gives us something to build on." The proof seemed to be in the faint glow her skin had taken. At least for her, it meant something. Good thing he'd drawn the curtains earlier.

The crystals. That shouldn't surprise her. "If that's the case, we may still work something out with them. We won't know that until we get to Pteryrina." That would be when they could make an accurate assessment. Neither of them knew enough about the sirens to do so beforehand.

Seru granted her a weak attempt at a smile. "For your sake, yes. Remember, I'm still Regent to the Clouds... as far as they're concerned. My agenda is Her agenda."

"And they seem to be aware that I'm an Atlis. Which means they know my purpose here, too." At least part of it. There had been a reason she'd avoided Pteryrina for days now. A couple of reasons, actually. Part of it so she could figure things out with Seru, and part... well, as things were progressing, she'd accept her role and all it included. Her diamond gaze fell to Seru's blue eyes. She wished staying here was a possibility. That it had even been one.

"Why Aurelia let both of us out of that cell," Seru returned, eyes boring into hers. "Delivering the fabled Atlis to Pteryrina. Imagine how that looks."

With the back of her hand, she stroked his cheek, not once taking her eyes from his. "Like a savior."

He leaned slightly into her touch, warm and soft.

For it to benefit Aurelia, information of their time in a cell had to be shared. A smile slowly crossed her face. He'd once told her that females held an elevated status amongst dragons. It was the complete opposite with sirens. While both societies were matriarchal, males had the most value. "Sirens revere males more than they do females."

"If that green one we met in Chicane is the only one left, you'll be hard pressed to save them."

He was right, but that had more to do with her role and duty than anything else. And maybe part of how she felt about saving those who were innocent. "He could always just breed with all of those who are of mating age." Not that she expected *that* would go over well. Still caressing his cheek, her lips curled up at the corners. "While it is something I lean toward, you still come first."

"I imagine that would take some convincing," he replied, doubt coloring every word. "You wouldn't sleep with him. Why would any self-respecting woman subject themselves to—" He cut himself short, shaking his head dismissively. "I'm not a siren, or a dragon. I'm not a free male. If not for my title, it's doubtful they'd respect me. Regardless, my standing by you appears as little more than a charade at Aurelia's hand. They'll like me significantly less if Mac tells them of our less-than-secret affair during our stay in his village. My being male won't buy me privilege with them."

"I don't even want to kiss him. Sleep with him..." Her nose wrinkled in disgust at the mere thought. Nope. No way. Gods, the idea alone made her want to throw up. She shook all of that from her head.

"You're making a lot of assumptions based on a little information." They didn't know if Mac had even made it there. If the male even intended to go there. Or what information the male would share about them given the opportunity? "Until we get there, we don't know what they'll think of us. Or if we can even change their minds."

"Am I?" His hands fell from her hips back to the edge of the bed. He leaned back and sighed. Impatient. And growing more anxious...

Thalasia cupped his jaw, brushing his cheek with her thumb. "Yes. Unless you've made a trip to Pteryrina recently? Or you've figured out how to read minds?" She paused. How had they gotten so far off track? "Two sides to every coin." Moments. She had to pray those moments would be enough. "Sirens may just surprise you." Something that all depended on their Elder. "I did."

"I'm not a mind reader," he admitted. "I observe and consider players, their motives, and the prices. Then use what I know and make predictions based on facts." He paused. "Does the touching help?"

He'd told her before that he didn't read minds. And she was fairly certain he hadn't been to Pteryrina... ever. The problem with predictions, facts changed when one wasn't looking. It had been days since they left Chicane. Neither of them knew what had happened since then. "A little." Not as much as she would prefer, but she enjoyed touching him.

"Really helps?" he asked skeptically. "Even with my clothes on." He allowed his question to linger a moment before looping back to her previous statement. "You surprised me because you're not from this isle."

With a sigh, she dropped her hand. Although she'd attempted to explain it before, she considered for a moment that she hadn't been clear enough. She opted to leave no room for misunderstanding. "No. I'd like nothing more than to shuck the clothes I'm wearing, but I put them on for your benefit. Crawling into a cold bath... I'd just steam the bathroom up with how hot my body is right now. Until it becomes painful, and that pain assaults me relentlessly. To where I'm of no use to anyone. Physical intimacy is the only thing that will help. Right now, it doesn't have to be the full act."

For a brief instant, she clutched the back of her neck, the sweat slick against her palm, before wiping it on the worn denim of her skirt. "You said it yourself, though. There are others that can jump between realms." It might take them more effort than it took her.

"You realize a good number of the nobility only wear clothing to court as a formality," he said. "Your clothes serve no benefit to me or you. Take them off." He lay back again, staring at the ceiling as he asked, "Physical intimacy is a matter of opinion... what it means exclusively to Atlis holds more value and context."

Stepping away from the bed, she took off her tank and skirt, tossing both aside. Where they landed didn't matter. "Atlis value a lot more than dragons, but you're not technically either." They didn't enslave people. Money wasn't a priority. And they didn't value magical power. With her arms crossed resolutely over her chest, rubbing against her bare skin, Thalasia moved deliberately across the room, her gaze fixed on the window. Yeah, the curtains were closed, which was fine.

"That's not really an answer," Seru prompted.

He hadn't technically asked a question. He posed a thought. "If you're asking my opinion, then it means a great deal. I have hope that it'll help strengthen our bond and push us toward closing this chasm between us. And that doesn't consider how it would address my pheromones."

"Does that mean it depends on *your* definition of physical intimacy?" The edge in his voice betrayed his annoyance.

"No. Nothing will change my belief that physical intimacy is a give and take, but I also understand your limited capacities. I can work within those boundaries... hoping when there is less of a sexual charge, we can figure the rest out." For a moment, she considered telling him exactly how important it was that they bridge this gap. Although there was already a slight difference between them, she didn't think it was enough. Their bond had to be as strong as they could make it, emotionally and sexually. She glanced over her shoulder at him.

"I'm not asking your belief... unless your belief is the rule." He sat up. "I want to know what *exactly* denotes physical intimacy within the confines of your being an Atlis and my being your Allimos. Specificity of what is and isn't going to... help *this*." He gestured to her person, not just the sweat collecting in a sheen on her skin, but the silvery glow. "You're obviously miserable..." he trailed.

Hadn't she explained it? Maybe not as well as she could. Her belief wasn't the rule. Thalasia walked back over to where he sat and kneeled down on the floor in front of him. "For now... oral. You service me." It was as blunt as she could get. She enjoyed touching him, and that wouldn't change, but this would work for both of them for the time being. "Sex, we have to figure out before the ritual. After the consummation period... what *we* are comfortable with."

Seru raked his hand through his mane. A deep sigh preceded his response, "No alternatives?"

Whatever had changed in the last couple of days didn't go unnoticed. Not that she could explain why. Only a couple of days ago, he'd been all too eager to distract her after a nightmare. Or his declaration to close the marks. Right then, he seemed less than thrilled at the prospect. Except she knew he was attracted to her. That had been determined the day they'd been left alone. Maybe the day after. She couldn't question what truth he'd actually shared with her over the last few days. It would undo what little patchwork they'd accomplished in the last hour. "No." Physical, emotional, spiritual. All three went hand-in-hand. "Seru, I *cannot* stress enough how much *we* need this." She already knew he had doubts about how much this would work. And she was doing everything in her power to ensure it did. At least so far as she believed it would.

"I know," he grumbled. "I don't have a good reason not to."

No, he didn't. Her gaze flicked briefly back to the window. There was one thing that had changed over these last few days. They'd ended up thrown in a cell. "What exactly happened to you in that cell?" The question tumbled out of her mouth before she could stop it. Not that she expected him to answer. It was difficult for him to answer personal questions.

His eyes found hers, which had gotten his attention. He tried to cover the reaction but failed. He shook his head, accompanied by a nonchalant shrug of his shoulders. "Nothing."

She shook her head. 'Bullshit,' was the simplest response. But they didn't need another argument to ensue because of that. "Something happened, Seru. I can feel the change in you. This... It's not the time to hide. *We* can't fix this if you won't talk to me."

"I'm not hiding and I am telling you the truth," he replied. "Just not all of it." He rolled his shoulders. Silence followed a sharp intake of breath. His talons curled into the edge of the mattress. "Nothing ever happened in the cell. If anything, it was a quiet reprieve from..." He closed his eyes. His brow knitted. "Why does it matter?"

"Because… it's the only place that things could've changed." And something like this impacted everything. All they'd been working toward. "Three days ago, not only were we making out like teenagers, but later you were all too eager to distract me from a nightmare. Two days ago, you talked about closing the marks. While we were in the Clouds yesterday… you spent half the day passed out. I know, I watched you." For a good while. He'd been so peaceful. "The only thing that changed after that… the cell." With a heavy sigh, she ran a hand across the top of her head. "You've spent days… days… telling me not to give Minerva power by focusing on my past." She'd been so busy trying to get answers, trying to understand the inner workings of the collar… none of the implications had crossed her mind if she delved too deep or in the wrong way. "Not only do I need to be stronger for this ritual, but we *both* need to be open to it. Everything… it all matters."

"I don't want to discuss it," he said stubbornly. "Let's just… do what needs done and get back to our other objectives."

Yeah, that was predictable. Rising from the floor, she walked back to the window. "You are my only objective." That's what he didn't get. It all led back to him.

"I'm not a problem that needs solving," he replied, his tone scathing and damn near venomous.

No. More stubborn than she was, but definitely not a problem. "I didn't say you were. My goal is to help you… free you… it hasn't changed." She gave a small shake of her head, then pivoted to face him. "Get mad or pissed at me all you want. It won't do any good. Might be better if you redirect it to yourself." She'd said it before. He was the only one standing in his own way. "At this rate, your stubbornness… your pride… it'll be your downfall. It'll be what keeps you here."

"I'm not mad at you. I'm frustrated," he corrected. "Your prodding about what I clearly don't wish to discuss isn't accomplishing any objective in a long list of them."

That made two of them. Extremely frustrated. As well as trying hard not to let her emotions get the best of her. Her fingers interlaced as she gripped the back of her neck, turning once more to face the window. Gods, she was over her pheromones. Amongst other things. "We can't afford any hindrances. You don't want to talk about it, fine, but you need to figure out how to deal with it. Get past it."

"It will pass on its own," he insisted. His tone mellowed; the tension lessened.

Gods, she hoped that was true. They had practically no time to bridge this gap. Physical intimacy would only take them so far. Just as much as replaying their wonderful memories in her head. Her eyes fell to the floor as she rubbed the achy muscles at the back of her neck. Tension had settled in her body. Something else that was probably a result of these pheromones.

He settled with a sigh. "How would you like to proceed?"

That was a good question. One she didn't exactly have the answer to. It all felt... clinical. Less personal. She'd been walking around naked for... how long now? And—a rush of hormones hit her so hard it sent her to the ground, her perfume suddenly more potent in the air between them. She had almost no time to react before she found herself on the ground. A cold sweat slicked her brow as a sharp, biting sensation tore through her, eclipsing any memory of the earlier sting. This time, she couldn't hold back the whimper.

Seru moved to her. He yanked her to her feet, setting her down as gently as possible while allowing her to lean against him as much as she needed. "I guess that answers that." He raked his talons through his mane.

Clutching his shirt in her hand, all she could tell herself was that it would pass. The last one had. This one should, too. Right? Her breath hitched, a desperate gasp for air in the suffocating darkness, her mind grasping for any escape.

He scooped her up, his arms strong and steady, and carried her to the bed, lowering her with great care into the rumpled sheets.

The throbbing eased, and she finally released the air she had held captive in her lungs. The tears that had sprung to her eyes rolled down her cheeks. She still had no words. No way to describe the agony that she'd just experienced. If what she knew about the pheromones was correct, without being handled, it would only get worse. Her eyes met his. "Please..." She didn't care how it sounded, but she'd rather have whatever came with him as an option than to go through that again.

He settled on the bed, kneeling beside her. Though irritation clouded his features, the concern in his eyes was undeniable. The conflicted blue slid from her, downcast. "Yes, fine..." he said, that barely audible whisper as if he hadn't spoken at all. He shifted on the bed, slipping between her thighs. Dipping his head low, he set his mouth on her.

The instant his mouth made contact, a wave of massive pleasure crashed through her. She balled up the covers beneath her hands as her back arched. Her toes curled as her legs slid against the fine material of his shirt. The light glow that had settled across her skin brightened ever so slightly. Waves of heat continued to pour off her, most noticeably from her inner thighs.

Not that Seru stopped. His hands shifted to her lower belly as he held her hips down. He relentlessly pursued her pleasure, leading her through repeated orgasms. She didn't know how much time passed or how many releases he'd given her. Countless moans passed her lips. There might have been a few rumbles or growls from him, but she couldn't tell. Her breath hitched with every touch, the world outside fading into a blur of muted sounds and colors.

As clinical as she thought it might be, it was anything but. Maybe she wasn't giving him pleasure, and at the same time, she very well could be... simply by allowing him to please her. It was a fleeting thought. The thought arrived and vanished as Seru helped her experience another wave of intense pleasure. As the lingering heat drained from her body, a wave of exhaustion washed over her, the day's worries dissolving as she sank into a deep, peaceful sleep.

Chapter Forty-Six

Cipriana shot Mac a furious, fleeting look, a silent message of her deep displeasure. Even with the tusks that jutted from the sides of his mouth, Chief Obrecht, the troll leader, seemed more open-minded than a purist. If that hadn't been the case, then she was positive negotiating a treaty would've been impossible. Just like her sister and brother-in-law had told her regarding the leader of the shape shifters. It was the very reason she agreed not to even waste time going there. Maybe she was just overreacting a bit, but this was her sister they were talking about.

Mac offered a sheepish glance, accompanied by a slight shrug.

As the Chief appeared more focused on where he walked than the two of them, Cipriana merely rolled her brown eyes at Mac. He just needed to learn to keep his trap shut. Instead of focusing on what had occurred, she checked out their surroundings. Something she'd done little of when they first arrived. The huts she could see seemed to be constructed from a woody material, perhaps bamboo or a similar plant. Nothing like what they used to build their homes, but still just as sturdy. The Chief's hut stood prominently at the village entrance; a sight they glimpsed after being halted by a handful of soldiers clad in impressive armor. Standing at an impressive ten to eleven feet tall, each of those males, just like the Chief, possessed tusks that jutted prominently from their mouths. Nothing like she'd ever seen before.

Cipriana glanced over her shoulder. As they strode deeper into the village, the clearing they had passed remained in sight. Six imposing towers formed a perimeter around the entire area, arranging the huts in three semicircles. They paused before a hut nestled within the inner curve of the semicircle, a position that offered the most shelter. As Chief Obrecht knocked, both she and Mac stood to the side, listening.

Not a moment later, the front door swung inward. On the other side stood a troll that looked awfully familiar. Not that she could place how. Standing at a formidable ten feet or more, he possessed a shock of dark red hair. The male bowed his head. "Chief Obrecht."

"Bruce. I expected you'd be on your way to the marketplace by now."

"I'm leaving here shortly."

Chief Obrecht gave a curt nod, his chin barely moving. "Good. These are our guests, the ones who'll be spending the evening with your family. This is Ambassador Cipriana and her mate, Maceron."

Mate? How had he gotten that? At no point had she referenced *that* word. When she'd introduced Mac, she'd purposely called him an associate. Nothing more.

"Of course, Chief. Cora and I will ensure they're well taken care of," Bruce replied.

"I'm positive you will." The chief turned to her and Mac. "You're in excellent hands here, so I'll take my leave." He lowered his head in a gesture of farewell, then walked away.

With a welcoming smile, Bruce moved out of their way. "Come on in. I'll introduce you to my mate."

"Thank you. And thank you for allowing us to spend the night in your home." Cipriana released Mac's hand and entered the hut, only to halt abruptly as Mac, with a gentle push, guided her deeper into the space. Her eyes widened. The female moving around the kitchen... was a shape shifter.

A breeze wafted in from the wide-open kitchen window over the sink, causing her dark gray fur to ripple softly. A radiant smile bloomed on her face as she turned to them, her other hand resting protectively on her significantly rounded belly. "Welcome to our home," the female said as she set a bowl of chopped-up fruit on the dining table. She moved into the front room, pressing herself against Bruce's side, her hand instinctively placed over her stom-ach.

Bruce beamed brightly, his arm wrapping around the female's shoulders as he affectionately kissed the top of her head. "This is my mate, Cora. Love, this is Ambassador Cipriana, and her mate, Maceron."

Cipriana just stared. As much as she tried not to, she couldn't seem to help herself. Her gaze darted between Cora and Bruce, a rapid back-and-forth. "You're... and he's..." Words. Words would be outstanding. She swallowed, her throat dry, and attempted to string together words that made sense. Still, she failed. It wasn't so much that the female was a shape shifter, and it was exactly the case.

A sly grin spread across Mac's face as he casually slung an arm over Cipriana's shoulders. "I believe that's her way of saying, It's wonderful to meet you both. And please, call me Mac and this beautiful female here, Cipriana. We're both pretty laid back."

"It is lovely to meet you both as well. Our son should be along soon, and dinner is just about ready." Cora tilted her head upward, her lips curving into a knowing smile as she lifted her hand to touch her mate's cheek. "You will be safe?"

With his hand engulfing hers, Bruce brought her palm to his lips and kissed the inside of her palm. "Always." He showered her with affection: a tender kiss gracing her lips, then her belly, followed by a gentle peck on her head, and finally, a lingering kiss returned to her lips.

"Say something," Mac whispered to Cipriana.

Her lips parted as if to speak, then clamped shut with a decisive click. Still, no words. Not only was the pair similar to her sister and brother-in-law, at least in some small way, it simply shook her to her core to see a shape shifter inside the troll village. And *now* the Chief's earlier response made so much more sense.

A firm, friendly squeeze came from Mac on her shoulder. "You'll have to forgive my silent companion here. She's usually... chattier."

"No worries," Bruce replied. "If you'll excuse me, I need to head off, but you'll be good here with Cora." He gave Cora another kiss before pulling away. "Is there anything you want me to pick up on my way home this evening?"

"It is alright," Cora said. Turning her attention back to her mate, she stroked his cheek. "Would you bring me some more of those sour candies? I ate them all again." She bit her lip, then leaned up to kiss him once more. "I love you."

"I love you, too." A grin spread across Bruce's face as he placed one more kiss on her belly. "Be good to mommy, little one. And yes, my love. More of the sour candies." With a last kiss planted on her head, he turned, strode toward the door, and departed.

As the male troll lumbered out of the house, Cipriana stared, then refocused her attention on Cora. "You're a shape shifter," she blurted. Oh, look, words. Even if it was stating the obvious.

"Smooth," Mac said.

"Shut up," she snapped at him. Ha! More words. Crude, but she'd actually strung complete sentences together.

"Darn, and here I thought I was hiding it better," Cora teased. "I am okay with questions; I am sure you have them. Though there are certain things I will not discuss in front of my son when he gets home. But there is always later when he goes to bed, too." She paused for a moment. "Um, please, make yourselves at home. In here, or in the dining room, wherever you would prefer. I just have a couple of things to finish up. May I get you both something to drink?"

"Well, I do, but mostly because you're a shape shifter, and he's a troll, and you're pregnant. And my brother-in-law is a shape shifter, too, and there are just some questions you don't really want to ask your sister, not with things of a more private nature." Each word tumbled out one after another at a breakneck pace. The words had been a jumbled mess in her mind from the moment they entered, and she hadn't meant to let them all spill out. With a sigh escaping her lips, Cipriana blinked. Yep, she could string things together really fast.

A smirk played on Mac's lips. "See, I told you she was chatty."

"Did you just call me a chatterbox?" Her eyes narrowed in anger as she crossed her arms, glaring at him.

"No. I said, 'chatty.' Big difference." A short, amused bark escaped him. He removed his arm from her shoulders, walked to the expansive wooden dining table, and sat down. "A drink would be nice, thank you."

"I can certainly understand the... awkwardness of asking your sister those things." The female let out a soft laugh. "Well, feel free to ask whatever you would like. My son is a full shape shifter. This pregnancy has been a brand-new experience in many ways." With her hand idly stroking her full stomach, Cora made her way back into the kitchen, her gaze flicking over her shoulder. "We have chilled tea, or I can make hot regular water and flavored water, or milk if you would prefer that?"

A silent communication passed between Mac and Cipriana as their gazes locked. *Milk?* She'd never heard of that. It appeared he hadn't either. "Um, tea is fine, thank you." She felt a pang of sadness, subtle yet undeniable, but couldn't quite pinpoint the cause. She'd kind of prattled a lot. Though from what Cora said, if her son was a full shape shifter, then it meant this was likely her first hybrid child. That was really what all of her questions related to, given her sister's relationship. As she crossed the room, a gentle breeze from an open window brushed her skin before she settled at the dining room table. "You said this pregnancy is different. How?"

"Flavored water for me, please," Mac responded.

Cora inclined her head in acknowledgment to both individuals. As she talked, she busied herself in the kitchen, gathering beverages. "Oh, different cravings, that is a big one. Certain foods I cannot stand this time, that I craved the first time around, not that they were usually available. Um, with Carson, I needed to sleep on my side; with this young, I have to sleep on my back or he crushes my ribs." The female let out a small, suppressed laugh. "He is also much bigger than my first son was, and is growing at a much faster rate. He is much healthier, too, and I have had fewer complications." Cora stopped briefly, her eyes darting toward the door. She glanced back at the pair, her hip resting lightly against the table as she brought her tea to her lips. "I almost lost Carson more than once. Of course, those I attribute to the more advanced care and better nourishment that are available here. I suppose I was lucky, though, that Carson's... birth father... actually cared if he survived the pregnancy—though more for the status of having a son than anything—so I was not denied medical care like many in Métamorphe."

Okay. Cravings. She glanced at Mac... he was giving her this look. One she didn't really like. Cipriana shook her head, the slight movement clearing her thoughts, and then she returned her focus to the female before her. "Could his father account for his size and growth rate?" It seemed better than saying that he was a half-breed or hybrid. While she didn't want to overlook the part about the females near miscarriage, it made her curious if that was common amongst shape shifters. Or could it result from other issues? There were some miscarriages that had occurred even in her own species. Not that a male had been around for eleven years.

"Thank you for the drinks," Mac added.

"You are welcome." Still standing, Cora savored another slow sip of her tea, its delicate aroma filling the air. "I think that could definitely be part of it. Canines do not get as large as trolls are. Felines are a different story, but even then, that depends on what type they are. You said your brother-in-law is a shape shifter?"

"Yes, he's a panther." Cipriana tilted her head. Although she'd given her sister and brother-in-law her support, sort of, it would be good to know more. Not that she'd asked Parthenia for more information. She figured it was safest if she knew as little as possible. "Gavin. His name is Gavin."

"And you gave me a dirty look," Mac stated, disappointment evident in his tone.

She had every right to be certain he could take care of her sister. The two of them intended to leave Prisma Isle. How else could she give them her blessing? Cipriana glowered at him. Of course, she gave him one. He deserved it. Instead of snapping at him, she refocused on Cora, letting out a deep, weary sigh. "I worry about them."

"I can understand that. It is very dangerous for mixed couples when one of them is a shape shifter."

"I've heard that. It was the reason we're avoiding Métamorphe." But they were going to get close to it, weren't they? Why hadn't she thought to have her sister and brother-in-law go this direction? They could've ended with the manticores, then gone back to Pteryrina and she and Mac could've gone the other way. It hadn't occurred to her to suggest otherwise. Despite the successful outcome, she had been preoccupied with her annoyance that Mac had insisted on joining her.

"From what I gathered, they're both very careful." Mac took a sip of his drink. He fixed his gaze on the cup for a beat, then his eyes flickered to Cora. "What's in this?"

"That one was made with strawberries, but several flavors are made here," Cora replied. "That is good on both accounts. Being careful. My son and I have not left these boundaries since we came here, almost eleven *solaris* ago."

The sound of running footsteps and gleeful laughter grew louder outside before the front door burst open, revealing a juvenile shape shifter.

A high-pitched male voice in the distance called out, "You know I let you win!"

"Ha, ha, in your dreams, Gregory!" Still chuckling, the young, male shape shifter turned around, his laughter fading as he froze, the door still wide open. His pale-blue eyes darted from her to Mac, then to Cora, and then back once more. "Hey," he said, easing the door shut behind him. He went immediately to Cora and kissed her cheek. "Hey, Mom."

"Hello, sweetheart." She pressed a kiss to his head, a soft sigh escaping her lips. "You are filthy. You are going to wash up before you help me in the kitchen."

"Sure thing. Sorry, Mom." He rubbed her belly, a soft chuckle rumbling in his chest. "Hey, little bro." Pivoting, he'd only taken two steps when his mother spoke up.

"Manners, Carson. This is Cipriana and her mate, Mac."

"Yes, ma'am." He changed his direction, turning and extending his hand. "Nice to meet you both. I'm Carson."

Her eyes flickered from the hand to Mac and Cora, a look of bewilderment on her face. What was she supposed to do with it? Pick it up? Stick her own out? Seemed ridiculous to do either. Cipriana tilted her head, a furrow forming between her brows as confusion washed over her.

"Good to meet you, too." Rising to his feet, Mac offered Carson a handshake and a broad, beaming smile. "You'll have to forgive her. They're a bit more formal where she's from."

He said it like it was a bad thing. Curtsies and bowing were appropriate whenever meeting someone new. With a frown, Cipriana sent a sharp glare toward her supposed *mate*. Arrogant ass. She shifted her focus to the young male. "It's wonderful to make your acquaintance." Then she copied Mac's handshake with the child, her hand firm and steady.

"No worries." Carson went to the sink and washed up. "I've got the rest, Mom."

"Thank you, sweetheart." She looked at Cipriana and Mac. "Please excuse me. I will be right back." With her hand still on her belly, the female disappeared down the hallway.

"So, you two are just here for the night?" he asked. With a few pieces of linen in hand, he retrieved an item from an odd contraption. He carried a tray with something dark that smelled rich and earthy, accompanied by bread, to the table.

"Yes, we're intending to meet with the manticores tomorrow." Or so she hoped. She didn't know how things would go based on what little information she had on the species.

"That should be fun," Mac muttered, pinching the bridge of his nose.

Good gods, he accompanied her why? A sigh escaped her as she rolled her eyes, then reached for the cup and took a taste of the tea. Oh, wow. That was freezing. How was that even remotely possible? Her gaze darted to the equipment the male used, just as the aroma of the food he retrieved filled the space. Her nose wrinkled. It smelled strange. "What's that? Well, both things." She gestured with her finger toward the square, metallic object, then followed with a motion indicating the platter of food.

"Cool. I've never met a manticore before." As Carson walked to the dining room with plates and utensils, his eyes briefly met hers. He pointed at the object. "That's a stove, what we used to cook things in. And that," he gestured to the platter in the center of the table, "is venison—deer. If you don't want that, my dad made fish. I like the venison better, and Mom's not supposed to eat fish right now; it makes her sick. What do you guys normally eat?"

"Fruit, vegetables... whatever we grow in our gardens. Sometimes we make them as stews. Or cook them over the fire." A stove? Something to cook food. How interesting? Rising, Cipriana went to investigate the stove, her eyes scanning its top before grasping the handle and giving it a tug.

Mac leaped to his feet, dashed to her side, and gave her a sharp tug backward. "Yeah. Let's not do something stupid."

"What're you talking about?"

"You realize that's hot, right?" He retreated a step. "But if you want to burn yourself, be my guest. I won't stop you." With a smirk, Mac folded his arms across his chest, his eyes glinting with amusement.

"Well, we have those, too. Obviously." The child gestured toward the table. "So, you cook over an open fire? And you've never had meat? Yeah, you should definitely be careful. Burns are no joke." With a nod, he indicated the round, raised bumps on the box's upper surface. "We cook stews and stuff up here, or things that need to be made in a frying pan. Never want to touch those when the stove is hot." Opening the door wider, he indicated the rack inside, where heat still emanated. "Or that—it gets hotter than the burners on top. It's where we make bigger meats, things like that, or sweet treats. Mom makes a mean cake."

"It took me quite some time to get the hang of using it," Cora said from the hallway.

Looking over his shoulder, Carson chuckled. "Oh yeah, I've heard some stories... that I'm pretty glad I don't remember actually happening."

Cora narrowed her sea-green eyes. "Be nice."

"Well, we eat fish, but it's a rare treat." One they hadn't had in a long time. Of course, she'd negotiated with Mac for that to change. Was this something else she should've considered? A... what did he call it... a stove? Yeah, a stove. It would certainly make cooking a lot easier. As it was, even making a cake took an extreme amount of time over an open fire.

"I can teach you how to use one, if you'd like," Mac stated. His eyes flicked from Cora to Carson, then back again. "Curious hands often equal minor burns."

"Yes, they do." Cora grinned.

"Yeah, I used to burn myself all the time. That was a long time ago, though."

Her gaze turned to Mac. She hadn't thought to ask how any of the food they'd eaten in his village had been made. And it wasn't something they'd seen with the dwarves, either. "You know how to use one of these?"

"We have a kitchen house in our village. Felix ensured I knew how everything in the village functioned, which meant I've worked in every role."

"We had a kitchen house where I came from, too. We either used an open fire or a mud stove, though nothing like this."

Carson glanced at his mother but said nothing.

"We have an arrangement with the fae, so ours are closer to this." Mac motioned to the stove. "Except larger."

Cipriana's eyes widened. "They come bigger?" How was that even possible? Their lives were rather simple. The most they had with anything was in their armory, except no one worked there anymore. Not since her father passed away.

"I think they can probably be made in whatever size is needed. I have never seen it, but my mate has told me the one where he works is quite large."

"Oh?" Cipriana tilted her head. "If you don't mind my asking, where does he work?" Maybe that's how she recognized him. She'd seen him somewhere in the marketplace. They had been there a couple of days ago.

"You planning to visit him?" Mac asked, a single eyebrow arching in question.

Her eyebrows drew together in a frown, and she gave him an exasperated roll of her eyes. There was something in his voice, although he seemed to tone it down. "I thought I recognized him. Nothing more."

"Even if she did, it wouldn't do any good," Carson commented.

"Carson!"

"Sorry." Going over to the table, the kid shut his mouth with a few pieces of fruit. "Just meant he's pretty attached, that's all."

Cora shook her head at her son. "Do not talk with your mouth full." With a sigh, she turned her attention back to Cipriana and Mac. "My apologies. My mate works at a place called Zancle's Rock."

"Oh, no! I really just..." Wow. Talk about talon in the mouth. Maybe she should've stated *why* to begin with, then it wouldn't have sounded like she found him attractive. No. Regardless of how he irritated her, she thought someone else was... a small glint in her eye as she glanced at Mac. Nope. She wasn't going there. Cipriana pressed her fingers to her temples, a familiar gesture of stress. "I think we were there a few days ago when we first started our journey. My sister, her mate, and I... well, and a friend of theirs."

Mac leaned down close to Carson and whispered, "Don't worry, kid. She's got her eye on me. No matter who she tries to fool." He sat down then, the rough wood of the chair creaking under him.

Cipriana sat down at the table once more, her eyes locking onto Mac with a fierce glare. Yeah, he was good-looking, but it didn't change his arrogance. Who would want to put up with that for a lifetime? "Maybe we should just eat."

Mac shut the door behind himself, Cipriana ahead of him. The bedroom furniture, mirroring that found throughout the house, was gargantuan, as if built for trolls. There was a small table on either side of the bed, each with a lantern; a dresser with four drawers against the wall; a round table in the corner with two chairs pushed in; and a closet. The bed had a dark-blue blanket on it with crimson stripes, and there were two plush pillows.

She glanced over her shoulder at him. "Do you have a preference for which side?"

"I'll take the right, so I'm closest to the door." It was probably a little macho, but he couldn't help it. While they'd held hands and kissed, there were things neither of them really shared with one another. Even more so, over the last couple of days, she hadn't asked him once about the crystal in his possession. Something he figured might come up at some point, especially as she'd gotten roped into making sure it got delivered to the dragons.

"Any reason?" she asked, strolling over to the left side of the bed.

He gripped the back of his neck, his gaze sinking to the floor in front of him. It hadn't been necessary to discuss before, even when they slept in the cave. But he also didn't want to sound sexist either, given all the progress they'd made over the last few days. But he wouldn't lie, either. "My... birth father. He taught me that a male protects his female, even when they sleep."

Cipriana stopped halfway to the bed. Turning toward him, her eyebrows knitted together. "I've never heard you talk much about your birth parents. I mean, a little about your mother, but I think this is the first time you've mentioned your father."

That wasn't what he expected her to say. Really, he thought she'd spout something off about her ability to take care of herself. Which he knew without a doubt she could do. Maybe he really was reaching past that tough exterior. Mac approached the vast bed, sank onto its edge, and propped his elbows on his knees. His eyes fell to his lap, the fabric of his trousers a dull blur. "I don't have many memories of them. Mostly bits and pieces." Including the day someone killed them.

The talons of her feet clicked against the hardwood floor as she crossed the room to where he sat. She perched on the bed next to him. "Is it painful to recall those you have?"

He wasn't sure how to answer that. When they'd spoken about his mother, he admitted as much to missing her; which he also missed his father. Over the last couple of days, he thought of them more than he had in the past. Not that he could attribute that to meeting her or to the loss of Felix. His shoulders slumped as he stared blankly at the floor. "I'm not sure. I mean, most of what I recall are the good times. Like my mom whenever she sang; or my father showing me how to scale a tree." His attention momentarily shifted to her. "Those used to come up to counteract the terrible memories. These last few days, they make me think about how much they would've liked you. It reminds me of everything they'll miss."

"Moving on without a parent can be hard, especially when... things are happening in your life that you don't quite understand or maybe you feel ill-prepared for."

"Exactly." His explanation hadn't really done it justice, but Cipriana had certainly summed it up perfectly. It was probably why he'd talked about their budding relationship with Parthenia and Gavin. Just the way those two stared at one another screamed love. While he wasn't ready to say that to Cipriana, he definitely didn't want their time together to come to such a quick end. Mac sat up. "I know I kind of hijacked your journey, but I'm glad you let me come along."

Cipriana rolled her eyes and let out a dismissive snicker. "You didn't really give me a choice. However, having you with me has proven... fruitful."

"Be still my heart," he teased. "That almost sounded like a compliment." At least in some small way; certainly, more than she'd given him up to that point.

Her nose wrinkled and a slight twinkle appeared in her hazel eyes. "I suppose it was."

The look on her face. Mac erupted in laughter as he wrapped an arm around Cipriana and brushed his lips across her temple. "Did it really taste *that* sour on your tongue?"

"No." She smirked. "I know I give you a lot of crap, but you have actually been really helpful. I'm glad you invited yourself along."

"That's good to hear." It was something he tried his best to do since he'd attended the meetings with the Elders by her side. The two of them hadn't outright described themselves as a couple, but it benefited them. And Cipriana never objected. His fingers traced the length of her arm, a gentle caress, while his brow creased in thought. "How come you've corrected no one on their assumption of us being together?"

Cipriana opened her mouth and snapped it shut. She pursed her lips. "I don't really know." With a sigh, her piercing, hazel eyes turned to meet his gaze. "When Kihrig said something, I noticed that he seemed to respect me a little more. Then with Obrecht... I don't know, there was just something in the way he mentioned it. Don't get me wrong, I am attracted to you, but I'm not exactly sure how to be a couple." She paused, angling toward him. "I hear the way you talk about your parents, and it's not something I've ever seen. Unless you count my sister and Gavin." With a slight scoff, she rolled her eyes. "My parents didn't have that. My mother was one of several breeding partners for my father."

Aside from acknowledging what she said, he didn't know how else to react. Felix had taught him about sirens. For a long time, he hadn't believed the expectations of males in the siren society. Maybe it was part of the reason he didn't care for females touching him. Something he didn't mind with Cipriana, or at least he wanted with her. The thought of numerous hands reaching for him sent a wave of icy dread down his spine. With his free hand, Mac swept across the top of his head, his fingers tangling in his hair. "Who says there has to be one right way? Every couple is different. What works for one may not work for another. As long as we're both honest with each other, I think we can figure out what makes us happy. That's all that matters in the end, right?"

"I suppose so." She bit her bottom lip. "I'm not really used to thinking about what makes me happy. Right now, I worry a lot about how being the Rising Elder will change my life. You know? Especially as I'll become responsible for the entirety of my species.

That's without taking into consideration these different treaties that we've negotiated and the impact that'll have going forward."

Mac gently cupped her chin, turning her face toward his until their eyes locked. "We don't have to rush anything between us. I know you have a lot on your plate, and I wouldn't do anything to interfere or hinder that." Quite the opposite. He'd do whatever was in his power to support her. She deserved nothing less.

"Even if it means our time together is limited? With what you know about Pteryrina, are you prepared to be the only male seen in the last eleven years?"

How did he answer that? Before he even met Cipriana, he considered turning the Elder position over to Maggie. Not that he couldn't manage if she refused, but she was better suited to the role. He rubbed the back of his neck. Moving to Pteryrina may not be the best move for him, but he'd prepared for it. As long as he got to spend time with Cipriana every day, it would be worth it. "I need to show you something."

"Okay?" She raised an eyebrow.

Mac stood and dug the darkened, orange crystal out of his pocket. He held it out to her. "Can you hold this?"

Leaning forward, she paused, her hand trembling slightly, before finally taking the object from his grasp. Her eyes narrowed in disbelief as Cipriana let out a sharp gasp. "Holy poppies! How do you deal with carrying this? It feels... horrid."

"Honestly, I'm not sure. Maybe it has something to do with my flames, but it doesn't really bother me." Not that it compared to the darkness that consumed the isle across the way. That had almost knocked him on his ass. It had been pretty noxious. He eyed the space between him and the door, a faint scent of dust filling his nostrils as he moved a little closer. This was something he hadn't been able to do since he'd taken possession of the crystal. Hopefully, as long as it wasn't in his grasp, this would work.

Steeling himself, Mac took a deep, steadying breath, trying to ease the tension from his muscles. It didn't normally take concentration, but it had been a while since he'd last utilized this ability. Closing his eyes, he found solace in the steady, comforting rhythm of Cipriana's heartbeat and her even breaths. The length of his hair grew until it tickled his shoulders. With a wince, he heard the snapping and popping of his joints and limbs as he became a few inches shorter, his reach diminished, and his facial features softened.

Even without the sharp intake of breath, he knew the change had completed; a silent confirmation settling around him. It was a strange ability, one that he never quite understood the purpose of, but nonetheless, he could switch his gender. Despite his dark, lustrous hair and the unchanged color of his eyes and wings, he now presented as and sounded like a female counterpart to himself. Mac opened his eyes.

Cipriana stared at him, blinking rapidly. "How?" she squeaked out.

"I can't really explain that," he said in a silvery voice. Although he believed it had something to do with why his parents opted to leave Pteryrina when they did. If many saw him as a girl until his true gender took shape, then it made perfect sense. Not that they ever mentioned anything about it before their deaths. "I know. It's a little strange."

"Strange is one way of putting it." She canted her head. "Do you switch like this often?"

"Usually, the only time I do this is when I head into the market-place. It lets me blend in a little better." As long as he wore a cloak to cover his wings, no one ever paid him much attention when he was a woman. It was a good reason to convince him this was a defensive ability of his, along with a few others.

"Is this how you were planning to get into Pteryrina in the first place? I mean, so you could cleanse the crystal."

Not initially. Then he'd gotten a whiff of Thalasia's pheromones and that plan changed, but he didn't want to tell her that. Beyond his first idea, he hadn't been sure; though this had been a consideration. "Nothing solid had really come to me until we met."

"Oh?"

Now he had to come up with something. His eyes darted to the multi-pointed star emblem on the band encircling her wrist. "What if you take it up to be cleansed while I wait at the bottom of the stairs or something? And you can mention me to the Elder, perhaps a few others. When you come back, we get it to the dragons, and then go back up together."

She narrowed her eyes, a thoughtful gesture as her finger tapped against her chin. The golden pools of amber and green shimmered, catching the light. "I think that sounds like a great idea."

"You had me worried for a second." He let out a huge breath as his shoulders sagged a touch. Nothing about the plan was half-assed or thrown together; at least not in the long-run, but she could've dismissed it without question. That was entirely her right.

"So, are you going to change back? Or do you intend to stay like that all night? I'm just asking because it might frighten our hosts in the morning." Cipriana snickered.

With a snort, he planted his hands on his hips and began a rhythmic sway, punctuated by deliberate poses. "Are you trying to say I might frighten them?" he gasped jokingly.

"No, not at all," she said, her words dripping with sarcasm.

"If you say so." With a wink, Mac executed the same steps he had previously taken. It took less effort to transition back into his true gender than it had for the initial switch. As he grew taller, his hair shortened, and his feminine charm vanished, Cipriana let out a loud gasp.

Dismounting the bed, she approached him, cradled his jaw in her hand, and caressed his cheek with her thumb. "Still, so strange." Her lips met his in a tender kiss.

"Mmm, if that's how you respond to the bizarre, then I'll take it." With the orange crystal back in his possession, its rough facets pressing into his palm, he pulled her close and kissed her. Gods, the explosion of her taste on his tongue left him practically breathless. Not that he'd take it any further than kissing; at least not until she was ready. He brushed his lips across hers one more time. "We should really get some rest," he murmured.

"Yes, we should."

Mac threaded their fingers together and led her over to the humongous bed. The two of them could easily fit on one side together, which suited him just fine. Even with the glint he noticed in her hazel eyes, they were going to rest. Nothing more; at least not tonight.

Fagonia slipped quietly through a window into the back bedroom of Vasilia's home. While it wasn't public information to the remaining sirens, she'd learned of the private selection of Cipriana as the next Elder. After these years, kissing Vasilia's ass and bowing down to her, *she* was supposed to be named next in line. Not some child! Then she could've done away with this silly notion of working with the other species. The only reason she even tolerated Markham's presence was that he'd been temporarily useful.

Since his Informants failed in their mission to collect that damn bluebird, it was an arrangement that wouldn't last much longer. Even her seitadi failed as well. Though seeing that so-called dragon flying in the sky... well, now, wasn't that a welcome surprise. A saint beast... remained on the isle? Not only that, he'd become attached to the bluebird. The fucker had devoured several of her precious babies. Though she had more where they came from. She'd sent a new pair to watch over the saint beast and bluebird once they'd fallen asleep. Which would've worked out wonderfully if the two hadn't disappeared in the morning.

Her seitadi had scoured the entire isle, but hadn't located either of them for nearly a whole day. She received word not too long ago that they'd been spotted in the marketplace. While she couldn't be positive, with what she learned of the bluebird, it stood to reason those two would head to Pteryrina. Sooner rather than later. Just meant she had to do whatever was necessary to keep them away for as long as possible.

Especially while she executed the next phase of her plan. And she had those creatures at her disposal that were quite expendable. Certainly, meant less of her own that she had to sacrifice. She had no problem allowing those guilers to be slaughtered by such a well-trained warrior. Only a few would be necessary with... addressing her niece.

Carefully measuring each step, Fagonia crept silently across the bedroom, weaving past the bed and armoire to use the door as concealment. She removed a dagger from a well-hidden sheath in her dress and waited.

It didn't take long before the bedroom door swung inward. Fagonia pressed her back against the cool, rough wall, her wings clamped shut as Vasilia ventured deeper into the room. The moment the female cleared the doorway, Fagonia darted forward. With her arm around Vasilia, she secured the female's arms and wings before pressing the blade to her throat.

"Fagonia."

"Here, I didn't think you'd noticed me." Her lip curled in a silent, mocking gesture. The woman had likely spent enough years observing her to recognize her distinct physical characteristics. No way Vasilia, the soon-to-be former Elder, spotted her and didn't fight back.

"Do you honestly believe I'm unaware of your antics?"

Oh, so that was the case. The woman knew she'd been leaving Pteryrina. No way she had knowledge of all the specifics. Even if she knew about her plans, it didn't matter. Nothing could stop what was coming. "So, you think you know what I've been up to?"

"Of course, I do. And I have taken action to counteract your plans. There are things in motion that you cannot stop."

"Naming that little girl as the Rising Elder will do nothing. She's weak and pathetic. And if you think that damn bluebird and her beast are going to make a difference... well, there are a few surprises in store for them, too." With a swift, brutal motion, Fagonia slit Vasilia's throat, cutting off her words mid-utterance. Blood splattered across the white duvet and stained her clothing as the female gurgled, clutching her neck in a desperate effort to stop the crimson flow.

Not that it would help. With a heavy thud, Vasilia collapsed forward, her knees making solid contact with the floor. It might be a life-threatening injury, but it wouldn't be enough to kill the female entirely. No. Good thing she knew exactly what it would take to complete the job. And she came fully prepared for it. After all, it wasn't the first time she had removed a pair of wings. In fact, it had been on that fateful day seventeen years ago when she'd first crossed paths with that fetid shape shifter.

"This might hurt." Fagonia's smirk widened as she kneeled, her hand finding the base of Vasilia's wing before she applied pressure and broke it. The crisp, sharp pop echoed beautifully through the air as the bone snapped. It wouldn't be enough. Her hand tight on the dagger, she tore at the wing, and crimson blood splattered the bedding, the floorboards, and her gown. As she worked, she thought back to the day she met Markham.

Fagonia had used the piercing screech of her seitadi to knock out Sanaya and Meteron. She strolled up to the two of them on the ground and scanned her surroundings. Nothing. Wherever their child was, she didn't see him. She had lost track of them for a few minutes. Of all the directions they could've chosen, why this one? So close to the enchanted fae forest. Her next actions would need to be swift.

There would be no point in questioning them further. The two had made it clear they would not give up the child's location. She crouched over Sanaya. "So pretty. Looks don't last. That's all you have."

The female's eyes flipped open. Fagonia sneered. "Oh good. I had hoped you would come around. Killing you wouldn't be any fun otherwise."

Sanaya's eyes flew open in shock, but before a sound could escape her lips, Fagonia's blade slit her throat. It wouldn't be the end-all of the female's life. "Don't worry. You'll still feel everything."

Fagonia grinned as she rolled the female to her side. The blood kept dripping from the open wound on Sanaya's neck as she pulled her wings free from her shoulder blades. The female attempted to struggle and scream, but no sounds came forth.

Rolling her shoulders, Fagonia cracked her neck as the female's body went limp in her hands. With blood coating her fingers, she jumped over to Meteron, who lay there unable to move. At some point, he'd come around as she took the life of his mate.

"Oh, good. I had truly hoped you'd get to witness this. She was lovely. You both could have avoided all of this."

Meteron hissed. "Demeter will—"

Feigning a yawn, she stabbed him in the heart and cut off his words. "Goddess, you can get wordy."

Grateful for the quiet, she yanked the knife from his chest, shoved him over, and rammed the blade into his shoulder blades repeatedly. She sat there for a moment, the metallic scent of his blood clinging to her skin. The soft rustle of leaves tickled her ears. Someone was coming. No one could know what she'd done. Fagonia grabbed the knife and shot into the trees. She flew away from the scene.

A masculine voice called out to her. "That was quite exquisite. Not you, so much, but what you did. I rather enjoyed watching it."

Pausing mid-air, she half glanced over her shoulder and smirked. "So glad you enjoyed it." Her words dripped with sarcasm. She cared not for his feelings. Disgusting, filthy, earthbound. Her gaze shot toward the sound when a fresh rustle of leaves broke the quiet. The fae weren't the only creatures they were close to. She flew farther from the scene and found herself a nice tree to watch everything unfold. She needed to see which creatures turned up and if the child came out of hiding.

"Oh, I did. It was quite entertaining." Nodding his head in her direction, the bear reached a paw up to touch the circlet crown atop his head. Reshaping himself, he pivoted and resumed his original course. Seven feet tall now, a foot taller than he had been before on all fours, a billowing black robe covered him from head-to-toe. It dragged along the ground behind him.

Hmm, this new form of his intrigued her. A shadow amongst the trees. She scoffed. Truly, she should wait to see what creatures came forth. Though ... her seitadi rested nearby. They could capture what followed for her and report back later. Fagonia leaped from the tree, soaring through the air as she followed in his wake. "You're quite a way from your village, furball."

"My path is no concern of yours, passerine. Move along, please."

"As my actions were no concern of yours, yet you felt it necessary to comment, regardless." She really didn't care where he planned to go. Or his reason for being there. But he'd piqued her curiosity all the same.

"I was merely paying a compliment where it was due. It is rare to find someone who enjoys malice as much as I do."

"Truly, if you were to pay a compliment, you would've stated something less obvious. Such as how their death came too swiftly." If she'd had her way, she would've prolonged it and tortured them for the information she sought. The location prohibited those actions.

He let out a low chuckle. "Perhaps I misjudged you. If you thought the deaths came too swiftly, why ever did you not take them somewhere more remote to prolong it? This isle is vast. There are many places where torture can be drawn out, information that is sought can be gathered, etcetera." He shrugged. "But, perhaps, a swift death is what you sought."

She perched in a nearby tree. 'He' misjudged her? Fagonia scoffed. Perhaps it was the other way around. *"I am aware of how vast the isle is; though one must learn to discern when the desired information cannot be collected. They would not reveal what I sought."* At least not on their own. Her *seitadi* would provide her with exactly what she needed.

"Sometimes, the way forward is not clear and experimentation is needed. But now, because of their swift death, the opportunity is lost. Or am I still misjudging things?" He waved a skeletal hand. "It is no matter, and not my concern. I have better things to attend to."

"And sometimes the way forward is nothing more than patience." She chuckled. Leaving him to his own devices, she launched herself into the air again, flying back in the direction she had traveled. Although something told her they would cross paths yet again.

He was still a filthy furball; even if they were currently on the same side. It didn't bother her that once again her dress was blood-stained. She'd only clove through half the bone; not that she would quit. No. It would be difficult, but if someone stumbled upon her too soon, they could resurrect Vasilia with The Reflection Pools. Even if she was missing one wing. While the woman hadn't put up a fight, it wouldn't surprise her if the female somehow clung to life.

Which meant she only had one option. Remove both wings. As no one expected to see the Elder for quite some time, well, she could certainly oblige.

Chapter Forty-Seven

Mac sat on the bottom two steps of Anemos, the pearly staircase that led to the silver gates of Pteryrina, feeling the cool marble beneath him. As discussed, Cipriana had gone up with the orange crystal. Originally, the plan had been for them to visit with the manticores that morning, but when they'd woken up, Cipriana had felt off. Not that she seemed sick, however, something certainly troubled her. It may have gone completely unnoticed if he hadn't paid so much attention to her mannerisms during breakfast. She'd been rigid, consistently crossing and uncrossing her ankles, and picked at her food. The truth had come out only once they'd left the troll village.

As he stared out across the white sandy beach, he hoped that whatever had shaken her earlier would be abated by the time she came back down. Until then, he focused on the rhythmic crashing of the waves, the stunning blue of the ocean, and the pleasant heat of the bright sun. Leaning back against one stair, he played out all the possibilities of what it could be like living here.

The sound of shifting sand reached his ears, which made little sense unless Parthenia and Gavin had returned as well. Sitting up, Mac scanned his surroundings in both directions, but he saw nothing. He was positive he'd heard something. Without hesitating, he shot to his feet and walked to the right side of the staircase. Still, nothing. He turned around to check the other side, and a deafening screech hit his ears.

Dropping to his knee, his hands instinctively went to cradle his head, pressing down on either side. His eyes darted all around, searching for the fucking black-winged bird causing the ringing in his eardrums. Instead, he found himself face-to-face with four dark guilers. Judging by the brutish-looking one, at least one of them had the earth element. Red splotches covered two of them, something akin to a rash, which made them fire. The last one bothered him the most. Aside from a few bony protrusions, nothing about the guiler identified their element.

Either way, he had to keep them from going up the staircase. A frenzy like he'd never felt before burned through him. Dropping his hands, Mac pushed to his feet and pounded his fists together. Emerald flames surged up his arms, casting an eerie glow. He didn't wait for the attack to come to him. A low rumble resounded in his chest as he charged straight for the fire guilers.

He slammed his knuckles right into one face of the creature, a green blaze quickly engulfing the pyromancer, a chartreuse color scorching through their veins. Their howls of pain didn't quite cover the consistent shriek blaring from high in the trees. Something wet trickled down his earlobes onto his neck. Not that he had much time to give it any attention as he dodged an incoming fireball, which charred the head of the railing. He didn't see the sharpened root that another launched at the same time. Unable to escape, the fallen branch tore a deep wound in his arm, crimson blood blooming across the gritty sand.

Before he had the chance to get back up, the geomancer sprang forward and punched him in the nose, knocking him back on his ass. He collapsed against the staircase, a sharp edge digging into his back. The sting barely registered as he rolled out of the way of another fireball. Two more attacks came at him, which he used to his advantage, and ducked them both, ending up on the ground. Blood from his broken nose pooled beneath him.

Before he could even shift his weight, a small, sharp object pricked the side of his neck. What was that? It was like he'd gotten stung by a small creature of some kind. With little time to analyze what happened, Mac rolled out of the way of another attack. He did it twice more as his legs refused to function. A touch of lightheadedness came over him during the third attempt, and the world seemed to spin in a dizzying dance. *Shit.* His tongue felt like lead as the blackness crept in, and he lost consciousness.

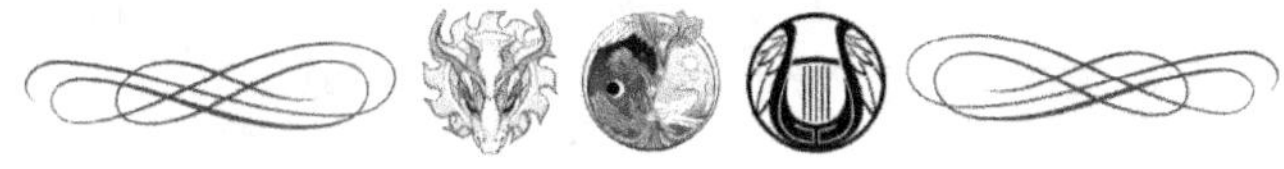

Seru focused on subduing his body's instinct and attempting to shake off the energy coursing from her to him. The vibration along his skin served as a constant irritation, distracting him from his thoughts. If this truly was her awakening, this problem wouldn't be resolving itself soon. If anything, it'd occur more frequently and more intensely with each pass. A chronic condition that required monitoring and near-constant treatment.

The thought was enough to have him rubbing his temples. The solution to pawn her off on another—to at least split the responsibility—crossed his mind again. And it wouldn't likely be the last time it did... Ione had been his initial option, but that only worked if they remained in the Clouds under dragon rule.

With each passing bout with Aurelia and the crystals—not to mention Thalasia's reaction to being in the Clouds for only a short while—that was bordering on the impossible. Ione had voiced her concerns regarding the eventuality that Aurelia would call the colors.

When she did, every clan, including Ione's, would be expected to rally their armies and answer that call. The ever-present issue existed in that the First had no army to call. Their ruse would be up the moment the call went out. An ethereal army only stood a chance when not actively withstanding the test of combat.

Though he had a contingency plan in the wings, he wasn't about to reveal that until absolutely necessary. Too many unpredictable variables made negotiating with the sirens a better option, assuming it could be done. That, he was at least certain they held some stakes in accomplishing.

"What's wrong?" Seru asked, breaking the silence as he caught her eyes on him. Clearly, they were both embroiled in their own thoughts—some about each other, others about their predicaments and ways to come out on top and remain there.

The quiet stroll provided an unwelcome window of reflection, one that left them both at the ready and waiting for the next encounter with enemy forces. There wasn't a chance they'd make it to Pteryrina without conflict of some kind. Too many enemies. Too many directions for them to travel. It was highly unlikely the other species—on and off the isle—didn't have plans of their own implemented to cease negotiations and incite further in-fighting.

"I'm concerned that we won't be able to bridge this gap before tomorrow evening. That we'll get to the ritual... and we won't be where we need to be."

Seru inhaled, readying himself for the conversation that she undoubtedly thought they needed to have. "And how do you think we should go about readying ourselves?"

The books offered their own solutions, but much of what they'd offered relied on the teachings passed down from Atlis to Atlis. As the Atlis, Thalasia's knowledge might surprise him and unlock better prospects. Or they might prove exactly what he suspected they would.

"I honestly don't know," she said. "I've replayed everything we've been through in my head. All we've been through. The good, the bad, the ugly. We have moments where we're reaching for one another. And then moments where we can't stand the sight of each other. While it seems we've become great at playing the part and fooling people, are we doing it to fool them or ourselves? Like the fact that we're holding hands. Is it because it's natural? Something we've done for days. Or is it because we want to? Because we just need to know the other is near."

She dragged a hand down her face. "I can tell you what my intuition is telling me about the ritual. I know you need something of value to set in place with my dagger. And I believe I can make you something that would work, but the rest... I don't have answers. It isn't like our situation is the same as any others who have come before us. Not to mention their inability to be upfront and honest about things."

She paused. "Neither of us seems all that inclined to... delve into our feelings. Or allow ourselves to feel what we do for another. We're both so accustomed to working alone because we don't trust easily, if at all, that I don't know how we get to where we're beyond how we started this journey, but closer to the times that we're unconsciously reaching for each other. Like when I'm curled up against you, just listening to the sound of your heartbeat. Or you grab my hand and stroke it. Or you pull me into your lap."

Thalasia sighed heavily. "I want to believe we can overcome this bridge, but I don't know how."

"Ever consider you're overcomplicating the matter?" he asked, his gaze lost to their surroundings, scanning the horizon and sky for their beauty as much as for potential threats.

"Possibly. But I also know that all the moving parts and complexities of the ritual should solidify our bond. What we've already..." Her words trailed off.

Moments like this left Seru wanting the sky. Being chained to the land in daylight marked them as a target for attack. Not that the untold treasure in Thalasia's bag wasn't enough to accomplish that on its own. With a relieved sigh, he relinquished his grip on Thalasia's hand, priming his muscles for the incoming fight. Five enemies, if his senses could be trusted.

Thalasia's stillness, the brief freeze, allowed him to know she'd sensed them, too. "If I tell you to fly ahead, you're going to refuse, aren't you?" Seru shot her a quick glance as he re-secured the dagger at the small of his back, covering it with his shirt just as swiftly.

"Yes, but I'll compromise. If I get hurt, I won't fight you on using your healing ability." As she spoke, she wrapped her hand around the hilt of the dagger she kept sheathed in her pants. As she pulled it free, she tightened her hold, and the weapon visibly grew, stretching longer and wider.

Seru sighed heavily with a shake of his mane. If that was her idea of a compromise, her knack for negotiation left much to be desired. Surely, she remained as much a tyrant as their opposition. "You're the target," he reminded her.

A slight frown crossed her face. Her eyebrows knitted together as she swung her blade in a circular motion.

Seru ignored her lack of acknowledgment, taking a moment to slip into that familiar state of calm he often found before and during the initial phase of the battle. When the beast wasn't in control, fights went much more quickly and smoothly. If their attackers remained on foot, they weren't the dark sirens from the lake, but likely guilers.

A quintet of elemental magic users stepped into view to confirm that theory. A lone aquamancer framed on either side by two pyromancers and two massive geomancers. His eyes couldn't help flitting to the skies to ensure no anemancers. No dark sirens. He tilted his head and narrowed his eyes at their opponents, waiting for them to make the first move while he decided on the best order to eliminate them. Fire, water, earth. Sure, save the best and biggest for last.

They formed a circle around the two of them. The two closest to Thalasia, one looked like a stack of large boulders, while the other had a slight reddish tinge to its skin tone, with a set of yellowish scales running the length of its arms. All five moved at once. Two toward her and three toward Seru.

Following suit, the earth and fire pair mirrored their counterparts. The four appeared to be safeguarding their watery partner, who siphoned a growing amount of water from the nearby river.

Seru evaded them both, swiftly dodging and stepping back until he determined their attack pattern. The pyromancer's attacks came swiftly and in quick succession, offering the much slower geomancer to build its strength for more precise and powerful blows.

The time between attacks allowed the geomancer to build an earthen shield around the aquamancer, who permitted it to borrow an insignificant amount from its whirling wall of water.

Out of the corner of his eye, he monitored Thalasia's combat with the other two. He didn't want to give them too much leeway and put her in over her head. But he also wanted to give them enough room for their siphoning to reach critical mass.

A ball of fire came at her, which she quickly counteracted with a stream of water, sending steam into the air as roots extended from the earth guiler in her direction. Aiming the water at the fire guiler, she dodged the topiary reaching for her ankles, using her blade to sever its branches while fending off the roots that erupted from the ground.

With a surge of water, Thalasia overwhelmed the fire guiler's blaze, drenching him entirely. She swung her weapon hard and chopped the vines as she shot into the air. In the instant it took the pyro to relight their fire, she soared above, decapitated him, and fed him to the grasping roots, which instead ensnared his falling form.

To his surprise, she dispatched the pyromancer with great ease. The succession of events at least indicated she'd formulated some manner of a plan prior to launching her assault.

The distraction of her progress, coupled with his repetitive dodging, granted the annoyed pyromancer on his side of the field enough time to catch the brush ablaze. Flames spread, climbing the bush and scaling the tree trunk. The heat did little to deter the growing sludge at the base of the clay wall from the combined earth and water. A lightning bolt loosed from overhead, lancing into the trickling stream of water, electrifying the conductive liquid in a blinding flash. The connection of earth and water severed as the aquamancer froze, paralyzed by the sudden shock. The water accumulation held as the will of the aquamancer warred with the saint beast's lightning.

At nearly the same instant, a stronger storm kicked up in the distance. The gusts generated by the fiery light show slammed into them. The pyromancer's flame snuffed out like a candle being blown out. Seru drove his heels into the dirt to stay his ground against the harsh wind. The immovable geomancer barely felt the sudden breeze, lumbering forth with a bellow as it advanced toward its fellow to aid with the barrier and fend off Thalasia's attack.

Seru guarded his eyes against the debris as Thalasia flew past, carried by the strong winds from the direction of the marketplace. He heard her land somewhere behind, but paid little mind as he watched the crimson storm in the distance. It formed far too quickly to—

Silver bolts impacted the residual charge of electricity from his earlier lightning bolt, tracing back through the channels until it reconnected with the source, serving him with a reversal strong enough to bring him to his knees.

The collar lit up at the influx of energy, Verie's dormant store waking at the disturbance. It constricted around his throat as icy spears drove inward. The chill spread through his veins, seeking to put a stop to his magic use.

"Are you okay?" Thalasia asked.

The band flared with blinding light. The bitter cold burned, seizing his muscles and stealing the breath from his lungs. It had been a long time since he'd triggered the collar, making the effect that much more devastating. He squeezed shut his eyes, trying to force his mana into a hasty retreat as the frigid cold raced to catch up. The white shone even there, too bright and unforgiving.

He couldn't see or breathe. Couldn't really feel much beyond the intense whiteout. But he could hear. The roar of the distant storm had quieted to the rush of ice and a thundering heartbeat. The faintest scrape of a leafy branch against silken cloth, the shift of soil underfoot to the wet, sick mud.

His hand grasped the hilt of the dagger at his back, drawing it to his side. His grip was shaky at best, and the dagger was little more than a shiny golden club inside its sheath. Better than nothing, which was exactly what he had in this state. Nothing. His strength and mana sapped, inaccessible. A brain could only do so much without the other senses, thoughts adrift in an ocean of white.

The steps stopped, pausing or taking to the skies. Seru's grip on the metal tightened. The hilt's raised design digging into his palm.

"You look like you could use some assistance."

The voice startled Seru. It was much closer than he'd anticipated. How had the person gotten so close without a sound? A low growl resonated in his chest. The strong male scent accented with a delicate perfume. Cloud-stepping meant dragon, though he didn't recognize the voice or the odd scent.

"We're okay," Thalasia replied.

"You needn't be afraid... I only wish to aid in your unbinding."

"Just out of the goodness of your heart? Or because you want something? You know, tit-for-tat." As she spoke, Thalasia stepped closer to his side.

Seru stilled, the words playing over in his mind. He felt the brush of Thalasia's jeans against his arm closest to her. Her shadow cast over him. "No one—dragon or otherwise—can 'unbind' me. Pedal your foolish nonsense elsewhere." Seru bared his teeth. He barked a bitter laugh. His muscles remained too rigid for movement, no matter how much he pushed his body to move. What he wanted didn't matter. But they needed to stall. Dragons didn't take kindly to insults or challenges of strength. "What makes you think your power can supersede that of the Matriarch? Have you gone mad? Down here on earth, where you've cowered for centuries."

Thalasia gently placed a hand on his shoulder.

Seru snarled a warning to her. The touch was well-intended, but to another dragon, it displayed weakness. It was bad enough that he still couldn't see. She was practically hyperventilating, her heart racing—prey to the other dragon. He didn't need to see how Thalasia fared against the unnamed dragon on her own. She was powerful in her own right. But not powerful enough if this dragon had stayed hidden and off the radar for so long. There was something very wrong about him, though he couldn't decide what. Curse the collar and its damning effects.

"One doesn't necessarily beget the other." The unknown dragon paused. "You're responsible for the silver magic," he said with a slight lilt to his voice. He seemed mildly bored by the realization. "You needn't be rude. We're not fond of your Matriarch. Here, let me help you."

There was a slight shift of Thalasia's leg against his shoulder. "Why?"

With each passing comment, the dragon in question read as increasingly more powerful. Could he be a former member of the Court from the age prior to Verie's ascension? Was the smooth voice even his own, or was it a mimicry of magic?

Didn't like the Matriarch—and wasn't ashamed to say so. That spoke volumes. He either thought himself superior or had a death wish. Seru thought carefully before deciding to accept the aid. Playing the game, the man desired until they could decipher more seemed the wisest course. At least until he stood a chance of actually challenging him. He extended his free hand, having sensed the male lowered to his level.

The dragon took hold of his outstretched arm.

Seru gasped at the sudden influx of energy and a searing burn where the man's palm connected with his forearm, even through the silk shirt. The male pulled him to his feet, his vision clearing almost instantly—to the point it dizzied him and threw him off balance for a moment. The energy blazed through him, targeting the collar—more specifically, the silver magic housed inside. Seru's brow furrowed as he marveled at the way the energy breezed past his magical signature, bypassed Aurelia's residual signature, and enveloped Verie's, effectively hampering it.

His hand shot to his throat, where the band had disappeared, fading to little more than an invisible string of magic looped around his neck. He felt the bare skin along his exposed throat for the first time in memory. He stepped back a single pace, withdrawing as he took in the dragon before him. But before he could speak, the dragon beat him to it.

"What are you? Your energy is... unusual."

As Thalasia remained in the same spot, her eyes flicked between him and the unnamed *dragon*.

He wanted to ask how the dragon had done it, but the words stayed locked behind his lips. He knew there'd be no answer. No actual answer, even if he'd dared to ask. Nevermind asking questions. How did he answer? Seru regarded the dragon carefully. All ivory and gold robes, several centuries out of style. His body language relaxed, but proud and expectant as he awaited Seru's response. Those serpentine blue eyes, as clear as a cloudless sky, watched him intently.

Shaking off the crawling sensation that lingered over his skin, he responded after far too long a pause. "I'm Seru." Best to leave off his title for now, lest it upset their new ally. He gestured beside him. "And this is Thalasia." He offered no more, no less. Though every part of him yearned to test the limits of the dragon's gift.

Seru's attention drifted to Thalasia, if only for a moment. She'd quieted. To the point, he figured she thought this fragile alliance was a real, terrible idea. Granted, she'd learned more of the dragons over the past several days than she'd known prior to a crash landing on the white sand beach. The dragon didn't bow, didn't offer any precursory formalities as he gave his introduction. Then again, because of their circumstances, neither had he.

"You may call me Luciel."

"How can I repay you for..." Seru lifted his chin, "unbinding me, as you put it?"

Luciel feigned offense as he breezed past them. "Let us call it even. Since we're headed in the same direction, why don't we walk together?"

Seru hesitated. It hadn't really been a question, rather a sound suggestion. He'd likely been able to scent their direction of travel prior to the guiler encounter. "You wish to see the sirens?" Seru trailed, suspicious, as he moved to follow. He barely cast their fallen foes a second glance before pausing.

Now seemed as good an opportunity as any. He called down a tremendous bolt of lightning, one with enough bulk and raw power to render the guilers' remains to ash. Twenty times more potent than what he'd pushed past the collar. Still not nearly the extent of what he was capable of. The soil cracked in a vicious spiderweb; the water evaporated in its tracks. A smile touched his lips as he took in the destruction, never bothering a second glance Thalasia's way. "Thalasia, the fire, if you please."

"Uh, yeah, sure." With flicks of her wrists, Thalasia sent water cascading over the blaze, stopping it in its tracks.

The trip promised the chance to decipher the dragon's affinity, the flavor of his power. A detail he hadn't revealed, courtesy of Thalasia's quick dispatch of the guilers prior to his arrival. The mysticism with the collar only revealed what Seru already suspected—the dragon was powerful and subtle. He knew magic Seru hadn't discovered in nearly 800 years. Had it been a secret passed down to him or one he'd concealed himself?

"No, I'm afraid I'm not terribly fond of their kind in the same way you appear to be," Luciel replied, content to walk at a brisk pace at the head of the group.

Seru quickened his pace to close the distance. He wanted to see the other male's face. Did he just admit to enjoying sirens as an entrée? He spoke so evenly, so plainly, without facial expression or other indicators. It was impossible to tell. The thought of him sensing the bond between him and Thalasia unnerved him a bit. Not that he'd ever let that show.

Into the mountains, towards manticore territory, then? What business could he possibly have there? Or perhaps, beyond to the sea? Though there were easier, more accessible routes if that were the case. Each answer Luciel granted brought new questions, effectively compounding the problem.

"Your friend seems awfully tense," Luciel commented.

Again, another powerful suggestion that he felt he should derive more from. Though what, he wasn't certain. Seru glanced over his shoulder, never quite taking his eyes off Luciel. The dragon's assessment proved correct. She wasn't just tense; her worry and distress were palpable. Likely flashing neon 'prey' signals to the dragon.

"So, Luciel, was there a particular direction you were going?" she asked.

"I'm merely wandering, Thalasia. I enjoy taking leisurely strolls around the isle. Don't you?"

"I prefer flying."

Luciel smiled at that. "It certainly has its perks," the dragon agreed.

Seru continued to watch them both. His eyes scanned Luciel from head to toe, searching for anything out of the norm. The lack of definitive detailing posed as suspicious as the non-answers. But how could he question it? The dragon had restored his power. Indebted was as severe an understatement as one could make. He owed the dragon, who purportedly wanted nothing in return.

"So does one's ability to enjoy an occasional swim."

"Feathers don't really allow for that."

"Hmm... so, it's your partner who holds the other string. Not this one," Luciel nodded in Seru's direction. "But another. Truly, how many dragons can one command?"

"Excuse me?"

Seru stiffened at the statement. If Luciel was the same drag-on who owned the strings Aurelia retrieved from beneath the lake—that made him a god.

Luciel slowed to a halt, turning to face her. He seemed no more bothered by her refusal to admit to the crime than he had been when he'd first arrived and announced his presence to them.

"Come, Thalasia." Seru suppressed a growl at the way he said her name. "Let's not play this game."

"You, or more specifically, one of your dragon friends, stole from me. Three strings and a coin." Luciel flashed the golden coin clutched between his talons, razor-sharp and more than capable of ripping out a few feathers and scales if the situation demanded.

Without saying a word, Thalasia closed the short distance be-tween her and Seru.

"Return my property and you're free to go... try to keep them from me and your present companion will have a choice to make," Luciel cautioned with that same slight smile and knowing eyes. "If it helps, I don't think you'll like the choice he makes should you opt to force his hand."

Without a second thought, Thalasia reached into her purse, produced the solitary string, and offered it. "That's all I have."

Seru's hand closed over hers and the string before Luciel could reach out to reclaim it, pressing it back to her person. The dragon tilted his head. "Surely, with a hoard as glorious as yours is, you won't miss a strand or two of gold."

Luciel gave a huff of surprise. "Surely, you don't mean to negotiate the terms of this arrangement." The blue eyes zeroed in on that fragile thread of magic still binding Seru to his master. The bind became taut, signifying the dragon's intention. What he'd done couldn't only be undone; it could render him further restricted—likely without magic or dead.

"No, just the timing," Seru offered. "Thalasia requires the use of your strands—both of them. Much as your other..." Seru peeled back his sleeve, revealing the ancient Draconic symbol for light emblazoned on his forearm. "Partner has agreed to grant her this one for a task. I imagine she's also brokered a similar deal with you." Though likely not for the strands. Luciel desired to reclaim his treasure on his own. "Give Thalasia time to obtain the other strand, time to complete her mission here, and I'll not only see the strands returned to you, but I'll also see to it the Matriarch's machinations are fulfilled on your behalf. It'll hasten your return to full power, and to you, I imagine that's far more valuable than a few silly strings."

Luciel considered Seru's offer. "Why go to so much trouble for her?" He inclined his head in Thalasia's direction. "You're far too powerful in your own right to seriously consider her your equal."

"Who said I was doing it for her?" Seru countered.

Luciel blew a breath through his nose. He shifted from one foot to the other, thinking. His attention shifted to Thalasia. "What do you intend to do with my possessions, Thalasia?"

"Repair a broken artifact," she replied simply.

"An artifact that just so happens to do... what?" Luciel returned, a tad disgruntled by her obvious evasion.

"It puts the barrier back in place."

He narrowed his gaze at both of them. First, Thalasia. Then, Seru.

"The barrier protects the sirens," Seru interjected. Now, he just needed a story Aurelia would find believable, if not backable. "They've been dying out and require protection while they reestablish their numbers." While they were both partial truths and not quite as intimately related as he made them seem, they should be enough. After all, sirens seemed to register as a food source to Luciel only moments prior. Why not use his assumptions against him?

Luciel curled a lip in disbelief. "All that trouble to preserve sirens?" he said, doubt coloring his tone.

"Sirens are the keepers of secrets; their capability of charm has proven useful in the past. If they go extinct, could you imagine the information that would be accessible, including that of the dragons, those things that make them look... less favorable, less trustworthy? While the barrier would be rebuilt so the sirens could reestablish their numbers, it would ultimately be to ensure things that are currently buried... stay that way. Unless you're looking for certain truths to come forward."

"I'm not my mother. I have nothing to hide," Luciel growled. "Sounds like the information they've compiled would prove useful if they were to meet a premature end."

"Everyone has something to hide." Thalasia paused. "I suppose that's why they've been meeting with the leaders across the isle for days now. Even more so why they've come to an arrangement with the Matriarch."

"What are you hiding?" Luciel asked, another head tilt accompanying the gesture.

"A growing lack of patience," Seru stated abruptly. His expression soured. The distaste and disdain practically dripped off him. "I've made my offer. Take it or leave it."

"If the siren information were that easy to access, someone would've done it already. That said, I'd be led to conclude either it's inconsequential or they're worth more alive than they are extinct. Regarding the strings, your contradictory statement in their number alone suggests that Seru's offer holds sufficient weight to their value."

"He's testing our ability to keep up," Seru muttered, unable to keep the irritation out of his voice. "Wants to see if we're agreeable to each mistake just as readily as the last."

"I won't deny reclaiming my former glory appeals to me," Luciel agreed. "But I'm still not sure I agree with your assessment of the sirens. Dead flyers can't very well share their secrets. They'd die on their lips with their last breaths. But then again, they're not rabbits—they can still be undone before they replenish their ranks. You may *borrow* my property, Seru. But if I get the slightest hint you intend to break your oath, the consequences will be yours."

Thalasia returned the string to her purse.

Without waiting for a further answer, Luciel transformed in a blinding light, taking to the skies. Heading toward the Clouds.

Seru stepped back wordlessly and retook their course to Pteryrina, if a little haphazardly. His focus clearly wasn't in the here and now, but somewhere swirling among his thoughts. Thalasia followed him.

Chapter Forty-Eight

With his mate's hand a warm pressure on his back, Gavin trekked across the forest floor on all fours, his breath misting in the cool forest air as they continued their journey. He'd camouflage when they moved out onto the open ground, but for now, he was staying fully visible. Their unhurried steps carried them through the forest; the path meandered alongside the lake before reaching the treeline. Gavin smiled over at Parthenia, his tail continually stroking her wings as they trekked along. He knew it had disappointed her a little how things had gone so far. She hadn't met with everyone, but she'd negotiated a few treaties. The nymphs, the sprites, and Milla, too. And the Elder of Migas and Mac. They would meet with the chimeras, then there were those Cipriana was meeting with as well. It was all better than nothing, and a good starting point, at least.

And no matter what happened over the next several days, until they could finally leave, he would never, ever regret having come on this trip with his mate. Seeing and experiencing all the new things he had, spending the time together with her... and what the nymph Queen had done for them. This trip would be something he would never forget as long as he lived. "What are the chimeras like?" he asked Milla as they walked. It was yet another species he'd never come into contact with.

"Well... under the right circumstances, they can be temperamental. Although they're normally calm and quite wise."

"I read that they've been at odds with the manticore for quite some time. Is that true?" Parthenia added.

"Yes, it is."

It seemed like most on the isle kept to themselves. With a few exceptions. Though he hadn't heard or read about many specific issues between the species yet. The dragons didn't like the sirens, but then again, they didn't really like anyone. Neither did Markham, though he didn't even like his own people. "Why is that?"

Milla stopped, raising her hand to signal a halt. A slight twitch of her ears preceded her hand reaching for the sheath at her hip and unsheathing a blade. With a gentle gesture, she brought her finger to her mouth, hushing them both.

Gavin shifted to the left, in front of Parthenia. His body stilled, except for the perking of his ears. Lifting his head a bit, he drew in a deep, silent breath. He frowned. Not Informants, but... There was a similarity to the dark guilers they'd fought before, but these were different. Not that he could discern exactly how just yet. His ears jerked as he focused on the subtle sounds of the footsteps drawing nearer, tracking the crunching of the leaves. Three... No... four... There was one... His gaze flicked up. In the trees, unlike the other three. Sensing his mate's eyes upon him, and the question in her mind, all he did was nod.

Parthenia spread her wings, ruffling her feathers to get herself ready.

Milla dipped her chin at both him and his mate and readied herself to attack.

As Gavin nodded to Milla, he brushed his tail over his mate's knee. He couldn't focus on his nerves and fear for her safety; he had to stay focused on their task—getting rid of these creatures before the things got rid of them. "Be careful, my love," he said, right before he camouflaged. Slinking closer to where he sensed the one, he scaled the trunk up to the first set of branches. It was then that he spotted it. It was... holy Hades, it was a... *hybrid*...had to be... Half guiler, half... feline shape shifter. How in the gods...

The creature was about a foot taller than him, even in its animal form. Fully black except for the stripes... cracks... in its skin, like a tiger's form. Only he couldn't even describe it in his head. The black parts of its skin looked dry, ashy, almost volcanic, appearing as if they would be hard and crumbling in nature. But with the orangish-red stripes, it looked like there was fluid movement to them. Its claws were the same... the same color, like fire, hard and razor-sharp like claws, but with a fluidity beneath the surface. Its eyes were like the shape shifter Informants whose eyes never strayed from black, except they were an orangish-red-like fire, too. Hades, had it crawled straight out of a volcano?

Giving himself an internal shake and forcing himself to focus, Gavin crouched down on the branch, preparing to spring—

The creature's head snapped in his direction and it lunged. He had no time to wonder if the creature could see through camouflage, or if it just smelled or sensed him, maybe heard him, before the thing was on him. The branch he was on snapped, a sickening crack ringing through the air, and both of them fell to the ground. As the creature landed on top of him, his skin burned. The smell of singed fur filled his nostrils. The heat was so overwhelming he could barely breathe. And that didn't even account for the pain. It felt like his skin was melting. Biting back a howl of agony, he got a paw up and swiped his claws across the creature's face.

Gavin's body spasmed involuntarily, and his heart fluttered with a sudden, surprising jolt. For a moment, he thought it was because of the creature on top of him, but no… his mate. She'd lost consciousness. There was nothing he could do for her at the moment; not with this *thing* on top of him. He dug his claws into the rough, unyielding hide of the guiler-hybrid, raking at its neck and face as he struggled to reach its core. He seized the creature's throat in his jaws, his tail making a firm grip on its ankle. With a powerful tug in opposing directions, a sudden crack echoed as the creature faltered, granting Gavin a crucial moment to escape its grasp and gain the upper hand. He resumed his struggle, feeling the sharp claws rake across his neck and belly as he finally tore through the tough, armor-like hide of its chest.

With one more swipe to the creature's chest, its heart stopped. Scorching, molten blood erupted and spilled onto him. Getting quickly off the creature's now-still body, he rolled in the grass to get as much off him as possible. Oh, Hades, that did *not* feel good on his side that had gotten burned. He needed to bathe. Despite the bile rising in his throat and the searing pain, he stood on shaky legs and scrambled as quickly as possible to Parthenia's side. He bit back a growl as he forced himself to shift to his humanoid form, retracted his claws, then wiped his hands on the grass to make sure he had no more of the thing's blood on them.

Damn, blood had matted the hair on the side of her head and her temple. Gavin gently brushed a stray strand of hair from her face before glancing behind him to check on Milla and ensure she was alright handling the others. A massive root had ripped the aquatic guiler's body in half, protruding from its center. The female continued fighting two other large rock-like creatures, one of whom was already missing an arm. Except it looked like—was it growing back?

He wanted to take his mate in his arms, but he couldn't do that until those things were dead. If they switched directions, she could get injured more. "Parthenia? Wake up, my love." His gaze flicked back to the ongoing fight between Milla and the other two guilers.

Yanking a dagger from a sheath on the other side of her hip, she attacked. Milla spun on her heel and lopped off a limb from the whole guiler just as he lunged toward Gavin. Stepping back around, she plunged the blade of her sword deep into the gut of the other guiler and hacked off its brand-new arm. Jerking her weapon from its belly, leaving a gaping hole, she charged at the other creature and hacked off its head. "Is she okay?" Milla hollered.

"She has gotten knocked out," he called back. Deep breath. Deep breath. She would be fine. Parthenia would be fine. With a grimace, he clenched his jaw and pushed himself up from the ground. Hades, his legs trembled. Chills swept through him despite the burn that covered his right side. Shit, he was woozy. Not good. He drew in long, slow breaths through his nostrils, the forest air crisp and cool, before turning to position his body defensively in front of his mate. He frowned as he watched a limb regrow on the creature. What in the gods? "Do you need help?" Oh, yes, he would be *loads* of help right now. "How do you kill them?"

She'd gotten the two things down to basically nothing, but they were slowly recollecting themselves. Milla rubbed her shoulder. "They have a master somewhere." She glanced at him. "If I leave you with a sword, can you keep them from pulling back together while I hunt for the master?"

He blinked twice. Even the head was regenerating. Forcing himself to concentrate, he looked at Milla. Master? "I have never even held a sword before, but I will do my best." He inhaled deeply, the scent of damp earth filling his lungs, and leaned his shoulder against the rough bark of the tree as he extended his hand for the sword. If finding their master was how to kill them, he would do whatever he needed to do with the sword; he had to protect his mate.

Milla reached for the curved blade sheathed between her wings, removed it, and held it out to him by the hilt. "Just hack at them. It won't stop them from regenerating until I kill the master."

With a nod and another deep breath, Gavin gripped the sword, his hand leaving the rough bark of the trunk. Alright, not the steadiest on his feet, but it would have to do. He'd had worse injuries. Just never with fire before. It made his stomach somersault.

He swallowed and took one more deep breath. Glancing down at his mate, he pushed away his nerves and fear. There wasn't time to fixate on that. Parthenia, she would be fine. Giving his assent once more to Milla, he crossed the ground to where the creatures half-stood. He'd watched what she'd done, so he at least had the concept in his head. Just hack at them. Alright, then. The sword felt so unnatural in his hand. Unlike a few of the others in Méta-morphe, he'd never even used a dagger before. If he'd ever needed to cut something, he'd used his claws. But he could do this. The metallic *shing* of the blade echoed as he dealt with each creature, the force of his swing preventing its head from reforming. Clumsy, but effective enough. He just had to keep at it until Milla found the master and killed it.

He continued his hacking, occasionally wiping blood from his eyes, a result of the claw strikes on his face as she searched for the master. Arms, legs, heads; he even hacked one of their torsos in half. They just kept regenerating. He didn't know how much time passed, but it felt like hours. Finally, the regeneration ceased, and their bodies disintegrated into piles of sand. Gavin shook his head a little, wincing at the wounds in his neck. Thank Hades for his species' quick healing. They'd likely stop bleeding by tomor-row, depending on whether there was something strange about the wounds the creature had inflicted. They'd just be tender for a day or two. It was the burn that was worrisome. He'd seen wounds like this, just never had them himself.

Moving back across the ground, he wrapped the arm holding the sword around his belly and used the trunk of the tree to kneel at Parthenia's side. He laid the sword on the ground in front of him, easily within reach if needed, then eased his mate's head into his lap. She was breathing, her heartbeat steady and normal—she just hadn't woken up yet. A concussion, maybe? Gavin gently brushed some hair from his mate's face to check out the wound on the side of her head. It didn't look too deep, but he was no healer. Hades, she had to be alright.

Sensing someone coming nearer, he flicked his gaze up and to the right, heightening his senses—Milla. As she emerged from the trees, her arm dangled at an unnatural angle. It didn't look broken, but her shoulder might have popped out of its socket. Her leather top was a little torn, with a bit of blood pooling at the spot. And there were a couple of bruises developing around her ribs. "Are you alright?"

"I'll live." Milla returned her sword and dagger to their sheaths on her hips. Stopping for a moment, she gripped her arm and gritted her teeth as she popped her shoulder back into place.

He opened his mouth but snapped it shut at the groan from his mate, the consciousness he sensed returning. His gaze dropped to Parthenia. He bit back a whimper at the throbbing he felt come from his mate. He even ignored all of his own pain and discomfort as he focused back on her. Hades, he hated how much her head hurt, but it could have been worse. Thank the gods she was at least waking up. "Lie still, love. You hit your head."

"Ow..." Parthenia muttered.

"I've called for one of my warriors to come offer aid. She'll be able to create a hollow in a tree for you to spend the night in, since I don't think either of you can travel farther for the evening."

No, they certainly weren't. He was doing a halfway decent job at not fixating on his own misery, more so to keep it from his mate as much as possible. Moving any more than necessary—definitely not on a list of things he wanted to do right then. He dipped his chin in response to Milla, but didn't take his eyes off his mate. "Thank you." Keeping still so he wouldn't jostle Parthenia, he brushed his fingertips over her cheek. "Just lie still. Keep your eyes closed if you need to. Milla said aid is coming. We are just going to stay right like this for now. Alright?" Inhaling and exhaling another deep breath, he worked on easing the pounding of his heart.

"Okay..." she mumbled. Slowly, her eyes opened, scanning over him. "You're hurt."

With pure, silent grace, a female swung from the branch above and landed softly on the earth. "Somebody call for aid?" A wide grin stretched across her face, her vibrant red hair flowing behind her as her tail swished rhythmically.

"I expected you would have arrived sooner," Milla said.

Gavin's gaze darted to the hybrid female briefly, and then he returned his attention to his mate. "I will be okay. I have been way more worried about you." He monitored the female out of the corner of his eye.

"Oh, tough guys are fun. Usually, the biggest babies with injuries." She shrugged and half turned to Milla, who glowered at her. "What?"

"Be nice." Milla held out her hand for the curved blade that remained in his possession. "This is Tam. She is an excellent healer, despite her issue with her tongue."

"You're such a goody-goody." Tam rolled her eyes.

"It is alright." Lifting his gaze to the female, his eyebrows furrowed. "I am not trying to be a tough guy." He carefully picked up the glinting blade—its cool metal a stark contrast to his warm hand—and with deliberate slowness, offered it back to Milla. It was difficult to hold back his wince at the movement. "I am just attempting to spare my mate. We feel one another's pain."

"Yeesh, that's gotta suck." The female smirked. "I kinda forgot about how that whole mate connection works. Don't have one, so no babies to piece back together for me."

Milla shook her head as she accepted the blade. "Goddess. What am I going to do with you?"

"You love me an' ya know it," Tam said as she removed a couple of crystals out of a leather pouch she had tied to a loop in her dark-green pants. "So, tough guy... ya want me to treat your mate first, then? These won't hurt. Won't heal everything, but my mom's one of those uppity-ups, so I get all kinds of cool shit to help with injuries."

With a slight groan, Milla narrowed her eyes. "I expect you will stay until morning and watch over them."

"Absolutely, boss-lady." Although Tam responded to Milla, her attention stayed on him.

"Yes, please, treat her first." And he was just going to sit there and concentrate on not making any sudden movements. With their fingers laced, he brought his mate's hand to his mouth, planting a kiss on the back of her hand.

"He has the worst of it. You should treat him first," Parthenia objected.

"Stubborn-ass couples," Tam muttered. "We're going with you first, and then him. Mmkay? Good. Glad we're all on the same page." She kneeled down by his mate. Leaning forward, she glanced over her shoulder at Milla. "You hanging around to babysit some more, or do you want me to treat you, too?"

"My injuries are minor. They'll be fine in a few hours."

"Oh? So, that's why you're nursing that arm, an' holdin' it close?" A slight nod from her drew attention to the arm Milla clutched to her side.

"Remind me again why I made you one of my warriors," Milla said.

"Because I'm fucking awesome!" The female chuckled and turned back to Parthenia. Tam pressed one stone to his mate's shoulder. As a low hum pulsed from the crystal, a white radiance surrounded Parthenia.

As the wound on the back of her head slowly closed, the tension on Parthenia's face softened.

Gavin let out a sigh of relief as the pain he sensed from her disappeared. "Good as new, my love," he said and kissed the top of her head. "Thank you," he commented to the female who had healed her. He moved to help his mate up, but paused, drawing in a sharp breath. The slightest movement sent a sharp, nauseating pain through him. Or pass out. Or both. Wrong arm. Wrong arm. That had been a mistake—it had tugged at the burn on his side. Or the claw marks in his belly. Maybe both. Swallowing hard, he switched arms and helped her sit up with his left arm instead.

"She should've healed you first," Parthenia declared.

"I was more worried about the possibility of you having a concussion. Besides, she asked my preference, and I will always care for you before I care for myself."

Tam got to her feet. "If you two are going to argue, I'ma just stand here and watch. Just so you know."

"We won't fight," Parthenia retorted. "Neither of us are prone to confrontation."

"Hold the lepoids." Tam's eyes widened. "Are you saying that the two o' ya have never argued? Not once?"

"We've never argued."

"Eh... give it time. I'm sure at some point, ya will." A smirk played on her lips as she strode over to where he remained on his knees. "Now, most of ya fur should grow back with this."

He seriously doubted that was true. They'd always been able to work anything and everything out before it even neared the point of an argument. "We have never had a reason to argue about anything. We hide nothing from one another, and we talk about everything."

Just as Tam had done with Parthenia, she pressed the stone to his left shoulder. A radiant-white glow surrounded him. The torn skin on his belly, a result of claw marks, mended itself, slowly stitching itself closed. The burn along his side cooled and vanished, with new fur sprouting as the skin regenerated.

"That is much better. Thank you for your assistance."

"Yes, thank you very much. It's appreciated," Parthenia echoed.

"Sure thing." Tam turned her attention to Milla. "Now, it's your turn, boss-lady. An' don't fight me on it."

"I wouldn't dream of it." Milla snickered.

"Course not, 'cuz then ya'd just hafta listen to me ask how ya planned to get your scimitar back in its sheath. It is restin' on your back, beneath your quiver." Tam approached Milla, who was standing nearby, and pressed the stone against her shoulder. The same white halo blanketed her, and the hole in her stomach knitted back together, the tendons around her shoulder reset, and restored everything to its proper place.

A sigh of relief left Milla's mouth. "Thank you."

"Any time, boss-lady. Now, I know ya got other shit to do," Tam responded as she returned the stones to her leather pouch. Her gaze lifted back to Milla. "I got this."

"Very well." Milla glanced between Gavin and Parthenia. "You are both in capable hands."

As Milla flew off into the forest, Gavin wrapped his arm around his mate and tucked her into his side, laying his head on top of hers. "Thank you again. My mate is Parthenia, and I am Gavin."

"Good to meet ya both. As she said, I'm Tam and if ya give me a few minutes, I'll get a hollow set up for ya. Won't be fancy, but it'll give ya a place to sleep for the night."

Parthenia snuggled in close to Gavin. "We appreciate it. Thank you very much."

Chapter Forty-Nine

As Thalasia and Seru approached Anemos, the staircase leading to Pteryina, the bitter scent of copper lingered in the air. Splotches of blood covered the bottom set of stairs, contrasting vibrantly against the wide, opalescent steps. A mix of black and green feathers clung to the thick crimson pools saturating the ground. The head of each balustrade on either side of the stairway appeared charred. Scorch patterns stained the white grains, banking the front of the staircase. Obviously, a fight of some kind had occurred.

Seru sighed. "Guess we can add rescuing Chicane's green-feathered protector to the docket." He strode to the bottom of the stairs, where he paused. "Are you coming? Or is there some other way in?"

She paused at what looked like an excess pile of sand; her gaze drawn between that and the black feathers. Thalasia dragged a hand across her face. "I'm coming." They had to go in through the front gate, not sneak in like they did last time. Dismissing her thoughts, she approached the staircase and climbed, her eyes fixed on the path ahead, avoiding the crimson stain.

Voices reached them before they had even made it halfway up. "Mom! Stop fussing over it!"

"I wouldn't need to *fuss* if you would allow yourself to get treated." The woman huffed. "Cipriana, what is so important that you needed to traipse down here with that gash across your head?"

Seru drew to a halt, allowing the procession of sirens the chance to notice their presence and identify them. "Greetings, Ambassador."

Before Thalasia even had the chance to open her mouth, Cipriana turned on them. "You two? Why am I not surprised that the two of you are here?" Her arms crossed protectively over her chest, her lips pulled into a frown. Her hair was matted to the back of her head, but the female showed no sign of concern.

"Cipriana! Is that how you greet guests?"

"Guests?" She peered over her shoulder at the woman she'd addressed as her mother. "She's an Atlis and I was advised not to trust him."

The two female guards flanking Cipriana exchanged a look and, without a word, fell to one knee, their fists striking their chests in a salute. "My liege," the women stated simultaneously.

"An Atlis," Cipriana's mother murmured, and then quickly followed suit of the other women.

Thalasia's eyes widened ever so slightly. All but the ambassador bent the knee and pledged their allegiance. This was an unexpected turn of events, at least to a degree. While she'd been taught the siren hierarchy with her position, this was the first time she had ever witnessed it in effect.

Seru blinked. Without stepping forward to supersede her as he had done at Court, he stayed in his place. "Contrary to your presumptions, Ambassador, we're here to broker peace with your people. Whether or not you personally deem us trustworthy has become irrelevant. Judging by the state of your doorstep, you're short on friends... and I highly doubt your list of new allies will appreciate your allowing the abduction of one of your more prominent guests. Better for all, you allow us to help you right the situation before word gets out."

"Rise," Thalasia said before things went too far. The two guards and the other woman all got back to their feet. "He's right. It's imperative we get a quick handle on the situation."

Cipriana's eyebrows squished together with a grimace. "Wait... wait, what situation? What abduction?" Ashen-faced, her shoulders drew in tightly. "Mac? Are you saying... he's not down there?" She gathered the fabric of her dress and started down the stairs, only to be halted by her mother.

"Who is Mac?"

"A male siren. I was going to tell you and Vasilia, but then everything got all messed up. That's why I..." Her words trailed off as tears welled in the corners of her eyes and she sat on a nearby step.

"My apologies, Atlis, and... companion." Cipriana's mother offered a faint dip of her chin. "Things have been in a bit of an uproar over the last hour."

"Thalasia and this is Seru." Obviously, the scene at the bottom of the staircase was only half of the story. Something more than Mac being kidnapped had occurred, but what? "Perhaps we can go inside. You can tell us what all happened while I heal her wound, then we can decide on an appropriate course of action."

While she maintained her position at Seru's side, she kept him in her periphery. She watched as he forced his gaze away and cleared his throat. This was whole new ground, not just because of deference to her, which he'd surprisingly managed well, but without his collar, too. The next few days certainly promised a lot of changes and adjustments rather quickly. Hopefully, they could figure out how to navigate it appropriately. "Would it also be wise to bring the Elder in on this?"

Cipriana's gaze lifted to Thalasia, then flicked to Seru, and back again. She wiped the tears from her face. "I am the Elder."

"Oh. I apologize; I wasn't aware of the change in leadership," Thalasia stated. Well, alright then. While that was certainly unexpected, it might also be something that benefited them.

"Recent change," Cipriana's mother said, her voice low. She held out a hand and helped Cipriana to her feet.

"I accept your assistance. Let's go inside and... figure things out." Cipriana paused. "Think we can use your house, Mom?"

"Of course. I'll send the girls out to the gardens."

Seru tugged at the collar of his shirt.

The envoy, led by Cipriana, made its way up the rest of the opalescent staircase toward the open silver gates. Poppies, rendered in exquisite detail, were woven throughout the design adorning the entranceway. They passed under an awning comprising the lyre symbol. The two golden-armored guards returned to their posts on either side of the pillars.

Clean lines of white appeared everywhere they looked, including the open-air temple just ahead of them. Crisp air surrounded them. As Cipriana and her mother continued on, Thalasia slowed her pace to put a small amount of space between them, while taking in the location of everything. To their right stood the library, its imposing columns reaching toward the sky. Two different gardens to their left with accompanying trees. Beyond that, even from where they stood, she could see the flash of red—The Poppy Fields, which they'd have to travel through to reach The Reflection Pools.

Keeping her voice low, she spared a momentary glance at Seru. "Are you alright?"

"Play your part here, so we can get what we can and leave," Seru replied, his voice dropping into gravelly undertones.

Leave? Oh, fun. He hadn't realized it yet. How many times had she told him *where* the ritual had to be performed? Even if they somehow found and rescued Mac in less than twenty-four hours, they'd still be returning here. And Seru was the one she'd decided to tie herself to for the rest of her life. Yeah, Ione was right. A different version of Seru, depending on his mood. At least she'd never be bored.

Thalasia scanned the area as they made their way toward the houses. From what she'd learned as a child, the armory would be in the same direction, just off to the side. As was everything else, the houses were also white on the outside.

Cipriana and her mother entered one of them, the door remaining open for Thalasia and Seru to follow behind. The older female quickly ushered three teenage girls with nearly identical features, except one who stood almost as tall as Seru, out the door. Cipriana's mother gave them a bow of her head. "I'll leave the three of you to speak privately."

"Thank you," Cipriana replied.

Seru gave a curt nod to the retreating woman. His eyes quickly found the newly appointed elder.

Gesturing toward the dining table, Cipriana sat in one of the six chairs around it. "Feel free to sit."

The house was modest, not a lot of furniture, but that coincided with what she knew about how sirens lived. It was a very open concept in the front room, comprising the table referenced on one side, an area for meal preparation behind it, and on the other side of the room was an enormous fireplace along with a few massive pillows for sitting. "I'm going to heal your wound while you talk," Thalasia said. She positioned herself behind Cipriana.

"I don't even know where to start."

"How did you meet Mac?" The female's prior reaction to his disappearance spoke volumes. It certainly didn't seem that the two had just met. Or maybe they had. Anything was possible. Thalasia hovered her hand at the back of Cipriana's head, allowing her power to flow through her and mend the bloody gash at the base of the female's skull.

"Gavin, my sister, and I got lost on our way to Chicane. Dark guilers attacked us, which Mac helped us dispatch. He then guided us the rest of the way. During our stay there, he volunteered to join us on our journey to visit the other Elders. Well, sort of. That kind of led to the suggestion of us splitting up. The Prime Warrior of the fae... Milla... she was going to lead Parthenia and Gavin through Verdant Grove while Mac and I headed in the opposite direction toward the dwarves." She let out a heavy sigh of relief. "Thank you. That feels better." Cipriana rubbed her eyes. "Do you both think you can really find him? I mean... Chicane can't lose another Elder so quickly."

Seru's eyes found Thalasia's at the mention of Mac's rise to leadership. "It seems many of the species on this isle are finding themselves under new leaders," he commented. "With all due respect, your motivations in this aren't strictly political. You care for Mac." Seru claimed a seat across from Cipriana, where the eye contact might be more agreeable despite their difference in size and stature. "Is he your... mate? Or, soon-to-be."

Yeah, definitely news to her. Though somehow, it shouldn't surprise her that the two times they'd crossed Aurelia that Felix's passing didn't once come up. To be fair, she hadn't trusted the female from the get-go. Information that hadn't gotten shared with Seru, either. So as not to make Cipriana feel crowded, Thalasia stepped around and shifted to stand next to Seru's seated position.

Cipriana's gaze dropped to her lap briefly as she fidgeted with her dress. Chewing on her bottom lip, she looked back at Seru and Thalasia. "I do care for him. I don't know if I can say 'mate' or even 'soon-to-be.' That isn't exactly how we've functioned for over a millennium, but it also seems to be our undoing." Her hazel eyes flicked to Thalasia directly. "I know you're supposed to... break the curse with him, and I'm not going to even pretend I like that idea, but I understand the necessity, too. I know that for us to thrive again, we have to make changes accordingly."

While she didn't openly say anything or allow her desires to cross her face, she completely agreed with the female. Adjusting to new circumstances was difficult, but often required to move forward.

The female refocused her attention on Seru. "I don't imagine it sits well with you, either. Sorry, that's none of my business." With a flick of her wrist, Cipriana brushed aside her own remark. "We both agreed that we'd take things slow, but yes... I believe the eventuality is that he and I would mate."

"Why would it bother me?" Seru asked, eyebrows raised as he settled back in the chair.

"Aren't you two together? I don't mean to overstep my bounds, but that's what my sister told me. That the two of you were a couple. Well, she said the two of you were in love, but it didn't seem like either of you saw it," Cipriana responded.

Words she hadn't actually mentioned to Seru, although Parthenia had said them to her. More specifically, it was in the way he kept glancing her way. Gods, that had been... four nights ago. It certainly felt longer. While she'd started the conversation, she figured she'd let Seru field this question.

"Both siren and dragon cultures involve complex interpersonal relationships. Whether we are or aren't has little bearing on breaking the curse or Thalasia's choice to partake in whatever it is exactly, you both agree the elder of Chicane offers." He shifted positions. "Monogamy isn't a factor—be it for repopulation or pleasure. If the Atlis wishes to court Mac, that is at her discretion. It has nothing to do with me." Seru rolled his shoulders and readjusted his clothing.

About what she expected of him. Thalasia held up a hand to stave off the obvious concern in the female's eyes. "Don't worry. I have no desire to court him." None. While she addressed nothing regarding the curse, that was a matter for another day.

Cipriana visibly relaxed at her words. "Okay. That's, uh, good to know."

"Why don't we get back to the matter at hand? What happened here today?" Sticking to the facts and boundaries they could work within served them better. Especially with all the obstacles that continued to pile up at their feet.

"Right. Well, Mac had the orange crystal in his possession. The night before we left Chicane, he and I spoke at length with Oriel, both regarding the crystal and the plan for how the invaders were going to be handled. Representatives for the Prime Warrior... were there, too. Oriel and I made an agreement that once we cleansed the crystal, I'd call on him and turn it over to them." She lifted the wrist with the band on it.

Seru tapped a pointed talon on the tabletop. His gaze drifted from the female to the landscape beyond. "Have you cleansed the crystal?"

"No. Someone struck me from behind. When I came around, the crystal was gone. I panicked and ran out into the clearing toward the staircase. I barely registered what they were telling me about our Elder."

While she didn't recognize the name the female had given, she strongly suspected Seru did. If the same person who had Mac had the crystal as well, what was Seru thinking about that? "Were you at The Reflection Pools?" It was the most likely place for the crystal to be cleansed.

"Yes." Cipriana's eyebrows furrowed.

Thalasia acknowledged the female's response, even the unspoken question, but she didn't intend to address it. There was a lot she knew about Pteryrina and the sirens that she'd kept to herself. It included those black-feathered birds. "This may seem like a strange question, but do you have any sirens unaccounted for?"

The female's eyes widened, taken aback. "I haven't checked, but you can't possibly think a siren had anything to do with this."

"It's a possibility I'd like to rule out." Her words meant nothing more than to reassure Cipriana. Thalasia bit the inside of her cheek. The truth of the matter was she had a strong suspicion a siren was involved. "How about Seru and I check out The Reflection Pools and see if we can ascertain any clues while you check in with your people?"

Seru didn't comment further.

"How do you even know about them?" Cipriana asked.

As much as Seru had loathed everything with her great-great-grandparents and what those two had put them through, it seemed their existence might actually come in handy. The corners of her mouth tilted upward. "My great-great-grand-parents, Adina and Aegeus, lived in Pteryrina for twelve years," Thalasia paused briefly, noting a minor look of confusion on the female's face. Right. She needed to use the more common term. "Twelve *solaris*. They ensured knowledge of this place was passed down through the generations."

The female sat there for a moment, her eyes darting back and forth as she appeared to process information. Cipriana gripped the back of her neck. "Fine, but nowhere else, and the two of you report back here in thirty minutes. No, twenty."

"We can do that." While she wasn't certain it would take that long, she could be wrong.

Seru rose from his seat. Without uttering another word, Thalasia went straight for the door. "Thank you," Seru paused briefly to offer his thanks to the female before following Thalasia.

She left with a clear destination in mind, her path set for the gardens. Although she waited until they got far enough away from the house before she said anything to Seru. "I take it you recognized the name?"

Nothing—Seru didn't respond. Okay. Having taken the path between the set of gardens, Thalasia hadn't bothered giving any attention to the food growing. More than likely, it resembled most of what she'd spent her life eating. Instead, she noted the portion of empty fields, which were minimal compared to the plush red that still covered the ground. Just as exquisite as had been described to her, and the fragrance—the remaining tension in her body eased. Easy to see why Seru liked them so much. The closer they got, the more the water's gentle, mystical trickling seemed to draw her in.

The Reflection Pools were buried in the center of The Poppy Fields—all nine pools, though only the bottom two currently flowed.

Seru slowed as they found themselves embraced by brilliant red poppies. Stooping down, he brushed his fingers over the silken petals. He grasped the hairy stalk of the stem of one poppy, easily plucking it free from its sisters, and brought the poppy to his face, inhaling deeply of its fragrance. The petals caressed his cheek.

"Wonderful memory?" Thalasia asked as she sat on the edge of the second pool, trailing her fingers through the water. The liquid embraced her hand, a conduit for her power, drawing the light to dance upon her skin.

He peered at her. Blue eyes unfocused, pupils dilated. If only for a moment. His gaze refocused. He managed a soft reply. "To a point." He stared at the flower a moment longer, nodding in her direction. "What are you doing with the water in those pools?"

"Nothing more than running my fingers through it. The restorative power in the water is responding to mine." He'd left her for a moment. Not that she needed to ask where he'd gone. Part of her conversation with Ione. The poppies here were the basis for the night poppies blooming in the Clouds.

"Atlis and sirens love their healing," he commented, tossing the bloom back into the sea of red.

"Among other things." Her gaze flicked from him to the droplets of blood on the ground. There wasn't much in the way of evidence. Not that she expected there to be. There had been a lot of questions swirling through her mind when they'd parted ways with Luciel, but she hadn't asked a single one of them. Truth be told, she didn't trust the sun god hadn't lingered nearby and watched them.

"Did you find what you were seeking?"

The short answer was no. Instead of giving him that, she opted to take a second and get a few of her questions out. "How are you doing without the band?"

His eyes slid back to her. "I'm fine." He tucked a stray piece of his mane behind his ear as he righted himself, coming to sit beside her.

His gaze trailed down her body, following to where her hand played in the water. He followed suit, caressing the back of her hand. The water itself was refreshingly chilly.

A shiver traced its way down her spine as the dappled light, suddenly more intense, warmed her skin where his hand met hers. Even her scent flared. It didn't take much. Her eyes settled on the contents of the pool. She watched as it hesitated before fully enveloping his hand, much as it had her own. Thalasia lifted her gaze back to Seru. They'd only been partially truthful with Luciel, especially regarding the lyre. "Exactly what kind of deal did you broker with Aurelia? Details, please."

Seru withdrew his hand. "I doubt the sirens would appreciate us defiling their pools," he murmured, pressing his sleeve to his nose. He turned his hand this way and that, marveling at the strange light until it faded. He inhaled. "She wants me back in the Clouds once we wrap up our business out here. Finish securing alliances," he said. "Though with each successive encounter, I'm more and more convinced she's given us leave so she might set in motion plans she doesn't trust me to see."

Thalasia gave the water a gentle shake before removing her hand, draping it across her leg. "What business exactly did you allow her to believe we needed to accomplish here?" The only task they had at the time they left the Clouds was the book. She was quite certain he'd mentioned nothing of the ritual. Not when it was something that benefited him so much. The first comment, she temporarily overlooked because if he thought they wouldn't be okay with their hands in the pool, then they'd hate what happened tomorrow night.

He crossed his legs at the ankles, leaning back to peer at their reflections on the water's surface. The removal of her hand sent a series of ripples through the images. "In line with our initial objective, I led her to believe we had a few loose ends to tie up, which promised us an advantage in the war to come." He leveled his gaze at her. Her eyes offered the same diamond sparkle and her skin fluorescence the same sheen of silver. Growing stronger by the day. "I didn't lie to her, but I didn't provide her specifics, either. Nor did she request them. I let her place her trust in me, or at the very least our presumed mutual self-interests, of her own accord."

Biting her bottom lip, her gaze shifted from him to the pool and back again. For the last couple of days, despite her agreement to give him details, she'd debated on exactly how much to show him beforehand of the ritual. Seeing how the water reacted to him restored her faith that it would work and would accomplish what they both desired since they first parted ways with Aurelia.

Thalasia reached over the lip, her fingers tracing the worn path until they found the familiar indent, and then she pressed the cleverly concealed button. Beneath the edge, the stone wall of the pool shifted, revealing eight moon phases with various shapes carved into the rock. "Sixteen items, currently fifteen in my possession. The last should come from you. Don't worry, I have an idea for that. We place the items together according to the moon phase of the pair in question. Full moon, waning gibbous, last quarter, waning crescent, new moon, waxing crescent, first quarter, waxing gibbous, and back to the full moon because the power of the moon is endless." She pointed each moon phase out as she spoke.

"I suspect by the completion of the ritual; the pool will be dry." Her eyes sought his back out. "I need to know you're fully committed to this. You'll have to be completely open to it. In the end, when it works..." Thalasia took his right hand within her own, turned it over, and traced an infinity symbol on the inside of his wrist. "A mark will appear here. We'll have the same, the inside of the infinity symbol specific to us together."

"And what does any of that have to do with my arrangement with Aurelia?" Seru asked. "Or was that question just a test before you decided to explain this ritual of yours?"

"It impacts everything, Seru." Releasing her hold on his hand, she reached for the button, closing it back up. "The lyre... this deal that was brokered with Luciel... what you've arranged with Aurelia, aside from the crystal." She paused. "You and I both know the lyre is merely a tool to provide a connection to the barrier that will seal the second I leave the isle with it fully intact in my possession. Unless you truly believe you'll be returning to the Clouds once we're done here in a few days." But she didn't think that was the case. Nor was she certain he completely believed the ritual wouldn't... as he had put it a few days ago, break a little magic.

Seru heaved a sigh, turning to brace his weight against the lip of the pool. "I'm playing the field, garnering as much information and as much of an advantage as I can prior to the battle. There may not always be a physical war game going on within the isle, but that doesn't mean it's ever been peaceful here. In truth, we don't always decide until the moment demands it. Keep them guessing, teetering on the edge by not knowing who you're going to promote until the last moment. Aurelia is but one side of this very complex puzzle. Your power and the lyre another. Luciel is yet another unanticipated but worthy consideration. Marius and the inhabitants of Candescent. Still another."

He shook his head. "And who's saying there aren't still others I've neglected to mention? I've not yet chosen my best way out of this situation because the pieces have yet to fall into place... though they're certainly getting there." His knuckles whitened as he gripped the basin. "If what you're truly asking is if I choose you, I do. But I don't choose to be marked—be it by you or one of your gods and goddesses—" he gestured as he spoke, "You know that's a firm no. And you know precisely why that answer is what it is, which is likely part of what's got you on edge. Your Atlis holy book doesn't offer an alternative. You've learned enough about me to know my methods have cost me dearly—as my brothers and my lovers have. I don't possess any friends, nor do I desire any."

Yes, she did. It was one of many things that had bounced around in her head over the last two days. While she didn't have a resolution with the current time restrictions, she had... something. "There's nothing I can do about the mark in our present situation. However, with some of the knowledge I've recently gained, I believe I may eventually sever the tie it creates. I won't tell you it'll happen overnight. There are a lot of complexities between our species to delve into. It's never been my intention to remove one tether of yours just to give you another."

"While I appreciate your intentions, that doesn't negate the fact that your option still requires that I subject myself to metaphysical chains for the foreseeable future. Reversible or not, with as rapidly as Luciel stripped down my current chains, I'm inclined to consider him a more viable alternative. Granted, that would likely require factoring in Aurelia—while I've insight into the vast majority of her motives and desires, I'd be a fool to underestimate her part in all this. As much as I enjoy your company," he admitted, running a hand through his mane, "I'm not like the shape shifters of Méta-morphe. I'm not some love-drunk puppy looking to be mated for life to one person and one person only. You can pretend the impli-cations of that won't and don't bother you, but they do and they will. You say you don't desire a family, but if that were wholeheart-edly true, would you have been so winded after discovering your family tree possessed many living relatives? I care for you deeply, but do I believe that's enough to see us through—not just the war and Prisma Isle, but to a sustainable future? No. I'm not even sure I live up to my end of the bargain in gratifying your budding urges... and if these past few days are merely your 'awakening,' I'm not disillusioned that this ritual will put an end to your increasing need of certain proclivities. Your heritage, as well as that of the sirens, stems from nymphs. I'm not a nymph, not even close. So, what happens if I agree to this arrangement half-assed? As I did at the start of all this. If long-term, your needs aren't met, if this thing we have doesn't work out?" He let those questions linger in the air between them for several moments. All the while, he studied their reflections. His and hers. "What happens if we supercharge ourselves and fulfill your lust-filled prophecy only to find ourselves at cross purposes? Will you kill me? Because I'll kill you."

Okay, that was a lot, and some of it she gathered was because of misunderstandings, but that was why they needed to get this out in the open. "One, if you were like a 'love-drunk puppy,' I would've slapped you. Repeatedly." She rolled her eyes and shuddered at the thought. "Holding hands is one thing, but good gods, they made me want to throw up. Second, the existence of family didn't bother me, but the secrecy that seems to be in bounds by my family. I don't want kids. After being stuck in your library for an hour with that boy... just confirmed it. Third, my... urges. I know that after the twenty-four-hour mark, the pheromones go away. Thank the gods for that. Beyond that, I don't know. I don't know what kind of sexual desires I'll have." Thalasia gripped the back of her neck. She replayed his other points in her head. "As for the cross purposes... no, I wouldn't kill you. That doesn't mean I wouldn't defend myself. Every couple has disagreements. It's only natural. Do I believe we'll always be on the same page? No. Do I believe we're likely to argue again? Yes. Do I think we'll attempt to kill each other... no." Regardless of what he believed. "As for Luciel... someone who could easily give it back as quickly as he takes it... the tie you get with me doesn't work like that. It gives you access to my power for one. And it allows us to feel what the other is feeling, which means if one or both of us are in a mood... we can always leave the other be for a bit."

"Your family and their long list of secrets don't seem to be news. Since you arrived here, we've operated under the assumption that we know precious little in terms of the whole truth. Having a new group of individuals to care for and support you, to whom you belong, is everything you've ever desired. They're more like you than I'll ever be. Do you honestly believe an Atlis belongs with a saint beast?" He rolled his neck and shoulders. "Zephyr is a... unique fledgling. He's afforded more privilege than most his age for superficial reasons. The only person he has to answer to is Aurelia and she seems quite content to let him run rampant. Once she's taken her mate and produced her own, I doubt she'll be so tolerant and dismissive. As Zephyr ages, he'll be seen as a threat. With no one to protect him, he'll likely be killed." His eyebrows knitted together. "Go away?" he asked, incredulous. "Somehow, I doubt that. There's a big difference between changing the role and eliminating your line. Who's saying this isn't just the beginning? Or, that there's not some invisible clause in stepping into your full powers as Atlis? Accepting the role in full is bound to come with certain expectations. If my options are being enslaved to another's will, the trappings of magical bindings, or killing you or dying trying, I will take my chances with the latter. Gods are fickle, but they have motivations of their own. If you can decipher and appeal to their desires, you can gain and maintain favor. Luciel is no different, though I relish the thought of what he's going to make of those who've forsaken him. I don't desire your feelings or you in my head," Seru growled.

She was fairly certain that somewhere in that jumbled mess, he was still saying he chose her. Something that hadn't changed anytime she'd asked. But that wasn't what she'd tried to explain or get him to understand. In order for them to do the ritual, she was going to offer some kind of explanation to the new Elder. It benefited her that Cipriana was desperate and the female's mother was on the side of the Atlis.

"I can't tell you if we belong together, but it's where we are. Whether by destiny's hand or a bunch of nosey buddies' idea of matchmaking, you and I... we're here together. In a jump feet first kind of situation. All or nothing because choosing me is choosing this." She gestured to the pool. "It's not something you can dip your toes in and see how the water fares. It isn't until a better deal comes along. And it doesn't mean I'll be inside your head. I'll *never* be inside your head. Yes, the emotions will be easier to feel, but that's part of the deal."

With a thoughtful touch to her hair, Thalasia pondered how to present everything with the utmost clarity. "I know we both care about each other a lot. And I know that doing this... comes with a lot of unknowns. But there are a few things I can say with absolute certainty." Her eyes found his, as she didn't want there to be any further misunderstanding about this. "Part of my arrangement with Aurelia is that when this is all said and done, I leave and I don't return." One of the few things they had ever agreed upon. "There are two rules they teach an Atlis from birth. Never reveal the truth, which I'll likely be altering, as that hasn't worked out really well. Not to mention the number of times I've broken it with you out of pure necessity. Protect the innocent. So, my plan, after we leave and get... our charges settled in their new home, is that we return Ione to her homeland, which may or may not be insane, and then we focus on getting you stabilized. And I'm expecting a few missions thrown in the mix somewhere, too. Since there's no actual way to know when a vision will pop up. Oh, and finding an uninhabited realm, at least one that only has animals. As for my family, comprising a multitude of species... hybrids, who's saying I'll ever feel like I belong with them? Even if I one day meet any of them, I may not like them; they may not like me. They could be total assholes. There's no telling." She let out a soft breath. "With you... I feel protected, like I'm always in the middle of a Seru donut." The corners of her lips tugged into a faint smile. "I also feel protective of you. When I put all of that together... I feel like I'm home. And I know, no matter how many times we argue or we disagree on something or how angry we get with each other, that will never change."

"No," Seru stated rather abruptly. "Ione is my... partner, my responsibility." His brow furrowed as he reached up to rub his head. "You may see to the strays." He remained silent regarding the rest. "What's a... donut?"

This was part of their problem. When she'd mentioned Ione, it hadn't been an *I* or *you* kind of thing; it had been *we*. Then he deflected, focusing on the menial as he'd done in the past. "Something from the human world," she muttered, gripping the back of her neck and flicking her gaze back to the pool. "Acceptance of the mark is accepting me as your partner, wife, companion... whatever term you want to use to coin it. You're accepting me and I'm accepting you. Rejecting it means you reject me." And they'd already discussed those consequences. "I just need... verbal confirmation for now. By tomorrow, the rest has to line up." Thalasia peered back at him. "I can tell you're still conflicted over it." It had even been in his face the night before—the concern mixed with the lack of desire. But he'd followed through on his promise. They'd only spent days together, and she'd started picking up on the differences in his moods and how his actions impacted them. Her course hadn't ever really strayed. Not that she hadn't entertained the idea of staying, but that was nothing more than a fantasy. "The fact remains, if this is our course, I need to make the arrangements while my body is still my own." The sexual hum beneath her skin still lingered. It had throughout the fight with the guilers and their conversation with Luciel. At least everything else for her had synced back into place—the healer and fighter in one.

He crossed his arms, shifting from side-to-side, unable to lay claim to his usual calm. He extended his arm to her; the wrist bared. "And how do you propose we conceal this... infinity symbol from the Matriarch?"

Her mouth slowly tugged at the corners. "Glamour." The answer was simple and complex at the same time. Perhaps he missed the part about him being able to pull on her abilities. That was one of the few things she expected he'd pick up like nobody's business. Hiding that was less of a concern than if it broke his bond with Aurelia.

"That might work on the average lesser dragon, but Aurelia's ascension is going to make her even more powerful, more dangerous. She already suspects... She's going to be ever more vigilant in her inspection once I've returned."

"The leather wristband I'm going to make you would be another option. Long-sleeve shirts are another." Which was something that he wore, anyway. The wristband. Yeah, she could see Aurelia's response now. Thalasia had to stop from rolling her eyes.

"The trace magic will not vanish simply because I cover the mark," Seru offered, dismayed.

"The only way to cover magic is with magic, but you didn't like that idea." Not that he offered any ideas of his own. "Although something to consider is that if it... affects your bond to her, the physical manifestation of the mark would make little difference." Thalasia folded her arms across her chest. "Not to mention, every dragon I've crossed has left me with the impression you're... rather powerful yourself. Are you saying that with her ascension, her power will exceed yours, the combination of ours, and that it would be impossible to... convince her of your allegiance even with the mark?" She gave him an incredulous look because she was fairly certain he could pull a rabbit out of his ass if he wanted.

"I'm saying our little adventures have provided her the opportunity to put a host of unknowns into play. While I appreciate your faith in my abilities, you're overlooking the fact that I trained her, from fledgling to just prior to your arrival. Our time together has allowed her to witness and experience my processes firsthand. The link transference between us grants her access to... more," he trailed.

"I figured that much out for myself. Somewhere between her comments regarding the elaborate ritual of the marks and Luciel's reference to the strings. While your training has given her some insight into your process, you've been able to manipulate her from the start. I don't think that's simply because she's allowed you to do so." Obviously, there were things she didn't understand. Their fighting pushed them to work less together and try to handle things on their own. She chewed on the inside of her cheek. "A lot of moving parts," Thalasia mumbled.

"No, it involved several hidden pieces in place before I knew her, knowledge procured under Verie's rule," he confirmed. "And her naivete. Our relationship—or perception of it. There's a chance that all has changed these past days. The real question is in degrees."

"Do you think it's possible she hates you?" She half shrugged. "Although that anger could've been more directed at me... maybe both of us." After all, he'd chosen her time and time again.

Seru eyed her from the corner of his eye as he stared out over the sea of poppies. "No, I believe she hates you because she loves me—at least so much as a dragon in the Clouds is capable of love."

"Oh, she doesn't hate me. She loathes me. Some of which I believe has been transferred to you. Her reference to the obscure ritual on prey kind of made that obvious." Uncrossing her arms, she leaned back a bit, her palm pressing into the lip of the pool as her fingers rested on the blades of grass next to it. None of that was the point, though. "But it's the unknown factors that have you concerned and how that will impact the things we know. So, what do you need that I can help with?"

"She sees you as beneath her—and beneath me—in terms of viable options," Seru replied. "Dragons don't have a penchant for sharing objects of desire, whether they're of precious metal, gemstone, or flesh. She'll, for all intents and purposes, ally with your sirens while having implemented plans to take you out in the fray. You can't not show, after all. The legendary Atlis, the savior of the siren flock." He paused. "I need you to follow instructions and stick to the plan, even the parts you'll know nothing about."

Maybe it was a good thing they'd made it to Pteryrina in one piece. She could collect the armor and weapons that had been left there for her after the completion of the ritual. "And the current plan is?" Because beyond figuring out exactly where Mac and the orange crystal had been taken, which they'd have to do in a matter of hours, the only other thing was when this battle occurred. Based on the current lack of information in that regard, they weren't likely to rescue Mac that quickly, and the timeframe on the battle she'd foreseen, also something there wasn't much to go on.

"I believe we have a siren to rescue before we worry about the upcoming fight and the Matriarch," Seru said, pushing off the lip of the pool. "We need to check back in with Cipriana before she sics her guards on us."

"That we do." Sparing a brief glance at the empty pools above them, she got up from the grassy embankment. One problem at a time. Hadn't they agreed to that at one point? It was almost amusing how they ended up back there on their own.

Chapter Fifty

Seru scrutinized the so-called home for their use. Although the outside of the house was white, the inside was an explosion of color. All the walls were bright red. The shelves and cabinets were a dark blue, close to the color of the night sky. With its fifteen-foot height, the ceiling featured two windows positioned at the top of the back wall. Each window had wooden shutters, both currently closed. A wreath of lavender and chamomile hung on the back of the door. It filled the room with a sense of calm. Directly in front of them, beneath one window, hung metallic moon phases.

A multitude of jars with various herbs, spices, fruit peelings, seeds, kernels, and roots filled racks, along with a few scrolls among the cubbies. Several flowers hung from hooks attached to the bottom counter. Aligning the shelves were also small vials of liquids in a variety of colors. It held jars of twigs, leaves, and small bones as well. More lined the wall closest to them, which contained books, tins, empty jars, gemstones, seashells, and a grater. Bowls of varying sizes, a couple more books, a few small knives, and a mortar and pestle sat on the counter. Four chairs surrounded the table. The other window was next to the empty fireplace. Oversized bedding lay on the floor just beyond the hearth.

Thalasia stepped a little farther into the building between the counters, eyeing everything around them. Minus the glaring color scheme, the sirens were being very accommodating—even overly so. The apothecary, which doubled as a home, was no exception. Thalasia looked like she was drinking the perfect cup of tea on a chill winter day, or so he imagined. Her eyes sparkled and a gentle smile curved her lips as she took in the shop, its shelves brimming with a vast array of medicinal goods. She brimmed with subdued excitement.

She picked up one jar with a few small, brown twigs inside it. Removing the lid, she sniffed, and her nose wrinkled. Returning the jar, she strode over to the table and scanned its contents. "Good gods," Thalasia muttered.

Seru offered a questioning glance before finding the source of Thalasia's annoyance. He peered over her shoulder as she flipped through pages of sketches. "Don't Atlis take part in the art of admiring and paying tribute to their partners?" he asked, clearly teasing her. He'd sketched her at least once since her arrival, though his drawing was a record, a visual accompanying his report.

A small smirk crossed her face. "Certainly makes me wonder if he sketched her just as much." She glanced back at him. "I need to head over to the armory and put something together. You gonna follow or wander?"

He canted his head to one side. Was that even really a question? "I'll explore later. For now, I want to see what the sirens' armory entails." He suspected it might want in the way of a veritable arsenal. Granted, the sirens preferred to live their lives in some semblance of peace, whereas the dragons preferred to sharpen not just their talons but all manner of martial arts and military skills they'd gained access to over the millennia.

She bit her bottom lip, a small snicker escaping her. "I suspect it won't compare to what you're accustomed to having access to." With a dip of her chin, Thalasia gestured back toward the door.

"I'm willing to bet you're exactly right," he said. "Let's hope your grandfather hasn't booby-trapped the armory like he did the cavern behind the waterfall."

Thalasia let out a small giggle. "I hope someone has been in there since he lived here." She grimaced as she slipped past him.

"Nothing like a dust and a cobweb-covered dull blade to the gut," Seru grumbled. If the sirens let their defenses slip so low, it's no wonder another species hadn't infiltrated and finished them sooner. Not that he'd encouraged much action in their direction, either.

Leaving the apothecary, Thalasia led him through the countless white homes, a majority of them abandoned. "Their numbers are fewer than a few. This place is like a ghost town." He followed Thalasia through the empty streets, scanning the endless line of hollow buildings.

"I didn't think it would be this... empty." She approached the armory, a large, lone building. She paused, her fingers gripping the handle, then gave a forceful pull to wrench the stubborn metal door open.

"What *did* you expect?"

"I expected the last male siren had passed, but I still figured there would be way more females than what I've seen." She stepped through the doorway. Torches lining the top of the walls slowly lit up, one after the other. Dust coated the worktables. Cobwebs had taken root in a multitude of places. From their vantage point, they observed a formidable array of weapons—spears, swords, and daggers—lined up against the far wall, with various pieces of armor strewn about the chamber. This didn't include the number of wooden cases stacked just beyond the worktables or the variety of cabinets against both walls.

"The curse is worse than you feared?" he asked absently. His eyes moved over the insubstantial armory, wondering who among them knew how to use these weapons. Beyond that, who still living—if any—possessed the skill to craft a proper weapon and suit of armor. Century-old hand-me-downs only went so far, no matter the craftsmanship. "Well, I'm certain the Matriarch will be glad to know we'll need to supply our new allies with armor and weapons that aren't on the verge of extinction themselves." He crossed his arms, lingering in the entryway. The way the torches lit reminded him faintly of their evening stroll out of the marketplace, where the drakes had fled.

"The results," she muttered. Thalasia strode inside. Her eyes darted from side to side. "Maybe one of the other new alliances Cipriana made can offer in that instance. Didn't she say that she and Mac went toward the dwarves?" Although she posed the question, she didn't look back at him.

"Yes, but while the dwarves make quality armor, the dragons are better versed in magic dampening and negation, which might prove useful against magic-rich opponents like the guilers." Seru watched her intently. "If you tell me what you're looking for, I may assist. My eyes are better in this light than yours." Though his not being trained as an Atlis might mean he missed what she considered obvious.

"I'm looking for the Atlis crest," Thalasia replied as she continued her slow walk, studying the walls with each step.

"Your lyre with wings?" Seru asked, stepping into the center of the room to gain a better view. "Or the moon phases like we saw at the pools?"

"The lyre with wings is the crest of the sirens. The moon phases are the link to the Commitment Ritual." She paused for a moment. "The Atlis crest will look like a pair of wings holding a sword with an intricately designed poppy flower embedded in the hilt."

He circled the room, inspecting the floors, walls, and ceiling. He checked the weapons and armor. Any sign that items hadn't gotten moved over time or at least moved less recently than the rest. If he'd hidden a symbol, he'd have ensured it was off the visible spectrum for one. But since sirens and Atlis had less accurate vision and didn't appear to filter through various lenses to improve or alter their vision, he presumed they'd hidden it somewhere out of sight. He felt in, around, and behind the armaments until he felt a series of engraved markings cut into the wall. Carefully, he cleared the rack of spears, tearing loose cobwebs and scattering dust. Once the cloud cleared and he got the rack down, the etching became visible.

Thalasia crossed over to where he stood. She bit her lower lip, her palm pressing against the cool, smooth crest. Her power bled into the lines of the mark. The crest lit up as it channeled energy outward into the edges of a long and wide imperceptible case. The current traversed up the middle and split open with a sharp hiss. White light spilled out as the two sides widened, revealing its contents inside a protective enclosure. On one side hung a leather top, skirt, and matching boots. Beside it rested a complete suit of armor with the Atlis crest embedded in the chest plate. Beneath the leather attire sat a sheathed sword and two double-antler-dragon-handled Bagua tomahawks. Above it hung a silver circlet with a full moon charm dangling at the center. Thalasia's eyes widened as she stared at the various pieces.

"Looks like you get a reward for all your hard work," Seru said, settling back as he watched her take it all in.

"Is it bad that I *really* want to take it all out now?" Thalasia rocked back and forth on the balls of her feet.

"No." Seru folded his arms across his chest. "Might as well try it on. Make sure it all fits *before* you require it."

Biting her bottom lip, she peered over at him, a twinkle in her eyes. Thalasia removed her purse from her belt loop and stripped her clothes. Once she had her boots off, the rest quickly followed.

With her bag safely tucked into her shoes, she then put on the leather halter and skirt.

Seru shook his head, opting to find himself a seat on one chest near the discarded spears.

Thalasia tugged the boots on, the leather creaking softly, before surveying her surroundings and then turning her attention to the armor. Her hand lingered in the air. After a moment, she switched directions and pulled down the circlet hanging above it all. She situated it on her head, the full moon settling perfectly against her forehead. "While I'm trying this on, would you mind looking for leather and some silver?" She glanced over at him. "Or are you going to sit there and make sure it meets your satisfaction?"

"Dare I ask what you want the leather and silver for?" he asked, pushing back to his feet.

"You'll see once I've put it together," she said as she worked on getting the armor on, piece by piece.

As much as he loathed the thought of being her errand boy, he obliged her. It allowed him the opportunity to better inspect the armory while he collected the requested items. Closer inspection didn't reassure him as to the sirens' ability to defend or attack. The outdated and unkempt weaponry and armor left a great deal to be desired.

"I wonder if Cipriana might offer insight into why no one got assigned to upkeep their armory or even the forges. They're critical tasks for any civilization, especially an isolationist society." Had their infighting left them fearful and sworn off weapons? They hadn't been difficult to find among the workstations. Scraps of leather and silver in various forms for detailing. Some barred, some long-dried liquid.

"She might... provided she knows. Of course, you may get information from others around here, too." As she got the last of the armor in place, she gazed over as much of it as she could see. Her weapons still hung in the hidden alcove. She shifted from foot to foot, stretching her wings along with a couple of other steps. Reaching forward, she took the blade in her hands, removing the sword from its sheath.

"The mother is the more obvious person to consult, but I doubt the newly appointed elder would approve of us undermining her authority," Seru admitted. "I'll stand out like a sore wing in Ptery-rina. As much as I'd like to sneak around and gather information." He rubbed his temples as he reclaimed his spot nearby, holding out the raw metal and strips of leather.

"No, she probably wouldn't." She looked at the sharp edge of the blade, tested its weight, and then effortlessly swished it through the air. Returning it to its sheath, Thalasia glanced over at him. "I suspect any male might stand out around here."

She crossed over to where he sat and collected the items he'd located for her. As she eyed what he'd retrieved, she hefted the blade over her shoulder and got it quickly locked in place between her wings. "Left wrist, please."

"You don't say." Somehow, he hadn't imagined Aurelia had overlooked that fact. She'd placed him in a situation where she knew his every move would be watched, effectively hampering his ability while facilitating her own. Serving double, the predicament illustrated in vivid color the consequences of his choosing Thalasia over her. He remained ever more restricted. Caged. With mild annoyance, he lifted his wrist for her. "Your bracelet, I presume."

"Yes, Seru. I'm measuring your wrist for a bracelet for me," she replied, her words dripping with sarcasm. With a slight smirk, Thalasia focused on using the leather he'd obtained to get a good measure of his wrist. It didn't take long for her to determine the excess and gather the information she needed so she could put it together. Leaving him on the chest, she located a nearby worktable. "Is this your way of saying you're not able to sneak around without being obvious about it? Or that you're unable to use your gender to your advantage?"

"I'm perfectly capable of both," Seru grumbled, dissatisfied. She'd witnessed his ability in the forest, light manipulation to disappear himself. A much-preferred tactic in-lieu of flirting with other winged females. One was more than enough, as far as he was concerned. As for the bracelet, it registered as another shackle in the making. Not unlike Ione's leather bonds, more symbolic, designed for comfort and appearance more than actual binding. Still a shackle. He forced his gaze away with a huff.

"I figured you might be." Thalasia sighed and set everything down. "It may not be what you prefer, but I figured it would be better than a chain or something. And since this requires something of value from you, this... was what I came up with. But if you have another idea, I'm all ears."

"How is any of *that*..." he gestured at her work-in-progress, "Anything even remotely of value to or from me?" He stood, then. A shake of his mane before heading for the door. He paused with his hand on the handle. "I'd rather not have a vote on such trivialities. We'll only end up arguing and nothing will get done."

He didn't meet her eyes. Instead, he glowered at the dusty floor. He hated dust, even without the accompanying drake. Opening the door, he stepped out. A slight, unnecessary flourish brought enough wind to sweep the offending dust from the armory out into the open. "I've changed my mind. I'm going to take that walk. Do try not to die, get yourself bird-napped, or find some way to maim yourself with your new toys." With that, he took her leave, pulling the door shut.

Seru wandered through the empty houses, soon finding himself with company.

A young female with honey-blonde hair and bright crystal-blue eyes ran up to his side. Folding her arms behind her back, she glanced up at him, doing her best to match his pace, but he had longer legs than she did. At first, she said nothing; she just peered over her shoulder at the other two young females following behind them. Her eyes flicked back to him. "Are you lost?"

Seeing as he had little idea where he was storming off to... No, he wasn't lost. He eyed the blue-eyed female for a moment, easing his pace so she wasn't scurrying after him with her claws skritching. "I suppose lost is a matter of perspective. Where is it you think I should be going?"

She shrugged. "I don't know you, so I can't say, but my sisters thought you might be. I told them you didn't look lost, that you just don't seem to have a direction of where you're going."

"Then, I'd say that makes you the victor," Seru replied, granting her a smile.

Offering him a toothy grin, she tilted her head. "I win a lot. They just don't like to admit that I'm smarter than them."

"You are not!" one female behind them called out. "You take that back!"

"No!" She stuck her tongue out and turned her attention back to him. "You have strange clothes. Do you always dress like that where you're from?"

"Perhaps you're each smart in your own way or your sisters have unique talents," Seru tried. This wasn't the Clouds. There was little point in championing one over the others. Besides, she appeared to have enough pride in herself. Seru glanced down at his present attire. "When I'm at Court or on diplomatic business, such as this, yes. In private or on my time," not that he got much of that, "I prefer much more practical attire. Expensive silk and embroidery are only for special occasions or the very wealthy."

"See!"

"Shut up, Ismena!" she hollered behind them.

"I'm gonna tell your mom, Blair," Ismena yelled back.

With a snicker, she rolled her eyes and returned her focus to his words. She silently mouthed *diplomatic business*. After a moment, her eyes lit up. "Oh! So, you've come about the treaties Elder Cipriana and Parthenia got sent to make." She canted her head back up at him. "Does that mean you're going to mate with the others? I'm not of mating age yet, but I guess you'd be okay."

"Yes, on the peace treaties. No, on the mating," Seru said. "I'm sure the last type of mate you'd want would be a dragon."

"Not really." Blair scrunched her nose. "At least you fly... and you're pretty."

"He's a male. We don't call them pretty!" Ismena exclaimed.

"But he has pretty beads in his hair!" With a huff, she flipped her blonde hair over her shoulder. "What do you know?"

"That they didn't say anything about mating with the treaties," Ismena smirked as she caught up with them, taking up the other side of Seru.

"You only know that cuz I told you," Blair retorted.

"I'm pretty sure your offspring wouldn't inherit the beads." He hid a slight smile. He wondered if they knew the truth, if they'd still think the same about them. "What *did* they say about the treaties?" Seru prompted. It was obvious, but they seemed more than willing to talk—at least so long as they could quarrel over who said what and voice their opinions.

"That we're getting help with the invaders." Ismena crossed her arms and glowered at the female walking beside him on his right. "I bet you didn't know that. Did you, Blair?"

"Yes, I did, Ismena," she responded, purposely drawing out the female's name. "I also know that we're supposed to be getting training, materials, and food, too." Blair stuck her tongue out at Ismena again.

The third female, who to this point hadn't uttered a word, whispered in Ismena's ear, "Weren't we just gonna ask him questions?"

"Hush," Ismena said, her gaze focusing back on Blair. "When did you hear that?"

"When they sent me away from the Elder's house." Her face brightened as if she'd successfully one-upped the female.

Trade deals were pretty typical of peace treaties. So were relief efforts. Help thy neighbor while also helping yourself. "What did you want to know?" Seru asked, directing his question to the shy, soft-spoken girl.

The female stared at him with wide eyes as she fidgeted. She opened her mouth and snapped it shut, then averted her gaze.

Ismena elbowed her in the side. "Lotus, say something."

Without looking up, she played with the skirting of the white dress they all wore as she spoke. "Are you... the dragons... gonna help?"

"That's a good question," Blair said and turned her attention back to him.

"If your elder allows it," Seru said, simple enough.

"How? How would you help?" Blair asked.

"And what would you want?" Ismena followed up, looking at him expectantly. When Lotus opened her mouth, Ismena elbowed her again, forcing her to shut it with a small grimace.

"We want for nothing in the Clouds. Ideally, we want to give. Food, building supplies, weapons, and armor," Seru said, only mentioning a few. "Dependent on the Matriarch's permission, maybe even magic. If all goes well, re-opening commerce isn't out of the question."

"Freely?" Lotus asked, her voice low.

"In exchange for clemency and a seat at the table once..." Seru trailed.

Tilting her head, Blair glanced from him to Lotus and paused. She leaned to the side and stared past them. Her jaw dropped. "Whoa."

The other two both turned their heads in the direction she stared. A plume of dark gray smoke rose into the sky above them. Both of them echoed her sentiment.

Smoke likely meant fire. More guilers or a chance that Mac's kidnapper wanted to make demands? Draw attention to where they weren't? With a heavy sigh, he retraced his steps back in Thalasia's direction. He turned back to the girls as an afterthought. "You three should get somewhere safe, where your leaders will know you're alright." With that, he ran toward the armory and the rising smoke.

The three girls flew off as he suggested. The minor cyclone of exhaust came from the armory itself. With the metallic door propped open, the board-covered windows they hadn't noticed before were agape. But there didn't seem to be any danger in sight—guilers or otherwise.

Seru's pace slowed as he realized what the smoke was from. With a shake of his head, he covered his nose and mouth with his sleeve before going in after her. The smog burned his eyes, but Thalasia was easy enough to locate as she cursed at the uncooperative forge.

"Motherfucker! Come on, you stupid piece of shit!"

"You really should leave this to the professionals," Seru stated, his tone muted by the cloth.

Thalasia glanced back for a fleeting moment before her focus returned to the metal hearth. "I've worked with forges in the past. And I've almost got this one up and running."

"Not before scaring the locals and damn near suffocating us."

"I opened the windows. And with one more tweak... ha!" Not only had she gotten it lit, but everything was now working the way it should. Thalasia took a few steps back and placed her hands firmly on her hips, standing her ground.

Seru shook his head, struggling to keep his eyes focused and his vision clear in the thick, black smog.

Her gaze shifted to him. She closed the distance between them and hooked her hand behind his arm. "Come on. We can step outside until all of this clears."

"You've also successfully ruined my clothes," Seru commented, more than tired of this place and her theatrics. Even those little girls were better behaved. No doubt, they and the smoke had raised the alarm and alerted the Elder and her guard, who'd likely meet them outside. This just kept getting better by the moment.

"To be fair, I didn't tell you to come back in here." She sighed heavily, ushering him outside. "If you feel you need a bath, there's a spring you can use, and I probably have some clothes in my bag you can change into."

Once they got outside, both Cipriana, who looked like she'd gone a round with the forge herself, and one of her guards stood there waiting.

Thalasia raised a hand. "There's no issue. I was just working on getting the forge up and running."

"Is that the cause of the smoke?" Cipriana asked. "And the disaster the two of you look like?"

"Yes. Really, it's nothing to worry over."

He coughed. "You didn't say you were going to fumigate the whole of Pteryrina, either." He let the bath comment slide. His concern didn't lie with the state of his clothing so much as the violation of their appearances and motives for being here. All of which she was casually tossing to the winds.

"Sorry. I didn't mean to startle anyone. Guess I didn't get it cleaned out as much as I thought." Thalasia sighed and dragged a hand down her face, only streaking the soot on her cheeks.

Cipriana stifled a chuckle. With a shake of her head, she cleared her throat. "It's fine." She waved it off and shot into the sky, her guard right behind her.

Those must be some legends for the elder to wave off the commotion so readily. Or, more than likely, her substantial inexperience. He sighed, dusting off what he could of his clothes. He'd cleaned the space once, only for her to turn around and soil it anew with thicker, greasier grime than before.

"At least I can amuse someone." Thalasia snickered. "Exactly how did you think I was going to work with the silver?"

"The sensible way, that amount of silver hardly requires—" he gestured broadly at the entire scene, "All *this*."

"I was going on a two for one. Figured if I got the forge going, it would be something that benefited them. I'll be another hour."

"Of course, you will," Seru said, resigned to this being a difficult stage in the last stretch of their journey.

"If you make it to tomorrow night, I'll be shocked." Thalasia spun on her heel and made her way back into the armory. "Gods, we both suck at showing we care," she muttered to herself. She crossed the armory's threshold.

He let her go on her way back to her work. A cycle that promised to keep replaying itself until they parted ways. He veered off back toward the apothecary, where they'd be staying. At the very least, he could strip out of his defiled clothing. There was little point in his sticking around here.

Chapter Fifty-One

Thalasia stepped into a white sundress with flowers on it. Unlike the one she'd worn the day before; this one had a halter that wrapped around her neck and hung looser. Despite their activities from the night before, a steady shimmer covered her flesh from head to toe. It was her body's warmth and thick scent that had her in another dress. Otherwise, it would've been shorts and a halter. The dress seemed like the better option as it clung to her body less. She got the back zipped up and glanced over her shoulder at Seru.

They still had hours to go, and she believed she should be nervous, but she wasn't. She couldn't quite put a finger on what she felt. A swirl of different things that there didn't seem to be words to describe. "I figure we'll see if we can find Cipriana. See if her siren count has changed at all."

"As you like," Seru mumbled, nuzzling into a mound of pillows.

A small chuckle left her mouth as she crossed over to where he lay and sat down on the edge of the bed. It was a good thing she'd found the stack of pillows in the closet. "Would you like me to leave you here to rest longer?"

"If that were an option, you'd have already left," he rumbled, prying his eyes open one eyelid at a time.

"You get annoyed with me anytime I go off somewhere on my own." She had to stifle another laugh. Not that her statement was amusing, but that he'd gotten himself nice and cozy in a nest of feathers.

"Might that have something to do with you always ending up in trouble?" he grumbled, forcing himself upright onto his knees. "Or that you end up precisely where I forbade you from going?"

Instead of starting the morning off with an argument, she consented with a simple answer. "Probably." She'd gotten distracted with the shape shifter. And too frustrated by his spectrum of moodiness to ask for an alternative to the yellow dragon. Thalasia rested her hands on her lap. "Now, if you'd like to go back to sleep, just say so. I can deal with the Elder on my own. Figuring out who's lying might be a bit more difficult." Depending on whether or not the Elder confirmed one of her sirens was unaccounted.

Seru stumbled out of bed and started hunting down his clothes.

Guess that answered that question. Gods, just don't let him be in a grumpy mood all day. Rising to her feet, Thalasia reached into her bag and withdrew a hairpin, its delicate prongs glinting. Sweeping her hair up into a semi-sloppy bun, she pinned it in place. For the last hour, she'd been nosy and gone through cabinets. Watching Seru for a moment, she recalled something the yellow dragon had said. Although it had been in a kind of bitchy way, the female had pointed out that he'd taken his sweet time leaving. What if he hadn't been able to?

"Something on your mind?" Seru prompted, securing the last of his clothes for their early morning venture.

For a second, she considered offering a generic response. He often gotten annoyed with her questions. Except it occurred to her that of all the people she had spoken with about him, he was the one person she hadn't asked. Probably because of his ever-fluctuating moods. "Your bond... is that what's kept you here? Kept you from joining your brothers?"

"My bond... which bond are you referencing?"

"The one to..." Her words trailed off. Her initial thought had been Aurelia because that was what kept him on the isle. Provided her comprehension of what she'd learned was accurate. The collar that used to be around his neck, even the bit of magic that remained—it hampered his energy, his power. If his ability to return required his power, then maybe the two worked in concert to keep him ever-present. "Um... Aurelia," Thalasia said.

"My bond to Aurelia is what sustained—sustains me from the point the Silver Queen was eliminated onward. My bond is independent of my brothers."

That just led to more questions. Why was his bond independent of theirs? What would it take for him to join them? Would something more than the eventual breaking of his bond to her—if the ritual was as successful as she believed—be required? Oh gods, what *if* she wasn't strong enough to sustain him? Why the fuck hadn't she thought of that before? Thalasia chewed on the inside of her cheek as each new question only incurred more.

No. She couldn't allow herself to *what if* the situation. Even without the ritual, she was powerful in her own regard. Plus, her gut had never steered her wrong. At least when she listened to it. And if anything, she'd be willing to bet Seru had thought about all of this, which meant he probably had some kind of contingency in place. Or a plan for one. "Sorry... my brain kind of... I'm not even sure what got it started. They should probably be saved for a later time?" Her last comment came out as more of a question than a statement.

He narrowed his eyes at her, remaining as still as a statue through it all. "You should eat something." He breezed past her to grab the door as if they hadn't even had the conversation. "We don't want to keep the Elder and her flock waiting."

As if that didn't say it all. "Uh, yeah. I was planning to swing by the gardens afterward." She realized earlier that she hadn't eaten since yesterday morning. Thalasia rubbed her forehead, the slight ache intensifying as she snatched her purse and made for the exit. "They've been up since the sun rose four hours ago." She was pretty sure they'd already been waiting.

"Stop worrying about problems you can't solve and focus on those you can," Seru reminded her. "Like how to appease your worshippers."

That was like asking her not to worry about him. Something she couldn't stop, but she could temporarily push the questions to linger in the back of her mind. Her nose scrunched up. "Can we please not call them that?" Watching the three females drop to their knees the day before had been both difficult and shocking. Still, after she'd verified the numbers, she'd been able to forge something more suitable for the three women.

"Do you have a better term?" Seru asked.

She pursed her lips and tapped her chin as she ran through alternatives. Bird and flock were definitely out of the question. And they weren't her wards or charges. She didn't want to be worshipped by anyone. It was the same concept as his errant term 'queen' a few days back. "Can't we just call them sirens?"

"They are that, just not only that in relation to you."

"Joy." Thalasia dragged a hand down her face. Bottom line, what they were called didn't matter all that much. She'd learned names and addressed them accordingly.

"You don't just get to pick and choose. You either intend to be an Atlis and all it entails, or you don't. Part of that involves fulfilling the role they assign you, not just picking out the parts you like and brushing aside those you don't."

This wasn't the first time she'd heard those words. The idea of being worshipped hadn't been one that ever sat well with her. Not any more than the acceptance of power. Both were there at her feet. This all-or-nothing situation wasn't lost on her. She'd already resumed her studies and training as time permitted. This was just another aspect that she had to accept. "You're right."

"So, which is it?" he pressed.

"All." Guess she hadn't made that obvious. "I'm all in." Yes, it was going to be complicated, and she'd have to accept things she didn't want, but she could fully commit to her role and everything it entailed. "Shall we go find the Elder now?"

He motioned for her to take the lead.

Why did she get the sense he hoped she'd go the other way? That couldn't be right. It didn't change her feelings about being worshipped or her acceptance of power. But she also understood one's feelings had to be pushed aside when something more important was at stake. Maybe he just wasn't all that excited about talking to the Elder. He had wanted to sleep more. Thalasia stepped past him, pausing for a moment in the apothecary's doorway. She peered at him over her shoulder. "Why don't you come back here and rest after we talk to Cipriana?"

"What is with you and obsessing over my rest?!" he snarled. "In case you've forgotten, your sirens—especially the Elder—expect us to locate Mac and return him."

"No, I haven't forgotten. But we have nothing to go on, and it isn't like we can spend the day scouting mountains and caves given the number that exists," Thalasia said. While she prayed, the female figured out which siren was missing; she wasn't hopeful. "Time is not on our side in this endeavor."

"No, but that doesn't mean we shouldn't give it our best effort."

Thalasia turned, folding her arms across her chest. Did he think she wasn't trying? There were things she'd done while he walked the day before. "Cipriana refused to accept the possibility yesterday that a siren is involved. I'm not banking on it miraculously changing this morning. I plan to have her introduce me to the sirens on the premise that maybe they saw something that would be helpful. And the missing siren might be determined, even if she doesn't see it."

Then, of course, they'd have to sneak into that siren's home in the hopes there might be some clue where they were hiding and keeping Mac. It wasn't like the two visions she'd previously had of the male offered any insight. She'd already looked. She rubbed her forehead. "The closest caverns are those bordering the manticore territory. We can scout those afterward." It seemed too convenient, but they wouldn't leave a single stone unturned. Not that she knew figuring who the siren was would be any more helpful. "Starting the search again after that... just depends on how quickly we rebound once the hormones leave my body."

"I'm sure the Elder won't mind lending a few of her people to continue and expand the search. If need be, I'm sure the dragons would love to hunt for Aurelia's favorite siren."

After what they'd seen of the place, she wasn't sure they had the people to spare. He'd said it himself; the place was like a ghost town. "Do you think she wants to involve the dragons? Considering not only is Mac missing, but so is the crystal?" Yeah. It hadn't been too hard to figure out that Cipriana relied on them because she didn't have very many options.

"If we serve every one of your charges based on what they want rather than what they need, then we're not doing the job, are we? They'll just go back to hating one another once you've left, and nothing will have truly changed. If she's extending the olive branch, she needs to make good on that. Just like if the dragons are sincere about being included, they need—more than any other group—to prove it." Seru dragged a hand through his mane. "Unless, of course, this is just another farce—for appearance's sake only. Suppose you don't care what happens afterward? Fine by me. It's your duty; you execute how you see fit."

"I'm not the one who has to be convinced. We can suggest it, but that doesn't mean she'll accept it." Maybe they could present an argument that would convince the female she needed to extend her options. Turn to the alliances made. "Okay. You and I need to present a united front. So, talk to the sirens to see if we can check out the responsible party. Based on what we saw of the fight, guilers are likely involved, so we can push her to reach out to those alliances since both sky and ground need to be covered. And see who she can spare to aid in the search." She had the female try the mate-link the day before, but it may not have been strong enough, or one or both of them were fighting it. It could be worth giving another try.

"This is your show," Seru returned.

"No, Seru, this is *our* show."

"I'm not the Atlis, Thalasia."

"No, but you are my Allimos, so own it." As much as she disagreed with Marius's assessment that the tasks belonged to the two of them, the male hadn't been wrong. They just had to agree on how to handle them.

"The only person who sees me that way in this equation is you. To the sirens, I'm merely a Draconic politician, maybe even a ruse or a spy."

"Only because we didn't introduce you any other way. If that's how you prefer, they see you..." Her words trailed off. The opportunity presented itself twice in just one day: when Cipriana asked if they were a couple and then again when she mentioned the private ceremony. "We're asking them to overcome hundreds of years of separation. Did it not occur to you that if the sirens saw one of theirs with a dragon as their partner, they would view it as a bridge?"

"Barring the fact that I'm not a dragon and you're not a siren, sure," Seru said. "It may just discredit you entirely. And just as soon as my being your Allimos gets back to the dragons, we can both surrender to our less than glorious fates as traitors. If you thought being trapped in the sky cell was bad, I'd hate to see how you take actual punishment into account."

"And you still think asking her to reach out to the dragons is a good idea?" Someone told the female *not* to trust them. Yet, she appeared to be doing so. They didn't just have to do what was right for the sirens, but they had to work within the boundaries created by the path they'd chosen to take. "You'll have to excuse me if I think that's nothing more than a bad idea. I get it; you want to believe that they want to reach out and help. Not me. I think if they saw how weakened a defense the sirens had, they would destroy what remains and overtake the entire sky for themselves. Then everything we've gone through would be for nothing."

"I don't." He paused. "What I think makes little difference. Do it your way."

Yep, she had a headache. And if she were anyone else or if he were someone else, she'd probably let it go. "What you think matters to me. What is it you think I'm missing? Because there's something." They had to rescue Mac and retrieve the crystal without the dragons finding out about their other tasks. Not to mention, she'd purposely left out information when she disclosed the ceremony to Cipriana, so the sirens had to remain partially in the dark. That was just the beginning of the convoluted web woven. It didn't consider the shape shifters, Markham and Minerva, or any other species on the isle.

"It shouldn't. Things will work out how they're supposed to be here, whether or not we interfere." He paused. "I'm honestly surprised the Elder didn't call on Oriel herself. If they're in league and Mac has the crystal—or at the very least, his captor does. Or did you miss the display at the lake, with his eyes and each crystal you passed to Aurelia?"

Sometimes she wondered why she offered the opportunity to input his thoughts. To be fair, there were times he gave them even when she didn't ask. "I didn't miss that; however, we don't know the extent of her agreement with him or their negotiations. Unless Aurelia shared that information with you." Since Aurelia didn't mention that Mac was the new Elder or that Felix had passed, that information probably hadn't gotten shared, either.

Seru laughed. "Your mistake is thinking Oriel is loyal to Aurelia. Cipriana has one of his weapons crafted into a signaling device—not hers. Oriel may be content to let Aurelia collect the crystals, but he has no intention of letting her use them."

"Aside from the purpose of the device, how much of the rest of that do you think Cipriana knows?" In the end, it was still Cipriana's decision. Thalasia turned around and opened the door. They were wasting daylight hours, something they couldn't afford.

"I'm not sure it much matters; Mac's so important to her, and Oriel cooperated so well... if her glorious Atlis can't find him, maybe the dragon can."

Thalasia narrowed her eyes at him over her shoulder. If she didn't know better, she'd swear he was goading her. Because the dragons were so much better, right? Yeah, she'd like to see him discern nuances and figure out a vision with no context, no information, nothing to go on—a pain-in-the-ass saint beast. Focusing on where she was going as they left the apothecary, the grip she had on her purse tightened as she spotted Cipriana heading in their direction.

"For someone who preaches resolution and trust, your actions say you're against it."

She halted in her tracks and faced him. "Trust goes both ways. Both parties have to bend to make it work."

"What makes you assume they haven't? We weren't here for their meeting. Cipriana didn't seem put off by him. Aurelia puts everyone off, but she's a powerful ally, nonetheless. However, I hardly see her involving herself in locating a missing siren so close to a battle—that doesn't mean she wouldn't allot resources. Though knowing Oriel and his lot, he might like it better if we didn't involve the Matriarch. You also don't need trust to use one another, which I hate to break it to you, Atlis, but that's how most of this isle operates. If you think you're just going to swoop in for a week and change all that, you're deluding yourself."

She shook her head. Didn't she say a few minutes ago that they hadn't been privy to their meeting? "No. I don't think it can be fixed in a week. Changes like that take months, sometimes years, to incorporate." Again, it was all information to present to Cipriana. Though if he wanted to give it to her to offer, sure, she could do that.

"So, why are you so against letting them figure it out on their own merit with supervision rather than doing it for them? Does being a hero mean that much to you?"

"What makes you think I'm not letting them figure it out on their own?"

He shrugged. "Prove me wrong." He meant that as a challenge.

What exactly did he think she'd contributed to any of the species thus far? She'd stolen a crystal from the manticore. She'd gone with him instead of Mac. The information given to the sirens had been minimal. She got a forge going and made a few weapons. Whoopee! A small feat among the number of things the sirens needed. Thalasia turned around just as the Elder approached.

"I'm not interrupting anything, am I?" Cipriana asked.

"Not at all." She had half a mind to leave him there on guard duty while she took a couple of sirens with her to scout the mountain-side. Something she was sure wouldn't go over well with him.

"Good. I thought we could go to the temple and talk."

"Lead the way." Typically, they would have flown to the temple, but she suspected Cipriana would walk there out of regard for Seru. Yeah, him flying would scare the shit out of the sirens here unless he did it that one way she'd seen when he followed her to the tree.

Seru stayed silent, letting her take the lead, just as he had promised.

They passed by the library on their way to the temple—a short staircase that led to two large, wooden doors. It was certainly in-teresting to see the stone building of the library from this side. The temple wasn't too far from it. A narrow flight of stairs ascended to a landing nestled between massive columns that encircled the stone structure. Intricately-woven poppies covered the base and top of each column. There was no roof over the temple. Cipriana led them through an open archway and into a long hall. They walked by one set of double doors and entered through the second.

Grains of white sand covered the ground. On the other side were rows and rows of stone benches. The temple itself had been semi-sectioned off into three parts. An altar sat at the height of the section to their left, including a statue of Demeter herself. In the area to the right, there was a long, angular stone slab with two poles. In the middle, someone had built a pyre. If she had to hazard a guess, she'd say they were making preparations for a death ceremony. Likely for the Elder who had just passed.

Cipriana strode a little farther in and clasped her hands at her back. She paced in a half-circle until she came face to face with them. "That thing you had me do yesterday to reach out to Mac, was that the mate-link?"

"Yes," Thalasia replied.

"I felt something earlier this morning. Like a flicker or a nudge. Does that make sense?" Cipriana asked.

"Yes." While she and Seru had something similar, she didn't think it was to the same degree. And it seemed more intentional than unintentional. All the same, it was a good sign. It meant the green-feathered siren was still alive.

"That's a good thing, right?" Cipriana started pacing again. Her talons dug into the sand with each step. "My mom said it was... that often in a true pairing, they could feel one another's emotions and sometimes got... images. I haven't gotten that. I'm sorry, I'm just horrible with this connection. Parthenia, it's like she was made for it." She stopped in her tracks. "I'm prattling, aren't I?"

"You're fine. To answer your first question, yes, it's a good thing." Yep. The female had it bad, even if she hadn't fully opened herself up to it.

"You should practice calming yourself, letting the connection manifest," Seru suggested.

"Calm myself. Um, yeah, that's something I can do." Cipriana nodded, her head bobbing up and down.

"We both believe you can." Was it interfering if she took the female's hand within her own and gave her a head start? Or recommended she spend some time in The Poppy Fields. It's what those flowers were for. She might need to lie in the fields herself before the ritual that night. Maybe she was sorting through her feelings about it.

"Right," Cipriana paused. "I went down the stairs with one of my guards. Those black feathers—do you know what they're from? I've never seen anything like them before."

"Yes. It's a creature known as seitadi." She didn't offer more information. Though if the female asked, she'd give it. But it might be the one thing that convinced her that a siren was involved. Thalasia bit her tongue hard. It was the only way to contain the laughter. When she thought about those large, black-feathered birds, she pictured Seru with feathers stuck in his snout. Not the time or place to think about that. Especially since they needed to find their master, who at least appeared to be working with guilers, and had the orange crystal. Given that it was still tainted, that bothered her.

"Okay," Cipriana said. "And the fire... well, the charring... guilers, I'm guessing? I haven't fought against a pyromancer, so I wasn't sure if that was the case or if it resulted from Mac's flames."

"Guilers, yes, I believe so." Raising an eyebrow, she glanced over at Seru. Since when did Mac have flames? If that was the case, how was he being detained? While she suspected he had theories, she didn't wish to verbalize the question in front of others. Something to ask later.

"Thanks," Cipriana replied with a slight shake of her head. "I'm presuming you're both going out scouting today."

"Yes. We'll return before nightfall." Technically, they'd return before the rise of the moon, but she didn't specify that information. Generic was better.

"Good. A couple of my guards have taken the forest bordering the manticore territory. So, you don't have to search there." Her eyes drifted to the ancient stone slab positioned at the far end of the temple. She turned her attention back to the two of them. "You both have... special abilities, right? I don't know what dragons can do, but my mom told me Atlis usually have unique powers."

"That's true." Where was the female going with this? It was a general question, but she wasn't sure she cared for the direction.

"I don't suppose either of you could... destroy that?" With a nod, Cipriana indicated the slab nestled on the far side of the ancient temple.

Thalasia gave Seru a sidelong glance to see if he wanted to take the opportunity. "Specifically, the slab?"

"Correct. We no longer need it."

"What is it?" Seru asked, scrutinizing the stone marker.

It hadn't been necessary for her to ask. That piece of construction had gotten established a year before her great-great-grandparents left. They had witnessed its use. Thalasia remained silent.

"We used it for public punishment. The offended would use a weapon of their choice on the offender," Cipriana replied as she diverted her attention from them, letting her hands fall to her sides.

The look on the female's face said it all. Someone used it in recent months. And it bothered the female. Thalasia reached out, clasped Cipriana's hand, and gave it a gentle squeeze. Even if Seru wouldn't, she would.

"That doesn't sound terribly out of order, presuming the one passing judgment is fair," he replied. "While fear isn't the only way to rule, consider the consequences of removing such a deterrent, even if you rewrite the law and it becomes antiquated."

"Maybe fear works for the dragons, but I don't require it to keep charge of my people." Cipriana crossed her arms. "While I respect the Elder who came before me, it isn't necessary for me to follow in her footsteps. As many of ours, it is an antiquated law. I'm rewriting them not only to consider the alliances I've made, but those I expect my sister has made as well. If I need to enforce them, I have a prison that still functions perfectly. Especially when people can get offended easily, regardless of the truth."

A faint smile crossed Thalasia's face. She was kind of proud of the female. She was curious if Seru would put his foot in it some more.

"Have it your way," Seru shrugged rather nonchalantly. "The artifact is siren. You should do the honors," he spoke, stepping aside to give Thalasia more than enough room to dispose of it however she saw fit.

Cipriana turned to Thalasia expectantly.

"I'll take care of it." Yeah, it was amusing. Though if he stepped in too much further, she would've intervened. Not only had he offered his opinion once, but he'd done it twice. No, wait. Three times. None of which the female asked. To the Elder, nonetheless. If her memory served her in current siren law, that alone would have constituted an offense. She'd gotten thrown in jail for asking questions. The issue had probably been about Aurelia's ascension.

Thalasia stepped around Cipriana and located a suitable position, angled away from the pyre. She spent a minute testing the air pressure, considering the position of the chunk of rock and the amount of energy required for the silver blast. After a thorough examination, she conjured a small, luminous orb in her palms, launching it at the stone and poles, reducing them to mere ash.

"Wow," Cipriana mumbled.

Brushing her hands off, Thalasia made her way back to where Cipriana and Seru waited. "If you require nothing else, we'll take our leave."

"Uh, no... nothing else." Cipriana's eyes darted back and forth between the two of them. Then she glanced back at the empty spot across the way, and her shoulders relaxed.

Thalasia gestured to the double doors they'd initially come through.

Seru gave a slight bow of his head to Cipriana. He waited a moment before responding to Thalasia's cue.

As they made their way down the hallway toward the exit, Thalasia eyed a few of the various depictions on the wall. Demeter, Persephone, and the first sirens. All of which was as she expected. She waited until they were outside the temple before she spoke. "Unless you feel the need to follow, I'll meet you at the gate in fifteen minutes."

Seru gave a resigned sigh. He branched off toward the gate.

That worked for her. Thalasia flew off into the sky toward the gardens. She'd gather a few pieces of fruit and head over to the armory, where she could retrieve her armor and weapons. Best to be prepared, just in case.

Chapter Fifty-Two

Parthenia and Gavin had made it to the Chimera territory earlier that day. They'd been there to negotiate a peace treaty for the sirens; neither of them expected to participate in a mating ceremony. It wasn't much, but they each currently worked on their part. It seemed to be something that would help solidify the terms she and Chief Elroy had already agreed to upon their arrival.

With a quick glance over her shoulder at her mate, a momentary turn of her head, she offered him a smile. The scent of rosemary filled the air as she, alongside the other females of the Chimera village, wove a crown. They assembled it in numerous stages, with each collective of women focusing on one level. And her mate helped the males remove the heads from the arrows. From what she'd gathered as part of their mating ceremony, the male would shoot his female with the headless arrows and then break them afterward. It was only a tiny portion of their ritual, but it seemed strangely romantic.

Her mate caught her looking at him. Beaming, he gazed at her a moment, then returned to his task, adding another arrowhead to the pile that had been removed.

She'd never actually seen a mating ceremony. What she had with Gavin had been private, but wonderful. Something she wouldn't ever change. Although sirens had traditional ceremonies, they hadn't performed one in a few centuries. The expectation for males to procreate with many females, coupled with their elevated standards, resulted in a complete absence of mating. It would be nice to see one. Her gaze shifted back to the group of women as they finished up their portion of the crown of rosemary. "What do we do now?"

"Well, we'll connect the layers with a twine of rosemary to pull it all together," one woman answered. "Why don't you help clean up the tables so that we can get this all set for the ceremony? I believe the men are almost finished."

"Of course. I'm happy to help." Parthenia stood and slipped between the tables, her fingers gently brushing against the smooth wood as she collected the small pieces, leaving the surfaces bare.

Her mate joined her, his arms encircling her waist from behind as he planted a tender kiss on her neck. "Hello, my love." He kissed her neck again, the warmth of his lips lingering, before gently releasing her. And then they began clearing the table together.

"How'd everything go over there?" Not that she had to ask. She'd snuck several peeks while she worked. Her gaze followed the tables as they converged, efficiently clearing away any remaining fragments. This was going to be a beautiful ceremony.

"Everything went well. There were just a few more needed, but I was told I could come to help you. I think because I could not stop staring over at you." He chuckled softly. "Something I have never done before, but it was fun. How did things go over here with you?"

"I've seen nothing that had so much detail to it. I mean, the spells and potions I put together are often particular in what they require to function." With a sprig of rosemary in her hand, she paused, its fragrant oils releasing a sharp, clean aroma. "I guess I have worked with something like it before. One misstep can mean disaster. Of course, this, you just do it again."

"Disaster in a... not-quite-so 'impending doom' fashion?" He chuckled as he brushed away the tiny bits of rosemary. "From what I saw of it, it is going to turn out lovely. I am sure it will be treasured. I never imagined a public mating ceremony could be anything like this." The corners of his mouth upturned. "Even though ours was private, I think it was perfect for us."

"As nice as it would've been to, I don't know, use one of our traditions or even start something new." She glanced over at him. "Ours was perfect." They didn't need anyone else to celebrate their joining. Why did anyone have to witness it or draw it out like a traditional mating for sirens? No. Simple and heartfelt. That was what mattered.

Gavin gently stroked her cheek, his fingers brushing against her skin, before collecting more rosemary sprigs from the table. "I think, in a way, we started something new. That was the first time I had ever danced, too."

With a slight tilt of her head, she bit her bottom lip. "Maybe you're right." They had started a new tradition—something they could carry on and teach to their young. "I think you danced beautifully. Maybe we'll get the chance to dance here, too." It was something she looked forward to doing with him. Not that they needed an excuse or even a reason just to want to be in one another's arms. Of course, they had limitations on how often they could dance since their mating ceremony. But soon, they'd be able to do it whenever they desired.

"Thank you. But I was only following your lead, love. If we get the chance while we are here, I want to take advantage of it. I am glad we got to be here to witness this."

"Me, too." She'd enjoyed everything they'd gotten to experience together over the last several days. It went beyond that. Every experience the two of them shared brought her joy. Her face glowed, a radiant smile spreading as she replayed the moment their eyes first met, a spark igniting within. All the time they'd spent together had been wonderful.

"Hey, Parthenia... Gavin, can you guys help us get these lanterns set up? We should start soon," one female said.

"Yes, we can do that." With a gentle smile directed at her mate, Parthenia then turned her attention and smile to the woman.

"We would be happy to." Taking Parthenia's hand, Gavin walked with her as they followed the female over. "I have not seen lanterns that look like that. Do they float away in the sky after they are lit?"

"That they do." The female grinned widely. "It's quite a sight with so many lanterns against the night sky."

"Is every mating ceremony performed at night?" If they released the lanterns every time, it made sense. She wasn't sure if that was the case.

"Always," the chimera answered.

"Is that purely so the lanterns can be seen, or is there another reason?" Gavin asked.

"The lanterns themselves symbolize the hopes, dreams, and wishes of the newly mated. It's done at night because of our connection to the stars."

"What about the arrows and the halo of rosemary? Do they represent something as well?" She hadn't ever learned much in her studies about chimeras—certainly nothing about the tradition of their mating ceremony. If they hadn't arrived when they had, then this may not have been something they'd have gotten to experience or learn.

"Yes, they do, too. The shooting and breaking of arrows signify their everlasting love, and the crown of rosemary is for the remembrance of the bride."

"That is beautiful. It sounds like everything possible is done to make this a truly memorable day."

"As it should be. It is two members joining as one," the female beamed.

"That makes sense," Parthenia replied. She glanced at Gavin as they prepared the lanterns. Though there were some minor setbacks, her anticipation for the dazzling sky illumination was immense. It would be exquisite. Maybe these were things she could tell Cipriana and Vasilia about, and they could incorporate a few of them into their own traditions. She wouldn't be around to see any of them, but she knew her sister would take care of the sirens—a prominent leader.

"It sounds like it will be a lovely affair. I am glad we got to be here to participate and witness it."

"I'm certain it will," the female said and went about getting the lanterns together. "Once we get these done, just follow everyone else toward the archway. That's where the ceremony itself will take place."

"Thank you. We'll do that." She ultimately agreed with her mate. Of all the issues they'd run into throughout their journey, she was glad they were here to take part and witness such a beautiful celebration. It seemed like the perfect way to close out their visits to the different leaders.

Gavin thanked her as well, and they worked on the lanterns. Once they finished them, he slid his arm around Parthenia's waist. He never strayed far from her side. "Is there any place in particular we are supposed to stand?"

"For the ceremony itself, you'll stand close to the front, per the Chief's request, and then at one of the front tables after we release the lanterns."

"That's so nice of him." From what she'd been able to assess based on her conversation with him, he was a wise male. Plus, he seemed determined that they reach an accord. She was sure there were things he left out, but she had as well.

"Yes, it is. We will have to thank him later, love." Gavin gently squeezed her waist and guided her across the dewy grass, following the path others had taken.

"That we will." Parthenia examined the circular archway, where branches were intricately woven together, their vibrant red blooms adding a decorative flourish. At the center, a large wooden target stood, where the female would position herself. It was intriguing to see another culture come to life before their very eyes.

At the front, Gavin embraced her from behind, his lips tenderly kissing the side of her neck. "This is all very exciting," he whispered. "The differences between all the species are so fascinating."

"Yes, it is." She smiled, lacing their fingers together. They both appreciated everything they'd seen of the various species. Nothing that she'd learned in books compared to what she'd seen over the last few days. When she first started this journey, she'd been quite unsure of herself, but that uncertainty had faded as she met with more leaders and successfully negotiated more and more peace treaties. There were a few they hadn't been able to meet with and at least one who declined to come to terms with them, but she wouldn't trade this experience for anything. Especially the night she and her mate got to be together fully. "It's like nothing I've ever seen before."

Everyone assembled, creating an aisle for the bride to walk down. A hush fell over the crowd as a dark-haired female, with the crown of rosemary upon her head, in a floor-length stunning red dress practically floated down the aisle toward the target. Arriving at her destination, she clutched the hem of her dress and pivoted to face ahead, her spine flush against the board.

Not a moment later, a male with large, dark-feathered wings swooped down from above and landed directly in front of the bride.

"Me, either." Gavin placed one more kiss against Parthenia's neck before straightening up. His fingers remained intertwined with hers, his thumb gently stroking the delicate skin on the back of her hand.

Parthenia leaned back ever so slightly into her mate as she watched the opening of the ceremony. Despite the number of arrows the males had broken the heads off of, the groom only selected three. He collected a nearby bow and took several steps back. As they'd been told would happen, he shot all three arrows at his bride. Once he finished, he strode forward, picked up the arrows, and broke every single one. Not once did she flinch or move as they barreled her way, each falling to the ground as they bounced off her body.

She wasn't positive how the act equaled the couple's everlasting love for one another, but she could certainly see the trust required between the two. Even more so, the tough hide of the bride's skin. Or perhaps it was something in the dress. Although they'd removed the arrowheads, it didn't make the item comfortable. From there, the bride and groom took one another's hands, and the chief appeared at the front of the altar.

Standing there with her mate, Parthenia didn't focus so much on the words exchanged between the couple; instead, she thought back to the one-on-one she and Gavin had together. There was no proper way to compare the two. Nor would she want to. Maybe it hadn't been as public as this one or as involved, but it had been just right for them. Where they spoke the truth of precisely what was on their hearts, vowing their eternal love to one another, she lifted their entwined hands and pressed a tender kiss to the inside of his palm, the gentle pressure a silent promise of forever.

A faint purr left her mate's mouth, and then he leaned down and pressed a gentle kiss to the top of her head.

Biting her bottom lip, Parthenia glanced up at her mate. Gods, she loved him so much. She returned her attention to the ceremony. From her peripheral vision, she saw the lanterns were being circulated and ignited. She gave her mate's hand a quick squeeze before the lanterns made it to them, along with a way to light it. It made sense that they'd release together as a group after the ceremony.

The newly mated couple kissed one another, and the surrounding group erupted into cheers, hoots, and hollers. Parthenia giggled ever so slightly. Something she was grateful she and Gavin hadn't dealt with, as it would've brought a flush to her cheeks.

Her mate caressed her cheek with their joined hands. 'I love you,' he mouthed to her.

'I love you, too,' she mouthed in return. Something she'd never tire of saying or hearing from him. Even if she was just reading his lips, the words meant much more than she felt she could ever explain. Though she was positive, he understood and felt the same way. With immense difficulty, Parthenia refocused her attention on the ceremony.

Lanterns had gotten sufficiently passed around and lit. The bride and groom, along with everyone else, hoisted their lanterns, the paper glowing as they prepared to set them free.

"As we set these lanterns free, let them not only represent all of your worries being carried away, but allow them to serve as a beacon of light for the wonderful future ahead of you," Chief Elroy stated.

On a silent count of three, every member there released their grip on their lanterns, letting them ascend into the night. Like a shower of brilliant stars streaking across the inky night, they illuminated the path to their most fervent aspirations.

Gavin's arms slipped back around her waist as they watched the spectacular sight before them.

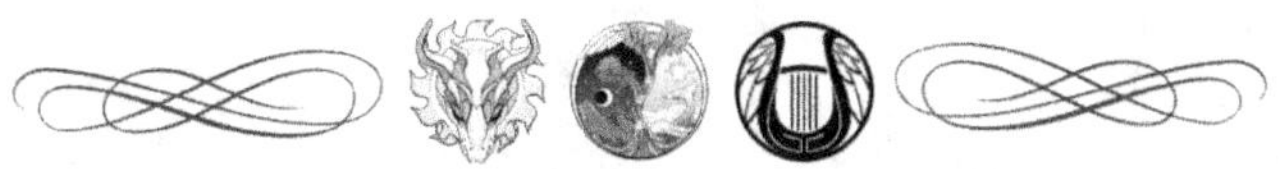

Thalasia rubbed the back of her neck, her bag swinging by her side, and gave Seru a look. "It's time." After they'd returned to Pteryrina unsuccessful, she'd suggested they each take an hour to themselves. She'd gotten out of her armor, bathed, and spent a good thirty minutes lying naked in The Poppy Fields. While it had helped, it just wasn't as much as she would've liked. Of all the emotions that swarmed through her that morning, nervousness hadn't been one of them. Instead, it seemed to be the one that had sat in the pit of her stomach, waiting for the right moment to show itself.

"Why are you nervous?" Seru asked. "You've been preparing for this your entire life."

Her eyes narrowed in skepticism as she lightly touched her forehead. In what reality did someone spend their life preparing to lose their virginity? Let alone to someone who cared for her but didn't dare show emotions, even in moments when it was just the two of them. Though he'd done it a few times lately, it was less and less. "I'm not nervous about the ritual *itself*." Had he even considered it would be more than that? She chewed the inside of her cheek and dropped her gaze to the ground. "Not everything can be prepared for, regardless of how much time you give yourself to accept it."

"If it's a problem, then call it off. I'm not the only one with a say in the matter. Who's saying your ancestors aren't full of shit? Or that you couldn't overcome the consequences? You're—we're—not them."

Her gaze snapped up to him. Call it off? If there was one thing she was *positive* of; it was that she had one shot. There was no second chance. No redo. That was something she'd accepted, along with her choice of him as her Allimos. He had good in him and the capacity to feel and express those emotions more than a cold fish. "I'm nervous about losing my virginity to you. While none of my ancestors ever wrote about their experiences, I had a pleasant conversation with my mother when I was ten and understood that some of what coincides with it can't be overcome. It's simply the way our bodies are built."

Thalasia inhaled and exhaled a deep breath. Her nerves had settled as much as she expected they would. She dragged a hand down her face. No, they weren't her ancestors. "Let's just go." Half turning back toward the door, she paused. "As an FYI, there is a shared kiss during the ritual."

Seru quickly covered his mouth. "What exactly is it you're worried about?" The touch of laughter bubbled to the surface. He stayed behind enough that he didn't need to move when she turned back. He smirked.

"Aside from the discomfort I've been told is associated with the initial penetration..." Her words trailed off as she peered over her shoulder at him. She'd amused him—maybe that was a good sign. She opened the door and exited the apothecary. "The full-blown intimacy."

"You were ready to jump me back at the inn. What's different now?"

"You've been a cold fish for days." He'd been into it; even in the cave, he'd been rubbing himself all over her. "Let me rephrase that. I've seen the emotion lingering there, but it's like you have resigned yourself to what was required."

"I am *not* a fish," Seru said, voice low.

"And I'm not a bird." She offered him a faint shrug as they headed toward the gardens. Thus far, she hadn't seen a single siren. From their current positions, even the gardens appeared blessedly empty. "I know you have the capacity for emotions; I've seen them. Without knowing whether any of that will come through, along with being my first time, being a little nervous just seems natural."

He stayed silent, trailing behind her like a shadow.

His lack of response was as she expected. She'd accepted what was in his limited capacity. While she hoped it would be something that changed, his attachments held him back. In the cave, he'd been upset because she'd shut him out. Now it seemed the opposite was true. She held her breath, her quiet demeanor unwavering until the pools appeared before her. "The only expectation I have of you is to keep your word. Regardless of what I believe I feel for you, I'd be a fool to hope for anything beyond your nature," she practically whispered.

Blue eyes glided in her direction.

Closing the distance between them and the pools, Thalasia sidled up to the grassy area beside the back of the second pool. The water level hadn't changed since they'd been here the day before. She removed several items from her purse: a gold, sun-shaped pendant with an amber amulet; a gauntlet with a sapphire amulet; two silver bands; a blue wooden rose; a hand-crafted smoking pipe with wings; a dreamcatcher; a bear-claw coin; a silver, crystal, crescent moon-shaped pendant; an inscribed dagger with a jeweled hilt; a charm bracelet; a bronze-colored pocket watch; a leather-bound journal with no discernible title; a compass, and the dagger her father gave her. "You'll need to strip, and I need to borrow the bracelet I made for you."

Seru unhooked the bracelet and tossed it her way. The leather band landed among the pile with the rest. Taking his time unbuttoning and untying the clothes, he rubbed at his wrist where the bracelet had been.

With everything out that would need to be locked into the grooves embedded in the pool, she tightened the strings of her bag and set it aside. She leaned over the cold, rough stone, her finger pressing the button to make the moon phases appear again. Her gaze lifted to the sky. It was all perfectly on track. Her heart and head aligned, evident in the shimmer across her flesh. Breathing in the air, rich with the sweet perfume of poppies, she pulled her dress over her head and let it fall away.

Out of her periphery, she watched Seru unbraid his mane. Careful to remove every bead, tucking them away in a small velvet pouch. He pulled the ties shut tight with his teeth, his gaze drawn to the curious reflection of her glow and the moon in the water.

In one smooth move, Thalasia climbed over the side and into the pool. The water lapped at her body, hitting just below her breasts. Turning to face him, she held her hand out. They both had to be in the pool before she set the pieces with their appropriate moon phase.

He finished securing the contents and concealing the pouch before accepting her invitation into the pool. The moon loomed overhead, casting everything in a silvery light. The water's surface shone their reflections like a mirror.

Her eyes settled on him for a moment before she retrieved each item, engaging them in place in the order of their associated moon phase. She started with the dagger and the bracelet she made for him and continued counterclockwise as she moved about. "Full moon, waning gibbous, last quarter, waning crescent, new moon, waxing crescent, first quarter, waxing gibbous, and back to the full moon because the power of the moon is endless," she muttered beneath her breath with each step.

With each set of items secured, a moon phase illuminated, accompanied by a low, steady hum. The gauntlet and sun-pendant, the two silver rings, the rose and pipe, the dreamcatcher and coin, the moon-shaped pendant and jeweled dagger, the charm bracelet, and pocket-watch. The last set, the book, and the compass, locked in with a click. Thalasia turned to face him; a whir reverberated in the pool, entirely illuminated by the connected moon phases, activating the latent magic in the water.

A shiver of iridescent black scales rode Seru's skin, reflecting dark rainbows in the moonlight.

Her gaze traced over his scales as she bit her bottom lip. Even if she couldn't say the words aloud, she could accept that somehow, she'd fallen in love with him. While his beauty at some point had drawn her in, it hadn't been what she noticed first. It had been his kindness and determination to comfort her. Maybe in the beginning it had started as nothing more than a ruse, but it had changed. Regardless of the way they easily pushed one another's buttons, he'd claimed her heart without trying. Though he had admitted nothing beyond caring, she was positive she'd claimed his as well. Thalasia stepped forward, took one of his hands in hers, and brushed a tender kiss across his cheek. "You're stunning." She led him to the center of the basin.

His features twitched into a half-smile, half-grimace. He didn't move to reciprocate. "I'm not your girlfriend. I don't require confirmation of how pleasing you find my physical appearance."

As snarky as ever. Not that she bothered with a response. As the sun dipped below the horizon, the moon reached its highest point. The orange and yellow hues of the sky faded, with pinks and purples taking their place. Her skin glowed more intensely, its luminescence connecting with the power of the full moon. Still holding his hand, Thalasia lowered her eyes to the small distance that lay between them. Using the power pulsating through her, she ran her finger through the water in the shape of an infinity symbol as she uttered the words in her native tongue to trigger the ritual.

Seru retreated a single pace. He took another step back and closed his eyes.

Her eyes snapped to Seru. The glow on her skin pulsed with renewed intensity, and the aroma emanating from her grew stronger. It hadn't yet reached its full shine, but it would. Shit. In all the planning for the ritual, neither of them had considered his beast. It appeared the figure-eight motion had triggered something with his magic.

While she didn't know if it would work as it had in the past, she reached forward and gently gripped his forearms, stroking her thumbs across his skin. The water began its retreat, building in a circle around them. Energy sparked between the items locked in place. The ritual had started, and there was no stopping it. Soon, a cyclone of power would surround them.

The beast raised its hackles, and armored scales pierced Seru's skin. The beast leeched the warmth from the air, causing a palpable drop in pressure and igniting a dazzling light display. Blue electricity flickered over every inch of him, sparkling outward where it merged with the conductive water, ready to deliver a potent shock. His hands balled into tight fists, muscles constricting.

His scales cut her palms, slicing her flesh, which healed instantly—something that had never happened before. Thalasia yanked her hands back. The last of the water receded, leaving them both dry as it meshed with the spiral pulsating around them. Energy from all sixteen items flowed into the cyclone, strengthening the electric current as its speed increased. There had to be something she could do or say; they were almost at the final stage. "Freedom! This is the way to—"

The sharp crack of several bones in her wings breaking silenced her mid-sentence. Thalasia roared, her fists clenching as a searing heat consumed her limbs, driving her down onto the unforgiving ground. A series of sharp cracks sounded in the confined area, coming from the blue growths on her shoulders. Her wings expanded, becoming significantly larger and longer. Rounds of cracks continued as the newly elongated bones in her wings mended, the cartilage stitching itself back together.

The beast let out a fearsome roar.

"Fuck," she muttered, catching her breath. Not that there was much time for it. The ritual went through stages. Sure as shit, her mother *never* once mentioned this. The whirring of the electrical current got louder as she got back to her feet. She could see the electric serpentine blue of the beast's eyes, although he was still in his human shell. Her eyes sparkled brightly, a shimmer reflecting across his skin. The light of the moon radiated above them. "We're almost—"

The electric charge from the cyclone reached out and licked across her flesh. Gritting her teeth, a jolt shot through her synapses.

Power, unlike anything she'd known before, surged through her body. The energy pulsed and crackled, a tangible force that buzzed around them. The luminescence of her flesh nearly matched the moon's brightness.

With an ear-piercing bellow, the beast forced its way through. It rocketed skyward, lashing out at the whirling water and electricity—the enemy attacking Thalasia—with its massive jaws. It snapped at the cyclone. Its scaly hide encircled Thalasia, cocooning her in the safety of its armored hide. Her brilliant light shone through the gaps like a silver beacon, bright enough to signal the stars.

The water in the cyclone had almost completely evaporated. Although the stone enclosed around them crumbled beneath the beast's heft, the magic of the pool stretched to accommodate his size. Even the artifacts remained sealed in place by the energy generated through the ritual.

As best she could, given how he'd coiled around her, Thalasia stroked her fingers along a single scale. "I know you want to protect me, but I promise I'm okay. Neither of us is hurt. And this is almost over, but I kind of need Seru back to stop it. Then, as soon as we can, we'll fly in a sky you've never seen before. Somewhere far away from here. To do that, I need Seru." The pain had wholly surpassed, at least to the point she no longer felt it. Her wings were tender, but it didn't surprise her after so many bones breaking and resetting. It would've been great if she'd known it would happen. They were right on the cusp of the last part.

The beast rumbled, waiting for something. When nothing happened, it burrowed its snout into its coils, sniffing her out.

With a quiet giggle, she let her fingers trail along the velvety sides of his snout. His hot breath tickled a bit. "I need Seru back."

The beast snorted at her request. Pressing further into her, it inhaled her scent and bumped her with its nose. A warm, wet tongue flicked over her, tasting the potent smell. Unlike Seru, the beast didn't seem bothered by her pheromones or the intense heat.

Him and that damn tongue—she had an inkling it was coming. While she couldn't quite see the entire energy that still encircled them, she could hear the slight vibration. It slowed, but it hadn't ended yet. "I'm about to get fucking bright. Two choices. Give me Seru back or shut your damn eyes."

The beast rumbled again. It didn't seem he was going back in without a fight, especially not with the offending magic still swirling about them.

This had been eye-opening about his protective nature—at least with her. Traveling to other realms with him was going to be fun. She pressed a soft kiss to a spot on his nose, right between his nostrils, which flared in response. It pushed back, perhaps a little too aggressively in its eagerness, as it knocked her back. Since he had coiled around her, she only fell back into him.

"I warned you." Thalasia, feeling a surge of warmth spread through her, pressed her cheek against his muzzle as her body glowed, radiating a luminescence as intense as the full moon. It enveloped them both.

It withdrew at the sudden flare with a sneeze.

With the last connection made, the centrifugal force around them slowed to a muted hum. The radiance across her skin dispersed, leaving a white halo covering her flesh in its wake—the ritual now complete. Her scent was so thick it blanketed the aroma of the poppies. As the surrounding energy settled, the artifacts fell to the ground.

The beast gave a victory roar, loud enough to echo across the isle. It lowered its massive head to the ground, growling and sniffing at the objects. Identifying them as a non-threat, it quickly shifted its attention back to her.

Yeah, she'd have to remember to return them to her bag, which she hoped remained on the part that hadn't gotten crushed beneath the beast. There would be time to test out some limits of her power later. "It's done now. We're safe and in one piece. Seru should join us for this victory."

The beast curled its lip at her suggestion, further revealing its most pronounced fangs. It sidled its head alongside her, granting her access to its unruly mane. It seemed more than content to lie there until she climbed on, unconcerned with curious sirens or anyone else who might've heard its earlier battle cry.

She wouldn't win this argument. Thalasia bit her bottom lip, but she couldn't leave the artifacts lying around. Or her bag. Hmm, well, there was something she could try. Another one of that theoretical knowledge, as she had only ever witnessed it. The image of all sixteen items, along with her purse, flashed through her mind as she lifted her hand and made a circling motion in the air with her fingers. A faint shimmer, like a pocket forming, appeared before her, followed by a soft whoosh as her surroundings vanished, confirming its success.

"Cool," Thalasia muttered. With a combination of wind control and her heightened reflexes, she pulled herself onto the beast's back without issue. Despite the blaze coursing through her body, she burrowed herself into his mane. For a moment, she considered telling him he'd require his human form soon, but she decided not to fret over it. The peak of her awakening was close, though.

Once she'd settled, the beast rocketed into the sky. Its massive underbelly skirted the tops of a few homes as it climbed higher. It shook from side to side and grumbled.

"Don't get so close to the roofs next time." The cat might be out of the bag. Thalasia sat up just a little to peek over him, spotting a few curious girls poking their faces out of windows. With a slight shake of her head, she curled back up to him, making herself comfortable.

The beast kept its head high as it wove through the sky, giving them the full view of Pteryrina. The village below had darkened with the sun's setting and illuminated with the power of the moon. Everything took on a silvery glow, mirroring Thalasia astride the beast. The poppies bobbed about, dancing in praise of the silvery goddess overhead.

Her lips tugged at the corners. Although it was only their third flight together, it was her favorite. Though she suspected they'd have many more. Maybe give him a chance to fly in every realm they went. Let him explore—true freedom; the thought alone brightened her smile. For the moment, she was content just to snuggle close.

The beast kept the moon in its sights, but kept its flight low. The bright light reflected well off its hide.

As much as she was enjoying this flight, they couldn't stay up here for hours. Though she would've been happy to do so, except she didn't know exactly when the peak—a blast of heat shot straight to her core, forcing a soft moan from her mouth as she wiggled against him. Got it—this wouldn't be like *anything* she'd experienced thus far. It would be more demanding, more concentrated, and ten times more potent, not only calling out to her Allimos, but driving her body as well, with a palpable energy. "Holy mother of gods," Thalasia mumbled. "We need to land. Either by the springs or in The Poppy Field."

The beast brought them down in the red of The Poppy Field. It lowered to its belly with a disgruntled sigh.

Yeah, she would've liked more time in the sky, too. Thalasia dismounted, another wave flooding her core as her feet hit the ground. "Seru..." she muttered.

The beast grumbled before granting her request. His dark rainbow scales retreated to return flesh and bone, a more human body to better match her own. Seru spilled onto the sea of poppies.

"Welcome..." Thalasia got out before another wave hit her, pulling a moan out of her simultaneously. Despite the compelling desire burning through her veins, she wouldn't assault Seru. Instead, she flopped down in the land of red right next to him. It seemed unnecessary to state the obvious regarding the beast. A reaction she certainly hadn't considered, but would be mindful of in the future.

He forced his heavy eyelids partially open. "I don't recall thanking you for that experience," he mumbled, struggling to push himself onto his knees and elbows.

"Supposed to be..." Her words trailed off again as another blast hit, pulsating outward from her body. With a groan, she dug her nails into the ground. "Welcome back," Thalasia muttered.

Seru got himself into a kneeling position with a grimace. His eyes shifted to her.

Another wave hit. A low grunt escaped her lips as her back arched and her fingers curled, the gritty texture of the earth sifting beneath her touch. Motherfucker, she wanted to strangle whatever god thought an awakening was a brilliant idea. Oh yeah, let the Atlis have to go through a torrent of hormones, where her body will become her own fucking personal volcano. Thalasia rolled onto her side. The poppies felt cool against the juncture between her thighs. "Take some energy," she panted out. "Can't stay here." At least not all night. She didn't think the females there in Pteryrina would even know what he was, but that didn't mean others across the isle wouldn't. Of course, there was a lot about the ritual that she hadn't known. Lack of information seemed popular among her ancestors.

"You need it more than I do," Seru insisted, looping his arm beneath hers and helping her to her feet. Gritting his teeth, he allowed her to lean against him for support as they found their footing.

Pheromones and heat continued to surge through her body as they walked, her leaning on him. As much as she tried not to, there didn't seem to be a way around it. "Hate gods," she muttered. It couldn't be any easier on him than it was on her, given how much it intensified their natural desire for one another.

"Ever met yours?" Seru mused with a bitter laugh as they stumbled towards the pools.

Thalasia suppressed a groan as a fresh wave of intense hormones surged through her body. Her fingernails dug into his skin, her grip tightening around him. "No," she muttered. Probably a good thing, too. At this rate, they'd be lucky to make it back to the apothecary. No way they'd get farther than that. Not until they burned the fire out of her body and the pheromones relinquished their hold.

He hoisted her up, attempting to get a better hold. As they neared the edge of the pools, he thrust out his free arm to brace them as he leaned her against the side. Once he ensured she was as comfortable as she could get, he started searching and feeling around.

Not all gods and goddesses made themselves known. They had their watchers, though. She'd met one of them, but didn't think it was necessary to share. Thalasia dug her fingernails into the rough hillside, the loose dirt crumbling beneath her grip as Seru held her upright. Somehow, she breathed through the surges. "What are you... looking for?"

Seru scrounged around a bit more. His frustration mounted as his hands continued to skid over little more than dried soil, rock, and debris. "The pouch," he barked, unable to keep the annoyance out of his tone.

Thalasia blinked. She'd seen him take the beads out of his hair and put them in a small velvet pouch. Had she seen what he'd done with the bag afterward? If it wasn't there... "Might have gotten pulled up with mine." Which she'd put in a one out of a hundred magic pockets.

"'Might have'?!" Seru growled as he turned on her. "Might have isn't good enough, Thalasia." He went back to searching, determined to locate the pouch.

An explanation would be great, but she was tired of asking him questions. Especially when she no longer expected answers. Ignoring the searing pain that lanced through her body, she hauled herself to her feet and summoned her strength. "Move!" she hollered.

He snarled at her, but heeded her request. Even though it meant settling back on his ass in the dirt, smudged from head to toe. He used the opportunity to tug his unruly mane back out of his face, the recently freed strands sticking to his sweaty face and neck.

Thalasia levitated the multitude of pieces that the beast had destroyed. While searching through the extensive number of magical pockets at her disposal. Thankfully, she didn't have to go through all of them—only five—before she located the items previously scooped up. While she was half-tempted to chuck them at his head, her body required the use of his for the next several hours. Everything that ended up in the pocket popped out, landing in front of him. Between that and her quick shift of the rubble, they located his bag.

Seru plucked the black velvet pouch from the pile. "Thank you."

Setting the mess back on the ground, Thalasia collected the artifacts and her pouch and returned them to a magical pocket, as she'd done before. They were safe there. Off-hand, she couldn't recall if he'd ever thanked her for anything before. Maybe, but if so, it had been days since it occurred. "You're welcome." The force of another wave, stronger than the ones before, made her push her hand against the rough dirt wall.

Setting about rebraiding the beads in his mane, he folded his legs in front of him, placing the pouch atop his thigh. He clasped one metal vessel between his teeth while he used both hands to secure another. One by one. He worked as swiftly as he could manage, but it took time to ensure all *seven* beads stayed in place.

Propping herself up again, she gripped her knees and dug her nails into her own flesh. Really, really kill whatever god came up with this awakening. Sitting on a volcano might be better than this. Though she was looking forward to it *all* leaving her body. Any desires beyond that, well, day by day.

Once he'd finished and checked the security of his items, Seru maneuvered to kneel in front of her, giving her his back. "Climb on."

For a second, she considered declining, but she was in no position to do so. Especially with the rate the heat and hormones assaulted her body. Shoving off of the barrier, she got onto his back, wrapping her arms around his neck in the most comfortable way possible. "Thank you."

Seru struggled not to stumble as he stood, but at least he didn't send them sprawling forward onto their faces. "You're welcome," he grunted. He settled her against him. Skin to skin, the heat alone threatened to boil them alive. "No chance you've got a change of clothes in that bottomless bag of yours?" He padded through the poppy fields toward the apothecary.

"Yes, I have more clothes... for later." As they were both currently naked and she was on his back, it was apparent he didn't intend for them to put anything on at that moment. With her bare breasts pressing against his shoulders and her calves gripping his hips, the heat coursing through her body intensified.

"We can't leave Pteryrina naked," Seru prompted. "We can't stay here," he re-emphasized. "The sooner we have clothes, the sooner we leave."

Thalasia clenched her jaw through a fresh wave and shuddered. Gods, she really hoped he'd accepted what the next twenty-four hours for them entailed. If he thought she'd wanted him back in the inn, yeah, that was nothing compared to how badly she wanted him right then. "One, the pheromones are only going to get stronger until we meet their demand. Two, given how sirens age and typically live, the likelihood that any of them know *what* you are by noise and sight is zero to none. Three, we still have yet to find Mac, and if we leave too soon, we'll absolutely convince Cipriana that we're not out to help them at all. Four, where exactly would we go?"

Seru readjusted her on his back. "Somewhere that's not in the open or anywhere near where we just created a saint beast sighting. Then we'll worry about *the pheromones,* and once you've had your fix, we'll find the missing siren."

"And you plan to get us out how?" Nevermind that the gates, which were under constant guard, were in the complete opposite direction he walked. While they could slip out through the secret passage in the library, it was completely visible from the gates. None of that accounted for the fact that her armor was in the armory; she'd left it there when she changed earlier for a reason. The only good news in any of this was that she'd advised Cipriana they'd be unavailable until late tomorrow night or early morning the day after.

"There are many ways out," Seru replied, shouldering the door as he ducked low to avoid any unwanted bumps or bruises. He traversed the length of the apothecary with relative ease. "Right now, I need you to find us clothes," he repeated, gingerly setting her on the bed. He turned to face her. "Think you can do that?"

Yep, it was a good thing she had that conversation with Cipriana. And that there'd be ways to sneak back in, convincing the female they'd never left. Thalasia wiped away the sweat beading on her forehead. "Sure," she said and rolled her shoulders. "Just take about ten steps back."

Seru backed off as instructed, but not before giving her a strange look to match the strange request.

Yeah, she would not answer why. He should be able to figure it out for himself. A shiver went down her spine, and she averted his gaze, looking around to see if his shoes were still there. Not that she didn't have any in her bag, just in case, but she needed the distraction. At least for a moment. As she'd done before, she called up her magic and searched through a multitude of pockets. Locating her bag on the seventh one, Thalasia retrieved it and left the other items behind. It didn't take her long to find a pair of black dress pants and a blue long-sleeve button-up made from sateen. She tossed both at him and tilted her head, studying his feet. "I didn't see your boots here."

"I don't require shoes," he said, shrugging into the shirt.

Worked for her. She dug into her bag again and grabbed the first sundress she put her hand on. It didn't matter what it looked like as long as it covered her. She pulled a dress that tied around the neck, matching the color of the shirt she'd given him. Well, that was unintentional. Tying the strings on her purse, she returned it to a pocket. It made it so much easier to carry that way. She got to her feet and tugged the dress on, getting it situated around her neck and zipped up the back.

"Isn't that redundant?" Seru asked, watching her disappear the bag. He'd stepped into the pants while she selected her dress.

"Only if I felt like I'd need to get into it right away." Which wasn't something she expected. Then again, she didn't expect his beast to make an appearance or for them to be leaving Pteryrina so quickly, either. "However, you intend to get us out of here. Think you can do it from here?"

"I was hoping to vanish us once we stepped outside. From there, it's on him," Seru said, referencing the beast.

"Alright. We're far enough off from anyone else; I don't think they'll notice us leave," Thalasia commented. And she was pretty positive the beast would enjoy flying anywhere. She threw her hand out, gripping the back of the chair in front of her tightly as another wave hit. "Motherfucker," she mumbled.

"Why would they?" Seru retorted. With a curse, he got to his feet, careful as he moved to support her. His hand rested on her back as she rode out another persistent reminder from her pheromones, waiting until it passed before releasing her and turning back around so she could retake her place on his back.

Gods, she couldn't wait for this to be over. Thalasia climbed onto his back, wrapping her arms around his neck again. She could feel the heat between them, even through the combined fabric. "They won't," she said. At least not until they noticed the pool—being dried up was one thing, but destroyed was something else entirely.

Seru's magic fell over them like a cloak. They shimmered before fading to nothing—at least to any eyes that might cross them tonight.

Huh, that was strange. Beneath the discomfort and fire raging through her was an inkling of... shock? Something she could analyze later. Hmm, what he'd done seemed close to her own cloaking ability, or at least what she had access to now.

Seru snuck them out of the front door and out into the open, where he relinquished control to the beast, never taking Thalasia from his back.

Chapter Fifty-Three

Thalasia turned to face Seru, the sleeping bag rustling slightly on the cold stone floor. Whether or not he cared if she told him, he was still absolutely stunning, especially under the white glow of her skin. Unable to hold back any longer, she quickly closed the distance between them and pressed her lips to his. Surprisingly enough, he responded to it. Not that she hadn't noticed how the heat of her pheromones impacted both of them.

Her tongue swept along the inside of his mouth. As the kiss deepened, her tongue explored the sharp points of his fangs. Something told her to be mindful of how she touched him. It was a sensation she'd noticed a few days back. She settled her hands on his shoulders. As their tongues entangled, his fingers skated down her spine. She moaned into the kiss. A searing wave shot through her, amplifying the palpable tension in the air between them. And she thought with skin-to-skin contact; it couldn't get hotter.

Upon reaching the frigid cave in the mountains, she instantly discarded her dress once the beast had returned to Seru. The biting cold of the cavern did little to cool the fiery passion that ignited between them. His hands slid to her ass. He cupped her, lifting her into his arms as her legs instinctively encircled his waist. He carried her over to the sleeping bag and slowly eased her back down onto it.

She unhooked her feet from his back, breaking the kiss. Seru nuzzled her neck, then traced a warm, wet path along the gentle curve of her breasts. He cradled one breast in his palm, his thumb gently tracing its curve, while his tongue swirled around the nipple of her other. Her back arched as her fingers skimmed the back of his arms. His thumb traced the pebbled surface of her nipple as he massaged her breast, his fangs lightly grazing the skin of the other before he latched on.

A gasp left her mouth and another wave hit to the point she wasn't sure which turned her on more. The endless bout of pheromones raging through her body or the things Seru was doing to it. Not that she didn't enjoy the attention he gave her breasts. It was as if, for the first time, she truly saw herself as a woman—a sexual being. Yes, she'd worn provocative clothes before, but recognizing something in yourself that others saw was utterly different. Maybe that was the whole point. To be fair, if she were going to determine exactly how much she did or didn't like sex, it would have to be when her hormones weren't in the driver's seat.

He slid down her body further, tracing an indistinct pattern along her abdomen with his claw. His head now between her legs, he pressed his hands down on her lower belly, hooking her legs over his shoulders, and licked up her slit. Thalasia gripped part of the bedding above her head. On a moan, her back arched as Seru drove his tongue into her sex. A wave of intense pleasure washed over her as an orgasm hit, something she chalked up to her pheromones, wondering if it was normal for a woman to climax so easily.

Unlike the last couple of nights, he didn't stay down there, which she didn't expect him to, especially as another wave hit. This one was more intense than any that had come before. Seru moved back up, and the tip of his cock grazed her entrance. Heavens above, that one simple action came so close to inducing another intense climax. She didn't imagine that happened with typical sex. He drew his hips back and pushed in slowly; the tension increasing as his shaft slipped further until it met an unexpected barrier. Following the same pattern, his hips recoiled and thrust forward, his length surging past any previous resistance. A low rumble slipped past his lips.

"Fuck," Thalasia grimaced. Her mother had told her it would be a pinch whenever the block broke. In what world was that a motherfucking pinch? And who in their right mind would like sex if it felt like that? She craved the anticipation, but the culmination left her breathless and gasping for air.

"Are you okay?" Seru asked, those deep-blue pools of his full of concern.

A small part of her wanted to say no, that he could get off of her. The central part of her remembered that obstruction only had to break once, and that was it. She brushed her knuckles across his cheek. They certainly had a strange relationship. She was almost positive that she liked his beast more than him, and vice versa. Not that she and Seru didn't care for each other; they did, even to the point she believed she loved him. Still, not something she could say out loud. "I'm okay."

With a nod, his lips fused to hers. Pure, unadulterated bliss surged through her as their kiss intensified, a symphony of pleasure echoing with every thrust. Holy shit. Thalasia moaned into the kiss. Yep, *okay* because she liked this. Every stroke of his shaft along the inner walls of her sex lit up her synapses. Even more so when she began lifting her hips to meet his. Her neck arched as she groaned, her hand balling up the soft fabric of the sleeping bag. Her fingers curled around one of his arms as his thrusts came harder and faster.

He gripped the bedding in his hands, his claws digging into the soft fabric. As he pounded into her, Thalasia adjusted her legs on his hips, her thighs parting further. With each matching thrust, she felt the penetration to her toes. Her thighs tensed, and the inner walls of her sex constricted. She let out a loud moan, and he growled. Her body trembled with a massive orgasm while his climax exploded outward. Neither of their hips stilled until they'd wholly ridden out their mutual release.

The two of them panted heavily. For the first time in days, Thalasia felt a slight reprieve from her pheromones. The temperature of her flesh dropped a notch. Although she knew this was far from over, it appeared to be giving them a moment to catch their breath. Her gaze met Seru's. With their ragged breaths finally evening out, she thought about checking if he was okay. But she didn't think he'd answer her honestly. What would she do if he wasn't? Her pheromones hadn't given them a choice in what her body demanded. Thalasia opened her mouth, and a fierce wave of heat washed over her, intensifying the inferno raging between them.

This pattern continued past the rising sun and well into the afternoon. A consistent surge and retreat of her pheromones kept their sexual activities going. Each stretch between dalliances was longer than the previous until nighttime when her pheromones finally departed. The change in the energy in the cave was rather noticeable. A palpable heat, still radiating from her, signaled the undeniable completion of her sexual awakening. So deeply exhausted, Thalasia fell asleep swiftly, mere moments after catching her breath from their final sexual embrace.

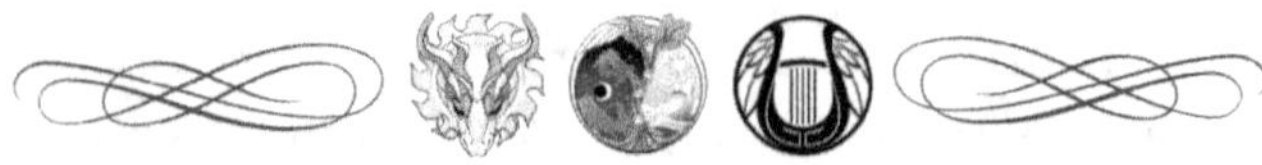

"I can't believe how much time has passed. I swear, it feels like we just left Pteryrina, and we're already heading back," Parthenia said as they left the chimera village behind.

Despite the smile playing on his lips, Gavin kept his focus from drifting too far into his musings. The past few days had been beyond excellent, especially the night they'd spent in the nymph kingdom. But he couldn't shake the nerves rolling through him. Now outside the protection the chimera territory offered, they were *way* too close to shape shifter territory for his comfort. "I know what you mean." He pressed his face against her neck, inhaling her scent for a fleeting moment. Catching her gaze, he paused before speaking. "I know it would be nice to enjoy the scenery on the way back, but do you think we should travel more quickly? At least until we get to another part of the isle?" He could run somewhere around 100 miles per hour. It wouldn't take them long at all to get safer than they were now.

She stroked his cheek. "Given how far we have to travel to get to Pteryrina, you're right. We should focus a bit more on getting there first."

Gavin purred as he leaned into her touch. "That would certainly make me feel better, love." With a soft nudge against her neck, he then trailed his tongue over the delicate skin where her pulse beat. Hades, he couldn't wait until the curse broke. He wanted to put another mark on her. A sudden shiver passed through him, one he couldn't explain. They needed to get out of here quickly. "Would you like to ride me or fly above?"

"You run faster than I can fly. I'll just ride you."

"Okay, love." Still, he hesitated, not that he could say why. He didn't like the sensations going through him, not at all. Nor did he like in the least what his instincts were telling him. To get his mate and run. His ears twitched as he scanned their surroundings. "Yes. Okay. That would be good." Gavin placed a kiss on either side of her mouth, then took a step back so he could shift. Not that he got the chance, though. Two ear-splitting shrieks pierced the air. In an instant, he was on his knees, fingers digging into his ears as if to block out a deafening sound. His mate was on the ground, too. He couldn't move. The shrieks persisted, sending agonizing pain lancing through his skull as his eardrums felt close to bursting. His vision blurred.

Despite Parthenia's desperate grip on her ears, a thin stream of blood continued to seep down her earlobes. A pair of arms came around her from behind and lifted her off the ground, her feet kicking into the air. Before she could belt out any notes to counteract the horrible squawks, a hand clasped tightly across her mouth.

"No! Parthenia!" Somehow, Gavin got up off the ground. He didn't have time to lunge fully. Fangs dug into the nape of his neck, lifted him off the ground, and flung him into a tree.

"You were supposed to let me do the honors," a familiar voice said. "I have been waiting for this day for months."

Four paws hit the ground at the same time Gavin's body did. Despite the shock that stole his breath, a snarl tore from his throat. His eyes, like twin voids of black, snapped open, and he tried to spring forward, but shifters swarmed him from all sides. Everything happened too fast to track anything, even who he fought against. Though his claws and fangs met flesh, it didn't seem to faze any of them. It felt not like moments, but hours before he was flat on his back on the ground, jaws locked around both ankles and wrists and staring up into the face of his father. Gavin was the spitting image of the male who had his paw pressed against his throat.

Parthenia thrashed against whoever held her. While they'd immobilized her wings, they hadn't quite gotten her arms. She clawed at whatever she could reach.

"Pin her arms," a familiar female voice called out.

Her eyes widened. The person holding her snarled, "Keep writhing, and I'll burn your flesh."

"Now, now. There will be plenty of time for that later," the female said.

Someone yanked her arms behind her back and placed a pair of restraints on her wrists.

No matter how hard the fangs bit down, sending rivulets of blood flowing through his fur, he struggled and fought as hard as he could. He could feel the crushing weight of his father's paws on his sternum and the constriction around his throat intensifying. A gasp escaped him as his lungs tightened, the crushing sensation on his ribs nearly breaking them, but he continued to struggle. Gavin experienced a sharp pang with every action taken against his mate. It only made him fight that much harder. His only priority was getting free so he could get to her. There had to be some way to get free, some way to help his mate. "Do not... hurt her! Let her go!" he growled out, his voice wheezing. Suddenly, his body ceased all movement. He couldn't move even a single bit, not even a twitch of his tail.

"That will no longer be necessary." The male voice held a hissing quality to it, almost as if a snake were speaking.

Gavin couldn't see whoever had just spoken. He couldn't even move his eyes to look around. Even as the jaws left his wrists and ankles, all Gavin could do was look up into the eyes of his father. He recognized the female's voice—Fagonia, Parthenia's aunt—but who in Hades's name was the male? There were Informants there, but that was not Markham.

Gembert moved his face right up to Gavin's, not that he lowered his voice any. "You have no idea how much I wish I could kill you myself." A malicious smirk spread across his face. "I just wanted to tell you one last time—you were a horrible son. Perhaps when your mother has this one, if the pregnancy does not kill her, the gods will bless me with one that is better than you." He laughed as tears filled Gavin's black eyes. "So pathetic. I wonder how you ever got a female at all, let alone one who is so attractive. Hmm, perhaps we will be allowed to visit her before she dies." With that, he moved back off.

"That is quite an intriguing idea," Fagonia said. "I believe this should take care of any further attempts with her mouth. Such a soft heart. Weak. I do believe I will allow them visitation. It would please me to watch them destroy that fragile little body of yours."

No! No! So close, they'd been so close. This couldn't be happening. Not after everything they'd gone through. Not after everything they'd survived. He found himself unable to move his lips, his tongue so engorged it seemed to fill his entire mouth. Talking wasn't possible, but in his mind, he was screaming.

"I believe that could certainly be arranged." A robed figure came into Gavin's view. "I echo your father's sentiments. You are a pathetic specimen. But I believe your view could be much better." A bony, desiccated hand pushed out from the folds of his robe. As the creature tightened its grip into a fist, Gavin was lifted off the earth, suspended a foot above it. With the new position, he stared straight at Parthenia. "I want to ensure you can watch as she is ripped away from you. And, as you will be separated, perhaps I can give you a small preview of what she may suffer."

His screams, which were only in his mind, just got louder at what he saw in his head. *No! No! No, no, no, NO!* He fought and struggled against invisible binds, though it was all internal. He'd lost all ability to move on his own, like he'd become a puppet or something. His attempt to protect her had failed. He couldn't save her. *Oh, gods!* His eyes flooded with tears, blurring his vision until the world became an indistinct watercolor. As the male—the creature—the thing, whoever he was, waved his free hand, though, his tears ceased entirely and disappeared, his vision thoroughly clearing. His eyes remained fixed on his mate. Oh, gods, please do not let her see what was being forced into his head right now. Gods, please, please—do not let that happen to her... *I love you. Parthenia, I love you. I love you so much. I am so sorry. I am so, so sorry.* They didn't have a telepathic connection. She wouldn't hear the words. But he sent her all of his love, too, so at least she would feel that.

"Nice try," a male said.

"You don't think I wasn't prepared for you to be less than cooperative, do you?" Fagonia asked. "Don't worry, big guy. I'll make sure she's well taken care of. If time permitted, I'd be happy to let your father at her first while you watched."

"If time permits, I believe he should be present for that. As you can see, as much as he would wish not to watch, he would have no choice but to witness every single moment," the creature commented. "Listen to every scream. Smell every drop of blood gouged from her skin and spilled from between her thighs." A low, hissing laugh filled the air. "It is a rather intriguing thought, is it not?"

The force of his growls and snarls, contained by an unseen pressure, caused his chest to heave more intensely, the ache deepening with each moment. There was nothing he could do: nothing but watch. Gavin kept sending every bit of his love to her, even though the horrifying images continued. His jaw clenched so tight he thought his teeth might crack; his body rigid with a fury he couldn't contain. The images weren't real. They weren't real. Oh gods, please, let them not become real. *I love you, my beloved. I love you so much. I am so sorry. Be strong, my love. Be strong. We will get free and come back to each other once again. Do not lose hope. I love you.*

"It certainly is. While I'm certain the show in his head is entertaining, perhaps a live preview would be better," Fagonia replied. "You know what I have always loved about these dresses? Easy access."

Lascivious growls filled the clearing. "I see time permits now," the robed figure said. "Good. The real thing is always preferable to a fantasy."

NO! NO! NO! Gavin's jaw clenched as he fought for air, a hot, furious pressure building behind his eyes with every failed attempt to fill his lungs. His breath hitched, a sob catching in his throat as he imagined the anguish she would face, an icy dread settling deep within him. That didn't stop him from straining against it, not that it did any good. The hold on his body and mouth remained, keeping him completely immobile. He couldn't even blink his eyes. All he could do was stare at his mate, his heart shattering. No, gods, no, this couldn't be happening. He continued to send his mate all of his love with as much force as he could muster. No matter what happened, there was absolutely nothing that could ever change his love for her. Not a single thing. *I love you, Parthenia. No matter what, I love you. I will always love you. We will get through this, my beloved. I promise. We will get through this. I love you so very much. Gods, I am so sorry...*

In his humanoid form, Gembert put his face back up close to his. Though Gavin was the spitting image of him, Gembert was larger and more muscular than he. Raised about a foot off the ground as Gavin was, they stood face-to-face. "Do not worry, *son*. I will show her what a real male feels like." With a malicious laugh, he patted Gavin's cheek a few times before striding across to where they held Parthenia. He licked his lips as he ran his claws slowly over her hips, ass, then up her spine, pushing the clothing more out of the way as he went. "So tiny. If I am not careful, I am going to break you straight in half."

"Do not block his view. I want to ensure he can see properly."

Fagonia readjusted and stood back. Her gaze flicked to Gembert. "Just stay away from the front. Trust me. This is all you want."

As Parthenia trembled, Gavin could feel the frantic thrumming of her heart echoing in his own chest. Then they repositioned her, giving him an even clearer view of what was about to happen. No, no, no, oh gods, no... He knew his father despised him, but this... Hades, how could he do this? And how was he even remotely surprised? The sight of Parthenia's tears soaking into the earth beneath her was like a dagger twisting into his heart, breaking it further with every drop. There was nothing he could do. He couldn't move or look away. Whatever the male had done to him continued to keep him from blinking and kept his tears at bay. He couldn't save her from this, comfort her, or even speak to her. Even as she pushed him away, he continued to send his love, his heart aching with understanding. It was all he could do, and he refused to stop. *Nothing will ever change the way I feel for you, my beloved.*

Nothing will ever diminish the love I feel for you. I love you so much, Parthenia. Stay strong, my dear. We will get through this, and we will be free again.

"Does her pussy have fangs or something?" His father chuckled. "No matter. The ass is always a tighter fit, anyway."

Nothing more than a smirk crossed Fagonia's face. "You deserve this. And everything else that's coming. Though I believe them fucking that pretty little ass of yours until you bleed... is a good start."

"As you deserve every bit of this, Gavin, and everything else that will follow. Did you think your transgressions would not catch up with you? Did you think you had escaped? That you were *free*? Oh, no. We have been watching you this entire time. And I have *so* much in store for you."

Every sensation coursing through Gavin at that moment had him feeling things he didn't think it was possible to feel. A scorching, white-hot wave of fury surged through his entire body. His sharp exhales were like icy daggers, each one a physical manifestation of his burning rage. He knew his eyes were so black they must have resembled pits of despair with no end. While her raw, physical torment was mostly distant to him, each choked-back scream, each heartbroken sob, and each fallen tear sent a jarring ache through his skull. His chest felt as though daggers had speared it repeatedly. Involuntary shakes rolled through him. Sweat poured off his body as he continued to fight to get free. There had to be a way to break this hold on him; there just had to. But it was no use. Nothing worked. All he could do was hang here, watching while his father violated her. He continued to send all of his love to her, and he prayed she could feel it all, regardless that she'd shut him out. If she couldn't... as soon as she opened back up to him, it would be the first thing she felt. *I love you. I love you, Parthenia. I am so sorry, my love. I am so very sorry.*

"Hmm... the live show is definitely so much better," Fagonia said. "Though I think you should bleed a little more before we cart you off."

Nothing he did budged the hold on him even a little. Oh, Hades, a muffled guttural shriek tore from his mate's throat as her body trembled, followed by ragged sobs that echoed in his ears, each sound amplified as if her pain were a shout. Gavin's body shook harder. With flaring nostrils, his breath grew more substantial and cloud-like with every exhale. The fury within him intensified even more, not that he knew how it was possible to feel more rage than he already had. His head felt as if it split in two. His fur stood on end as if bolts of lightning had struck him. Though he didn't stop sending every bit of his love to his mate in waves, it didn't stop his screams in his head. He just couldn't help it. Were his voice not impacted, they were so loud he imagined he'd bust his eardrums. *NO! NO! NO! STOP THIS! LET HER GO! LET HER GO! LET HER GO!*

The robed figure let out a loud, hissing laugh. "Hm. In your current state, you appear to be having difficulty shielding your mind. Should I let her hear how much this is hurting you? Should I let her hear your screams?"

"Oh, I believe that means we should *all* hear it. While I can't very well give you a chance to use your song... we can definitely hear his screams. Hear him beg for mercy on you." Fagonia glanced at Gavin. "Mercy, that will never come."

"Oh, yes. I think that means we should most *definitely* hear it." The robed figure laughed.

A roar, the first sound from him, erupted and sent tremors through the trees, causing their smaller branches to bend low. It went on so long his throat felt like it scratched worse than raw before it trailed off. Tears poured down his face. The last thing he ever would have wished to do was amplify his mate's pain... but he couldn't stop his screams, yells, words. He'd long lost the capacity to hold any of it back. Everything he'd screamed in his head began spilling out of his mouth; his voice strangled as he practically choked on the words. "NO! NO! NO! STOP THIS! STOP! LET HER GO! LET HER GO!"

"She feels *way* too good for that, *son*," Gembert called out. "I am so very far from finished fucking her. And I think the others want a chance at her tight little hole, too. I fear it is a bit... mangled now... but I think they will be okay with that."

"PARTHENIA!" Gavin shrieked. "I AM SORRY! I AM SOR-RY! I AM SO SORRY!" he sobbed out. "I LOVE YOU! I LOVE YOU! NO MATTER WHAT, I LOVE YOU!"

"How *sweet*," Gembert said, his voice full of sarcasm. "You may *love* her, but I certainly *love* how her tight little asshole feels." All that came back at him was another mighty roar. "Oh, Gavin. I do not think you hate me nearly as much as I hate you."

Gavin's heart stopped in his chest, missing several beats. The roar of fury that erupted from him was so powerful it could have made mountains tremble. The flow of his tears could have filled an ocean. "NO! NO! NO! I WILL KILL YOU! I WILL KILL YOU!" And he was going to kill each of the other males who were roaring with laughter as Gembert's fangs pierced his mate's neck.

"Oh, shit, he fucking marked her!" one informant called out.

"Fuck, yeah! Bite her harder!"

"I want dibs next," another growled out.

He laughed. "Oh, will you, Gavin? You are so certain of that. How amusing that you think you will ever have the chance."

"Don't you dare close your eyes." Without impacting the hold Gembert had on Parthenia's neck, Fagonia yanked on her hair, forcing her to open them again.

A keen, sharp cry of profound suffering tore through the air, coming from him. Gods, this was all his fault. This was all his fault. He should have gotten her away from here quicker. They should have gone in a different direction. Put her on his back and raced out as fast as he could, taking her somewhere that was as safe as they could be until they were off the isle for good. Protected her. Protected his mate. He hadn't been able to. He had failed her... in the worst possible way. "I am so sorry, my love," he sobbed. "I am so sor—" Gavin shrieked, the sudden, intense pain overwhelming him. What he was receiving from her extended far past the physical; it was the crushing weight of her emotional torment, more agonizing than her physical hurt. Her emotions hit him like a tidal wave, and they ripped him apart.

Gembert didn't take his eyes off Gavin's. A malicious smirk spread across his face. With his hold still on Parthenia's hair, he pulled her back up a little and turned her head so she was staring straight at him. "I want to make sure you get a good look at my face. For as long as the rest of your life lasts, I never want you to forget the face of the male that took something *so special* away from the two of you." Releasing the grip from her hair, Gembert backed away. "Who is next?"

Morfran stepped forward. He was larger even than Gembert, by almost a foot and at least a hundred pounds. "Me. I called dibs, remember? Or did you not hear over their screams?" He laughed. "Hades, she is tiny. Do you think I will fit, or will I split her right down the middle?" He grabbed hold of her waist and dug the tips of his claws in. "Shall we find out?"

"NO! NO! NO! GODS, PLEASE, NO!" he wailed. His voice, rough and jagged, carried the weight of his suffering. Gods, please, *please,* let this stop, let this stop. How could he have let this happen? This was every bit his fault, and he would never forgive himself. "Parthenia... Parthenia, look at me. Look at me, my love. It is okay.

It is going to be okay. I love you. I love you so much. No matter what, *no matter what*, I will always love you. Nothing can ever, *ever* change that, okay?"

Fagonia smirked as she peered at Gavin. "Perhaps if you beg a little more, we'll let her go." She tapped her chin. "Hmm, you know, I thought about it and... no. This... it's just the beginning of what I have in store for your little bitch."

Never had such potent anger, such deep and consuming despair, taken hold of him. He let out another roar that shook the very ground beneath them. "If it is the last thing I ever do... I will *kill you*, you heartless *bitch*," he snarled.

"Neither of you is ever going to be free again. And this... this will be the last view you have of your *precious mate.*" The robed figure sneered the last two words. "Violated, again and again, her blood spilled by others. Hmm. Perhaps Morfran should mark her, too. It is sometimes done on both sides, is it not?" His mouth opened, but instead of words, another roar erupted from Gavin. The male laughed. "You deserve every single bit of this, Gavin. And everything else that is coming after. You knew what you were doing. You had to know this was coming."

Gavin couldn't shut out the laughter or jeers from the other Informants. His father still stood near to where they restrained Parthenia. He couldn't shut out the smirk on Gembert's face, either. The sounds of his mate's sobs and screams. The acrid scent of her blood mingled with the salty sting of her tears. Her pain, gods, she was in so much pain. And he couldn't stop it. He couldn't do a damn thing. More tears streamed down his face, hot and fast. "This is not your fault, my love. It is not your fault. I love you. I love you so much. I will always love you. Gods, I... I am so sorry..." Gavin shrieked again, a visceral sound, as an intense, full-body spasm overtook him, pure anguish coursing through his veins.

"Is that what was done?" Fagonia sneered. "I rather enjoyed that display. Perhaps he should. Perhaps then my niece will finally understand her shortcomings."

"Mmhm. And perhaps Gavin will as well. It is what a shape shifter does to their *true mate* during times of intimacy. *True mate* is such an archaic term for stupidity." He hissed out a chuckle. "The highest form of mockery and torture that could have been done to him. Something that is supposed to be *sacred*, so wondrously defiled. I am rather glad I could witness it." He turned his gaze to Morfran. "When you finish inside of her, mark her, too."

His guttural roar then twisted into a piercing shriek, amplifying with his mate's escalating pain. *"STOP THIS! STOP THIS! STO—"* Another shriek left him. He couldn't put a name to the sensations that overtook his nerve endings. A chilling wave washed over him, leaving him breathless and hollowed out. His ribcage felt like it was moments from shattering. His vision blurred and flickered. He couldn't tell if it was because of his tears, because of the pain, or because his body was shaking so hard. His throat burned. He was still screaming. He wasn't sure how much time passed before it trailed off. *"Please... please... please..."* he gasped out.

Tilting her head, Fagonia peered at the robed figure and then back to Parthenia. "Tragic. I don't think she will last beyond this male."

"Good." He smirked. "I wonder if she will even last until he has finished."

Gavin's mouth didn't close, but words failed him. He simply couldn't get any more out. A choked gasp escaped his lips, his throat raw and burning. All he could feel was a searing, all-consuming pain. Each moment of what they'd done to his mate burned through him like fire, shredding his nerve endings. He could feel the agony through every inch of his bones. He continued to send all of his love to his beloved mate as much as he could muster. *I love you. I love you. I love you.*

Gembert got in Gavin's face. All he did was stand there for a minute, smirking in the wake of all of his wails. "You are going to be dead before too long. Since I cannot kill you myself, I can at least be grateful that someone has assured me they will bring your remains back home. I cannot wait to crush your bones beneath my feet before we feast on what is left of your flesh." With a quick swipe of his hand, he gouged his claws down each side of Gavin's face.

"Hm, perhaps I was wrong. She looks like she still has a little fight left in her."

"Perhaps. I wonder how long it will last."

It didn't matter that his father stood right in his face; Gavin still knew the moment someone gripped Parthenia's hair. He felt the rapid, anxious bobbing of her head as she struggled to hold on to what was about to be taken, a familiar dread washing over him. "NO!" He'd heard the words from the robed figure; he'd seen Morfran's nod, but no... no... no... Not again... *Not again!* That was sacred... something he'd never thought of sharing with anyone but his mate. They may have only known each other for around seven months, but it had always been Parthenia for him, his Parthenia, his beloved mate. Even before they'd met for the first time, even before he'd ever laid eyes on her, his soul had been searching for hers. The marking... that was *only* for them, between him and his mate. Wasn't his father having already done it bad enough? "NO! NO! NO! GODS, PLEASE, NO!" he choked out, the sounds and sensations of her agony completely breaking him.

"Oh, yes." Gembert laughed. "Please excuse me. I would hate to block your view. Trust me, you do not want to miss this." With a hard pat to Gavin's cheek, sending blood spattering from his injuries, Gembert shifted out of the way and turned to watch.

Another earth-shattering roar of fury erupted from him, causing the leaves on the nearby trees to tremble once more. The tree closest to him shuddered as a fissure ripped its way up the middle.

"Well... just as I expected. Truly weak. For shame. I was looking forward to seeing her pretty little ass torn asunder repeatedly."

"As was I."

Gavin gasped for breath as his lungs felt as if they'd constricted. At that moment, he couldn't seem to draw in any air. Each thrumming beat of her heart resonated deep within him, a deafening echo in his mind. It felt like his entire body had been lit on fire and left to burn. She was barely hanging on, right on the edge of unconsciousness. Gavin continued to send her all of his love, not that he knew if she could feel anything, but he sent it all the same. "I am sorry..." he whispered. "I am sorry... I am so sorry, my love. I love you... I love you so much."

"Pity. It appears the rest of you will miss out until we return home."

As her body slackened and she lost consciousness, Gavin's fury erupted in another bellow, cleaving a second tree nearly in half. He didn't know how long it lasted before the reverberations trailed off into a choking sob.

"Just that long, then." The figure laughed. "That show was so very entertaining."

He remained paralyzed, unable to shift his weight. He could only stare, his gaze fixed on the broken body of his mate. Another choked sob escaped his throat. The blood, a thick, crimson tide, covered her from the twin marks on her neck to her taloned feet. But it didn't prevent him from seeing the black and purple bruises on her shoulders, hips, thighs, and waist. Her hair dripped with sweat, plastering it to her mangled skin. "Let her go... please... Do whatever you want to me... Torture me further, take my life... Just let her go... please... let her go... let her go..." he pleaded.

"As amusing as it is to hear, it does not matter how many times you beg for mercy. It will never be given to either of you. Mercy is the very last thing you deserve."

"He's right. Beg all you want, but letting her go is the furthest thing from my mind." Fagonia eyed her men. "Take off with her, but make sure her blood doesn't leave a trail."

The larger guiler grunted in response and hoisted Parthenia's battered body over his shoulder. Requiring no further instruction, he turned and started into the forest.

As they took Parthenia away, he sobbed harder than ever before, not that there was much sound to it any longer. He couldn't feel a single thing from her—not even the tiniest of flickers. Were it not for the immobilization on his body, he would have collapsed to the ground. Waves of exhaustion and agony washed over him, intense and rhythmic. His lip trembled. His body shook, sweat visibly dripping off every inch of him. He could barely see from the number of tears that cascaded down his face.

"Would you care to know what I intend to do? How much more I plan to destroy that fragile little body of hers?" Fagonia asked.

Gavin bit his lip, the metallic taste of blood a desperate attempt to silence the "no" that threatened to escape. They would tell him and likely give him every detail. Nothing had ever made him feel this murderous. He had not once ever relished the thought of taking a life. But he wanted to kill them all. Every one of them.

"I think that means you definitely should." The robed figure smirked. "Be sure to leave nothing out."

"To start, I have a special set of shackles waiting. Not only will they restrict her movements by binding her wrists, ankles, and wings... should she move the wrong way, they'll constrict. I'm quite eager to see them slowly cut off her circulation. When she comes around, I have a scourge waiting. Tell me, did you get the pleasure of seeing the results last time? The pieces of her flesh that were ripped from her body?"

No, no, no, oh gods, no... Gavin bit his lip even harder and felt it swell. Not that it did much to stifle the noise of his strangled, mournful cry. As hard as he tried to keep the memories out of his mind, he just didn't have enough strength left to do so. And his ability to shield his thoughts was even less than before. The pain he'd felt from her while it had happened... the wounds, even a couple of days after she'd received them... Gavin wept harder, his breathing labored. His chest felt tight and strained, making each breath a desperate, painful effort.

The robed figure tilted his head a bit. "Oh, now that is *very* interesting. Not only did he see the aftermath, he *felt* it while it was occurring." His hissing laugh echoed around the clearing. "I wonder how that is possible. Does that mean you not only had to watch while your *mate* was violated, but you felt it, too?"

"Oh my. Had I known that, I would've allowed them to play with her some more. We may not have heard her screams, but we certainly would've heard yours." Folding her arms across her chest, Fagonia extended the talons along her fingers. "I wonder. Does this mean the marks on your face... could she feel those in return? Or is it only one way? Perhaps we should test this theory."

"I believe we should. I certainly relish the thought of experimenting further than I originally planned. I wonder if it will be the pain inflicted on them, or the pain inflicted on each other, that will end up breaking them."

Gavin let out another roar of frustration. His vision blurred, and a wave of dizziness washed over him. With a violent shudder that shook him to his core, and the unbearable agony gripping him, he fought back a wave of nausea. Something wet trickled down the back of his throat. The force and intensity of his screams had drawn blood.

"That is an excellent question. Though how do we test this theory without getting them too close to one another? We don't want to spoil our other plans." Fagonia canted her head. "You know... I allowed your men to play with her. Perhaps I shall allow mine. They don't care too much for sex, but they enjoy watching things... burn."

Gavin wailed, the noise long and drawn out. He couldn't even pause long enough to swallow as more blood oozed down the back of his throat. *"Please... no... no... gods, please... no..."* he choked out, his words barely audible through his sobs.

"We could always compare notes along the way. Perhaps not as enjoyable as seeing them witness one another's torture firsthand, but for experimental purposes, it would do." Reaching up a skeletal hand, he stroked where his chin would be through the opening of his hood. "Hmm. I do rather enjoy witnessing feathers burn. The way they curl in on themselves before disintegrating." He glanced at Fagonia. "Have you had the pleasure of witnessing flames lick across bare flesh? It is a delightful sight. While the stench can initially be quite bothersome, before too long, they all smell like venison roasting over an open fire." He chuckled and turned his head back toward Gavin. "Gavin has seen that many times, have you not?"

"Please, no... please... no... Anything... I will do anything... please..."

"You should have thought about that long ago. It is far too late now."

"Not recently. And they certainly weren't alive when I did. I believe the notes will do... and after her lashing, I'll be happy to leave her in the care of my men. It would be intriguing to see how it impacts him as they burn her flesh." She smirked. "In the meantime, I believe we should allow one of your... males... to have a little more fun with her. Truly, does it matter if she's passed out?"

Lust-filled growls left all the Informants, their eyes darkening all over again. It didn't matter how many choking sobs or pitiful begging and pleading left him. None of it made any difference.

"No, it does not matter in the least. A hole is a hole, whether the brain attached to the body is conscious or not." He waved his hand toward his Informants. "Take your pick; then I believe it is past time we part ways for now."

"I concur." Her gaze flicked across those gathered. "I believe I'll take you." She looked back at Gavin, confirming it was the perfect decision. "Oh yes, I believe you'll do just nicely."

A wide smirk spread over Caith's face as he walked over to where Gavin still hung suspended in midair. A dark-gray panther, standing over nine feet tall with deep-purple eyes. "Do not worry, Gavin. I will take excellent care of your female. And perhaps, if the urge just strikes me, I will leave my personal mark upon her. Something... a little more permanent than the biting. What do you think?"

Another earth-shattering roar left him. Gavin hadn't been able to hold it back. It just made them laugh all over again. A sharp snap echoed behind him, and then a heavy thud, the sole sign that a tree branch had broken free. *No... no... oh, gods, no... He couldn't... he wouldn't do that... Two males had already marked her... They wouldn't allow another to brand her permanently...*

"Now that was just plain rude," Caith growled as he wiped the spittle from his cheek. Pulling his arm back, he punched Gavin in the face as hard as he could, effectively knocking him out.

Chapter Fifty-Four

Mac eyed the cool, smooth silver bands, their tight grip around his wrists and ankles a constant reminder of how they anchored him to the rough stone wall. Limiting his movements as much as possible, he looked for any way to remove them. When he'd first come around a couple of days earlier, like anyone in his position, he jerked against his bindings. It didn't take long to discover that the more he struggled, the tighter each shackle got, including the ones around his wings. For the first time since he'd woken up, he was by himself.

At least, that was how it appeared. In the dimly lit cavern, his gaze scanned the shadows, darting from one spot to another. His nostrils flared, catching the musty odor that permeated the air. Gods, he prayed, he'd never become accustomed to that awful stench. Not that he could put his finger on the cause; nor was he certain he wanted to know. None of the irons keeping him in place had a keyhole, which meant he couldn't pick them. Maybe with enough luck, he could get the leather mask off his face.

Mindful of each direction he maneuvered his head, he focused on trying to catch the buckle on the jagged rock behind him. The deep thudding of approaching footsteps reverberated from the tunnel to his right. He halted, drawing in a breath and focusing his hearing on the subtle whispers of the environment. It could be guilers returning. He had seen a few of them aiding some female siren. A woman who looked familiar, but he hadn't been able to place thus far.

It had to be guilers—they were the only ones that made sense. If the siren had come back, it would've been the clicking of talons resounding against the walls. Damn it, definitely not enough time to get this thing from his mouth. Those foul beings seemed to work with the bitch. As much as he despised it, he'd have to play the waiting game—his eyes narrowed. Even without clear details, he could make out the shapes of the creatures emerging from the shadows. One of them carried something or someone over their shoulder.

His gaze never left their forms as they continued their approach. He could finally make out enough minutiae of what they had with them. His eyes widened. His heart rate sped up. It was a siren. *Oh, dear gods, please don't let it be Cipriana.* The female who held him captive had offered no kind of information, not even her name. Despite his best efforts, he hadn't been able to determine what she wanted from him. Why capture another siren? What purpose did it serve?

Three males entered the shallow alcove. Two of them had bright-red, scaly skin, while the other looked like a freakishly gigantic pile of rubble. Not that he paid them much attention. No, his focus was on the female over the massive guiler's shoulder. It was Parthenia, covered in a multitude of bruises. Crimson splotches bloomed across the back of her white dress. His eyebrows furrowed. What in all the gods had they done to her?

Mac scrutinized all he could as the men removed the binding from Parthenia and worked to get her hooked up to the shackles attached to the uneven wall opposite him. He glimpsed the nearly black discoloration along the back of her thighs. A knot settled in the pit of his stomach. It couldn't mean... no way another female would allow *that* to happen. What other explanation could there be? Especially given the location of what he assumed was blood on her dress. For someone to be violated like that—all of that was before he even spotted the bite marks and purple hue to her skin on both sides of her neck.

Wait a minute. If Parthenia was here, then where was Gavin? These guilers had been the only footsteps he'd heard. Did that mean... had they killed the male? Oh, gods. No, he couldn't think like that. It was imperative he remained positive that he would find a way out and that Parthenia's mate was alive. He didn't think Parthenia would survive otherwise, and if she didn't... the pain his own mate would endure at her loss—he wouldn't let that happen.

The guilers finished the transfer, leaving Parthenia's limp body to hang from the wall, her head lolling to the side. Mac stared intensely at the men until they left the alcove, and then it was just him and

Parthenia. His attention turned back to the cuffs around his wrists. As carefully as he could muster, Mac repositioned his head, taking in every angle of the bindings. There wasn't any overt keyhole that he could decipher. He couldn't transition to his female form or call his flames, which obviously indicated that the cuffs were imbued with some kind of magic.

The sound of talons clicking against the stone floor, along with an additional pair of footfalls, drew his focus away from the shackles. Mac listened closely to the way the second set of steps echoed off the tunnel. It wasn't like anything he'd heard before. Okay, their captor had come back, but who did she have with her? He peered toward the tunnel's mouth, his eyes blazing with animosity at the woman who had just stepped through. He regarded the towering feline shape shifter that followed behind her.

"Oh, good. She's already chained up for you." The siren briefly glanced at Mac.

He received barely a sliver of attention from the feline, his eyes passing over him without pause. The male focused on Parthenia. "Mmm. So, it would seem." He strode across the stone floor and violently ripped the dress from her, exposing a disturbing tapestry of bruises and blood, a dark stain pooling between her thighs, and deep claw marks scarring her hips and shoulder. "I think that was just getting in the way." The male let out a growl as he grazed his claws along her sides and across her ass.

What the fuck was she letting him do? What the fuck had they already done to Parthenia? He had noticed none of that when the guilers carried her in and chained her up. Glowering at the two of them, Mac strained against his bindings, the mask muffling his yells. He didn't care if the metal bit into his flesh; he'd do whatever was possible to stop this from happening.

The female smirked. "Here I thought it would be less enjoyable without her *mate* being forced to watch."

Gavin had been... oh, gods. The very notion of Parthenia being defiled sent a searing heat through his veins, making his fists clench. Maybe she wasn't his mate, but that didn't matter. He glared daggers at the shape shifter, struggling harder to call on any of his abilities.

Glancing over, the shape shifter laughed. "That is rather amusing. Does she mean something to him, too? Or is he just too squeamish to watch?" His tone held a teasing note as he turned back to the female. His hands rested on her mangled hips.

The bitch didn't even bother with an answer. She simply waved it off dismissively as if it didn't matter. Mac let out a muffled growl, the sound rough in his throat, as he pulled with all his might at his shackles. Not that it stopped the male shifter from assaulting Parthenia. *NO!* Oh, gods! This couldn't be happening. It just couldn't.

Refusing to cave, Mac continued to wrestle with his restraints as the male's filthy noises reverberated off the walls. Something wet trickled down the inside of his forearm, but he didn't care. He kept trying to get free. Once he did, he was going to tear that motherfucker apart limb from limb, and then he'd rip into that bitch who just stood there. How could she allow this? How could she do nothing?

The sounds from the shape shifter only got louder and more aggressive. Still, Mac struggled against his restraints, the metal biting into his flesh with each tug, the coppery tang of blood sharp in the air. While he knew that if he didn't stop, eventually his hands would go numb, he simply couldn't. The mask may have subdued his snarls, but he glared at the shifter, promising to end the male's life if he got loose.

Mac bucked against the wall, the tethers around his wings rattling as he struggled to escape, even as it seemed the abuse on Parthenia ended. Fresh bruises covered her body, and more blood stained her alabaster skin. His chest heaved and his nostrils flared as he yielded to his inability to save either himself or his sister-in-law.

The shape shifter just stood there as if he was admiring what he'd done. Without looking away from Parthenia, he scraped his claw against the stone wall in front of her to sharpen it. "I will need a piece of thin metal, as hot as you can get it."

"I believe I can take care of that. I'll be, but a moment." With the flash of a black cloud, she disappeared.

His eyes widened. Why did the male need hot metal? Why was he sharpening one of his claws against the stone? No! No! The male had to be done. Although his fingers tingled, Mac pulled on his restraints as he screamed against the mask.

The female stepped back into the cave, her brutish henchmen in tow. She glanced at Mac. "His chains will need to be reset, but before you do, let him watch this."

Kneeling down on the floor, the male pulled Parthenia's legs up and rested one knee against his shoulder. With his sharpened claw, he carved something Mac couldn't see into Parthenia's right inner thigh. Blood immediately welled up, dripping onto the floor.

Each time his claw left her skin, he wiped at the crimson flow. "I have never put my permanent mark on another. This is quite an enjoyable experience."

Once he had finished, he remained where he kneeled. A malicious smirk covered his face. Without looking away from it, he held his hand out behind him for the metal he'd requested.

Nothing. He hadn't been able to do a damn thing to stop the male from hurting Parthenia. A single tear traced a path down his cheek, a silent testament to the pain she was experiencing and the anguish she would face upon waking. Gods, he had to get them out of here.

Without hesitation, she placed the requested sliver of heated metal in his hand. "Deal with him. I believe he's seen enough."

The male used the red-hot end of the piece of metal to trace over the carvings he'd made with his claw. He took his time. Without going so slow that the metal would cool down, ensuring he branded every single bit of it. Her pale skin bubbled and darkened as blisters appeared. The mark looked charred by the time he finished. His fangs grazed against her disfigured skin as he licked fully over the brand, growling as her blood coated his tongue. Dropping her knee from his shoulder, he stood up before handing the poker back over. "Be sure to let Gembert's disappointment know that this female no longer belongs to him."

Mac tried to fight off the large guiler's attempt to knock him out. His prior exertions, along with diminished blood flow, had sapped his strength to a mere whisper. A sharp sting bloomed on his skin, followed by a whisper that dissolved into the roaring in his ears, and then nothing.

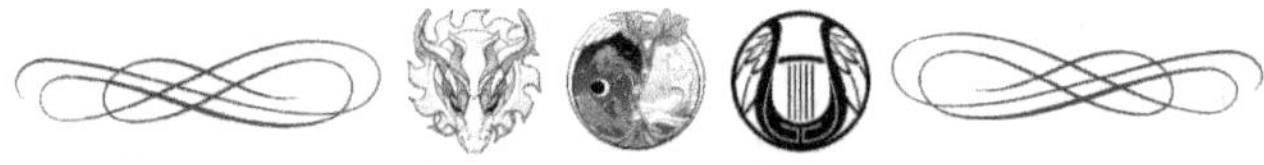

A small groan left her mouth as Parthenia stirred. Oh, gods. Her entire body ached—not just the places she'd been awake for, but a new throbbing on the inside of her right thigh. A hollow ache settled in her chest, and the corners of her eyes stung as the past replayed itself, heavy and suffocating. Gods, please... she didn't want to think about any of it, remember any of it. She took a ragged breath, fighting the pain and constriction in her chest, and banished the intrusive thoughts. She had to focus.

Keeping her eyes averted from the cuffs around her wrists, she turned her head with a slight wince. While the mask no longer covered her mouth, her neck still hurt. She couldn't move much at all. Someone had chained her to a wall. Her talons didn't even touch the floor. Not that it would do any good if they could. Her ankles had been bound as well. She also suspected her wings had been bound, just as they had upon her capture. The jagged rock dug into her abdomen while she fixed her eyes on the dimly lit, immense cavern ahead. A musty scent, like old earth and damp leaves, filled her nostrils as she looked in the opposite direction. It appeared just as dark, though the possibility of an entryway existed. Maybe a way out. Either way, she couldn't see much. And her mate's scent was nowhere around. What had they done with him?

"It's best if you limit your movements," a familiar voice said from somewhere behind her.

What in the world? Despite the twinge that still lingered at her pulse point, Parthenia managed a glance over her shoulder and spotted the shadow of another person hanging on the wall opposite her. "Mac? What happened? Where are we? Is my sister okay?"

"As far as I know, Cipriana is fine. I got kidnapped... maybe a day or two ago. All I can tell you is that we're in a cavern somewhere."

Her aunt had worked with some skeletal creature to separate her and Gavin. If she and Mac were in the same place, why had Fagonia nabbed Mac? Before she could ponder it further, a scent she recognized wafted into her nose.

"Ah, I see you've finally awoken."

"What have you done with him? Where is Gavin? Where is my mate?" Parthenia pulled at the cuffs that held her in place. As cold steel clamped around her wrists, beads of sweat formed on her brow. She had to get to him! She had to get out of here.

"That disgusting creature is not in my possession."

"Let us go!" Mac growled out.

While she applauded his words, the only way they found freedom was if they escaped. Something she wasn't certain was even possible. She'd never get back to Gavin. All she felt from him was anger, fear... not just for her, but for him as well. It wasn't supposed to be like this. They had been so careful; taken every precaution possible. Keeping the memories of their capture locked in the back of her mind, Parthenia glared at Fagonia. "If you hurt him, I swear by all the gods, I will rip your head from your body."

"Isn't that sweet? You can try all you want, but you'll never free yourself from your binds."

"What are you doing, Fagonia? What did we ever do to you?"

"Nothing really. I am simply repulsed by your choices." Fagonia smirked. "Instead of wondering what will happen to him, you should be concerned with what I'm about to do to you."

A deafening crack in the air assaulted her ears before she replied. A moment later, she felt the sharp, biting sensation of the whip's spikes against her skin. With a sickening tear, a piece of metal gouged out a large section of flesh from her shoulder. She screamed at the agony that tore through her body. Her vision blurred, a hot, stinging sensation accompanied by the sting of salt on her skin. This hadn't been her first time with the scourge, but this was different. The lashing was more intense, more painful than usual. Either Fagonia had more power behind the weapon, or the bruises that already covered her body made it much more tender.

The familiar, menacing whistle of the whip echoed in her ears again. Wrapping her fingers around the chains, she tried to brace herself, but to no avail. The metallic part of the scourge tore into her shoulder blade, a sharp, searing pain. Parthenia cried out as a warm trickle of blood seeped down her back, the rough cuffs chafing her wrists. Even the one around her waist shrunk. If it got any tighter, it would likely break a bone in one of her wings, if not both. More tears streaked her face.

Gods, she couldn't hold anything back. This was much worse than what she was accustomed to receiving. Gavin had to be feeling all of her pain. She didn't know how to stop it. Or if she could. The lashes continued for hours. That much time hadn't likely passed, but she had thought they wouldn't end. Parthenia tried to count them, to keep track somehow, yet she couldn't. The relentless throbbing had escalated to a point where she could barely function. Not any more than the number of times she heard Mac yelling at Fagonia to stop. The metal restraints around her wrists and ankles had tightened so severely that she had lost all sensation in her extremities.

Same with the one around her waist. That one was the worst. She knew the second it happened. The scourge had come across her spine. As the sharp claws raked across her skin, another scream tore from her throat, instantly followed by a sharp pinch and a sound like thunder. The sound roared, a powerful force that she felt not just in her eardrums but deep within her soul. The cuff that held her wings against her back snapped one of her bones. A desperate, pleading wail escaped her, a sound so thin and reedy it seemed to fray at the edges, a last-ditch effort against the encroaching void. It had been pain like no other.

"It would seem she has had enough. For now."

"You bitch!" Mac spewed. "I'm going to tear you..." His words trailed off, becoming muffled.

"While I enjoy listening to your threats, I prefer your silence more," Fagonia said. "Loosen her cuffs and turn her around. I have other business to attend to." The sound of talons clicking against the concrete floor echoed all around.

Despite her attempt to see who aided Fagonia, she noticed little. Her vision swam, and the room tilted precariously as the world slowly faded. She was a prisoner of her body, the blood loss and cut-off circulation rendering her numb. A sensation washed over her as invisible hands unlocked her bonds, eased her down to the ground, and then refastened the chains to her wrists, positioning her against the unyielding stone. Wincing, Parthenia hissed at the sting that burned over her wounds. Her eyes welled up, the realization dawning on her as tears streamed down her cheeks. Here she thought she had nothing left to give.

How had she missed the smell of brine and sulfur when she inhaled earlier? Whatever cave she sat in, wherever they had taken her to, it was near the sea. Which also meant salt coated the cavern walls. She had to find a way out of here before the scars on her back became the least of her problems.

Just as she thought she had a moment to breathe, to determine a way out, a fresh wave of agony coursed through her body. It was as though each bone, from her ankles up to her arms, had fractured sequentially, causing overwhelming agony. Writhing in pain, her scream resounded all around her as it bounced between the cave walls. More salt from the stone made its way into her back as her wrists unwillingly tugged against the cuffs and chains that bound her. It seemed like forever before the sensations stopped. Though no bones of hers had broken.

With just the cuffs around her wrists to bite into her skin, it left only one option. This was something she had gotten from... her chest tightened. Her breathing grew labored, as if all the air had been violently expelled from her lungs. She turned her head, as it was all she could do as she gasped for oxygen. With her wrists chained above her head, there was no room for her to claw at her throat. She could feel... oh, gods, Gavin! It seemed as if he was choking on water. She could do nothing to help. Not him. Not her. Nothing. It felt like forever had passed before she could draw anything into her lungs.

The cuffs around her wrists were so tight again. Her head lolled against her arm as ragged breaths left her mouth. "Help... please...." she croaked out. She could barely move, let alone fight back in any way possible. With Mac chained up across the wall, there had to be someone out there who would help. Perhaps the ones who had undone her chains before. She hadn't noticed them the first time. All she had registered earlier had been their hands. Two guilers approached her cautiously and slowly unlocked the cuffs restricting circulation to her wrists. She collapsed to the ground. The cold stone pressed into her cheek.

If she was going to escape, this would be the time. Despite her freedom from physical restraint, she lacked the energy to even raise her head, making the use of her voice to influence them impossible. A vile sensation came over her. It was as if bugs crawled over her skin, no, inside her body. Then something coiled around her heart as it crushed the life out of... no... this wasn't happening to her... it was happening to...

Parthenia cried out her mate's name as tears sprang forth. Whatever evil had made its way inside his body left, but she hardly had a second to register the relief. Her stomach churned violently, forcing her onto her hands and knees as she vomited. Even once she completely evacuated its contents, she continued to heave. It was some time before she collapsed to the stone floor again. Her cheek was wet and sticky, covered in a mixture of her sweat, vomit, blood, tears... gods, what he had gone through.

As the last vestiges of light receded, an icy dread enveloped her, the fight draining away, leaving only a hollow despair. They would never escape.

Chapter Fifty-Five

Her cheek stung. That was the first thing she noticed as she came around. Parthenia blinked, and the blurriness receded, allowing her vision to sharpen. She didn't know how long she'd been out. Or how she'd gotten back against the wall. Or… she didn't tug on the cool metal wrapped around her wrists. They would only tighten. Multiple attempts had proven that. Lifting her head, she took in her surroundings. Nothing about the cave had changed.

Even Mac still hung on the opposite wall. A leather mask covered his mouth. His wrists, ankles, and wings had been bound the same as hers. His emerald-green eyes softened as sorrow and knowledge filled them.

Parthenia averted her gaze. Something told her he'd witnessed whatever they had done to her inner thigh and more. Like most of her body, the throbbing hadn't stopped. So much of her hurt that she couldn't pinpoint one place that didn't. She didn't want to think about what he might have seen. Nor could she stand the sight of the pity that burned in his eyes. She swallowed, her dry throat rasping, and fought to keep the tears from spilling down her cheeks. "We need to find a way out of here."

"I wish you luck in that," Fagonia said as she stepped into the alcove through the entryway.

Parthenia hissed at the female. It didn't matter what either she or Gavin went through. They would both fight with every fiber in their being. They would fight. And they would find a way back to one another. "Nothing you do will ever make me stop loving Gavin. His love for me will never wilt. It reaches higher than the tallest mountain and goes beyond the deepest part of the ocean.

My love for him has only one equal: the endless sky. We will love one another long past when the seas dry and the rocks decay. Our love will continue from this life into the next. Our hearts beat only for one another. Our souls belong only to each other. Nothing you can do will ever change that."

"Hmm, I wonder if he would feel the same way if you were not so pretty? Do you think he would still love you, then?"

"Nothing—"

With a stinging slap, Fagonia's hooked nails tore into Parthenia's skin, her fingers digging into her cheeks. "If your love transcends everything, then I suppose you will both die for each other. I expect Markham will deliver nothing less than the most painful torture before he takes his life."

Her eyes grew wide, and a shiver traced a path down her spine. No, she couldn't have heard the female correctly. There hadn't been time to give the male's name, let alone offer some image of forewarning to her mate before Fagonia's claws struck her. A searing pain shot through Parthenia as her cheek bled and flesh ripped. A lone tear made its way down her dampening face. Fagonia's hands had never looked like that before.

"Oh yes, my dear. I tossed your pathetic excuse for a male to the bear. If you both feel everything the other does, then I shall certainly make it as painful as possible as I destroy that beautiful face of yours." Fagonia swiped her claws across the other side of Parthenia's face.

She tried hard not to struggle against her restraints. Not to move at all, but she couldn't seem to stop it as her head jerked from one side to the next. With every involuntary twitch, the shackles dug deeper into her skin, a painful reminder of her restraint. She didn't know how many times Fagonia's elongated nails hacked into her jaw, cheeks, and forehead. Eventually, her agonized cries became rough and strained.

A stark crimson bloomed across the front of her dress, a vibrant contrast to the ruby trickles weeping from countless cuts marring her face. Her head lolled to the side as she attempted to blink the crimson fluid free from her eyes. Parts that had already swollen. Once again, she no longer felt her wrists or ankles, nor the pain of another broken bone in one of her wings.

"I am *sure* he will still love you now." Fagonia sneered and turned away. "Clean this mess up and loosen her cuffs. Do *not* forget to re-chain her."

"May we play with her before we do?" one of the guilers asked.

"I do not care what you do, as long as she remains alive. Do you understand?"

The other guiler smiled wide. "Yes, we do."

The swelling in her face and the blood that had entered her eyes made it impossible to see clearly. But she could hear noises coming from Mac. She couldn't make out any words with the covering still across his mouth.

"Do you have something to say?" Fagonia asked. "No? Do not fret. The best part of the show happens tomorrow."

The sharp click of talons on the stone floor resounded as the guilers adjusted her bonds. She didn't give their earlier question to Fagonia much thought, as it seemed they would leave her alone. Except they didn't. Once they had her cuffs in a loose state, one toyed with the pendant around her neck.

"This is lovely."

"Leave it alone," Parthenia said through gritted teeth. She had worn it since they left Pteryrina. As Cipriana had known about Gavin and he traveled along with them, she hadn't seen the need to hide it. Though her face was streaked with blood, she would break free from her restraints if any of those deceivers attempted to take it. Wait—there was a way. Her voice. Provided she could belt out the right notes beyond the scratchiness in her throat.

"No worries. I prefer to play with something else entirely. Shall we begin?"

She opened her mouth to attempt some manipulation and completely stilled. A pair of hands came upon the back of her neck and unfastened the top of her dress. It hardly occurred to her that something was different about the attire they worked to remove. Her muscles locked rigid, a guttural whimper escaping her lips as her vision narrowed to a single, desperate point of escape. Oh, gods... gods, no... please... males had already... even Gavin's father... Tears welled in the corners of her eyes as she closed them tight. Not again. Please, not again.

Her chin quivered as the fabric tore from her skin, a rush of cool air caressing her exposed flesh. "Please..." Parthenia pleaded in a whispered voice. This couldn't happen again. It just couldn't.

Near her outer thigh, heat radiated. Her eyes snapped open. She hadn't seen what caused it. A feverish hand suddenly pressed into her skin, its heat shocking. Parthenia screamed, the searing heat of the fire burning her flesh. Her thigh contracted and bubbled at the contact from the scorching touch. A choked sob escaped her lips as the burning sensation intensified on her untouched limb, each tear a desperate plea. Her body quaked as she cried out in anguish.

She clutched the chains tightly. It was the only way to keep her wrists still, so the cuffs didn't restrict her circulation. Once again, the blaze left her body, though she didn't expect the reprieve to last long. Parthenia took shallow, rapid breaths. It was all she could do to mentally prepare—

A searing heat enveloped her, constricting her chest with an invisible, crushing force. She wailed at the agony coursing through her veins. No amount of mental control could've prepared her for the constant, excruciating pain wracking her body. She had no time to breathe through one before they set upon searing her flesh again. Full sobs streaked her face as she pleaded with her attackers to stop.

Demeter, please make them stop. I can't—one scorching hand came in contact with her lower belly while the other followed seconds later to her collarbone. A hoarse sob escaped her as her lungs seized, a crushing weight settling in her chest. She didn't know how much longer she could hold on. How much more she could take.

The places where her flesh had already blistered sent her synapses into overdrive. Though both of their hands lifted from her skin, she cried out again. It felt as if claws ripped at the fresh wounds across her stomach and collarbone.

"Look, she bleeds."

"Perhaps we burned too deep."

"I do not think so. They seem to have come from something else."

"Then shall we continue?"

"Yes. Let's."

"Please..." Parthenia croaked. She had to go to her happy place. Images of Gavin flooded her mind. Of their time together. Curled up in one another's arms. Sitting in his lap as they read. Their lovemaking. Relentless, grabbing hands snatched away the last fading sparks and left her adrift in despair. She could've handled anywhere... or so she thought... except they went for the place where she was most vulnerable—her wings. With a strangled sob, she felt the unyielding heat consume the very foundation of her flight, a hollow emptiness spreading through her. A scream, so piercing it chilled her to the bone, tore from her throat.

She could take no more. Her last breath hitched, a ragged whisper lost in the encroaching blackness that swallowed her screams. The last thing she saw was the concrete floor as her body fell against it. She barely noticed the blood seeping from her wrists as she passed out.

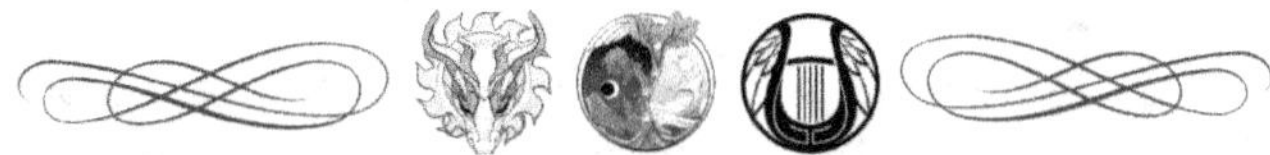

Cipriana stared at the rubble where the second reflection pool used to be. How could this happen? How was this even—Thalasia, that's how! The female had gotten *her* permission to utilize the pool for some kind of ceremony. She hadn't expected a result like this.

"Is it even possible to repair this?" Fantasia asked.

Her sister had been the one to get her about ten minutes earlier. When Fantasia mentioned there was a problem, *this* wasn't even close to what she'd imagined. A dry pool, sure. They'd been drying out for years. Cipriana dragged a hand down her face, sighing with exhaustion. "I don't know. They're magical, sacred pools. It isn't exactly like *we* built them." Uncertain what to do or how to handle this, she turned around and started toward her mother's house.

While she hadn't knocked or gotten too close to Parthenia's apothecary, she'd tried twice to see if she could hear anything. Yes, Thalasia had told her that they'd be unavailable for a day or two, which led her to conclude those two were off screwing while Mac was still missing. To make matters worse, Parthenia and Gavin hadn't returned yet, either. To be fair, her sister and brother-in-law probably wanted a little more alone time together. Except they could've gotten it here. It made little sense why they were still gone.

Her hand paused on the doorknob. She prepared to seek her mother's advice again. Most of everything she'd learned recently about the Atlis had come from her mother. It contradicted what little she'd found on her own. While she trusted the woman's opinion, was she naïve to give so much to someone she didn't honestly know? Cipriana lifted her wrist, and her gaze fell upon the five-pronged star Oriel had given her.

Mac had been gone for three days. Her sister and brother-in-law could potentially be missing. Was it better to continue to lean on Thalasia and Seru or call Oriel, admitting someone stole the crystal? For the second time, her fingers gravitated toward the item, hovering over it. She groaned and dropped her hand. Twice, and neither time could she pull the trigger. Rubbing her eyes, Cipriana opened the door to her mother's house and closed it behind her. Her gaze drifted across the way.

Her mother stepped out of the kitchen. "So? What was the issue?"

"One pool is destroyed." She didn't see any reason to beat around the bush. It wasn't like she could go back in time and change her decision. Instead, she had to accept the consequences and figure out how to move forward.

"Destroyed? I don't believe that."

Cipriana strode farther into the house and plopped down on one chair around the table. "Well, believe it. There's nothing but debris left." She watched as her mother's eyes darted back and forth. Something brewed in the woman's head, but what? Could her desire to understand what happened be related to it? There had been that loud roar last night. Everyone in the village had heard it. The entire isle might have heard it. Not that she knew for sure it came from Seru. The only dragons she'd ever met were the four in Chicane Village.

"I'm sorry, Cipriana. I imagine that weighs heavily on you," her mother said as she sat down in the chair opposite her.

"Yes, but it isn't just because we have one pool left. The Reflection Pools are sacred pools given to us to protect. For centuries, we've done just that. Then, over the last seven years, not only have we allowed them to dry one at a time, but now we just give people the opportunity to demolish them outright. I'm pissed, Mom!" Though she wasn't sure if she was angrier at herself or her mother. After all, *she* had been the one to follow her mother blindly. Each decision she made impacted every siren in the village.

"I know, sweetheart, and I'm sorry. Technically, as the Atlis, Thalasia outranks you. According to our laws, you're required to give her pretty much anything she wants."

Her brows furrowed. That couldn't be right. She'd been going through the laws for the last couple of days, deciding which ones needed to be changed and which ones she'd do away with, period. Not once had she come across a single law about an Atlis. That left only one other possibility—the Elder journal, which she'd given to Devin to hide. Cipriana covered her face with her hands, then ran them over the top of her head. "'Anything' sounds like a bit much."

"Then trust your gut. All I can do is offer you my opinion. It's your choice whether or not to take it. No one else can make these decisions for you." Her mother stood, patted her shoulder, and headed back into the kitchen.

Trust my gut, Cipriana thought to herself. That seemed to be part of the problem—her gut gave her conflicting responses. She could use Mac to talk things through, except they had discussed Thalasia already. What had she told him? That maybe she'd been quick to judge the female. Okay, for now, she'd give the Atlis a chance to prove herself.

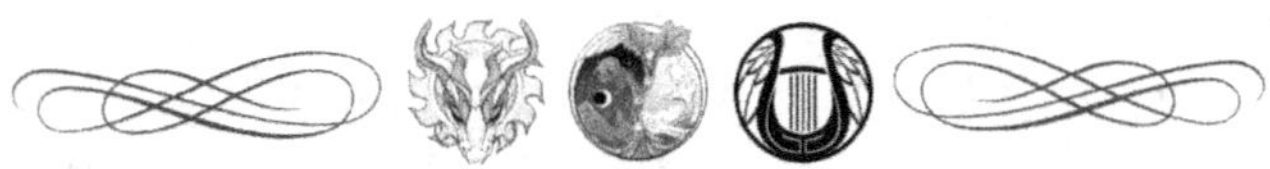

The cool, grainy wall against Parthenia's cheek felt nice, not that it did much to relieve the incessant throbbing that covered her body. In a few places, she felt more pain than others—the back of her arms, calves, neck, and back. None of which the guilers had touched, which meant... oh, gods... Gavin. There was even an endless pounding along the sides of her skull. It was like someone had smacked her upside the head a few times with a branch. Her hair might be matted, too. Not that she could tell for sure.

Parthenia peeled one eye open at a time. It was the only way to acclimate to the ambient light of the torches lining the wall of the cave. They hadn't bothered her so much the first time she'd come around, but the steady thump in her skull currently suggested otherwise. She blinked. Was her left wing spread out? That couldn't be right. She tried to recall the position she'd been in last—whatever it had been, she didn't think it applied any longer. Not with the jagged rock pressing into her face.

"Mac?" she called out, her voice hoarse.

"I'm here, Parthenia."

Part of her wanted to ask, and part of her didn't. Not that she truly had to do it. She could feel it—only one of her wings had gotten fanned out. This couldn't be happening. No way Fagonia hated her this much. A stinging sensation of tears welled up at the edges of her eyes. *Demeter, please, please get us out of here. Please don't let this—*

"About time. I was worried those last wounds had claimed your life. It's good to know that's mine for the taking," Fagonia hissed.

Something sharp trailed across her wing, ruffling her feathers; likely a dagger or something similar based on how it felt. It didn't hurt, but she tensed up. Parthenia attempted to soothe her cracked, thirst-stricken throat. "Please... Aunt Fagonia... please..." Not once had she ever called the female 'aunt,' but she'd try anything to stop this.

"Oh, I'm *Aunt Fagonia* now, am I? Do you really think that'll work? Hmm?"

The edge of a sharp blade scraped against the rough stone wall, just under her wing. She didn't like that. Her eyes darted wildly around the room, a desperate plea caught in her throat as her limbs trembled. Clenching her jaw, Parthenia tried not to flinch. "Please..." she stated through gritted teeth. What little hope remained that she and Gavin might survive this, find their way to freedom... it slowly slipped away. Not if—

Her eyes widened; a sharp glint of metal caught her attention moments before it plunged into her wing, tearing through feathers and burrowing deep into her flesh. A guttural cry tore from her throat, each ragged breath a testament to the agony searing through her.

"As much as I enjoyed watching Markham torture your mate, I think I'm going to enjoy this more," Fagonia whispered in her ear and yanked the dagger out.

"Stop it!" Mac yelled. "You'll kill her!"

"That's the point," Fagonia retorted. "It's almost a shame that I need you. Otherwise, I'd be happy to make you bleed."

"You won't win. They'll find us... and rip you to shreds," Mac said. "Just hold on, Parthenia. Hold on!"

"Keep telling yourself that." Her aunt cackled.

With each savage yank of the blade from her flesh, Parthenia cried out in anguish, feathers scattering as the woman inflicted deeper wounds. A soft, broken sob escaped her lips, her shoulders slumping as she lowered her gaze to the floor. No matter how much she begged, Fagonia didn't stop. With each plunge of the knife, the female continued to inflict further wounds upon her wing, a grim, repetitive motion. Parthenia wept, a torrent of tears for the vanished dreams of her and her mate, the unborn children, the unbuilt home, and the overwhelming sense of loss. While she knew she'd see him on the other side, where they'd spend an eternity dancing, chasing one another around a lake, and making love... she wanted more. More time, more nights curled up in one another's arms, more kisses—she wanted everything they'd ever desired together to come true.

Her head drooped forward, tears making glistening trails down her cheeks. She'd lost count of the number of times Fagonia had stabbed her wing. She wasn't even sure how many times she'd screamed. Though she'd heard a male voice hollering across the way, it had been some time since she'd been able to make out the words. A chilling frost prickled her skin, and an icy dread seeped into her bones.

Fagonia grabbed her by the hair and yanked her head back. "I'm not done with you yet, but I promise... it'll be over soon. Well, that depends on how long you can survive once I remove a wing. I'm looking forward to finding out."

A snarl resounded from somewhere behind her. "You keep fighting, Parthenia! Keep fighting, my love. I'm coming for you!"

"Gavin..." she whispered, her voice rough and barely audible. She couldn't see him, but she swore she heard him. He'd gotten free, and he was going to save her. Maybe he was here already and fighting with her aunt. Her wing felt as light as a feather, and a wave of warmth spread through her, banishing the lingering ache. Her head rolled to the side, leaning against her arm; not that she could feel her fingers. They'd gone numb—

Parthenia hadn't registered the soft whoosh in the air. She felt a searing pain as the sword's edge sliced through her wing, its force driving her violently against the unforgiving stone of the wall, all before she could even see it. A crack echoed around the cave as she wailed in agony. Fire seared through her veins as if fueled by her blood. Just when she thought the torture had ended, that it was finally over—a sickening pop reverberated off the walls as the remnants of her wing were torn from her shoulder.

"Keep fighting, my love! Keep fighting!" her mate instructed. The last things she saw before she slipped into the abyss were his exquisite emerald-green eyes.

Chapter Fifty-Six

As she chewed on the inside of her cheek, Cipriana clasped her hands behind her, the faint scent of lavender from her clothes filling the air. Every few seconds, her gaze darted to Thalasia and Seru. Thalasia and Seru had addressed the destruction of the second pool earlier that day. Her concern now was that they'd yet to locate Mac. If the matelink existed between her and Mac, she hadn't yet gotten enough of anything to aid in their search. While they knew who was responsible, she had no way of tracking Fagonia. Well, she did, but it wasn't in her possession.

To make matters worse, Parthenia and Gavin had yet to return, either. She worried the shape shifter's leader had found them. What would that mean for her sister? Although her mother had convinced her not to call on Oriel, she'd nearly done it twice. Maybe it was time she involved him and admitted Fagonia stole the crystal.

A swooshing sound pulled her gaze upward, toward the open entrance of the temple situated overhead. Her mother swooped down towards them, a sudden rush of wind accompanying the movement, and though the landing was quick, her mother's taloned feet contacted the ground smoothly. "You need to go to the gate, now," her mother urged.

A chill swept down her spine. It wasn't just the tone of her mother's voice, but the look in her eye. "What is it? Is it Mac? Parthenia? Gavin?" Her eyes widened as she silently pleaded for more information.

"Just go," her mother stated, and then flicked her gaze to Thalasia and Seru. "The two of you should go as well."

Nothing more needed to be said. Cipriana rocketed into the sky, abandoning the temple as if her very existence was at stake. Without hesitation, she headed straight for the nearby open gates. She didn't even notice whether Thalasia and Seru followed her. Both Ariadne and Khryseis stood with their backs to her, just within the entryway to Pteryrina. Whatever the problem was, she couldn't see it, even as her feet touched down. "What's going on? Did something happen?"

"Our apologies, Elder," Ariadne said as she stepped aside.

"Oh, gods." Cipriana gasped, her hands immediately covering her mouth in shock. Her gaze landed on a vibrant brown wing, just a few steps from their doorway. It looked like someone had partially shredded it and picked at it with the way the feathers stuck out at various angles. Kneeling next to it, Pallus had a blade and a piece of parchment in her hand. Dropping her hands from her mouth, her eyes wide, Cipriana pointed to what Pallus held. "What's that?"

"They were both found with the wing, Elder." Pallus pushed up to her feet and ascended the few stairs between them. She offered the papyrus to Cipriana.

Despite her urgent need for a moment to compose herself, the frantic beating of her heart left no room for calm. If she was right—the wing looked like it belonged to Parthenia. Shakily, Cipriana accepted the sheet of parchment and scanned over the note. Every fiber of her being resisted the overwhelming desire to shriek and weep uncontrollably. She swallowed the lump in the back of her throat and peered over her shoulder at Thalasia and Seru.

Seru held her eye contact. There was a sudden blaze of blue in them. "You should sit down," he insisted, muffling the sharp edge of his voice with his hand.

While Cipriana noticed the change in Seru's eyes, she didn't further analyze it. Her mind was a whirlwind of thoughts, struggling to comprehend the possibility of the truth. Not just at the significance of her sister's wing, but the whereabouts of her sister's mate, along with to whom the note was addressed and who had sent it. Her shoulders tightened, and her chin trembled. Her eyes grew moist, and tears gathered at the edges as she extended the letter to Thalasia.

Despite the insistence to sit, she just couldn't do it. All she could think about was her sister's captor. What had the female put her sister through? Had the woman tortured Parthenia? Oh, gods—the tear slipped free.

Thalasia grabbed the paper a moment before Cipriana tumbled down, landing ungracefully on her posterior. It wasn't very Elder-like, but she couldn't stop the stream of wetness down her cheeks. Nor did she much care. The threat of losing her sister...

The note in hand, Thalasia read it over. Her jaw clenched, and one of her hands curled into a fist. Unfurling her fingers, she clasped Seru's forearm, allowing him to read it over as well.

Thalasia,
You seem to be at a loss for finding your friends. I thought I'd help you out. Come alone to Kenos Ridge at first light, or it'll be more than blood on your hands.
Fagonia

Seru's eye color reflected off the parchment, turning it a pretty shade of cerulean. His eyes slid to Thalasia. The answer to the sender's last request was going to be a no, and the look he gave her said as much.

"You have to get her back... you have to. I don't even... oh, gods..." Cipriana's words trailed off. Why couldn't she get the terms out? She had to collect herself. For her sister's sake. Swallowing to wet her parched throat, she wiped at her face and focused her attention on Thalasia and Seru. "Her mate... they were together."

Thalasia dipped her chin in a silent acknowledgment and flicked her gaze to the three guards standing nearby. "Can one of you cloak yourselves?"

"I can, my liege," one of them replied as she stepped forward. "Ariadne at your service."

Getting low on her haunches, Thalasia clasped Cipriana's shoulder. "We're going to borrow one of your guards and get her back. I promise we'll get both of them."

"We should get her somewhere safe first," Seru suggested softly, nodding in Cipriana's direction. "With people she trusts."

Wiping her face, Cipriana got to her feet. Normally she'd agree, especially after someone had killed Vasilia. Assessments were still in the works, but it wasn't impossible to believe Fagonia had orchestrated this whole thing. "I'm not leaving. These are my people. What kind of Elder would I be if I ran at the first sign of trouble?"

Thalasia stood. "He's right. There's too much at stake."

"And I suppose you'd tell me I need to stay away from what's coming our way as well." She folded her arms across her chest. She knew all about the so-called invaders. Even fought a few of them herself, alongside Mac, her sister, and Gavin.

"I would," Thalasia replied.

Cipriana took a long, cleansing breath and finished wiping her face. Yes, she was still young and figuring things out. There had been no time to study with Vasilia and learn everything her new role entailed, but that didn't mean she had no support. "I didn't back down from the last altercation I got into, and I won't back down now."

"If we have time to spare once all the hostages are found, I'd be more than willing to run through a few training exercises—with *all* of you." The color in Seru's eyes changed again, his gaze shifting between her and Thalasia. "Then, we'll discuss who gets to join us on the front lines and who remains to defend our respective homes and those too weak to fight. One is no less noble than the other."

Cipriana brushed the last of the wetness from her face. Whether or not he believed it, either of them, her not joining the front lines, was non-negotiable. Though he had a point she hadn't considered. The invaders could attempt to breach their gates. It might be safest if they were closed once she got her family back. If the Seelie's Prime Warrior held to her word, they should arrive within the next day or so. Not information she intended to share. She turned her attention to Thalasia. "I don't care what happens to Fagonia. You do *whatever* is necessary to bring them home."

"Understood," Thalasia said. She glanced from Ariadne to Seru. "We should head off now. We can strategize on the way and cloak once we're closer."

Seru heaved a sigh.

Cipriana watched as the three departed, careful to step around the remains of her sister's wing. It would need to be cleaned up. No way could she allow them to return and still find it there. This gave her something to focus on and keep her mind temporarily occupied. *Demeter, please bring them back.*

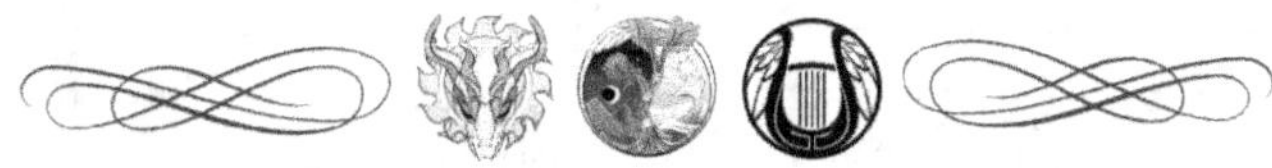

Thalasia glided effortlessly through the canopy, the wind rustling her feathers. While Seru had been reluctant, he'd finally agreed to follow the plan she'd come up with to fight Fagonia. It hadn't taken a genius to piece it all together. Between the seitadi attacking her at the lake and the charred railing from the attack on Mac—it was highly probable Fagonia had guilers at her dispatch. She didn't expect Fagonia to hold up her end and fight alone. It also meant freeing Parthenia and Mac wouldn't be easy. Although she certainly had faith, he and Ariadne could get those two out. That left Fagonia to her.

She dropped a bit, shifting her weight and taking in the vibrant green landscape as she soared. Her gaze swept the surroundings, watchful for any seitadi, poised to strike or simply observing. It had been part of the reason she'd parted ways with Seru and Ariadne a short time ago. It was better not to take any chances. The entrance to Kenos Ridge came into sight. A half-mile away, she could make it out from her current location with no problem. Her gaze zeroed in on the female standing at the cave's mouth. The corners of her lips curled upward. Oh, she hoped it wouldn't be too easy to take the female down. She was itching to try out some of her new powers.

Slipping out of the forest alongside the mountainside, Thalasia angled her body, turning to the front entrance. The plan was to draw Fagonia out, and she could only do that if she remained in the air. While she believed there was a high probability the female had also worked with Markham, it was nothing more than conjecture. In the hours she, Seru, and Ariadne had watched Kenos Ridge, nothing had come up to support it. So, she didn't mention it.

As intended, Thalasia approached the cavern's opening from the front. Her gaze fixed on Fagonia, she paused several feet from the entrance, remaining suspended in the air. The female looked different from the last time they'd almost run into one another. Both her hair and feathers were darker, as well as her eyes. Not that it mattered in the least bit. "I'm here, as you requested."

"I see. You even followed directions and came alone."

Why did it seem like the woman was trying to taunt her? Miserably, she might add, but still trying. "Of course, I did. Now, are you gonna make this easy and just give me my friends? Or are we going to do things the hard way?"

"Oh, where would the fun be if we did things the easy way, Thalasia? Given the way you roamed all over the isle, you should know that better than anyone." Fagonia smirked.

"I guess it's the hard way, then." That, indeed, confirmed her theory. The seitadi had been watching her and Seru since the beginning, a suspicion she'd purposely neglected to share with him. There wasn't time to give that too much thought. She had to keep her wits about her.

"I was hoping you'd say that."

That said it all. The first move was about to be made. Thalasia heightened her senses without taking her eyes off the broad-shouldered siren. She spotted the red, beady eyes before they even came into view—six sets in total. That meant she had to be smart about her next maneuver. The last thing she wanted was for Fagonia to realize she'd seen her pets. Or that she had already formulated a plan of attack. She had to get the siren away from the cave's mouth so Seru and Ariadne could sneak inside.

Thalasia remained suspended in the air, her magic skillfully unlatching the belt and securing her sword in its scabbard. Her eyes narrowed as she watched the eyes get closer. The six massive birds suddenly erupted from the cavern, their powerful wings beating as they zoomed straight for her. Without wasting a second, she yanked the blade from the sheath between her wings and darted backward. Getting further away was vital. So, she didn't put too much distance between her and the squawkers; she didn't fly at full speed.

But she also didn't want Fagonia to think she was flying scared, either. Thalasia peered over her shoulder and located the six birds. Aiming, she called a bolt of lightning from the sky. The air ripped with a loud crack and a brilliant flash as she tagged a seitadi. Her mouth upturned as a multitude of feathers exploded into the air, and the creature fell toward the ground. One down, five left to go. She circled back and dove straight for them.

It benefited her that they flew in a V-formation. Once she'd gotten close enough, she lopped the head off one and stabbed another before it could open its golden beak. With three dispatched, she put the second part of her plan into motion and cloaked herself. Thalasia tucked her wings in tight and swooped under the three seitadi that remained. If her studies proved accurate, the creatures had extensive eyesight and shitty hearing. Far enough below the confused birds, she let her wings out slowly to steady her flight. She peered back toward the entrance to Kenos Ridge and watched as Fagonia took to the air.

"Tricky, tricky," the female mumbled. "Here, I thought you'd fight fair."

Really? Thalasia thought to herself. Maybe if she expected the female to do the same, but seeing that as highly unlikely, this was the better option. Her gaze flicked toward the cave's mouth. While she'd accomplished the first part of the plan, there was no telling if Seru and Ariadne had gotten into the cavern. She'd simply have to trust—the whoosh of wind drew her attention. Her eyes snapped in its direction. A black ball of something barreled at her. Dropping as quickly as possible, she didn't quite move fast enough to avoid it completely. It grazed the top of her wing, eliciting a wince.

As she removed her cloak, she activated her bond with Seru and invoked his healing touch. A small part of her wondered if he could sense that. If so, it would probably make him more smug than usual. Whatever, she had a siren to deal with.

"There you are. Now... shall we try this again?" Fagonia smirked. Her eyes grew dark, and a blade as black as night materialized in her hands.

Well... at least she knew how the female was using the crystal. Thalasia called on her magic. With a fierce crackle, three bolts of lightning struck the remaining seitadi, their dark feathers erupting in a final, devouring burst. Without pausing, she lunged for Fagonia. The edges of their swords clashed as they pressed in against one another.

With a swift motion, Fagonia raked her long nails down Thalasia's face. The proximity between them was so great that contact was inevitable. While she made use of Seru's healing power, she tossed jolts of electricity at the female and knocked her back. She pressed her assault on Fagonia, showing no mercy. Swinging her blade in a downward trajectory, their swords connected. Thalasia sent bolts through her cutlass, disintegrating the weapon in Fagonia's hand.

Firing a current of light at Fagonia, it crackled along the female's flesh and sent her stumbling backward. Thalasia grabbed hold of one of her tomahawks. She knew exactly how she planned to end this. As Fagonia shook herself, the surrounding air thrummed with power before she conjured a new blade and hurled a black, electrified orb her way. Instead of trying to evade the thing, Thalasia sliced it in half with her sword.

A crack of thunder echoed as she directed a bolt of lightning toward the weapon Fagonia gripped. As it struck, turning the item to nothing more than ash, Thalasia threw her charged tomahawk toward Fagonia's left side. It went wide, creating the illusion that she missed her target, except she hadn't.

"Here, I thought you'd be a challenge," Fagonia hissed. "You may have some unique abilities, but you're still nothing except a siren."

"Try again," Thalasia smirked as the tomahawk came back around on the female's other side. "I'm an Atlis, you bitch." With a grip on the weapon's handle, a crackling net of pure energy ripped through Fagonia, exploding her into a shower of fleshy fragments.

A faint grimace crossed Thalasia's face as the chunks fell to the ground, landing along the treeline and shore. Hmm, not something she'd considered when she decided on this course.

With a small shrug, she scanned the remnants in search of the crystal. Spotting the darkened item, Thalasia dove toward the forest. Her feet sank softly into the warm sand as she moved forward, hurrying toward the artifact.

Thalasia's eyes narrowed as she scanned the treeline. While she'd gone for the crystal, her senses remained heightened. It hadn't been a foregone conclusion, but she had believed in the strong possibility Fagonia worked with the shape shifters. Proof now stared her in the face. She saw only two. Surprising, unless others hid further back than she could see.

With unwavering focus, she channeled her energy to gather the crystal, its surface humming faintly as she secured it in a magically woven pouch. An electrical charge crackled across her blade. She lunged at one canine and swung her blade down in an arc, slicing his chest open, currents of lightning sweeping through his body.

The first canine died instantly at the stroke of her blade. The second got behind her, and she pivoted to face him. Using her wings, she leaped into the air, bringing the blade down from over her head. The shape shifter jumped back before the edge of her sword made contact. Thalasia stepped forward, aiming her weapon at the male's gut. Again, he avoided her attack.

This continued for a minute. No matter which way she maneuvered or how she charged at him, he kept evading her. Tired of this little game, she opted for a guaranteed result. Just as she'd prepared to call a bolt of lightning from the sky and be done with it, something pricked her in the neck. Thalasia felt around and yanked out a blow dart as she swayed, stumbling backward. "Motherfucker," she muttered.

Damn bitch, got her again. The same way, too! Her sword felt heavier than usual. If she tried hard enough, she could probably use it against the canine. Screw that. With a deep breath, Thalasia called upon the ancient magic that resided within her. A bolt of lightning struck the shifter, quickly frying his ass. The shocked look on his face as he collapsed kind of amused her. The acrid smell of burned fur made her nose wrinkle. "You stink."

Thalasia staggered over to the nearest tree and leaned against its trunk. Shit... Seru had always told her he could withstand most poisons or drugs... hadn't he? Was that something of his she could use? Fuck, she didn't know. Perhaps a gentle nudge and a quick look around would help her pinpoint the origin of the pesky object. Yes, that plan seemed quite solid.

From her vantage point, she scanned the forest and attempted to reach out to him. She saw nothing except green. The area was densely populated with trees and various shrubs. How far inside the thicket had she ended up? Where was the shoreline? If she could spot that, she could make her way in that direction. At least that way, if Seru didn't feel her nudge, then she'd be in his line of sight. Or so she hoped.

Thalasia inhaled deeply, striving for mental clarity as she raised her eyes. The fuzziness of her sight obscured her ability to clearly make out the exact edge of the shoreline. She rubbed her eyes and tried again. Perhaps, she thought, as she pushed off the rough bark of the tree, her heavy footsteps echoing on the forest floor as she moved, using each trunk to steady herself during her brief pauses.

Her sword was becoming so burdensome, but she probably wouldn't be able to get it back in its sheath. She pressed the tip of the blade into the ground, using it to help prop her up. "Hey, that worked." Thalasia giggled. Was this how drunk people felt? Like their brains were swimming, but their limbs took too much energy to function. Wasn't she supposed to be doing something?

With a waver in her step, Thalasia found another tree and leaned her tired body against its trunk, sliding down to rest. Try as she might, she couldn't go any farther. Her eyes drifted shut, the sword falling from her grasp, and she passed out.

Chapter Fifty-Seven

The wide mouth of the cavern led deeper into Kenos Ridge. Unyielding darkness greeted them. Its earthy scent blended in with the salty taste of the sea air carried by the muffled sound of the wind. From their current position, they could see nothing in the depths of the hollow tunnel—nothing except the endless passage of the abyss.

Seru *almost* let the female go first, if only to appease his curiosity. Exactly how well sirens could see in the pitch-black? But he didn't want to have to rescue her, too, if she ended up walking off a ledge or tripping over her talons. He silently took the lead, allowing her to fall in wherever she chose.

With one hand resting on the hilt of the blade at her hip, Ariadne ran her fingers across the jagged wall and sniffed the air.

Seru followed the metallic scent of blood. Chances were the missing siren—the one with the brown wing, anyway—was still alive. Her captor, Fagonia, couldn't bait Thalasia and Cipriana or escalate her threats with a corpse.

With how the female clutched her blade, Seru wondered if sirens felt as out of place in their current environment as they did in the water. He decided it was best not to ask and continued forward, trusting Thalasia's desire to try out her new powers meant she'd make quick work of Fagonia.

The natural brine of the sea coated the caverns. Salt and wounds didn't mix well. He felt the female stalling occasionally behind him to inspect their surroundings, scenting at the substance coating the walls, speeding her gait to catch up and falling back into step

It produced an odd symphony of scritch-scratching as her talons struggled to find purchase on stone.

"Doing alright back there, siren?" he called, not much caring whether she bothered to respond. Sirens and caves didn't mix well, either. The stony underground was a much better hideout for snakes or many reptiles and mammals—vampire drakes for one.

His eyes drifted to the ceiling, where he found bare roosting sites. The tortured screams of Parthenia must have scared them off. Pity. He so wanted to see if the siren withstood their tiny fangs. At least, the opportunity to see whose vocalization trumped whose would have been interesting. The darkness concealed his amusement well.

"Fine," the female replied, her voice low. A half a mile ahead or so, they could make out the outline of an entryway with the slight flickering of orange flames bouncing along the edge. Her nose wrinkled as the stench of sulfur and burned flesh and feathers drifted their way. There was a faint echo of footsteps approaching from the other side of the suspected alcove.

Guilers—five of them. He considered asking the siren's preference, but it seemed she didn't hold the same regard for him as she did for Thalasia, so instead, he let loose a bolt of blue lightning. The jagged bolt of electricity crackled and snapped before splitting three ways. Each slammed into their target with enough force to send a shudder through the entire cavern as the three lumbering geomancers burst into a rain of rubble and dust.

He stepped aside, gesturing her forward with a self-satisfied grin, fangs and all. It left what he presumed to be pyromancers for her. He wanted to see how well the sirens of Pteryrina trained their guards. The duo provided the perfect opportunity to see those skills in action, where the stakes were real and not just a failed exercise accompanied by tender muscles.

Ariadne didn't hesitate as she procured the blade from its sheath. The sharpened edges of the sword glinted with white light. She took advantage of the cave's perimeter and leaped into the air, darting toward the two remaining guilers. The creatures threw a multitude of fireballs at her, which she successfully dodged before landing on the other side of them. With both pyromancers facing in her direction, she doused one in a cacophony of water and chopped off the hands of the other.

Seru waited in the wings, watching the fight unfold. He wanted to see what she was made of. She'd made quick work of the pyromancers, but the geomancer trinity swiftly rebuilt. The rubble and dust tumbled together as if he had never destroyed them at all.

They posed a renewed threat, and she was most certainly within their grasp.

Both heads, now cut off from the guilers, Ariadne turned to the three stone creatures. She encased them in water, restricting their movement. She bounded for the alcove several feet behind her.

Not bad... Seru rolled his shoulders. Following suit, he stepped back into the shadows, waiting to see what transpired next.

As she neared the opening, she narrowly missed being seared with a blaze of fire by pressing her body against the cool stone wall. A hulking figure stepped out from the alcove with a large boulder in hand that it threw at Seru. It then turned its attention to Ariadne and emitted a continuous stream of flames from its hand, which she counteracted with a current of water.

Seru bit back an irritated growl. Of course, they were standing on earth... the guiler of earth, and fire likely sensed the vibrations of even the softest of steps. So naturally, it knew exactly where he was and where to hurl its attack. Though dumb enough to choose earth.

He hit the boulder with another jolt of electricity, more intense and longer-lasting than the last. Unless the guiler intended to re-build its weapon from dust, that one wasn't coming back. A new one, however, was fair play.

The battle between the creature's fire and Ariadne's water kept going as it hurled fireball after fireball at Seru. Some of them flying directly past him, aimed at the other geomancers, neutralizing their watery encasements.

The steam from the jet stream of fire and water created sauna-like conditions in the tunnel. The heated mist reminded him of the luxurious bathhouses and spas in the Clouds. Burning brimstone only heightened the effect, calling forth a memory of volcanic clay face masks and exfoliants.

Cynric came to mind.

The fiery male who lorded over the volcanic region in the south, where the Clouds obtained many of its scale care products and the home of one of their best fighters. The same fighter who made use of infernal magic, not unlike the guiler used.

Water didn't put out the fire—a lack of oxygen did.

Remembering a long-ago battle between Cynric and Verie, Seru called on his storm magic, creating a powerful vortex in the tunnel. The wind kicked up, taking flame, stone, and water as the suction began.

Getting low on her haunches, Ariadne buried her blade into the ground, which wasn't an easy feat. She grabbed the hilt and held on tight as she cut off the flow of water.

The creature barreled forward, running right toward Seru, only to get swept up in the powerful whirlwind. The vortex carried the guiler and his counterparts back toward the mouth of the cave, where it spat out the remnants. As the wind in the tunnel quieted, Seru came up behind Ariadne. "You may pull your sword from the stone." She'd passed the test. And they had a severely wounded siren who had yet to be discovered.

She stood and retrieved her weapon, returning it to its sheath. Ariadne dipped her chin in thanks as they closed what little distance remained between them and the hollow's entrance. The opening was wide enough that they could both go through at the same time. Faint tendrils of smoke licked at the air from the once-lit torches as they stepped into the alcove.

Mac hung from the left wall, restrained by cuffs around his wrists, ankles, and wings. Muffled sounds came from the leather mask secured across his mouth. Other than places where his wrists and ankles appeared red and inflamed with a few cuts, he looked utterly unharmed.

On the right, Parthenia lay on the floor in a crumpled mess. Her hair was a tangled mess, matted with dried blood. Her eyes were shut, and her breathing was shallow. Grimy dirt and dark bloodstains speckled her once-white dress. Bruises covered her from head to toe. Blisters had formed over the flesh and feathers along the base of her right wing. Her right wing and back had chunks ripped from them. One could also see a multitude of reddened, crisscrossed markings there. Several cuts across her cheek, a few of which had become scars.

"See if you can't free Maceron," Seru said, crossing Ariadne's path to retrieve Parthenia. He checked her over carefully; they could do little in the field to save her. For the time being, he shrugged out of his shirt, trying his best to secure and cover the worst of her injuries. He needed Ariadne to free Mac and keep her head until they'd returned to Pteryrina. She may not do it if they'd left her to tend to Parthenia; like Cipriana, she was too close, too intimately involved with Parthenia to remain objective.

He stood and lifted the wounded siren with little effort, cradling her against him. The sooner they met with Thalasia, the better. While his rapid rate of healing transferred to her, it wouldn't do Parthenia any good. Not that he had the faintest idea where to begin, even to try healing anyone or anything. He'd never healed in his entire life, only destroyed. A niche he fully intended to maintain.

He stepped around Ariadne and Mac, trusting they'd get themselves together and follow once possible. Parthenia needed at least some form of relief, or she wouldn't make it. That meant reconnecting with Thalasia, who by now had dealt with Fagonia.

Ariadne rushed across the room and made quick work of the leather mask.

"Seru!" Mac hollered, though his voice still came out strained and somewhat hoarse. "Shape shifters... she was working with them! They're supposed to... help with Thalasia!"

Seru paused in the entryway, turning back to address Mac. With Parthenia limp in his arms, he raised a brow. "Yes, we've long suspected Markham and his Informants pursued Thalasia in league with... some greater scheme."

'Help' certainly wasn't the term he would have chosen. One shifter had already sunk its claws into her the night of Marius's visit. If that hadn't confirmed it, the pack that chased them into Adina's death trap behind the waterfall had. "We need to go," Seru spoke levelly, resuming his course toward the exit.

Mac groaned. "Get these off... now..."

Five static-fueled clinks echoed through the tunnel. Not too long after, the whooshing sound of wings flapping followed suit. Mac landed noisily behind Seru. "Give me Parthenia. You need to get to Thalasia like yesterday's news. Fagonia... she was expecting them to fight alongside her against Thalasia."

Ariadne touched down, her feet hitting the ground with finesse.

Seru leveled his gaze at Mac. He'd already grown bored by this game. "Thalasia can take care of herself. She already has access to any and everything she could need from me," he explained. "*She,* on the other hand," he dropped his gaze to Parthenia. "Requires medical attention. We'll find Thalasia outside."

He continued walking, carrying the injured siren. "And if you *ever* tell her I said as much; you'll wish we'd let that woman carve you into mincemeat."

Letting out a heavy sigh, Mac rushed around so that he walked alongside Seru. He scoffed and muttered something under his breath about choices.

Ariadne stayed behind both males as they made their way toward the exit.

Seru felt Thalasia nudging at his shields, like a shy knock on a door, the kind one second-guessed hearing. With a frown, he let down his shields, just enough to help her get at whatever she seemed to be blindly feeling for between them. They really would need to carve out time to get her up to par on shielding. She needed to learn to use the connection and when and how to draw on it if she needed it. There would be times he could shield, and she could break her way in—to a certain point—if the situation required. Truthfully, at present, her attempts were clumsy at best.

When no other contact came, it gave him pause. Had Mac felt something he hadn't? Mac was her prophesied counterpart—at least in terms of the curse. With it still unbroken, did they feel a connection? As they exited the cave mouth into the glaring light outside, his gaze drifted back to the male beside him.

He begrudgingly left the fortified haven of his shields, sending out his flare of energy towards Thalasia to gauge her condition. When his energy met nothing but emptiness, cold and dark, he prickled.

A low-burning ember of silver energy wavered at the end of the connection. He'd shared a connection with his brothers. Felt each of them succumb to various ailments and states of consciousness before the ultimate severance of those bonds at their demise. This sensation was... different. Odd. Not right somehow.

Without a second thought, he stilled just long enough to unpack the mangled female into Mac's unsuspecting arms. He let loose the beast, which rocketed into the sky in pursuit of Thalasia's scent.

The beast found Thalasia strapped to a feline's back. It looked upward and froze for only a few moments, eyes wide, before it started forward. The beast spared no time in descending upon the feline, cutting off all escape routes by encircling him in its massive coils. The forest floor cracked and groaned beneath its coils, the sharp *snap* of trees breaking like twigs reverberating through the air. It bared ferocious rings of teeth, dripping with thick saliva laced with venom at the shifter. The growl that followed blasted the feline with its scorching breath.

The feline held still, making no move to shift. It didn't show any sign of aggression back at the beast.

The surrounding air crackled with electricity; blue bolts sliced past the feline, nicking him in places while severing the bonds holding Thalasia to his back. With its head pressed low to the ground, the beast revealed its menacing jaws and razor-sharp teeth, bringing them uncomfortably close. The feline could likely see his own reflection staring back at him through the beast's oversized teeth. If he were smart, he'd have abandoned Thalasia for the slimmest chance at the forest. However, immobilized as he was, he made easy prey. The beast devoured the shifter with ease, swallowing him whole.

It slid its snout closer to the unconscious and still unmoving Thalasia. It nudged her ever so slightly. Its breath disheveled her blue waves and feathers. A low grunt at the strange addition intermingled with her usual scent, and another nudge came, rolling her onto her side as the beast attempted to get a response.

"Holy shit," one siren mumbled.

The beast ignored the sirens. They weren't close enough to be a threat, not yet anyway. It continued to rumble at her, prodding at her body from various angles until it eventually came to rest its massive head down beside her.

A single blue eye positioned directly above her. The beast laid its snout alongside her and heaved a disheartened and defeated sigh. The rumble tapered into something akin to a whine.

Mac glanced at Ariadne with a slight shrug. "Here, take her." Without giving her a chance to object, he carefully handed Parthenia off to the female.

"What are you doing?" she hissed.

"Either something stupid or crazy, possibly both," he said. Mac inched just a little closer, but not too close. "Hey, buddy. I don't think she's going to wake up soon. Maybe you just take her back to Pteryrina?"

The unwelcome approach earned the green siren a nasty snarl as the beast raised its head to intercept him. Tightening its coils around Thalasia, the beast encased her with its armored scales. It threatened Mac back with a burst of electricity.

He backed up without hesitation. "Alright. Would you be willing to take Thalasia back to Pteryrina? We kind of need her to heal our friend here."

"Do you think that's going to work better?" Ariadne asked.

"I don't know. I'm taking guesses here." He gestured to the beast. "It isn't exactly like Seru, and I get along," Mac mumbled.

As if in response, the beast forcefully swung its tail through the space between them, nearly knocking Mac off his feet and felling several more trees. Thalasia was hurt; that much it understood. The warbling, green crunchy only agitated it. It shielded her as best it could, fending off anything that came too near. When Mac stayed his place, the beast took it as a sign of non-violence and wound into a more comfortable position to monitor and guard her.

Mac grumbled. "Case in point."

"I see," Ariadne said as she returned Parthenia to his arms. "We'll just have to wait it out." She retrieved the sword that had fallen, leaning it against the trunk of an untouched tree.

A lot of time passed before Thalasia finally stirred. A low groan came out of her mouth. "I'm gonna kill that bitch," she muttered as she peeled one eye open. "Hi, big guy," Thalasia said, her words coming out soft and warm.

The beast's nostrils flared, and it eagerly pressed its snout into her. A flick of its tongue scented her to see if the foul smell was gone, to check if she'd returned to normal. In its excitement, the beast's tail swept through the wreckage, destroying the debris that had built up around them.

"Yes, it's all gone." She stroked her hand along the side of his muzzle. Thalasia propped herself up on her elbow with a slight giggle. "You did good, big guy."

"Uh, Thalasia?" Mac called out.

The beast raised its scales at the sound of Mac's voice, responding with a growl. The siren annoyed it. And while eating him offered substantially more raw mana than the shifter had, the beast stayed close to Thalasia. If it couldn't eat her, eating Mac somehow seemed like a bad idea, though the why likely escaped it.

"Hey, big guy. Don't worry about him." Thalasia slowly pushed herself into a sitting position.

The beast reluctantly lowered its scales and dialed back its growl to a more muted warning. It loosened its coils around her, allowing fresh air and the sky overhead to come back into view. Plenty of room to spread her wings, but not enough that it couldn't restore its protection of her if either of the sirens tried anything it didn't like.

Several minutes went by as she moved each limb, including her wings, until she got to her feet. She ran her hands across the beast's scales. "Think I can get Seru back shortly?"

The beast gave a drawn-out rumble, giving her one more bump with his snout. It retreated with little resistance, leaving Seru seated at her feet. He heaved a sigh of his own, reaching out a hand to steady her in place of the beast's massive side. "One of these days, I'm just going to let you keep him."

A wide grin spread across her face. "That could be fun."

Mac's gaze flicked from her to Seru and back again. Not that he said anything; he merely shook his head.

"Give me a minute, and I'll heal her enough so you can take her back to Pteryrina."

"'Fun' is not the descriptor I would choose," Seru cautioned. "He might protect you now, but wait until you piss him off. If you think I'm bad, he's catastrophic." Seru pushed to his feet, none too concerned about walking her toward the injured siren in the nude. Priorities. Healing the nearly dead and wounded came before clothes. "You need to work on your shielding," he said as he allowed her to put as much of her weight on him as she chose.

"While that is the plan, I don't think you can shield against tranquilizer darts. I'm all ears if you have a way around it."

"What's a tranquilizer dart?" Mac asked.

"Knock-out drug."

Seru gave her room to reply to Mac before releasing her and addressing her request. "No, but if you can bypass the first few layers of shielding, you might bolster your resistance. Buy yourself valuable time. Maybe even prevent yourself from passing out. Listening will not hone your skills," he added. "Only practice and proper training can accomplish that."

"Training is already on the agenda," Thalasia said as she scrutinized the varying injuries across Parthenia's body. "A lot," she tacked on as she continued to study everything.

"Whatever you do, Mac, don't move." Using him for support, Thalasia got down on her knees.

"Got it—stand perfectly still," Mac echoed.

Ariadne, who'd remained quiet, pushed up off the tree and watched as everything unfolded.

With her focus on the crisscrossed lashes across Parthenia's back, Thalasia lifted her hands. A soft white luminescence flowed from her hands, a gentle balm that painstakingly mended the individual gashes across Parthenia's back.

Seru lent her his strength and stability. At least, what he could muster following the beast's protective rampage. She needed it more than he did. She was their heroine and savior. He was content to be a support structure and fade into the background for this part of the mission.

The white light left her hands several minutes later. Thalasia got to her feet with a little more ease than she'd gotten down. "Are you okay to carry her back to Pteryrina?"

"I'm good."

"Alright. We'll be right behind you."

With a quick acknowledgment, Mac took off into the air.

"Here's your weapon, my liege." Ariadne held out Thalasia's sword with a slight bow of her head. "I'll follow with him and ensure he doesn't falter."

"Thank you, Ariadne," Thalasia replied as she accepted her blade and returned it to its sheath. The female quickly followed Mac.

"Tell me they don't pray to you as well," Seru beseeched her, more than a little spent. His energy would bounce back soon enough. His patience made no such promise. Somehow, all the time and energy spent playing their roles for the sirens left him agitated and uncomfortable than playing his role at court.

He was glad neither Mac nor Ariadne asked a single question about the beast's appearance or actions. That the beast hadn't eaten either of them surprised him more than a little, not that he said so aloud. They had more significant concerns than the beast's ability to differentiate between friend and foe. He remained by Thalasia's side until she was ready, hoping he didn't cough up a shifter-sized hairball soon.

"Your guess is as good as mine." She shrugged. "Knowing you outrank the Elder and how everyone is going to treat you... two different things." Thalasia peered over at him. "Want me to dig out clothes for you?"

"If they do, you're on your own," Seru proclaimed. "I didn't sign up to watch them line up to kiss your feet or sing your praises at morning choir." He watched a question appear and fade just as quickly in her eyes. "Not really..." he offered after a moment, rubbing at his eyes. "We have to fly back, don't we?"

"Yes, we do."

"Sure, you don't want to just keep him this time?" Seru asked with a shake of his head, "Bet he'd keep your worshippers at bay."

Thalasia laughed. "And see how he'd react trying to go through a gateway? I don't see that ending well."

"That's simple. He'd just rip it off the hinges and call it a day." Or give them both indigestion by eating the damned thing.

"Kind of like him trying to eat the whirl of magic during the ritual. Wouldn't get him very far."

"You'd be surprised what he's eaten. He's not terribly picky. Anything magical is fair play. The rest basically just disintegrates."

She giggled. "Are you gonna tell me he's gotten more than feathers in his maw?"

"I'm sure he's gotten whole sirens stuck in his fangs on more than one occasion. Dragonhide—mostly the scales—is worse," he grimaced as he recalled the experience. "Didn't stop or deter him."

"He's a force to be reckoned with." She grinned. "Shall we?"

Seru shrugged in response. "If we must..." He'd let her take off first and gain some distance before giving the reins back over to the beast. She didn't want its over-eagerness to knock her out mid-flight. He'd banged her up enough for one day.

"Seeing as we now have a shape shifter to find, I think we must." Before she took off, she glanced back at him. "And thank you."

Seru drew back, feeling even less comfortable. "You don't need to thank me."

"Oh, I wasn't. I was thanking him; it probably would've worked better if he was at the forefront, though." Her words carried a hint of sarcasm. Thalasia shrugged. "I'll see you there." Without a word, she rocketed skyward, her wings beating a frantic rhythm until she was a speck above the emerald canopy, and then she banked hard, heading for Pteryrina.

He wondered if she realized the beast failed to understand even the most basic social norms. The only expression of gratitude it understood was... Oh, wait. Seru closed his eyes and allowed himself to fall back into the darkness, granting the beast permission to spring forward. With a ferocious roar, it gouged a crater in the dry ground as it launched itself in pursuit.

Chapter Fifty-Eight

The trip back to Pteryrina highly amused her. Thalasia couldn't remember the last time she'd laughed so hard. While she'd flown off first, it quickly became a race, which the beast won hands down. As fast as she was, he had size and speed over her. It eased her in a good way. She still had to heal Parthenia, but she thought it best to get the cursed business out of the way. Going through each individual injury would take time. This, well, it should be a quick kiss—provided the beast didn't make an unexpected appearance.

As an audience wasn't necessary, Thalasia and Seru joined Mac and Cipriana on the far side of the temple. Both Mac and Cipriana walked several feet ahead of them. Stepping through the third set of doors, Thalasia glanced at Seru. "Are you good with this?"

"Does it change the course if I'm not?" he asked.

She really wanted to say yes. In a way, if she opted not to break the curse, it would change the course. It would subject the sirens to continuing as they had until the eventuality of them dying off happened. Her guilt over causing the extinction of a species would pick away at her. The more it did, the harder she'd push to redeem herself until she got him killed, herself killed, or both.

If she told him no, and stayed the course even though she *still* didn't want to kiss Mac, then she'd give the sirens a fighting chance to survive. Maybe they'd even thrive. Thalasia let out a heavy sigh. "There's no good way to answer that."

"Precisely," Seru said. "When you encounter no-win situations, it's often choosing between two evils. You pick the consequences you can live with and move forward. This is your calling. That makes it your choice, Thalasia. While I appreciate your concern, asking destruction to choose life would be like asking a savior to kill. It's not in you, no matter how you might argue otherwise, for you to let them all die over a moment's discomfort." He looked ahead to Cipriana and Mac. "I'm pretty sure your two—what do you call them? Charges?—up there will agree with you while struggling to come to terms with the personal reassurances once all is said and done. Worst case, three-to-one. I'm overruled either way. So, make peace with your decision and do what you came here to do."

Either 'charges' or 'wards' worked, but that really wasn't the point. The bottom line: he was right. But they'd both known that. The only consequences she could ever live with would be to follow through. It didn't matter what she wanted; it mattered what was best for the whole. That was the life she'd chosen. Thalasia peered at Seru. Not that she hadn't gotten something she wanted out of all of this. For that, she was grateful.

She looked back to Mac and Cipriana, both of whom had stopped in the middle of the arena. Returning her gaze to Seru one last time, she gave him a small nod. "Just do what you can to keep him in check; *he* may not agree with you." All Mac had done earlier was say her name, and the beast hadn't reacted kindly. Almost similar to when Santos had done it.

"Just try not to use your teeth or take off on a celebratory flight without him, and I think he'll manage," Seru replied, stepping back to remain at the edge of the arena. He found a wall to lean against, folded his arms across his chest, and crossed his legs at the ankles. His eyes never left her as she headed off to join Mac and Cipriana.

"I wouldn't dream of it." She cracked a faint smile at him over her shoulder. Not that she was sure it would do any good, but she sent a silent prayer that the beast didn't make an appearance, or if he did, he didn't eat Mac. She didn't think Cipriana would take well to that. Leaving Seru behind, tucked against a wall, felt wrong, but she also understood the necessity. Although her feet moved, her steps were slow, not quite hesitant or uncertain, but minimally apprehensive. Still, it didn't take her long to catch up to the other two.

Mac glanced from Seru to her as she approached. "He's not coming over?"

"No. We both agree it's best that he's not too close." He'd still be able to see and hear everything from where he stood.

"I guess that makes sense." Mac gripped the back of his neck and his gaze dropped to the ground. "I get this isn't easy for anyone here, but... I don't know. I guess I just wanted him to know... that you chose right with him."

Thalasia raised an eyebrow. "Okay." She wasn't sure what that had to do with anything. Or where this brief interlude was going, provided it even had a direction.

"I feel bad about how I treated him when we first met. You know, I was kind of rude... well, to both of you, really."

Somehow, Thalasia kept the amusement from her face. It had been rather obvious that Mac didn't like Seru, and vice versa. Not something she expected would change. "He can hear you just fine from over there." She glanced at Seru out of her periphery.

Seru placed his head in his hand.

"Oh," Mac said.

Thalasia held her hand up to stop Mac from tacking on anything else. It was kind of amusing to pick up on some of Seru's emotions, or at least a glimpse, and she agreed. "Let's just get this over with." Still, other things had to be done.

Letting out a slight breath, Mac nodded. "Yeah." He pressed a tender kiss to Cipriana's lips, and then closed what little distance there was between him and Thalasia. He lifted her chin, a soft kiss meeting hers, his tongue exploring the delicate line of her bottom lip.

A tiny, swirling vortex of energy, like a miniature tornado, rapidly swirled around his and Cipriana's feet. Yep, that was enough, which was good. She really didn't want to have to give more. Thalasia took a step back, allowing the power of breaking the curse to do its work.

A gust of wind blew through the arena, rolling the grains of sand along the ground. As the whirlwind continued to build around Mac and Cipriana, the gusts became a torrential wave that spread through all of Pteryrina. It wrapped around every siren in a burst of light, an electrical current they could see even from where they stood. It all died down rather quickly, then completely disappeared, as if it had never occurred.

A powerful bolt of blue lightning struck the sand near Mac's newly formed feet with a deafening crack. Attempting to retreat, he stumbled on his unfamiliar feet, landing ungracefully on his backside. The sand where the bolt had struck melted and reformed into sheets of broken glass.

Yeah, he deserved that, Thalasia thought to herself. And the tumble just made it that much sweeter. Her lips curled in amusement. She turned her attention to Cipriana, who'd quickly moved to help Mac back to his feet. "I'm going to go address Parthenia's injuries and see what information I can garner about where they might've taken Gavin."

"You can do that? I mean, even though she's..." The female's words trailed off.

"Yes, I can." Without further explanation, Thalasia turned on her heels and started back in Seru's direction. Before she could get too far, Mac called out her name. Reluctantly, she glanced back over her shoulder at him.

"There's... a, um... can you..." He rubbed the back of his neck.

Good gods, he could attempt to shove his tongue down her throat in front of Cipriana, but he couldn't get a string of words out? Things would go quicker if she dug around his cranium for the information. Not wasting any time, Thalasia slipped into his head for whatever he... Oh, well, that made sense. "I'll take care of it." She noted the relief that crossed his face and strode toward Seru.

Seru uncrossed his arms and legs once she started in his direction. He took a few paces to meet her once she'd passed the halfway point. "I can't decide if that kid has balls or is simply too stupid for his—and her—own good," he said with a shake of his head. "What do they want now?"

"Maybe a little of both," she said as they made their way toward the exit. "He wanted to make sure I knew about the location of one of Parthenia's wounds." There had been a lot, and with where that injury was located, it wouldn't have been one she'd thought to search for. What exactly was she going to find happened when she got into Parthenia's head?

"A little?" Seru uttered in disbelief.

"Alright, a lot," she conceded. "I also think he's egotistical." And he wondered why she didn't want to be with Mac. Even if it meant she could've parted ways with her visions, it didn't matter. She'd take Seru's turbulence of moods any day of the week, and then some.

"What about her?" he asked, throwing a glance back at Cipriana.

For starters, the female was too accommodating, afraid to piss people off and be the bad guy. A lot of which she'd taken full advantage of during the time she and Seru stayed there. While there were some things she could understand, others she couldn't. "I think this role is going to chew her up and spit her out."

"I agree," Seru replied. "They're also a horrible match."

That one was a little hard to agree on. How many times had he said *they* made a horrible match? Hell, how many others repeated the same thing? If she were going to spend time to assess Cipriana and Mac together, she'd have to watch them together, see how they functioned. Thalasia exited the temple and started for the infirmary. "Whether or not they do, that's not our problem."

"I thought saving the species was part of your mission?" Seru fell into step with her.

"No, my mission was breaking the curse. I've given them the opportunity to utilize their new alliances to thrive." Though it did kind of defeat the purpose of going through all of that trouble to break the curse if she didn't help. And she would enjoy slapping Mac around a bit, knocking some of that ego out of him. As well as pushing Cipriana to take a hard look at her world and adjust accordingly. Thalasia frowned. "Damn it," she muttered with a faint groan. "I'll have a conversation with them. Just don't be surprised if I smack Mac."

Seru snorted. "I'm surprised you didn't already."

"Not like I've been around him much. Though if he'd gone any further with that kiss, I was gonna make him scream like a little girl." Fucker wouldn't have forgotten it. Thalasia snickered. She *definitely* would've enjoyed that.

"That would have almost made this trip worthwhile," Seru said, a slight smile twitching onto his lips.

"Oh, come on. You didn't get any amusement from him falling on his ass after your bolt struck close to his feet?" Because she did. Thalasia paused at the door to the infirmary. "Though, if it would make you feel better, I can certainly go back and kick him in the gonads. Might lose some punch now, but I can still do it."

"That won't be necessary," Seru said, sobering as they entered the medical building. He stopped next to Thalasia. "Why would anyone dedicate an entire structure to mending the weak and dying?"

"It's also for keeping track of pregnancies and ensuring they come to term, among other things." She strode past the desk at the front of the building, her footsteps echoing down the hall as she made her way to the first room on the left. The door was wide open. They had laid Parthenia out on the bedding, angled enough to keep pressure off her shoulder. "This is going to take a bit of time. I'm going to have to heal each wound individually."

"Not in recent history," Seru added in disbelief. His eyes roamed the structure as he trailed behind, surveying the layout and roving over supplies and foreign instruments.

No, he was right, but it didn't mean it wouldn't change. Although it depended on the age of the building. Who knew how long it had been there? As Seru nosed about and checked out the various tools and treatments sirens used, Thalasia went to work on healing Parthenia.

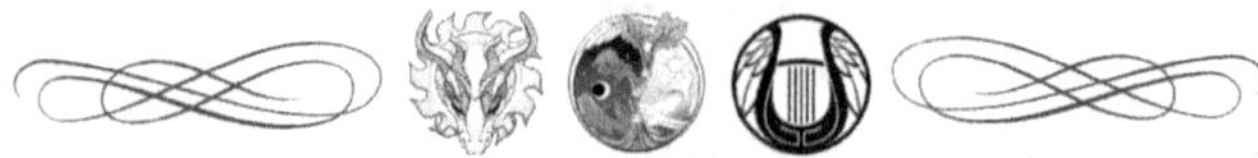

Tucked against Mac's side, Cipriana's eyes scanned the charred debris that had been the Elder's home. Most of the destruction was confined to the back of the house, with minimal impact elsewhere. This had been Mac's way of keeping her away from the infirmary. Not that she knew why, nor had he explained why. So much had changed in the last week, even in the last few days, and there was still more to come. Decisions to be made, laws to be addressed... not to mention an upcoming battle that she had been *instructed* to stay out of.

Not just by the Atlis, who according to her mother outranked her, but by Seru, who her mother suggested could be the Atlis's partner. Which she hadn't confirmed, nor was it a question she intended to ask. They'd rescued her sister and Mac, but Gavin wasn't there with them. She feared what this meant for Parthenia. If Seru and Thalasia didn't find him alive—something diverted her focus, drawing her gaze toward the gates. A flicker of surprise crossed her face as she let go of her mate, her eyebrow lifting slightly as Pallus drew near. "What is it?"

"There is a small group that has requested entry and to speak with you, Elder. One female stated her name is Milla, and that she is the Prime Warrior of Two Rivers, the Seelie kingdom."

"She's here?" Mac's brows furrowed.

Cipriana peered up at him and gave her guard a small nod. "We're right behind you." Her gaze followed the female as she pivoted, a momentary wobble in her step as she made her way back to the gates. Yeah, they were all trying to get accustomed to the change in their feet and weight. Either learning to walk barefoot or with shoes, something they didn't require before. She and Mac strode alongside one another as they made their way to the entrance.

As she approached, Cipriana scrutinized the other three Seelie that joined Milla. She had met none of them before, but all of them donned armor and weapons. It seemed the female was keeping true to her word. Cipriana inclined her head, a gesture of subtle respect. "Milla, it's good to see you again."

"You as well, Elder, if I was advised correctly," Milla replied with a returned bow. "This is my second-in-command, Samara, and two of my finest warriors, Leiland and Tamiane." As Milla introduced them, each of them offered a slight nod of his or her head. "If we may enter, there are some things I believe we should discuss."

Acknowledging the other three, Cipriana returned her attention to the Prime Warrior. "You have been and yes, of course." With a wave, she encouraged them to move through the imposing silver gates.

Leiland walked by Tamiane, following behind Milla and Samara as they entered. Stopping when they did, he stood behind and just slightly to the left of Milla, hands clasped behind him.

As she didn't want to be too far from the infirmary whenever Thalasia and Seru finished, she opted to stop them in the middle of the vast space between the gardens and the library. It wasn't as if too many sirens would overhear their conversation. Most were tending to daily chores. Though she was grateful Mac stayed with her and that he didn't automatically drape his arm across her shoulders. "My apologies. Normally, we'd go somewhere more private. However, that building suffered damage a few days ago, and we have yet to begin repairs."

"I see," Milla said. She glanced over her shoulder at Samara, as if taking a mental note, and then refocused on Cipriana. "When last we spoke, you and I discussed the possibility of some additional training for your forces. If you are still interested, I would like to begin. I believe the battle is only days away."

'Forces' made it sound as if she had so much more than she did. Up to this point, she'd been able to keep information generic enough that it didn't clue anyone in how few of them remained. Cipriana clasped her hands together, her shoulders sagging a bit. "I have to be honest with you. I have three guards, that's it. My *force* is so minimal that our most prominent protector and her partner wanted to get me somewhere safe. For me to stay out of the battle."

"Advice I would humbly suggest you take, Elder. But we can work with that. I am adept at training." Samara glanced briefly over her shoulder before focusing back on Cipriana. "If you are amenable, Leiland and Tamiane can stand guard at the gates."

"It might not be such a bad idea," Mac added.

Really? Hiding? And he had to agree with not only Thalasia and Seru but the Seelie as well. Cipriana did her best to hide her growing frustration. Instead of trying to address the suggestion, she flicked her gaze to the two mentioned for guard duty. It was important that she do right by her people. "Yes, thank you. I can certainly accept that. My guards haven't had training in a long time." It had been easier when their gates were closed, but with them open... and so many new alliances... it would be necessary.

"As well, if you would acquiesce, I will have some of my warriors hold a position along your shores to protect against a breach," Milla suggested.

"Uh, yes, thank you." She hadn't expected that at all. Truly, she wasn't sure what she could ever offer that would allow her to repay the kindness. While she'd spoken through others to the female, they hadn't spoken about an alliance.

With another bow of his head, Leiland and Tamiane turned and made their way back to the gates. Once they'd reached them, Leiland shifted to his animal form. Close to the same height in this form as he was in his humanoid one, his wings spread wide for only a moment before tucking in against his back. His armor shifted with him; his clothing disappeared.

Samara focused on Cipriana. "It would be prudent to get started sooner rather than later. Is there a particular place you would like me to work on the training?"

That was a good question. Not anywhere around the pools, and definitely not the temple. Cipriana bit the inside of her cheek. A brilliant idea flashed into her mind, and her eyes widened with excitement. Her gaze flicked to her three guards upon their approach. "This is Pallus, Ariadne, and Khryseis," she gestured to each. "Ladies, this is Samara. She's going to run you through some training exercises. If you could show her to the clearing by the armory, I think that'll be a good place to do so."

Samara offered a slight dip of her head to every female present. "If you will lead the way, we can get started."

Standing there, Cipriana watched as Ariadne confidently took the reins, guiding the group toward the cluster of abandoned dwellings and the armory, precisely as Thalasia and Seru emerged from the infirmary. She flicked her gaze back to Milla. "Excuse me for a few minutes. I need to speak with them. I'll be right back."

"Of course."

Cipriana quickly reduced the distance to them, with Mac rapidly gaining on her. It had taken long enough. Hopefully, those two got whatever they needed to find Gavin.

Seru leaned into Thalasia as they exited the infirmary. Thalasia angled a little closer to him. With a huff, Seru draped his arm around Thalasia's shoulders, pulling her in close as he deliberately slowed their pace. He pressed his nose into her hair.

Cipriana halted in her steps. Unprepared for the sudden impact, Mac crashed into her, and they both landed heavily on the ground. It seemed a small price to pay for not encountering any awkward emotional conversation or whatnot going on between Seru and Thalasia. Enough of them had occurred already with her sister. It took her and Mac a few minutes to untangle their legs and get back to their feet.

Somehow, the two of them stood. Cipriana did the best she could to brush it off. The good news was the only witnesses were Milla… and whatever Seru and Thalasia saw. Not that they'd gotten close enough that she could even hear bits of what Seru and Thalasia spoke to one another. Though if it really was something person-al—*I need you to listen carefully,* she heard inside her head. What the fuck? The voice sounded *a lot* like Thalasia. It seemed idiotic to ask, but she kind of had to know for sure. *Thalasia?*

Yes, it's me. Do I sound like someone else?

Nope. The attitude wasn't necessary. *Okay, so why are we talking like this?*

Because it's necessary.

"Are you okay?" Mac asked.

"I'm fine." Her tone held a little edge to it. Cipriana did what she could to keep it out of her voice, but her frustrations only continued to build with everything going on. Yeah, she was just fucking dandy. She had a mate who couldn't keep his tongue in his mouth, new feet she didn't know how to manage, someone had brutally tortured her sister, and her sister's mate was missing. That didn't include whatever the fuck was going on with Thalasia and Seru. *Alright, I'm listening.*

Cipriana remained statuesque as she waited for Seru and Thalasia to join her and Mac. Yeah, she wasn't going to the two of them. Not to mention, it had gotten a little quiet in her head. While she considered herself a fairly patient person, this was getting ridiculous.

I'm going to send the Seelie away; advise them we've already accepted aid from the dragons and do not require their help.

Excuse me? Cipriana asked mentally, doing as much as she could to keep her face neutral.

You're going to send your guards to a cave in the cliff-side just outside of the manticore boundaries. It'll be under the guise of securing provisions in a place where the sirens will hide. Whoever is handling their training at the moment will continue to do so in secret there. I have already made the arrangements with Milla.

This seemed completely unnecessary. She'd already made arrangements with Milla. Cipriana bit the inside of her cheek to calm her annoyance. *Can you tell me why?*

That's not information you require.

Sure, she didn't need to understand why. Nobody wanted to explain anything to her. She was just the Elder, the one responsible for the sirens, but why should anyone tell her anything? Cipriana bit back a groan.

Express some annoyance with me once Milla and her people have departed, just do not mention this. And don't overplay it.

At that point, she surpassed annoyance, but she'd happily express how pissed off she was at Thalasia. No doubt about that.

Thalasia adjusted her positioning against Seru, standing straight with her head high. Seru retrieved his arm, restoring it to his side as he straightened to resume his full height and usual posture. Back straight, eyes forward. The female leaped into the air and took flight, quickly crossing the clearing. She touched down on the ground in front of Milla, landing with the true grace of a siren. "Milla, I take it. The Prime Warrior of the Seelie."

What the fuck was she doing? Cipriana left Mac's side and hastened to the spot where Milla and Thalasia stood. It took a significant amount of effort not to run, especially as she might've tripped over her own two feet.

"That is correct," Milla replied. "I presume you are the protector Cipriana spoke of."

"Yes. Whatever arrangements the two of you made, we don't require them. We have all the aid we need."

"Should that not be Cipriana's decision? It is my understanding that she is the Elder. Is that not correct?"

"She is, however, I'm the Atlis, protector of these lands. I'm responsible for the sirens. As such, I'm in charge and these decisions are mine, not Cipriana's. She has overstepped her bounds in accepting your help."

Cipriana narrowed her eyes. The two of them spoke as if she wasn't even standing there. Had she somehow become invisible without realizing it? Thalasia was about to undo everything she'd just done. She didn't care what that stupid hierarchy stated, or that it wasn't something she could change. Fighting to suppress her anger, Cipriana tightened her jaw. "Excuse me, Atlis, but may we speak privately for a moment?"

"Now is not the time, Cipriana," Thalasia said.

"As my decision is being questioned, it would seem a perfect time." Cipriana crossed her arms. It had been a sound decision, and a reasonable one. Then she heard in her head, *I apologize for the invasion. However, I would like to confirm that your Atlis here has touched base with you regarding our assistance with your people.* Could everyone just get into her brain?

Yes, she has. Not that she understood why.

Excellent. Her mind went quiet after that. At least it wasn't as long as it had been with the so-called decision-maker.

Thalasia turned ever so slightly so she could face both females. "You already have an arrangement in place with the dragons. Or has that slipped your mind?"

Her brows furrowed with a slight shake of her head. How did she know about that? That didn't matter right then. "I haven't forgotten, however, the Seelie were present at that meeting. Milla had two representatives there."

"You are correct," Milla responded. "However, I did not agree to an accord with the dragons. My people joined to see what plans were in place to take action against the ever-growing threat of the guilers on the isle."

Chewing on the inside of her cheek, Cipriana thought back to that night where she'd sat around the fire with Mac, Keir, Islay, and Oriel. Damn, Milla was right. The Seelie could have spent more time training with her guards, but she hadn't yet committed to it. Most of her focus had split between Mac and Oriel. "This is something that affects us all. Wouldn't it make the most sense for all of us to come together?"

"Under normal circumstances, yes, it would. These are not normal circumstances. I am certain your dragon friend," Milla gestured her head in Seru's direction, "can concur—the dragons and the Seelie do not work together. Our... philosophies differ too greatly for us to reach anything that would be agreeable and beneficial to both species."

"I see," Cipriana replied, not bothering to hide her disappointment. Her initial impression of Aurelia hadn't been all that great, and now this with the Seelie. Were both species more concerned about their own self-interests than to swallow their pride over something like this?

"My people and I will take our leave." Milla offered nothing more than a curt nod to both her and Thalasia before walking toward the gates.

Out of her periphery, Cipriana caught sight of her guards returning with Samara, who quickly caught up with her associates, including the two that they had stationed by the silvery entrance. She watched as all four of the winged Seelie left. She turned her attention to Thalasia. "That's something that would've been nice to know beforehand."

"Yes, it would have, and I'm certain over the coming days, you and I will get on the same page."

Sure, they would. Just like they agreed to the terms of the pool, right? And every other way she'd accommodated the Atlis. Cipriana bit her tongue. She should've just called Oriel, but she'd hesitated both times. Too late to regret that decision now. There was other business at hand, and she still wanted to check on her sister. "The crystal still needs to be purified and handled."

"I'm going to take care of that now. I'll ensure it gets to Aurelia on your behalf."

Cipriana blinked. Was she joking? If the look on Thalasia's face was anything to go by, the short answer was no. "Then what exactly am I supposed to do?" The fury had cooled within her, but only for a short while. Now it was back full-force.

"There's a cave in the cliff-side just outside the manticore boundaries. It's empty and extensive. Begin taking provisions there for our people. After Seru and I return with Gavin, you'll take everyone there and seal the gates. It'll be the safest place during the battle." Without another word, Thalasia gave a slight nod to Seru and disappeared through the gardens.

Wait until after Seru and I leave to send your guards to the caves. Make sure they have provisions with them. Cipriana heard in her head. Gods, she was already exhausted. She dragged a hand down her face, the exhaustion weighing heavy on her skin. Letting out a heavy breath, she started toward the infirmary. Her sister was her priority.

"Cipriana—"

"Don't," she said, cutting Mac off. "You stood there and said *nothing,* did *nothing.* I thought you were supposed to have my back." Cipriana waved her hand dismissively at him, the gesture brushing past his face as she continued toward the infirmary, walking by Seru. Useless males, both of them—neither had opened their mouths. Strange, at least for the dragon, especially given the opinions he'd been all too happy to share with her just a few days ago.

Whatever. She no longer had the desire to appease him or the Atlis. Once she'd checked on her sister, well, then she'd do as Thalasia requested—but only because it benefited her. As she considered it more, she couldn't help but wonder if that entire show was for Seru's benefit.

Maybe she had misjudged the Atlis, not that it meant she completely trusted the female. It just meant that while those two were off rescuing Gavin, she and her guards would prepare for war.

To Be Continued...

In Book Five

Silencing the Shape Shifter

Silencing the Shape Shifter

*S*eplugh, Year 977

As dawn broke, Markham began his journey, the crisp morning air filling his lungs. He wouldn't reach his destination for hours, but that was for the best. Scarcely anyone ventured near where he was going, and there must be no prying eyes for what he hoped to accomplish this day.

As he walked, the crisp leaves shattered under his massive paws, and his long, hooked claws gripped the ground with each stride. Each time one of his paws lifted from the earth, the soft soil seemed to knit itself back together, erasing his presence. He could have no evidence of his pursuits. The only way anyone would know where he was going would be if they were following him, and he was certain that wasn't the case. Using his magic, as it was now, wore him down more than he would ever admit. His abilities were minimal as well, when they should be great. The time to fix the troublesome situation had long since passed.

Perhaps with this new magic, that would finally become a possibility.

Chicane Village, home of the guilers, was many miles from his village and on the outskirts of Prisma Isle. He hoped it wouldn't take him too long to find the one he sought.

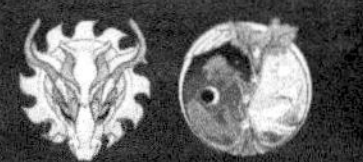

The air grew thick with the varied scents of guilers as Markham approached the village. He cloaked himself in his camouflage before he got any closer, ensuring none of the creatures noticed his arrival. If they caught wind of him, they would defend themselves or they would scatter, and he couldn't have either. He had to watch them without being seen until he found the one he sought.

An elder one, a creature who camouflaged himself with mud and twigs, wore a distinctive red crystal. Whispers and ancient tales spoke sparingly of the rare celestial fragments, hinting at their immense magical power.

Markham needed that crystal, and he would have it before this day was through. No matter what it took. He had spilled gallons of blood already in search of the information he required. If it had been false, he would spill gallons more until he found the treasure he desired.

The air crackled with an unseen energy, and Markham knew it was emanating from someone nearby. It was close. Conscious of the need to remain unheard and thus undetected, he glided between the trees, his deliberate slowness a shield against revealing his invisible state as he approached the captivating source of energy. After several minutes, Markham caught sight of a singular form on the edge of the treeline. The creature was strolling along the edge of the forest, collecting small sticks. Every bit of information he'd been able to get regarding the thing rang true. This must be the one he pursued. The horribly camouflaged protrusions from the being's spine told him that much. He could almost smell the energy, even from this distance. Staying cloaked in his camouflage, he left the shelter of the trees and moved around behind the creature. The thing could run into him or it could run into the trees. Either way, it wouldn't escape.

Markham kept his voice low, almost a whisper. Though no one else was near, he knew it was unwise to push his luck too far. "Do not scream and do not run. It will not go any better for you if you do." A look of displeasure crossed the creature's features as it deliberately placed the bundle of twigs onto the earth. Clearly, it didn't want to bring attention to the situation, anymore than he did.

"Good choice." A subtle, unseen smile played on Markham's lips. "You are going to come with me now, or I will bring your entire village to its knees." With a slight tilt of his head, his eyebrows drew together and his forehead wrinkled as he concentrated. He should have been able to catch every single bit of thought from the creature's mind, but he could only get snippets. Always just snippets. It was frustrating and annoying. "You would not care so much about that, though, would you? Just... one..." His head tilted to the other side. "Hmm. Who is this... Felix? I wonder what he looks like." He extended the mental tendrils of his mind, seeking to scrutinize the creature's thoughts more. He barely held back a growl when he got nothing else.

The creature slowly turned toward him, following the sound of his voice. A look of amusement settled on its face. "You may take me. The rest, it is inevitable."

The corners of his mouth curled upward. "Is it? I look forward to hearing all about it." With a swift movement of his paw, he rendered the creature unconscious, securing it by the scruff of its neck just before it met the earth. Markham had no way to camouflage the creature, so he would just have to stay inside the trees and be cautious. Not that he was *not* cautious. In no way did he want to put the thing in his mouth, so moving on two legs was going to have to suffice.

The journey from Chicane Village to his cave took several hours, much longer than he would have liked. He had to weave through the dense trees, carefully navigating around each territory, until he reached a quiet clearing. Nestled between the shape shifter and manticore territories was his secret haven. With a deep breath through his snout, Markham savored the noxious perfume of wickedness wafting from the cave's maw. Mentally dropping the protection spell on the entrance, only long enough to cross the threshold, he fixed it firmly back in place as he carried the creature inside.

Outwardly unassuming, his cave's interior was a magical marvel, expanding to the dimensions of a spacious hut. Carrying the thing fully inside, Markham propped it up against the wall. He no longer had any use for his camouflage now, so he removed it, fully revealing his black bear form for whenever the creature awoke. His shadows were practically leaping, eager for some fun, but he stifled their desperate calls. Their time would come soon enough.

Using what magic he had, Markham coaxed the iron chains from the walls, but only just far enough that the creature wouldn't be able to move much. The shackles, as if with a will of their own, snapped shut on its wrists, ankles, neck, and waist, pressing it against the wall. Markham leaned down and inspected the protrusions from the being's back, using a claw to scratch a bit of the mud off that coated them. The tiniest bit of red gleamed through.

A loathsome grin spread across his face. Oh, yes, this was most certainly what he'd been looking for. *Finally.*

With a flick of his paw, the creature shed its camouflage of mud and twigs, which clattered to the cave floor. Markham ignored the liquid as it dripped, some of it even soaking into the fur of his back paws. As he gently scraped a claw over the surface of the ruby-red gem, an electric sizzle pulsed through the air. *Oh, what he could do with this!*

The creature stirred. As its eyes fluttered open, it gave a small glance over its shoulder, its gaze falling on Markham standing behind it. As it was tightly chained, there was little it could do. He saw a flicker of understanding dawn in the creature's eyes, tinged with a hint of mild astonishment. It didn't struggle, beg, or yell. Its voice remained calm as it spoke. "I offered to come quietly, and this is how you treat a guest. Really, I had hoped for better manners."

Even though Markham chuckled quietly, the sound seemed to bounce off the cave walls, filling the space. "You will find I have little of those at my disposal. Besides, you said I could take you yet declined to specify a preferred mode of travel. My way was just the easiest one. Now. Tell me about this crystal attached to you. What can it do?"

"Tell *me*, why would I go about helping you?"

Markham's left shoulder rose slightly in a gesture of indifference. "It may lessen the pain of your death. But it is truly your choice whether you give me any information or not. I am sure I can discover all of its secrets on my own." That was time he would rather not spend on such a trivial task. Again, the sharp tip of his claw rasped against the gem's smooth exterior. He sensed the potent energy within it beginning to swell and grow. "With this crystal, why ever would you choose to hide in such a place as... *that?* You could have accomplished so much."

"You will have to learn its secrets all on your own. As for hiding, those are my reasons and mine alone."

"Hmm. Maybe. Or perhaps taking possession of it will enhance the abilities that I already have. We shall see." With the crystal in his gaze, his claw made another pass across its striking red face. There was really only one way that would suffice in parting it from the creature who wore it. Grasping the biggest chunk of crystal tightly, Markham wasted no time in wrenching it away from the creature, the rough stone scraping against his fur. Blood gushed down its back, and more than just skin tore away with the gem, but he could deal with the mess later.

The being balled its fists up, grinding its teeth together as it attempted to bite back its scream. Despite the effort, it was futile; a gasp of agony ripped from the creature's throat, and it slumped, almost imperceptibly, against the wall. Markham ignored it, choosing instead to focus on the crystal he clasped in his paw. With every second he maintained his grip, the sheer force entering him intensified, causing him to practically drool with eager desire. He hadn't missed how, at the moment he'd taken possession, it had darkened slightly in color. It still held the bright shade of red, except for the tiniest tendril of black that had snaked its way throughout. While that was interesting, it wasn't enough to hold his attention for very long. An explosion seemed to take place inside his mind, an electric tingle beginning to flow through every inch of him. *Oh, yes... this was **exactly** what I've been searching for.*

A rush of information was flowing from the creature's mind into his. Though he didn't think it was necessary, Markham gripped the back of its skull and closed his eyes as he absorbed every bit. The creature's name came to him. Jaha. And Felix... was the Elder of Chicane Village. Jaha had been playing its part on Prisma Isle for hundreds of years, since before the formation of the barrier. It had camouflaged itself to be indistinguishable from the many who'd originally fled from the neighboring Candescent Isle. It had come here after Felix's sire and had just been biding its time for all these years. Its sole mission was observation and absorption of knowledge, destined to be shared with its kin, restoring their former might and reclaiming their ancestral birthright.

Markham's expression shifted into a self-satisfied smirk. That wouldn't happen now.

Felix, he was the only one that mattered in Chicane. Jaha had truly not cared if the others of the village perished, so long as Felix remained unharmed. Felix could get Jaha's people here, so they could tear this isle apart as had been done long ago to their world. Despite Jaha's intention to resist, Markham's chains rendered his struggle ineffective. Locked up as it was, there was little room for the creature to move at all.

"Interesting. Very interesting. So many secrets you have been holding inside this tiny mind of yours, Jaha." Markham's chest rumbled with amusement as he dropped the creature's head from his grasp. "I must thank you for this gift you have given me. I assure you, I will have many great uses for it."

"Enjoy it... while you can... shape shifter..." the creature croaked out. "It will not... last." Fire ignited inside it. The flames it had conjured writhed around its form, a searing inferno that simulta-neously snapped the telepathic link between them. The blaze soon buried the screams that erupted from it.

Markham's gaze remained on the body until it was only a pile of ash. The now-empty shackles clanged against the stone as the chains snaked back into the wall. His shadows beneath the floor were disappointed, but he quieted them with the promise of bring-ing them another to ease their hunger soon. Removing the crown he wore from the top of his head, Markham stared into the empty eyes of the skull that adorned the center. If done right, that would be the perfect place for this marvelous gem he held in his hand. Oh, yes, that would do nicely.

Markham's gaze drifted to the far back corner of the cave, where a table overflowed with a towering stack of books and scrolls. Every single piece of history of the shape shifter species was gathered here, as well as the journals of every leader Métemorphe had ever had. It would have been a dreadful waste to destroy all of it when he'd taken leadership from his brother. Not to mention, so many of Oc-tavius's journal entries had been a significant source of amusement. But it wouldn't have been beneficial—to him, at least—for their history to be taught. For anyone in the village to know that things had ever been different.

With a fluid motion, he traversed the floor and then morphed into his humanoid form. It was only within the confines of this cave, when he wished to record new things, that he ever took this form. He favored his bear form, despite the minimal distinctions between it and his other shape. The pronounced claws and teeth made ripping creatures apart so much more enjoyable. However, paws made penmanship too difficult; he needed his fingers to write.

He picked up one book and opened it to a blank page. Laying it flat, he removed a quill pen from an inkwell. It would be pertinent to record every detail that had occurred on this historical day.

As he wrote, Markham spoke to her in his mind. Despite being torn apart four centuries prior and separated by countless realms, their bond remained as strong as ever. He relished the grin that cov-ered her face, as well as her enjoyment from what she'd witnessed through him. They mirrored his own as he watched their progeny through her eyes.

Do you see what I have gained, sister? With this new power, every-thing we have been working toward for so many years will finally come to fruition. The gateway will be open once more. We will be together again soon. I will bring you home, and the four of them will come with you. Together, we will create an empire that will demolish everyone and everything that stands in our way. And no one will ever rip us apart again.

About the Authors

Author of the Love's Worth Series, **Brigit Rosé,** lives in a world of romance. She has taken her life experience and made it into one endless love story. When she's not writing, she's singing loudly and off-key, hanging out with friends, or playing with her 2 fur babies. She can usually be found with a kiss in one hand and a twist of line in the other, exactly the stories she likes to read and write. If you'd like to know more about Brigit, you can find out more on her website: https://kbfennerrose.com

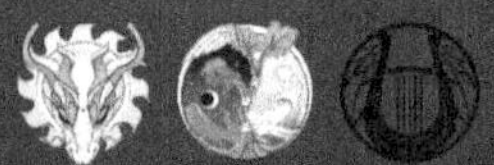

Nikki Haras has had a passion for writing since she was a small child. She will use whatever means necessary to get the words down that swirl inside her head, bleeding ink onto the page and breathing life into the characters who demand to tell their stories. When she's not immersing herself in her fantasy worlds, she's a full-time mom of three children and three fur babies, but you can usually always find her with a cup of coffee in one hand and a pen tucked into her messy bun. Always plotting the next amazing scene, fantastic new story, or immersive fantasy world to bring to life. To find out more about Nikki Haras and her upcoming book releases, you can find her on Facebook.

Under Krys Fenner

The Atlis Chronicles
Blood Sacrifice
Hunted

Co-authored

Prisma Isle Series
Perfectly Reckless
Chaotic Tranquility
Rebel Tides
Siren's Curse
Prisma Isle Puzzle & Coloring Book
The Empyreal Den Chronicles
Blood & Bondage

Coming soon